Ronald Firb

Born in Clarges Street, Piccadilly in the January of 1886, Arthur Annesley Ronald Firbank was the son of a wealthy MP and the grandson of a man who started life as a Durham miner. Firbank went up to Trinity College, Cambridge, where he never sat an examination or took a degree. It was at Cambridge, however, that he discovered the Catholic faith, an obsessive passion for the rest of his life. He had privately published a slim volume of fiction before Cambridge, but his first novel, *Vainglory*, was published in 1915, with a frontispiece by Rops. Firbank's subsequent books were illustrated by such artists as Nevinson and John. After The Great War, Firbank was an accepted figure in London's bohemian society. No private view or first night was complete without him. In the 1920s he began to drink heavily and to travel abroad. He developed a lung disease and died in Rome in 1926, discouraging friends from visiting him in his last weeks because of the poor quality of his wallpaper.

PICADOR*Classics*

Photograph of Ronald Firbank courtesy of Bassano Studios

The Complete Firbank

With an introduction by
ANTHONY POWELL

PICADOR *Classics*

published by Pan Books

Odette

In all the world to the dearest of mothers

Caprice

To Stephen Hammerton

The Flower Beneath the Foot

To Madame Mathieu and Mademoiselle Dora Garnier-Pages

First published as *The Complete Ronald Firbank*
1961 Gerald Duckworth and Co. Ltd
This Picador Classics edition published 1988 by
Pan Books Ltd, Cavaye Place, London SW10 9PG
9 8 7 6 5 3 2 1
© Thomas Firbank 1961
ISBN 0 330 29871 2
Printed and bound in Great Britain by
Richard Clay Ltd, Bungay, Suffolk

Contents

Introduction

by ANTHONY POWELL

RONALD FIRBANK was born on 17 January, 1886, at 40 Clarges Street, Piccadilly, an adequately fashionable, even slightly raffish, address, satisfactory to a person of his own socially sensitive temperament. Like everything else about him, the family background is unusual. He is the classic, the ultimate, example of the 'third generation type,' that trio of descending individuals in which the grandfather makes the money, the son consolidates the social position, the grandson practises the arts (or sometimes merely patronises them) in some 'decadent' manner, thus expressing the still existent, yet by now failing and feverish, energy that suddenly, unexpectedly, welled up in the race.

Joseph Firbank, the writer's grandfather, began his wage-earning life at the age of seven in a Durham coal mine. There he worked underground for some fourteen years; then became a labourer on the new railways everywhere in process of construction. This change of employment took him to the Marches of Wales, where he rose with remarkable speed to the position of buying the land required by the railway companies; soon becoming one of the largest railway contractors in England. Justice of the Peace and Deputy-Lieutenant, he was appointed High Sheriff of Monmouthshire in 1885. It is a notable example of the fluidity of class divisions in this country, often thought of as so immutable in Victorian times. Joseph Firbank's son, Sir Thomas Firbank, M.P., lists in *Who's Who* membership of five clubs (including White's and the Carlton), recording at the same time his recreations as 'very keen on all outdoor sports and athletics, music and objects of art.' Sir Thomas married the daughter of an Irish clergyman. Lady Firbank was also, so it appears, greatly attached to 'music and objects of art.' Their son, christened Arthur Annesley Ronald, was born in the year of his grandfather's death.

Few details seem available about Ronald's childhood. There

was another brother, who subsequently married and had a family; a sister, who died unmarried not long ago, leaving the nation a collection of ladies' dresses in all the fashions of her day. One would like to know more of home life at the Firbanks'. In the light of how Ronald himself developed, it seems likely that there were unusual features; perhaps, rather, efforts to achieve absolutely conventionality were so rigid, that determination in itself created an abnormal atmosphere. Ronald—it is perhaps not an impertinence to call him by his christian name, since he once complained that to be addressed as 'Firbank' gave him a sensation of goloshes—did not go to school until his arrival at Uppingham at the age of fourteen; preceded there, not long since, by at least two other authors of distinction, Norman Douglas and E. W. Hornung, creator of Raffles. The place was evidently uncongenial. In fact he survived Uppingham only two terms. His education was completed under a private tutor at Buxton; later in Touraine. In France, apparently, the bizarre notion took shape in his parents' minds that Ronald would make a suitable candidate for the Diplomatic Service. It is hard to resist the impression that they had either taken little trouble to discover what their son was like, or held unusual views as to how best the country's foreign policy should be conducted abroad.

Even before going up to Cambridge in 1905, Ronald produced a 'slim volume,' containing a short story, *Odette d'Antrevernes,* and a piece called *A Study in Temperament.* He paid for this publication himself; and, like Proust, Galsworthy, and other writers who subsequently achieved celebrity, his early books—indeed, the great majority of his later ones—were published at his own expense. Conceived under the influence of Maeterlinck and Francis Jammes, the best that can be said of this early production is that, for an author of nineteen, the writing has a certain smoothness. There is no vitality whatever; no evidence that matters would go any further. One would expect this to be a first and also a last book.

Cambridge was approached through Scoones the crammer's, where Ronald appears to have been mildly victimised by the other pupils, who included an uncle of Miss Nancy Mitford's. Then came Trinity Hall. This Cambridge college, the house *par excellence* of hunting, racing and rowing men, was another of those unaccountable choices for his son on the part of Sir Thomas Firbank. However, Ronald seems on the whole to have enjoyed the university, where he liked to read poetry aloud to himself, and possessed a certain ready-made status as author of a published book. He took no share in the athletic activities of the college, except for occasionally getting into shorts and trotting about in the neighbourhood for the good of his figure; nor did he sit for any examinations. He contrived to complete five terms of residence.

At Cambridge, as might be expected, Ronald was drawn towards the aesthetic tastes of the Nineties—then at about their lowest ebb, both in relation to the state into which *art nouveau* had by that time developed, and also the lack of esteem in which the period was held by those who claimed go-ahead ideas. Although always afterwards reticent upon the subject, it appears established beyond doubt that at some moment during his undergraduate days he was received into the Roman Catholic Church. His keen interest in the less demanding side of religious life may be gathered from his books, in which the clergy always play a prominent rôle. He also fell under the literary influence of Huysmans, whose stylistic mannerisms can sometimes be recognised in his own writing. Like Huysmans, too, Ronald's attraction towards Catholicism was tempered by a taste—*croyant*, no doubt, rather than *pratiquant*—for Transcendental Magic and the deities of ancient Egypt. At the university he is spoken of as having already developed his capacity for making striking remarks, his torturing shyness, and the physical habit of writhing his body, and grasping his head, as he stood or sat.

Any idea of the Diplomatic Service was now wisely abandoned, but, probably under the enthusiasm of recent conversion, he toyed with the possibility of office at the Vatican. In 1910, the year after Ronald came down from Cambridge, his father died. The will revealed the unpleasant fact that the Firbank fortune had steeply declined, dwindled in fact to no more than a comfortable income; a situation which—with some of the diffidence of his son—Sir Thomas had scrupulously concealed from the rest of the family. His widow was immediately overcome with financial forebodings of the worst kind. It was, indeed, a disagreeable shock for everyone. For a time Ronald lived with his mother in Curzon Street. Then he set up on his own; also beginning to embark on the extensive travels which played such a part in his life. Now, he entered, too, the world of the Café Royal and the Eiffel Tower restaurant. Those who wish to learn something of how he lived, and the people he knew in London, both at this period and later, are recommended to read *Ronald Firbank: a Memoir,* by Ifan Kyrle Fletcher (Duckworth,

1930) which gives an excellent account of his habits and conversation.* Indeed, that book collects together most of what is known about him, containing personal reminiscences by Lord Berners, V. B. Holland, Augustus John and Sir Osbert Sitwell. It is a mine of Firbank lore. The memoir is also illustrated with reproductions of Ronald's portraits by Augustus John, Wyndham Lewis, Alvaro Guevara and Charles Shannon.

War broke out in 1914. Ronald, who—it need scarcely be said—was totally unfit for military service, found even civilian life in the circumstances of world conflict exceedingly hard to endure. He went to live in Oxford. There he made an important change in his own personality. Hitherto, he had always been known as 'Arthur Firbank'; now he switched to 'Ronald Firbank.' It was a thorough metamorphosis. In 1915 appeared his first novel, *Vainglory*, with a frontispiece by that good old Nineties bourgeois-shocking illustrator, Félicien Rops.

It may be convenient here to list together Ronald Firbank's subsequent books. *Vainglory* was followed by *Odette* (a new edition of *Odette d'Antrevernes*) with four illustrations by Albert Buhrer, 1916; *Inclinations*, with two drawings by Albert Rutherston, 1916; *Caprice*, with a frontispiece by Augustus John, 1917; *Valmouth*, with a frontispiece by Augustus John, 1919; *The Princess Zoubaroff:* a *Comedy*, with a frontispiece and decorations by Michel Sevier, 1920;† *Santal*, 1921; *The Flower Beneath the Foot*, with a decoration by C. R. W. Nevinson, and portraits by Augustus John and Wyndham Lewis, 1923; *Prancing Nigger*, with an introduction by Carl van Vechten and frontispiece by R. E. Locher, 1924; *Concerning the Eccentricities of Cardinal Pirelli*, with a portrait by Augustus John, 1926. *Prancing Nigger*, the first of Ronald's books to be accepted by a publisher without payment, appeared in America under that title; then in England the following year under the name originally intended, *Sorrow in Sunlight*, with end-papers designed by C. R. W. Nevinson. *The Artificial Princess*, written shortly before *Vainglory*, was put away and forgotten, appearing posthumously in 1934, with an introduction by Sir Coleridge Kennard.

By the time the war was at an end Ronald Firbank had already

---

* See also pp. 199–208 of Grant Richards' *Author Hunting* (Unicorn Press, 1960).

† *The Princess Zoubaroff* was performed at the Irving Theatre Club in 1952 with the late Brenda Dean-Paul—a tragically Firbankian heroine in real life—playing the lead.

become one of the accepted figures of that curious, exuberant, talented, rather amateurish London bohemia, which, having its roots in the pre-war era, now luxuriantly expanded into the historical period known as the Twenties. The Firbank Legend began to take shape. His unusual appearance; his preference for drink, rather than food; his excessive shyness (which on one occasion caused him to get under the table while lunching tête-à-tête with a friend), all became famous. No Private View or First Night was complete without him. He was particularly delighted with Florence Mills and her Blackbirds—that Twenties solution of the colour question, and, up to date, far the most satisfactory one. Ronald's travels began once more ('Off to Haiti to-morrow, I hear the President is a perfect dear'), and his drinking bouts tended to increase in volume. He had never been easy to deal with; as time went on his friends found him quite impossibly touchy. His health was bad. There were warnings on all sides, not only from fortune-tellers, who played a great part whenever he made plans. Finally, on 21 May, 1926, he died in Rome, having discouraged his friends from visiting him, owing to the dreadfulness of the hotel bedroom's wallpaper. He was interred (though later the body was transferred to a Catholic burial ground) in the doctrinally inappropriate, but romantically incomparable Protestant cemetery.

In the autumn of that same year—if I may be permitted a brief autobiographical excursus in order to put in perspective my own association with Ronald Firbank's writing—I began work in a publisher's office in London. While up at Oxford, I had heard of Firbank, though never, I think, read any of his books there. They were, indeed, hard to obtain, already possessing 'first edition' value, due in some degree, no doubt, to their attractive production and the artists who had illustrated them. In London I came across many people who had known Ronald, all of them those few years older than myself—years more especially underlined at that particular moment by the division between those who had seen, and those who had been too young to see, war service—which made Ronald seem to belong to a world of fantasy, one utterly beyond recall. I do not think I have ever met anyone of exactly my own age who had met him, although that would, of course, have been perfectly possible. This point seems worth making in tracing the establishment of the Firbank myth. Certainly this myth was flourishing by the year after his death.

Introduction

In due course I read some of Ronald Firbank's books, and, since they were all hard to find, suggested that my firm might reprint some of them. No great enthusiasm was stimulated by this proposal. Even when it was found that a capital sum had been left in his will to guarantee the expenses of republication, a limited edition of one hundred copies was felt to meet the case. There was genuine surprise in the office when this edition was 'over-subscribed' by booksellers, before publication, to the extent of about twice that number. 1929, therefore, may be said to have been the year of the Ronald Firbank revival. Since then, there have been several editions of most of his books; and, even if 'out of print,' never a time when they have all been hopelessly unprocurable, even in the second-hand market.

Ronald Firbank is not a writer to be critically imposed by argument. He must be approached, as Rilke advocates for all works of art, in a spirit of sympathy; and—if one is going to bring up heavy continental artillery—it is also, where Firbank is concerned, well to remember Valéry's words that 'the problems [of the arts] are always indefinite, the results are always debatable, and the final approval always uncertain.' Either you find entertainment—even food for thought—in the Firbankian Universe, or you do not. Some readers complain that they have no idea what the whole thing is about; others, that they know what it is about, but are not in the least interested. There is no persuading either of these schools of thought. In any case, it would be a mistake to claim too much. Ronald Firbank's range is limited; his narrative devious; his characterisation stylised. Not everyone finds amusement in the preoccupations of his *dramatis personae*, those society ladies and ecclesiastics, lesbians, crowned heads and blackamoors, promenading against their backcloth of cathedral close, Greek mountains or Caribbean sea. Such fleeting figures are not to be enjoyed in a mood of severity. Certainly any attempt to explain why they are funny would be otiose to a degree.

What, then, is the point of Ronald Firbank's writing? Why should he continue to be reprinted, when all kind of apparently worthier figures sink into oblivion? This is not easy to explain in a word. I think it might be said to have two main causes; first, his mastery of technique; second, the fact that his daydream is a more popular one than might on the surface be expected.

Ronald Firbank, at his own particular level, is an interesting

example of the coming into being of the 'modern movement' in art
—in this case, writing. That movement was largely born, so it
appears to me, among persons whose natural tastes were, in the first
instance, directed towards nineteenth-century aesthetic character-
istics in their most lush and heavy-handed form. To realise this,
one has only to think of so eminent a performer in the 'modern'
field as Picasso, starting life by admiring the Pre-Raphaelites; a
later 'experimental' writer like James Joyce producing (in *Portrait
of the Artist as a Young Man*) a sentence like: 'Yes, these were noble
names on the dusky flyleaf and, even for so poor a Latinist as he,
the dusky verses were as fragrant as though they had lain all those
years in myrtle and lavender and vervain; but yet it wounded him to
think that he would never be but a shy guest at the feast of the
world's culture and that the monkish learning, in terms of which
he was striving to forge out an aesthetic philosophy, was held no
higher by the age he lived in than the subtle and curious jargons of
heraldry and falconry.'

From such examples it is possible to grasp that the great inno-
vators had to innovate or die. There could be no half measures.
Accordingly, Ronald Firbank must have seen that the manner of
Odette d'Antrevernes—although, no doubt, in one sense always dear
to his heart, even to some degree recurrent, like an incurable
malady, in *Santal*—was at bottom valueless for expressing the
many odd facets of life which perpetually obsessed his mind. He
therefore made an onslaught on the actual technique of writing.
The effect of this onslaught is by no means to be lightly dismissed.

His innovations were chiefly in the sphere of dialogue. Those
already familiar with his novels need not be reminded of his extraordinary facility in giving the impression of a crowd of people
'making conversation' in a room: others, perhaps belonging to
a generation that has not yet encountered Firbank's style, may
be surprised on reading his books to observe the mark left by him
on writers so different as Mr. Evelyn Waugh and Miss I. Compton-
Burnett; and it would be interesting to know whether Mr. Ernest
Hemingway, too, ever dipped into the Firbank novels in his early
days. To dwell on such prosaic professional aspects of the writer's
craft would no doubt be deprecated by Ronald Firbank himself,
but I shall return to the subject when the books are considered
individually. The point I want to make at this stage is that, although
rightly regarded in many ways as a ninetyish figure, Ronald Firbank

is also an adjunct of escape from Victorian writing, whether of the Nineties or earlier.

His books are, in fact, a picture of himself—what went on inside him, the daydream, almost absolutely uninhibited, of a shy, lonely, observant, witty, hopelessly *insortable* man, deeply devoted to the arts, but lacking some of the innate toughness required by those who practise them successfully. Some of that toughness he certainly lacked, but by no means all. In his solitary, some might say rather snobbish, certainly over-alcoholic life, he disciplined the sentimentality of his earliest work into a hard, often sparkling flow of words. What he lacked in powers of designing a pattern for what he had to say, he largely made up by presenting a world, in the last resort absolutely original; one that causes a cavalcade of wishfulfilment myths to sweep gaily past the reader's field of vision.

Vainglory, his first published novel, in a manner he was to make his own (and, indeed, *The Artificial Princess,* too) plunges straight into the Firbank style:

> Mrs. Henedge lived in a small house with killing stairs just off Chesham Place.
>
> 'If I were to die here,' she had often said, 'they would never be able to twist my coffin outside my door; they would have to cremate me in my room.'
>
> For such a cottage, the sitting-rooms, nevertheless, were astonishingly large. The drawing-room, for instance, was a complete surprise, in spite of its dimensions, being ocularly curtailed by a somewhat trying brocade of drooping lilac orchids on a yellow ground.

In *Vainglory* are to be found almost all the Firbank ingredients, especially that curious sense of reality that so often eludes more determinedly matter-of-fact novelists. One knows immediately what Mrs. Henedge's house was like; indeed, one is halfway to knowing Mrs. Henedge. The author himself appears in *Vainglory,* under the name of Harvester.

> 'It's here; Harvester's *Vaindreams*!'
> 'Not exactly the kind of book, is it, to take to her?'
> 'Why not? He has such a strange, peculiar style. His work calls to mind a frieze with figures of varying heights trotting

all the same way. If one should by any chance turn about it's usually merely to stare or sneer or to make a grimace. Only occasionally his figures care to beckon. And they seldom really touch.'

'He's too cold. Too classic. I suppose.'

'Classic! In the *Encyclopaedia Britannica* his style is described as *odd spelling, brilliant and vicious*.'

There are, in fact, many unexpected echoes to be detected by the trained ear in Ronald Firbank's work. Some of the dialogue recalls *Plain Tales from the Hills*. There is from time to time more than a touch of Saki mannerisms; although to suggest any comparison with Clovis or the Unbearable Bassington would no doubt have set the author of *Vainglory* writhing. It is clear that he knew Henry James's books well. More interesting is the obvious familiarity with Shakespeare—and that side of Thomas Hardy which might be said in some degree to derive from Shakespeare's clowns and grotesque situations.

'A hundred maidens would have had him if he'd asked 'em,' said the wide woman.

'Didst ever know a man, neighbour, that no woman at all would marry?' enquired Humphrey.

'I never did,' said the turf-cutter.

'Nor I,' said another.

'Nor I,' said Granfer Cantle.

'Well, now, I did once,' said Timothy Fairway, adding more firmness to one of his legs, 'I did know of such a man. But only once, mind.' He gave his throat a thorough rake round, as if it were the duty of every person not to be mistaken through thickness of voice. 'Yes, I knew of such a man,' he said.

'And what ghastly gallicrow might the poor fellow have been like, Master Fairway?' asked the turf-cutter.

'Well, 'a was neither a deaf man, nor a dumb man, nor a blind man. What 'a was I don't say.'

'Is he known in these parts?' said Olly Dowden.

'Hardly,' said Timothy; 'But I name no name . . . Come, keep the fire up there, youngsters.'

The above passage is from *The Return of the Native*. That which follows is taken at random from *Prancing Nigger*; or, to use the title its author preferred, *Sorrow in Sunlight*:

Introduction

'I dats way wondering why Bamboo no pass dis evenin', too; as a rule it is seldom he stop so late out upon de sea,' the young girl ventured.

'After I shall introduce you to de world (de advantage ob a good marriage; when I t'ink ob mine!), you will be ashamed, sh'o to recall dis infatuation.'

'De young men ob Cuna-Cuna (tell me, Mammee), are dey den so nice?'

'Ah, Chile! If I was your age again . . .'

'Sh'o, dair's nothin' so much in dat.'

'As a young girl of eight (Tee-hee), I was distracting to all the gentlemen,' Mrs. Mouth asserted, confiding a smile to a small, long-billed bird, in a cage, of the variety known as Bequia-Sweet.

'How I wish I'd been born, like you, in August-Town, across de Isthmus!'

'It gib me dis taste fo' S'ciety, Chile.'

'In S'ciety, don' dey dress wid clothes on ebery day?'

'Sh'o; surtainly.'

'An' don't dey nebber tickle?'

'In August-Town, de aristocracy conceal de best part ob deir bodies; not like heah!'

It must surely be allowed that there is something in common between Hardy's treatment of Wessex peasants, and Firbank's of West Indian negroes. Both these bursts of dialogue are at once realistic, esoteric, funny, sad, a trifle cruel.

Vainglory was followed by *Inclinations*, the story of the visit to Greece of two spinsters, Miss O'Brookomore and Miss Collins. Count Pastorelli and Miss Dawkins, the Australian girl, are good minor characters. By this time Ronald Firbank was at home with his own style. The next novel *Caprice*, which takes place in a cathedral town, is in some ways, I think, the best thing he wrote. The dialogue is splendid, although, with increased self-assurance, the tone of the gossip-column sometimes looms ominously close. *Valmouth,* of which a 'musical' was staged not long ago, has perhaps worn less well than some of the earlier novels. It is probably Ronald Firbank's best-known work (or at least competes for that place with *Prancing Nigger*), and certainly he made a great effort in writing it to overcome some of his weaknesses. There are enjoyable passages, but the material has settled down to a certain routine. Mrs. Yajñavalkya, the masseuse of indeterminate Afro-Asian origins, introduces a coloured element that was to play an increasing part in Ronald Firbank's imaginative world. Mrs. Yaj lives, undoubtedly, but she is a figure of somewhat coarser clay than other of his perhaps less completely realised conceptions. Possibly this is because Mrs. Yajñavalkya is a success, a power figure, a person without that fundamental melancholy that is at the heart of the Firbankian world. *The Flower Beneath the Foot* (a beautiful title) was written before *Valmouth*, though published later. It clearly belongs to an earlier manner, and might be described, broadly speaking, as Ruritanian in setting.

'Her great regret you know . . .' the murmur came, 'she is . . . God forgive her . . . the former Favourite of a king; although, she herself declares, only for a few minutes.'

It would be possible to quote endlessly. There is a foreshadowing of *Finnegans Wake* (although further verbal convolutions would have taken place) in the association of ideas contained in the description:

The moon shone out now high above the trees. In smoke-like dreamy spirals streamed the elms, breaking towards their zeniths in incredible *ich diens*.'

Indeed, Joyce, in his earlier, more ornate manner, comes to mind more than once, for example, in *Cardinal Pirelli*:

She had been freshening a little the chasuble worn last by his Eminence at the baptism of the blue-eyed police-pup of the Duquesa Dun Eden, which bore still the primrose trace of an innocent insult.

Perhaps the Surrealists—and their patron saint, Hieronymus Bosch—are closer in spirit than Joyce (who indeed hated Surrealism); certainly in such a fancy as that in *The Artificial Princess*, when:

A girls'-school passed with its escort of Nuns, and fantastic Demons flying above them (invisible) criss-cross through the air . . .

A final word should be said of an edition of Ronald Firbank's works collected in one volume. Nothing could be more convenient for a bedside book; to open at any page and read for a time against a pile of pillows to prepare yourself for suitable dreams. It is not, however, 'fair' to the author to jog through this volume from cover to cover in a pedantic mood, then complain there are repetitions, samenesses, and a too consistent display of fireworks. Ronald Firbank's books, like his style, were designed to appear in exquisite *format*; to be read almost at a sitting. That should be borne in mind. People not too irretrievably 'engaged' will find much there to amuse them.

Odette: A Fairy Tale for Weary People

IN the long summer evenings, when the shadows crept slowly over the lawn, and the distant towers of the cathedral turned purple in the setting sun, little Odette d'Antrevernes would steal out from the old grey château to listen to the birds murmuring 'good-night' to one another amongst the trees.

Far away, at the end of the long avenue of fragrant limes, wound the Loire, all amongst the flowery meadows and emerald vineyards, like a wonderful looking-glass reflecting all the sky; and across the river, like an ogre's castle in a fairy tale, frowned the château of Luynes, with its round grey turrets and its long, thin windows, so narrow, that scarcely could a princess in distress put forth her little white hand to wave to the true knight that should rescue her from her terrible fate.

Just until the sun disappeared behind the trees, veiled in a crimson cloud, little Odette would remain in the shadowy garden, then quickly and mysteriously she would slip back into the old grey château; where, in the long, dim drawing-room, before two wax candles, she would find her Aunt Valerie d'Antrevernes embroidering an altar cloth for the homely lichened village church, that one could see across the rose garden from the castle windows.

'Where have you been, my child?' her aunt would ask her, glancing up from the lace altar cloth that fell around her in a snowy cloud.

And Odette, in her pretty baby voice, would reply: 'I have been listening to the birds saying their evening prayers,' and then silently she would sit on a low hassock at her aunt's feet, and tell herself fairy stories until Fortune, her Creole nurse, should come and carry her off to bed.

Sometimes of an evening the old Curé of Bois-Fleuri would come to visit Madame d'Antrevernes, and little Odette would watch them as they talked, wondering all the while if Monsieur le Curé had really seen God. She had never dared ask.

Her aunt always sat in a high armchair of faded blue tapestry, embroidered in gold, with the family arms on a background of fleur-de-lys, and her pale, beautiful face, as it bent over the lace altar cloth, made little Odette think of angels and Holy Saints.

Odette had always seen her aunt thus, bending over an altar cloth for God, so whenever she thought of Madame d'Antrevernes it was with a peculiar reverence that almost approached to awe.

One evening, when little Odette lay awake in her deep four-posted bed, watching the firelight dance upon the strange tapestry figures that covered the walls, she heard Fortune, her old nurse, talking to one of the servants. She caught her aunt's name, then her own, and without realising that she was doing wrong, she listened to what Fortune said.

She did not really understand what she heard, for she was watching the firelight as it shone upon the tall faded-looking lady in blue, who was regarding with outstretched arms the sky which was full of angels. All about the lady, in a field of red and white flowers, lay sleeping sheep. Her aunt had once told her that the faded-looking blue lady, whom Odette had imagined to be the Lady Virgin herself, was Joan of Arc receiving the message from heaven to deliver France.

So as Odette watched the firelight dancing upon the faded tapestry, she listened, without knowing that she was listening to the voice of Fortune, who, in the next room, sat gossiping with another servant.

'She never seems able to forget him,' she heard Fortune say. 'Ever since the day that Monsieur le Marquis killed Monsieur d'Antrevernes in a duel, Madame has never recovered.

'She had scarcely been married a month, sweet soul, when her husband was brought home to her dead ... and so beautiful he looked as he lay in the great hall, his eyes wide-open and smiling, just as if he were still alive. ... Madame la Comtesse was in the rose garden at the time with Monsieur le Curé—no one knew where she was, and when suddenly she entered the hall, her hands all full of summer roses, and saw her husband lying dead before her, she gave a terrible cry and fainted straight away. ... For days after she hung between life and death, and then, when she at last got well again, she always seemed to be thinking of him, always seemed to be living in the past. Sometimes she would sit for hours in the garden staring in front of her, and smiling and talking to herself so that I used to feel afraid. Then, a few years later, when the father and mother of the little Odette were drowned on their way back from India, Madame seemed to wake up from her long dream, as it were, and went to Paris to fetch Mademoiselle Odette from the convent of the Holy Dove.'

Little Odette had fallen asleep berced by the lullaby of the old servant's voice, and when next morning the risen sun shone in a shower of gold through the diamond-paned windows of her room, and all the birds in the garden below were rejoicing amidst the trees, little Odette had forgotten the conversation she had overheard the previous night as she lay awake watching the firelight dancing upon the faded blue gown of the Maid of France.

⚏ *II* ⚏

SOMETIMES of an afternoon Monsieur le Curé de Bois-Fleuri would call at the château and ask Blaise, the long valued butler, whether Mademoiselle Odette d'Antrevernes was at home; and Blaise would smile at Monsieur le Curé and ask him to be seated whilst he went to see.

Then slowly, slowly, Blaise would traverse the great hall, pass under the torn and faded flags that drooped sadly like dead things from the massive rafters and shaking his silver head and murmuring to himself he would disappear on the great staircase lined with armour.

And the old Curé would sit musing on the past, his eyes fixed on the torn flags that had once been borne in proud splendour at Pavie and Moncontour.

Then the little Odette in her flowing robe would trip eagerly down the wide oak staircase, and making a low reverence to the Curé, she would take his hand, and together they would walk out into the rose garden that faced the south side of the château.

There, by a broken statue on a rustic seat they would sit surrounded by clustering roses, and the Curé, with his soft, low voice, would tell little Odette beautiful stories about the Saints and the Virgin Mary.

But the story that Odette found the most wonderful of all, was the account of the child Bernadette beholding the Holy Virgin in the mountains. This, for her, was the most perfect story in the world, and with her quick, imaginative mind she would picture the little peasant girl Bernadette returning to her parents' distant dwelling, when suddenly in a ray of glorious light, the Holy Mary herself appeared on the lonely mountain path, like a beautiful dream.

Oh! how Odette wished that she could have been little Bernadette! And she would delight to surmise what the little peasant girl looked like; whether her hair was brown, or whether it was gold— and Odette was terribly disappointed when asking the Curé this question, that he only shook his head and said he did not know.

So the days slipped by quietly as on silver wings. Madame d'Antrevernes always in her high blue chair, her altar cloth between her hands, and little Odette on a faded cushion dreaming at her feet.

Then one beautiful evening in August, as little Odette watched the two twin towers of the distant Cathedral flush purple in the setting sun, and the great round dome of St. Martin's Church loom like a ripe apricot against the sky, a wonderful idea came to her. She, too, would seek the Holy Virgin. She, too, like little Bernadette, would speak with the Holy Mary, the Mother of the Lord Seigneur Christ.

☒ *III* ☒

IT was the evening of the eventful night. For one whole week Odette had prayed steadfastly, and now this evening she was going to speak to the Holy Mary in the rose garden, when Aunt Valerie and Fortune, Blaise, and Monsieur le Curé were all fast asleep.

She felt terribly excited as she kissed her aunt good-night, and trembling with a beautiful holy fear she allowed Fortune to undress her and put her to bed.

Then for two long hours she watched the moonlight fall upon the dim blue figure of Joan of Arc, for the frail summer fire that Fortune lit of an evening had long ago burnt itself out, and now the room was filled with mysterious shadows and strange creakings of furniture, so that it was all Odette could do not to be afraid. At last she heard the gentle rustle of her aunt's gown as she passed her door, and Odette could see the yellow light from Madame d'Antrevernes' candle glint like a fleeting star through the keyhole. Soon afterwards she heard the slow steps of Blaise cross the Picture Gallery, and then a sudden silence fell upon the château only broken by faint nocturnal noises from the garden.

Odette sat up amid her pillows listening. She felt her heart beating, beating, as if it were trying to escape.

Then silently she slipped from her bed, crossed to the window, and looked out.

Perhaps the Virgin was already waiting for her in the garden?

But she saw no one.

Far away she could see a few lights shining like fallen stars in the town of Tours, and through the trees upon the lawn she saw the Loire glittering like an angel's robe beneath the moon.

'How wicked to expect the Holy Virgin to wait for me,' thought Odette, 'It is I who must wait for Her.' And fastening a fair silver cross about her neck, she noiselessly opened the bedroom door, and found herself standing alone upon the great dark staircase.

To get to the garden it was necessary to cross the Picture Gallery; for the Picture Gallery was at the top of the great staircase.

Odette trembled as she passed down the long still Gallery where the portraits of her ancestors peered eerily from the panelled walls. But she was comforted by the thought that Gabrielle was at the other end.

It was the picture of Gabrielle d'Antrevernes, one of the beauties of the court of Louis XIV, that Odette loved most. And she never tired of looking at the long pale face, the sea-blue eyes, and the dull gold hair capped with pearls, of her beautiful ancestress.

Odette adored the tired languid-looking hands, full of deep red roses, that lay like two dead doves upon the silver brocaded gown, and she would weave beautiful tales about Gabrielle, seated on her favourite cushion, peering up at the portrait, her great eyes lost in thought.

But this evening she did not linger as her custom was but with a friendly smile to the beloved Gabrielle she hurried by, her cautious feet all a-pit-a-pat, a-pit-a-pat, on the parquet floor.

Then she went down the broad staircase between the pale armour, beneath the brooding flags, and so to the glass door that led to the garden.

The door was locked, and oh! the dreadful creak it gave as Odette turned the key! and a pair of little exploring mice rushed helter-skelter, tumbling about on the slippery floor.

Odette tremulously turned the handle, and suddenly she found herself alone after midnight in the garden.

Her heart beat so that she thought she was going to die. But oh! how beautiful the garden looked beneath the moon! The roses seemed to look more mysterious by moon-shine. Their perfume seemed more pure. Odette bent down and kissed a heavy crimson rose all illumined with silver dew, and then quickly she picked a great bouquet of flowers to offer to the Virgin. Some of the flowers were sleeping as she picked them, and Odette thought, with a little thrill of delight, at their joy on awakening and finding themselves on the Holy Mother's breast.

Then, her arms full of flowers, Odette went and knelt down by the low marble seat, where so often Monsieur le Curé had spoken to her of the Saint Mary and of Jesus, her Son. And there, with her eyes fixed upon the stars, she waited. . . .

In the trees a nightingale sang so beautifully that Odette felt the tears come into her eyes, and then far away another bird sang back . . . and then both together, in an ecstasy, mixed their voices in one, and the garden seemed to Odette as if it were paradise.

Suddenly a low moan, like the sound of a breaking heart, made Odette start to her feet.

Could it be that the Holy Mother was in pain? She looked about her.

Yes, there it was again . . . a long, low cry . . . it came from the other side of the wall, it came from the road.

Odette hastily collected the flowers in her hands, and ran swiftly down the avenue of lime trees, her untied hair drifting aerially behind her as she ran.

Then once upon the white road, she looked about her expectantly, but there was no one to be seen. The river ran the other side of the road like a silver chain, and far away in the town of Tours a few lights burnt like candles in the dark. She stood still, listening intently; yes, there again, quite, quite close, was the long, sad cry.

Odette ran forward to the river bank from where the sound seemed to come, and there, her face buried in her hands—a woman lay.

'Oh! Oh!' cried the little Odette, the tears rolling down her cheeks, 'the Holy Mother is in pain,' and stooping down, she timidly kissed the sobbing woman at her feet.

Then as the woman uncovered her face with her hands, Odette

sprang back with a startled scream. There, on the grass, amongst the pale-hued daisies, lay a woman with painted cheeks and flaming hair; a terrible expression was in her eyes.

'Who are you? What do you want?' she asked Odette brutally; and Odette, afraid and trembling, began to sob, hiding her face in her hands so as not to see the dreadful eyes of the woman at her feet.

She felt the woman staring at her, though she did not dare look, then suddenly she heard a laugh, a laugh that froze her blood.

'Why, you have no shoes or stockings,' said the woman, in a frenzy of mad laughter. 'What are you doing here in your night-gown on the high roads? You've begun early, my dear!' And she rocked herself to and fro, laughing, laughing, laughing, and then suddenly her laughter turned to tears. All her poor thin body shook with terrible sobs; it seemed as if her very heart was breaking.

Odette uncovered her eyes and looked at this shattered wreck of a human soul, and an immense unaccountable pity seized her, for suddenly she bent down and kissed the woman on her burning lips.

The woman's sobs grew quieter, as she felt Odette's pure cool mouth upon her fevered face. 'Who are you?' she kept asking her, 'Who are you?'

And Odette in her baby voice whispered back, 'The Holy Virgin has sent me, in order to make you well!'

Presently the woman calmed herself, and sat staring at the shining river, as though she had quite forgotten that Odette was beside her.

'Tell me what is the matter,' Odette said at length, 'and I will try to help you.'

The woman looked at her kindly: 'How should you understand what is the matter?' she said, 'You, who have lived always with good people, far away from the temptations of the world, what have you to do with the likes of us?'

'I do not understand,' said Odette, looking at the woman with great questioning eyes.

'And may you never understand, little one,' said the woman, kissing her. 'When I was but a wee mite I heard the preaching folk tell of God and the Angels. You must be one of them, I think?'

'Oh! no. Oh! no,' said Odette. 'I am not an angel, but I have been sent by the Queen of Heaven to save you here tonight.'

The woman looked at her curiously. 'You came only just in time,' she said, and again her eyes strayed towards the river.

'Let me give you this silver cross,' Odette said, changing it from her own neck to the woman's. 'Keep it always, for it is holy, and is a sign that Jesus came into the world to die for us.'

The woman took the cross into her hands, and seemed to weigh it. 'Is it really silver?' she asked.

Odette smiled at her. 'Yes, and is it not beautiful? It was given to me by my mother before she went away to India; I do not remember her giving it me, for I was then only a tiny creature. But Aunt Valerie has often told me that when mamma hung it around my neck, she cried, and kissed me, and told me to love the Holy Virgin, for that faith, and love, were the only things that were beautiful in life.'

The woman looked at her sadly. 'I will keep it in memory of you, little one,' she said, 'It may bring me luck,' and she got up as if to go.

'Will you promise never to do things that the Holy Mary would not approve of?' asked Odette, taking the woman's hand, and gazing earnestly into her eyes.

'I will try, little one,' the woman said, and she stooped and kissed Odette passionately; the warm tears falling from her eyes upon Odette's upturned face.

Far away in the East, the day began to Dawn. A flush of yellow like ripe fruit spread slowly across the sky. The birds in the trees piped drowsily to one another, and the bent cyclamens by the river-side lifted their fragrant hearts in rapture to the rising sun.

The woman and Odette stood side by side watching the breaking day, then, as a clock struck away across the meadows from some church tower, the woman shivered, and looked down the long white road that followed the river bank.

'I must go,' she said.

Odette looked at her. 'Where to?' she asked.

'I don't know,' answered the woman. 'I am going to try to find work—honest work,' and taking Odette in her arms she kissed her again and again. 'Good-bye, little one,' she said. 'And since you pray to the Holy Mother, perhaps sometimes you will pray for me.'

And then, with a tired, sad step, the woman walked slowly away down the long white road, her shadow falling beside her as though it were her soul.

'Oh, Holy Virgin, Mother of Our Lord Seigneur Christ, I thank Thee for having brought me here this night,' prayed the little

Odette. 'Take into Thy protection, dear Mother, this poor woman who has need of Thee, and bring her safely to Thy beautiful Kingdom in Heaven, for the sake of our Lord Jesus. Amen.'

Then little Odette returned thoughtfully to the great grey château. And as she passed down the avenue of over-arching limes a thousand thrushes sang deliriously amidst the branches.

But Odette felt somehow changed since last she passed the castle gates. She felt older. For suddenly she realised that Life was not a dream; she realised for the first time that Life was cruel, that Life was sad, that beyond the beautiful garden in which she dwelt, many millions of people were struggling to live, and sometimes in the struggle for life one failed—like the poor woman by the river bank.

And Odette turned as she walked, and looked behind her, to where, by the roadside, and dying beneath the golden sun, the red roses that she had gathered for the Holy Mother, shone in the morning light like drops of crimson blood.

The Artificial Princess

IN WHICH A LADY BEGS ANOTHER TO PERFORM A SERVICE

'YOU take the white omnibus in the Platz,' murmured the
Princess, 'but do not forget to change into an ultramarine on
reaching the Flower Market, or you will find yourself in the "Abat-
toirs." Had it been any other day, I would have sent you in the
incognito glass-coach—the one my poor sister used when she ran
away with the little chorister—but I have ordered that, since it is
my birthday, the royal horses shall pass the day lying down.
To-night, they shall be led out to see the fireworks, and possibly the
stars. . . . But, Baroness, you are not eating any of these delicious
sweets—that purple one looks irresistible. I think it is a crystallised
Orchid; or this wee pink one; I think it is a Wild Rose. In spite of
the Revolution the dear President never forgets my birthday.'

The Baroness Rudlieb declined, and then accepted; it was a way
of hers. . . . Seated at the piano she had accompanied the Princess's
directions to a brilliant Rhapsody by Liszt, her eyes fixed theatrically
upon a Coronation of the Virgin that adorned the ceiling. In silence
she swallowed both sweets, and then expressed herself by a bewildered sigh.

The Princess's economies were ridiculous. The white omnibus!
And then a vulgar blue one! It was an indignity, but it was characteristic of the Princess to be so mean.

'A hired landau,' the Baroness ventured to suggest, 'would look
less conspicuous. . . .'

The Princess lifted her shoulders slightly. 'No, dear, I think you
had better take the bus.'

There was a firmness, honey-sweet, about the voice that was not
intended to disguise the pill.

At Court the Princess was considered exquisite—a Largillière . . .
but her mother, the Queen, had never doubted her to be a Minx.

'We have never heard of the painter,' the Maids of Honour
would say, curtseying, and opening very wide their eyes: but the
Mistress of the Robes, who was considered intellectual (she had

written several volumes white-washing famous Sinners, and an extravaganza to be performed that evening in the Princess's honour), had more than once declared that the Princess possessed all the delicacy of expression, and radiancy of colouring, only to be found in the later manner of a Minx.

'I know; I like his pictures; they are so exquisitely unreal,' the Queen usually agreed. 'I admire the fantastic grandeur of his backgrounds, his looped-back portières, and towering storm-clouds . . . so sweet!' She was the first cynical Queen to reign just there for many hundreds of years; indeed, she may have been the very first, for her predecessor could only be judged from her postures in a masquerade, embroidered in certain medieval tapestries, representing the extreme exclusiveness of Semiramis, Queen of Babylon and her own particular set. The Queen in consequence was often misunderstood; many people considered her to be extremely foolish. 'But intellect,' they said, 'was seldom found under a yellow fringe.'

The Princess was seventeen—except on those days when she went to play at Mah-Jong in the Casino. On these occasions she would powder her hair in front, put on diamond earrings, and say she was twenty-two. 'Such fascinating insolence!' The amiable beauties who frequented the place adored her.

People either admired the Princess very much, or they didn't admire her at all. Like a Virgin in a missal her figure lacked consequence—sex.

'My tall-tall schoolboy,' her mother would usually call her in her correspondence with neighbouring Queens.

Realising to the full the drawbacks of an extreme finesse, the Princess's choice of gowns was nearly always indiscreet; but happily reckless toilettes suited her.

To-day, the wicked thing wore masses of lace with twists of riband termed 'Inspirations' and no particular sleeves; her slender arms like the stem of flowers fainting away to the pointed finger-tips that seemed to evaporate and lose themselves in æther.

Evidently she was not at all plain; she looked like some radiant marionette.

The Baroness was a thin weary person, with the air of a passée Madonna. She had that faint consumptive colouring that connoisseurs so admire, and nervous mystical hands that might have belonged to an El Greco Saint. Her nose, ever so little to one side, suggested ruse, a capacity of deception. In her day it was said that she had provoked great passions, and it was known that she possessed love-letters in three different languages which she kept on her dressing-table in a silver box. In a woman whose appeal had been so gloriously universal, graciously unhampered by politics, her charm was naturally elusive. But probably her secret lay simply in her untidiness; she had made it a study. Untidiness, with her, had become a fine art. A loose strand of hair . . . the helpless angle of a hat; and, to add emphasis, there were always quantities of tiny paste buttons in absurd places on her frocks that cried aloud to be fastened, giving her an air of irresponsibility which the very young Courtiers seemed to find quite fascinating.

Super-sensitive, exquisitely impressionable, it was part of her temperament to fall under a new influence every quarter of an hour. She could draw all the beauty from a face, and for the space of a Rainbow make it her very own. Often the fugitive marvels of the Sunset would linger with her in an afterglow entirely personal, and some of her lunar effects were extremely fine. Unfortunately, she was equally sensitive to ugliness, and she had made many enemies among plain people through an almost telegraphic abruptness, excessively wounding, and it had been often remarked that, after chatting with the King, or dining with the Prime Minister, her beauty invariably waned.

'She is so splendidly feminine,' the Courtiers would say. 'What fastidious joie de vivre!' 'She is a Cobra,' thought her maid, who understood her to perfection.

She had put on that morning, in honour of the Princess's birthday, a cloth costume, in a new and mysterious art-shade, embroidered capriciously with sprays of Oleander-flower in brightest pink. A sly short train, much ruched, coiled serpent-like about her Louis XV heels.

Seated on the edge of a threadbare music-stool, she appeared now to delicate advantage; her indeterminate profile, fugitive against the insinuating masterpieces upon the walls. Mechanically, with a heavy black fan, she stirred up the air. From the piano, surrounded by Iris, an idol in a professional pose, considered her with a look of golden indulgence; in life, only a diplomatist could look so much, and mean so little.

The Princess raised her eyes sleepily to an oval portrait of an ancestress, known to history as 'Queen Beryl the Bad.' The Queen, with a star in her hair, clad in a French dinner-gown, was leading, by a chain of frail Convolvulus, a prancing war-horse. The portrait was by Nattier.

'It is two o'clock,' remarked the Princess. 'All the town is at siesta; it is an hour more secret than midnight,' and she slightly shivered.

'You forget the Queen, dear,' sighed the Baroness. (The Baroness was privileged to call the Princess 'dear' whenever she chose.) 'She went out motoring only an hour ago. It would be *so* awkward if I should meet her!'

'Mamma is too wrapped up in herself,' returned the Princess, 'to be really dangerous, besides, you could open your sunshade when you see her coming.'

The Queen had a passion for motoring. She would motor for hours and hours with her crown on; it was quite impossible to mistake her ... she was the delight of all those foreigners, and especially Americans, who came to her Capital to study Art.

'To tell the truth, darling,' began the Baroness, 'I have a severe headache; I noticed it this morning when I got up; I fancy, before evening, we may expect a storm.' And throwing down her fan, and removing some rings, she commenced a melancholy fugue.

'A storm!' mocked the Princess, lighting a cigarette and heightening a trifle the blind (to sit in a strong light was against all her principles), 'alas! there will be nothing so interesting; but if you *must* play, dear, couldn't you manage to be a little less sinister.' And she added mysteriously: 'You may play that to me, if you like, after *he* is dead.'

Outside, under the Palace windows, the sun shone down on the meek boughs of the lime trees that waved about a green pool where a Dolphin bubbled heedlessly and warmed the strangely shaped beds and borders, strictly floral, which, woven through the grass, suggested patterns on an Oriental shawl. Here and there where the foliage dipped, you could see the blue-washed Wellen Range, hill over hill, along whose veins flashed the splendid automobiles. Overhead the sky was so pale that it appeared to have been powdered all over with poudre-de-riz. The scent of Lime flower wafted through the open windows, filled the long corridor-room where the Princess sat, surrounded by faded royal furniture, and mingled pleasantly with Tea Cigarettes from China, which it was her pleasure to inhale.

What an elegant view! What deceptive expanse! Who could have guessed that behind the swaying curtain of the trees, stood the curly wrought-iron gates, with prowling Sentinels in gay plumed hats, and sun-fired swords; while beyond, the white town, with its countless Spires and gold domed Opera House, its Theatres and spacious streets, its Cafés, from whence, sometimes, on still nights, you might hear the sound of violins, trailing capriciously, like a riband, upon the wind. Who could have guessed at such gaieties, looking down from the Palace windows at the quiet Dolphin, as it bubbled heedlessly, amid its reeds and lilies; staring foolishly up at the Royal window-panes, indifferent to the swirling dance of Butterflies, or to the occasional leaping of a Carp. What an elegant view! What deceptive expanse! So much, contained in so little, suggested a landscape painted delicately upon a porcelain cup or saucer, or upon the silken panel of a fan.

'This cigarette . . . my nerves . . . the hour,' faltered the Baroness with uncourageous fingers pressing her heart.

'Nonsense, Teresa!' the Princess said, quite sharply, 'I had not thought you such a coward. See! here is the letter; take it, there is no danger. It is as obscure as the second part of "Faust"; indeed it is a good deal more so.'

The envelope, lilac, narcissi-scented, was addressed to:

St. John Pellegrin,
Villa Montoni.

'Villa Montoni!' The Baroness rolled up her eyes in resignation to the barocco ceiling, tucking as she did so the envelope into a fold of her gown. 'Of course,' she said, 'darling, you must do just as you please, I never advise anybody, but if I were you, I certainly should not dream. . .'

'The Villa is two miles beyond the town,' continued the Princess, nestling her head deep into an incredibly shaped cushion, 'but the tram passes the gate. It is surrounded by a low wall which is plastered all over with inartistic announcements in the worst possible taste. There are pomegranate-trees on either side of the door; such stately ones; he also keeps pets. Lovely plump pigeons that take his letters; and run little errands of mercy for him through the sky. Only last night I noticed two of his birds fly over the Palace with a pair of stockings. His garden they say is full of tropical flowers even in the winter, and it is rumoured that strawberries ripen there all the year. Do not forget to take a basket with you nor, in your emotion, to admire the fruit.'

The Baroness fixed enormous eyes on a Crucifixion by a pupil of Félicien Rops—a pale woman seen stretched upon a Cross in a silver tea gown, with a pink Rose in her powdered hair; the pearls about her throat bound her faster to the cross, and splendid lace draped her bleeding hands and feet. At the foot of the Cross lay a fan, a letter, and a handkerchief, tortured into a knot till it looked like a white flower; behind her spread the sky grey and ashen, gashed with flame, whilst rain-drops fell slowly, slowly, as though scattered through fingers ... For a moment the Baroness seemed lost in thought, imagining the martyred woman's lover.

'He must have been very young to be so cruel,' she told herself. 'I should not be surprised if he were quite a boy. *She* might be any age; a powdered wig is so deceptive. What secretive eyes! I do not like her look!—I am wondering,' she said at length, after a pause just long enough for an Angel to pass, flying slowly, 'what I shall wear. I hope the man is shy and not at all forward; think! dear, if he should molest me! I cannot forget poor Gilda's fate in that very faded Opera we saw last night.'

'Hush!' the Princess exclaimed, drawing in voluptuously a long slow breath—a breathing exercise known familiarly to herself and the Baroness as 'a soul flutter.' 'He is a Saint, you forget that! And if that were not sufficient, his mother, I believe, was an *Italian Countess.*'

The Baroness looked less suspicious, it was a comfort to think that the creature had not begun life as an acrobat or with a concertina, she began to feel almost excited.

'Should I,' she enquired, 'wear the little gown I wore at poor Eulalia's funeral, or dare I wear a heavenly thing—Scenes from the Decameron painted upon chiffon, and an enormous sombrero with silver strings?'

'I do not mind what you wear,' replied the Princess, 'but oh, Teresa, whatever you put on, do not return without his promise that he will come to my party to-night. How I should care to be a new Salomé! And why pray should I not be? Indeed the position in which Fate has placed me, to hers, exactly corresponds. Let us review the situation, and you will see that all I need is to develop my style.'

The Princess loved colouring her retrospect. She would do it indeed aloud by the hour, ignoring altogether that the patient Baroness had nearly always been present at the original occurrence.

'When dear Papa died at Montreux seven years ago,' she began, —'he died holding a bottle of absinthe,—Mamma erected a mundane-looking angel to his memory and accepted his brother's, the King's invitation to weep away the remainder of her life at Court. How pretty Mamma looked as a widow, with her thin rouged cheeks, and her black feather boa! and how dreadfully she worried over her pink pearl earrings with permanent clasps that would not take off. In doing so she mercifully quite forgot poor, poor Papa. What an unenjoyable journey that was; Mamma prostrate with presentiments. Each time the basket of Arums and Orchids (eked out with Gypsophila) that the Station Master at Montreux had presented her with, rolled to the ground, Mamma screamed, and said she was certain that she would be assassinated within the year, which naturally reminded her of the fatal gala performance given to poor Aunt Caroline—*requiescat in pace*.

"Did you never hear of the Duchess of Malfi," my Governess asked mysteriously, in tones that robbed us of our circulation, and without any more warning began to recite: "What would it pleasure me to have my throat cut with diamonds? or to be smothered with Cassia? or to be shot to death with pearls?" Personally, I was almost paralysed by the idea of a long drive on our arrival through crowded thoroughfares in an open landau, and being stared at, in an ugly crêpe hat trimmed with crêpe buttercups, my hair in a knot like a Chinaman's tail. It was a beautiful June evening, the blues and reds of the sunset combining in an exquisite mauve. The sky was then decidedly mauve, which, as night came on, turned to subdued violet. We passed through fields of white clover, bounded by canals of purple water, and hurried by windmills that turned and turned in the dusk like revolving Crucifixes. The white oxen returning from the fields were washed in violet light, and the pink powder on the end of my governess's nose turned violet too. As we drew near the Capital, Mamma became terribly unstrung, and began to laugh immoderately.

'The King met us at the Railway station with his Crown on, and at the sight of him, poor Mamma lost all control of herself and laughed till she wept: "He looks like a piece off a chess-board!" she gasped. "How totally sweet!"

'The train was late, and the King already annoyed.

"Quiet your mother for the love of God, and a box of chocolates, little cat-thing," he whispered to me, and turning to Mamma he said: "The public has been standing since daybreak to catch a glimpse of you, while many people have gone to the expense of taking balconies to watch the Procession pass. They will certainly feel disappointed if you do not look stricken, shed public tears, and behave in a general way as though you are very much upset.'

"Can you not see that I am?" cried Mamma ... "But, really ... an ovation? How delightful! No; of course I shan't disappoint them. Is my hat on straight? How does my veil droop?" And all the way back to the Palace she flung herself about amid a storm of sympathetic applause. She went down to dinner that night in a lovely black cashmere, sewn with sparkling Lilies, an *uraeus* diadem of diamonds outstretched wingwise in her hair. I was standing at the window as she entered watching the sentinels pace slowly to and fro; the night was so still that I could hear them swear. I think the moon looked like a piece of Majolica-Ware as it hung above the trees, and I remember the fire-flies darting in the garden below were a new experience for me; you see, dear Papa would never stay anywhere unless there was a Casino; he loved the dazzling life of Casino Towns, and would find poetry in the cool shuttered rooms, whilst outside the sun poured louis on the sea. In the afternoons Mamma and I would go and drink tea in lace frocks in the public salons, and listen to the Viennese band, and even in those days, she held a gay little court. She would often scold me for looking too old and said that no nice girl ever looked more than eight; and she would never take me about with her unless I carried a silly woolly lamb until I was past fourteen.

'It was foolish of me, but I confess I felt just a wee bit lonely that first evening as I stood at the window recalling it all. How gloomy the Palace seemed! I missed the glamour, the feeling of possible adventure that you get at twilight in a large hotel, for not unfrequently (as Mamma knows!) I would manage to find at least *one* small boy to pay me his respectful love. It was the hour when we were accustomed to music, when it was my habit to hide behind a curtain or a tub of flowers and watch the people as they wandered down to dine. One could hear often the waves of the sea, like some great chagrin, unclasping themselves without, and when a door opened catch a glimpse of it, stretched like a strip of tight silk, across a window as a blind.

'How gloomy the Palace seemed! How still! You know, dear, when we first came, they put me all alone up a horrid tower; the same apartments poor Queen Beryl had before they dragged her out to die.

"How foolish of us to come and live in such a Barrack," I exclaimed bitterly, for in spite of Mamma always grumbling about dinner in Restaurants—"Snatching Meals" she used to say,—I knew she really loved it, when suddenly, behind me, I heard the movement of her gown.

'Directly I saw her smart frock I knew why we had come. She read my thoughts, and pressing a finger to her lips, and pointing to heaven with her fan, she hurried from the room without a word.

'Six months later the Crown jewels had been all re-set and Mamma was Queen. She was married quite quietly in a corner of the Ballroom . . . before an Empire table, without a bridesmaid, without a flower. Just the Lord's Prayer in B and a chapter that sounded as though it were taken from Jean Cocteau or Maurice Rostand mumbled over their heads! Of course I have never believed it to be properly binding. And I am sure that he will think so too. And when I asked Mamma why she wasn't married in State at the Cathedral, she told me not to ask questions, but that it was on account of the roof.

"That is what I call perfect candour!" I said, "but you cannot deceive me; you wished to escape the Procession."

'Whereupon she displayed vexation and screamed: "Impudent!" in French, and predicted that one day I should make a *mésalliance*, and that is why I have gone and engaged myself to that horrid-horrid Crown Prince, but of course nothing, nothing, nothing shall ever make me marry him.'

The Baroness smiled, twisting her mouth sideways like La Taxeira in an invalid rôle . . . the monotony of these daily outbursts! 'The resemblance *is* remarkable,' she agreed, tactfully, 'your mother, like Herodias, *did* marry her brother-in-law, but somehow I had never thought of them together before. I don't know why!'

'Ah! but you will,' the Princess declared, 'after *he* has denounced her. Moreover there is something in Mamma's appearance that

35

recalls Herodias, especially in the afternoon when she wears her furs. You will never know how bored I am, Teresa, nor how I long for a little excitement, and now that there seems to be a faint chance of having some, it would be cruel of you to spoil any trifling amusement the dear Devil sends my way. Charming Man! He neglects our Court ever since Fräulein Anna Schweidler giggled so disrespectfully at a Black Mass. She attributes her laugh to nervousness, but you know what Anna is! She should never have gone.'

'After all,' said the Baroness soothingly, 'it is delicious to lie still. Excitement, particularly when it is diabolic, always tells. Not that life is really so very dull . . .'

'Naturally,' replied the Princess rather spitefully, 'as one grows old, one likes to be quiet,' and seating herself, with the unreasonable look of an Iphigenia, upon a brittle, tattered and ornate throne, she began to hum a certain air by Strauss.

These cast-off Thrones were one of the features of the Palace. Whenever a throne began to look worn-out or the silk got 'shrill,' it was hurried off to a spare bedroom in the visitors' wing and used as a chair. Whenever a Grand Duchess came to stay, she was sure to be late for dinner, leaning back on her seat in a regal pose before her dressing-table, her combs arranged 'en couronne,' forgetful of time, the Queen's temper and the cold soup—dreaming, dreaming. . . . The Princess also shared the same weakness. Leaning back now, her index finger pressed against her cheek, she felt like a married woman, as she studied herself attentively in a mirror. 'Alas!' she presently exclaimed. 'Why are present-day sins so conventional—so anaemic? A mild, spectacled priest could trample them out with a large pair of boots. I prefer a Prophet who will insult me! It is then a pleasure to retaliate. I have always suspected mine to be a Salomesque temperament. Naturally, it would be treason to speak with candour of the King, but he would make a superb Herod. He has the same suspicious walk and the incurable habit of prodding curtains and expecting an ambush round every corner. So silly of him! and a constant disappointment as well. He is an old darling, and spoils me, but really his character is frightfully weak. What ever will History say? But he never troubles about that, and he will certainly be made into an Opera after he is dead, and I daresay I shall be dragged into it, too. And now, since Fate has placed us—how events repeat themselves—King, Queen, Princess—improbable people like ourselves, with a Prophet at our very gate, and the whole

Court languishing for something new, it would be ungrateful not to take advantage of the opportunity and make hay whilst. . .'

'Hay!' The Baroness looked sceptical. 'I am afraid you deceive yourself, dearest,' she said, 'about this man, he may not be all you suppose; I have made enquiries, and even quite foolish people think him foolish . . . And then remember, darling, that you *really are* affianced to the young man from Bucharest—The Crown Prince. If it should get into the papers . . . this adventurousness may end in some dreadful scandal. I cannot forget an old maxim of my mother's! "You cannot," she used to say, "be too careful until after you are dead." Remember how jealous your fiancé looked in his yellow uniform at the Review only the other day; I am sure he could be terrible when roused.'

'Do not speak of him, I hate him, and will never marry him, I would rather die,' declared the Princess, dramatically.

She had been brought up on this speech, so to say, from her earliest years. It came in most of the Classical plays at children's matinées, and sometimes the heroine would speak it from her closet whither she had been confined in disgrace, or sometimes through the keyhole of her dungeon, to an invisible person without, usually her mother, trembling lest her outraged lord should surprise her in forbidden intercourse. If the play happened to be an opera this scene gave splendid scope for a long duet.

'I would rather die,' repeated the Princess.

'Think of yourself alone with him, on a desert island,' the Baroness said, drearily, after a sententious pause.

'Ah! Don't, Teresa, how can you be so cruel.'

'Cruel! My dear, it is the only way to think about a man. Consider, what would a young girl of parts, fresh from her convent, do under similar circumstances. The first day on the Island she would (if she were at all distinguished) refuse to speak to him, and withdraw to some Oasis with a book. The second day, she would find herself watching him out of the corner of her eyes; still, she would not admit it. And when he tried to tell her that the desert winds had given her an infinitely better complexion than her married sister— who went out far more than was good for her—she would force a tired, distrustful smile and go away to write letters for the afternoon-tide. But the third evening, after she had finished dessert, and there were a few stars shining, she would probably feel a nervous flutter, a positive emotion at his approach. And why? Simply because he would be the *only man* . . . and the uglier he was, the more terrible the fascination! And fascination is really far more binding than love. I contend the Desert Island is the proper way of looking at every wealthy man; especially if he be a Prince. All you need, dear, is just the will to shut your eyes to everybody else and tell yourself there is only *one* man, and that you have been lucky enough to secure him all-to-yourself, and then, with a little coaxing, Love is bound to come . . .' And the Baroness, looking wise, took out her powder-ball and used it with an elegance that could not have been exceeded even in the flowery days of the Petit Trianon.

'Dear Teresa,' exclaimed the Princess. 'You are so wonderful! But you have had so many experiences. I feel I could never really love anyone unless he was pale, but pale . . . with violet rippling hair, and had eyes, blue, but blue, as skies in May, and could boast a big-big, Oh,' she abstrusely broke-off,' 'have you ever loved anyone just like that, Teresa?'

'Several,' answered the Baroness, recklessly. And as the Princess expressed a wish to know more, she was obliged to rise to her feet. These sentimental talks she usually learned to repent.

From the mantelpiece came a sudden 'whirr' from an unconcerned Sèvres shepherdess; a coquettish silence, followed by the florid chiming of a clock.

'Very well, dear,' she said, 'if you really wish me, and I absolutely must, I will be ready in an hour. Nothing discreditable, I hope, may come of it. I shall put on all my amulets; it would be difficult to harm me when I'm wearing my Winged Victories—and long earrings are being worn just now.'

'Bless you,' the Princess purred transported; and she added, sweetly: 'Remember the jewelled girdle that shall be yours if you set your nets with tact.'

The Baroness blinked as she withdrew. 'Nets! Alas! I have none, but the jewelled girdle . . . you spoil me, dear.'

'Poor Teresa,' reflected the Princess, sounding idly a harp with jade stops and rose-red strings, 'she is a dreadful hypocrite, but I am very fond of her all the same.'

When the Baroness returned an hour later she was all feathers and nerves. She was looking angelic in a gown three shades of grey, with silver embroideries and improvised knots and falling tassels, partly concealing the 'heavenly aquarelles,' which was perhaps just as well. Quantities of tiny painted buttons ran hither and thither, quite aimlessly, going nowhere, all undone. Like yellow butterflies the Winged Victories hovered from her ears, and a string of filmy stones, obviously spells, peeped furtively, like watchful eyes, waiting to operate at a moment's warning, in ways best known to themselves. She was looking pale, and unusually weary, under an enormous structure of feathers and orchids, weighed down on one side in artistic collapse. In her delicate Greco hands, cased in stiff white kid, she carried the frailest of wicker baskets and tucked under her arm an elaborate sunshade of geranium pink.

'How nice you look!' the Princess said, as she kissed her on either cheek. 'And, oh! What a smart hat. And how sensible of you to wear grey—it is always *safe*. Black, if it is well-made looks so fast. And now, don't forget, dearest, to bring me back in your basket an enormous water-melon, the kind they have in Palestine; and, if it were possible, I should so love a light green Rose. Up to now I have seen them only in hats, when they look like cabbages, or in paper sometimes at bazaars.'

The Baroness seemed too overcome, with the perils of her mission, to articulate; a soul-flutter was her only comment. She received her mistress's embrace with a nervous calm, never lifting her eyes higher than the royal shoe. When at length she had actually disappeared the Princess gave vent to her relief and performed a riotous valse. Up and down the room she whirled, past the famous Master-pieces (hung by a gardener, one might have said, skilled in Herbaceous lore) past Madonnas and frowning Queens, and Favourites shivering on sofas in airiest batistes and 'Awkward Surprises,' and 'Storms at Sea,' and enormous paintings of bouquets of flowers, all satiny, on varnished boards, over which the gold dust poured. Presently, exhausted by her transports, she collected her hairpins and seated herself on a conventional Empire stool, with a conventional book, from a conventional Aunt, with conventional love, for a conventional birthday. The conventional book was 'The Home Life of the Queen of Sheba.'

'So far,' she told herself, 'it isn't a bit amusing to be a débutante. I believe I almost wish I were back in the Schoolroom again with old Miss Littleclaud, although I called her such an odious woman at the time.'

But what was that heavy persistent perfume that lingered amorously on the air, enfeebling the moral senses, undoing good resolutions—supposing any to have been made? The Princess sniffed.

Lime Flower? No. Acacia Blossom? Hardly. Tuber Rose? Perhaps. She rose suddenly to her knees, her mind full of a horrible suspicion. Could it be what the Queen most abhorred, what the King most objected to; what she herself most particularly disliked because she was forbidden to employ? Could it possibly be . . . *scent*?

Yes, it was, indeed, and of a particularly execrable kind—'Vieille Cocotte' she pronounced it. A woman with such a pocket handkerchief could have no prestige.

Pacing to and fro, she pondered the matter. Here was some mystery brewing; some intrigue to unveil.

Teresa? It was unthinkable. 'Knowing, as she knows,' she murmured, 'Mamma's horror of all essence she would never dare. . . .'

But there was no mistaking it; the room was drenched with the pungent smell. It *was* Vieille Cocotte! You could get it at the Casino in small green bottles tied up with gay-gay ribands, at an unusually beautiful Kiosque with 'Madam Carmen' painted across the door. Madam Carmen, a remarkable looking person, sat there all day long, in a paste necklace and earrings, smiling always at her own amusing thoughts, her face so powdered that it seemed to be smothered in flour. But how had the Baroness managed to procure the guilty stuff? And now, through a spiral of inconsequences, the Princess recollected. Last night at the Theatre the Baroness had begged leave during an entr'acte. . . .

'I love,' she had said, 'wandering on the terrace at night. The City looks really queenly with its white houses, glittering water, and arching trees!' and with the smiled permission she had gone.

'Artistic creature!' the King had said, quite loudly, as she left the box.

On her return, her manner had seemed strange—she must have procured it then.

The Princess crossed to the windows and flung them open. How irritating the Dolphin looked below as it stared up at her, bubbling needlessly, its mouth wide open like a person who had committed a fault. Beneath the shadow of the trees men were erecting a vast Marquee, and bringing forth refreshments for the ball. Trays laden with sparkling sweetmeats and champagne bottles, reclined imprudently in the sun (how irresponsible those impassive bottles would make folk when the stars came out!) and a forest of empty glasses packed tight together like flowers grown for sale, suggested Dutch gardens glowing with all the colours of rarest Tulips. Scattered over the lawn were majestic dishes, and piles of plates, more gorgeous even than the flower beds they were set among. 'Let the crockery be representative!' the Queen had said, 'as the Ambassadors will be here.' And she had also added: 'Do not turn on the fountains before you perceive the first guest.'

Oh! What a variety of porcelain there was! Looking down upon it it was like assisting at a fancy dress ball. There was gala Dresden (which showed the imperfections of their own national faïence) and Crown Derby and Biscuit, and Urbino, and Delft. There were things Japanese, and things Chinese, and whole regiments of mysterious pots and pans which, unless turned over and their marks examined, refused to be known. There were festoons of flags, too, to correspond, and hampers of roses (white Miss Missingham and dark red Mrs. Steeple) all the way from the King's country seat in the Wellan Range, whose Ogreish towers and sinister Minarets, just visible, served to scare the disobedient children in the capital beneath.

Fluttering out upon the balcony, the Princess became absorbed. There was something exquisitely Eastern about all these bustling servants that suggested slaves. 'I am afraid the sunset will be a failure,' she remarked presently regarding anxiously the sky. And as she spoke a bird skimmed past her with a satin quilt.

O Charity! She watched it, spellbound, soar above the trees. In some cosy cottage garden *his* gift would fall like a bolt from the blue. Only the Flemish Primitives could do justice to the surprise.

How the elder Brueghel would have delighted in the scene. . . . The fence, the rows of stiff hollyhocks, the invalid at her casement, the children rolling in the dust, the father busy digging, the immodest courtship in the back-yard, and the sudden appearance of the struggling bird over the low thatched roof.

What an admirable Primitive it would have made! What scope for amazement! for flinging up of hands! And to think of it all wasted. She sighed, and turned her eyes to heaven at the loss.

Although the Princess had been expensively brought up, she could not prevent herself from uttering a scream. Gazing down upon her from the floor above, her Grandmother (an old lady almost past everything but making mischief) stared straight into her eyes. In her great mob cap she looked like some dreadful gargoyle. Could it be an evil omen? How often the King had said at the noonday-meal, that his mother had been the Ruin of the Country....

'My dear,' the old lady called down in her crotchety voice, 'did you notice that irregular looking bird? I'm afraid it means *we are about to have a War.*'

With an unamiable reply, the Princess returned to the Corridor-room, but the scent of Vieille Cocotte did not soothe her; it dawdled ridiculously, lingering on as its name implied, and it was some time before it could make up its mind to depart and escape by the window.

Ablaze with suspicions, there was to follow for her a period of considerable suspense.

Of course! She might have guessed it. The Baroness would try and dazzle the Saint. In imagination already she saw her seated on the Saint's knee, a perfervid arm about the prophet's neck. It was not to be endured. Deliberately, she cast her glance about for something to destroy. Marie Leszczinska, in her robes of Fleur-de-lys, stared at her from over the fireplace in cold dismay.

Stiffening her fingers, and dilating the pupils of her eyes, the Princess examined herself carefully in a mirror. What fatal beauty! What a wonderful expression! But, of course! Only dull relations or stupid courtiers could fail to notice the very close resemblance....

*   *   *

Ten minutes later the whole palace was in an uproar. The Princess had commanded a warm bath à la reine de Saba, and before she had it, she wished to *speak with the King.*

❧ *II* ❧

IN WHICH THE DEVIL HIMSELF INTERVENES

IN the Platz under the Linden trees stood the white omnibus, less white than the Princess had supposed. Catching her skirts closely about her the Baroness seated herself in the furthest corner, shielding herself from the public gaze behind the pages of the Court Gazette.

How the bees hummed among the Linden flowers, and how dull it was hiding behind the Court Gazette! After a few moments the

Baroness made a window in her newspaper—a long Gothic one—
and peered out.

The Platz seemed almost deserted. There was an afternoon atmosphere about everything difficult to define. Even the equestrian
statue of the King, with his fierce expression and brandished sword,
seemed to unbend a little to the influence of the hour, while his
bronze charger, so imposing by moonlight, looked almost gentle
as it pranced into the blue-pale air.

In the shadow of the Linden trees a few children played, in subdued manner, the National game—Whipping Tops—and near by a
Vendor of Images appeared asleep before his tray.

Birds flew past and butterflies loitered, and in their formal
borders, the town flowers languished in stately rows. How close it
was! Small risk to get down and sit on the bench outside . . . but to
manœuvre one's hat twice through that narrow door . . . No!
better sit still and essay to be amused as best one might. How stout
the conductor was! . . . really there was lots to see.

Beneath the great *West* door of the Cathedral (where she had
ripped her gown at the Coronation of the first Queen), a lady, all in
raptures and a guide book, stood admiring the façade, whilst a
gardener, too young to be allowed a can, busy watching her, seemed
to be watering his feet, and almost along the very rails of the tram
from behind his remarkable structures, an artist, in a shady hat, sat
painting the Image-seller.

The Baroness would have given a crystal rosary to know whether
the Image-seller was only posing or actually asleep. 'I shall never
know,' she reflected mournfully, and just as she thought she
detected an eyelid tremor faintly, the tram cruelly carried her away.

In the Flower Market she descended.

It was a delightful spot, with its lazy fountain designed from an
early drawing of Verrocchio, round which, under monster parasols,
the market-women clustered before their fragrant wares, idly dreaming, perhaps, of deceiving their husbands, or posing to Foreign
artists at a shilling an hour. But in Medieval times, so history said,
this delightful spot had been used for other ends than flowers.

'My little dressmaker lives quite close,' the Baroness murmured,
' and I do so want a tinsel rose . . . and a few yards of spangled net.
I hear she has some transcendently foppish gauzes just now, and the
smartest plumes. But, alas! I suppose I haven't time.' She could not

resist, however, purchasing a beautiful bouquet of 'Cottage' lilies—a suitable offering she considered for the Saint.

The charming caress of her frock, the cottage-lilies, and the strange afternoon atmosphere, gave her a vague and soothing sensation wholly delightful. Contrary to what might have been supposed, the Baroness did not 'glide'; far from it, she walked as if the heel of one shoe were a trifle higher than the other; not that this was so; it was merely style. Catching sight of herself in a shop-window, she reminded herself of an Angel of the Annunciation—a Carlo Dolci.

But there was no time to indulge in roadside-sensations, and putting up her lorgnon she peered about her for the blue tram.

There it was; and *what* a conspicuous blue. 'Really, my dear,' she said to herself, 'it is too crude.' The Mistress of the Robes had a dinner-gown in exactly the same shade.

'There are already two people inside; it is crowded,' she murmured, as she got in.

In a corner of the tram sat a Priest, reading a Book of Hours—not her own dear, charming, delightful Monsignor Parr, but such a *hard*-looking man, who looked as if he might be a little relentless towards his Penitents; and although she rustled her gown a great deal, and changed her position twice, he *never* looked up from his book. The other occupant was an impressionable-looking youth in a blue smock, picturesquely patched in conventional places. (. . .) He had profusions of golden hair, and eyes as hard as flints.

'He is charming,' thought the Baroness. 'I think him all too sweet.' And lowering her eyes at his insistent stare, she commenced a long voyage on the silver laces that adorned her gown.

She was at Thebes, and preparing to start for Tunis, when he suddenly interrupted her innocent pastime and asked her the name of the flowers she was wearing in her hat.

To talk *chiffons* to such a person was out of the question, so she answered a trifle stiffly: 'I beg your pardon, did you ask for the time? It is not yet half-past four.' Can he be mad, she wondered, looking at him with interest. Psychologically, an imbecile was not to be despised.

'He has pretty eyes,' she told herself, 'and looks wonderfully robust (. . .) but I cannot afford to risk anything just now in returning glances with a lunatic,' and with an annihilating look at the golden-haired youth, she left the interior of the tram and climbed on top.

How delightful it was on top!

The branches of the chestnut trees drooped above her listlessly, wrapt in summer haze. Here and there the town doves, looking like plump white pearls, threaded through the heavy foliage, cooed capriciously as they plumed themselves, dropping down feathers and platitudes on the passers-by.

They were inadequately supported by the State, and would certainly have died long before, but for the charitable assistance of foreign tourists. They lived to be photographed; posing for picture-postcards, and 'souvenirs,' hovering, and doing their best, over the heads, or at the feet, of anybody who would throw them sufficient corn—As indifferent to the Nationality, as to the quality of the hand that threw; more callous even than the pert *meretrix* who flaunted beneath them when evening fell. They were not particular, but they were acutely bored with their professions, and took it in turns, when, for a livelihood, a bourgeois destiny obliged them to disport themselves and show the lining to their wings. Sweet things! They had never heard of Venice.

To be up among the cream and pink chestnut flower, like a bird, had seemed to the Baroness a foolish dream. Yet suddenly, unexpectedly, it had happened.

The warm wind, passing across the Flower Market, brought with it, in rhythmic waves, the scent of narcissi and violets, and above, great fleecy clouds hung low in the sky as though they were going to fall. Opening her parasol, the Baroness looked about her vaguely expecting to see the Queen.

The Queen always insisted while motoring on mending her punctures herself, and it was no uncommon sight to see her sitting with her crown on in the dust. Her reasons for doing so were complex; probably she found genuine amusement in making herself hot and piggy; but it is not unlikely that the more Philistine motive of wishing to edify her subjects was the real cause. She had been called a great many things, but nobody had ever said she was proud; this was her pride. . . .

But the Queen was nowhere in sight. Indeed, nobody of any note seemed to be about. A few pious persons threaded their way towards the Cathedral on emotions bent. A girls'-school passed with its escort of Nuns, and fantastic Demons flying above them

45

(invisible) criss-cross through the air; (these summer days! how irksome they were . . . even quite fervent prayers would fall swooning to earth, too tired to rise) whilst at the corner of 'Looking Glass Street,' over the new Beauty Shop, where, unembarrassed, you might buy other things as well, they were hammering the Royal Arms up over the door.

'Surely these things ought to be done at night,' the Baroness mentally reflected, as she watched the swaying emblem, when suddenly the refined sound of horses' hoofs, and a superb rumble of heavy wheels, broke the apathy of the hour (such a magnificent noise, dear reader, could only be produced at great expense, and indicated an elegant establishment, a number of servants, flattering friends, and family skeleton, none of which, of course, just then, one was privileged to see) and the Mistress of the Robes clattered by in her painted coach. She was off to attend a last rehearsal of her play and was evidently so late that the most she could hope for would be to arrive in time to witness all her characters lying dead in each other's arms.

Fortunately for the Baroness, it was impossible for the great woman to see sideways without turning her head, for her profile was entirely hidden behind a huge Leghorn hat, perched completely on one side, smothered with Jericho roses and Autumn leaves. Severely perpendicular, she carried in her dimpled hands an imprudently small parasol in the loveliest shade of sunset silk. Two black pages in powdered periwigs, and liveries couleur de rose, displayed their vocation by clinging with amazing agility to the swaying splashboard, ducking and bobbing in the most ingenious fashion so as to avoid being wound up in the meshes of her voluminous veil that streamed behind.

As she swept past the Baroness she suddenly let fall her sunshade and stretched out an impulsive arm with considerable coquetry, the palm of her hand turned inwards, as if—any student of the theatre would recognise the movement—to ward off some disgraceful proposition made by an indelicate person, invisible to the eyes, yet mentally no doubt an abomination of sin. She was evidently fussing over a stage gesture for her forthcoming play.

'I call her impossible,' reflected the Baroness. 'I daren't think what are her thoughts; but I always knew she had a criminal mind.'

The tram, after several false starts on account of absurd people who *would* come late, gesticulating wildly as they waddled up with enormous baskets of flowers, or vegetables, at last got under way, and the Baroness endured as best she might the jolting motion, and the uninventive naïvetés of a playful breeze. 'This is life,' she told herself at each fresh jolt. 'This is life.'

But the opportunity that came with solitude was not to be missed, and producing her faithful vanity-bag she administered to her complexion. 'He may be very handsome,' she told herself, 'or he may be only a frump; but in any case there is no harm in looking my best.'

The young man who came and sold her a sordid-looking ticket, seemed a dear, and almost made amends for the trouble it was to find her purse. He had brown, delicate hands (the backs amply strewn with fine blonde hair) and a reckless look about his eyes.

'Quite too graceful,' she described him.

'Cripples' Gate?' he asked her, with a charming smile.

'No! No! The Barrier.' And whilst he clipped her ticket *with a bell*, she could not help asking him a thousand questions. Who lived in that great-big-ugly house? (It was her own.) Was the Queen really liked? And didn't it get just a wee bit monotonous always being on a tram? And why was the tram painted blue? ? ? Surely heliotrope or palest amber would attract more passengers? What! colour made no difference! No? How strange! She felt quite sorry when the time came for her to alight and say farewell to the conductor.

To her dismay, the Princess had looked at an old time-table, and it was necessary to change her tram and take a pink. It was too tiresome; she would have some time to wait.

But, oh! How lovely it was to be in the Country again! !

'I would love to sit down on some shady bank,' she thought, 'and put daisies in my hair, and throw away this heavy-heavy hat, and drown it in a lilied-pool; and people passing by would think some poor unhappy woman was wearing it underneath."

Now, at that moment, the Devil, who had felt wounded, slighted, pained, at the Princess's complaints that afternoon, was hurrying incognito towards the Palace disguised as a sleek black Crow. Recognising the Baroness, with some faint surprise, he circled above her, deeply meditating. Here was a woman who interested him. He had long kept his eye upon her. He admired her languid style, her way; more than once, moreover, he had been vastly entertained by some of her conversations with Monsignor Parr.... He would have been pleased to have nominated her an extra Perpetual-lady of the Bedchamber (with the Eternal precedence of the Marchioness), at his own Infernal Court.

'Where she is,' he murmured, 'she is wasted.' But, as he was well aware, she belonged to that slithery type, which, alas! too often slipped through his fingers by the merest riband. How many delightful creatures had eluded him at the last moment by a sudden whisk! Here was an opportunity not to be missed. Wheeling several times above her, he plucked a feather from his breast and willed . . .

Ambling up and down beneath, the Baroness was growing impatient for the pink tram. Such unpunctuality was a scandal! It was monstrous! It was a perfect bore!

Already the sun had dipped below the hills, and the sky was streaked with crimson like a china rose. Just where the sun had dipped there lingered a mild yellow glow, producing that curious *Sunday effect* only to be found in Turner's water-colours; it made her think immediately of *Chepstowe*.

The sudden sound of an automobile behind her made her turn— if it should be the Queen!

To be found wandering at shut of day on the high-roads would require considerable explanation, and as she herself (to use her own expression) had more than once declared: 'I always feel that nobody ever believes me as soon as I start to explain.' She looked about her. How much lively gossip might yet be avoided if only by chance she could hide. Such an adventure, too, would delight the Princess; with a little embellishment it would make the most piquant story. 'The growing dusk, the rising moon, and there, my dear, was I . . .'

Already the Baroness indeed had begun to exaggerate, She had seen half a dozen cars go by, and had some interesting information to give about the occupants of each . . . 'and little did they guess, the wicked things! that at that very moment there, my dear, was I . . .'

But there was not a second to lose. Happily, there was not far to go; over there behind those Silver Fir she would find safety; an ambush there was even nearer, but—'No! No! "she shuddered", *not* that dreadful ditch.'

To pick up her things and rush blindly towards the advancing automobile was due partly to that femininity for which she was admired. 'One is so handicapped,' she panted, as she flew, 'with the wind snatching at one's hat. How exhilarating it is to feel oneself pursued! but oh! oughtn't I to be going the *other* way?'

It was impossible to doubt. To rush past the automobile would give the impression of a person steeped in guilt. Her chief chance was to stand still and look dazed and feign to be the sole-survivor of an accident. Promptly she struck a pose. Putting up her lorgnon, with a wretched look of broken bones, she began to stare very hard into a hedge.

'Theresa!' Through a thin veil of dust the bright countenance of a young man whom her husband had often sworn to kill, smiled at her in delighted surprise.

Although the Baron had often sworn vengeance, he was constantly offering his victim cigars and lending him his box at the Opera. It was difficult to know what quite were his intentions.

'Thérèse!'

'Max!' she gasped. 'Oh: You sweet thing! No, I'm not hurt—only very much shaken ...'

He led her with solicitude to the car. 'Poor dearest!' he said, 'she is dazed.'

His manner was so charming, she felt it would be almost rude to resist. Besides it was delicious to give way to him, and nothing could be more to her taste than an escapade when frankly egotistical. But the letter ... duty ... it was demoralising.

'My dear,' she said, realising that she was being carried off all willingly-unwillingly like a creature in a Rape. 'I have a tiresome errand; a note to leave; I cannot go with you another yard,' and as she spoke there was a flash of diamonds, and the Queen whirled by in a cloud of dust. Like a shot Cameo she passed—all glimmering stones and pale mimosa hair, and wide dilated eyes.

'Never mind,' he exclaimed: 'Give me your note; the chauffeur can take it, and we will steal an hour ... one little hour.'

She demurred, consulted a pet Saint (a neglected long-shelved creature, one of her own discoveries: St. Aurora Vauvilliers). 'Oh! dear St. Aurora, watch over me in this imprudence, and keep me from all calumny, Amen.' And, since she was about it, she added a few urgent words for a certain tardy frock: 'delivered by to-night, dear Saint,' *etc*. Then, acquiescing feebly, she rearranged her hat. 'I suppose your man could leave it just as well as I?' she murmured. 'And certainly the country, this evening, looks irresistible.'

There arose a fleeting dialogue as to time and place.

'I don't mind,' she said. 'But we must be careful to avoid the Romantic Valley; half the Court have gone there to a picnic. And we must be careful to avoid the road to Fort Little; it is just the hour when the Officers are likely to be hastening towards the Capital—gracious knows for what! And we must be careful to avoid . . . but, really, I don't mind; everywhere in my present mood is equally delicious.'

He proposed Sand Dunes, Lanes; those towards Vermillionville? The Sea Shore . . .

She became suddenly wildly romantic.

'There is an old haunted Inn on the Wellan road,' she began, 'with a parlour hung in flapping tapestries, and a painting by Vermeer in the front hall, and an entrancing garden beyond, full of Hollyhocks and Fruit blossom, and a running stream . . . We might go there for an hour; the Fête, at the Palace, does not begin till quite late to suit the moon. Nobody well can miss me. From the number of invitations sent out the Banquet is certain to be a terrible crush; last year it was dreadful!'

They pulled up before a signpost, looking like a very thin Pierrot, as it pointed a white arm backwards, towards the Capital. The wind had fallen and the Roses on the hedges hung motionless on the thick blue air, as though posing for a study in Still-life for a Flower painter who had failed to come. Along the fertile Wellans, the fields lay like spread silks. In pale stripes ran the Cuckoo flower; in wavy lines coiled the Daisies; here and there, weary with sweetness, stretched patches of ruffled Clover, and once or twice, something more richly brittle—a speckled Orchid. Above, wrapped in evening haze, rose the loftier slopes, like rubbed-out charcoal where they touched the sky.

While he gave directions to the man, she meditated how she should fill her empty basket with fruit for the Princess. Doubtless, one would find Cherries, and Melons, at the Inn. 'Little fool, she will never know,' she thought. 'But the Green Rose—alas!' and she tittered.

Observing the chauffeur for the first time, she was pleased with his unintelligent expression; he had the obtuse look of a village Barber in a Comic Opera; she could see him dancing in a pair of sabots between two windmills, whilst the Prima Donna chatted archly at a lighted window, staring vivaciously into the boxes.

'Here,' she murmured, proffering him a whole sheaf of dainty, pansy-coloured notes, 'this is for your pains. Be careful not lose the letter, nor to soil the envelope. There is no answer, but remember to say that the Baroness Rudlieb would be glad if the Saint would kindly telephone *to her* whether he is able to accept ... I think that is all. Do not bandy words with other servants, but when you have done your duty go and watch the moonrise from a hill.'

They set off at a reckless speed. 'Indecent haste, disgraceful empressement,' thought the chauffeur—whose face was his fortune —and looked about him for the nearest Tavern where he could get a drink. A sleek black Crow followed the Car for a while cawing 'lost—lost.'

How helpless the Baroness looked in the hurrying twilight! An unfinished masterpiece, suggesting delicious possibilities. Her plumed hat seemed sliding from her head, and her heavy coil of chestnut hair looked so loosely wound that anybody uninitiated in the Craft-mysteries of an experienced maid, would have said that it *must* fall as inevitably as a shower of Autumn leaves. O Magical Untidiness! O never-failing Charm! 'She looks like a Nun come into a sudden fortune,' he thought, 'did one ever see such a frock!' and the little empty basket in her tired white hands went straight to his heart. She leaned against his sleeve with the lightness of a moth. How wonderful the trees were, as they swept past them in the failing light, and the blue chain of hills reaching endlessly beyond, how peaceful!

'I can so well understand,' she mused, 'why the Saints flew to the hills. Some day I shall do the same, as St. Aurora did.'

And her thoughts returned to the adventurous history of Aurora de Vauvilliers. Aurora, who till the age of thirty-nine had been a celebrated courtesan when (by celestial design) an overturned carriage, and some injured limbs, had put a finish to her irregular mode of life. Aurora who had vowed (should she ever recover) to mend her ways, and make an expiatory pilgrimage as far as Palestine (with commissions to gather Roses at places of interest for the good Nuns of Forbonnais, and to fill bottles with water from well-known founts for the dear Monks at Istres). Aurora who had contemplated setting up a shop ... Aurora who had set sail one languid summer evening with just a faithful maid and a Book of Hours ... Aurora who, before she had been at sea a week, was captured by Pirates, and after enduring untold horrors made her escape on a loose board disguised as a man. Aurora who was tossed about for many days on a pitiless sea. Aurora who was cast at length upon a desolate shore, where she led for five years the Simple Life. Aurora who returned at length to her own dear France, with wonderful silver hair, more captivating than she had ever been before. Aurora who became the rage, attended fashionable assemblies, and who, whilst on a round of visits to the Châteaux in Touraine, had expired quite beautifully, one All Hallows Eve, at the Castle of Loches.

How often had the Baroness pondered the life of this adorable being (as set forth in the sympathetic biography of Monsignor Parr) and found extreme profit thereby in her own self-scrutinies.

'After all,' she murmured to herself, excusingly, '*we* may have an accident, too. He is driving very badly. . . .'

She leaned back, her face almost grey, the sins and sorrows of all the world gathered for an instant in her tired green eyes.

The warm air swept past them; the scent of flowers rose up from the fields. A startled cow grazing knee-deep in the long blue grass—like a creature in a Noah's Ark—looked up with a martyred glance expecting milk-pails, effrontery. Above hung a solitary star. What a lonely existence! The Crow followed yet, murmuring 'lost—lost.' Its effect was Japanese against the clear pistachio of the sky. On the outskirts of a wood a white goat fled into a thicket. 'Stop, stop,' she cried, 'I think I see Pan,' and round a bend suddenly appeared the Haunted Inn, with Pink Hollyhocks sleeping before the door. How dark it was inside. The Vermeer (a chaste Suzanne) was in eclipse. He ordered Champagne in the tapestry parlour, and they wandered out into the garden while the landlord groped for the wine.

She had exaggerated the beauties of the garden. It was full of Yews, strange lichened Statues, brown Owls . . . there was an air of witchcraft about the place; from the little stream floated up a thin mist.

She began to feel anxious; after risking so much, she was almost afraid that he was going to be dull. The twilight she felt sure laid too great stress on the *Madonna* side of her, he needed encouragement; she gave an artificial shudder, and took his arm. 'Everything seems so creepy,' she remarked, 'so immaterial in this light—black upon rose!'

They sauntered away down a meditative-looking path that twisted and twirled like a by-way in a legend.

How dim it was under the trees, and how still. It was exceptionally sweet of Nature to allow her to trouble the silence sola, with the silken murmuring of her gown.

The Statues in the dusk looked terribly emotional as they clung to each other in immortal love. How fervent they seemed. Quite candidly, it was absurd to be alive and yet more cold than they. How dark it was! The ground sank away in profoundest purple under their feet; profoundest purple with a phosphorescent flicker, here and there; fortunately atmosphere left no stain . . . or what would Zellie say—without actually *leaning* she felt she might exact from him a further slight measure of support. It was a most disappointing path. Instead of hurrying to a comfortable summer-house (as she had certainly supposed) it went only a short way before it began to repent. In a moment they were back again before the Inn. A light twinkled from the parlour window. All around the Statues showed unflagging in the dusk. . . .

'Have we made the most of our opportunities?' she asked herself doubtfully as they wandered in.

Inside, all was candle-light and gloom. The parlour at any other time, and with anybody else, would have been disenchantment, for where was any tapestry? But the simmering wine, and the mellow light were things to be grateful for.

After all one did not expect to enjoy these adventures much at the *time*; it was only afterwards, from a sofa, in recollection, to the sound of a piano that they began to seem delightful; and just now, the landlord, she was afraid, was likely to be a thorn. He lingered insufferably.

Seating herself at the table, she drummed her fingers with impatience.

'What a pity,' she murmured desperately, 'that Goya never painted Fans.'

*   *   *

Far off, in the Palace, the Princess, who had obtained the King's word, that she might ask, during dessert, for anything she pleased, had risen from her bath, and was dancing a Tarantella before the Mirror, in just a bracelet and a rope of pearls.

ᛘ *III* ᛘ

THE Mistress of the Robes had lost her temper. The première danseuse from the Opera House, who was to have taken part in her al fresco extravaganza, refused to dance in the dew. 'I cannot do so,' was all the reason she gave.

'Obstinate creature,' the great lady stormed. 'Amateur!' she taunted her, but all in vain.

Nothing could have been more inconvenient. Failure, fantastic and Dureresque, stared at her and chilled her to the marrow. There could be no Ballet ... the Ballet could not take place.

Oh! everyone knew how fond the King was of a little dancing, especially after a Banquet ... to think that an abandoned wretch had it in her power to refuse to wobble her clumsy legs. To postpone the play at the eleventh hour and fifty-ninth minute, whilst a double throne, upholstered in gamboge, stood gaping before the sweetest of stages, was impossible.

Heaven alone could solve the embarrassment, and rolling up her eyes, she prayed with all the fervour of an horticulturer, for rain, or sudden hurricane. 'A steady downpour, dear Christ,' she implored, 'a Second Deluge!'

But unfortunately the weather was adorable; above, the night was a marvel of serenity, the air clearer than beaten silver; around her stood the trees motionless, like massive candelabra tipped with stars.

The Overture had already commenced. The Mistress of the Robes was in despair. Whenever she closed her eyes, she could see a skeleton dancing in the moonlight, clapping grave-bones, and cutting capers too harrowing to describe; it was no wonder, for she was thoroughly unstrung. It was remarked that in her agitation she had misquoted Lucretius during supper, and dropped her fan into the soup.

'All this strain will take her an extra month at Carlsbad,' a voice was heard to lament. 'I shall not get my holiday this year.'

Standing now midway on the flight of grassy stairs (the King was so tired of marble!) that led to the gardens, chatting with dangerous politeness to the French Ambassador, as she drew on her long white gloves, the Mistress of the Robes was the cynosure of all eyes.

'You mix them with olives and a little cognac,' she was telling him. 'Naturally it is a speciality, but it is quite my favourite dish.'

Flushed to the colour of a Malmaison, she was looking conspicuous in silver tissue and diamonds, her long train spread, shimmering, over the steps behind, with the exquisite restraint of a waterfall in a poem. Above, from the fortifications of a lofty tiara, an Ostrich feather fluttered in her hair, as from a Citadel. What radiancy! The moths caught themselves in her crown, and beat their soft wings against the crystals on her gown; with a scream she felt their cold caress upon her throat and breast.

'Flatterer,' she breathed, trying not to hiss. 'Personal magnetism indeed! Charms exposed? Help me, or I shall faint'; and the Ambassador bending gallantly over her, removed them one by one.

'He is taking liberties with her, before all the world,' murmured those who did not understand.

Clearly she was a Rubens, with her ample figure, florid colouring, and faintly pencilled moustache, a Rubens on the verge of becoming a Jordæns from a too ardent admiration of French cooking, and a preference for sleep. To all suggestions, kindly meant or otherwise, she would reply, indiscriminately: 'It is too sweet of you, still! I wrote the play, and you must admit that I know best.' And to the well-meaning entreaties of the extremely épanouie wife of a Court official 'to do a little Moorish dance,' she answered evasively, 'Thanks, dear, I dare say I could flop about myself.'

'How waspish!' murmured those who were standing near enough to hear.

She was not popular like the late Mistress—a polite woman— who, when one had said that she was too fond of gay colours, and was always insinuating the untruest things about everyone, was an angelic creature who would exclaim: 'thank you *so* much,' even for a pin.

On the terrace above the Rose Garden where the stage was set, stood a tumult of Servants, Operatic in liveries that included all the colours that may be found in a child's paint-box between white and black. How self-conscious they looked! fidgeting, whispering. Like a Chorus waiting outside some Cathedral for the Prima Donna; their poor hands aching for somebody at whom to point. Above them towered the Palace, looking like yards and yards of purple satin, stitched upon blue; a puff of air, one felt, would fill the whole thing out like a sail: the lack of perspective and needless quantities of Stars suggested an ambitious drop scene. Behind the servants, gleamed the startled eyes of the Princess's horses; their behaviour during the fireworks had caused censure and surprise. 'They will go into disgrace for a fortnight,' said the lugubrious Lord Chamberlain, which meant they might run about exactly as they pleased. 'There,' he added, addressing the horses in rebukeful tones, 'should be your model,' and he waved a soft white hand, and some wonderful cameo rings. Through the trees, a bronze horse leapt lightly into the night, bearing a dainty Queen arrayed in wind-blown draperies and stone-rosettes. She carried a fan, and an enormous key. The key was so fantastic, that people had come from all parts of the world to look at it, obliging the King to throw open his gardens on Thursdays from two to four. After a pedantic controversy, it was agreed that the key opened nothing more particular than the doors of her heart.

There were Roses in the Rose Garden, which was remarkable where all was paradox, and from every Rose bush hung a Chinese lantern; between these, the Maids of Honour tripped about, looking like Easter Lilies, they were enjoying themselves immensely, and giggled a great deal; but nobody smiled at the absurd antics of the King's Dwarf. A young boy, with a tired white face, wandered about among the Terminal figures and the Rose trees, playing in the remotest fashion upon a violin. No voice could reach the silver region where he *began*, and he would trail deliciously away until he evaporated imperceptibly into silence.

In the chiaroscuro of a shrubbery, a Society Crystal gazer, swathed in many shades of violet, was predicting misfortunes by the light of the Stars.

The summit of her dreams was to look 'uncanny'; this (for she succeeded perfectly) was her solitary secret.

'People won't come to one in a peach-charmeuse trimmed with Point,' she had often lamented. 'One requires Moonstones, Veils, and a ghoulish cut to one's skirt . . . it is so tiresome not to be able to wear out one's professional clothes in the street.'

She wore, this evening, an Amethyst chain, a high Aigret in her hair, and concealed her face behind a Mauve Satin Mask. The Maids of Honour shivered, and quarrelled about their turns: 'She is not very definite, and muddles her dates,' was the verdict of those who had already been.

Under the quivering detail of the Limes, the Stone Dolphin bubbled heedlessly, it looked in the moon-mist like a large white Rose. The night was so warm that conversation languished, many people chose to nibble ethereally-tinted sweets, and sip Elixir Vitæ, and say nothing at all, waiting until the extravaganza should begin, but a select group of Matrons, Mothers to Maids of Honour, or Pages in Waiting, drew themselves aside to gossip with Monsignori, or whispered scandals about the Statues, dispassionately, behind their fans.

In spite of the Princess's wish that there should be 'no old people much,' the Queen had replied: 'My dear they *have* to come!'

Here and there, from a tree, hung a caged Nightingale—professional birds, with trained voices, and a grand manner of rounding off their notes with a marvellous shake. The wild Nightingales, unable to express their sentiments with such perfect finish, were silent from respect.

A loud crash of porcelain, and a smothered scream from behind the brocaded curtain, was a signal that the extravaganza was soon to begin.

The Mistress of the Robes closing her eyes saw flowers of alabaster and flame, and felt the earth as it revolved beneath her. Quite perceptibly she slipped a yard.

The King and Queen sat on a dais apart, the King with glazed eyes, the Queen amiably austere (so far everything naturally had to be a little stiff) watching a continuous stream of Mothers and débutantes trip forth by twos from a lighted Marquee, as from an Ark. The débutantes dipped a careless knee, while their mothers bowed down and enjoyed a delicious grovel. The Queen felt herself growing more beautiful every minute, it consoled her to be worshipped. Life with the King and his tiresome old mother was not all Violets, and when the ceremony was over she was feeling quite her best.

The Princess reclined gracefully at the Royal feet, looking incomparable in a Louis Quinze skirt, with the most interesting paniers, a corsage of a later period, and a cluster of wired gardenias (worn like a married woman), festooned with pearls. It was one of her Infanta Nights. One longed to make her stand up to see what she really had on. Her hair, like the tower of Pisa, leaned all one way, caught together by a gemmed stiletto, smouldering fire. Now and then she would hold up a rose-red fan, painted by Conder, slantwise across the night: it pleased her to watch whole planets gleam between the fragile sticks; she had a capacity for dreams.

The Queen's expression was distinctly worried.

'I keep wondering, Theodore,' she kept saying to the King, 'whether there will be enough for them all to eat! I had not meant the refreshments to be served until *after* the play, and it looks as though everything would be consumed *before*. It is mortifying to be obliged to think constantly of expense, and to have to bargain, but now that the Army is being increased, and the uniforms have been changed from lemon and silver to periwinkle and violet, one must do what one can. But never forget this, dear, I will walk with you to the last under the same parasol.'

The King appeared unaffected by this fond outburst; if anything he seemed a trifle vexed.

'To-morrow,' the Queen went on, 'we will begin our economies. The Court shall have *Rabbits* for dinner. So good for them.'

'Nonsense!' growled the King, who looked like a tired Viking under an elaborate arrangement of jewels. 'It is bourgeois to think seriously about one's food; but if you meditate economy, let it not be in the *Cuisine*, Madam, for we forbid it,' and with a look of fixed horror he stared up into the hollow of the moon, murmuring 'Rabbit' in a deranged voice, as if it were a plot, or the name of a poison.

Although the Queen was a Colonel in several dashing regiments, she looked quite fearful. She wept and laughed with an equal facility and found an equal enjoyment in doing either; if she had any choice she preferred to weep; it was more refined.

'I am sure I do my best,' she murmured, leaning back carefully on her throne, on account of her puffed hair, 'and I am tired of doing it; tired, *tired*. It is impossible to scramble along on our small income. There are *not* enough taxes, although of course one cannot say so. My poor friend, you will never really be popular and you may just as well get what you can. If not, I dare say, one day, I shall be forced to pawn my pearls!' And dilating the pupils of her eyes she gazed wanly up at the tall-tall windows of the Palace, so large in winter, so tiresome in times of war.

The Queen loved to provoke a scene in public; it was a means to an end.

She desired to create a permanent pose, to be symbolical.

She wished History to speak of her sadly as 'ill-used,' 'ill-starred,' 'the wretched Queen of a Tyrant.' She sought the warm tears of posterity, at the risk of being considered unsympathetic during her own life; to kindle enthusiasm, to leave a glamour, these were her ambitions; if it were not for the pain of it, she would have liked to have been executed.

'Mon Dieu! Que de cancans!' murmured the Princess, lowering her fan and fidgeting with the bouquet at her heart: 'Tell me, Papa, are the wires turning my Gardenias brown?'

'No, little-cat-thing,' replied the King, bending amicably over her.

'I am afraid *there is something* . . .' thought the Queen and she said quite icily: 'How often have I told you that I object to the child being called by any other name than Mary. *Another word,* and I will make the girl a Nun.'

'A Carmelite, dear, perhaps?' enquired the Princess unruffled, 'or a Poor Clare. Tell me, for I should like to know.'

The King threw a look of complete indifference at the Queen, and the conversation came to a close. The King had a glass eye, and it was difficult to say which was which.

'He has only one eye, and I never know which is looking at me,' the Queen would sometimes complain. 'His stare is quite a Medusa's one; it is most uncomfortable. Ah! If that were the least of my grievances I might bear with it. But, unfortunately,' . . . and she would float away into a delicate psychology of her wrongs.

In Court circles men were mostly 'sorry for her' and thought her 'far too good' for the King.

'He is getting senile,' they would say. 'What a pity she is so constant. She lives for History—it will have nothing to say.'

The Queen was considered very lovely, but the relations of the King's first wife, and especially the Dowagers of the ancient régime, never ceased whispering about the individual style of her dress.

Rumour had it that she slept in a hat garnished with Roses, Plumes and Pearls. 'Her style seems a little too "emancipated," ' certain ladies would purr, 'and smacks too much of "*those women*" or at best "a Prima Donna." Ah! Poor King Theo!' And they would sigh.

To-night, the Queen was looking like a column in a white velvet dinner gown, with a delicate spiral of silver leaves that wound up her dress, towards her hair. Except for her hands, Providence had been unusually kind. Her hands, large like a gladiator's, were her most sensitive point; it was useless to bury them in rings, or squeeze them in gloves; she was obliged to carry a perpetual muff. Her feet ... but one could only suppose. There was a donjon, rumour had it, prepared for the Bootmaker who should reveal her size.

But the play had already begun, and by degrees all chatter ceased.

Everybody modelled their expression from the Queen. The expression was not too difficult to imitate, for it was elementary ... a languid interest.

Under the Rose Trees the critics sat upon the ground. They had been presented with diamond scarf pins by the Mistress of the Robes as soon as they arrived, so they knew just what they had to say. 'In her play,' wrote one, 'four persons faint at the same moment. With what economy of means does she bring this about?—A simple telegram.'

Notwithstanding the lateness of the hour, the Baroness had not yet appeared. When the Princess turned her head towards the Palace, she could see her Teresa's window ablaze with light, and now and then caught a glimpse of her passing shadow across the blind.

'She is probably putting on an over-emphasis of rouge,' she thought, 'and painting circles under her eyes. Poor dear! She is always so extravagant on gala nights.'

From the attic leaned her grandmother, looking, as earlier in the day, exactly like a gargoyle. A lighted candle beneath her chin threw the light uppermost à la Gerard Dow. Overcome with delight at the Fireworks she had waved her handkerchief at the Roman Candles, Flower Pots and Catherine Wheels. Beside her stood a Parrot, and a faithful maid. The Parrot's reflections, limited to 'Rubbish!' and 'Oh, how sweet!' could be heard plainly in the garden below, and the actors, perplexed, thought the critics must be composing their notices aloud.

On the stage, a pretty actress, in a pearl satin nightgown, and a bandeau of orange blossom, was dictating to herself an impassioned telegram. She was a huge success. Unquestionably she had learned her art from frescoes and tapestries; her poses were those of the figures on the best embroideries.

'Superb,' everyone agreed. 'Prodigious.' And the King was pleased to say: 'She is a lovely Nymph.'

An immoderate laugh made the whole Court turn. The Mistress of the Robes was enjoying her own play.

'It is so witty,' she cried. 'What satire! And, oh, do look at the Paramour behind the curtain.' And, leaning against a young attaché, she collapsed into his arms a heap of quivering diamonds.

Under the trees, wrapped in nature's indigo, an orchestra, composed entirely of Zithers, commenced a serenade, and just then the Baroness appeared gliding between the Chinese lanterns that adorned the grass. It was a conspicuous entry, for, at a sudden silence from the parrot, everybody had turned on their chairs. The women, with their long necks curved, looked like spiteful swans. The Baroness seeing the whole Court turn towards her, imagined herself irremediably lost.

She had foreseen an ordeal; and was prepared to meet it. To be a taper in a wind showed inexperience, a shallow nature. Praise to St. Aurora, she had greater strength than that. She knew the power of being aloof, the effect of night-shade on sugar for the soul. A puff of air could not quench the electric force, the wrap of dreams, that flowed within. On returning to the Palace she had sprayed her face with spirits of Roses and read a chapter from *The Way of Perfection* of Theresa of Jesus. Under such circumstances, St. Aurora she found was too exciting, but the sublime Theresa never failed to restore her to complete peace.

After reading her words of blue-pale fire, she felt as though the waves of the sea had swept over her, obliterating any traces of emotion, reinforcing her, leaving her cheeks waxen as delicate shells.

Only for an instant, startled at the flash of stones as long necks curved enquiringly towards her, did her soul misbehave itself, and the stronger feelings flit to the surface, above the elaborate look-of-peace she had laid on as with a trowel. For a moment she lost her mask, and her guilt tripped forth, a ripple, and was gone, She felt suddenly a little masculine, that she was wearing his lips, his eyes, his way. . . .

It was irritating. To compose herself she thought of Carpaccio's St. Ursula in Venice, a woman without a trace of expression, with the veiled, crêpe-de-chine-look of a Sphinx. 'Whoever said the Sphinx *had* a secret?' she wondered; and at this wonderful thought she was lifted into realms of abstract speculation, and was saved.

She wore a gown neither blue nor green, like the egg-shell of a thrush, and a wreath of flat silver Vine leaves fastened across her hair. In her gracile fingers, long like a bunch of ribands, she carried a bouquet of full white tulips, and slung from her waist an enormous fan of sea-gulls' wings. She walked very slowly, with the artful unconsciousness of a Prima Donna wandering in a forest before a crowded house, examined, spied upon, through countless malicious glasses.

'Can she be in love *again*?' whispered the Lord Chamberlain. 'Impossible!' cried the Court Physician, 'only yesterday she declared that she was tired of love.' 'Tired of love?' The Court Matrons positively sniffed. 'She cares only about Statues now,' said a Maid of Honour. 'She has married herself to a Marble Pan in the middle of a wood; she told me so last night.'

'She is frightfully made up,' murmured the King's favourite.

'Her eyes are full of belladonna,' remarked the Queen's favourite.

'She is growing old,' whispered others.

'In the blue twilight of a garden all is permissible," smiled the Queen.

The Princess moved aside. She had not seen her Teresa to speak to, since her return, though she had sent her a thousand messages.

The Baroness had crept into the Palace by a side door, used as a rule by the Royal Family as an emergency exit in times of Revolution. She had gone straight to her room, rung for her maid, and locked herself in.

At that moment, it chanced that the Princess with her hair half-finished was seated at her bedroom window amusing herself by frightening the passing Bats with a rope of pearls. It was a pastime she never wearied of.

She was arrayed in a Chinese wrapper, embroidered with Junks riding on a sea of flowers, whose foam turning to Plum-blossom, blew right in at the open doors of the Pagodas, that peeped provokingly through wisps of cloud. The wrapper was a birthday gift, from a Sailor cousin; a boy with the glamour of foreign sea-ports in his eyes.

The night was full of Bats and purple Butterflies, they trembled by in a shadowy stream.

She had startled not a few, when the stealthy frou-frou of silken petticoats beneath her window aroused her girlish curiosity.

'Some Marguerite perhaps hurrying to her doom? The wear and tear to one's heart must be simply tremendous.' She leaned suspiciously out; curiosity with her was strongly hereditary . . .

The trees in the garden had turned to blackened-emerald; the air seemed smeared with bloom.

The footsteps wavered, ceased. Someone with a marvellous shadow (what bravura in the angle of the hat!) was concealing herself behind a statue.

'Poor darling,' murmured the Princess with a seraphic smile. 'Trust me! I shall not move.' And folding her hands, she warbled plaintively some words by a Court Poet.

> 'I am disgusted with Love,
> I find it exceedingly disappointing.
> Mine is a nature that craves for more
>   elusive things,
> Banal passions fail to stir me.
> I am disgusted with Love.'

It was not really a popular air with vulgar persons, but it was a privilege to hear her sing; judging from the timbre of her voice one might have supposed her to be a child of six. She paused, and picking up the rare first edition of Unlikely Conversations, flung it out into the night.

There was a movement.

'Teresa?' the Princess called, surprised.

The Baroness, for it was she, wavered, looked up, gave a stage-start and vanished, apparently into a sentry-box.

A quarter of an hour later came a gentle knock at the Princess's door.

'Sesame!' called the Princess, who was mixing something in a jar, but it was only a maid with a note in the Baroness's flower-like hand—all loops and tumbling blossoms and faint stems bearing unformed buds. Tearing the envelope, she read: 'Patience, dear, he is capricious, but *I believe* that he will come.'

A basket of unripe fruit accompanied the note.

'How is the Baroness,' enquired the Princess; 'I hope not tired?'

'She has asked for ice, and hot water,' the maid had answered, 'and seems very much upset.' And this was the beginning of the thousand messages.

'Am I dreadfully late?' murmured the Baroness, as she hurried up. 'I did all I could to be in time when I heard there was a creature practising Black Art in the shrubberies. Are her methods really those of the witch of Endor, as they say they are. And, oh, ma chère *where* is she?' and opening wide green eyes, and pretending to be a little out of breath, she fearfully scanned the shadows.

The Princess was accustomed to intricate temperaments, everyone at Court had one; ignoring the Baroness's remarks she said in calm but firm tones: 'Do not be tiresome' Teresa, but come and tell me all about him.'

At such direct mode of speech, the Baroness visibly winced.

'Come and tell me all about him.' Exactly what one house-maid would say to another after an evening out. After all, it was scarcely astonishing; the Princess's lineage was perplexingly mixed.

'My dear,' the Baroness murmured in her most mundane voice. 'What more is there to tell? My maid wore holes in her shoes, running to and fro on our enigmatical correspondence. As I said, I cannot possibly describe him, but I daresay he would like look a Donatello in his bath.'

The Princess evinced interest.

'We must stir him up to say dreadful things about Mamma,' she cooed. 'How like Herodias she looks to-night! And how step-Papa's glass eye shines! I am sure something terrible is going to happen.'

'Not necessarily,' murmured the Baroness, uneasily, catching at the heart-shaped, sensitive leaves of a Headache Bush. She felt that she was standing in a Quagmire, and to recover her equilibrium she *imagined* Pico de la Mirandola saying his prayers. She put him in a window with a distant view of Florence seen through the casement; the Tower of the Signoria, the dome of the Cathedral, and just the tip of Santa Maria Novella all visible through the stems of the tall white lilies that grew upon the sill. From the way she lit the picture the hour would be Tierce.

'Modern landscapes are all sky,' she murmured, taking an invisible step backwards to admire her work, 'but here you really see the town.'

'Would you say that his eyes were stern?' queried the Princess in a Baa-lamb voice that would have rejoiced the Queen. Like an invalid, she could harp cleverly upon a single string.

'Il est bon, il est doux,' the Baroness gurgled, seeking refuge in Massenet. 'But see,' she murmured, 'His Majesty is observing us'; and she added in louder tones, to be heard by all: 'Tell me, dear, do you think the Nightingale's song is really sad?'

On the stage, standing at her dressing-table, draped like an altar with rows of flickering candles, rocking gently in a drowsy breeze that seemed to spring straight from the heart of a bouquet of Sweet-briar, the pretty actress, suddenly become the most vivacious of widows, was recklessly throwing objects into a satin-lined box, preparing to leave for Venice there and then with the Paramour.

This was the climax in the play, and the Baroness's interlude on the subject of Nightingales was greeted with a loud 'Sh!' and an 'à la porte' from an insignificant page.

Under the Rose-trees, wearing their diamond scarf pins, the critics wrote indefatigably.

'Nature, by some mechanical process,' wrote one, 'can produce dew, but it takes Art to produce tears.'

The Princess, drawing her Teresa's arm through hers, ambled lightly away, hoping, by a few naive questions, to arrive at the truth. But the Baroness was not to be duped.

They seated themselves on a low seat overlooking the Japanese garden.

It was quite a charming garden.

None of the flowers grew in the earth, but lived in celibacy in China pots, packed closely together, and divided symmetrically by formal paths made out of porcelain tiles, in patterns of rose and gold. In the centre a miniature lake, dotted with sacred lilies, lapped the smooth shores of an Island, presided over by the Goddess Kwannon, in a tight frock, and still tighter shoes.

She stood ever before the doors of a shuttered temple, whose gates were far too small to let her in, looking down into the unemotional waters of the lake with narrow sidelong eyes; the temple was pleasantly situated at the foot of an artificial mountain capped with snow.

Through the garden, lanterns glimmered, strangely huge, and fountains spurted, strangely high, and all the flowers in their lonely bowls, stiffly in bloom, smelled strangely sweet.

A City of Flowers, and Lights!

Whole troops of phantom eerie things, fluttered noiseless down the porcelain streets.

'What voluptuous flowers!' murmured the Baroness with a wave of her fan, 'and what a languid night; not since I was a girl have I seen a more audacious moon.'

But the Princess was anxiously watching the airy movements of a

Page, as he tripped towards her, bearing a note on a cushion, at an angle considerably higher than his head.

He wore the dainty trappings of a page in a Benozzo Gozzoli, and was paid a large wage to look wilful, and to stand about corridors and pout. The expression, as was natural, ended in a sulky frown.

'Thanks, little dear,' said the Princess taking the note. And whilst the child lingered for the answer, the Baroness, with great sweetness of manner, retied his sash.

'Not bad news, I hope?' she enquired carelessly as she finished her bow.

'It is from the Bravados, dear. They have thrown me over; it seems that they have trouble of their own. I engaged them just to stroll about and to be at what they term, professionally, "a beck and call."'

The Baroness took the Princess's hand in her own, and sympathetically pressed it.

'You *poor* thing! *How* awkward! But I daresay they were only dreadful Meissonier-people after all.'

At that moment, a barbaric blast of trumpets from the King's Heralds, sustained as long as their breath would permit, announced the arrival of a belated guest.

For a timid person such an entry must have been extremely trying.

The Baroness pressed a hand to her heart. 'Mercy!' she exclaimed, 'it must be he! Hold me, dearest, I believe I'm going to faint.'

'Don't, dear, until something has actually happened,' the Princess implored, darting forward to meet her guest.

'Very well,' the Baroness called after her, 'I will put it off until after supper, and choose a more frequented spot'; and wreathing her arms about a sundial, resting in the moonlight, she unburdened herself in an intimate soliloquy, raising the dial to the dignity of a Mute Confidante in a 'periwig' play.

'It would look so strange,' she meditated, opening a fan that was a sensuous delight, 'to faint and then to eat a substantial supper; and after my long day I can no longer disguise it from myself—I feel slowly sinking. How I reproach myself for this afternoon! . . . little puss! She will dredge the truth from her poppy-haired Saint, before it were possible to exclaim "Spinoza!" Great Booby! . . . probably not even a picturesque man, or he would live in a cave on a sun-parched plateau and swathe savage skins as Iokanaan about his loins. He would have no chance against the machinations of the Princess. She would flatter; she would bleat; she would make him feel that it was he that held the crook—until he began to make use of it, when—becoming suddenly contralto—she would spring.'

Some words from an 'Everywoman's Criminal' fluttered to her mind.

'Spread the threads of your Cobweb with enough sequins, scintillating enticingly like a lamp-lit street. Carefully veil the Monument at the end. Amuse your victim. When you have gone far enough, turn suddenly and thrust!'

Hush! What was that? Voices surely upon the dilettante breeze. . .

'The Baroness was enchanted with your garden; and thank you so much for your heavenly flowers.'

His silly look of amazement, reproduced upon the air, caused the first Autumn leaf to fall.

She shivered. It was merely, of course, that she was overwrought.

'My mind is a bonfire; my feet are brass,' she told herself. 'Only a salamander could feel as I. A little supper. A little champagne,' she mused, 'and I shall feel less enervated. And then, a long, delicious faint in some nice man's arms.'

She smiled, a faint unholy smile, and with a charming sigh wandered slowly away examining the moon's disk through her lorgnon; it looked like a disembodied spirit above the big top-heavy trees.

'Surely,' she murmured as she walked towards it, 'I think I see the violet cassock of Monsignor Parr.'

The Princess, in the meanwhile, had powdered her neck and arms with poudre Rachel and captured her Saint midway on the flight of natural stairs.

She was surprised, and not displeased, to notice that he wore a Gardenia in his buttonhole, and that his hair—a dusky gold—seemed decidedly waved.

'He looks clever,' she thought, as she rushed up to him.

It was an unfortunate meeting-place, for the chaperons, grouped about the steps in tiers, were idling the hours, patiently awaiting the first streaks of dawn.

'Griffins!' murmured the Princess, shuddering her paniers, but never wavered. 'Did you get my message!' she asked sweetly, as he kissed her hand. 'It was delightful of you to come. This is my birthday: isn't it provoking to have to be a débutante?' And, looking into his eyes, she threw him a bewitching glance intended to be demure.

It had been her intention to lead off with a little speech, previously prepared. But somehow (oh, why?) things seldom turn out just as you suppose . . . and the rows of staring chaperons were decidedly disconcerting.

'Where can she have picked him up?' asked a tired dowager. 'Who is he?'

To recollect the speech by message was out of the question, so she continued hurriedly: 'But won't you take me to the buffet; I am sure you must need refreshment, and *I* am longing for an ice. When I knew you were coming I wired for Lampreys; I thought they might tempt you. What is a Lamprey? Well, really, I scarcely know; surely a sort of *Locust*,' she enquired with a searching look. 'But we will go and see.'

The play was over. Everyone was circling about the Mistress of the Robes to congratulate her on her success. She stood simpering depreciatively between two Rose trees, trying to convey—by a sorrowful surface smile—that there were greater depths in her than she allowed the world to see.

'I wrote the play between dinner and prayers,' she was telling everyone; and allowing the smile to fade, looked sadly away to the Palace, as though it were a hospital.

'Your theories on death?' asked Madame Storykoff, the wife of a rising Privy Councillor, catching her mood. (She was on the staff of four newspapers and considered 'dangerous.')

The great woman looked at her.

'I think when wicked people die they become sheep,' she replied airily, and, pivoting slightly, indicated her disapproval by the angle of her bust.

The English Ambassadress, Melissa, Lady Lostwaters, trailed slowly across the scene.

'Can you tell me,' she was enquiring, vaguely, 'has anybody seen him? I am looking everywhere for *Sir Oliver* Scott.'

Nearby the King was bestowing the Order of King Sigismond II on the principal actors, in 'recognition' of their Art.

In her riding habit and a feather boa, contentedly sipping champagne, the very pretty actress stood chatting with extreme animation

to the Prime Minister. 'I do hope the horses won't bolt,' she remarked
a little anxiously, 'or behave badly in any way. I am so suspicious
of quadrupeds ever since the shock I sustained once on tour! It was
when I was playing "La Dame aux Camélias" in the desert. In the
middle of the great scene—you remember where I have the trying
interview with *his father*—I noticed creeping up behind the Audience
an enormous lion. Just fancy! Of course I said nothing; I remained
true to my author.'

'Did it spring?' enquired the Prime Minister.

'Of course it sprang,' answered the actress; 'well, naturally!'

And the great man listened spellbound to her narrative, supporting himself against a tree, his mouth ajar, till his wife observing him,
and fearing a pernicious influence—for she knew his frailness—came
and dragged him away.

Just then, a loud peal of laughter, and clapping of hands from a
Pavilion, came floating across the garden. The King's Favourite, an
intensely plain, rather impudent-looking woman, already, perhaps,
sur le retour, was singing comic songs accompanying herself on a
guitar. She was the type of person who, in a former age, would have
probably ended her career on the scaffold, or by being poisoned; for
nobody liked her.

Among the majestic or dove-like Beauties of the Court, beauty in
time became a weariness, and the Favourite's plainness positively
a distinction—hence a danger. 'Odd,' 'weird,' 'bedraggled,' were
the courtesy-titles usually used to describe her, whilst many spared
their brains in finding descriptive symbols and pronounced her merely 'vulgar.' One could suppose her dangling a ball-slipper over a cliff
and murmuring, 'Shall I?' in a voice irresistibly cajoling. Her
sallow cheeks, alert eyes, and malicious mouth, made a vivid
contrast to the frail vestal type that the Queen admired.

'She is the only distinguished woman at Court,' the King was in
the habit of saying. 'She is so *Spanish.*'

In her gold trailing skirts, the Favourite pirouetted amidst a ring
of bottle-nosed Dowagers who were urging her on to wilder follies,
garnering up the while a stock of conversation to last them over
many a drowsy evening. 'She is calling the Attachés "pets,"' they
murmured, delightedly, fanning themselves at a tremendous pace,
and they thrilled.

The Queen watched the lady from a distance, and presently,
smiling suavely, wandered away into the chiaro-oscuro of the

Shrubbery to enquire of the crystal gazer the date and hour of the Favourite's fall.

Meanwhile, in the Refreshment Tent, the Princess was exploring her Saint. 'How delicious these Lampreys are,' she was saying, making a charming grimace. 'Put some honey with them; aren't they far nicer than Locusts?' And holding out a hand, powder-white: 'Oh, do give me some more Champagne.'

They were drinking Champagne out of Limoges enamel Ewers, decorated by Jean Limousine, and Suzanne Court, with scenes from the lives of Castor and Pollux.

The Champagne was completely spoiled, but there was intoxication in the delicate naked figures, in their rumbling cars, seen through the sparkle of the wine.

From the garden came a lazy ripple of strings, like waves breaking uncertainly on some veiled coast, a pause, a troubled stillness, and in a key infinitely remote, the violins broke imperceptibly, inevitably, into a slumberous Valse.

The Baroness peered in at the tent door, sweeping aside like a handful of Honeysuckle the voluminous fringes that adorned the entry. She was looking for a partner . . . For an instant she hovered on the threshold, admiring her pose in an unexpected mirror.

Behind her, showed reflected in the glass, a patch of lamp-black sky crowded behind the unschooled draperies of a tree, while beyond, fluttering in the rhythm of the dance, like figures on a bas-relief, the Maids of Honour in their long white frocks appeared and disappeared between huge tubs of flowers.

The Baroness hastily dropped the fringe, such a full background made her feel quite dizzy. She was looking extremely pale. News had just reached her that the Princess's note had not been delivered.

The better for wine, it seemed the chauffeur had left the letter at some Inn, to be delivered by some stable-boy, at some time during his convenience, who, in turn, had entrusted the letter to a van passing the Saint's doorstep on the course of its rounds, laden with the creations of the 'Maison Greuze.'

At the Schloss of the Countess Elsassar, the wife of the Chancellor of the Exchequer, the van had been driven back to the capital almost by swords to fetch a piece of passementerie, and the driver had been so harassed thereat that he had forgotten altogether the Princess's note. With the unopened letter scorching her bosom the Baroness was at a loss.

To screen herself, she felt, could best be done by warning the Princess of her mistake. Yet how?

Already the Princess seemed to have commenced a pious flirtation. 'When I asked her to describe you,' the Baroness could hear her say, 'she said: "he has a long straight nose, a determined chin, and would look like a Donatello when in certain lights." '

'What on earth am I to do?' wondered the Baroness. 'Nothing perhaps, until after I've had some supper; it will choke me, I know, and I'm certain to be dull. I shall go in with another woman'; and catching up her train over her arm, and calling herself 'Coward,' she left the tent looking more helplessly untidy than she had ever looked before.

She stepped straight into the arms of the King and the English Ambassadress, who were patrolling slowly up and down in deep confabulation. The Ambassadress was complaining, in French, of the mice at the Embassy whilst the King was telling her of some quite wonderful mouse-traps, intermixed with the history of the house. Detaining the Baroness, they forced her to join them, too. Their ill-assorted shadows, falling on the grass, suggested Early Abyssinian Art,—'persons returning from a lion-hunt.' Music came towards them on little puffs of air, strange languid, passing suavely through the myriad small openings of boughs and brambles, twining round the sleeping heads of flowers, blown through the philharmonic fingers of the statues; the violins, heavy, stifling as black velvet, made everybody long to sit down.

The Conductor's wand, mesmeric, swayed sensuously to and fro, falling, climbing, till his hands seemed full of stars. With a delicious dissonance the Valse unexpectedly ceased.

The dancers crushed streaming by into the tent, where a frugal 'Theatre Supper' was being served. The battle for precedence before the mirror was, in several cases, the commencement of a life-long feud.

There came a babel of voices: 'Such a cat! I would, dear, if I could only move my poor hips.'

'Insolence!'

' . . . As if I were no more than the wife of an Aide-de-camp!'

'Above social littleness.'

'Those "Isolde" cocktails make one very amorous!'

'Would you mind not hurting me with your fan?'

'Oh! Be careful there, Countess, of some horses' offal.'

'I hear that your wife and my wife . . . but I fancy there's nothing in it . . .'

The Princess turned to her companion. 'I am afraid our Court life must strike you as dreadfully hollow,' she said.

'Not at all,' he answered, 'I'm enjoying myself immensely.'

The Princess staggered. Was it possible that this man had a common nature? She would not believe it.

'You are a dear, excellent creature,' she murmured, touching his arm, 'and you think of us far too well. If you could see us in the searching light of morning you would condemn us in fiery words. But you must come to lunch . . . Although, even now, I daresay if you look about you will find bribery and corruption in our very midst.'

In a hurricane of silver, and swinging chains, leaning solidly on the arms of two of her most formidable critics, the Mistress of the Robes approached the buffet; flushed and triumphant. Apparently, she was revealing the plot of her next play. 'In the last act,' they could hear her say, 'she confesses her guilt; she departs, and crossing a rickety wooden bridge, falls into the river and is drowned.'

'A merciful end,' the Baroness breathed, glancing up into the blue of the night.

Certainly the affair was now beyond ker keeping: the Princess must be allowed to discover the error as she might.

'The man must be a hardened opportunist,' she reflected, sinking with wan philosophy to a seat.

A wild Hawaiian melody, evoking exuberance and glamour, fell engagingly upon her ear.

'You are not dancing, Baroness?' An elderly gentleman with a toothbrush-moustache and a sapphire ring made blandly question.

'I? Oh, Sir Oliver,' the Baroness started.

'You prefer, perhaps, looking on?'

The Baroness nodded, her glance following some shooting stars that slipped suddenly down behind the palace.

'There,' she observed with half-closed eyes, 'went Ursa Major!'

'Never! Ursa's over there . . .'

'What; Ursa is?' she murmured, wondering if her own fall from royal favour and grace would be equally rapid.

It seemed indeed quite certain that a season of disesteem was upon her; 'I shall let my house and go abroad,' she brooded, bestowing a smile of sleepy sadness at her rings—London! Paris! Madrid! perhaps further still! 'Tell me, Sir Oliver,' she demanded, 'have you ever been to Greece?'

'More than once,' Sir Oliver dryly replied, 'I even married, *en secondes noces,* a Lesbian . . .'

'A native of Lesbos? Just fancy that!' the Baroness marvelled, appraising a passing débutante, a young girl in a mousseline robe of palest Langue de chat.

'*Née* a Demitraki.'

'A demi what?' the Baroness abstrusely twittered, blinking at the intermittent lightning in the sky.

'A Demitraki.'

'Hark.'

'What is it?'

'Only,' the Lady answered, raising her face into the soft dream morning, already pointing, '*a cock.*'

'A cock?'

'Chanticleer,' she added suavely, for the sake of euphony: 'Chanti . . .'

* * *

'Cock-a-doodle, dooooooooooooooooooooooooocoooooooooooooooo ooooooooooooooooooooooooooooooooooooooooooooooooooooooo'

'(Cluck-cluck?)'

'Cock-a-doodle. . . .'

Vainglory

'A ND, then, oh yes! Atalanta is getting too pronounced.' She
spoke lightly, leaning back a little in her deep arm-chair. It
was the end of a somewhat lively review.

On such a languid afternoon how hard it seemed to bear a cross!
Pleasant to tilt it a little—lean it for an instant against somebody else.
. . . Her listener waved her handkerchief expressively. She felt,
just then, it was safer not to speak. Tactfully she rose.

On a dark canvas screen were grouped some inconceivably
delicate Persian miniatures.

She bent towards them. 'Oh, what gems!'

But Lady Georgia would not let her go.

'A mother's rôle,' she said, 'is apt to become a strain.'

Mrs. Henedge turned towards her. 'Well, what can you do, dear?'
she enquired, and with a sigh she looked away sadly over the
comparative country of the square.

Lady Georgia Blueharnis owned that house off Hill Street from
whose curved iron balconies it would have seemed right for dames
in staid silks to lean melodiously at certain moments of the day. In
Grecian-Walpole times the house had been the scene of an embassy;
but since then it had reflowered unexpectedly as a sympathetic
background, suitable to shelter plain domesticity—or even more.

Not that Lady Georgia could be said to be domestic. . . . Her
interests in life were far too scattered. Known to the world as the
Isabella d'Este of her day, her investigations of art had led her
chiefly outside the family pale.

'It is better,' Mrs. Henedge said, when she had admired the massive foliage in the square, and had sighed once or twice again, 'to
be pronounced than to be a bag of bones. And thank goodness
Atalanta's not eccentric! Think of poor little Mr. Rienzi-Smith
who lives in continual terror lest one day his wife may do something
really strange—perhaps run down Piccadilly without a hat. . . . Take
a shorter view of life, dear, don't look so far ahead!'

'I was thinking only of Monday.'

'There will be eleven bridesmaids besides At'y!'

'They will look Satanic.'

'Yes; it's perhaps too close to picture them!'

'I don't know, yet,' Lady Georgia said, 'what I shall wear. But I shall be very plain.'

'The cake,' Mrs. Henedge said, beginning to purr, 'is to be an exact replica of the Victoria Memorial.'

'Do you know where the honeymoon's to be spent?'

'They begin, I believe, by Brussels——'

'I can hardly imagine anyone,' Lady Georgia observed, 'setting out deliberately for Brussels.'

'I suppose it does seem odd,' Mrs. Henedge murmured, looking mysteriously about her.

The room in which she found herself was a somewhat *difficult* room. The woodwork by Pajou had been painted a dull, lustreless grey, whilst the curtains and the upholstery of the chairs were of a soft canary-coloured silk striped with blue. Here and there, in magnificent defiance, were set tubs of deep crimson and of brilliant pink azaleas. Above the mantelpiece was suspended a charming portrait of Lady Georgia by Renoir. No one ever warmed their hands there, or before the summer wilderness of plants, without exclaiming 'How wonderful it is!' In this portrait she was seen promenading slowly in an economical landscape, whilst a single meagre tree held above her head its stiff branches lightly, screening her from the sun by its just sufficient leaves. On the opposite side of the room hung a second portrait of herself with her husband and her children—a lovely Holy Family, in the Venetian manner, and in between, all round the room, at varying heights, in blotches of rose and celestial blue, hung a sumptuous *Stations of the Cross*, by Tiepolo. Upon the ceiling, if one cared to look so high, some last few vestiges of the embassy might be seen—quivers, torches, roses, and all the paraphernalia of love. . . . But the eyes, travelling over these many obstacles, would invariably return to the Venetian portrait, spoken of, as a rule, somewhat breathlessly as the *Madonna in the Osprey*.

Glancing from it to her hostess, Mrs. Henedge had not observed the remotest resemblance yet. She was waiting. . . . Except, she considered, for dear Lord Blueharnis, a fine, dashing St. Joseph, with blue, slightly bloodshot eyes, and the darling children, and the adorable Pekinese, it was decidedly a *Madeleine Lisante*. Striking, as it most unquestionably was, of Lady Georgia herself, it was not a

76

satisfactory portrait. But how, it might pardonably be asked, was it likely to be? How was it possible for a painter to fix upon canvas anyone so elusive? He must interpret. He must paint her soul, taking care not to let her appear, as an inferior artist *might*, an over-dressed capital sin.

Lady Georgia's face, indeed, was as sensitive as a calm sea to the passing clouds. She had variety. Often she managed to be really beautiful, and even in her plainest moments she was always interesting. Her nature, too, was as inconsistent as her face. At first sight, she was, perhaps, too individual to make any very definite impression. . . . A single pink flower on her black frock, this afternoon, made her look, somehow, very far away.

Who can she be angling for, Mrs. Henedge wondered, and for whom is At'y becoming too pronounced! Was it for poor Lord Susan, who was sick, so everyone said, of the world at three-and-twenty?

At this notion she caressed, with a finger of a creamy glove, a small bronze of a bird with a broken wing.

Mrs. Henedge, the widow of that injudicious man the Bishop of Ashringford, was considered, by those who knew her, to be Sympathy itself. His lordship, rumour reported, had fallen in love with her at first sight one morning while officiating at a friend's cathedral, when she had put him in mind of a startled deer. She was really only appropriating a hymn-book, as she had afterwards explained. Their marriage had been called a romance. Towards the end, however, the Bishop had become too fe-fi-fo-fum-Jack-in-the-Beanstalk altogether. She had had a horrid time; but still, she was able to speak of him always as '*poor dear Leslie*,' now that he was gone. To-day, perhaps, it might be said of her that she had deserted this century for—she had hardly settled which. Wrapped in what looked to be a piece of Beauvais tapestry, she suggested a rumble of chariots, a sacking of Troy. As Lady Georgia observed, quite perceptibly, she was on the brink of . . . Rome.

But reflections were put to flight, as some of the angels, from the famous *Madonna,* and several of the Pekinese came whirling into the room.

'It ran away in Berkeley Square.'

'She had been having ices.'

'On her head were two very tall green feathers.'

'The policeman went away with her parasol.'

77

'She was on her way to see us.'

The children were very much excited. 'Hush, darlings!' Lady Georgia exclaimed. 'And when you're calmer, explain who it was that ran away from Berkeley Square!'

'Grandmamma did!'

'Who would have thought,' said Fräulein, appearing, 'that a one-horse cab could do *so much mischief*!'

They were returning from the large heart of Bloomsbury, where the children were frequently taken to learn deportment from the Tanagras in the British Museum. After posing meaningly as a Corinthian, or practising sinking upon a camp-stool like an Athenian, they came home, as a rule, rampageous.

'This afternoon they are uncontrollable!' Fräulein murmured, attempting to hurry them away. But Mrs. Henedge, with an arm about a child, was beginning to expand.

'Her complexion,' she observed, 'is as lovely as ever; but she *begins to look older*!'

As a foreigner, Fräulein could fully savour the remark. She had succeeded, only lately, to Mademoiselle Saligny, who had been dismissed for calling Marie Antoinette a doll. Unfortunately, as Lady Georgia had since discovered, her Teutonic scepticism varied scarcely at all, from the Almighty to a can of hot water; but this was more pardonable, she considered, than labelling Marie Antoinette a doll. Distinguished, or harmless doubts were these!

'It's really rather an escape!' Lady Georgia murmured, as soon as they were gone; 'my mother-in-law's dictatorialness is becoming so impossible and in this warm weather she's sure to be out of sorts.'

She stretched out a hand, listlessly, towards a red, colossal rose. So many talismans for happiness fettered her arms! She could hardly move but the jingling of some crystal ball, or the swaying of some malachite pig, reminded her of the fact that she was unhappy. 'I can't bear,' she said, 'James to arrange the flowers, he *packs* them down into the vases.' She got up and loosened some. 'And when Charles does them,' she murmured, 'they're invariably swooning away! Come and see, though, all I've been doing; our lease, you know, doesn't expire until two thousand and one. And so it's quite worth while to make some little improvements!'

But Mrs. Henedge seemed disinclined to stir. Seated upon a sofa entirely without springs, that had, most likely, once been Juliet's bier, it appeared she had something to confide. Something was troubling her besides '*the poor Guards, in all this sun!*'

'My dear Georgia,' she said, 'now that you've told me your news, I want to tell you of a most exquisite discovery.'

Lady Georgia opened wide-wide eyes. 'Is it some new thing, she inquired, 'about Mrs. Hanover?'

Mrs. Henedge looked about her. 'It's rather a secret still,' she continued, 'and although in many ways I should have liked to have told Ada, she would probably immediately tell Robert and he, in confidence, would, of course, tell Jack, and Jack would tell *everybody*, and so——'

'Better say nothing to Ada!'

Mrs. Henedge heaved a sigh.

'Do you remember Professor Inglepin?' she asked. 'His mother was a Miss Chancellor . . . Fanny. Well, quite lately, whilst in Egypt, the Professor (he terrifies me! he's so thin, he's so fierce) came upon an original fragment of Sappho. And I'm having a small party at my house, on Sunday, with his assistance, to make the line known.'

Lady Georgia became immediately animated. The Isabella d'Este in her awoke.

'My dear, how heavenly!' she exclaimed.

'Exceptional people,' Mrs. Henedge hinted nervously, 'are coming.'

'O—h?'

'Mrs. Asp, Miss Compostella, the Calvallys!'

'It will be delightful!'

'Well, you won't blame me, dear, will you, if you're bored?'

Lady Georgia closed her eyes. 'Sappho!' she exclaimed. 'I'm wondering what I shall wear. My instinct would dress me, I believe, in a crinoline, with a yellow cashmere shawl, and a tiny turquoise bonnet.'

Mrs. Henedge became alarmed. 'I hope we shall be all as *Ingres* as possible,' she said, 'since there's not much time to be Greek. And now that I've told you, I must fly! No, darling, I can't even stay to look at the improvements; since the house is yours for so long, I shall see them, perhaps, again. I'm going this evening with the Fitzlittles to the Russian dancers.' And she added melodiously from the stairs: 'I do so *adore* Nijinsky in *Le Spectre de la Rose*.'

Vainglory

MRS. HENEDGE lived in a small house with killing stairs just off Chesham Place.

'If I were to die here,' she had often said, 'they would never be able to twist the coffin outside my door; they would have to cremate me in my room.' For such a cottage, the sitting-rooms, nevertheless, were astonishingly large. The drawing-room, for instance, was a complete surprise, in spite of its dimensions, being ocularly curtailed by a somewhat trying brocade of drooping lilac orchids on a yellow ground.

But to-day, to make as much space as possible to receive her guests, all the household heirlooms—a faded photograph of the Pope, a bust of *poor dear Leslie,* some most Oriental cushions, and a quantity of whimsies, had been carried away to the top of the house. Never before had she seen the room so bare, or so austere.

As her maid exclaimed: 'It was like a church.' If an entire Ode of Sappho's had been discovered instead of a single line she could have done no more.

In the centre of the room, a number of fragile gilt chairs had been waiting patiently all day to be placed, heedless, happily, of the lamentations of Thérèse, who, while rolling her eyes, kept exclaiming, 'Such wild herds of chairs; such herds of wild chairs!'

In her arrangements, Mrs. Henedge had disobeyed the Professor in everything.

Professor Inglepin had looked in during the week to ask that severity might be the key. 'No flowers,' he had begged, 'or, at most, placed beside the fragment (which I shall bring), a handful, perhaps, of——'

'Of course,' Mrs. Henedge had replied, 'you can rely upon me.' And now the house was full of rambler roses and of blue sweet-peas.

A buffet, too, had arisen altar-like in her own particular sanctum, an apology to those whom she was unable to dine; nor, for toothsome curiosities, had she scoured a pagan cookery-book in vain. . . .

Glancing over the dinner list whilst she dressed it seemed to her that the names of her guests, in neat rotation, resembled the cast of a play. 'A comedy, with possible dynamics!' she murmured as she went downstairs.

With a tiara well over her nose, and dressed in oyster satin and pearls, she wished that Sappho could have seen her then. . . . On entering the drawing-room she found her beautiful Mrs. Shamefoot as well as her radiant Lady Castleyard (pronounced Castleyud) had already arrived, and were entertaining lazily her Monsignor Parr.

'Cima's Madonnas are dull, dull, dull,' Mrs. Shamefoot was saying, looking over the Monsignor's shoulder at her own reflection in the glass.

Mrs. Shamefoot, widely known as 'Birdie,' and labelled as politics, almost compels a tear. Overshadowed by a clever husband, and by an exceedingly brilliant mother-in-law, all that was expected of her was to hold long branches of mimosa and eucalyptus leaves as though in a dream at meetings, and to be picturesque, and restful and mute. As might have been foreseen, she had developed into one of those decorative, self-entranced persons so valued by hostesses at dinner as an ideal full stop. Sufficiently self-centred, she could be relied upon to break up a line, or to divide, with grace, any awkward divergencies of thought. Her momentary caprice was to erect with Lady Castleyard, to whom she was devoted, a window in some cathedral to their memory, that should be a miracle of violet glass, after a design of Lanzini Niccolo.

It was therefore only natural that Lady Castleyard (whose hobby was watching sunlight through stained glass) should take the liveliest interest in the scheme—and through the mediation of Mrs. Henedge was hoping to kindle a window somewhere very soon.

A pretty woman, with magnificently bold shoulders and a tiny head, she was, as a rule, quite fearlessly made up. It was courageous of her, her hostess thought, to flaunt such carnational cheeks. Only in a Reynolds or in a Romney did one expect to see *such a dab*.

'Tell me! Tell me!' she exclaimed airily, taking hold of Mrs. Henedge. 'I feel I must hear the line before everyone else.'

Mrs. Henedge, who did not know it, pressed to her lips her fan.

'Patience!' she murmured, with her subtlest smile.

Monsignor Parr gazed at her with heavy opaque eyes.

Something between a butterfly and a misanthrope, he was temperamental, when not otherwise . . . employed.

'I must confess,' he observed, 'that Sappho's love affairs fail to stir me.'

'Ah, for shame!' Mrs. Henedge scolded, turning from him to

welcome an elaborate young man, who, in some bewildering way of his own, seemed to find charming the fashions of 1860.

'Drecoll?' she enquired.

'Vienna,' he nodded.

'This is Mr. Harvester,' she said. She had nearly said 'Poor Mr. Harvester,' for she could not endure his wife.

Claud Harvester was usually considered charming. He had gone about here and there, tinting his personality after the fashion of a Venetian glass. Certainly he had wandered. . . . He had been into Arcadia, even, a place where artificial temperaments so seldom get— their nearest approach being, perhaps, a matinée of *The Winter's Tale*. Many, indeed, thought him interesting. He had groped so. . . . In the end he began to suspect that what he had been seeking for all along was the theatre. He had discovered the truth in writing plays. In style—he was often called obscure, although, in reality, he was as charming as the top of an apple-tree above a wall. As a novelist he was almost successful. His books were watched for . . . but without impatience.

'Cleopatra,' he said, 'was so disappointed she couldn't come.'

'I thought I saw some straw——'

'Miss Compostella,' the servant tunefully announced.

'Ah, Julia!'

A lady whose face looked worn and withered through love, wearing a black gauze gown, looped like a figure from the Primavera, made her way mistily into the room.

Nobody would have guessed Miss Compostella to be an actress; she was so private-looking. . . . Excessively pale, without any regularity at all of feature, her face was animated chiefly by her long red lips; more startling even than those of Cecilia Zen Tron, *cette adorable Aspasie de la décadence Vénitienne*. But somehow one felt that all Miss Compostella's soul was in her nose. It was her one delicate feature: it aspired.

'How was I?' she murmured, when she had shaken hands. 'I was *too nervous* for words!'

'You were completely splendid.'

'My dear, how beautifully you died!'

Miss Compostella was experimenting, just then, at her own theatre, with some tableaux inspired from Holbein's *Dance of Death*.

'Two persons only,' she said, 'were present at my matinée. Poor things! I asked them back to tea. . . . One of them is coming here to-night.'

'Really! who can it be?'

'He plays the piano,' she said, 'composes, and he has the most bewitching hair. His name is Winsome Brookes.'

Mrs. Shamefoot tittered.

'Oh, Winsome's wonderful,' Mrs. Henedge exclaimed. 'I enjoy his music so much. There's an unrest in it all that I like. Sometimes he reaches to a pitch of life. . . .'

'His tired ecstasy,' Claud Harvester conceded, 'decidedly is disquieting.'

Miss Compostella looked at him. She admired terrifically his charming little leer; it was like a crack, she thought, across the face of an idol. Otherwise, she was afraid, his features were cut too clearly to make any very lasting appeal. . . .

Nevertheless, for her general calm she could have wished that it had been next year.

Each day she felt their position was becoming more strained and absurd. She had followed Claud Harvester closely in his work, until at length she stood beside him on a pinnacle at some distance from the ground. And there they were! And she was getting bored. It disgusted her, however, to be obliged to climb down, to have had her walk for nothing, as it were.

With a smile that might, perhaps, have been called pathetic, she turned towards her hostess, who, with a deeply religious eye upon Monsignor Parr, was defending her favourite Winsome Brookes from Mrs. Shamefoot's innuendoes.

'But why, why, *why*,' she enquired, 'do you think him dreadful?'

'Because I think he's odious,' she replied.

'Children irritate you, dear, I know, but he will do great things yet!'

'Can one ever say?'

'The most unexpected thing in my life,' Monsignor Parr broke in gently, 'was when a certain cab-horse from Euston ran away!'

'Thanks for your belief in us,' Mrs. Henedge exclaimed gratefully, rising to greet an indolent-looking woman who brought with her, somehow, into the room, the tranquillity of gardens.

Mrs. Calvally, the wife of that perfect painter, was what her hostess called a complete woman. She was fair, with dark Tzigane eyes, which, slightly dilated, usually looked mildly amazed. Like some of Rubens' women, you felt at once her affinity to pearls. Equanimity radiated from her leisurely person. She never became alarmed, as her friends well knew, even when her husband spoke of going away and leaving her to live alone in some small and exquisite Capitol.

She would just smile at him sensibly, pretending not to hear. . . . Secretly, perhaps, his descriptions of places interested her. She would have missed hearing about the White Villa, with its cypress-tree, between the Opera House and the Cathedral, and she let him talk about it like a child. She did not mind when the town chosen was Athens, which was near Malta, where she had a cousin, but she had a horror of Bucharest.

George Christian Calvally accompanied his wife, unhappy, perhaps, at playing, if even for only a few hours, an oboe to her violin. His face was delicate and full of dreams. It was a perfect *grief face*.

'My dear Mary,' Mrs. Henedge exclaimed affectionately, leading the sympathetic woman to the most sylvan seat she could find, a small settee, covered with a chintz all Eve's apples, and a wonderful winding snake, 'had you to be very strategic?'

'Oh, not at all,' Mrs. Calvally replied: 'but what do you think followed us into the house?'

Mrs. Henedge looked alarmed.

'Oh, nothing so dreadful . . . Only a butterfly!'

Mrs. Shamefoot, who was listening, became positively ecstatic.

How nice it was to escape, if even for a second, from the tiresome political doings of which she was so tired. Not that she could always catch everything that was said, now that she wore her hair imitated from a statue of the fifth century. . . .

But the inclusion to-night, however, of Winsome Brookes was something of a trial. Without any positive reason for disliking him, she found him, perhaps, too similar in temperament to herself to be altogether pleased.

He came into the room a few minutes later in his habitual dreamy way, as might one upon a beauty tour in Wales—a pleasant picture of health and . . . inexperience. From the over-elaboration of his dress he suggested sometimes, as he did to-night, a St. Sebastian with too many arrows.

A gentle buzz of voices filled the room.

Vainglory

Mrs. Henedge, admirable now, was orchestrating fearlessly her guests.

Mr. Sophax, a critic, who had lately lost his wife and was looking suitably subdued, was complimenting, just sufficiently, a lady with sallow cheeks and an amorous weary eye. This was Mrs. Steeple.

One burning afternoon in July, with the thermometer at 90, the ridiculous woman had played *Rosmersholm* in Camberwell. Nobody had seen her do it, but it was conceivable that she had been very fine.

'Tell me,' she said to Mr. Sophax, 'who is the Victorian man talking to that gorgeous thing—in the gold trailing skirts?'

'You mean Claude Harvester. His play the other night was a disaster. Did you see it?'

'It was delightfully slight, I thought.'

'A disaster!'

'Somehow, I like his work, it's so lightly managed.'

'Never mind, Mr. Harvester,' Lady Georgia was saying to him, 'I'm sure your play was exquisite; or it would have had a longer run.'

He smiled.

'How satirical you are!'

She was looking tired, and not a bit wonderful; it was one of her lesser nights.

'I wish she would give her poor emeralds a rest,' a lady like a very thin camel was observing to Monsignor Parr.

A flattering silence greeted the Professor.

'I'm afraid you must feel exhausted from your field day at the British Museum,' Mrs. Henedge said to him half hysterically, as they went downstairs.

The success of the dinner-table, however, restored her nerve. To create a slight atmosphere she had made a circuit of the table earlier in the evening, scattering violets indiscriminately into the glasses and over the plates.

For a moment her guests forgot to chatter of themselves. They remembered Sappho.

The Lesbian wine (from Samos. Procured, perhaps, in Pall Mall) produced a hush.

Claud Harvester bethought him then that he had spent a Saturday-to-Monday once, in Mitylene, at 'a funny little broken-down hotel upon the seashore.'

Vainglory

It had been in the spring, he said.

'In the spring the violets in Athens are wonderful, are they not?' Mrs. Calvally enquired.

'Indeed, yes.'

She spoke to him of Greece, but all he could remember of Corinth, for instance, was the many drowned lambs he had seen lying upon the beach.

'*Ah! Don't speak to me of Corinth!*'

'What a pity—and in Tanagra, tell me, what did you see?'

'In Tanagra . . . ?' he said, 'there was a kitten sunning himself in the Museum, beside a pile of broken earthenware—handles of amphoræ, arms and legs of figurines, and an old man seated in the doorway mending a jar!'

'How extraordinary!' she marvelled, removing with extreme precaution an atom of cork that had fallen into her glass. 'Really! Is that all?'

'Really all,' he murmured, looking with sudden interest at Miss Compostella, whose face, *vis-à-vis,* he thought, still bore traces of his comedy.

He could appreciate her subtle mask quite enormously just then; now that she had recalled to him his play. How very delightful she was!

'Surely,' he reflected, 'her hair must be wired?'

Probably, as his wife had hinted once, her secret lay simply in her untidiness. She had made it a study. Disorder, with her, had become a fine art. A loose strand of hair . . . the helpless angle of a hat. . . . And then, to add emphasis, there were always quantities of tiny buttons in absurd places on her frocks that cried aloud, or screamed, or gently prayed, to be fastened, and which, somehow, gave her an air of irresponsibility, which, for simple folk, was possibly quite fascinating.

'She's such a messy woman,' Cleopatra had said. 'And, my dear . . . so unnatural! I wonder you write plays for her. If I were a man, I should want only . . .'

And she had named the impossible.

'I feel I want to go away somewhere and be ugly quietly for a week,' Miss Compostella was confiding to George Calvally, as she cut a little wild-duck with her luminous hands. 'The effort of having to look more or less like one's photographs is becoming such a strain.'

He sympathised with her. 'But I suppose,' he said, 'you are terribly tied.'

'Yes, but you know, I love it! Next month I'm hoping to get Eysoldt over to play with me in Maeterlinck. . . . It isn't settled, there's some incertitude still, but it's almost sure!'

'Her Joyzelle!' he began to rave.

'And my Selysette!' she reminded him.

'Now that Maeterlinck is getting like Claud Harvester,' the Professor, without tact, put in, 'I don't read him any more. But at all events,' he added graciously, 'I hope you'll make a hit.'

'A hit! Oh, I've never done anything so dreadful,' she answered, turning her attention towards her hostess who, beneath her well-tipped tiara, was comparing the prose of a professional saint to a blind alley.

'But what does it matter,' Lady Georgia enquired, leaning towards her, 'if he has a charming style?'

In the vivacious discussion that ensued Mrs. Steeple, imprudently, perhaps, disclosed to Winsome Brookes her opinion of Miss Compostella.

'Oh, Julia's so stiff,' she said, 'she will hold herself, even in the most rousing plays, as though she were Agrippina with the ashes of Germanicus, and in depicting agony she certainly relies too much upon the colour of her gown. Her Hamlet,' and she began to laugh, 'her Hamlet was irresistible!'

And Mrs. Steeple laughed and laughed.

Her laughter, indeed, was so hilarious that Winsome became embarrassed.

'Her H-H-Hamlet was irresistible!' she repeated.

'Do tell us what is amusing you!' Miss Compostella enquired.

But Mrs. Steeple appeared to be too convulsed.

'What has Winsome been saying?' her hostess wished to know.

In none of these disturbances did Mrs. Shamefoot care to join. Mentally, perhaps, she was already three parts glass. So intense was her desire to set up a commemorative window to herself that, when it was erected, she believed she must leave behind in it, for ever, a little ghost. And should this be so, then what joy to be pierced each morning with light; her body flooded through and through by the sun, or in the evening to glow with a harvest of dark colours, deepening into untold sadness with the night. . . . What ecstasy! It was the Egyptian sighing for his pyramid, of course.

As might be feared, she appeared this evening entirely self-entranced. Indeed, all that she vouchsafed to her neighbour, Mr. Sophax, during dinner, was that the King had once been 'perfect to her' in Scotland, and that she was fond of Yeats.

'If you cannot sleep,' she said to him, 'you've only to repeat to yourself *Innisfree* several times. You might be glad to remember. . . .'

As Mrs. Henedge had explained, it was only a fragile little dinner. She was obliged to return to the drawing-room again as soon as possible to receive her later guests. It occurred to her as she trailed away with the ladies that after the Professor's Sapphic postscript they might, perhaps, arrange some music. It would bring the evening to a harmonious close.

There was Winsome, fortunately, to be relied upon, and Mrs. Shamefoot, who sang the song of Thaïs to her mirror very beautifully, and later, she hoped, there would be Mrs. Rienzi-Smith, who composed little things that were all nerves . . . and who, herself, was so very delightful. . . .

In the drawing-room she was glad to find that wonderful woman, Mrs. Asp, the authoress of *The Home Life of Lucretia Borgia*, refreshing herself with coffee and biscuits while *talking servants* to Mrs. Thumbler, the wife of the architect, and the restorer of Ashringford Cathedral.

'She was four years with Lady Appledore,' Mrs. Asp was telling her, taking a bite at her biscuit, 'and *two* at the Italian Embassy, and although one wouldn't, perhaps, think it, I must say she was always scrupulously clean.'

'My dear Rose,' Mrs. Henedge said, sailing up, 'I do hope you haven't been here long?' She seemed concerned.

'I—I—I, oh no!' Mrs. Asp purred in her comfortable voice, using those same inflections which had startled, so shockingly, the Princess H. of B. when, by telephone, she had confessed: 'Yes . . . I am Mrs. Asp. . . . We're getting up a little bazaar and we expect you royalties to help!'

'And there, I believe, is Mira?' Mrs. Henedge said, turning towards a young girl who, seated in a corner, seemed to be counting the veins in her arms.

'I admired your valsing, the other night,' she said to her, 'at the de Lerens'. It's so brave of you, I think, to like dancing best alone.'

Mira Thumbler was a medieval-looking little thing, with peculiar

pale ways, like a creature escaped through the border of violets and
wild strawberries of a tapestry panel.

As a rule nobody ever noticed her (in spite of a few eccentricities,
such as dancing singly at parties, etc., sufficiently manifest, possibly,
to have excited attention). She was waiting to be found. Some day,
perhaps, a poet or a painter would come along, and lift her up, high
up, into the sun like a beautiful figurine, and she would become the
fashion for a while . . . set the New Beauty.

'These apparent icebergs,' Mrs. Henedge thought, as she touched
Mira's charming and sensitive hand, 'one knows what they are!'

'My dear, what a witty frock!' Lady Georgia said to her, fingering
it. 'Is it that little Miss Finch? It's a perfect psalm!'

'The cupids are imitated from a church frieze,' Mira explained,
holding out the stiff Italian stuff of ruby and blue woven with gold.

'I have seldom seen anything so splendidly hard!' Lady Castleyard
admired. 'You're like an angel in a summer landscape, reposing
by the side of a well!' And holding her coffee-cup at an angle, she
surveyed the room, a bored magnificence.

'There's no plot,' Mrs. Asp, who seemed utterly unable for
continuity, was confiding to a charmed few, 'no plot exactly. It's
about two women who live all alone.'

'You mean that they live just by themselves?'

Mrs. Thumbler was unable to imagine a novel without a plot,
and two women who lived so quietly! . . . She was afraid that poor
dear Rose was becoming dull.

'I wonder you don't collaborate!' she said.

'Oh no. . . . Unless I were in love with a man, and *just as a pretext*,
I should never dream of collaborating with anybody.'

'You would need a sort of male Beatrice, I suppose?'

'How amusing it would be to collaborate with Mr. Harvester,'
Mrs. Steeple murmured, glancing towards Miss Compostella, who
just then was looking completely flattered, as she closed her eyes,
smiled, and lifted, slightly, a hand.

'Certainly I adore his work,' Mrs. Asp admitted. 'He pounces
down on those mysterious half-things . . . and sometimes he fixes
them!'

'Do you know Mr. Harvester?' Mira asked.

'Of course I know Mr. Harvester. . . . He scoured Cairo for me
once years ago, to find me a lotus. Why?'

'I should so much like to meet him.'

'My dear, what an extraordinary caprice!' Mrs. Henedge exclaimed, disengaging herself to receive a dowager of probable consequence, who, in spite of a crucifix and some celestial lace, possessed a certain poetry of her own, as might, for instance, a faded bacchante. It needed scarcely any imagination at all to picture her issuing at night from her cave on Mount Parnassos to watch the stars, or, with greater convenience, perhaps, strutting like the most perfect peacock, before some country house, over the rose-pale gravel; as charming as the *little stones* in the foreground of the Parnassos of Mantegna.

Lady Listless, or Atossa, as her friends respectfully called her, had the look of a person who had discovered something she ought not to know. This was probably brought about by being aware of most people's family feuds, or by putting merely two and two together. In the year her mistakes came to thousands, but she never seemed to mind.

'I've just been dining with the Barrows,' she said solemnly to Mrs. Henedge, keeping her by the hand. 'Poor little Mrs. Barrow has heard the Raven. . . . She came up hurriedly last night from the country and has taken refuge at the Ritz Hotel.'

'It's hardly likely to follow her, I suppose?' Mrs. Henedge enquired anxiously.

'I don't know, I'm sure. The hotel, it appears, already is particularly full. . . . The last time, you remember, they heard it croak, it was for old Sir Philidor.' And looking exceedingly stately, she trailed away to repeat to Mrs. Shamefoot her news: 'Violet has heard the Raven!'

'To be painted once and for all by my husband is much better than to be always getting photographed!' Mrs. Calvally was saying to a Goddess as the Professor came in.

'I know,' the Goddess answered: 'some of his portraits are really *très Velasquez*, and they never remind you of Whistler.'

'Oh, beware of Mr. Calvally!' murmured Mrs. Asp, flitting past to seize a chair. 'He made poor Lady Georgia into a greyhound, and turned old General Montgomery into a ram—he twisted the hair into horns.'

An unwarrantable rush for places, however, announced that the critical moment had come.

'Well, darling,' Mrs. Thumbler, triumphant, explained to her daughter, excusing herself for a sharp little skirmish with Monsignor

Parr, 'I was scarcely going to have him on my knee!' And with emotion she fluttered a somewhat frantic fan.

'I think your *young musician* so handsome,' Mrs. Asp whispered to Mrs. Henedge, giving a few deft touches to a bandeau and some audacious violet paste. 'With a little trouble, really, he could look quite Greek.'

'Is your serial in *The Star*, my dear Rose, ever to be discontinued?' Mr. Sophax, who stood close behind her, stooped to enquire.

'Don't question me,' she replied, without turning round. 'I make it a rule never to be interviewed at night.'

Next her, Lady Listless, perched uncomfortably on Claud Harvester's *New Poems*, sat eyeing the Professor with her most complacent smile. She knew hardly anything of Sappho, except that her brother, she believed, had been a wine merchant—which, in those times, was probably even better than being a brewer.

'But if they had meant to murder me,' the camel-lady was mysteriously murmuring to Monsignor Parr, 'they would not have put chocolate in the luncheon-basket; my courage returned to me at that!' when a marvellous hiss from Mrs. Asp stimulated Miss Compostella to expand.

'My dear, *when an angel* like Sabine Watson . . .' she was heard to exclaim vaguely above everyone else.

Julia, just then, was in high feather. George Calvally had promised to design for her a beautiful poster, by the time that Eysoldt should arrive, with cypress-trees and handfuls of stars. . . .

But the Professor was becoming impatient.

It would be utterly disgusting, Mrs. Henedge reflected, if he should get desperate and retire. It was *like* Julia to expatiate at such a time upon the heavenliness of Sabine Watson, who was only *one*, it seemed, of quite a troop of angels.

To conceal her misgivings she waved a sultry yellow fan. There was a forest painted upon it of Arden, in indigo, in violet, in sapphire, in turquoise, and in common blue. The fan, by Conder, was known perversely as *The Pink Woods*.

'I'm not going to inflict upon you a speech,' the Professor said, breaking in like a piccolo to Miss Compostella's harp.

'Hear, hear!' Mr. Sophax approved.

'You have heard, of course, how, while surveying the ruins of Crocodileopolis Arsinoë, my donkey having——'

And then, after what may have become an anguishing obbligato, the Professor declaimed impressively the imperishable lines.

'Oh, delicious!' Lady Listless exclaimed, looking quite perplexed. 'Very charming indeed!'

'Will anyone tell me what it means,' Mrs. Thumbler queried, 'in plain English? Unfortunately, my Greek——'

'In plain English,' the Professor said, with some reluctance, 'it means: "Could not" [he wagged a finger] "Could not, for the fury of her feet!" '

'Do you mean she ran away?'

'Apparently!'

'O-h!' Mrs. Thumbler seemed inclined to faint.

The Professor riveted her with his curious nut-coloured eyes.

'Could not . . .' she murmured helplessly, as though clinging to an alpenstock, and not quite sure of her guide. Below her, so to speak, were the rooftops, pots and pans: Chamonix twinkling in the snow.

'But no doubt there is a *sous-entendu*?' Monsignor Parr suspiciously enquired.

'Indeed, no!' the Professor answered. 'It is probable, indeed, that Sappho did not even mean to be caustic! Here is an adventurous line, separated (alas!) from its full context. Decorative, useless, as you will; a water-colour on silk!'

'Just such a Sapphic piece,' Mrs. Asp observed, with authority, 'just such a Sapphic piece as the *And down I set the cushion*, or the Γέλως παιδοφιλώτερος, or again the *Foolish woman, pride not thyself on a ring*.'

'I don't know why,' Lady Georgia confessed, 'it thrills me, but it does!'

'Do you suppose she refers to——'

'Nothing of the kind!' the Professor interrupted. 'As Mrs. Asp explains, we have, at most, a broken piece, a rarity of phrase . . . as the poet's *With Golden Ankles*, for instance, or *Vines trailed on lofty poles*, or *With water dripped the napkin*, or *Scythian Wood* . . . or the (I fear me, spurious) *Carrying long rods, capped with the Pods of Poppies*.'

'And isn't there just one little tiny wee word of hers which says: *A tortoise-shell*?' Mrs. Calvally murmured, fingering the huge winged pin in the back of her hair.

'I should say that Sappho's powers were decidedly in declension when she wrote the Professor's "water-colour," ' Mrs. Steeple said disparagingly.

'I'm sure I don't see why!'

'Do you remember the divine Ode to Aphrodite?' she asked, and rapidly, occult, archaic, before anybody could stop her, she began to declaim:

'Zeus-begotten, weaver of arts deceitful,
From thy throne of various hues behold me,
Queen immortal, spare me relentless anguish;
    Spare, I beseech thee.

Hither haste, if ever of old my sighing
Moved thy soul, O Goddess, awhile to hear me,
From thy Father's house to repair with golden
    Chariot harnessed.

Lovely birds fleet-winged from Olympus holy
Fluttering multitudinous o'er the darksome
Breast of Earth their heavenly mistress hastened
    Through the mid ether;

Soon they brought the beautiful Aphrodite;
Softly beamed celestial eyes upon me;
And I heard her ask with a smile my trouble,
    Wherefore I called her.

What of all things most may appease thy frenzy?
Whom (she said) would Sappho beguile to love her?
Whom by suasion bring to heart adoring?
    Who hath aggrieved her?

Whoso flies thee, soon shall he turn to woo thee;
Who receives no gifts shall anon bestow them;
If he love not, soon shall he love, tho' Sappho
    Turneth against him!

—Lady now too come, to allay my torment;
All my soul desireth, I prithee grant me;
Be thyself my champion and my helper,
    Lovely Dione!'

'Exquisite, dear; thanks.'

'Christianity, no doubt,' the Professor observed, with some ferocity, to Monsignor Parr, 'has invented many admirable things, but it has destroyed more than it has created!' The old pagan in him was moved.

'You have been stirring our antenatal memories, Mrs. Steeple,' Claud Harvester said.

'Have I?' she laughed.

'Mr. Brookes has promised to play to us,' Mrs. Henedge said hurriedly, with sufficient presence of mind.

'Can he play *Après Midi sous les Pins*?' the camel-lady wondered.

'Certainly,' Winsome snapped, lifting from the piano a photograph of two terrified-looking little boys, which somehow had been forgotten. 'I can play anything when I have the music!'

'Poor Mr. Calvally . . . he looks always so atrociously sad!' Lady Listless murmured, staring about her.

'It's unfortunate,' Mrs. Rienzi-Smith said to her, 'that the Professor seems so displeased.'

'Well, what more could he want? We were all on footstools before him.'

'What am I to play to you?' Winsome asked of Mrs. Henedge. 'A fanfare? A requiem?'

'Oh, play us something of your own. Play your "Oakapple," from *The Suite in Green*.'

But, 'to break the ice,' as he put it, he preferred the exciting *Capriccio Espagnol* of Rimsky-Korsakoff to anything of his own.

'But didn't you hate waiting for Othello to press the pillow?' Lady Castleyard was questioning Miss Compostella. 'I should have got up and screamed or rung the bell, I'm sure I should!'

'Really? I think it's almost the only moment in the play that gives an actress an opportunity to see where are her friends,' Julia replied.

'Just as I've observed,' Mira Thumbler murmured maliciously to Claud Harvester, 'that a person who begins by playing the Prelude of Rachmaninoff seldom plays anything else——'

'Oh no,' he said. 'When Winsome plays like that, I want to live in a land where there'd be eternal summer.'

Mira looked amused.

'All places, really,' she said, 'have glamour solely in essence, didn't you know, like a drop of scent!'

She paused a moment to listen to her neighbour. 'So appallingly badly kept,' the Goddess was describing Valhalla. 'In the throne-room, for instance, the candles leaning in all directions ... and everything else the same!'

'Tell me,' Mira said, turning towards Claud Harvester abruptly, and speaking with sudden passion, 'why are you so *genial* with everyone? Why? It's such—a pity!'

'Good heavens,' he exclaimed, startled, 'what is the matter?'

But she had moved away.

'No, something of your own,' Mrs. Asp was begging Winsome, rather imprudently.

'I will play through the first act of my *Justinian,* if you think it wouldn't be too long.'

'A few of the leading themes, perhaps,' Mrs. Henedge suggested.

'Very well. I will begin with the folk-song of the Paralytics.'

'That will be delightful.'

'You must imagine them,' Winsome explained to Lady Listless, who was sitting next to the piano, 'grouped invalidishly about the great doorway of Santa Sophia. The libretto directions will say that there is a heavy violet moon, and that it is a warm June night.'

Whilst listening to the music Lady Listless would allow her aspirations to pass unrestrainedly across her face. They passed now, like a flight of birds.

'And here,' Winsome murmured airily, without ceasing, and playing with delightful crispness of touch, 'is the *pas* of the Bare-footed Nuns.'

Lady Listless became rhapsodical. 'It's almost as delicious,' she breathed, 'as the Sugar-Plum Fairies' Dance from *Casse Noisette.*'

Mrs. Asp also nodded her approbation. 'The finale was distinctly curious,' she exclaimed. 'Just like the falling of a silver tray!'

'And this,' Winsome explained, folding his arms and drooping back shyly, 'is the motive for Theodora.'

'My dear young man,' Lady Listless objected, 'but I hear nothing ... nothing at all.'

'The orchestra ceases. There's audible only the movement of her dress——'

And, suddenly irresponsible, he began to play 'Summer Palace—Tea at Therapia,' which seemed to break away quite naturally into an exciting Czardas of Liszt.

'But how amusing!'

Mrs. Henedge, slightly anxious now, judged that the moment had come to ask Mrs. Shamefoot to sing. Winsome was hardly serious. It was perhaps a pity, she reflected, though it couldn't be helped, that her dear Mrs. Shamefoot cared only for the extremely exalted music of the modern French school. Just then, *a dose of Brahms*, she felt, would have done them all more good, but doubtless Mrs. Rienzi might be relied upon to bring the evening to a calmer close with some of her drowsy gipsy dances.

'And when she died she left everything for the Capuchin Fathers,' Mrs. Shamefoot was telling Monsignor Parr as Mrs. Henedge approached.

'Sing, dear . . . ?' she said. 'Oh, I don't really know if I can. . . . The room is so hot. And there are so many roses! I don't know which look the redder, ourselves or the roses. And I have been chatting all the evening. And my voice is just the least bit tired. But if you simply insist, and Dirce· will play my accompaniment; and if——'

And ultimately, as was to be hoped, she rose and fluttered over the many prayer rugs to the piano.

Seldom, George Calvally thought, watching her, had he seen a more captivating creature.

'Do you think her as graceful as she passes for?' he could hear Winsome Brookes enquire.

'Graceful?' the camel-lady answered. 'No, really! She's like a sack of coals.'

'Ah! je suis fatiguée à mourir!' Mrs. Shamefoot sang. 'Tous ces hommes ne sont qu'indifférence et brutalité. Les femmes sont méchantes et les heures pesantes! J'ai l'âme vide. . . . Où trouver le repos? . . . Et comment fixer le bonheur! O mon miroir fidèle, rassure-moi; dis-moi que je suis toujours belle, que je serai belle éternellement; que rien ne flétrira les roses de mes lèvres, que rien ne ternira l'or pur de mes cheveux; dis-moi que je suis belle, et que je serai belle éternellement! éternellement!

'Ah! tais-toi, voix impitoyable! voix qui me dis: "Thaïs ne sera plus Thaïs! . . . Non, je n'y puis croire; et s'il n'est point pour garder la beauté de secrets souverains, de pratiques magiques, toi, Vénus, réponds-moi de son éternité! Vénus, invisible et présente!" . . . Vénus, enchantement de l'ombre! réponds-moi! Dis-moi que je suis belle, et que je serai belle éternellement! Que rien ne flétrira les roses de mes lèvres, que rien ne ternira l'or pur de mes cheveux;

dis-moi que je suis belle et que je serai belle éternellement! éternellement! éternellement!'

'Exquisite, dear; thanks!'

'Oh, she's heavenly!'

'Edwina never sang so!'

'If she becomes invocatory again,' Mrs. Asp whispered, beating
applause with a finger upon a fan, 'I shall have my doze—like
Brünnhilde.'

'You would be most uncomf'y,' Mr. Sophax observed, 'and then
who would finish your serial for *The Star*. . . . No one else could.'

It was too true. . . . Nobody else could draw an unadulterated
villain with the same nicety as Mrs. Asp. How she would dab on her
colours, and then with what relish would she unmask her man; her
high spirits during the process were remarked by all her friends.

But there was to be another song, it seemed, for with her back
to the room and a glow of light flooding her perfectly whitened
shoulders, it was unlikely that Lady Castleyard would yield immediately to Mrs. Rienzi her chair. With her head slightly inclined, it
was permitted to admire the enchanting fold of her neck and the
luxuriant bundles of silvered hair wound loosely about her head,
from whence there flew an aigrette like a puff of steam.

'An aigrette,' Mrs. Asp calculated, 'at least sixteen inches long!'
No; there would be at least two more songs, she felt sure.

'They tell me,' she said to Mr. Sophax, shaking long tearful
earrings at him, 'that the concert at Jarlington House, the other
night, was a complete success, and that Lady Castleyard played so
well that someone in the audience climbed over a great many poor
toes and tried to kiss her hands. . . . Atossa says that he received
quite a large cheque to do it!'

But a troublesome valse, that smouldered and smouldered, and
flickered and smouldered, until it broke into a flame, before leaping
into something else, and which was perhaps the French way of
saying that 'still waters run deep,' cast for an instant its spell, and
when it was over Mrs. Henedge decided that she would ask Mira
Thumbler to dance.

Not unlikely it would be giving an old maid her chance. Indeed,
at seventeen, the wicked mite was far too retiring. Nobody ever
noticed her. So many people had said so! And her poor mother
with nothing but daughters; her only child a girl. . . .

She found Mira lolling beneath a capacious lampshade looking inexpressibly bored. Her hostess gathered by her silhouette that the temptation to poke a finger through a Chinese vellum screen, painted with water-lilies and fantastic swooping birds, was almost *more* than she could endure.

'My dear, won't you dance for us?' she asked.

Mira looked up.

'Oh, forgive me, please,' she exclaimed, 'but I should feel far too like . . . *you know*!'

She smiled charmingly. . . .

'The daughter of Herodias?' Mrs. Henedge said. 'Nonsense! Don't be shy.'

'Anything you might ask for . . .' George Calvally murmured kindly, who was standing near.

'Do you mean that?'

'Of course I mean it!'

She considered his offer.

'Then,' she said, 'I'm going to sit to you for my portrait. Oh, it's stupid and dull of me, I suppose, to have so few features—just a plain nose, two eyes, and a mouth—still!' She flung a hand up into the air to be admired. She smiled. She looked quite pretty.

'I shall be immensely flattered,' the painter said.

And so—after what seeemed almost incredible adjustments—Mira danced.

On their way home he spoke of her lovely Byzantine feet.

Mrs. Calvally yawned. 'It's extraordinary that a little skimped thing like Miss Thumbler should fascinate you!' she said.

∞ *III* ∞

JUST at the beginning of Sloane Street, under the name of Monna Vanna, Mrs. Shamefoot kept a shop.

It was her happiness to slap, delicately, at monotony by selling flowers.

Oh, the relief of running away, now and then, from her clever husband, or from the fatiguing brilliance of her mother-in-law, to sit in the mystery of her own back parlour, with the interesting Dina or with Jordan, her boy!

She found in this by-life a mode of expression, too, for which her nature craved. It amused her to arrange marvellous sheaves of flowers to perish in the window before a stolid public eye; and some of her discords in colour were extremely curious. Often she would signal to her friends by her flowers, and when, for some reason, at the last Birthday Mr. Shamefoot had been carefully overlooked, in a freakish mood she had decked the window entirely with black iris.

But notwithstanding politics, it was declared that in all England nobody could wire Neapolitan violets more skilfully than she.

It was her triumph.

In a whole loose bouquet she would allow a single violet, perhaps, to skim above the rest—so lightly!

On her walls hung charming flower studies by Fantin Latour, and by Nicholson, intermingled with some graceful efforts of her own—impressions, mostly, of roses; in which it might be observed that she made always a great point of the thorns. And when there was nobody much in town these furnished the shop.

This morning, however, Mrs. Shamefoot sat down to make a wreath—she hardly knew for whom; but since to-day was only Monday, she had a presentiment that one might be needed. . . .

With her dark eyes full of soul she commanded Dina to fetch her one. She fancied she might make ready a lyre, with some orchids and pink lilies, and numberless streaming ribands; something suitable for a disappointed débutante, and hardly had she commenced her work when Mrs. Henedge came into the shop.

'My dear Birdie, who ever expected to see you!' she exclaimed. 'I thought you fluttered in only now and then, to see how everything was getting on——'

She seemed embarrassed.

Mrs. Henedge had looked in early indeed solely to implore Dina to persuade her mistress to take back some of the rambler-roses from her last night's party, but now, as she put it, they were face-to-face her heart *failed* her.

'What is the cost of those catkins?' she enquired, pointing, in her agitation, at something very fabulous-looking indeed.

They might go, she reflected, to Winsome Brookes. Often she would thank him for music by a cake on a small shrub, and Rumpelmeyer's to-day was not in her direction.

Mrs. Shamefoot became vaguely flurried.

'I don't know, dear,' she replied. 'When I try to do arithmetic clouds come down upon me like they do in *Tannhäuser*.'

With a gasp, Dina crossed over to a book—she seemed to be suffering still from lack of breath. The pretty creature lived in a settlement *William Morris*, some paradise on the confines of the Tube, from whence she would appear breathless each morning, and would stay so, usually, until the Guards went by. When this occurred she would commence her duties by flying to the window to sprinkle water from a Dresden can over the grateful flowers, admiring, meantime, the charms of the cavalcade through the handle of one of Mrs. Shamefoot's psychological baskets, or whatever else might be in stock.

After this, she would calm down slightly for the day. But unfortunately, even so, Dina lacked sense. Even in the afternoon she would say: 'The roses this morning are two shillings each.'

'I did so enjoy last night,' Mrs. Shamefoot said to Mrs. Henedge, 'though, when I got back, for no reason . . . Soco simply stormed at me; but I was splendidly cool. I said nothing. I just *looked* at him.'

'You poor darling,' Mrs. Henedge said sympathetically: 'What an unhappy life!'

In silence Mrs. Shamefoot stuck a lily in her lyre.

'It is sometimes,' she said, 'rather unpleasant. . . .' She began suddenly to cry.

'They are not catkins at all,' Dina observed, apparently herself somewhat surprised. 'They're orchids.'

But Mrs. Henedge ignored her. She was determined to have nothing to do with them.

'There,' she exclaimed, 'went poor little Scantilla stalking along. Did you notice her? She had on a black jacket and a vermilion-magenta skirt——'

'Half-mourning!'

'Exactly.'

'I dare say she's off to the wedding,' Mrs. Shamefoot said. 'Lady Georgia and At'y are coming in, I believe, on their way. The wedding is at Holy Trinity.'

Mrs. Henedge looked out at the stream of carriages through the flowers. The seldom coarse or unspiritual faces of the passing crowd . . . veiled by plum-blossom, had an effect, she thought, of Chinese embroidery.

'I can't quite forgive Nils for getting married,' Mrs. Shamefoot murmured, twirling in the air a pale rose with almost crimson leaves. 'I used to like to talk nonsense with him. He talked agreeable nonsense better than anyone I ever knew.'

'I'm more concerned for Isolde,' Mrs. Henedge said. 'I pity her, poor child, married to a charming little vein fickle thing like that!'

'Oh, what does it matter!' Mrs. Shamefoot queried. 'When I took Soco I married him for certain qualities which now, alas! I see he can have never had.'

'That's just what's so sad! I mean, I'm afraid you did something commonplace after all.'

Mrs. Shamefoot became discomposed.

'Oh, well!' she said, 'when I got engaged I was unconscious, or very nearly. I had fallen sound asleep, I remember, off an iron chair in the park. The next day he had put it in the paper; and we none of us could raise the guinea to contradict . . .'

'Have you sent Isolde the——'

'No, . . .' Mrs. Shamefoot confessed.

To nine brides out of ten she would make the same gift—a small piece of Italian gauze.

When the recipient, holding it to the light, would catch a glimpse of her fiancé through it, she began to realise something of its significance.

'What did you send?' Mrs. Henedge wondered.

A tenth bride invariably was interesting.

'I sent her,' Mrs. Shamefoot said, 'a Flemish crucifix, with ruby nails for the hands and feet. . . .'

'Dear Biddy. . . . *I* ran only to a pack of cards; supposed once to have belonged to Deirdre. I got them in Chelsea.'

But Dina at the telephone was becoming distressing.

'Hullo! Yes! No! To whom am I speaking?'

The 'To whom am I speaking?' characterised, as a rule, her manner.

'An order,' she said, 'for a shower of puff-puffs for Mrs. Hanover, to be at Curzon Street to-morrow morning by nine o'clock. If the flowers are not delivered by then she will expect them at the Law Courts.'

'Poor thing!' Mrs. Shamefoot murmured; 'send her a lovely spray, and tell Jordan to be there by eight.'

Jordan lately had been imported from the country, only to exclaim, the first time it rained: 'It's too-wet-for-to-go-far!'

It had been very disheartening.

Mrs. Shamefoot considered her lyre; in its way, it was going to be as wonderful as the anchor of peonies she had made for the late Lord Mayor.

'Do you remember it, dear?' she said, beginning to laugh. 'It was so *huge*, so perfectly huge, that it had to be tilted sideways to get it out of the shop.'

But Mrs. Henedge was considering an amazingly elegant landaulette—a landaulette that seemed to her to positively whistle with smartness.

'Here comes Lady Georgia, now,' she exclaimed, 'and Mrs. Mountjulian, "Emily" is with her——'

'Oh, she's getting sinister and *passée*.'

'Perhaps; but only sometimes! It's not so long ago that she was tinting her toes with blackberries to be a nymph! You'd never credit it, dear, but we were the same age once!'

'I shall hide behind the counter,' Mrs. Shamefoot said, 'if she comes in.'

'For the love of heaven, mind the lyre!' Mrs. Henedge screamed as Mrs. Mountjulian entered.

Mrs. Mountjulian was long and slender, like an Imari vase, with a pretty, lingering manner which many thought tiresome.

As Miss Emma Harris the world had found her distinctly aloof. As the Duchess of Overcares, however, she had been very simple indeed; it had been a new form, perhaps, of pride. And now, as Mrs. Mountjulian, she was becoming 'aloof' again. To add a dash of picturesqueness to her career, her husband, it was said, was doing his utmost to get rid of her; and although she had been in an aeroplane disaster, a fatal gala performance, two railway accidents and a shipwreck, she always came back—smiling.

'We've come to rifle you of your nicest flowers,' Mrs. Mountjulian said.

'Oh, I need nothing,' Atalanta explained. 'Only to smooth my hair.'

In a muslin frock with a broad blue sash, and a bridesmaid's bouquet of honeysuckle and meadow-sweet, she was looking engagingly pronounced. She needed only a mop and a pail to be altogether delightful.

'Isn't she *voyou*?' Lady Georgia said nervously. 'I'm really afraid to be seen with her.'

'My dear, you look a dove!' Mrs. Henedge murmured.

'Properly managed, nothing need ever clash,' Mrs. Mountjulian assured Dina, singling out for herself a savage, multicoloured leaf.

But Lady Georgia appeared transfixed.

'For whom,' she asked, 'is that heavenly lyre?'

' "For Time sleeps not, but ever passes like the wind . . ." ' Mrs. Shamefoot replied vaguely.

'St. Catherine!'

'To the Queen of . . . Naples.'

They smiled.

'Oh, do choose,' Atalanta said, glueing down her hair inventively, with a perfect sense of style. 'There's sure to be a struggle at the church. And Isolde will have a *crise des nerfs* or something if we aren't there soon. Besides, Victoria's getting impatient: I can see her dangling a long leg from the car into the street.'

'It was too bad really of Mrs. Fox foisting her on to us,' Lady Georgia said. 'Prevent her, do, from getting out.'

She was looking, perhaps, annoyed, in arsenic green with a hat full of wan white flowers.

'Blueharnis insists that you come to us for the Ashringford races,' she said to Mrs. Shamefoot, as she said good-bye, 'and stay at Stockingham for as long as you can.'

'How sweet you are! If only to lie in the garden, I'll come.'

'At present I'm revolving a Tragic Garden,' Lady Georgia told her, 'with cypress-trees, and flights of stairs.'

'I'm admiring your pictures,' Mrs. Mountjulian said, dawdling. 'Those clouds—so stationary—surely are Cézanne? and the Monticelli . . . ! And that alluring Nicholson. . . . Only last night I was talking to Sir Valerian Hanway; you know whom I mean? And he said: . . . "It's an anxiety for a poor man to own beautiful things. Where would be the pleasure of possessing a Velasquez, and having to hold a pocket handkerchief all the time to the roof to keep out the rain?" '

'If she thought to embarrass me,' Mrs. Shamefoot said as soon as they were gone, 'I'm afraid she failed!'

'Poor woman!' Mrs. Henedge considered it diplomatic to say. 'Either she is growing old, or her maid is getting clumsy. . . .'

'I should imagine both,' Mrs. Shamefoot observed, returning to her lyre.

'I'm delighted, at any rate, that we shall see something of each other in Ashringford! We must contrive to conquer all difficulties to obtain the window.'

'Otherwise,' Mrs. Shamefoot said, 'I shall try Overcares!'

'It's not so *obvious,* of course!'

'And the Bishop, I know, is not unfavourably disposed.... But somehow, dear, a manufacturing town is *not* the same.'

'Indeed it isn't!'

'Besides, there were so many sickening stipulations——'

'The Bishop of Overcares is the most paralysing man I know,' Mrs. Henedge said, 'and she . . . Mrs. Whooper——'

'A terror!'

'A perfect terror!'

'Well, it's so nice of you to help me.'

'And might a tiny nosegay be left for Mr. Brookes? Lilies he likes. . . . Just five or six; I'm making, unavoidably, in the opposite direction, or I'd drop them on his doorstep myself.'

Mrs. Shamefoot stood a moment pensively watching Dina remove the dark hearts that stained from Winsome's lilies before continuing her wreath.

It would be quite too extravagant, she feared, when finished, for the penniless young man for whom her débutante had died. He could never afford to buy it.

What should be done?

Remove a few of the orchids? No!

Allow the father it? Certainly not.

Die and use it herself? Soco was so dilatory. . . .

She remained dreaming.

'Be so good,' she called to Dina presently, 'as to fetch me the scissors.'

And, shaking her head sadly under her heavy hat, she cut a string to the lyre.

∞ IV ∞

13 SILVERY PLACE was the address of Mrs. Henedge's latest genius.

'A young boy,' it was her custom to describe him.

With a few simple words she could usually create an interest.

The young boy, gentle reader, was Winsome Brookes.

Standing at his window, hairbrush in hand, we find him humming some bars of *Cimarosa*, whilst staring up at a far-off Fuji of clouds. The attitude was essentially characteristic. When not exercising those talents of his, Winsome Brookes would spend whole hours together grooming fitfully his hair.

'Don't mind me,' his gracious lady often said to him, 'if you care to calm your hair. I know that with you it takes the place of a cigarette.' And at Chesham Place, sometimes, she would supply the needful weapons.

Just now, however, with two invitations for the same afternoon, he was looking pestered. . . .

'Will you not make, Andrew, that appalling noise?' he murmured distractedly, without turning round. 'You make me shudder.'

'It's extraordinary,' Andrew answered briskly, waving, as he spoke, a file, 'but ever since that Arabian ball, the paint clings to my finger-tips, as if to the cornice of a temple!'

Winsome removed an eye from the street.

'Well, need you point at me like a finger-post?' he irritably enquired.

'I consider your friend to be half a minion, and half an intellectual,' Mrs. Henedge, who had never taken to Andrew in the least, had said once to Winsome Brookes. 'That violet muffler, and the no collar . . .' was the official reason, but in reality, a lurid sketch of herself leaning upon the arm of an Archbishop of Canterbury whilst smiling across her shoulder into the eyes of Monsignor Parr accounted for the antipathy. She had come upon the trifle altogether suddenly at the Grafton Gallery and had decided at first it must be a Forain.

'I wish your breakfast would come,' Andrew exclaimed disinterestedly, stretching himself out upon the floor—a *nature morte*.

'And so do I,' Winsome complained. 'But what is one to do? I order an egg, I wait an hour for it, and in the end most probably they'll bring me some fearful thing that looks like an auk's.'

'A hawk's?'

'Oh, my dear friend. . . . An auk's. The great auk!' Winsome rolled his eyes.

Let us follow these bright ornaments.

The rooms of their occupants are sometimes interesting.

Taking for granted the large, unwieldy furniture, the mournful carpet, the low-spirited draperies, the brown paper of the walls, the frieze, in which Windsor Castle appeared again, and again, and again, and which a patriotic landlady (a woman like a faded Giotto) would not consent to hide lest it might seem to be disloyal, let us confine our observations to the book, the candlestick, the hourglass, or the skull.

In a litter upon the mantelpiece—some concert fixtures, a caricature of Owen Nares, an early photograph of Andrew in a surplice, a sketch of Mildenberg as Clytemnestra, an impression of Felia Litvinne in Tristan, might be seen, whilst immediately above, usually quite awry, was suspended a passionate engraving of two very thin figures wandering before a retreating sea.

Winsome, indeed, to Andrew's amusement, cared only for quite independent landscapes of disquieting colour. He found beauty in those long, straight roads bounded by telegraph poles, between which some market cart would trundle through the pale midday.

Upon the piano, swathed in a scintillating shawl, rose up a modern figurine with a weary gesture, which, upon examination, was not lacking in signs that the original must almost certainly have possessed the proverbial kind heart of a black sheep. Beside it, against a stack of music, was propped a mask of Beethoven in imitation bronze, which, during the more strenuous efforts of the player, would invariably slip, giving, often, the signal for applause.

While in a corner, intriguing the eye, reposed a quantity of boards: polished yellow planks, the planks of Winsome's coffin. These, in the event of a party, could be coaxed to extend the dinner-table. 'If you're going to be ten for supper to-night,' his landlady would say, 'you'll need your coffin boards stretched out.'

But as much as he was able Winsome sauntered out to dine.

In her cooking, he found his landlady scarcely solicitous enough about his figure. . . . So manifest, of course, at concerts. In her supremest flights the good woman would seldom get beyond suet.

And even this was in her most Debussyish vein. . . . And the question of concerts was occupying largely his thoughts just now.

Continually he was turning over in his mind the advisability of being re-baptised, this time—Rose de Tivoli. For musical purposes it sounded so much more promising, he considered, than Winsome Brookes. . . . Two persons would come to hear Rose, whereas only one, and perhaps not even one . . .

But if Winsome Brookes had talent, Rose de Tivoli had genius! Could he possibly be Rose?

Mrs. Henedge was inclined to think so. She had been, indeed, most hopeful:

'I'll take the Aeolian Hall, one afternoon,' she had said, 'and you can give the concert——'

To be—or not to be Rose! It was one of the things that was troubling him most.

'Ah! here comes breakfast now,' Andrew observed, as Mrs. Henedge's floral gift was ushered in upon a tray.

> ' "I offer ye these violets,
> Lilies and lesser pets,
> These roses here pell-mell—
> These red and splendid roses,
> Buds which to-day uncloses,
> These *orchids dear* as well." '

' "These opening pinks as well," ' Winsome corrected. And returning impassively to the window, he leaned out.

Everywhere, between the houses, those old and dingy houses, whose windows would catch the sunrise with untold splendour, showed plots of garden, like snatches of song. Sometimes of a summer morning, leaning from his window, it would not have astonished him greatly to have surprised the Simonetta of Boccaccio at the end of the shady place leaping lightly, with uplifted arms, between the trees, pursued by Guido degli Anastagi and his pack of hounds. . . . Nor were visions all. Across the street the Artistic Theatre, a brilliantly frescoed, Asian-looking affair, aspired publicly heavenwards every day. It was the adornment and the scandal of the place. Too late, now, to protest about the frescoes; they were there!

Winsome sighed. At that moment his gracious lady bored him badly.

For just as the bee has a finer nature than the wasp, so had Andrew the advantage of Winsome Brookes.

By nature mercenary, and, perhaps, a trifle mean, a handful of flowers suggested to him nothing very exactly. . . .

> 'The courtyard clock had numbered seven
> When first I came; but when eleven
> Struck on my ears, as mute I sate,
> It sounded like the knell of Fate.'

Winsome turned.

Nothing diverted Andrew more than to investigate Winsome's books.

With a *Beauty and the Beast* he was almost happy.

The entrance, fortunately, of breakfast put an end to the recitation.

Whilst Winsome breakfasted Andrew indulged himself by venting his indignation on Miss Compostella's poster for the *Dance of Death* at the theatre over the way.

'It's enough to make me cart the Magdalen back home!' he exclaimed.

'Perhaps some day,' Winsome said, 'I may go for curiosity to New York, but until then——!'

For Andrew frequently would model strange, unusual figures that were ostensibly Church pieces had they been more subdued . . . His Mary Magdalen, for instance, might be seen in the foyer of the Artistic Theatre, where, even there, it was usually abused. . . .

'The Eros looks at least sixty!' he observed, criticising the poster. 'And Death in that small toque's absurd. Surely Death required a terrific Lewis and a Romney hoop to conceal the scythe.'

'But Death isn't a woman!' Winsome objected, cracking the top of his egg.

'Indeed? Death is very often a bore.'

'Only for Adonis,' Winsome murmured absently.

' . . . Do I disturb you?'

'No, come in. Not in the least!'

'I thought,' Andrew said coldly to the intruder, 'that you went to the Slade!'

'Certainly; but not to-day! I shall run round later on, I dare say, for lunch at the British Mu-z. . . .'

'How fascinating!'

'I want you to come upstairs,' the young man said plaintively to Winsome, 'and tell me what Titian would have done. . . .'

'Me?' Winsome said.

'Yes, do come.'

'Knowing you,' said Andrew, 'I should say that most likely he would have given her a richer background, and a more expensive silk.'

'How can I?' the young man queried, as he withdrew, 'when the model has only a glove?'

'Why will you appal him?' Winsome asked; 'he has the soul of a shepherd.'

'Impossible.'

'What are you saying?'

'Nothing; but when I look at your landlady's frieze,' Andrew said limply, 'I've a sort of Dickensey feeling coming on. I get depressed, I——'

Winsome swallowed his coffee.

'Then let's go.'

'Il tend à leurs baisers la plume de sa main,' Andrew began to warble inconsequently as he escaped downstairs.

∞ *V* ∞

'I WONDER you aren't ashamed, Sumph,' Miss Compostella said to her maid, 'to draw the blind up every morning on such a grey sky.'

'Shall I draw it down again, miss?'

'Yes, please do. No, please don't. Come back to me again when I ring.'

'And the shampoo?'

After the final performance of any play it was the maid's duty to perform this office to precipitate from the mind a discarded part.

'Washing-out-Desdemona,' Sumph called it, dating the ceremony from then.

'It's hardly necessary,' Julia said, 'after such a light part. And, candidly, I don't quite agree with this romance-exhorting haste. For five whole weeks now, I'm only myself.'

'Lord, may it keep fine,' prayed the maid, lowering an inch the blind.

She was as stolid a mortal, it is probable, as ever graced a bedside or breathed at heaven a prayer.

'A light part,' she said, 'becomes a load during fever. And none of us are so strong as my poor——'

'But after Hermione,' Julia objected, 'I remained a week. . . .'

'After Hermione,' the woman replied, 'you could have gone ten days. After Hermione,' she repeated loftily, 'you could do as you pleased.'

Sumph, indeed, worshipped Shakespeare. . . . Stratford, it appeared, was her 'old home.' Consequently, she was scarcely able to endure her mistress to appear in those pieces—pamphlets, or plays of domestic persecution—in which all that could be done was to waft, with one's temperament, little puffs of rarefied air, now and again, across the footlights.

And yet it must be said that Sumph was a bad critic. It was just in these parts that her mistress most excelled.

Julia sat up and smiled.

Round the bed in which we surprise her hung a severe blue veil suspended from oblong wooden rings. Above it, a china angel upon a wire was suspended to complete the picture.

At the sight of her tired mistress set in bolsters the devoted woman was almost moved to tears.

'Oh, be quiet,' Julia exclaimed. 'I know exactly . . . I remind you of Mrs. So-and-so in some death scene. . . .'

Sumph straightened her cap, a voluminous affair drawn together in front in a bewildering bow.

'You do,' she said, 'miss. Of Mrs. Paraguay, or la Tazeira, as she was to become. She achieved fame in *Agrippina at Baiae*, in a single night. Never will I forget her pale face or her white crinoline. She was marvellous. It was that first success, perhaps, that drove her to play only invalid parts. Ah, miss, how lovely she looked with the treasures of half the Indies in her hair. . . .'

'Indeed?' Julia observed. 'You're hurting my feet.'

The woman turned away from anything so brittle.

'Tell me truthfully,' Julia queried, 'how am I looking?'

'Beautifully weary, miss.'

Miss Compostella sank back.

Like some indignant Europa she saw herself being carried away
by the years.

'Sumph,' she said feebly, 'what do you think of Mr. Harvester?'

'As a poet, miss, or as a man?'

'. . . As a poet.'

'His poems are very cold and careful, miss; just what one would
expect.'

Julia turned her face to the wall.

Since her mother's death, caused, no doubt, by a flitting forth
with an excursion ticket to Florence (Mrs. Compostella had succumbed almost immediately in the train), Julia had taken a charming
house for herself in Sacred Gardens. The address alone, she hoped,
would be a sufficient protection, and so spare her the irksomeness
of a chaperon. And here, somewhat erratically, she lived with the
invaluable Sumph, whom she ill-treated, and of whom, in her way,
she was fond.

'Mr. Harvester came round last night, miss, just after you had
gone,' Sumph said; 'and I'll confess to you I flew at him. At the
totally unexpected, as they say, it's oneself that speaks.'

'Indeed, it ought not to be.'

'Surrounded as we are,' said Sumph, 'it's best to be discreet.'

'I'm afraid you were very rude to him!'

'Oh, miss, why waste words on a married man? I'd sooner save
my breath and live an extra day.'

'Are you so *fond* of life?' Miss Compostella painfully enquired, her
face turned still towards the wall.

'And an old gentleman, with the wickedest eye, called also, and
asked if you was in.'

'Did he give no name?'

'He left no card, but he called himself a saint,' Sumph answered
slyly.

Mr. Garsaint's political satire, *The Leg of Chicken*, which was to be
played in Byzantine costume, was to be given at the Artistic Theatre
in the autumn; unless, indeed, Miss Compostella changed her
plans, and produced *Titus Andronicus,* or *Marino Faliero,* or a wildly
imprudent version of the *Curious Impertinent* at the last moment,
instead. For if there was one thing that she preferred to a complete
success, it was a real fiasco. And Mr. Garsaint's comedy would
probably be a success! What British audience would be able to
withstand the middle act, in which a couple of chaises-longues,

drawn up like passing carriages, silhouetted the footlights from whence the Empress Irene Doukas (a wonderful study of Mrs. A.) and Anna Comnena lay and smoked cigarettes and argued together—at ease? And even should Mr. Garsaint's dainty, fastidious prose pass unadmired, the world must bow to the costumes, foreshadowing as they did the modes of the next century.

'How tiresome to have missed him!' Miss Compostella exclaimed, sitting up, and blinking a little at the light.

In the window hung a wicker cage of uncertain shape that held a stuffed canary. It had had a note sweeter than Chenal's once. . . . And there it was! Poor, sad thing!

'Angel! Sweet! Pet! Pretty!' Julia would sometimes say to it by mistake.

Through the vigilant bars of the cage she could admire a distant view of a cold stone church by Vanbrugh. The austere and heavy tower, however, did not depress her. On the contrary, she approved its solidity. Flushed at sunset, it suggested quite forcibly a middle-aged bachelor with possessions at Coutts. At times she could almost think of it as *James.* . . .

'And there are several hundred more letters waiting for you in the next room, miss,' Sumph said.

To Julia's enquiry for a man with ecstasy to stage-manage, she had received several thousand applications.

'Go to the next room,' Miss Compostella directed, 'and choose me two with your eyes shut.'

It was in the 'next room' that Miss Compostella sometimes studied her parts . . . though for modern comedy rôles she usually went 'upstairs.'

She sank back now and waited.

With five weeks at her disposal, with the exception of a complaisant visit to Stockingham for a race party, it was her intention to lie absolutely still, preferably at a short distance from London, and explore her heart.

For indeed the dread of Miss Compostella's life was that she had not got one. Unless that sorrowful, soft, vague, yearning, aching, melting, kite-like, soaring emotion was a heart?

Could that be a heart?

From the mantelpiece came a sudden 'whirr' from an unconcerned Sèvres shepherdess, a coquettish silence, followed by the florid chiming of a clock.

Noon; or very nearly—for as an object submits meekly to its surroundings, Julia's timepiece, invariably, was a little in advance.

She held out long arms, driftingly.

It was noon! Sultry noon—somewhere in the world. In Cintra now . . .

She lay back impassively at the sound of Sumph's Olympian tread.

A gesture might revive a ghost.

It was irritating to discover that one recalled Polly Whatmore in *The Vicar's Vengeance*, or Mrs. Giltspur in *The Lady of the Lake*.

The indispensable woman, holding the testimonials of the men of ecstasy, approached the bed.

"And Mr. Harvester is here, miss,' she said sedately, lifting up her eyes towards the quivering angel. 'Should I show him into the next room, or shall I take him *upstairs*?'

Julia reflected.

'No,' she murmured; 'put him in the dining-room and shut the door.'

'Yes, miss.'

'And, Sumph . . . offer him a liqueur, and something to read—of his own.'

'Yes, miss.'

'And, Sumph . . . I shall be getting up now in about half an hour.'

She waited—and recast her arms expressively.

'Claud . . . ?'

But the worst of it was, she reflected, that with a chair upon Mount Parnassos (half-way up) he was somewhat inclined to *dictate*. . . .

∞ *VI* ∞

TO Ashringford from Euston is really quite a journey.

Only an inconvenient morning train, or a dissipated evening one—described in time-tables as the Cathedral Express—ever attempt at concentration. Normal middle-day persons disliking these extremes must get out at Totterdown and wait.

As a stimulus to introspection, detention cannot be ignored.

Cardinal Pringle, in his Autobiography, confesses that the hour spent on Totterdown platform, seated in deep despondence upon his trunk, came as the turning-point in his career.

Introspection, however, is not to be enforced.

'It will hardly take us until five o'clock, Violet,' Mrs. Shamefoot observed to her old crony, Mrs. Barrow of Dawn, fumbling, as she spoke, with a basket, 'to drink a small bottle of champagne. Is there nothing particular here to see?'

She looked out at the world, through a veil open as a fishing-net, mysteriously.

Where were the *sunburned sicklemen of August weary*! The *ryestraw hats*! Surely not many yards off.

Mrs. Barrow put up her sunshade.

'Oh yes,' she said, 'a cousin of Oliver Cromwell is buried not far from here; and in the same graveyard there's also the vault of a Cabinet Minister who died only the other day.'

Mrs. Shamefoot produced with perfect sympathy a microscopic affair.

'In this heat,' she observed, 'champagne is so much more refreshing than tea.'

Mrs, Barrow accepted with gratitude.

It may be remembered from some exclamations of Lady Listless that just lately she had 'heard the Raven.' It was said, however, about Dawn, that whenever she wished to escape to town for a theatre or to shop she would manage to hear its croak.

'I do hope,' she exclaimed, 'that Sartorious won't be at Ashringford to meet me; it's perfectly possible that he may.'

'Well, there's no good in singing a dirge over what can't be helped; the connection's gone.'

'What tactless things trains are!'

Mrs. Shamefoot shook a panoply of feathers.

'What is that curious watch-tower,' she asked diplomatically, 'between the trees?'

Mrs. Barrow began to unbend.

Life, after all, seemed less raw after a glass of champagne.

'I don't know, dear,' she said, 'but I think the scenery's so perfectly French.'

'Isn't there a hospital near here—for torn hearts, where love-sick persons can stay together in quarantine to enjoy their despair and help each other to forget?'

'I don't know, dear,' Mrs. Barrow said again, 'but I believe there's a sanatorium for nervous complaints. . . . All the country round Totterdown belongs to Lord Brassknocker.'

'Oh, he's dreadful!'

'And she's such a thorough cat.'

'And poor Lord Susan!'

'Poor, *poor* Lord Susan.'

'I can almost feel Ashringford Cathedral here,' Mrs. Shamefoot remarked. 'Aren't the hedges like the little low curtains of a rood-screen?'

'Exactly!'

'And aren't the——'

'My dear, what a dreadful amount of etceteras you appear to bring,' Mrs. Barrow replied with some aridity.

Mrs. Shamefoot's principal portmanteau was a rose-coloured chest, which, with its many foreign labels, exhaled an atmosphere of positive scandal. No nice maid would stand beside it.

A number of sagacious smaller cases clambered about it now into frantic streets, and sunny open piazzas, like a small town clustering about the walls of some lawless temple.

Mrs. Barrow was appalled at so much luggage. She had been to the ends of the earth, it seemed, with only a basket.

Mrs. Shamefoot re-helped herself to Clicquot.

She was looking to-day incomparably well, draped in a sort of sheet *à la* Puvis de Chavannes, with a large, lonely hat suggestive of *der Wanderer*.

'The relief,' she exclaimed, 'of getting somewhere where clothes don't matter!'

'But surely to obtain a window in the Cathedral *they will*. You'll need an old Ascot frock, shan't you, for the Bishop?'

'Violet, I'm shocked! Can such trifles count?'

'Well, I dare say, dear, they help to persuade.'

'Bishop Pantry is quite unlike Bishop Henedge, isn't he?'

'Oh, quite. The present man's a scholar! Those round shoulders. He will probably die in his library by rolling off the final seat of his portable steps.'

'But not just yet!'

'You have read his *Inner Garden*!'

'Oh yes. . . . And *Even-tide,* and *Night Thoughts*, and the sequel, *Beams*. But they're so hard. How can it be good for the soul to sleep upon the floor, although it mayn't be bad for the spine.'

'Besides, to tread the spiral path means usually a bother . . .' Mrs. Barrow observed. 'There are the servants! And to get a girl to stay in Ashringford——'

Mrs. Shamefoot fixed her eyes upon the hills that slid back, she thought, with a fine monastic roll.

'And is he very plain?' she asked.

'I should never say so. It's a fine Neronian head.'

'Lady Anne is charming, isn't she?'

Mrs. Barrow hesitated.

'Sartorious,' she replied, 'thinks her wily.'

'But she is charming?'

'Oh, well,' Mrs. Barrow said evasively, 'she doesn't shine perhaps at the Palace like dear Mrs. Henedge. I suppose we shall never replace *her* again! Fortunately, however, she's devoted to Ashringford and comes there nearly every summer. Since she's taken the Closed House she's thrown out fourteen bow-windows.'

Mrs. Shamefoot snapped the lid of her basket.

'Who are these condottieri?' she enquired, as an imperious party drove up with considerable clatter.

Mrs. Barrow turned.

'Don't look more than you can help, dear,' she exclaimed, in a voice that would have piqued a stronger character than Mrs. Lott, 'it's the Pontypools.'

'Ashringford people?'

'Theoretically.'

Mrs. Shamefoot smiled.

'Sartorious——' Mrs. Barrow began.

'Thinks them?'

'Totally dreadful. They're probably reconnoitring. Mrs. Pontypool is usually spinning a web for someone.'

'The dowager's very handsome,' Mrs. Shamefoot remarked, 'in a reckless sort of way, but the girl's a fairy!'

'Oh, don't swear! Don't, don't swear!' Mrs. Pontypool was adjuring a member of her family, with brio, stepping, as she spoke, right into Mrs. Barrow's arms.

'Is it quite true,' she asked, shaking hands, 'that the connection's gone?'

'Quite!'

Mrs. Pontypool sat down. 'It needs heroism in the country,' she explained, 'to keep sight of anybody.'

'Certainly. Crusading, and without a car——'

'Crusading, dear Mrs. Barrow! Yet how did one's ancestors get along?'

'I don't know,' Mrs. Barrow said. 'It's so rare, isn't it? nowadays, to find anybody who had a grandmother.'

'In the times I mean,' Mrs. Pontypool said, undismayed, 'women went for miles in a sedan-chair, and crossed continents in their tilburies, and in their britschkas, and in their cabriolets!'

'Heroic!'

'Less heroic, surely, than those women one sometimes sees who fasten their bath-chairs to their lovers' auto-bicycles.'

'And where have you been—if it isn't indiscreet . . . ?'

'We've been spending a few hours at Castle Barbarous.'

'I hear Lord Brassknocker is going to open his pictures to the public,' Mrs. Shamefoot said. 'He has, of course, a very fine Ruisdael, an attractive Sisley and a charming Crome, but really the rest of the collection is only fit for the Sacristy scene in *Manon*.'

'A Last Supper at *two tables*,' Mrs. Pontypool said confidentially, 'struck one as—scarcely——'

'Not if it was Veronese.'

'It was Rubens.'

'The busiest man who ever lived most certainly was Rubens.'

'Was it a party?' Mrs. Barrow asked, less from curiosity than because she would be glad to have something to say to Sartorious during dinner.

Oh, the trial of those dreary dinners at Dawn. . . . What wonder was it that Mrs. Barrow should sometimes become peevish or invent things that were untrue or, in her extremity, hear the Raven's croak? Had she been neurasthenic she would have probably sometimes screamed at the sight of her Lord enjoying an artichoke, slowly, leaf by leaf.

'Was it a party?' Mrs. Barrow asked again.

'Only old Mr. James and little Mrs. Kilmurry,' Mrs. Pontypool replied. 'Such a strange old man, who strolled once with the Tennysons in the Cascine in Florence.'

There was a pause—just long enough for an angel to pass, flying slowly.

'Was Lord Susan there?' Mrs. Barrow enquired.

'He very seldom is,' Miss Pontypool said.

'Unfortunate young man,' Mrs. Pontypool exclaimed, playing

with the tails of her stole: 'perpetually he's on the verge of . . . and, although I'm told he's gun-shy, in my opinion . . . and I would willingly have sent a wreath, . . . only where's the use in sending one the day afterwards?'

'But you've heard nothing?'

'No. . . . Naturally the Brassknockers don't care to talk of it before they're quite obliged; but Lady Brassknocker did strike me as being so unusually distrait. Didn't you think so, Queenie?'

'I really didn't notice,' Miss Pontypool said. 'Where's Goosey?'

'To be sure! I thought if Lord Brassknocker could only see the boy he might take a fancy to him,' Mrs. Pontypool said.

'Really, in what way?' Mrs. Barrow wondered.

'Who can tell? Lord Brassknocker's a very important man.'

'He is a very rich one.'

'Poor child! What is one to do with him? In any other age, of course, he could have ambled along in the retinue of some great lady.'

'Oh, be thankful,' Mrs. Barrow began.

'As it is, with a little influence, he's hoping to get into some garage.'

'Poor young man,' Mrs. Shamefoot said, with sympathy, 'such a bending life!'

By the time the train had reached Totterdown Mrs. Barrow congratulated herself that she would be artichoke-proof now, positively, for nearly a week.

In the railway carriage, Mrs. Shamefoot was sufficiently fortunate, too, to secure the seat opposite to herself for a magnificent image of the god Ptah.

The terrific immobility of Egyptian things enchanted her, particularly in the train.

Often the god had aroused her friendliest feelings by saving her from the strain of answering questions, or expressing hopes, or guessing whether the carriage would be there to meet them, or whether it would not, or from the alternative miseries of migraine brought on by feigning to read, for, as Mrs. Shamefoot was aware, she might be called upon to remove a dressing-case, but how seldom did it occur to anyone to deplace a god.

But Mrs. Pontypool was not to be suppressed.

'I once met a Mrs. Asp,' she said, 'who was writing the life of

Hepshepset, wife and sister of Thothmes II, who, on becoming a widow, invented a hairwash and dressed as a man.'

The beautiful summer's day had crumbled to dusk as the twin towers of the Cathedral and the short spire (which was, perhaps, an infelicity) came into view.

How desolate it appeared across the fields of wan white clover, now that the sun had gone! Saint Apollinaris in Classe never looked more alone.

'Ashringford is quite a healthy place, isn't it?' Mrs. Shamefoot enquired anxiously, turning towards Mrs. Barrow.

Mrs. Barrow opened her eyes.

'One wouldn't care to say so,' she replied, 'there's usually a good deal of sickness about; *of a kind.*'

'I consider it a regular doctor's town!' Mrs. Pontypool exclaimed; 'the funeral horses are always on the go.'

Mrs. Pontypool looked humane.

'Poor animals!' she said.

'You see the Ashringford houses are so old,' Goosey explained, 'and so stuffy, and the windows are so small. It's as if the Ashringford people had made them themselves by poking a finger through the brick.'

'Which makes us all delicate, of course, and the climate doubly treacherous,' Mrs. Pontypool said. 'Although at one time I fancy it used not to be so bad. I date the change to Bishop Henedge. He was so High Church. His views were so extremely high! Quite unintentionally, perhaps, he attracted towards us the uncertain climate of Rome. I should advise anyone visiting Ashringford for the first time to do precisely as they would there.'

'And what is that?' Mrs. Shamefoot demanded doubtfully.

'Wear an extra flannel petticoat.'

Much to Mrs. Barrow's disappointment, there was no Sartorious to meet the train; only a footman—Lady Georgia's chauffeur attended to Mrs. Shamefoot and her maid.

'I wonder she keeps him,' Mrs. Barrow observed, as she climbed into her brougham. 'From the marks on his cheeks he looks as if he had been in more than one break up.'

'My regards to Lady Georgia,' Goosey called after Mrs. Shamefoot to say.

'My dear, at nineteen has one regards?' Mrs. Pontypool said. 'Silly, affected boy!'

Mrs. Shamefoot was glad to be alone. How wonderful it was to breathe the evening air. As she sped towards Stockingham over a darkening plain, patched with clumps of heavy hyacinthine trees, almost she could catch the peculiar aroma of the Cathedral.

'As indefinable as piety!' she exclaimed, drawing on her glove.

∞ *VII* ∞

LADY ANNE PANTRY was sitting in the china-cupboard, a room fitted with long glass shelves, on which her fabled Dresden figures, monkey musicians, and sphinx marquises, made perfect blots of colour against the gold woodwork of the walls.

Heedless of her sister-in-law, she was reading her morning letters whilst massaging her nose.

'Such a dull post, Anne,' that person exclaimed, lifting up an incomparable, tearful, spiritual and intellectual face from the perusal of a circular.

'Mine is not,' said Lady Anne.

'Indeed?'

Lady Anne rustled her skirt.

' . . . Mrs. Henedge,' she said, 'it appears, has quite gone over to Rome.'

'But is it settled?'

'Since she's to build in our midst a bijou church for Monsignor Parr. . . . Such scenes, I expect, there'll be.'

'Certainly. If it's to be another Gothic fake.'

'And Lady Georgia asks if she may lunch here to-morrow and bring a Mrs. Shamefoot. Mysteries with the Bishop. And there's been *almost* a murder at the workhouse again.'

'How very disgraceful.'

'And the Twyfords are coming—at least some of them. Less tiresome, perhaps, than if they all came at once.'

'I love her postscripts——'

'To-day there isn't one. And that brocade, you remember, I liked, is seventy shillings a yard.'

'Too dear.'

'And I said *a spot,* Aurelia; I did not say a *cartwheel* . . .' Lady Anne murmured, getting up to display her wares.

Vainglory

Lady Anne had turned all her troubles to beauty, and at forty-five she had an interesting face. She was short and robust, with calm, strong features, and in the evening she sometimes suggested Phèdre. Her voice was charming, full of warmth and colour, and although she did not sing, it might be said of her that she was a mute soprano.

Aurelia Pantry extended a forlorn and ravishing hand.

'Aren't they fools?' she exclaimed, spreading out the materials before her.

She spoke habitually rather absently, as though she were placing the last brick to some gorgeous castle in the air.

It was the custom at the Palace that the Bishop's eleven sisters should spend a month in rotation there each year.

Aurelia, who was the most popular (being the least majestical, the least like Eleanor), corresponded, as a rule, to August and September.

Of the Bishop's eleven sisters, indeed, she was the only one that Lady Anne could endure.

Eleanor, Ambrosia, Hypolita, Virginia, Prudence, Lettice, Chrissy, Patsy, Gussy and Grace were all shocking, hopeless and dreadful, according to Lady Anne.

But Aurelia, who was just a little mystic, added a finish, a distinction to the Palace; especially got up in muslin, when, like some sinuous spirit, she could appear so ethereal as to be almost a flame.

'I think, of course, it's perfect,' Miss Pantry said, holding her head aslant *like smoke in the wind*, as she considered the stuff, 'but the design limits it.'

'I should call it hardly modest myself.'

'There's something always so inconsecutive, isn't there, about a spot?'

'But a spot, Aurelia; in theory, what *could* be quieter?'

'Nothing, dear,' Miss Pantry said.

'And yet,' Lady Anne murmured, 'when one's fastening one's mind on one's prayers, one requires a little something.'

'I cannot see why it should be easier to sink into a brown study by staring at a splash.'

'Often, I think it helps.'

'Of course you may be right.'

'Shall we take it down into the Cathedral, Anne, and try?'

'This morning I've so many things to do. There's always one's small share of mischief going on.'

'I would never take part in the parish broils if ever I could avoid it.'

'I cannot be so impersonal, I'm afraid.'

'But surely a little neutral sympathy——'

'To be sympathetic without discrimination is so very debilitating.'

'Do you never feel tired?'

'Oh yes, sometimes.'

'I adore the country,' Aurelia said, 'but I should die of weariness if I stayed here long.'

'No, really, I like Ashringford. I abuse it, of course, just as I do dear Walter, or anybody whom I see every day . . . but really I'm fond of the place.'

'That's quite reasonable.'

'And if sometimes I'm a wreck,' Lady Anne explained, 'I look forward to my St. Martin's summer later on.'

'But Canterbury's so dreadful. It's such a groove.'

'The proximity of our English Channel would be a joy.'

'It's only seldom you'd get a whiff of the sea.'

Lady Anne's eyes skimmed her lawn.

A conventional bird or two—a dull thrush, a glossy crow—cowering for worms; what else had she, or anyone else, the right to expect? Sun, wind and quivering leaves made a carpet of moving shadows.

'It's with Stockingham,' she said, 'at present, that I've a bone. I shall scold Lady Georgia when she comes. To tell a curate his profile is suggestive of Savonarola is so like her. But it's really a mistake. It makes a man a firebrand, even when he's not. He gets rude and makes pointed remarks, and offends everybody. And I have to sit at home to talk to him.'

Aurelia looked interested.

'Probably a creature with a whole gruesome family?' she indirectly enquired.

'Unhappily he's only just left Oxford.'

'Ah, handsome, then, I hope.'

'On the contrary, he's like one of those cherubs one sees on eighteenth-century fonts with their mouths stuffed with cake.'

'Not really?'

'*And he wears glasses.*'

'But he takes them off sometimes——?'

'That's just what I don't know.'

'Then, as you will hardly need me,' Aurelia said, 'I'll go over to the Cresswell Arms and see Chloe. Poor dear, it's very dull for her all alone.'

'How is Miss Valley getting on?'

'So well. She asks if she can come up one afternoon to examine the tapestries when Walter's out.'

'By all means, but the tapestries are too fantastic, I should imagine, to be of any service to her. Historically, they're quite . . . untrustworthy.'

'Does it matter? Besides, the Archdeacon believes that Mrs. Cresswell was an Ely anchoress and not an Ashringford anchoress at all.'

'That's nonsense,' Lady Anne said; 'she belongs to us.'

'I don't know why you should be so keen on her,' Miss Pantry said. 'Of course, she *may* have been a saint, but from some of the little things I've heard, I fancy you might ransack heaven to find her——'

'I won't hear anything against Mrs. Cresswell. Her career here was an exquisite example to us all.'

'Well, I'm sure I hope so, dear.'

'And perhaps, Aurelia,' Lady Anne said gently, 'if you're going to the Cresswell Arms you'll call at the workhouse on your way, and find out what actually took place. I won't ask you to stop in Priest Street with a pudding. . . . And if you should see Miss Hospice in the garden, will you send her up to me?'

For some time after Aurelia had left her, Lady Anne stood in the window looking out upon the Cathedral. There was usually a little scaffolding about it. . . . If she had a voice in the matter it should never be allowed to come away. Her spirit shrank from the peculiar oppressiveness of perfection. And the Cathedral was very perfect indeed. How admirable, through the just sufficient drapery of the trees, were the great glazed windows that flashed like black diamonds in the sun. The glass, indeed, at Ashringford was so wonderful that sticks and umbrellas were left (by order) at the door. . . .

Lady Anne looked up at the large contented towers and fetched a sigh.

They were lovely.

Without veiling her eyes, they were as near perfection as she could conveniently bear. Placed at the end of the tennis lawn too, they had saved her from many a run.

Miss Missingham, in her *Sacerdotalism and Satanism,* has called the whole thing heavy, '*Very weighty indeed,*' although she willingly admits that at twilight the towers, with their many pinnacles, become utterly fantastic, *like the helmets of eunuchs in carnival time.* But then, if there was not much spontaneity about them on the whole, they had taken so long to build. Stone towers cannot be dashed off like Fragonard's *Inspiration*.

At the Pilgrims' Depot in the busy High Street there is to be obtained an anthology of 'Last Words,' culled chiefly from the lips of the womenkind of the Episcopal set. If the sayings of these ladies were often salty and frequently pointed, the Palace, it should be said, faced a Gothic arch.

Built around two sides of a quadrangle, it was, according to local taste, an ugly, forlorn affair, its bricks having been masked by stucco in 1785. Here and there, where the stucco had chipped away, the brick peeped out as if some rare fresco lay smothered underneath. From a flagged courtyard a classic staircase of divine proportions swept, exteriorly, to a broad balcony above the ground floor (spoken of sometimes as the loggia), which created, perhaps, something of a grand-opera effect.

It was here, recumbent upon a deck-chair, propped up by piles of brilliant cushions, that Mrs. Henedge, in her day, preferred to drink afternoon tea, surrounded by the most notable Church dignataries that she could find.

It was told that at one of these courts she had had as many as three bishops simultaneously handing her toast.

What wonder was it that persons should linger in delighted amazement at the wrought-iron gates until they formed a substantial crowd?

Carts would draw up, motorists stop, pedestrians sit down.

Lady Anne, on the contrary, preferred to hold her receptions out of sight.

To many, unquestionably, it was a blow.

She preferred, when not indoors, her tennis lawn, with its high clipped hedges, behind which the Cathedral rose inscrutably, a soft grey pile elongating itself above the trees, from whence would fall, fitfully, the saintly caw-cawing of the rooks.

Lady Anne's eyes fell from the wise old towers.

Vainglory

Framed in the expiring windows of the china-cupboard, the glimpse of Ashringford was entrancing quite. Across the meadows could be seen the struggling silver of the broad river, as it curled about Crawbery, invariably with some enthusiast, rod in hand, waiting quietly upon the bank. Nearer, hither and thither, appeared a few sleepy spires of churches, too sensible to compete with the Cathedral, but nevertheless possibly more personal; like the minor characters in repertoire that support the *star*.

She turned as her secretary, Miss Hospice, entered.

With a rather cruel yellow at her neck, waist and feet, and a poem of fifty sheets, on *Verlaine at Bournemouth*, at her back. What is there left to say——

Lady Anne was fond of her secretary because of her wild, beautiful handwriting, that seemed to fly, and because she really did enjoy to snub the Bishop's sisters. And others, too, liked her. Perpetually, she would make those pleasant little pampered remarks, such as, on a sultry August night, 'B-r-r-r! it's cold enough to light a fire!' Now that Aurelia was at the Palace, she should have been away on holiday, but, somehow, this year, she wasn't.

Lady Anne had discovered Miss Hospice some years since, lost in the advertisements of *The Spectator* seeking, as she had explained, the position of guardian angel to some elderly literary man.

Intelligent and sympathetic, Nature had appeared to indicate the way. The short hair, the long wavy nose *à la* Luca Signorelli, that seemed scarcely willing to sustain the heavy gold glasses, the figure, as flat as Lower Egypt, and the dazzling eyes like Mrs. Aphra Behn—for a really ticklish post, all was right. With complete clairvoyance Lady Anne had secured this treasure for her own, whose secretarial uses had now quite reached their zenith. Miss Madge Hospice was Lady Anne's barbed wire.

'I was wondering what had become of you,' Lady Anne said to her as she came in. 'Where on earth have you been?'

'. . . Wading through fields of violet vetch. It's so delicious out.'

'Had you forgotten to-day?'

'I don't think so: I've told Gripper again to sponge the stretchers, but he's so lazy, you know he never will.'

The bi-weekly Ambulance Classes at the Palace, so popular socially, were, it must be owned, on a parallel with the butter-making at Trianon.

'That's thoughtful,' Lady Anne said. 'And now, here are so many letters to answer, I really don't know where to begin.'

When a few minutes later the Reverend Peter Pet was announced they were entirely engrossed.

'Savonarola!' Lady Anne exclaimed. Miss Hospice continued conscientiously to write.

'Is it possible that anybody cares a straw what he says?' she queried.

'A curate should be quiescent; that's the first thing.'

'But tactlessness is such a common complaint.'

'He has referred to the Bishop as *a Faun crowned with roses*,' Lady Anne said severely.

'I *heard* it was *Satyr*.'

'And his encounter with Miss Wookie. . . . Well, not since the last election have I heard anything so scurrilous.'

'And is he absolutely charming?'

Lady Anne arranged her descriptions; when the introductions came about there was often some confusion.

'He's fair,' she said, 'with bright green eyes. And such gay, attractive teeth.'

'You make me curious to see him.'

'I should hate to shake his faith in his vocation,' Lady Anne murmured, 'but——'

'Have you dropped anything?'

'Only my little bit of lace. . . .'

And although very likely Lady Anne was the most sensible woman alive, she would scarcely have had the claim had she not crossed first to the mirror and——

But oh, *Vanity*! is there any necessity to explain?

∽ *VIII* ∽

'HOW fond I am of this sleepy magic place!'

'In town,' Mrs. Shamefoot said, 'the trees so seldom forget themselves into expressive shapes.'

'Well . . . You haven't answered my question yet.'

'Because I don't know!'

Lord Blueharnis looked bored.

'Is it grey,' Lady Castleyard wondered, chiming in, 'or white; or would it be blue?'

She settled herself reposefully, as if for ever.

'That Sacharissa style,' Atalanta remarked, bending forward, 'of rolling your hair is so enslaving.'

'I wish you would *not* look down my neck like an archer of Carpaccio.'

'Tell me what you're guessing.'

'The colour of the cuckoo's egg. . . .'

'If I recollect, it's a mystic medley of mauves.'

Mrs. Shamefoot prepared to rise. 'We shall get appendicitis,' she exclaimed, 'if we sit here long.'

Lord Blueharnis prevented her. 'Oh, what charming hands! . . . Don't move.'

'If you admire them now,' Mrs. Shamefoot said, sinking back, 'you would worship them when I'm really worn out. My hands never look quite so marvellous as when I'm tired.'

'But . . . fresh as you are; mayn't I see?'

'How perfectly idiotic you are.'

'For years,' Lady Georgia's voice came falling to them through the dusk, 'she couldn't get rid of it. In the end, quite in despair, and simply prostrate, she exchanged it for a string of pearls.'

'Might one learn what?' Lord Blueharnis enquired, half turning.

'Number 39. . . . Her great, comfortless house.'

'Darling Georgia! Why will she always withdraw to the gladiators' seats?'

'Away, too, in all the dew.'

' "Up in those tracts with her, it was the peace of utter light and silence." '

'How fascinating your *cabochon* tips look, dear, against the night.'

'Little horrid—owl—thing, I wonder you can see them at all.'

'How astonishingly acoustic it is.'

'These marble tiers are very cold.'

'I don't suppose the Greeks wore any more than we do.'

'Though, possibly, not less.'

'Aren't you coming down to recite?'

'Oh no; when Miss Compostella comes, we'll get her to do it instead.'

'I shall come up and fetch you,' Mrs. Shamefoot said, 'if Mr. Aston will lend me a hand.'

And, with the indifference of Madame Valpy about to climb the scaffold, she rose.

She was wearing an imaginative plain white dress that made her appear like a broken statue.

'Good-bye,' she murmured, 'Dirce,' her voice harking to the period of her heels—Louis XV.

'Be very careful. I've had Aase's Death Music running in my head all day. . . .'

And now beneath her lay the Greek theatre like an open fan. All around the glimmering sweeps of steps the sullen elms gave a piquant English touch.

'How perfectly fairy!' she exclaimed, falling breathless at the top.

Like some thin archangel, Lady Georgia stooped to help her rise.

'I adore the end of summer,' she said, 'when a new haystack appears on every hill.'

Beyond the dark proscenium and the clustering chimneys of the house stretched the faint far fields. No lofty peaks, or Himalayas, but quiet, modest hills, a model of restraint.

'Isn't it soothing?' Mrs. Shamefoot said.

'I suppose so; but it quite makes me cry to think of you fastened up over there in Ashringford, with a stiff neck, till the day of doom.'

'I always respond,' Mrs. Shamefoot replied, 'to the sun.'

Lady Georgia opened wide, liquid eyes. 'I shall hardly ever dare to come and look at you,' she said.

'But I should be entirely flattering, dear, for you.'

'Would you? Many people are so thoughtless about their lights.'

Mrs. Shamefoot wound an arm about the neck of an architectural figure.

'Don't you agree,' she said, 'that there's something quite irresistible about stained-glass caught in a brutality of stone?'

Lady Georgia seated herself stiffly. 'Caught,' she exclaimed. 'When I die, I should prefer to leave no trace.'

'But you follow, darling, don't you, what I mean?'

'For anyone that needed a perpetual retreat,' Lady Georgia said, 'Ashringford, I should say, would be quite ideal. The choir's so good. Such peaceful voices. . . . And there's nothing about the Cathedral in any way forbidding! One could really hardly wish for anything *nicer*. The late Bishop often used to say it suggested to him *Siena*, with none of the sickening scent of hides.'

Mrs. Shamefoot became ecstatic.

'We must make Dr. Pantry promise a two-tier window,' she said. 'and Dirce can take the top.'

'Sharing a window,' Lady Georgia said, 'in my opinion, is such a mistake. One might just as well erect a Jesse-window and invite a whole multitude to join. It may be egotistical, but if I were going down the centuries at all, I should want to go alone.'

'Unfortunately,' Mrs. Shamefoot murmured, 'it's too late to alter things, without behaving badly. . . .'

'That could be arranged. There's not the same rush now for monuments that there used to be.'

'Just at present there's almost a revival. . . . There are so many Art Schools about, aren't there? Everybody one meets appears to be commemorating themselves in one way or another. It's becoming a craze. Only the other day my mother-in-law had designed for Soco a tiny triptych of herself as a kind of Madonna, with a napkin drawn far down over her eyes.'

'Really?'

'Of course it's only a firescreen; it's *certain* to get scorched.'

'But still——'

'And with some scraps of old Flemish glass Lady Faningay has set up a sort of tortoise-shell window to a friend; so pretty. . . . She would have it.'

'Oh, that dreadful réchauffé of fragments. I've seen it.'

'But you understand, don't you, dearest, my poor motives, what they mean. . . .'

'I should be disappointed,' Lady Georgia said, 'if you did not, with Mrs. Cresswell, become the glory of the town.' And with a sorrowful, sidelong smile she turned towards Ashringford, admirable in a gay glitter of lights.

Faint as rubbed-out charcoal where it touched the sky, loomed the Cathedral, very wise and very old, and very vigilant and very detached—like a diplomat in disgrace—its towers, against the orange dusk, swelling saliently towards their base, inflated, so the guide-books said, by the sweet music of Palestrina. Between them, an exquisite specimen of irony, careered the short spire, which was perhaps an infelicity that would grow all long and regretful-looking towards the night.

'Since you've climbed so far,' Lady Georgia said, 'I shall repeat to you a somewhat saturnine little song of Mrs. Cresswell.'

And opening her fan, she said:

> 'I am disgusted with Love.
>   I find it exceedingly disappointing,
>   Mine is a nature that cries for more ethereal things,
>   Banal passions fail to stir me.
>   I am disgusted with Love.'

'How heavenly she is!'

'Such an amusing rhythm——'

'I do so enjoy the bypaths,' Mrs. Shamefoot said, 'of poetry. Isn't there any more?'

'No. I believe that's all.'

'Of course her words condemn her.'

'But that she should have arrived at a state of repugnance, possibly is something.'

'Isn't it unkind,' Lady Castleyard interrupted, advancing towards them, 'to recite up here all alone?'

'Dearest Dirce, how silently you came!——'

'Like a cook we had on the Nile,' Lady Georgia observed, 'who once startled me more than I can ever say by breaking suddenly out of the moon-mist so noiselessly that he might have been treading on a cloud.'

'Well, won't you come down? A stage and nobody on it is shockingly dull.'

'This evening, I really don't feel equal to Euripides,' Lady Georgia murmured, 'although perhaps I might manage the *Hound*.'

'*The Hound of Heaven*? My dear, what could be more divine?'

Mrs. Shamefoot looked away.

Star beyond star, the sky was covered. The clouds, she observed, too, appeared to be preparing for an Assumption.

∞ IX ∞

WHEN Aurelia left Lady Anne she set a straw hat harmlessly upon her head, powdered her neck at a tarnished mirror with crystal nails, selected a violet parasol, profoundly flounced, slipped a small volume of Yogi Philosophy into her wallet, took up, put down, and finally took up the cornflour pudding, gave a tearful final glance at her reflection, put out her tongue for no remarkable reason, and walked out into the street.

Oh, these little expeditions through the town! . . .

Hypolita habitually got over them by horse when, in a bewildering amazon, she would swoop away like a valkyrie late for a sabbat.

'One can only hope that heaven will wash,' Aurelia murmured meekly, as she prepared to trudge. Which optimism, notwithstanding the perfect stillness of the day, fluttered her aside like a leaf.

It was disgraceful the way her linen came home—torn.

'Torn, torn, torn,' she breathed, twirling her sunshade with short, sharp twirls that implied the click of a revolver.

But to reach the laundry she was obliged to pass the Asz—that river spoken of, by vulgar persons, often, as *the Ass*.

Between solemn stone embankments and an array of bridges spaced out with effigies of fluminal deities, a sadly spent river coiled reluctant through the town. Sensitive townsfolk felt intensely this absence of water, which, in many minds, amounted almost to a disgrace. Before the Cathedral, just where, artistically, it was needed most, there was scarcely a trickle.

As a rule Aurelia was too completely preoccupied with her own sensations to observe particularly her whereabouts, but instinctively, as her foot touched the bridge, she would assume the tiresome supercilious smile of a visitor.

This morning, however, she paused to lean an arm upon the parapet to rest her pudding.

Has not Mrs. Cresswell (in a trance) described heaven as *another* grim reality? Aurelia stood, and remained to drum a tune.

'Oh, I could dance for ever,' she exclaimed, 'to the valse from *Love Fifteen*!' And she lingered to hum, by way of something more, Priscilla's air from *Th' Erechtheum Miss*. How giddy it was! What abandon there was in it. Happy Priscilla, hardworking little thing; from her part song with Bill, love, manifestly, was sometimes simple and satisfactory.

Aurelia peered down.

The creak of oars whispered up to her with wizardry.

There was often a barge to be towed along. Here came one now, lifted over the sun-splashed water, with a mast, long and slightly bent, like the quill of an ostrich feather. The stubby willows, that mirrored their cloudy shadows from the bank, sobbed pathetically, though too well bred to weep.

'It gets emptier and emptier,' she mused. 'I suppose the weeds absorb the water!'

'Oh, beware of freckles!'

Aurelia turned.

'Who could have foreseen,' she said, 'that our intercession for fine weather would produce all this heat!'

'If two of the churches, in future, were to apply, I consider it should amply suffice.' And Mrs. Henedge, leaning leisurely upon the arm of Winsome Brookes, and sharing the weight of half a mysterious basket with Monsignor Parr, nodded and was gone.

With her gleaming strings and veils she suggested, from behind, the Goddess Hathor as a sacred cow.

'I'd rather go naked than wear some of the things she wears,' Aurelia murmured critically, as she watched her out of sight.

But a ripple of laughter from some persons at the toll made Miss Pantry fix her eyes perseveringly into space.

The peals of laughter of the Miss Chalfonts were as much a part of Ashringford as the Cathedral bells. Constantly they were laughing. And nobody knew why. Along the crooked High Street they were often to be seen, almost speechless with merriment, peering in at the shop windows, a trio interlaced, or standing before the announcements of the Lilliputian Opera House, where came never anything more extraordinarily exhilarating than Moody-Manners or Mrs. D'Oyley Carte. Tourists avoided their collision. And even the delicate-looking policeman in the market-place, when he became aware of their approach, would invariably disappear.

Rossetti, long ago, had painted them, very pale, in bunched-up dresses, playing cats'-cradle in a grey primeval waste. And the reaction, it was politely supposed, had completely turned their brain.

'They will laugh themselves to death,' Aurelia murmured, as she wandered on.

The scent of the bushes of sweetbrier from innumerable gardens followed her along the sentimental esplanade that faced the Asz as far as the gates of Miss Chimney's school for backward boys. Here Vane Street, with its model workhouse, began, the admiration of all. Debt, disaster, held few terrors, while gazing at this winter palace. . . . With a chequered pavement below, and an awning above, a man, trusting to philanthropy, might reasonably aspire to lounge away what remained to him of life, inhaling the suavest of cigarettes.

Vainglory

Deferring her errand there until her return, Aurelia wound up Looking-Glass Street towards the laundry. With its houses, that seemed to have been squeezed from tubes of multi-coloured paint, it was not unlike, she had often heard, a street in one of Goldoni's plays. Miss Hospice catches the peeping Brueghelness of it in her *Scroll from the Fingers of Ta-Hor*, in which, steeping herself in deception and mystery, she attempts to out-Chatterton Chatterton with:

'Poor Pale pierrot through the dark boughs peering
In the purple gloaming of a summer's evening,
Oh his heart is breaking, can't you hear him sobbing,
Or is it the wind that's passing among the yellow roses? . . .'

An imperfect scarab that owed its existence chiefly to loitering in Looking-Glass Street, or thereabouts.

Choosing her way along it, Aurelia perceived, midway, a lady with a pair of scissors, who, in an abstracted attitude, was inducing a yew-tree peacock to behave.

'Good-morning,' the lady with the scissors cried, 'I am so glad. . . . I was just coming round to enquire.'

Miss Wookie was always *just going* somewhere. At all hours one would find her in a hat.

'To enquire?' Aurelia halted.

The lady leaned classically against her bird. In its rather dishevelled state, it resembled a degenerate swan.

'People are circulating such dreadful stories,' she said.

'Indeed!'

'Such shocking stories. Poor mamma! This morning she seems quite pulled down.'

'Some new nervousness, no doubt.'

'She has sent me out to tidy this. As if I were in a condition for gardening!'

'To fulfil a ritual, if one isn't quite oneself, does often only harm.'

Miss Wookie considered her work. 'I clip the thing,' she said, 'in the wrong places. . . . In profile it has almost the look of a turkey. So unnatural!'

'Whatever happens, it could always be a blue-bird.'

'We hear you're going to pull down half of the Cathedral,' Miss Wookie said tragically, 'and put in a Russian ballet window. Is it *true*?'

Aurelia appeared astonished.

'It's the first I've heard of it!' she exclaimed.

'The Palace, of course, always is the last to hear of anything,' Miss Wookie said, 'but I assure you all Ashringford's talking. And, *oh, Miss Pantry*, Mr. Pet has been saying the most frightful things about us. About me, and about mamma.'

'He's a horrid, conceited boy,' Aurelia comforted her.

'Come in, won't you? I'd like you to hear the truth.'

Aurelia blinked. 'It's very kind,' she said, 'but with this nasty, sticky dish——'

'Never mind the dish,' Miss Wookie murmured, unlatching the gate.

'Sycamores,' the shelter of Mrs. Wookie, the widow of Brigadier Percy Wookie of the Ashringford Volunteers, to whom there was an explanatory tablet in St. Cyriac's which related, like a page torn from Achilles Tatius, how and where, and by whose manicured extremities he fell, was a bleak brick cottage, with "1839" scrawled above the door. A short path with a twist like a lizard's tail led up to the entrance, where an unremarkable tree with a long Latin name did its best to keep out the light.

'Poor, poor, poor, *poor* mamma!' Miss Wookie repeated rhythmically, as she led the way in.

Mrs. Wookie was usually to be found reclining upon a sofa, agitating a phial of medicine, or embroidering martyrdoms imaginatively upon a stole. Interrupted in any way, she would become as flurried as a canary when a hand is thrust into its cage.

But to-day, because she was unwell, her daughter had given her, by way of distraction, a party frock to pull to pieces, and now the invalid was aggrandising perceptibly the aperture to an evening gown in a posture rather more at ease than that of Whistler's Mother.

The morning-room at the 'Sycamores,' mid-Victorian and in the Saracen style, would most likely have impressed a visitor as an act of faith throughout. Upon the mantelshelf, however, between much that was purely emigrant, stood two strange bottles.

Being in the City-of-Random-Kisses to receive a legacy, and by proxy (alas) a blessing; and caught in a shower of perhaps predetermined rain, Miss Wookie and her guardian angels—handsome rural creatures—had sought shelter beneath the nearest arch.

It was noon. All three were completely wet.

'Christie's . . .' Miss Wookie observed the name, whilst the angels shook the water from their hair, and flapped the moisture sparkling from their wings. And reassured by the six first letters, she had gone inside.

'What else?' she can recall remarking, prepared for a waiter to pounce out upon her from the top of the stairs.

And then, instead of the prosaic bone, as afterwards she explained, and the glass of lemonade, and the quiet rest, and the meditation on the unexpected behaviour of poor Aunt Nettle ... Miss Wookie had found herself calling out in a sort of dream for the vases, until, for the life of her, it would have been impossible to stop. And when, ultimately, she reappeared in Ashringford, the legacy all gone, it never occurred to Mrs. Wookie to part with her *famille rose* again.

'Family Rose' the bottles had become to her—and accordingly as dear.

'I see that bodices are getting more and more scamped, Kate,' Mrs. Wookie remarked, as her daughter came in, 'and so, my dear, I hope I've done what's right.'

Miss Wookie stood still. 'Oh, Tatty,' she said.

'With the scraps of stuff I've taken,' Mrs. Wookie announced, 'I can make four small pincushions; or two large ones.'

'I didn't know how selfish you could be.'

'Don't be absurd, Kate. You may be sure I'd not allow you to appear in anything unbecoming. And if you go out, my child, to-night, don't forget, like last time, to order yourself *a fly.*'

'I'm so glad,' Aurelia murmured, coming forward, 'you're able to sew.'

With her needle suspended in the air, Mrs. Wookie fluttered off to a favourite perch.

'I was very poorly first thing,' she said. 'Kate tried to persuade me to send for a physician. But I wouldn't let her.'

'Luckily an attack is quickly gone.'

Mrs. Wookie began to twitter. 'And one of these days,' she observed, 'I'll go with it. I hardly expect to survive the fall of the leaf; I don't see how I can. ... Shall you ever forget last year, Kate? Round Ashringford, there're so many trees.'

'Possibly all you need's a change of scene. Scheveningen, or somewhere——'

Mrs. Wookie floated to the floor. 'A few minutes more or less on earth,' she said dejectedly, 'what does it matter? And packing upsets me so. Besides, I wish to die here, beneath my own roof.'

'But what pleasure would it give you?'

'None, Miss Pantry. But I wish to die there.'

'You may be right,' Aurelia assented; 'the strained atmosphere of tuberose and trunks of a health resort in autumn is often a little sad.'

'And Ashringford in autumn,' Miss Wookie said, 'isn't so bad. Of course the leaves come down. The worst of it is, one can get no grapes; I can get no grapes.'

Mrs. Wookie looked pathetic. 'If I could only see Kate married,' she complained. 'It comes, of course, of living in a cathedral town. Curates are such triflers.'

'One little wedding, Mrs. Wookie, oughtn't to be so difficult. Consider, with five or six daughters to dispose of, how much more tiresome it would have been!'

At such a notion Mrs. Wookie's nose grew almost long.

'In the forties,' she crooned, 'we were always dropping our things, and we fainted more. Of course, in the country there are many ways still. One can send a girl out with a landscape figure, sketching. That always works. . . . Alice, Grace, Pamela and Teresa, my nieces, all went that way.'

'Oh, Tatty, Teresa married a menial. She went away with a chauffeur.'

'How very disgraceful!' Aurelia remarked.

'I suppose it was. Particularly as he wasn't their own.'

'Be quiet, my dear; we live too near the laundry as it is.'

'Besides,' Miss Wookie said, striking her chord, 'I don't intend to marry. I should be sorry to let myself in for so many miseries. . . . An habitual husband would, also, bore me to death.'

'Hush, Kate! It's just those infantine reflections that circulate and get twisted, till they arrive, goodness knows how, to the ears of that dreadful Mr. Pet.'

'I'm sorry you find him so troublesome,' Aurelia said.

Mrs. Wookie glowered. 'I wonder I'm alive,' she exclaimed, 'from the reports they bring. Not only am I affronted, but the Cathedral, it seems, itself, is in peril, and the name of our city also endangered. For a whim, if not from sheer madness, Dr. Pantry, it appears, has petitioned the Archbishop to contract the See of Ashringford into *Ashingford*. Merciful heaven, why can't he leave it alone?'

'I dare say if Mr. Pet had his way he would boil us down to *Ash*,' Miss Wookie observed.

Her mother closed her eyes.

'If that happened,' she said, 'I should leave Ashringford.'

Driven out with her Family Rose, and followed by her servant Quirker, and by Kate, she saw herself stumbling at sunset like the persecuted women on her stoles. And night would find them (who knew) where the cornflowers passed through the fields in a firm blue bar.

'That Mr. Pet is a disgrace to his cloth,' she murmured, rallying. 'Indeed, I'd rather we had Mr. Cunningham back again. He wasn't a great preacher, but he neither droned nor gabbled, and he could be wonderfully voluble when he liked.'

'Oh, my dear, but he was so unbalanced. He would do his American conjuring tricks in the vestry before the choir boys. . . . Such a bad example.'

'Still, it's an ill wind. . . . And Miss Wardle and her set seem quite satisfied with his successor.'

'She would be. If you asked her for her hymn-book she'd imagine it was being borrowed for some felonious purpose.'

Aurelia looked interested. 'I don't see what one could do with a hymn-book,' she exclaimed.

Mrs. Wookie's nose grew long again.

'Don't you?' she answered. 'Neither do I.'

'Besides, fresh from a Cornish curacy, what can he know?' Miss Wookie wondered.

Aurelia corrected her.

'From Oxford, I fancy, isn't he . . . ?'

'The man's a perfect scourge, wherever he's from,' Miss Wookie declared. 'Not half-an-hour ago he dashed down this street like a tornado. I was standing with Quirker at the door. You know I collect motor numbers, which obliges me frequently to run into the road. . . . I have such a splendid collection. I hope I'm not so vulgar as to bang a door, still, when I saw him coming, I confess I shut it!'

Mrs. Wookie joined her hands.

'He must have discovered about Mrs. Henedge and Monsignor Parr,' she said. 'How shocking, should there be a struggle.'

'What should make you think so?'

'They've gone to pace out the site of the new church. . . . Monsignor Parr has been hurrying to and fro all the morning, like St. Benedict at Monte Cassino. And his employees already are entrenched at the corner of Whip-me-Whop-me Street at Mrs. Cresswell's old Flagellites Club.'

Aurelia raised her eyes.

'Surely in such a sweet old house it would feel almost vulgar to be alive!'

'I don't know,' Mrs. Wookie replied. 'I do not care for Mrs. Cresswell. She repels me.'

'In any case, if anything should happen, Mrs. Henedge will be quite secure. That fair-haired pianist accompanied her. You remember him, don't you, mamma?'

'I remember him perfectly. Nobody in the world ever got over a stile like Mr. Brookes.'

'To see her continually with that perverse musician or with that priest is enough to make poor good Bishop Henedge burst his coffin.'

'Alas, Ashringford isn't what it used to be,' Mrs. Wookie complained. 'The late Bishop was, in many matters, perhaps not a very prudent man . . . but he had authority. And a shapelier leg, my dears, never trod the earth. He obtained his preferment, one may say, solely on their account. He had such long, long legs. Such beautiful long, long legs.'

'And,' Miss Wookie murmured, flinging her flower, 'a really reassuring way of blowing his nose! To hear him do it was to realise immediately the exact meaning of *conviction*.'

'But in the official portrait,' Aurelia objected, 'he appears such a little gasp of a man!'

Mrs. Wookie became belligerent.

'That topsy-turvy thing in the Town Hall! I was fond of my husband, but I'd scorn to be painted in evening-mourning pointing at his dead miniature. His portrait indeed! His widow's rather, basking on a sofa, with a locket.'

'Apparently Mrs. Henedge admires the baroque.'

'Well, her new church will be dedicated to it,' Miss Wookie assured.

'So ornate?'

'Mr. Thumbler has gone to Italy to make the drawings. . . . The exterior is to be an absolute replica of St. Thomas in Cremona, with stone saints in demonstrative poses on either side of the door.'

'And the interior, no doubt, will be a dream.'

'It is to be lit entirely by glass eighteenth-century chandeliers,'

Miss Wookie said, 'and there will be a Pompeian frieze, and a good deal of art leather work from the hand of one of Lady Georgia's young men, who did some of the panelling at St. Anastasia's once, although, of course, he was rather *restricted*.'

'Art leather,' Aurelia said, 'sounds to me a mistake.'

'If it's half as delicate as at St. Anastasia, it should be really rather lovely.'

'Let us hope that it may——'

'And then there are to be some very nice pictures. In fact, the pictures will be a feast. Madame Gandarella, the wife of the Minister, has presented a *St. Cecilia Practising* and a more than usually theatrical Greuze. And Baroness Lützenschläger is to give a Griego. Nobody knows quite what it represents—long, spiritual women grouped about a cot. The Clalfonts, also, are offering a Guardi for the baptistery. But as there was never any mention of one, they ran no very terrible risk. And last, though hardly least, Lord Brassknocker is sending to Paris to be framed a mysterious pastelle entitled *Tired Eyelids on Tired Eyes* which, as Mrs. Pontypool truly says, is certainly the very last thing she looks.'

'Kate hears everything,' Mrs. Wookie said; 'thread me a needle, Kate.'

'And when everything is complete, the Grand Duchess Ximina will stay at Stockingham to unveil the leather. The Cardinal Pringle will appear to sprinkle the pictures and to bless it all.'

'If the Grand Duchess stays at Stockingham,' Mrs. Wookie said, 'I suppose they will prepare the State bed.'

'Poor woman,' Aurelia murmured. 'It's as hard as a board.'

'Elizabeth——' Miss Wookie began, but Aurelia rose.

'How pretty the garden looks,' she said.

Miss Wookie smiled.

'It's only charming,' she observed, checked in her little tale, 'on account of the trees.'

'Tut, Kate. I'm sure in the spring, when the laburnums are out, and lilacs in bloom, the garden's hard to beat.'

'It has been always summer,' Aurelia said, as she took her leave, 'when I've stayed here before.'

Down an alley and through an arch led her straight to Washing-tub Square.

Notwithstanding the eloquence prepared, it was with relief that she perceived her laundress docilely pinning some purple flowers against a fence, while close by, in the dust, Miss Valley was kneeling, with her arms about a child.

At her approach the Biographer lifted loose blue eyes that did not seem quite firm in her head, and a literary face.

'I shall have to commence my life all over again,' she said. 'Six weeks wasted! This child—employed in the laundry here'—and she began to shake it—'this carrier of dirty linen . . . is Reggie . . . Cresswell—a descendant of the saint. . . .'

And because Miss Valley seemed in such distress, and because, after all, she was a friend, Aurelia let fall her dish and, with a glance right and left, first, to make sure that 'nothing was coming,' sank down upon the road, by her side.

'But can you not see,' she murmured sympathetically, taking Miss Valley by the hand, 'that an apologia is just what everyone most enjoys?' And then, drawing Reggie to her, she exclaimed: 'Oh, you dear little boy!'

∞ X ∞

'AND your own tomb, dear Doctor Pantry, what is it going to be?'

'My own tomb,' the Bishop replied demurely, 'will be composed entirely of encaustic tiles that come from Portugal—a very simple affair.'

Mrs. Shamefoot sighed. 'It sounds,' she said, 'almost agitating.

'Ah, these old cathedrals, my dear Mrs. Shamefoot, how many marriages and funerals they've seen!'

'I suppose——'

'Ashringford may not have the brave appearance of Overcares, or the rhythm of Perch, or the etherealness of Carnage, or the supremacy of Sintrap; but it has a character, a conspicuousness of its own.'

'It stands with such authority.'

'To be sure. You'd hardly believe there was a debt upon it.'

'No; indeed one would not.'

Lady Anne broke in. 'There is often,' she remarked, 'a haze. Although I couldn't bear the Cathedral without a few sticks and props—I should miss them frightfully. It's curious the way the restorations hang fire, especially with the number of big houses there are about. Don't you agree with me, Mrs. Roggers?'

'Decidedly,' the Archdeacon's wife exclaimed, beginning to docket them upon a glove. When revealing no small mishap, she quite omitted Stockingham from the list.

At this gust of tact Lady Anne appeared amazed.

'If Mrs. Shamefoot wishes to explore the Cathedral,' the Bishop said, 'it will be well to do so before the excursion train gets in from Perch.'

'Then you had better take her across.'

'But you'll come with us.'

'I must remain here for Lady Georgia. Should Mrs. Henedge be out or telling her beads she'll be back directly.'

'Very well, we will not be long.'

'And be careful,' Lady Anne adjured her husband, with fine frankness, 'not to commit yourself. No rash promises! The Cathedral's all glass as it is. It will be like a conservatory before we've done.'

'What are those wonderfully white roses?' Mrs. Shamefoot inquired of the Bishop, as she trailed with him away.

In a *costume de cathédrale,* at once massive and elusive, there was nostalgia in every line.

'They bear the same name as the Cathedral,' the Bishop replied: 'St. Dorothy.'

Mrs. Shamefoot touched the episcopal sleeve.

'And that calm wee door?' she asked.

'It's the side way in.'

'Tell me, Doctor Pantry, is there a ray of hope?'

'Without seeming uncharitable, or unsympathetic, or inhuman, what am I to say? With a little squeezing we might bury you in the precincts of the Cathedral.'

'But I don't want to be trodden on.'

'You might do a great deal worse than lay down a brass.'

'With my head on a cushion and my feet upon flowers. Oh!'

'Or a nice shroud one. Nothing looks better. And they are quite simple to keep clean.'

'But a brass,' she said, 'would lead to rubbings. I know so well! Persons on all fours, perpetually bending over me.'

'I can see no objection in that.'

'I don't think my husband would like it.'

'Naturally; if Mr. Shamefoot would mind——'

'Mind?' She began to titter. 'Poor Soco,' she said; 'poor, dear man. But a window's more respectable. Though I'd sooner I didn't borrow an old one.'

And with an effort she manœuvred her hat through the narrow monastic door.

Darkness, and an aroma of fresh lilies, welcomed her, as though with cool, invisible hands.

Here, most likely, would she dwell until the last day surprised her. And, like twelve servants, the hours would bring her moods.

She sank impulsively to her knees. A window like a vast sapphire —a sumptuous sapphire, changing back—chilled her slightly.

Must colour change?

Here and there the glass had become incoherent a little, and begun to mumble.

'One could look for ever at the pretty windows!' she murmured, rising.

The Bishop seemed touched.

'We must try and find you a corner,' he said, 'somewhere.'

She turned towards him.

'Oh, you make me happy.'

'I said a corner,' the Bishop replied. 'Perhaps we can find you a lancet.'

'A lancet! But I should be so congested, shouldn't I? I shall need some space. A wee wheel-window, or something of the kind.'

The tones implied the colossal.

'A lancet would be rather limited, of course, but does that matter?'

'Wait till you see the designs.'

With a sensation of uneasiness Doctor Pantry began to pivot about the font.

'In Cromwell's time,' he explained, 'it was used as a simple washtub.'

'Oh, what a shame!'

'And from here,' he said, 'you get such a curious complication of arches.'

Around the pillars drooped stone garlands that had been coloured once. From them a few torn and marvellous flags, that looked more as if they had waved triumphant over some field of scandal than anywhere else, reposed reminiscent.

'What shreds!'

'Certainly, they are very much riddled.'

But she lingered apart a moment before the tomb of an Ashringford maiden, lying sleep-locked upon a pyre of roses, with supplicating angels at the head and feet.

'Do I,' she whispered, 'detect romance?'

The Bishop bent his head.

'Alas,' he said, 'the entire *bibliothèque rose*.'

'And how sweet something smells.'

'Many persons have noticed it. Even when there has been barely a dry leaf within doors.'

'Why, what?'

'It emanates from the Coronna Chapel, where Mrs. Cresswell is.'

'Is it there always?'

'It varies. On some days it's as delicate as a single cowslip. On others it's quite strong, more like syringa.'

Mrs. Shamefoot scanned the shadows.

'But Mrs. Cresswell,' she enquired, 'who was she—exactly?'

'Primarily,' the Bishop replied, 'she was a governess. And with some excellent people too. Apart from which, no doubt, she would have been canonised, but for an unfortunate remark. It comes in *The Red Rose of Martyrdom*. "If we are all a part of God," she says, "then God must *indeed* be horrible." '

'Nerves are accountable for a lot. Possibly, her pupils were tiresome. . . . Or it was upon a hot day. In her *Autobiography* she confesses, doesn't she, to her sensibility to heat?'

Doctor Pantry smiled.

'What a charming book!'

'I love it too. It's a book that I adore.'

'I have the 1540 edition.'

'Have you? how rare!'

'Indeed, it's a possession that I prize.'

'I should say so. I can repeat, almost by heart, the chapter that commences: "What can be more melancholy than Stonehenge at sunset." Her cry of astonishment on beholding it from the window of Lord Ismore's coach is the earliest impressionary criticism that we have. She was asleep, wasn't she, when a sudden jolt awoke her. "The stones," she said, to little Miss Ismore, whom she was piloting to Court, "the stones are like immense sarcophagi suspended in the air. . . ." '

'Admirable!' the Bishop exclaimed.

'And Miss Ismore in her way was interesting too. Eventually she married Prince Schara, and retired to Russia with him. And kept a diary. Each night she would write down the common-places of the Czarina, with the intention of one day revealing them in a book; as if she hadn't sufficient incidents without! Before her death, in Moscow, where she was poisoned, one gathers that the influences of childhood, although most likely smothered, were not entirely put out. And she would wear her heavenly tiara at the opera as if it were a garland of thorns. Really, the Princess was one of the very first persons to get Russiaphobia.'

'Russiaphobia; what is that?'

'Wearing one's rubies and emeralds at the same time,' Mrs. Shamefoot said in a hushed voice.

The Bishop waved aside a hanging.

'There is usually,' he explained, 'a slight charge asked for entrance to the Coronna Chapel. But to-day you're with me!'

She stood awed.

'How seductive she is; though, somehow, I should call her inclined to be too rotund for a saint! A saint should be slim and flexible as a bulrush. . . .'

'The effect, no doubt, of her fine gaiety! Her exuberance was wonderful. She was as gay as a patch of poppies to the last.'

'I suppose, in her time, there were a few flower faces, but the majority of persons seem to have been quite appallingly coarse.'

'It has often been remarked that she resembles Madame de Warens. . . .'

Mrs. Shamefoot became regretful.

'If only Rembrandt might have painted Madame de Warens!' she said.

'You have not yet been to our small gallery in the town?'

'I didn't know there was one.'

'Oh, but you must go——'

'I will, but not before my own affair's arranged! Wait; a lancet, did you say? Or a wheel-window, or a chancel-light—I'll be confused.'

'Before I can make any definite promises,' the Bishop said, 'an unworthy world is sure to demand a few credentials.'

'Dear Doctor Pantry, were I to proclaim myself a saint you'd probably not believe it——'

'Indeed, I assure you I've no misgivings.'

'I cannot conceive why, then, there should be any fuss.'

'You have never yet come across our *Parish Magazine*?'

'I dare say if I stayed here long enough I'd get horrid too.'

'No; I don't think you ever would.'

'I might!'

'I assure you every time it appears I find myself wishing I were lying in the sanctity of my own sarcophagus.'

'Dear Doctor Pantry, don't say such shocking things! I will not allow it. Besides, I could compose the notice myself.'

'Indeed, I fear you'd have to.'

'Behind a white mask and a dark cloak. Quite in the manner of Longhi. Thus: "The beautiful Mrs. S., who (for the next few weeks) wishes to remain unknown, desires to remove from St. Dorothy one of those white windows (which resemble prose), and replace it by," etc., etc., etc. Or, to slip away the west window altogether. . . .'

'But the west window . . . the pre-Raphaelite window. . . .'

'It's a blot to the Cathedral. I cannot make out what is written beneath; but isn't it to say that in the end the king marries the kitchenmaid and they lived happily ever after?'

'To remove the west window,' the Bishop said, 'when everyone is alive that subscribed for it, I fear would be impossible.'

Mrs. Shamefoot peered about her. Once only, long ago, in the Pyrenees, could she recall a similar absence of accommodation.

'Perhaps,' she said half shyly, 'I might share the Coronna.'

'Share the Coronna!'

Doctor Pantry turned pale at the impiety.

'Why not? Two triangles when they cut can make a star. . . .'

'I fear your Niccolo in Ashringford might be unapprehended.'

'After all, what is the Dorothy window but a wonderful splash of colour?'

'Have you tried the Abbey?' Doctor Pantry asked.

'What, Westminster?'

'With a husband in the Cabinet. . . .'

Mrs. Shamefoot smiled sedately.

'But I'm not a public person,' she said. 'An actress. Although, of course, I do sell flowers.'

'With such an object in view, Heaven forfend you should become one.'

Mrs. Shamefoot closed her eyes.

'To be an actress,' she said; 'to ruin one's life before a room full of people. . . . What fun!'

'Every good preacher,' Doctor Pantry observed, 'has a dash of the comedian too.'

'Do you often go to the play?'

'The last time I went,' his lordship confessed, 'was to see Mrs. Kendall in *The Elder Miss Blossom*.'

'Oh, she's perfect.'

'Although Lady Anne saw Yvette Guilbert only the other day.'

Mrs. Shamefoot looked sympathetic.

'I can imagine nothing more sinister,' she said, 'than Yvette Guilbert singing "Where-are-you-going-to-my-pretty-maid." It will haunt me always.' And she paused meditatively to admire a stone effigy of the first Lady Blueharnis, stretched out upon a pillow like a dead swan.

'How entirely charming the memorials are.'

'I'm so glad that you like them.'

'Somehow, some people are so utterly of this world,' she mused, 'that one cannot conceive of them being grafted into any other.'

But a sound of unselfconscious respiration from behind the Blueharnis monument startled her.

'Macabre person! . . . Fiend!' she said.

Winsome looked up sleepily.

'I came,' he explained, 'to collect a few books for Mrs. Henedge.'

Mrs. Shamefoot blinked.

'That looks,' she observed, 'like going.'

'I don't want to be too hard on her,' the Bishop said, 'but I think she might have told me first.'

'I cannot say,' Winsome said. 'In the country one is always grateful to find anything to do.'

'Have you been here long?'

'Since yesterday. Already I could howl for staleness.'

Mrs. Shamefoot glanced at the Bishop.

'Very likely,' she said; 'but to run away the moment you arrive, just because it's the most appealing place on earth . . . I should call it decadent!'

And, indeed, after a few hours nearer Nature, perpetually it was the same with him. A *nostalgie du pavé* began to set in. He would miss the confidential 'Things is very bad, sir,' of the newspaper boy at

the corner; the lights, the twinkling advertisements of the Artistic
Theatre . . . the crack of the revolver so audible those nights that
the heroine killed herself, the suspense, the subsequent sickening
silence; while the interest, on lighter evenings, would be varied by
the 'Call me my biplane,' of Indignation as it flew hurriedly away.

Mrs. Shamefoot picked up a rich red-topped hymn-book.

'And so,' she said, 'the aloe, apparently, has bloomed!'

'No; not yet. But there's nothing like being ready.'

'And when do you think it's to be?'

'I hardly care to say. Though, when the change is made, you can
be certain it will be done quite quietly.'

'In Ashringford,' the Bishop said, 'nothing is ever done quite
quietly!'

'But that's so silly of Ashringford!' Mrs. Shamefoot exclaimed.
'When my sister 'verted, I assure you nobody took the slightest
notice. But then, of course, she was always going backwards and
forwards. . . . She made excursions into three different religions.
And she always came back dissatisfied and grumbling.'

'The world is disgracefully managed, one hardly knows to whom
to complain.'

'Many people,' the Bishop remarked, 'are very easily influenced.
They have only to look at a peacock's tail to think of Brahma.'

Mrs. Shamefoot turned her eyes towards the entrancing glass.

How mysterious it was! Like the luminous carpets that veil a
dream.

She became abstracted a moment, lost in mental measurements,
unhappy and elaborate-looking, in her mourning, as a wasted
columbine.

'Well, since you're here, Mr. Brookes,' she said, 'you must
absolutely try the organ. And Doctor Pantry has never heard me
sing.'

∞ XI ∞

FROM a choice of vivid cushions she placed the least likely
behind her head.

'I'm ready!' And with a tired, distrustful smile she looked away
towards the house as if it were a hospital.

At her feet crouched an animal who, hourly, was assuming an expression as becoming, and as interesting, she believed, as the wolf of St. Francis. Her hands full of dark clematis, clutched and crowned. . . .

'There'll be the funnel of the jam factory, and a few chimney-pots for background,' Winsome said. 'Do you mind?'

'My dear, what can I do? In the end, these horrid encroaching shapes will drive me out.'

'One, two, three; do smile . . . less. I'd rather work a water-wheel than be a photographer.'

Mrs. Henedge relaxed.

'I wish,' she murmured, 'instead, you'd decide about being Rose.'

'I will. But in these wilds the very notion of a début makes one shiver.'

'My dear Mr. Brookes, when you give your first concert I will lead you on to the platform and stay by you all the time!'

'Well, I'm vacillating. I only need a push.'

'Oh, be careful of the tail.'

And, indeed, an animal who had bitten a poet, worried a politician, amused a famous actress and harried a dancer was not to be ignored.

How was it possible, it may be asked, for anything in Ashringford to have come in contact with such celebrities? By what accident had these Illustrious crossed his path? Incidentally, St. Dorothy was responsible for all.

And now that Miss Compostella was awaited at Stockingham, and with a Rose de Tivoli within reach, there appeared every likelihood of lengthening the list—a poet, a politician, a pianist, *two* famous actresses, etc., in anticipation—he counted them over upon his paws, surveying, meanwhile, the newly planted scene; for his lady cared only for those airier sorts of trees, larches, poplars, willows, so that, in the spring, the garden looked extraordinarily inexperienced and green.

'I shall have to chloroform him,' Mrs. Henedge said, 'if he does it again.'

'He might be grateful. One can never tell.'

'Why, what's wrong?'

'I've so many moods. You cannot like 'em all. . . . I'm never characteristic!'

'Poor Mr. Vain! Never mind if you're bored. Relax! Recoup! The country's very good for you.'

'That's what everyone says. Mrs. Shamefoot said the same to me this morning.'

'Oh, have you seen her?'

'In the Cathedral. Do you know, if I stopped here long, I'd start a Satanic colony in your midst just to share the monotony.'

'My dear, there's one already.'

'Direct me——'

'No; stay here and be good. I've something to tell you that will please you.'

'Me?'

'Yes. Old Mrs. Felix said to my maid: "I think Mr. Brookes so beautiful. He has such a young, romantic face!" '

'What else did she say?'

'She said nothing more.'

'Hooray!'

Mrs. Henedge raised a finger. 'S-S-Sh! or you'll disturb Monsignor Parr. He's half asleep in a rocking-chair making his soul.'

'According to Monsignor Parr, heaven will be a perpetual concert. Do you think that true?'

'I believe he has been *favoured*. . . . In fact, in the little powdering closet, before it became my oratory, something picked him up, and danced round him. . . .'

'Oh! When?'

'Only the other day. My dear, yes! And *twice* in the month of Mary!'

'Zoom—zoom!'

'Read to me.'

'What shall I read?'

'Get the Lascelles Abercrombie, or the Francis Jammes——'

' "La maison serait pleine de roses et de guêpes"—that's adorable.'

'It makes one dormitive, too.'

'Let's talk of it.'

She sighed shortly.

'With so many tiresome cats about, it ought to be protected.'

'Still, with a bronze-green door at night and a violet curtain in the day——'

'I know!'

'And what is it to be?'

'I suppose we shall adhere to the original plan, after all, and call it John the Baptist.'

'Oh, don't!'

'And why not, pray?'

'For lack of humour,' Winsome said, 'I know of nothing in the world to compare with the Prophet's music in *Salomé*. It's the quintessence of villadom. It suggests the Salvation Army, and General Booth. It——'

'You don't like it?' she interrupted him.

'Not very much.'

'If you're going to be childish, I propose you should take a walk.'

'There is nowhere attractive to go.'

'My dear, there are the walls. They are not Roman walls, but they are very nice walls.'

'I find it rather boring, the merely picturesque.'

'Then I'm sure I hardly know——'

'I've an irresistible inclination to attend Mrs. Featherstonehaugh's fête in the Close—*admittance a shilling*.'

'Keep your money, my dear boy, or look through the fence.'

'Ah, Rome!...'

'Well, I'm going indoors. I've letters.... Perhaps you want to write to Andrew, too? I expect he must miss you.'

'Poor Andrew! He goes stumbling along towards some ideal; it's difficult to say quite what.'

'The more reason, then, to write to him.'

'Oh, stay; another minute, please; and I'll be g-good——'

'Then put your tie straight, my dear Rose.... And, *mind Balthasar's tail*!'

∞ XII ∞

'HAIL, angel!'
     'Darling!'

'Dearest!'

'I've been thinking about you so much, dear, all day.'

'Well, I find myself thinking of you too....'

George Calvally had collided with Miss Thumbler, holding 'a marvellous bargain,' a score of music and a parasol.

'At the corner of Vigo Street,' she confessed, 'my *ear* began to burn, so frightfully.'

'Are you going anywhere, dear?'

'I was in the act,' she said, shivering, and growing strangely spiritual, 'of paying a little bill.'

'Then——'

He looked up. Overhead the sky was so pale that it appeared to have been powdered completely with *poudre-de-riz*.

'The proper place,' he said, 'to feel the first hint of autumn, I always think, is the angle of Regent Street, close to the Piccadilly Hotel.'

'How splendidly sequestered, dear, it sounds!'

And already, quite perceptibly, there was a touch of autumn in the air.

In the shops the chrysanthemums mingled with the golden leaves of beech. Baskets of rough green pears lay smothered beneath blue heather.

'How sweet, child, you look!'

'I'm so glad. Have I changed since yesterday? Sunday in town leaves such scars.... Have I my profile still?'

'You've got it. Just!' he assured her.

For the dread of Miss Thumbler's life was that one day she should find herself without it.

'And do you like me, dearest, so? Mamma considers me quite ghastly in *crêpe*; she seems to fancy it may somehow cause an earthquake in Cremona, and bring down a doom upon papa....'

'You're wonderful. You should never, never wear anything else.'

'And it's scarcely a second since I commanded a muslin sprinkled with showers of tiny multi-coloured spots like handfuls of confetti flung all over it!'

'Darling!'

'Dearest!'

Now that George Calvally had lifted Mira up into the sun, she had become more melodious perhaps.

Continually she would be tying things round her forehead, to her mother's absolute astonishment, or perusing, diligently, the lives of such characters as Saskia, Hélène Fourment, Mrs. Blake....

Sometimes, when the mood seized her, she would wander, for hours, through the slow, deep streets of the capital, in a stiff, shelving mantle, with long, unfashionable folds. At other times, too, she would meet George Calvally, swathed like an idol, and they would drive together in a taxi, full of twilight, holding each other's hands. Oh, the mad amusement of Piccadilly . . . the charm, unspeakable, of the Strand . . . the intoxication of the Embankment towards St. Paul's.

'Darling, what would you care to do?'

'At the Coliseum,' she said, 'they're giving *George Dandin,* with the music of Lully. Shall we go?'

He laughed.

'On such a glorious afternoon it would be ungrateful to stay indoors.'

'But Professor Inglepin, dear, has designed the dresses, and his sense of costume is simply . . .'

'Angelic one, he's getting . . .'

'Though, certain busts of Bernini, George——'

'Oh, mind. . . . There's weariness!'

Holding a pink-purple flower to her nose, her eyes closed, Miss Compostella swept by them, in some jewelled hades of her own.

'How magnificent she looked!'

Mira turned, serpentine.

'Was that the first sign of autumn, do you suppose?'

'Listen. I've something to ask you, child.'

With her scroll of music she caressed, sympathetically, his arm.

'It's about the church your father's setting up.'

'Dearest, he says *it's the last he ever means to build.*'

'Mrs. Henedge has asked me to undertake the frescoes. . . .'

'That's joy!'

'But you must help.'

'You mean . . . give me time, dear, I'll see.'

'Darling! Decide.'

'Wouldn't Rosamund——?'

'Impossible. Every five minutes she needs a rest! Besides——'

'Rubbish, besides!'

'But I need *you.*'

'What will Mary say?'

'What difference can it make to her?'

'I suppose not. She left, just now, the sweetest note, with tickets for the Queen's Hall.'

'She's very fond of you, I know.'

'Oh, George, it makes me miserable to think of her.'

He hailed a taxi.

'How would the Wallace be?'

'The Collection!' he exclaimed. 'Isn't it indoors ... dear! And surely it's the most *stagnant* place on earth?'

∞ XIII ∞

'WIERUS, Furiel, Charpon, Charmias!'
The very air seemed charged with tragic thoughts. The play of colour from her aura was so bright it lit the room.

'Charmias!' she called compellingly.

Stretched out upon an Anne settle, watching her, Lady Castleyard lay, in a rather beautiful heap.

'Can you see anything?' she enquired. With a bottle of pact-ink overturned upon the dressing-table, she had retreated to the background, to be 'out of the way.'

'Selah! ...'

Lady Castleyard took up a mirror.

'If the devil won't come,' she said, 'we can't force him.'

Mrs. Shamefoot seemed piqued.

'Not come? Why, he's taken all the wave out of my hair.'

'It certainly *is* less successful, from the side.'

'What would you advise?'

'I should take what the Bishop offers you. Don't break adrift again.'

'You'd accept Ashringford?'

'Well. . . . One may as well as not!'

She collapsed, disheartened.

'I'm like a loose leaf,' she moaned, 'tossed about the world.'

'Don't be so foolish; probably it's more amusing for the loose leaf than for the rooted tree.'

'And you no longer care to join?'

'Birdie, when I've squared my card losses, and my race losses, and my dressmaker, and redecorated our new house a little, I'll have nothing over.'

'There's Lionel! ...'

'Oh, he's so prodigal; I know I'll die in a ditch.'

'Then it's clear, of course, you mustn't.'

'Besides, Biddy, you couldn't expect me to climb away into the tracery lights; it would be like singing Souzouki in *Butterfly*.'

'And you forgive me?'

'I bear no bitterness.'

Mrs. Shamefoot moved towards the window.

The gardens looked almost heroic in the evening light. If the statues, that lit the sombre evergreens of the walks, did *not* suggest Phidias, they did, at least, their duty.

'When the birds fly low, and the insects turn, and turn,' she said, 'there's rain!'

Lady Castleyard closed her eyes.

'I like a storm,' she murmured, 'particularly at night. Sometimes one can catch a face in it—somebody one's been wondering about, perhaps, or who's been wondering of you. And one meets in the explosion.'

With a string of pearls Mrs. Shamefoot flicked at a passing bat.

'We should dress,' she observed, 'for dinner.'

'Sir Isaac is strolling about outside still, isn't he?'

Mrs. Shamefoot peered out.

Already the sun had dipped below the hills, using, above Ashringford, the golds and purples of Poussin that suggested Rome. In the twilight the old, partly disused, stables looked strangely mysterious and aloof.

'And Sir Isaac?'

'Yes, he's there still; like a tourist without a guide-book. But he's not going to be stitched into a Poiret model by eight; nor has his head been ruffled recently by the devil.'

'Is that a Poiret shimmering across the bed? . . . What does Soco say?'

'My dear, he never looks. In the spring he goes striding past the first violet; and it's always the same.'

'I wish he'd take up Lionel until my ball-room's done. His idea of decoration never varies, and it's becoming so wearisome. Horns at intervals! . . .'

'How appalling!'

'We shall be all spears and antlers when you come.'

'Have you that same artistic footman still?'

'Oh, heavens; yes!'

'I adored him. He would clap his hand to his forehead whenever he forgot the . . . potatoes in an attitude altogether *Age d'Airain*.'

'Biddy, see who it is; there's somebody at the door.'

'It's me!'

'Who's me?'

'It's Sumph.'

'Who's Sumph?'

'It's me.'

'I know.'

'I'm Miss Compostella's maid.'

'So Julia's *here*.'

'Opst!'

'And when did she arrive?'

Sumph smiled. 'I've been buzzing about the house,' she said, 'this last *half*-hour.'

'Indeed!'

'Miss Compostella sent me downstairs after a cucumber. Travelling disorients her so. And I must have missed my way.'

'I believe she's in the Round Tower.'

'The housekeeper did say. But had she been the mother of Roxolana, Duchess of Dublin, she could hardly have been more brief.'

Mrs. Shamefoot became concerned.

'When you find your way again,' she said, 'give your mistress these, with my love; they're certain to cure her.'

'The poor soul was stretched out like some dead thing that breathes,' Sumph murmured, 'as I came away.'

Nevertheless, at dinner, nobody could have guessed Miss Compostella's recent critical condition. Had she returned that moment from a month at Mürren one would have wondered still what she had employed.

'It's only now and then,' she informed Lord Blueharnis, inclining towards him, 'that I ever venture; wine has to be utterly exquisite, or I make a face!'

Falling between Dean Manly and Mr. Guy Fox, she resembled a piece of Venice glass between two strong schoolroom mugs.

'I expect he'll fall in love some day with somebody,' Lady Georgia exclaimed, injuring a silence, 'and marry; or don't you think he will?'

'Marry; who?'

'Claud Harvester.'

'Why should he? If Claud can be the Gaby Deslys of literature now, he doesn't seem to mind.'

'But would he be literature?'

'Why, of course!'

'*Love's Arrears*,' Dean Manly said, 'was an amazing piece of work.'

Miss Compostella turned upon him.

'I'm Maggie!' she said.

But Mrs. Shamefoot took compassion upon the Dean's surprise.

'He's become almost *too* doll-like and *Dorothy* latterly,' she enquired, 'hasn't he?'

'Of course, Claud's considered a cult, but everybody reads him!'

'And Mr. Garsaint's comedy?'

'With the exception of Maria Random, Anna's maid, the cast is quite complete.'

'I suppose Anna Comnena had a maid?' Mr. Guy Fox remarked.

Lady Georgia stiffened a candle that had begun to bend.

'I want you to tell me, presently,' she said, 'about young Chalmers. I used to know his mother long ago. She was a great hypocrite, poor dear, but I was very fond of her, all the same!'

But Miss Compostella never put off anything.

'Oh, well,' she said, 'of course he's wonderfully good-looking and gifted, and rather a draw; but I dislike playing with him. Directly he comes on to the stage he begins to perspire.'

'And that nice little Mr. Williams?'

'*He* joined the Persian Ballet.'

Mrs. Guy Fox put up her lorgnon. Her examination of the purple Sèvres dessert service and the James I spoons, she intended, should last at least two minutes; her aversion to the word *perspire* was only equalled by her horror of the word *flea*. . . .

And indeed Mrs. Guy Fox was continually upon the alert.

Ever since her sisters-in-law had been carried off by peers, she had looked upon her husband as a confirmed stick-in-the-mud. It was unreasonable of her, Mr. Guy Fox complained, when it was hardly to be hoped that Fortune would repeat herself with him.

'No, really, I ask for nothing better,' Mrs. Shamefoot said to the Dean, 'than to waste my sweetness on the desert air. . . .'

'And I see no reason why you should not,' he replied. 'The Bishop, I'm confident, doesn't intend to be disobliging.'

'Yes; but you know he is!'

'I wish it were in my power to be of service to you. But you're negotiating, I believe, with five or six cathedrals, at the present time?'

'Not so many. I've Overcares in view, though to be surrounded by that unpleasant Gala glass would be a continual strain. And then, there's Carnage. But somehow the East Coast never appealed to me. It's so stringy.'

'Even Ely?' he enquired.

'Oh, Ely's beautiful. But how sad!'

'Ashringford, also, is sad. Sometimes, in winter, the clouds fall right down upon us. And the towers of St. Dorothy remain lost in them for days.'

'A *mariage mystique* would be just what I'd enjoy.'

'Has it occurred to you to become identified with some small, some charming church, the surprisal of which, in an obscure alley, would amount almost to an adventure?'

'But I'm so tired,' she said, 'of playing Bo-Peep.'

'Still, some cosy gem!'

'A cosy gem?'

'St. Lazarus, for instance——'

'I'm told it leaks. There are forty-two holes in the roof.'

'Or St. Anastasia.'

'St. Anastasia is quite unsafe. Besides, I can't endure a spire. It's such a slope.'

'St. Mary Magdalen?' he ventured.

'I have her life upstairs! Did you know she was actually engaged to John the Baptist? Until Salome *broke it off*. It was only after the sad affair at the palace that Mary really buckled to and became what she afterwards became. But her church here is so pitch dark, and it's built, throughout, with flints. I couldn't bear it.'

'Or Great St. Helen's!'

She shuddered.

'There's the graveyard,' she said. 'I'd never like it. I don't understand the tombs. And I hope I never shall! Those urns with towels thrown over them cast shades like thirteenth-century women.'

'It's unaccountable to me,' the Dean said, 'that you should care to tie yourself in consecrated ground, when you might be an Independent. A Theodoric!'

'I hope you'll make it plain to Doctor Pantry,' Lady Georgia said to him, as the ladies left the room, 'that she's fading fast away.

She has scarcely tumbled a crumb between her lips now for weeks. It almost breaks my heart to look at her.'

Miss Compostella twined an arm about her friend.

'If *I* worship anything,' she confessed, 'it's trees. . . .'

'Come outside; the flowers smell so sweet in the dark.'

The tired cedars in the park had turned to blackened emerald, the air seemed smeared with bloom. Here and there, upon the incomparably soft grey hills, a light shone like a very clear star.

'How admirable, "Orgy," it is!'

'Though to my idea,' Lady Georgia said, 'the hills would undoubtedly gain if some sorrowful creature could be induced to take to them. I often long for a bent, slim figure, to trail slowly along the ridge, at sundown, in an agony of regret.'

Mrs. Guy Fox drew on a glove.

'I'm quite certain,' she remarked, 'that Lord Blueharnis would not require much pressing.'

Lady Georgia made her gentlest grimace.

'I wish,' she said, 'he would, for his figure's sake. He is getting exactly like that awkward effigy of the late Earl in the Public Gardens.'

'Mrs. Barrow of Dawn vows she can fall in love with it a mile away.'

'Poor Violet! Cooped up half the year with an old man and seven staid servants, it cannot be very gay.'

'They say if she's absent, even an hour together,' Mrs. Guy Fox said, 'he sends a search party after her. And he's so miserably mean. Why, the collar of pearls he gave his first wife strangled her!'

'I heard she died in torment; but I didn't know from what.'

Mrs. Shamefoot held the filmy feathers of her fan slantwise across the night. It pleased her to watch whole planets gleam between the fragile sticks.

'Nobody,' she exclaimed, 'would do for me the things that I would do for them!'

'. . . One can never be sure *what* a person will do unless one has tried.'

Lady Georgia drew a scarf devotionally about her head.

'Julia has offered to speak some scenes from tragedies to us,' she said.

'Gladly, Georgia, I will, when we're full numbers.'

'Here come our husbands now!'

'At the risk of seeming sentimental,' Sir Isaac declared, 'I want to tell you how good your dinner was; it was excellent.'

'All millionaires love a baked apple,' Lady Georgia murmured, as she led the way with him towards the Greek Theatre.

' "Que ton âme est bien née Fille d'Agamemnon," ' Miss Compostella declaimed dispassionately, by way of tuning up.

In sympathetic silence Mrs. Shamefoot followed with the Dean.

The statues stood like towers above the low dwarf trees, dark, now, against the night. Across the gardens, from the town, the Cathedral bells chimed ten. Ten silver strokes, like the petals falling from a rose.

She sighed. She sought support. She swayed. . . .

∞ XIV ∞

ALAS, that conviviality should need excuse! While Miss Compostella, somewhat tardily, raised the Keen for Iphigenia, Lady Anne conducted a dinner conference, for women alone.

A less hospitable nature, no doubt, would have managed (quite charmingly) upon tea. But Lady Anne scorned the trickle.

Nor was it before the invitations were consigned to the pillar-box in the Palace wall that she decided, in deference to the Bishop, who was in Sintrap, to add the disarming nuance. To append which, with a hairpin, she had forced the postman's lock.

For indeed excess is usually the grandparent to deceit. And now, with a calm mind beneath a small tiara, she leaned an elbow, conferentially, upon a table decorated altogether recklessly by Aurelia, with acacia-leaves and apostle spoons.

She had scarcely set her spark.

'No, really! . . . I can't think *why* she should have it,' Miss Wardle exclaimed, leaping instantly into a blaze.

'She's very handsome, isn't she? And that's always something. And when you're next in Sloane Street you'll observe she has a certain wayward taste for arranging flowers.'

'If those are her chief credentials, I shall not interfere. . . .'

'Nobody denies her her taste for flowers,' Mrs. Pontypool exclaimed. 'Though, from her manner of dress, one wouldn't perhaps take her to be a Christian. But handsome! I must say, I don't think so. Such a little pinched, hard, cold, shrivelled face. With a profile like the shadow of a doubt. And with a phantom husband too, whom nobody has ever seen.'

'To be fair to her, one has read his ridiculous speeches.'

'If a window is allowed at all, surely Miss Brice should have it?'

'But why should the Cathedral be touched? It's far too light as it is. Often, I assure you, we all of us look quite old. . . . The sun streams in on one in such a manner.'

'Besides, when she has already nibbled at Perch, why must she come to us?'

'Nibbled! One fancies her to have stormed Overcares, Carnage, Sintrap, Whetstone, Cowby, Mawling, Marrow and Marrowby, besides beseeching Perch.'

'If she could only bring herself to wait,' Mrs. Wookie wailed, 'Mrs. Henedge might cater for her at St. John's. . . .'

'St. John's! From what one hears, it will be a perfect Mosque.'

Lady Anne refused a peach.

'I've begged the Dean to propose something smaller to her,' she said, 'than St. Dorothy, where she can put up a window and be as whimsical as she likes.'

'That's common-sense. It wouldn't matter much what she did at Crawbery.'

'Or even in the town. So many of the smaller churches are falling into dilapidation. It's quite sad. Only this evening Miss Critchett was complaining bitterly of the draught at St. Mary's. Her life, she says, is one ceaseless cold. A window there, that would shut, would be such a blessing.'

'And the building, I believe, is distinctly Norman.'

'Call it Byzantine to her. . . .'

'It's a pity she won't do something useful with her money. Repair a clock that wanders, for instance, or pension off some bells. Whenever those bells near us begin to ring they sound such bargains.'

'Or fence in St. Cyriac, where my poor Percy is,' Mrs. Wookie said pathetically. 'It really isn't nice the way the cows get in and loll among the tombs. If it's only for the milk——'

'What is your vote, Mrs. Pontypool?'

'Oh, my dear, don't ask me! I mean to be passive. I mean to be neutral. I shan't interfere.'

'But isn't it one's duty?'

'Well, I'm always glad of any change,' Mrs. Barrow said. 'Any little brightness. Nothing ever happens here.'

Miss Wookie became clairvoyant. 'If I'm not much mistaken,' she said, 'it's an expiatory window she intends us to admire.'

'That's perfectly possible.'

'Indeed, it's more than likely.'

'For some imprudence, perhaps. Some foolish step. . . .'

'Ah, poor thing . . . !'

'And in any case the window, for her, will be a kind of osprey!'

'One could understand a window in moderation, but apparently she's quite insatiable.'

'When my hour comes,' Mrs. Wookie said, 'I shall hope to lie in the dear kitchen-garden.'

Miss Wardle groped about her, and shivered slightly.

'I'd like my cloak,' she murmured, 'please, if you don't mind.'

And indeed it was a matter of surprise, and a sign of success, that she had not sent for it before.

For any gathering that might detain her beyond her own gate after dark it was her plan to assume a cloak of gold galloon that had hidden, once, the shoulders of the Infanta Maria Isabella.

How the garment had reached Miss Wardle's wardrobe was unknown; but that she did not disown it was clear, since frequently she would send a footman for it midway during dinner. It was like the whistle that sounded half-time at a football match, bucolic neighbours said.

'What is the feeling about it in the town?' Lady Anne enquired.

'Until the decision is final, people hardly know which way to object. But Mr. Dyce says if she has the window, he'll show up the Cathedral.'

'Really! Horrid old man! What can he mean?'

'Insolency!'

'And Mr. Pet. . . . But, my dear, fortunately he's such a rapid preacher. One misses half he says.'

'The text he took on Sunday was Self-Idolatry, the Golden Calf. . . .'

'I thought it was to be green!'

'What, the calf?'

'No, the window.'

'Perhaps he'll go before it's all arranged.'

'Very likely. I hear he finds Ashringford so expensive. . . .'

Mrs. Pontypool scratched her smooth fair fringe.

'I suppose,' she said, 'poor young man, with exactly twopence a year, he'd find everywhere ruinous.'

'And then, I wonder, who will take his place?'

'Oh, surely Mr. Olney will.'

'He's such a boy. . . .'

'My dear, age is no obstacle. And his maiden sermon came as a complete surprise! Of course, he was a trifle nervous. He shook in his shoes till his teeth rattled. And his hair stood on end. But, all the same, he was very brilliant.'

'Oh, don't!' Miss Pontypool murmured.

And indeed, notwithstanding a certain analogy between her home circle with that of the Cenci, she was almost an Ingenious. She would say 'Don't!' 'Oh, don't!' 'My dear, don't!' apropos of nothing at all.

'Oh, don't!' she murmured.

'I recall a song of his about a kangaroo,' Mrs. Wookie said, 'once. At a hunt ball.'

'Garoo-garoo-garoo, wasn't it?' Aurelia asked. 'Disgraceful.'

'My dear, *don't*. . . .'

'How fortunate for that little Miss Farthing if he should come. Although she'd have to change her ways. As I've so often tried to tell her, one should wear tailor-mades in the country, instead of going about like a manicure on her holiday.'

'I don't believe there is anything in that,' Miss Hospice said.

'I'm not at all sure. Whenever they meet he gives such funny little gasps. . . .'

'Mr. Olney needs a wife who could pay *at least* her own expenses.'

'What has he a year?'

'He owns to a thousand. But he has quite fifteen hundred.'

'Besides, he's too pale, and his face lacks purpose.'

Lady Anne rapped her fan with pathos.

'Any side issues,' she said, 'might be settled later.'

'Well, I don't see why she should have it,' Miss Wardle repeated. 'To the glory of Mrs. Shamefoot, *and* of the Almighty. . . . No, really I can't see why!'

'Had she been a saint,' Mrs. Wookie observed, 'it would have been another matter.'

'There's not much, my dear, to choose between women. Things are done on a different scale. That's all.'

'Hush, Aurelia! How can you be such a cynic!'

'All the same,' Miss Pantry said, 'trotting to the Cathedral solely of a Sunday, and caring about oneself, solely, all the week, is like crawling into heaven by weekly instalments. . . .'

'Indeed, that's charitable,' Miss Chimney, who was dining at the Palace as a 'silent protest,' was constrained to say.

'But it's such a commonplace thing to do, to condemn a person one knows next to nothing of!'

'Mrs. Shamefoot was at St. Dorothy for the Thanksgiving, wasn't she?'

'I believe so. But Miss Middling sat immediately before me. And with all that yellow wheat in her hat I couldn't see a thing.'

'I remarked her rouging her lips very busily during a long Amen.'

'Well, I couldn't quite make out what she had on. But she looked very foreign from behind.'

'That was Lady Castleyard. Mrs. Shamefoot's little jacket was plainer than any cerecloth. And on her head there was the saddest slouch. . . .'

'Then she shall have my vote. For counting the pin-holes in it made me positively dizzy.'

'And you may add mine.'

'And mine. . . .'

'I forbid anything of the kind, Kate,' her mother said. 'Lady Anne will return it me, I'm sure.' And extending a withered hand in the direction of the vote she slipped some salted almonds into her bosom.

'Oh, Tatty!'

'I shall put your vote with mine, Kate,' she said, 'for it grieves me to see you are such an arrant fool.'

'*Don't!*'

'Where's the good of stirring up Karma for nothing?' Aurelia wondered.

Mrs. Barrow shook her head sceptically.

'I've too little confidence,' she said, 'in straws and smoke, as it is, to credit the pin-marks of a bonnet. It was her maid's.'

'How agnostic, Violet, you are! I shall have you going over to Mrs. Henedge before you've done.'

'Why, she wears the Cathedral even now'.

'I thought she had dropped it. She is getting so tawdry.'

'There's a powder-puff and a bottle of Jordan water, or Eau Jeunesse, of hers here still,' Aurelia said. '*Besides* a blotting-book.'

'I'm not surprised. She appears to have entirely lost her head. The last time I called upon her, the cards *In* and *Out*, on the hall table, were both equally in evidence.'

'It's safer to keep away from her,' Mrs. Wookie murmured. 'I've maintained it all along.'

'No doubt, in our time, most of us have flirted with Rome,' Mrs. Pontypool remarked, 'but, poor dear, she never knew where to stop.'

Lady Anne accepted a conferential cigarette from Mrs. Barrow of Dawn.

'Since the affair appears a decided deadlock,' she pronounced, 'I move that we adjourn.'

Miss Valley manœuvred, slightly, her chair.

'I'm so eager to examine those Mortlake tapestries of Mrs. Cresswell,' she said, 'if they're not away on loan.'

'They're on the Ponte di Sospiri,' Lady Anne replied, 'that connects us to the cloisters. But at night, I fear, it's usually rather dark.'

'Impressions I adore. And there's quite a useful little moon.'

Aurelia appeared amused.

'Even with a young moon,' she said, 'like a broken banana, and Lady Anne's crown, and my carved celluloid combs, and all the phosphorescent beetles there may be (and there are), trooping in beastly battalions through the corridors of the Palace, and the fireflies in the garden, and the flickerings in the cemetery, and, indeed, the entire infinity of stars besides, without a little artificial light of our own, one might just as well stop here.'

Lady Anne looked at her.

'Don't be so ridiculous, my dear, but lead the way!'

'If the electric isn't in repair I refuse to stir.'

'I'm taking the Historian to inspect some curtains,' Lady Anne announced, 'if anyone would care to come.'

'Historian? . . .'

Mrs. Pontypool revealed her Orders.

Quite perceptibly she became the patroness of seven hospitals, two convalescent homes, with shares in a *maison de santé*.

'We must have a little chat,' she exclaimed, 'together, you and I!

All my own family had talent. Only, money, alas, came between them and it.'

'My dear, don't!'

'Indeed, it was getting on for genius. And even still my brother (her uncle) will sometimes sit down and write the most unwinking lies. Of course, novels——'

Miss Wardle fastened her cape.

'I should hate to prostitute myself,' she remarked, 'for *six* shillings.'

'Or for four and sixpence cash. . . .'

'Some people publish their works at a guinea,' Miss Valley murmured, as she followed Lady Anne towards the door.

The Ponte di Sospiri, whither Lady Anne advanced—built by a previous bishop, to symbolise a perpetual rainbow—broke, quite unexpectedly, from the stairs with all the freedom of a polonaise.

Behind their hostess the ladies trooped, as if Miss Pantry's timely warning had made it imperative to wade. The concern, indeed, of Mrs. Barrow was such that it caused a blushing butler to retreat.

'My dear Violet!' Lady Anne began, 'the only time, I believe, I ever——'

But Mrs. Wookie intervened.

'There is somebody,' she remarked, 'thumping at the gate.'

'It is probably only the post.'

And turning to the tapestries Lady Anne commenced the inspection, starting instinctively at the end. And the end, as she pointed out, was simply frantic Bacchanals. After (*à rebours*) came the Martyrdom, spoken often of as 'I've had such a busy morning!' the saint's final word. A model, in every particular, of what a martyrdom should be. And indeed nothing could have been simpler, quieter, or better done. There was no squeezing, fainting, crushing or tramping. No prodding. . . . The spectators, provided, each, with a couch and a cup of chocolate, were there by invitation alone. Although, in the market-place (as one might see), tickets were being disposed of at a price. And in the centre of all stood Mrs. Cresswell, leaning with indifference upon a crosier, inset with a humorous and a somewhat scathing eye.

And so, in the dim light, the fourteen panels ran: growing, as they receded, less and less serene, until, at the opening scene, the atmosphere was one of positive gloom.

'It was the "Marriage."''

'What do people marry for?' Miss Wardle said. 'I've sometimes wondered.'

'My dear, don't ask me.'

'One marries for latitude, I suppose.'

'Or to become a widow.'

'I'd give such *worlds* to be a widow,' Miss Pontypool declared.

'It's a difficult thing to be,' Mrs. Barrow assured her.

'I'm that disgusted with Love,' Miss Valley volunteered in her chastest Cockney voice.

'I find it dreadfully disappointin',' Lady Anne supported her.

Mrs. Wookie sighed.

'Mine,' she said, 'is a nature that cries for more ethereal things.'

'Banal passions,' Miss Wardle whispered faintly, 'fail to stir me.'

' "I'm that disgusted with love," ' the ladies chanted charmingly all together.

'If that is Mr. Cresswell,' Mrs. Barrow remarked, 'I'm certainly not surprised.'

'He's so worn,' Miss Chimney observed critically, 'and she's so *passée*.'

Aurelia touched the tapestries with her thumb. 'It's probably only the stuff.'

'And who would this be?' Miss Valley queried, trailing towards an easel with a little quick glide.

'That!' Lady Anne said. 'I suppose it was Walter once.'

'If I were getting painted,' Mrs. Pontypool announced, 'again I'd try Mr. White. He doesn't reject beauty. And he reveals the sitter's soul.'

Miss Chimney showed some sensitiveness.

'Anything nude, anything undressed, anything without a *frill*,' she said, 'revolts me somehow so. I'm sure in the winter, when the trees show their branches—well, I go, when I can, to the South.'

But the appearance of the Miss Chalfonts upon the stairs, closely entwined, their eyes astream, their bodies racked by laughter, a single superb boa shared more or less between them, caused a commotion.

'We rang and we rang,' Miss Clara said.

'I'm so sorry. But, at all events, you've dined?'

Miss Blanche quite collapsed. 'Why, no!' she said.

'Do you abominate almonds?' Mrs. Wookie asked.

Miss Constantia placed a hand before her eyes. 'If there's anything on this earth,' she said, 'I've a horror of, or an aversion for, it's that.'

And her gesture seemed to make vibrate all those other objections latent in her too. All those other antipathies, *less* than almonds, that were hereditary, perhaps. She began suddenly to droop. She stood there, dreaming.

'Unwind, can't you,' her sister said, 'and let me out.'

Miss Chalfont commenced to turn.

'It's not from coquetry,' she confessed gaily, 'that we're last. But the nearer one lives, somehow, the later one's sure to be.'

'To be frank,' Lady Anne said absently, 'you might be stopping in the house.'

They were free. . . .

Their garments, the ladies noted, were white and sparkling streaked with green.

Never, Miss Valley affirmed, had she encountered so many charming Ideas. Even at a Poet's dinner.

'Now I know,' she said, 'exactly where to tie a necklace. On my arm.'

'We were getting rather nervous about the vote,' Miss Clara said, 'so we decided to bring it ourselves. It's the first engagement we've kept for I don't know how long!'

'And which way is it?'

Miss Clara indicated the Cathedral.

'I would read them my essay on Self-Control,' Miss Hospice murmured, 'if you thought it would have any effect.'

'It would probably make them infinitely worse. It might even kill them outright. And then it would be murder,' Miss Valley said.

Miss Hospice smiled sedately.

'My publisher, at any rate, could be found,' she said. 'I've had the same man always. Byron had him. And Coleridge had him. And Keats. I should be really ashamed to flutter from *firm to firm* like some of those things one sees. . . . I simply couldn't do it. And God looks after me! He has never abandoned me yet to sit up night after night in a public-house to libel His saints by Christmas.'

'My dear, I congratulate you! To compose an essay on Self-Control when one is so strangely devoid of it oneself was an admirable *tour de force*.'

But the Miss Chalfonts were becoming increasingly unstrung.

'Oh, hold me!' Miss Blanche sighed, sinking, slowly, like the

Sienese Santa of the frescoes, to the floor. Miss Clara and Miss Constantia made a movement, which, although a miracle of rhythm, was ineffectual upon the whole.

With quiet complacence Mrs. Wookie took a chair.

'They're off!' she said.

'If Lord Chesterfield could only see them now!'

'Don't!'

'By birth they may be County,' Mrs. Pontypool murmured. 'But by manners——'

'Indeed, by manners——'

'By manners!...'

'Crazy creatures,' Mrs. Wookie crooned, 'crazy-crazies!'

Mrs. Barrow agreed.

'That a certain Signor Calixfontus,' she said, 'followed St. Augustine over here and married a savage—and ran through his life before most people would have cared to be seen about at all, is no excuse for his descendants to behave like perfect idiots.'

'Or to drape themselves in those loose misfits.'

'Lampshades!'

'It's Vienna!'

'Teheran!!'

'Vienna or Teheran,' Mrs. Pontypool said, 'or the Edgware Road, *I've* never seen such a riddle!'

But Lady Anne was looking bewildered. 'When Saul was troubled,' she said, 'David played to him. Didn't he?'

Miss Valley nodded.

'There's a Rembrandt,' she said, 'about it at the Hague. I remember it so well. Chiefly because of David, who is tucked away in a remote corner of the canvas, almost as if he were the signature.'

'And has he got a golden September-skin like Hendrickje Stoffels?' Aurelia asked.

'Yes; and a smile like sad music.'

'Oh, but I know it!'

'Well, won't somebody go to the piano?'

'Miss Wookie will,' her mother said. 'Won't you, Kate? And, perhaps, sing some little song besides. She knows such shoals. What was that one, my dear, that despairing, dismal one about the heliotrope? *When Heliotropes Turn Black.* It's the true story of a sailor. Or he might have been a coastguard. And he goes away. And he comes back. And, of course, he finds her dead.'

'A fugue and a breath of air,' Lady Anne said, 'should be quite enough. Come into the drawing-room and the Miss Chalfonts can have some supper there while we play cards. A little fruit, a little wine. . . . Poor Miss Blanche is simply sinking.'

Miss Wardle disappeared altogether into her *point d'espagne*.

'O heavens!' she said.

Lady Anne's drawing-room, that had belonged, upon a time, to Mrs. Henedge, who had 'rescued' it from Mrs. Goodfellow, who had come by it from Mrs. Archer, who had whipped it from Lady Lawrence, who had seized it from Mrs. Jones, of whose various 'improvements' (even to distant pretty little Saxon Ethel) it bore some faint chronological trace, was picking up, as well as might be expected, to be a trifle Lady Anne's. Although there were moments even still in the grey glint of morning when the room had the agitated, stricken appearance of a person who had changed his creed a thousand times, sighed, stretched himself, turned a complete somersault, sat up, smiled, lay down, turned up his toes and died of doubts. But this aspect was reserved exclusively for the house-maids and the translucent threads of dawn.

It appeared quite otherwise now.

Upon an oval table that gleamed beneath a substantial chandelier a solitary specimen of Lady Anne's fabled Dresden was set out, equivalent, in intention, to an Oriental's iris, or blossoming branch of plum.

It was her most cherished *Rape*.

With as many variations of the theme in her cabinets as the keys in which a virtuoso will fiddle a gipsy dance, it revealed the asceticism of her mind in refraining from exhibiting them all. So situated, it is certain Mrs. Henedge would have exposed the lot.

Eyes beseeching, arms imploring, fingers straining, raiment blowing, an abduction, of necessity, must be as orthodox as a wedding with a Bishop to babble it off.

Mrs. Wookie wished.

'That's precisely my fear for Kate,' she said, 'when she runs out to take a motor number. Somebody, some impulsive foreigner, perhaps, visiting the Cathedral, might stop the car and capture her, and carry her away, possibly as far as Ringsea-Ashes, before she could resist. And there, I should hope, Mr. Walsh would marry them before they went on.'

'She'll have many a million, I dare say, before that occurs,' Miss

Wardle observed. 'People aren't handcuffed, seized, gagged and pinioned. Are they?'

'Still, foreigners visit the Cathedral—even blacks. While I was watering my garden to-night I saw a Moor looking at me through the fence.'

Mrs. Pontypool sighed.

'Ashringford's getting *too* discovered,' she said. 'It's becoming spoilt. Mrs. Fulleylove was telling me at the Dean's that Lolla's to finish abroad. "And what will she gain by it?" I said. She could pick up quite enough languages from the tourists in the Close.'

'All that would be good for her.'

Miss Chimney looked fiendish. 'I detest all foreigners,' she said.

But, from a withdrawing-room, Miss Wookie was being borne rapidly away upon the wings of a perfectly hysterical song.

'Can nobody stop her?' Mrs. Barrow asked. The human voice, in music, she considered far too explanatory. And what did it matter *what* the heliotropes did, so long as they were suppressed.

'Her *coloratura*,' Mrs. Wookie observed, 'most surely improves. Although, to vibrate like Fräulein Schuster isn't done in a day.'

Notwithstanding, upon the veranda, Miss Valley and Aurelia were sketching out a valse. Gently, with gowns grasped, through the moonlit spaces they twirled, the Historian gazing up abstractedly at the Cathedral towers.

'I lay you ten to one she gets it!' she cried.

'Of course, if she persists she'll prevail.'

'I wish she were dead.'

'Surely the world is large enough for us all.'

'But I need a *Life*.'

Aurelia glanced about her timidly. The solemnity of their shadows startled her.

'Though, indeed, when my investigations are over in these parts, I hope never to set foot in Ashringford again. Never, Never, Never, Never, Never, Never!'

'Some of the Spanish saints were so splendid, weren't they?'

'Oh, Aurelia—not another.'

'But try a man this time.'

'Man, or woman!' Miss Valley said.

'Or edit letters. Those of King Bomba to the Queen of Snowland require revision badly.'

'And drown the text in the notes!'

'Make an anthology.'

'*Euh*, that's so messy!'

Aurelia reversed. 'Mrs. Shamefoot won't die,' she said, 'unless we kill her.'

'Luckily, there's the climate. The air here has been called a moist caress.'

'It's a poor prospect anyway.'

'How I wish she were dead!'

'She's like some heavy incense, don't you think?'

Miss Valley became visionary.

'At the back of her mind,' she said, 'in some strange way, she's convinced her spirit will be caught in colour, and remain merged in it, as long as the glass endures.'

'Has she said so?'

'Certainly not. But in our profession naturally one knows. . . . And my intuition tells me that if an atom of her, a teeny-weeny particle, *isn't* woven into the window, she'll be very cruelly chagrined.'

Aurelia blinked, uncertain.

'And when would one know?' she enquired.

'Not, of course, until after she were dead.'

'I call it really rather disgraceful.'

'Why . . . ?'

'Because, by the time she'll have done, St. Dorothy will be too disturbed to be nice. Nobody would go into it unless they were obliged. All the tranquillity would be gone. I'd never enjoy a quiet minute there again.'

'My dear, that's selfish. Besides, you're scarcely two months in the year here ever, are you?'

'I should still think it horrid.'

'Nonsense. Beyond a little vanity, it's hard to explain exactly what the idea indicates. But I'm sure it points to something.'

'Earthiness. The extremes of it. Earth spirit!'

'Oh, more. And even if it did *not*, Mrs. Shamefoot can furnish an opera-box as very few others can. And if one can furnish an opera-box one should be able to fill in a window.'

'I can imagine her asleep in a rather boring Louis the Sixteenth bedroom with a window on Sloane Square.'

'Why not in Sloane Street? Over the shop. Though if you

troubled to get a directory, you'd see she doesn't live that end of town at all.'

But Miss Pontypool was singing now.

'Paris! Paris! Paris! Paris! O Paris! Cité de joie! Cité d'amour. . . .'

'It's the arietta of *Louise*.'

'I knew it couldn't be David.'

Like a riband flung in carnival the voice trailed away across the night.

'Poor girl! If her lines are cast in Ashringford. . . . For an instant she brought almost into this ghastly garden the glamour of the Rue de la Paix.'

'Is it policy? The Miss Chalfonts will be on the floor.'

'What does it matter, if they are?'

But, peeping through the window, Aurelia was unprepared to find the Miss Chalfonts listening intently while the tears were streaming from their eyes.

∽ *XV* ∽

THE municipal museum in Ghost Street was rarely, if ever, thronged, especially after noon.

'You can have the key,' the wife of the custodian said, 'if you want it. But there's nothing whatever inside.'

And the assertion, sometimes, would spare her husband the weariness of struggling into a pair of black and silver trousers and vague historic tunic that was practically a tea. For in Ashringford, the Corporation, like a diver in a tank, was continually plunging back into the past.

'Since it pleases visitors to catch a last glimpse of this vanishing England,' the Mayor had said, '*and if Stratford can*; why . . . !'

And after the customary skirmishing of the Board, and reconciliatory garden-party, a theatrical tailor had been beckoned to, from Covent Garden, who had measured half the town.

And now, beneath the grey horse-chestnut trees, where stood 'the Fountain,' round which, of a summer morning, the 'native' women clustered, chatting charmingly, as they sold each other flowers, or posing, whenever they should be invited, to anxious artists for a shilling an hour, an enchanted American, leaning, observant, from a window of the Cresswell Arms, might almost fancy that, what with the determined duennas thronging to the Cathedral, and darting chambermaids holding long obtrusive envelopes, and tripping shepherdesses and dainty goose-girls, and occasionally, even, some pale, ring-eyed powdered-nervous Margaret, with empty pitcher and white-stockinged feet, it was still the threshold of the thirteenth century.

'There's nothing in the museum, whatever,' the woman repeated. 'Nothing at all.' And she added almost desperately: 'It's where they keep the rubbish.'

But Mrs. Shamefoot was not accustomed to be baulked.

'There're the sepulchral urns, and the tear-bottles, at any rate,' she said, 'and there's a good skeleton, I believe?'

'Yes, marm. There is that.'

'Well, then . . .' And pushing apart the light gilt gates, she swept inside. And even if it were only for the fascinating fanlight on the stairs, she was glad that she had come.

And there was also a mirror! The unexpected shock of the thing brought a flush of pleasure to her cheek. She had hardly hoped to find so much.

'Marvellous woman,' she exclaimed, going up to it, with an amicable nod, 'where've you been?'

She was looking bewitching beyond measure, she believed, bound in black ribands, with a knot like a pure white butterfly under her chin.

And, to her astonishment, there were mirrors, or their equivalents, upon most of the walls.

'The habit of putting glass over an oil painting,' she murmured, 'makes always such a good reflection, particularly when the picture's *dark*. Many's the time I've run into the National Gallery on my way to the Savoy and tidied myself before the Virgin of the Rocks. . . .'

And selecting a somewhat spindle-legged settee she glanced yearningly around.

It was the room of the Blueharnis Bequest.

In a place of prominence, unmistakable, was the Dehell portrait of the donor, leaning against a door, in full uniform, the arms folded, the eyes fixed, dangling a sword.

What could have happened?

Anxiously, for a clue, she scanned the pendant of his wife, a billowy, balloon-like creature, leading by a chain of frail convolvulus a prancing war-horse. But the mystery still remained.

Near by, upon a screen (being stored for her), was the *Miss Millicent Mutton* of Maclise. Here, in a party pinafore, *Mrs. Henedge* was seen riding recklessly upon a goat clasping a pannier of peaches and roses while smiling down at an angelic little boy who, with a thistle and a tambourine, was urging the nanny on.

Eventually, authorities affirmed, the canvas would find its way to the South Kensington Museum, where (besides being near to dear Father . . . and to old Father . . . and the Oratory) there was a room ready waiting to receive it where it would be perfectly happy and at home.

And as one work will beget another, Mrs. Pontypool, not to be outdone, had contributed an ancestral portrait of a lady, reclining upon a canopy, plainly prostrate, beneath the hot furnaces, and the fiery skies, of Manchester. . . .

But, for the most part, as was but fitting for a Cathedral town, the mildly Satanic school of Heironymus Bosch was chiefly to the fore.

Yet, whimsically wistful, an elderly frame in curtains was waiting to be found. Leisurely, Mrs. Shamefoot rose.

That something singularly wicked was concealed beneath the hangings she had no doubt.

And indeed it was '*Le thé à l'Anglaise, chez Lucrezia Borgia,*' in which an elegant and radiant Lucrezia, tea-pot in hand, was seen admiring the indisposition of her guests like a naughty child.

A glass of flowers by Fantin brought her to herself.

'If I could feel it were all arranged!' she murmured. 'Unless this window-quibbling ceases, I'll soon be in my grave. And Soco, I'm confident, could not be counted upon, even for the simplest cross. He'd marry again. The brute!'

She looked out across a half-wild garden to the Asz. Beyond the broad bridges, the peaked hayricks, sprinkling the hills, stood sharp, like pyramids, against the sky. There was something monstrous and disquieting in their shapes that thrilled her. To be an Independent upon some promontory, she mused, above the sea; a landmark; perhaps a shrine! . . .

White birds, like drifting pearls, would weave their way about her, examining her with their desolate empty eyes.

Or to be a lighthouse; looped in lights!

Although to search out some poor face when it the least expected it would be carrying ill-nature, perhaps, to a rather far extreme. Better some idle tower. But in England towers so seldom mellowed rightly. They were too rain-washed, weather-beaten, wind-kissed, rugged; they turned tragic and outlived themselves; they became such hags of things; they grew dowdy and wore snapdragons; objects for picnics; rendezvous of lovers, haunts of vice . . . ; they were made a convenience of by owls; they were scarred by names; choked by refuse, and in the end they got ghoulish and took to too much ivy, and came toppling down.

She stood oppressed.

Over the darkly gleaming water of the Asz a boat passed by with cordings like the strings of some melancholy instrument. From the deserted garden below an odour of burning leaves loitered up to her. The long pink Infidels flared stiffly from the shade.

'Heigh-ho,' she yawned, 'one can't play fast and loose for ever. . . .' And she turned away, dolefully, through the damp deserted rooms.

A piece of tessellated pavement, a sandalled foot, detained her. 'Street!' she murmured, stooping down, enthralled.

The frou-frou of the custodian's skirts disturbed her.

'Such a mixture of everything as there is; a country Cluny!'

'I dare say, marm. I've never been round the worruld; I've lived in Ashringford, man and boy, these sixty years.'

'Indeed; that's why you look so young!'

'I beg your pardon, marm?'

'I say, that's why you look so *young*!'

And startled by his historic attire, she trailed slowly towards the door, gazing back at him across her shoulder, with one arm stretched before, the other lingering behind, in the attitude of a nymph evading a satyr upon a Kylix.

It was a relief to hear voices! Chatting beneath an immaterial study of the sunset breeze, she beheld the ample form of Sumph.

'And in Act IV,' she was saying, 'the husband *pretends* to go away. But, of course, he doesn't! He goes only a' little distance. . . . And the "curtain" should be beautiful! Lovely it ought to be. The birds all singing as if their last hour had come. And Miss Compostella and Mr. Chalmers——'

'Is your mistress anywhere about?' Mrs. Shamefoot interrupted her.

Sumph smiled.

'Why, no,' she said, 'she's not. I'm here with Mrs. Henedge's maid, just taking a look round.'

'Really? . . .'

'Whenever I'm able I like to encourage anything that's Art.'

'And how do you like Ashringford?'

'I like it. It puts me in mind of the town Dick Whittington came to when all the bells were ringing.'

'You've been up the tower!'

'It didn't seem worth while. They told us beforehand we could never see *back there*. . . . But we watched them pull the bells. Quite a receipt of their own they seemed to have. Such swingings and pausings and noddings and rushings. You should have seen the dowdies run! And in such bonnets. As Thérèse remarked, it was an education in botany.'

'Oh-h-h!'

There came a cry.

Mrs. Henedge's maid was before the Borgia *thé*.

Nodding sympathetically to Sumph, Mrs. Shamefoot disappeared.

∞ XVI ∞

'EVER since the accident,' Lady Georgia said, 'she has been going about in such heavens of joy. I've seldom seen anyone so happy.'

Mrs. Guy Fox passed a hand across her eyes.

'It fell,' she remarked, 'so suddenly; I was in my bath.'

Miss Compostella helped herself to honey.

'I fear St. Dorothy's badly damaged.'

'Half of it is down.'

'Oh no, dear; not half.'

'It's as if the gods granted it to her,' Lady Georgia declared; 'she's been so brave.'

'Such gusts of wind! The way they pulled the bushes——'

'How did it happen, exactly?'

'A pair of scissors, it appears, was left upon the scaffolding, and caught the lightning's eye.'

'What a dreadful thing!'

Mrs. Fox shuddered.

'That the Cathedral should submit to be struck,' she said, 'strikes me as being so strange. It never has before.'

'Lady Anne has twice 'phoned.'

'. . . Surely not already?'

'Before breakfast, too!'

'Polite. . . .'

Lady. Georgia rolled her eyes.

'What is one to do with a person,' she demanded, 'who cannot feel the spell of a beautiful supreme thing like Tintoretto's *Crucifixion*?'

'And where is she now?'

'Oh, my dear, she's wandering exultant about the house. She's been doing it since six.'

'Leave her,' Mr. Guy Fox advised. 'Perhaps presently she'll come down and have a good cry.'

'Darling Biddy, she's been divinely patient. But the strain was becoming too much for her. It was undermining her health.'

'Holding ten cathedrals at arm's-length must have been terribly tiring.'

'I had an idea it was quite the other way. In any case, thank Heaven, the wrangling's over. Done.'

'I wouldn't say that. But clearly a difficulty is removed. They're sure to secure her for the Restorations.'

'My maid has asked if she may go over and see the ruins,' Miss Compostella said.

'She should take the bridle-path through the fields,' Lady Georgia murmured, rising to welcome Mrs. Shamefoot as she came in.

Over a rug that suggested a summer morning Mrs. Shamefoot skimmed, pale in cloud-white laces, her hands buried beneath the flimsy plumage of a muff, like some soul who (after a tirade or two) would evaporate and take flight.

'You may kiss me,' she murmured wistfully, 'but kiss me carefully.'

'I heard you at the telephone as I crossed the hall.'

'Lady Anne re-rang.'

'I hope she was pleasant.'

'No. She was only half-charming, if you know; she was nice, without being nicer. . . . But one feels she's climbing down. Of course, I told her, without the approbation of all Ashringford, I wouldn't for the world ... and, on her side, she spoke of making a ragoût with the remains.'

'She's so tasteless,' Lady Georgia exclaimed. 'But there it is, many people seem to imagine that a stained-glass window is nothing of the kind unless some over-good-looking young saint is depicted in bathing drawers and half-an-inch of water.'

Mrs. Shamefoot raised her muff beneath her chin.

'Soco's so silly,' she said. 'He'd fire at anything like that with his revolver. And, oh, Mr. Guy Fox ... I've got to scold you. Standing beneath my window and calling me by my name millions and millions of times was fearfully indiscreet. ...'

'I thought you'd be interested to know.'

' "It's down," you said, "it's down." The servants must have wondered what you meant! Though it's really rather odd; when your voice disturbed me, I was having such a curious-funny dream. People were digging me up for reliques. ...'

'Here's your coffee, dear.'

'All I need, darling, is a Railway Guide. I must return at once to town; I'm so busy!'

'Remain until to-morrow,' Miss Compostella said, 'and travel back with me.'

'But, Julia, you're not leaving us so soon!'

'I must. You know I'm in despair with my helmet for the Garsaint piece. I do not care about myself in it at all: it's too *stiff*. And the crown; I'm sure the crown's too timid.'

But Mrs. Guy Fox was reading aloud some extracts of a letter from her son, a dutiful diplomat who, even when fast asleep, it was said, suggested the Court of St. James.

'Just now,' she read, 'the Judas trees along the banks of the Bosphorus are coming into flower. The colour of these trees is extraordinary. They are neither red nor violet, and at evening they turn a sort of agony of rose.'

'Delicious!' Lady Georgia said, staring at Atalanta in dismay. There were moments, especially in the early morning, when she alarmed her mother. Moments when she looked remotely Japanese. ...

'No; there's nothing in the paper at all, except that the Wirewells have arrived,' Lady Castleyard said, stepping out upon the lawn.

Mrs. Shamefoot joined her.

After the gale a yellow branch lay loose beneath each tree, making the park appear to be carpeted by some quite formal silk. The morning was fine with courageous crazy clouds.

'You're tired?'

'A little,' Lady Castleyard confessed. 'All this death makes me melancholy.'

'I expect it's merely Lionel!'

'Lionel? But I'm not tired of Lionel. Only, now and then, I long rather for a new aspect. . . .'

'Do you suppose, if there were no men in the world, that women would frightfully mind?'

'I don't know, really. . . . What a pity to leave that gloriously bound book out all night!'

They turned aside through a wicket-gate into an incidental garden.

At periods, upon the enclosing walls, stood worn lead figures of cupid gardeners, in cavalier hats and high loose boots and cunning gloves, leaning languidly upon their rakes, smiling seraphically over the gay rings of flowers that broke the grass.

'Age holds no horrors for me,' Mrs. Shamefoot said, 'now, any more. Some day I'll have a house here and I'll grow old quite gracefully.'

'Surely with age one's attractions should increase. One should be irresistible at ninety.'

'A few of us, perhaps, may. You, dear Dirce, will——'

'But in Ashringford! You used always to say it would be at Versailles, or Vallombrosa, or Verona, or Venice; a palladio palace on the Grand Canal. Somewhere with a *V*!'

'I remember . . . ; although I was tempted too rather, wasn't I, towards Arcachon. And that's an *A*!'

'Poor Soco. He'll be so surprised. . . .'

'It's a pity, whenever he speaks, he's so very disappointing.'

'Still, there'll be the bill. . . .'

'Well, he could scarcely have seriously supposed I'd throw myself away upon a lancet! Besides, I believe I'll be desired somehow more when I'm gone. What good am I here?'

'My dear, you compose in flowers. You adorn life. You have not lived in vain.'

They were in the dogs' cemetery.

Lady Castleyard tapped a little crooked cross.

'One fears,' she said, 'that Georgia must have poisoned them all for the sake of their epitaphs.'

'Here come the children!'

'And remember, Frank,' Fräulein was warning Master Fox, in her own wonderful Hanoverian way, 'not to pursue Mirabel too much towards the end. It makes her hot.'

They were preparing to play at Pelléas.

Lady Georgia insisted that her children should practise only purely poetic games. She desired to develop their souls and bodies harmoniously at the same time.

'Remember the chill she caught as Nora!' Fräulein said. 'And, Dawna, must I re-implore you not to pick up the sun-money with your hands? Misericordia! One might think your father was a banker.'

'I do so love the sun!'

'Do you, dear?'

Obviously, it was an occasion to kiss and form a group.

∞ XVII ∞

'CERTAINLY I should object to milk a cow,' Miss Compostella said. 'Why?'

Sumph smiled.

'I see so many,' she said. 'One, the prettiest possible thing, the very living, breathing image of the Alderney that you engaged, miss, to walk on in *The Princess of Syracuse.*'

'It would be the signal,' Miss Compostella said, 'often for a scuffle.'

'And don't I know it!' said Sumph.

'Although to me it was always extraordinary that Miss Elcock, who almost fainted whenever she encountered it in the wings, would become indifferent to the point of being tossed the instant the curtain rose. She was too preoccupied about appearing young, I suppose, to care about anything else, her own part included.'

'Oh no, miss. She was a great, great actress. Watching her in certain scenes, how cold my hands would grow! The blood would fly to my heart!'

The invaluable woman grew nostalgic.

'I fear you don't delight in the country, somehow, as you should.'

'I don't know, miss. Ashringford amuses me. I find myself dying with laughter here several times a day.'

'Indeed——'

'Naturally not in the house. It's too much like a sanatorium for that. Every time I come to you along the corridors I feel just as if I was going to visit some poor sick soul and had forgotten my flowers.'

Miss Compostella gave an arranging touch to a bouquet of blue berries above her ear.

'I hope you passed a pleasant afternoon,' she said, 'among the ruins.'

'It was lovely. I sat on a piece of crumbled richness in the long grass for over an hour. Afterwards I took tea at the Closed House with Thérèse. She was so busy with her needle. "I shall need a frock for my conversion," Mrs. Henedge told her the other day, "and another for my reconversion, in case that's necessary." "But fashions change so quickly, madame," Thérèse said to her. "And so do I," she said; "I can travel a long way in a week." Chopping and changing! But it's to be quite a decided little frock for all that. Very plain. With some nice French buttons. The *other* is one of those curious colour contrasts. . . . So sickly. But rather smart. A discord of lemon, pink, and orange. And I came back, miss, to Stockingham, by way of the Asz, in spite of Signora Spaghetti, "Never walk by the water-side," she said to me, when I was a child. That's why we left Stratford. Because of the Avon.'

'But surely the Thames——'

'Bless you, no!'

'And you saw nothing of the Bishop?'

'His pinched white face frightened me. It gave me such a turn. . . .

> 'Weep, willow, weep,
> Willow, willow, weep,
> For the cross that's mine is difficult to bear.'

Miss Compostella interposed.

'You needn't pack up everything,' she remarked.

'It's my impatience! I could sing when I think we're returning home to-morrow. If it's only to escape the housekeeper here. For we had quite a quarrel just now. . . . "Where's your wedding ring?" she says. "I never wear it," I replied. "It makes one's hand look so bourgeoise. And don't you go flinging your nasty aspersions over me," I said, "for I won't have it." '

'Quite right.'

'My word. I was very carefully brought up. My mother was most tyrannical, especially with us girls. Why I wasn't even allowed to read *The Vicar of Wakefield* until after I was married. . . . Not that I didn't belong to a Rabelais-lovers'-Society by the time I was twelve.'

'What, in Stratford?' Miss Compostella wondered, taking up with lassitude the manuscript of a play left with her by Mrs. Shamefoot (before the accident), in the expectation of obtaining an interest at the Palace by overwhelming Miss Hospice by an eternal and delicate debt of thanks.

It was a *Tristram and Isolde*.

'*Brangane and Isolde*,' she read. '*Deck chairs. Isolde making lace. Soft music.*

BR. But what makes you think he's so fond of you, my dear?

Is. He presses my hand so beautifully.

BR. You know he does that to *everybody*.

Is. O-h?

BR. Take my advice. *I* should never marry him.

Is. Really? Why not?

BR. He would leave you.

Is. Nonsense!

BR. He has ears like wings. . . .

Is. Is that all?

'Not such a bad beginning,' Miss Compostella commented. 'But why must Isolde be so impatient to confide to the waves her age? "I'm exactly nine-and-twenty." I cannot see that it helps. And why, oh, why,' she murmured, rising to her feet, 'when Tristram enquires for her, should Brangane lose her head so, and say "She's out, she's not at home, she isn't there"? Were she to reply quite calmly, almost like a butler, "The family's away," or "I expect them home in about a fortnight," it should be amply sufficient.'

A lazy ripple of strings surprised her.

'What is that——?'

'I don't know, miss, I'm sure. It sounds like *Pippa Passes*.'

'Well, go and see.'

'It brings back to me the reading Mrs. Steeple gave at the Caxton

Hall when I, Miss Falconhall and her fiancé received Press tickets.
... Coming away, foolish fellow, he slipped on a piece of cabbage-
stalk and snapped his coledge bone.'

'Can you make out who is serenading us?'

'It's the Honourable Mrs. Shamefoot,' Sumph informed. Pacing
beneath a magnificence of autumnal trees, Mrs. Shamefoot was
strolling slowly up and down with a guitar.

'She's been on stilts all day,' Sumph said.

Miss Compostella coiled an arm across her head.

'Give me a phenacetin powder,' she exclaimed, 'at once. For what
with the crash the Cathedral made in falling, and your silly jabber,
and her guitar ... !'

∞ XVIII ∞

'THE little turquoise flower you admired, my beloved, on Wednesday, is known as *Fragment of Happiness*. You will find it again
in some of *Dürer's* drawings. Oh, George! ... On my desk there
is an orange-tree. How it makes me yearn, dear, for the South! I
count my oranges. Eight poor, pale, crabbed oranges. Like slum
cripples. I think of Seville now. Yes. To-morrow. Absolutely.
But, dearest, *downstairs*, Rosalba Roggers sometimes sallies up.
She saw us together last time and begged so to be told who my
wonderful big child was with the tragic face. Five o'clock, dear.
And don't be late as you usually are.   M.

'*P.S.*—I will carry some of your troubles, if you will send them
to me with your thoughts.

'*P.P.S.*—You say I blush! When, I wonder, shall I learn to have
a mask of my own?'

'Minx!' Mrs. Calvally exclaimed. 'The snake. . . .'

She seemed stupefied, stunned.

'I merely opened his paint-box,' she began, stammering to herself.
'Mamma! . . .'

And, as if to demonstrate that domestic drama is not entirely
tired of its rather limited tricks, her little son Raphael entered the
room at that minute and rushed right into her arms.

He came. . . .

She stooped. . . .

'My dear!'

And now she was calm again, complacent, with all her old tranquillity of gardens.

'Oh, how ugly! . . .'

'Where, my precious?'

'And is it a present, too?'

For the artist's anniversary Miss Thumbler had despatched a door-knocker, wrought in bronze, that represented a woebegone, wan Amour.

'By all means,' Mrs. Calvally had said, 'let us put it up. I will call a carpenter. And some of the mirrors, as well, need glueing. . . .'

And the gift decidedly had eclipsed her own humble offering of the Hundred Best Pictures, in photogravure, that did not appear to have aroused in him all the interest that they might.

'Mrs. Asp and Mrs. Thumbler are in the drawing-room.'

'Are they, my pet?'   •

'And Mrs. Asp is concealing such a lovely-looking thing. All wrapped up. It must be something for papa.'

'Come along and let us see.'

'Don't sigh, mamma. It bores me to hear you sigh.'

'I'm so sorry George isn't in,' Mrs. Calvally said, as she lounged leisurely round the huge Ming screen that began her drawing-room. 'But he went out, quite early, almost before it was light, to make a Canaletto of the space before White Hall.'

'I believe he's unusually busy. . . . So I hear!' Mrs. Asp announced.

'No. Not so very. . . . He's making Mrs. Jeffreys at present in all her jewels—or, at any rate, more than he usually likes. And the old Duke of Spitalfields. And the cartoons of a country church. . . .'

Mrs. Thumbler began to purr.

'And he obliges Mira,' she said, 'nearly every day. And in such varieties of poses! Even as Absalom, swinging from a tree.'

'I know. He raves about her. He told me he looked upon her almost as an inspiration,' Mrs. Calvally replied, confident that the 'almost' would be repeated to haunt Miss Thumbler for days.

'All the same, quite between ourselves, I confess, I wish he didn't. It's making her so vain! Lately (I'm ashamed to tell you) she's taken to wear *a patch*. A crescent-moon-shaped affair above the lip that gives her such an o-ri-gi-nal expression. Really, sometimes in the street . . . Well, I won't go out with her again. I let her take the dog.'

Mrs. Asp untied an ermine stole.

'My dear,' she exclaimed, 'do be careful. When it comes to dragging a dumb animal about as a chaperon one gets generally misunderstood.'

'But what am I to do? Mira's so sensitive. I dare hardly say a word. Although those pen-and-ink embroideries Mr. Calvally made for her, charming as they are, are only fit for the house.'

'I wasn't aware he had ever made her any,' Mrs. Calvally said. 'I'm sure he never made pen-and-ink embroideries for me!'

'Occupation,' Mrs. Asp reflected airily, 'is an admirable thing, especially for a man. It restricts restlessness as a rule.'

'How you comfort me! He talks of a farm-house now near Rome.' Mrs. Thumbler shuddered.

'I should hate to keep an Italian cow,' she said. 'I should be afraid of it!'

'But *we* should be Byzantine. Just peacocks, stags and sheep. . . .'

'The danger of Italy,' Mrs. Asp observed, 'is, it tends to make one florid. One expands there so. . . . Personally, I go all to poppy-seed directly. I cannot keep pace with my ideas. And then I fall ill, and have to have a nurse. Shall I ever forget the creature I had last year! My dear Mrs. Calvally, she looked just about as stable as the young woman on the cover of a valse. Unfortunately, I was too exhausted to object. But I simply couldn't endure her. She made me so uneasy. A habit of staring vaguely into space whenever she spoke to me would make me shiver; I began to believe she must be in league with the doctor; that she was hiding something, keeping something back. . . . At last, one day I collected all my strength together and sat up in my bed and pointed towards the door. After that, I took a nun, who was quite rapacious for martyrdom. But all that was ever allowed to her was, sometimes, to get cold feet.'

'And what are you doing now?'

Mrs. Asp relaxed.

'At present,' she said, 'I'm preparing a *Women Queens of England*.'

'Isn't it idle—to insist?'

'Not as euphony. *The Queens* of England, somehow, sound so bleak. And, really, rather a brigade. . . . More like history!'

At the portentous word Master Raphael rolled down upon the floor.

Mrs. Asp considered him. She was old-fashioned enough to

believe it necessary for a young thing, when it gaped, to know exactly where to place its hand.

'Does he take after his papa?' she asked.

'I hardly know. He loves to flick his tongue up and down the rough paint of a picture, and to cool his cheek along the shrubberies on my fans.'

'He promises!' Mrs. Asp declared.

'But so wicked. Yesterday Princess Schara came to show George a fan. You know her husband used to paint the most wonderful fans. Poor man, in the end he became so decorative that he died! His last fan—would you care to see it?—is such a muddle that very few people can discover what it means. And now Raphael has made it utterly impossible.'

'Most modern fans are so ill and sickly,' Mrs. Thumbler observed, 'I hope nothing will happen to your courageous little boy.'

Mrs. Calvally lit—one of those . . .

It was a caprice of hers that could still charm, thrill and fascinate a wayward husband.

He had studied her too, thus, at three different angles on a single canvas. More vagabond, possibly, than the Charles, or the Richelieu, or the Lady Alice Gordon of Reynolds, but, nevertheless, with not one whit less style.

'How stately the studio is,' Mrs. Asp said, a little confused. 'A perfect paradise!'

'I regret I've nothing to show you much that's new. You've seen his joy-child for the top of a fountain, I expect, before?'

But Mrs. Thumbler did not seem cast down.

'I admire your plain black curtains,' she said, 'and, oh, where did you get these?'

Continually, Mrs. Calvally would design an eccentric frame for her husband's pictures. It was a pathetic attempt, perhaps, on her side, to identify herself in his career.

For, indeed, she was notoriously indifferent to art.

She was one of those destined to get mixed over Monet and Manet all their life.

The exhibition of some 'lost' masterpiece, in Bond Street, was what she most enjoyed, when, if not too crowded, she could recline upon a sofa and turn out the lining to her purse.

'I'm such a wretched, wicked housekeeper,' she would say. 'And were it not for an occasional missing Gainsborough, George, I should never know what I had.'

'Bristling with intellect,' Mrs. Asp pronounced, laying down the fan, 'and I seem to catch a face in it, too. Little Mrs. Steeple's! . . .'

'Oh, quite——'

'Poor thing! She says Sir Samuel has become so vigorous lately. It nearly kills her every evening waiting for his slap.'

'We were at Smith Square on Sunday,' Mrs. Calvally said, 'and sitting at her feet found Julia's new man—Charley Chalmers!'

'And I suppose a god?' Mrs. Asp enquired.

'Not at all. It's a doll-like, child-like, Adamy sort of face, and very healthy.'

'Dear Julia, I've seen nothing of her since the Sappho supper-party Mrs. Henedge gave in the spring.'

'I hear she's been safely landed now about a week.'

'One can hardly credit it!'

'She sent us a jar of Ashringford honey,' Mrs. Thumbler said, 'recently. Perfectly packed, in half-a-field of hay.'

'She takes a kind of passionate pleasure in her bees. And Mr. Brookes helps her in them, muffled up in all the newest veils.'

'He's been away now so long. He might be almost learning to be a priest,' Mrs. Asp remarked, as Lady Listless came in.

'I heard a thrush singing in the park,' she said. 'It was so attractive. I don't know what came over me! Are my eyes still wet with tears? I held back one to bring your husband (I saw the many-happy-returns in *The World*), but I lost it. It rolled, unluckily, under the wheels of a miserable motor-bus. But I managed to get another! So I carried myself as if I were Lily, Lady Ismore, and got nearly safe with it, when it fell down as the lift stopped.'

'You should have warned the boy!'

'I did. . . .'

'The incredible thrush!' Mrs. Asp exclaimed.

'Very likely it wasn't totally the thrush. I won't be positive. It may have been merely the reaction after Mr. Hurreycomer's Private View. His *Susanna*! . . . Have you seen it? . . . A young woman (my dear, his wife) splashing herself in some perfectly lilac water. . . . And the Elders. . . . Oh, they are all portraits. . . .'

'Tell me about the Elders,' Mrs. Calvally begged.

'Your husband. *Most* prominent.'

'But George isn't forty!'

'Are you sure?'

'It's incredible, in any case, that an insignificant stupid thing like Carla could interest even Elders,' Mrs. Asp remarked, getting up. 'Moreover,' she continued, drawing on a glove, 'she revels in making herself needlessly hideous; it appeals to her sense of truth. Added to which,' she rambled on, 'his candid studies of women are simply hateful. . . .'

'Brutal!' Mrs. Thumbler opined.

'Has anybody seen my stole?'

'And, remember, Rose,' Mrs. Calvally said, returning it to her, 'for Friday, it's *you* who've got the tickets!'

'I shan't forget. But since it's likely to be a debate, don't expect to see me smart. I shall simply wear my old, soiled, peach-charmeuse. . . .'

'My dear, don't bother to dress!'

Mrs. Asp hesitated.

'I trust that nobody of yours,' she said, 'is ill or stricken, for there's a strange old man seated on the stairs, with such a terrific bag of tools!'

Mrs. Calvally chuckled.

'I conclude it's only the carpenter,' she explained, 'who has come to pass a screw through Miss Mira's charming consumptive Amour!'

∞ XIX ∞

'DON'T the hills look soaked through and through with water?' 'My dear, I don't know!'

'If you don't object, I'll go back, I think, to bed.'

'What can you expect at the fall of the leaf?'

'But, except for the evergreens, all the leaves are down.'

'Well, last winter, it rained so, and it rained so, that the drawing-room became a lake. All my beautiful blue silk chairs . . . ; and a few goldfish I'm attached to were floated right out of their bowl, and swam upstairs into Thérèse's room.'

'Ashringford's becoming dreadfully disagreeable.'

'Patience. The sun will come up presently. Even now it's doing something behind the Cathedral. It usually takes its time to pick a path across St. Dorothea.'

Now that she had actually abandoned it, St. Dorothy, for Mrs. Henedge, had become St. Dorothea.

'Hannah was telling us the night it fell she noticed devils sort-of-hobble-stepping beneath the trees.'

'My dear, she tells such lies. One never can believe her. Only the other day she broke the child's halo off my plaster Anthony and then declared she didn't.'

'The most wonderful name in all the world for any child,' Winsome said, 'is Diana. Don't you agree? Your gardener intended to call his daughter Winifred, but I was just in time!'

'There now, there's a pretty motive for a walk. Save Mrs. Drax's baby. It's to be christened Sobriety, to-day, at half-past-two. Such a shame!'

'But I should miss Goosey.'

'Winsome, lately, has taken quite a fancy to Goosey, while risking their necks together upon the scaffolding of St. John's.'

'You see so much of him. The Miss Chalfonts, in comparison, aren't to be compared.'

'Don't ever speak of them!'

'Why not?'

'I've such a shock in store.'

'Yes; what is it?'

'The Miss Chalfonts have scratched.'

'Scratched! . . .'

'Their Guardi.'

'What does it matter if they have? I've really no need for any *more* pictures. People seem to think that St. John's is going to be a Gallery, or something of the kind.'

'And I've something else to tell you.'

'Sit down and tell me here.'

'While we were leaning from the campanile an idea occurred to me. Another opera.'

'Bravo! You shall kiss my hand.'

'I start *fortissimo*! The effect of the Overture will be the steam whistle that summons the factory hands. *Such a hoot!* . . .'

'But you'll finish what you're doing?'

Since his arrival in Ashringford he had been at work on a *Gilles de Raie,* an act of which already was complete. The sextet between Gilles and his youthful victims bid fair, Mrs. Henedge declared, to become the most moving thing in all opera. While the lofty theme for Anne de Bretagne and the piteous *Prière* of the little Marcelle seemed destined, also, to be popular.

'I'm so glad, for, naturally, while the building's in progress I have to be on the spot. And I do so hate to be alone. . . . I cannot bear it. I like to have you with me!'

'Still, you've got Monsignor Parr. . . .'

'Dear, charming, delightful Monsignor Parr!'

'Are there any more new designs?'

'No. But Mr. Calvally is constructing some confessionals for us utterly unlike the usual *cabines-de-bains*. . . . And apropos of them, I've something serious to say to you. I'm sorry to have to say it . . . for I'd really much rather not!'

'I'm listening.'

'It's about *Andrew*. Those Dégas danseuses he sends to you . . . on letter cards. . . . I know, I know, *I know*! And, perhaps, if he didn't scribble over them . . . But—how very often have I said it?—I never liked him. That violet muffler. And the no-collar. . . .'

'Why, what?'

'Here is a card that came for you. When I saw it I assure you it made me feel quite quaint and queer. *I thought it was for me!*'

'Oh, but you couldn't!'

' "My dear old Sin, do ask me not to write to you again. Or answer my letters properly." '

'I wish Andrew wouldn't correspond with you in that coarse way. Ever! At least not while you're at the Closed House. What must the postman think?'

'That's nerves! You mustn't begin to worry like Lady Brass-knocker. Her apprehension of the servants is a disease.'

'But a postman isn't a simple servant. One doesn't dismiss him. I like my letters. Here is one from Atossa Listless. She says Lady Castleyard and Mrs. Shamefoot are going to Cannes. And there's another difficulty apparently: whether the window shall open, or *not*."

'How capricious the Palace is.'

'Mrs. Shamefoot is ill with strain. Lady Listless says she speaks of nothing now but death. She says it's almost shocking to hear her. Nothing else amuses her at all. . . . And it gets so gloomy and so monotonous.'

'Probably the casino——'

'That's what they try to hope. At present she's continually cabling

to India about her pall. After the coffin she says she'll have violins—
four: Kubelik, Zimbalist, Kreisler, and Melsa. . . . And no doubt
Dina will send a splendid sheaf of something from the shop.'

Winsome tossed back his hair and half clouded his eyes. He glazed
them.

'Wait!' he murmured, moving to the piano.

Mrs. Henedge obeyed, expectant, upright, upon the tip of her
chair. She knew the signs. . . . Her fingertips hovering at her heart
caged an Enchantress Satin Rose.

> 'Lillilly-là, lillilly-là,
> Là, là, là.
> Lillilly, lillilly, lillilly-là,
> Lillilly-là, lillilly-là,
> Lillilly, lillilly, lillilly-là,
> L-à-à-à. . . .'

'Well; really! . . .'

'I couldn't help it. It just broke from me. It's *The Song of the
Embalmers*. . . .'

'. . . I call it lovely! Poor Mrs. Shamefoot. That lillilly, lillilly,
lillilly. One feels they are really doing something to the corpse.
It's sitting up! And the long final l-à-à-à. It's dreadful. Don't they
fling it down?' And with finger rigid she pointed towards the floor.

'It's good of you to like it,' Winsome said, with some emotion.
'And here's Goosey?'

'Never lend your name, or your money, or your books, or your
umbrella, or anything, to anybody—if you're wise,' Goosey Pontypool remarked over his shoulder to Winsome as he pressed Mrs.
Henedge's hand.

'But it isn't raining?'

'It doesn't matter. Here, they pour down dust upon you as you
go by.'

'It's a sign,' Mrs. Henedge said, 'that the houses are tenanted.
Thérèse will sometimes say to me that that melancholy Miss
Wintermoon must have gone away *at last* when suddenly up flies her
window and a hand shakes a duster into the street.'

'In Ashringford there's chatter enough indoors. You'd be surprised?'

'Well, I never know what goes on, except when the sow gets into
the Dean's garden. And then I hear the screams.'

'I hear everything.'

'Which, invariably, you exaggerate!'

'It's no crime to exaggerate. It's a sign of vitality rather. Health. . .'

'Whisper what you've heard.'

'That Mr. Pet is to marry Miss Wardle and Mr. Barrow's to be made a peer.'

'Upon what grounds?'

'For doctoring the Asz. You know it used always to ooze away; he's just discovered where. While she was watering her rhododendrons he noticed. . . . Anyway, he's going to Egypt officially soon to do something to the Nile!'

'How delightful for her!'

'She's advertising for a cottage at Bubastis, a bungalow, a villa. . . .'

Mrs. Henedge became staid.

'I suppose she'll get like Salabaccha now,' she said. 'Ah well!'

'Even so, it's much more wonderful for Jane. . . .'

'I'm at a loss to conceive anyone . . .'

'I don't know. Miss Wardle isn't, perhaps, what you'd expect. When I called at Wormwood she said: "I was so sure we should find plenty in common. *I could feel it through the window.* I've often watched you pass." '

'Those complicated curls of hers remind me of the codicils to my poor dear Leslie's will.'

'Who arranged the match?'

'St. Dorothy. She was expatiating on her escape . . . "I heard a noise," she said, "a sound. But country servants are so rough. Aren't they? Breaking, dropping, chipping things. . . . I haven't a dish that isn't cracked. . . . So, if I didn't hurry immediately to look out, it was because . . . because . . . because . . . because . . . Because I was in the middle of my prayers."

' "Had it fallen a *leetle* more your way," he said, "there would have been an end to them." '

' "Oh, Mr. Pet," she said, "What difference could that have made to you?" '

'So simple!'

'Well, if it's true, it's the best thing possible. Now, perhaps, we shall get rid of them *both*.'

'I believe it's not at all unlikely. Wormwood's to be let; not noisily. But, at the land agent's, nobody could mistake the exaggerated description of the conservatories and the kiosk by the lake.'

'Mrs. Shamefoot's searching for a house hereabouts, isn't she?'

'Oh, Wormwood's hardly what she wants. It isn't rustic enough. It doesn't thrill.'

'Besides, she's already made an offer for the Old Flagellites Club.'

'It should suit her. That long flaying room would make an exquisite drawing-room. And there's a sheltered pretty garden at the back.'

Winsome began twisting across his eyes a heavy, heliotrope veil.

'Don't let me interrupt you,' he murmured, 'I'm merely going to peep at the bees.'

∽ XX ∽

LADY BARROW lolled languidly in her mouse-eaten library, a volume of medieval Tortures (with plates) propped up against her knee. In fancy, her husband was well pinned down and imploring for mercy at Figure 3.

How eagerly, now, he proffered her the moon! How he decked her out with the stars! How he overdressed her!

Coldly she considered his case.

'Release you? Certainly not! Why should I?' she murmured comfortably, transferring him to the acuter pangs of 9.

And morally she could have started as her maid came in.

'Yes, what is it?'

'Sir S'torious is looking everywhere for your ladyship.'

The difficulty the servants seemed to find in saying 'Sir Sartorious,' without a slovenly contraction, was frequently distressing.

Grigger, his man, would quite break down, while the housemaids tripped, and the chauffeur literally sneezed.

'Say that I'm busy.'

Lady Barrow closed her book.

Something would have to be done.

'Had it been a peerage, was elocution compulsory, there need have been none of this fuss,' she exclaimed.

And with her finger-ends pressed to her eyes she began to conjure up his latent baptismal names:

'Sartorious, Hugh, Wilful, Anne, Barrow. S,H,W,A,B. *Schwab!*' she murmured.

And loosening a pencil from her wrist, she put them sharply to the test.

'Sir Sartorious regrets——'

'Sir Hugh and Lady Barrow regret——'

'Sir Wilful and Lady Barrow much regret——' Or even 'deeply——'

'Sir Anne—— *San*——' She shuddered. Lady Barrow walked towards the door.

'Wilful!' she called, in what her maid later described as a light silvery voice, 'I'm here! . . .'

But the silence oppressed her. 'Presently,' she reflected, 'perhaps, will do. It'll be something to discuss during dinner. Although, indeed, after what's occurred, I hadn't intended to say very much to him to-night.'

And apathetically she looked away across the cloud-shaded hills.

How well she knew the roads round Dawn! Here and there a tree would lift itself above the rest. . . .

The forlornness of it!

Up to the very house crept the churchyard yews, whose clipped wide windows never held a face.

And, somewhere, in the dark, dipping branches of a cedar, lurked the Raven. . . .

'I'm *all* romantic feelings,' Lady Barrow murmured. 'I always was. I always will be.'

And from a lavender cardboard box she slipped a smart sombrero piled up with wings and wings and wings.

'What is the good?' she murmured, dispirited, as she tried it on. Still, in every shadow, of every room, Lady Barrow would store a hat.

'I never intend to lose sight of town clothes,' was the explanation that she gave.

But to-day it was not essentially in vain. Scarcely had she poised it than she saw Lady Georgia's car coming up the drive.

'I'm perfectly ashamed,' Lady Georgia began, 'not to have been over before.'

'Say nothing of it!'

'And so, thanks to Sir Sartorious, one may curtail one's domestic troubles. Like poor Mrs. Frobisher——'

'Who is Mrs. Frobisher?'

'She was our nearest neighbour with a soul.'

'The Asz is in arrears. A short while ago even my cook went down. (Sartorious, if anything goes wrong . . .) And there were we! All of us upon our knees to her, flattering her, from the bank.'

'And a Mrs. Luther Gay—such a shocking thing—sprang quite suddenly off her lawn——'

'And one of the Olneys, too, was driven home from the Dean's dance, drenched. And with her heavy head, and her thin neck, and her poinsettia-pink arms——'

'So long as it isn't bathing.'

'And then there was Captain Hoey.'

'Cards!'

'And Azeza Williams.'

'Love!'

'And little Miss Chimney.'

'Despair!'

'And Admiral van Boome.'

'I heard——'

'It makes one long to get away. The responsibility is beginning to tell.'

'And so you're positively off?'

'Yes. We've got rid of Dawn to such a very pretty widow—a Mrs. Lily Carteret Brown. . . .'

'Who, at all, is she?'

'I couldn't be sure. But after a career of dissipation she seems delighted to settle down.'

'And where *is* the great man?'

'Sartorious? He's packing.'

'Packing!'

'All great men are prosaic at close quarters. Didn't you know?'

'Dear Violet——'

'Not since we were married have we been away together once.'

'It should rekindle happy memories.'

Lady Barrow shook the dancing, whispering things upon her hat.

'When we were first married,' she said, 'I was very, very wretched. I would weep, weep, weep at night! And in the morning, often, my maid would have to put my pillow-case out upon the window-ledge to dry. Fortunately, it was in Sicily, so it never took long.'

'And later, what are your plans?'

'I had the project of Paris.'

'Mrs. Henedge goes there too, in connection with the festas at St. John's.'

'My dear, she's always covered in embroideries; one never sees her in anything else.'

'She was superintending her building just now very busily as I came through the town.'

'How is it getting on?'

'Fairly fast. . . . It will have a very fine front. And, of course, nothing at all behind.'

'I believe it's only going to be very large——'

'Exactly!'

'When once they're gone she'll almost regret her workmen's blue sleeves.'

'It must be a little lonely for her sometimes.'

'I can't conceive when! She's for ever dancing round her yclept geniuses. . . . Making their death-masks, or measuring their hands. She never leaves them alone one minute.'

'Of all the discoveries, Mr. Brookes appears to be the best.'

'The least anxiety, perhaps——'

'That requiem he sent Biddy showed style.'

'Where is she now?'

'At Cannes. Lady Ismore caught sight of her in the casino the other day, in magnificence, brilliance, beauty. . . .'

'One either admires her extremely or not at all.'

'Of course, she's continually criticised.'

'Sartorious thinks her colourless!'

'How? . . .'

'Pale. I don't know. He believes she makes up with chalk.'

'What an idea.'

'I suppose we shall receive cards for her vitrification before very long.'

'Not until the spring. She wants the sun.'

'She used to hate it.'

'Poor Mrs. Frobisher's girl was to have taken part in the cortège.'

'Cortège!'

'She's to be supported. Children singing; scattering flowers.'

'What does Dr. Pantry say?'

'For the moment he objects. The *panther skins* upset him. . . .'

'Lady Anne would never hear of it!'

'On the contrary, she adores processions. They are quite her weakness.'

'Depravity!'

'Biddy will be charming. I shall persuade her, if I can, to wear a crinoline.'

Lady Barrow beamed.

'Take her to Madame Marathon,' she said.

'I've never heard of her.'

'Of course, she's rather expensive. You pay her ninety guineas for a flicker of a gown. . . .'

Lady Georgia's gesture was sublime. 'Look. *All that for a shilling!*' she murmured as she rose.

∞ XXI ∞

'HAIL, hyacinth! Harbinger of spring . . .' Miss Hospice hesitated.

Before being whirled away, before descending deeper, it would be well to decide in what situation it was to be.

Should it be growing or cut. Should it be lying severed. Besmirched. Should it be placed in some poor weary hand, withering upon a quilt. Should it wave upon a hill-top, or break between the slabs of crumbling marble of the theatre tiers beneath the Acropolis; the soul of a spectator. Should it be well wired, writhing in a wreath. Or, should it be a Roman hyacinth, in which case, should she trace Christianity to its sources, musing on many a mummery by the way?

She raised a delicate witty face.

Or . . . should she seek another flower instead? Above her the branches of the chestnut-trees rocked rhythmically. A warm wind rippling round St. Dorothy stirred the dark violet of the bougainvillæa along the wall.

'What have you found?' Lady Anne enquired.

She was seated before the Palace, a panther skin upon her knee.

'Only——'

'Then come and help me, do. To make it less schismatical, I believe I'm going to take off the tail.'

'Oh no. Give it a careless twist.'

Lady Anne snapped her scissors.

'It's such an infamy!' she declared.

'Mrs. Shamefoot will say you tried to slight her if you harm a hair.'

'I begin to think we've made a mistake. . . .'

'Well, she's in the saddle now. The window's up.'

'I fear it'll cause a good deal of horror, scandal and surprise.'

'I don't see why it should.'

'It must be altogether impossible or why aren't we allowed to go near? Why must it be concealed behind a thousand towel-horses, and a million screens? Oh, Madge, you haven't a conception what I shall endure when the curtains come away. My dear, I shall probably have to sit down. All my amusement in the procession's *gone*.'

And Lady Anne buried her face in her panther skin because of the sun.

'No doubt it's better than we expect. Kitty Wookie got a glimpse from the organ loft.'

'She's such a cunning creature. What does she say?'

'She says it's a thing quite by itself. Apart.'

'What does she mean by that?'

'She says, of course, it's entirely without reticence. . . .'

'For instance!'

'Apparently, the features are most carefully modelled. The ennui of half the world is in her eyes—almost, as always. And she is perched upon a rather bewildering throne, in a short silver tunic, showing her ankles up to her knees.'

'Aurelia always said it would jar.'

'It depends. Miss Wookie's easily scared. Very likely it's exquisitely lovely.'

'I wouldn't willingly offend the Segry-Constables or the Nythisdenes or the Doneburning'ems or the Duke.'

'I should tack a pocket to my libbard skin and let it make very little difference. . . .'

'Walter has told her she shall sleep a night in the Cathedral whenever she likes.'

'He might have offered her the pink room here for the matter of that.'

'It wouldn't do. She wishes to watch the colour roll back into the glass again.'

'What a curious caprice!'

'I call it simply shallow.'

'I'd die of terror. Mrs. Cresswell—they say, constantly . . .'

'Oh, nonsense! At most she'll confront the dark.'

'For a nervous soul what could be more appalling?'

'You forget she isn't timid.'

'It's hard to tell. She gave me the saddest, the whiptest, look last night as I passed her in the lane.'

'Those tristful glances of hers are so irritating. Especially when everyone tries to kill her with kindness.'

'That's probably why she does it.'

'Well, I'd be so glad if you'd leave a book for her at the "Four Fans" whenever you go for a walk.'

'Such an address almost makes one flurried."

'Still, poor thing, one understands intuitively, she wouldn't choose the Cresswell Arms. . . . And to stop, on the contrary, at Stockingham, where Lord Blueharnis I believe . . . And the Flagellites, of course, is overrun still by a firm from . . . And, frankly, I'm not altogether sorry. For, if there's anything I dislike, it's a house-warming.'

'In Ashringford what egotists we are.'

'Are we?'

'Tell me where the book is I'm to bear.'

'It's here; Harvester's *Vaindreams!*'

'Not exactly the kind of book, is it, to take to her?'

'Why not?' He has such a strange, peculiar style. His work calls to mind a frieze with figures of varying heights trotting all the same way. If one should by chance turn about it's usually merely to stare or to sneer or to make a grimace. Only occasionally his figures care to beckon. And they seldom really touch.'

'He's too cold. Too classic, I suppose.'

'Classic! In the *Encyclopædia Britannica* his style is described as *odd spelling, brilliant and vicious.*'

'All the same, dear, if you wouldn't mind carrying it across.'

'Shall I allude to the tail at all while I'm there?'

'Too late! I fear it's already off.'

Lady Anne turned.

She was sufficiently alert to feel the vibration from a persistent pair of eyes.

'May I come in?'

With her weight entirely on one foot and an arm raised towards a gilt rosette Miss Wardle was leaning against the wrought-iron gate.

'By all means do.'

'Might I have a word with the Bishop?'

'Unhappily, he's gone round to Miss Spruce.'

'Something serious?'

'I trust not. She has sent to him so often *in extremis* that really——'

'Then perhaps I'd better confess to you.'

Lady Anne glanced away.

Clouds, like scattered cities, dashed the blue.

'You needn't,' she said. 'I guess. I sympathise. Or will try to. You mean to leave us for St. John's!'

'St. John's is still without a roof.'

'But ultimately, I understand, it will have one.'

Miss Wardle drew a deep breath.

'No,' she said, slightly shocked, 'it's not that—I'm married!'

'Already!'

'I can scarcely credit it either.'

'To Mr. Pet?'

'*Lippo Lippi* man! He's too sweet to be true.'

'I'm delighted. I'm glad you seem so happy.'

'... He's twenty-three.... Five for elegance. Four for luck. Three for fate!'

'Of course, now, he'll need a little change?'

'A change! But Peter raves about Ashringford. He says there's nowhere like it.'

'No honeymoon?'

Mrs. Pet opened a black parasol.

'Oh no,' she said. 'A honeymoon must always end in a certain amount of curiosity. So we've decided not to have one, but just stop here.'

'It's really refreshing to find anyone nowadays who tries to avoid a fuss!'

'Peter, you see, insisted that the wedding should be quite—quite —quiet. For although you mightn't think it, he's as sensitive, in his way, as anybody in the town. And so I simply walked from Wormwood to Violet Villas with a travelling-clock and a bag.'

'How dull. And surely a trifle dusty?'

'It was my first small sacrifice,' Mrs. Pet said, sitting down. 'As a girl I used always to say I would be married in my *point d'espagne*.'

'You must make up for it at the unveiling. A dot of gold ... against those old monks' stalls. ...'

'I'm very uncertain yet whether I shall go.'

'Indeed, I don't feel up to it myself.'

'After all, one isn't always inclined for church!'

Lady Anne fetched a sigh.

'I've a tiny favour to ask,' she said.

Mrs. Pet twirled, quite slightly, her parasol.

'If you wish to be really charming exert your influence! Keep your husband at home.'

'I'm afraid I don't understand.'

'During the little masque amuse your husband indoors.'

'But I've no influence with him at all!'

'Have you none . . . ?'

'Hardly any.'

'At any rate promise to do what you can.'

Mrs. Pet stared, reflective, across the *mors-in-vita* of the Cathedral green.

'I realise my limitations,' she said.

'But you mustn't!'

'According to *The Ashringford Chronicle* there'll be almost a procession.'

'Oh, nothing half so formal. . . .'

'And one of the Olneys, it appears, as the curtains fall away, will break from behind a pillar with a basket of orchids, and say: "*Accept these poor flowers.*" '

'Not in the Cathedral; only in the porch.'

'And those foolish, silly Scouts are to fire off minute-guns from the walls.'

'I haven't seen the *Chronicle*.'

'Sometimes,' Mrs. Pet protested, 'I have no loftier wish than to look upon the world with Kate Greenaway's eyes!'

Lady Anne shivered.

'I'm all nerves,' she explained, 'to-day, and here's Hypolita and the Bishop!'

It was Hypolita's turn.

Aurelia had gone away to a pale silver palace in Bath, where she was casting into purest English the *Poemetti* of Pascoli.

'We looked in for a moment at the Four Fans,' Dr. Pantry said. 'Well! . . .'

'Mrs. Shamefoot wasn't quite up, but I spoke to her under the door.'

'Anything new?'

'She sent her love! ... She will make her vigil on the eve of the day.'

'Surely if she spends a night in the Cathedral somebody should be within call?'

'Things change so, don't they,' Hypolita said, 'when the daylight goes? Frequently, even the shadow of a feather boa ...'

'Who would look after her?'

'One of the students, perhaps——'

'Ah, no flirtations!'

'It should be an old, or *quite* an elderly man.'

'What elderly person is there?'

'In this neighbourhood there're so many. There's such a choice!'

The Bishop was affected.

'I don't mind being ninety.'

'You, Walter? Certainly not.'

'Mr. Poyntz, perhaps. ...'

'He'd need to raise a bed.'

'Still, on Sunday he manages wonderfully well without.'

'I'm down in the garden every morning by five ...'

'My dear, what ever for?'

'Besides, she refuses! She desires to be alone.'

Lady Anne gazed at her sister-in-law in dismay.

How was it possible that one did nothing to such a terribly shiny nose?

She considered it etched against the effortless chain of hills, designed, apparently, to explain that the world was once made in a week.

The morning was so clear the distances seemed to shrink away— one could even trace the racecourse, to its frail pavilion, by the artificial fence.

'It will be so nice when it's all over,' she exclaimed.

'All over, Anne?'

'The unveiling——'

'Life was never meant to be quite easy!'

When Hypolita began upon *Life* she simply never stopped.

Dr. Pantry raised his wife's wrist and examined the watch.

'Are you coming, my dear, to——'

'Oh, my dear, very likely!'

'Then make haste; the bells will begin directly. ...'

But to-day she invented an entirely new excuse.

'I must run indoors *first* to wave my white hairs,' she said.

∽ XXII ∽

A SMART, plain sky stretched starless above St. Dorothy. The night was sulty, sweet and scented.

Miss Thumbler shrugged her pretty, crippled shoulders and pressed volcanically her hands.

'Beautiful!' she murmured. 'But how walled in!'

'Answer me!' he said.

'Oh, George . . . haven't I enough already? Of course I cannot recall all the trifling ins and outs. Although, I believe, he kissed me, once, in the Vermeer Room at the National Gallery!'

She turned away.

These continual jealous scenes. . . .

Only a few hours back there had been an aria from *Tosca,* in St. John's.

There came a babel of voices.

On the lawn and in the lighted loggia the total town was waiting for Mrs. Shamefoot to pass. And as usual everyone was turning on the hose.

' . . . Vanna! Mrs. Nythisdene got a palm there . . . ages ago. She said . . . she could see her . . . plainly . . . in the little room behind the shop . . . tearing the white lilac out of a wreath . . . and wiring it up for . . .'

'Her dull white face seems to have no connection with her chest-nut hair!'

' . . . with *him* to Palestine last spring. Oh, dear me, I thought I should have died at Joppa!'

'You mix them with olives and a drop of cognac.'

'What could be more tiresome than a wife that bleats?'

'His denunciations of the Government nearly brought the lustres down.'

'I can't get him to come with me. He doesn't like the pendant lamps.'

' . . . above-board, when one can!'

' . . . Half the profits.'

'Ce gros Monsignor Parr!'

' . . . A day together.'

' . . . Rabbits.'

' . . . As tall as Iss'y.'

' . . . Precedence!'

' . . . A regular peruke.'

' . . . An interesting trio!'

'A tiara swamps her.'

'She will become florid in time. Just like her mother.'

'Don't!'

'For him a *tête-à-tête* would be a *viva voce*. . . .'

' . . . glare.'

' . . . lonely!'

' . . . no sympathy for——'

' . . . Idolatry.'

' . . . a top!'

'I heard a noise. A sound. But country servants are so rough. Aren't they? Breaking, dropping, chipping things. I've scarcely a dish that isn't cracked. . . .'

' . . . escape!'

' . . . *is* such a duck in his . . .'

'The only genuine one was Jane.'

' . . . poison.'

' . . . fuss. . . .'

'My husband was always shy. He is shy of everybody. He even runs away from me!'

'"Let us sell the house, dear," she said, "but keep the car! We can drive round and round the park in it at night. And it looks so charming for the day."'

Lady Anne trailed slowly up and down. She seemed worn-out.

'I'll go on,' Hypolita said. 'Life's too short to walk so slow.'

'As you please. But there's no escape from Eternity,' Mr. Pet's voice came, unexpectedly booming out.

At which vision, of continual middle age, the younger Miss Flowerman fainted.

On a litter, in the garden, where the stairs streamed up towards the house, Miss Spruce surveyed the scene with watchful, wondering eyes. It was cruel to be an invalid with her energetic mind. . . .

Still, a good deal came her way.

'Come now, and meet him, and get it over!' Mrs. Henedge was exhorting Winsome Brookes.

It was her first appearance anywhere since the change.

Attended by George Calvally, Mira Thumbler, Winsome and Monsignor Parr, she would have responded willingly to an attack.

From beneath a black bandeau sparkling with brilliants and an aigrette breaking several ways she seemed to Miss Spruce like some radiant Queen of Night.

'Anybody born in 1855 I've no desire to meet,' Winsome declared.

'Hush! Remember your *future!*' the relentless woman murmured, dragging him towards Lord Brassknocker to be introduced.

' . . . Belongs to the Junior Carlton, the Arts, and to several night *cabarets.*'

'Sir Caper Frisk was explaining to me that cocktails——'

By the great gold gates that closed at dusk the choir was waiting to give three cheers.

'Poor mites! I hear they've been told to give four,' Mrs. Wookie said.

'What are we waiting for?'

'I haven't a notion.'

'The moon——'

'It must have been the year that Drowsy-Dreamy-Dora won the Derby. . . .'

'The old Duke begins to look a bit hipped.'

'One tooth missing. And only half rouged. On one side only. I'd not call her pretty.'

'Pan?'

' . . . descended from *a waiter.*'

'If anything takes him to town it's the cattle-show.'

'I loathe London.'

' "Sable, sable, indeed!" I said. There's no depth to the skin. Nothing to fathom. It might be crocodiles.'

Monsignor Parr drew in his feet. He had been so very nearly asleep. All his life he had waited for something attractive to happen. Usually, now, he would sit huddled up like a Canopic jar saying nothing at all.

' . . . too tired to make converts. . . .'

' . . . totter from party to party. . . .'

'How do you do?'

' . . . sorry.'

'If my father marries again it will be to some sweet soul to stir the fire.'

' . . . does enjoy a rubber!'

'The lanes round Dawn are so narrow. And Sir Sirly and Lady James. . . . Well, there's hardly room for us all. . . .'

'Only Miss Knowle and Mrs. Lloyd!'

' . . . sheet-lightning?'

'Naturally, for the moment,' Mrs. Shamefoot was confessing, 'it's the least bit gorgeous, perhaps. But one has to look ahead. Posterity?'

'Such a pity not to have gone halves. You and Lady Castleyard together. A Beaumont-and-Fletcher——'

'So, actually, you've come!'

'What a wonderful wrap. My dear, what skins!'

'In case you should feel faint at all in the night you'll find a lobster mayonnaise and some champagne in the vestry!'

'Dear Lady Anne, how could you dream of such a thing?'

'In the grey of dawn, when a thousand grinning fiends peer down on you, you may be very glad of a little something. . . .'

Above the toppling timber, and the long low vineries, towered St. Dorothy. Urging each quivering leaf, and every blade of grass, to strain higher, *higher.*

'I hope you've a nice warm pair of stockings?' Mrs. Wookie wailed.

Mrs. Shamefoot stretched wearily above her head some starry spangled stuff.

'The mornings,' she observed, 'are still quite chilly!'

'I'm looking everywhere for Kate. It's like searching for a needle in a bundle of hay.'

'It ought not to be!'

'You'll find Miss Wookie in the drawing-room, playing Siegfried's Journey.'

'I must make sure she's ordered our *fly.*'

'A representative of the *Chronicle* would so much like to know——'

'Not now. Just when my spirit cries to be alone everything that's earthly seems to pass between!'

'He merely desires to ask you how you are.'

'How I am?'

'How you feel.'

'I feel such a strange sadness. You might tell him.'

She moved away.

Miss Thumbler had apparently consented to dance.

Stiffening her fingers and thrusting out her chin, she began slightly to sway, as though pursuing an invisible ideal.

'Sartorious always said she had a horrid mind!'

'I'm delighted she's so busy.'

'Really——'

'She's been doing her utmost to *will* the tower down upon us this last half-hour.'

'You mean——'

'I'm afraid so.'

'Could anyone be so rough?'

'No, I haven't yet finished,' Miss Valley was saying. 'Alas, a little fame! One buys it at such a price. . . .'

Beneath the big blue Persia-tree, the Miss Chalfonts lay quite still. They had attained their calm.

'It might be almost the Hesperides!' Lady Georgia declared.

' . . . foot's on the wane!'

'In a gloomy corner she is still quite pretty.'

Mrs. Shamefoot held up her fan.

' . . . the crops!'

'Ah, here comes our dreadsome friend!'

'Leave him to me,' Miss Valley said. 'I'll undertake to tame him.'

'Use some of your long writing words to him, my dear!'

'Shall I? Would you like me to?'

'Few people are worth untidying one's hair for,' Winsome Brookes observed.

'Mrs. Shamefoot!'

'Yes, my angel.'

Master Guy Fox was staring at her with great goo-goo eyes like a morning in May.

'Mr. Pet says you've done something to be ashamed of.'

'I? . . . Oh, good heavens!' Mrs. Shamefoot began to laugh.

'We've such trouble,' his mother said, 'to get him to close his mouth. He gapes. But at Eton, probably, there are instructors who will attend to *that*.'

'There are certain to be classes——'

'Perhaps even oftener than any other!'

And the Dean smiled sheepishly and tried to look less like a wolf. It was a favourite expression of his when addressing youth.

'What would you like to do eventually if you live to be a man?'

Almost nervously St. Dorothy chimed the hour.

'I would like to hang in a large gold bird-cage in the window.'

'Is that all?'

'And be a bird!'

'And not a wild one?'

'Supported?'

'Kept!'

'Oh, you lazy little thing.'

'I wish my boy had his quiet tastes,' the Duchess said. 'A child in the Life Guards runs away with so much money!'

'O-o-o-h. . . . When that Miss Thumbler bends so far it makes me quite afraid.'

'I long to see La Taxeira in a new set of attitudes.'

'Has she fresh ones?'

'Oh, she's unearthly!'

'They say she never dances without her Pompeian pavement!'

'Dear Lady Barrow, I've had no opportunity before! . . . We seem, now, surrounded by water as we are . . . quite to be floating. The Castle is my *yacht*.'

'I do so love a wreck.'

'From our upper stories, I must tell you, the Asz has almost a look of the sea! One has an impression of chestnut-trees and swans, and perfectly pink roses.'

'Some day, perhaps——'

'Unfortunately from my room, sir, there is really nothing to admire. . . . A view over tiresome chimney pots. And that is all.'

'I adore tiresome chimney pots.'

'Where is everybody going?'

'Indoors. There's such an absorbing . . .'

Through the wide windows of the drawing-room someone could be heard to say:

'Town Eclogues! . . . Epistle from Arthur Grey the Footman. Words by Lady Mary Wortley. Music by Chab-bon-nière.'

'Delightful!'

'So suitable!'

'Ingenious!'

'Ingeniousness *is* so rare!'

'And so enchanting!'

'Prevent the Pets——'

'Dear Peter,' Mrs. Pet murmured, tapping her husband lightly, 'he is everything I admire, and like and love.'

'I wonder I'm not in strong hysterics,' Lady Anne confessed.

'Before the Monsignor wakes wouldn't it be well to uncover the piano?'

'Uncover it? . . .'

'Remove that cope!'

'How can I, while——'

A. G. declared:

' "Though bid to go, I quite forgot to move:
   You know not that stupidity was love!" '

'Afterwards, then! . . .'

'You have the sweetest heart!'

'Should you hear the organ sounding in the night,' Mrs. Shame-foot remarked, 'you'll realise it's *me*.'

'How piqued!'

'An over-sensitive person in the country is always a strain.'

'Try.'

'Oh, I'm sure I never could——'

'I should never, never, no never, have believed it to be so difficult to enlist a *prima donna*.'

'Flatterer!'

'You wouldn't fail us!'

'My poor repertoire,' Mrs. Henedge explained. 'If I sing anything now it's *Divinités du Styx*.'

'Gluck!'

'Jeanne Grannier *en vacances* couldn't equal her!' Lady Georgia affirmed.

Up the steps, from the garden, clitter-clatter, with the agility of an antelope, came Mrs. Budd, whose claim to being the oldest woman in Ashringford nobody seemed likely to dispute.

The piano had lured her from beneath the shadow of the trees. She stood mumbling and blinking in the light, leaning on the arm of Reggie Cresswell of the choir.

'Her son is sexton here!'

Mrs. Shamefoot held out a hand.

'I'm so happy——'

'Here, Reggie,' Winsome said.

'Oh, what a darling!'

'We want him to sing.'

'Sing?'

'*Come away Death*, or something.'

'Shakespeare is all very well in his way—and in his place.'

Reggie looked shy.

'He's been crying!'

'Tears!'

'What is the matter?'

'Mr. Pet——'

'What did he do, dear?'

'I aroused his provocation.'

'You aroused his . . . that surely was very indiscreet.'

'Yes, miss.'

'Reggie's all feelings. Aren't you, Reggie?'

'Yes, miss.'

'Reggie will do anything for sixpence,' Mrs. Budd said. 'He is a true Cresswell.'

'She introduced the parlour or salon,' Miss Valley observed. 'She helped, too, to give afternoon-tea its vogue: the French five o'clock. She was also one of our original vegetarians. Oh, my dear, she took the silliest things. Her adoration for apricots is well known. She would tin them. And sometimes she would sleep for days on days together——'

'So sensible.'

'And her love for animals! Even as a girl she would say: "And I shall have a doll and a bird and talk to it." '

'Why not them?'

'Because she prefers a solecism! And then, her fondness for flowers. . . . "How beautiful violets are," she says, "in a room, just as the day is closing. I know of no other flower *quite* so intense." '

'There's a sensuousness, a concreteness in her ideas. Isn't there?'

'She was so human. So practical. An artist in the finest sense.'

'You'll quite miss her when you've done.'

'I dare say I shall.'

'And afterwards who will take her place?'

'I've scarcely settled yet. I never care to arrange anything at all ahead. I dislike a definite programme. Perhaps, a Judas Iscariot——'

' "Vapours of Vanity and strong champagne," ' Arthur was beginning to drawl.

Mrs. Shamefoot glanced about her.

The moon shone out now high above the trees. In smoke-like, dreamy spirals streamed the elms, breaking towards their zeniths into incredible *ich diens*.

'Between us all,' the Bishop said, 'I was afraid we should lose the key!'

She took it, seizing it slightly.

There were ribands attached, countless streaming strings.

'How charming!'

'It has been circulating about like one of those romances of Mrs.——'

'Am I to lead the way?'

'A coterie of ladies, first, expect a little prayer.'

'A prayer!'

'Lady Victoria Webster Smith insists on something of the kind.'

'You know she has never really got over her *mésalliance*. . . .'

'What am I to do?'

Mrs. Shamefoot raised her face.

Above her, silver-white, a rose dangled deep asleep.

'There's one thing I've done,' she said, 'I've sent to the Inn for a hat.'

'Indeed!'

'One feels securer, somehow, beneath a few fierce feathers.'

'You're not afraid.'

'Certainly not.'

'Permit me to say you look bewitching.'

'This unfinished rag——'

'Has teased——'

'When she comes it will be as if a Doge espoused the Adriatic!'

'Hark . . . to your soulless flock! . . .'

'In Ashringford, if souls are rare, we've at least some healthy spirits.'

'Dear Dr. Pantry, everybody's wondering where you are!'

'You seem upset.'

'Lady Anne is over-tired, I fear. These warm airless nights. . . . Just as Miss Pontypool was commencing her second encore——'

Mrs. Shamefoot slipped away.

In the garden all was dim.

Vainglory

Along a walk laced with weeping violet fuchsias she skimmed, glancing apprehensively from side to side.

There appeared to be a good deal going on.

In the chiaroscuro of the shrubberies marriages were being arranged. . . .

On a garden bench in a shower of moonlight an Ashringford matron was comparing shadows with her child.

'And why *not,* pray?' she seemed to ask.

'Marry. . . . Have a substantial husband? Oh no, I couldn't, I couldn't, I really couldn't.'

'Well, dear, there's no need to get so agitated. It wouldn't be— just yet.'

Round and round a great gloomy bush of thorn Miss Thumbler was circling in the oblivion of a dance, while, threading here and there, Lady Barrow annulled a thousand awkward calls. . . . 'Your poor husband.' 'Your interesting son.' 'Your gifted girl.' 'Your delightful wife.'

Observing her the Miss Chalfonts were assailed again. Monsignor Parr, revealing his mind, moved a finger from forehead to chin, and from ear to ear. And through the gilded gates that closed at dusk Mrs. Henedge's dog had found a way and was questing inscrutably about. . . .

'He ought to be muzzled!' Mrs. Wookie declared.

'Come now. Just once more!' Mrs. Henedge was entreating still.

'But I'm so tired,' Winsome said, 'of meeting other people. I want other people to meet me.'

'Really, and what should you say to them?'

'Nothing; I don't know.'

Mrs. Shamefoot hurried on.

A dark cloud like an immense wild bird had drifted across the moon.

Were the gods, she wondered, taking any interest in her affair?

'Oh, don't spoil it,' someone she did not recognise implored. '*I think Alice and Dick are holy.* They're each eighteen. And they're in love! . . .'

Mrs. Shamefoot turned aside.

Before her, serene, soared St. Dorothy.

It was a joy to admire such beautifully balanced towers.

'No, I never once lost hope!' she informed a grimacing, ghoulish gargoyle of a sprite.

Those demons, imps, fiends and fairies with horns like stalactites and indignant, scurrying angels and virgins trampling horrors beneath their firm, mysterious feet, and the winged lion of Mark and the winged ox of Luke and the rows and tiers of things enskied above the cavernous deep doors were *part of her escort now*!

And within, elusive, brittle, responsive to every mood, in every minute, and every year improving. . . .

'Shall we go?'

'Certainly. Let's.'

Figures flitted by.

She bolted in.

The utter void unnerved her.

'A collier,' she reflected, 'would laugh at me. He would say . . . He would *call it light*! . . .'

She sank across a chair.

In the dark nothingness the flags drooped fearfully. . . .

Imaginatively, she strove to hold her man.

'Bill?'

She admired his full lips, his tip-tilted, inquisitive nose. She thought he had a soft Italian face. . . .

Marble quarries!

Dirty, disgusting coal!

She recalled visiting marble quarries. Soco and she together. 'Oh dear! . . . That slow sad drive. Up, and up, and up! And when the road turned, such a surprising view. . . . Then the coachman invited somebody on to the box . . . I remember I said nothing!'

'A footstool!'

She lay back on her chair . . . relieved.

How still it was. . . . She could almost hear the worms nibbling the carved images of the saints!

'My poor maid must be searching everywhere for me in vain. . . .'

Which little hat would she bring? Lately, she had become so revoltingly stupid. . . . What had come over her at all? She was so changed. . . .

She could make out the Ashringford Juliet now borne as though a leaf on a misty-shadow sea. And, more massive, the Blueharnis monument of course! Over the canopy crouched an occult, outrageous thing, phosphorescent in places. Beyond, an old statesman was reclining, his head resting upon a confused heap of facts.

He had a look of Soco.

Where would he be while she was vigiling here?

The club. . . . Savoy. . . .

Never in her life had she though so much about him before. Twice in two minutes!

That pretty Miss Chance. . . .

Oh, well! . . .

And in future, this was to be her home!

Had she chosen wisely? . . . By waiting, perhaps——

Cupolas and minarets whizzed and whirled.

After all, Overcares had its points. . . . It rose with brilliance from its hill. It made a deep impression from the train. One dropped one's paper, one changed one's place, chatter hung suspended in the air. . . . Dear Dorothy was in a hollow rather. The trees shaded it so. Sintrap, too, had style. And Mawling. . . . But, there, there was nothing to regret. Placed in the midst of the town. Stifled! All about it stood such fussy, frightful shops. Post-cards, bibelots, toys for tourists. . . . And a cab-stand and a horse-trough and a pension. And, besides, the stone was changing yellow—almost as if it had jaundice. And Mrs. Whooper had said . . .

Did such trifles matter now?

To be irrelevant at such a minute. . . .

At the Inn to-night she had thought ten thousand thrilling things were taking place about her.

How long ago that seemed!

She had spent the day at Flagellites in a corner of the orchard listening to the ecstasy of the bees. And then Pacca had come to rouse her. And she had returned to the Inn through the cornfields by the Asz. How clear the river ran! Every few yards she had paused to stand entranced. And a young man with a fishing-rod and in faint mourning had entreated her earnestly not. 'I could not watch you do it,' he had said. 'Not that you would spoil my . . . At least!' And his hands were quite hot and clammy. 'What is a flaw more or less in an imperfect world?' he had asked. And he had accompanied her back to the Inn. And she had wept a little while she dressed. . . . And a white-winged moth had fluttered into the lamp. And she had gone to close the window. And everywhere the stars had sprung out like castanets and then gone in again. And the sunset had been heroic.

And she had waited so anxiously for to-night!

Mortifications had paved the way to it.

Was it only to suffer aridity and disappointment?

Such emotions were experienced best at home.

And would vignettes give way to visions?

Bill again.

'No, no!'

Or Satan. . . .

With dismay she waved her fan.

She was aware once more of leering lips. A tip-tilted, inquisitive nose. . . .

'Then the coachman,' she began, speaking in her agony aloud, 'invited somebody on to the box I remember I said nothing——'

∞ *XXIII* ∞

EVER since Mr. Calvally had taken a total adieu of his wife the building operations in Ashringford had practically ceased.

'It is certainly unfortunate,' Mrs. Henedge complained, 'that the daughter of my architect should run away with my painter—the husband, too, of my most valued friend!'

She was in town again, for someone, of course, must be brought to finish the frescoes at St. John's.

'If only I were able,' she declared, 'I would finish them myself!'

For, after all, what was there, when one came to consider?

A torso . . . an arm of a centurion . . . a bit of breast-plate . . . a lady—*if any lady* . . . a few haloes . . . and a page.

Carefully she arranged the items in a list while waiting for the *School of Calvally*, Andrew who had failed to come.

From her writing-table, whenever she looked up, she caught the reflection of her car in the downstairs windows of the house opposite.

'When I invited him to my fireside,' she reflected, 'no doubt he thought it was to roast him. But I was in such a tremor, I hardly remember what I said. I might have been bespeaking paste pearls——'

And she recalled the casual words of the master.

'Andrew can't draw,' he had often said; 'he gets into difficulties and he begins to trill!'

And on another occasion he had remarked: 'All his work is so pitch dark—that little master of the pitch dark. . . .' And had not she too foolishly mistaken his *Ecce Homo* loaned about at pre-impressionist shows for an outing of Charles I?

And here was she sitting waiting for him?

'Poor Mary,' she reflected. 'I ought to have gone round to her before. Though, when I do . . . she is sure to set upon me! She will say I threw them together.'

And, perplexed, she picked up a pen, a paper-knife, a letter-weight——

A postscript from Lady Twyford peeped at her.

'In recommending to you Martin as chauffeur,' she read, 'I feel I should say that his corners are terribly *tout juste*.'

What could be better in her present mood? She would have preferred to fly.

'I adore an aeroplane,' she breathed; 'it gives one such a tint——'

She rang.

'Thérèse? *My things!*'

'Oh, London. Native place! Oh, second string to my bow! Oh, London dear!' she prayed.

Whose uplifting was it?

As Martin sped along she was moved.

'The way the trees lean . . . the way the branches grow——' she addressed the park.

How often, as a child, had she sat beneath them, when, with hands joined primly across her solar plexus, the capital, according to nurse, was just a big wood—with some houses in it.

She found Mrs. Calvally propped up by a pink pillow shelling peas. It brought to mind her husband's disgraceful defence.

'How could I ever have been happy with her,' he had asked, 'when her favourite colour is crushed strawberry?'

'I had no idea,' Mrs. Calvally said, 'that you were in town.'

'I felt I could not pass——'

'Everyone has been so good to us.'

'Yesterday,' Raphael said, who was lying upon the floor, 'a cat, a peacock-person, an old lion and a butterfly all came to enquire. And to-day, such an enormous, big, large, huge, terrific——'

'Yesterday, dear, will do.'

Mrs. Henedge raised an eyebrow.

'I was afraid,' she said, 'I should find you in one of Lucile's black dreams——'

'Tell me all your news!'

'In the country what news is there ever? This year we fear an epidemic of yellow flowers will spoil the hay. . . .'

'I am sure the country must be quite a sight.'

'. . . I prefer my garden to everything in the world.'

'There is a rumour that it has inspired an opera!'

'I fancy only a consecration. Mr. Brookes is certainly to be Rose. A Christmas one! He makes his début this winter.'

'And *the other*, when is that to be?'

'One can only conjecture. . . . It occurred to me that very likely Andrew——'

'Oh, Andrew! An-drew can't draw. He never drew anything yet.'

'Run away, dear; do.'

'Besides, he's going to Deauville to decorate *a Bar*. . . . Scenes of English Life——'

'My dear, all Europe is very much alike!'

'And all the world, for the matter of that.'

'I heard from George this morning.'

'Really, what does he say?'

'Oh, it's only a line. So formal, with the *date*, and everything. And there is a tiny message, too, from her.'

'Poor demoniac——'

'Of course I haven't seen you since!'

'No——'

Mrs. Calvally settled her pillows.

'She came round like a whirlwind,' she began.

'. . . Manner means so much.'

'A tornado. I was just putting on my *shawl*. You know how he loved anything strange——'

'Well!'

Mrs. Calvally paused.

'I think there must be thunder about,' she said. 'I've been at the point of death all day.'

'And where are they now?'

'In Italy. Trailing about. And he went away with such an overweight of luggage. . . .'

'I expect he took his easels!'

'This morning the letter was from Rimini. It appears it reminds them of Bexhill. . . . And the hotel, it seems, so noisy.'

'How painfully dull it sounds.'

'Quite uninteresting!'

'I think it sounds jolly.'

'Shall we evoke Morocco with a rose and lilac shoe?'

'What would be the good of that?'

'No good at all, my treasure, only it might be fun.'

Mrs. Henedge struggled to her feet.

'Evoke Morocco!' she said. 'I fear I haven't time. I've a dentist and a palmist, and——'

She surveyed half nervously the shoe.

There was hardly any rose and scarcely any lilac. It was *a crushed strawberry*.

∽ XXIV ∽

'TO-DAY I'll have threepennyworth!'

In a flowing gown tinged with melancholy and a soupçon rouged Mrs. Shamefoot stood ethereal at her gate.

She laughed lightly.

'And, perhaps, I'll have some cream. . . .'

With the movement of a priestess she handed him a jar.

'That jar,' she said, 'belonged, once, to . . . So mind it doesn't break.'

And while the lad ladled she studied with insouciance the tops of the chimneys across the way.

The sky was full of little birds. Just at her gate a sycamore-tree seemed to have an occult fascination of its own.

Whole troops of birds would congregate there, flattening down each twig and spray, perpetually outpouring.

'Before I came here,' she enquired, 'were the birds so many?'

He shook his head.

'There was only an owl.'

'It's extraordinary.'

'Shall I book the cream?'

'What is the matter with the bells?'

'They're sounding for the Sisters.'

'Are they ill? Again?'

'They died last night—of laughter.'

Vainglory

'What amused them, do you know?'

'They were on the golf links. . . .'

'Death, sometimes, is really a remedy.'

'Soon there'll be no call for a dairy. What with the river——'

'Indeed it's more like somewhere in *Norway* now!'

'Not that, in milk——'

'Crazes change so, don't they?'

'A nice deep pail of——'

'Since yesterday, has anyone else? . . .'

'It's a pretty jar,' he said in a subdued voice. 'What is it?'

'That's Saxe,' she said, as she carefully closed the door.

The long flaying room was flooded by the evening sun.

'One needs an awning,' she murmured, setting down the cream.

Before the house stretched a strip of faint blue sand. There were times when it brought to mind the Asz.

Only last night she had trailed towards the window, and with the tip of her toe . . .

She turned, half charmed, away. There could still be seen the trace . . .

'I think the house will be the greatest success!'

Of course, the walls were rather carpeted with pictures——

There was the *Primitive,* that made the room, somehow, seem so calm. And a *Blessed Damozel*—that fat white thing. And a Giorgione, so silky and sweet. And a Parma angel. And the 'study-of-me-which-is-*such*-an-infamy!'

'I must have blinds,' she exclaimed.

It was tiresome there were none now since Georgia was coming in to tea.

How prim the cups were upon their china tray!

She had placed them there herself. . . .

In a bowl beside them floated a few green daisies with heavy citron hearts.

And if they chose to make eyes at the cherries, what did it matter, since the background was so plain?

She glanced at her reflection.

'O mon miroir, rassure-moi; dis moi que je suis belle, que je serai belle éternellement!'

She paused, causelessly sad.

Even here, the world, why . . . one was still in it——

'We should pray for those who do not comprehend us!' she

murmured. And, of course, that would end in having a chaplain. Or begin by having one.

A camera study of her sister, Mrs. Roy Richards, a woman whose whims would have made the theme of a book, or a comedy *en famille*, with her seven children standing round her nearly naked, had arrived, only lately, as if to recall her to herself.

'Not since the last famine . . .' she murmured, tucking it into a drawer.

'Ah, there!' One could hardly mistake that horn. . . .

She lifted the wooden pin in the door and peered through the grill.

'Who knocks?'

'A sinner.'

'A couple,' Lady Castleyard corrected, 'of the very worst. Regular devils.'

'Come in. Unfortunately, my Gretchen has gone out.'

'I hear you are achieving sainthood by leaps and bounds!'

Mrs. Shamefoot embraced her guests.

'I fear . . . it's far more gradual.'

'It must be so desolate for you, dear, here all alone, cut off from everybody.'

'I love my solitude.'

'Whatever do you find to do, in the long evenings?'

'I'm studying Dante——'

Lady Georgia rolled her eyes.

'I imagine you keep a parakeet,' she said. 'Where is it?'

Mrs. Shamefoot busied herself with the tea.

'Have you noticed the birds?' she asked. 'Such battalions. . . . And before I came there was only an owl!'

'I admire your garden. Those tragic thickets of thorns——'

'I think the autumn here should be simply sublime.'

'I will witness it, I hope, from my roof-top! I'm like an Oriental when I get up there. I'm sure I was one, once.'

'How, dear?'

'Oh, don't expect me to explain.'

'Jack would insist still that you had saved the country.'

'Locally, of course.'

'He's so enchanted with the window. He has got me to change our pew. "Poor Biddy," he said to me, "she looks really royal. A kind of grandeur——" '

'Several young men in town seem struck by it too. They like to sit before it. I believe they even kneel. . . . So annoying! Often, just when I want to be there myself.——'

'I'm glad you go somewhere. It's wrong to withdraw yourself too completely. Without a servant even!'

'My servant, Gretchen, ran, silly child, to the post office about a week ago.'

'I wonder you let her. . . .'

'I needed stamps.'

'Stamps!'

'Soco had scribbled. . . .'

'What are his views?'

'He speaks of a visit. He has never seen St. Dorothy. I received such a volume from him this morning, quires and quires and quires, all about nothing.'

'You must bring him to Stockingham when he comes. We're giving *The Playboy of the Western World* in the Greek Theatre. . . . I don't know how it will be!'

'Julia's Pegeen——'

'I see she's reviving *Magda*.'

'So she is. But you know nothing lasts her long.'

'And her strange maid, apparently, is going on the stage. She is to take a part of a duchess.'

Lady Castleyard yawned.

'I love your room,' she said. 'It's so uncommon.'

'I want to show you my mourner's lamps.'

'Where are they?'

'In my bedroom.'

'Your bedroom, Biddy. I expect it's only a cell.'

'It overlooks the grave-ground.'

'Oh, how unpleasant!'

'I don't mind it. I like to sit in the window and watch the moon rise until the brass weather-cock on the belfry turns slowly silver above the trees . . . or, in the early dawn, perhaps, when it rains, and the whole world seems so melancholy and desolate and personal and quite intensely sad—and life an utter hoax——'

Lady Georgia rubbed away a tear.

'I don't know!' she said.

'A hoax! You wonder I can isolate myself so completely. Dear

Georgia, just because I want so much, it's extraordinary how little I require.'

'Don't the neighbours tire you?'

'I hardly ever see them! I am afraid I frighten Lady Anne. . . . Old Mrs. Wookie made me some advances with a *face-cloth* she had worked me for my demise. . . . And I've become quite friendly with the Pets. He has such character. Force. I am leaving him a lock of my hair.'

'S-s-sh! How morbid! Shall we explore the cell? I've never seen one yet.'

'I'd sooner not be over-chastened,' Lady Castleyard confessed. 'It might spoil me for the antiquarians. . . . And the last time I was here I unearthed such a sweet old chair with hoofs.'

'Poor Mrs. Frobisher found four Boucher panels there once.'

'I'm quite sure it was once!'

Mrs. Shamefoot slid aside some folding doors.

Ashringford, all towers, turrets, walls, spires, steeples and slanting silver slates, stretched before her in the evening sun.

'I'll come as far as St. Dorothy with you,' she murmured, 'if you like. It's just the time I go for my quiet half-hour.'

Inclinations

PART I

Ø. I Ø

'"HAIR almost silver—incredibly fair: a startling pallor."'
Otherwise, unmistakably, there was a close resemblance.
It is true, whenever she began a new work she said the same.
There were the Ducquelin, the Pizzi, the Queen Quickly periods
. . . and that curious autumn evening when she had experienced the
impulse of an old and wicked Cæsar. . . .

'And here am I rusting in Yorkshire!' she exclaimed.

In the twilight her face showed vague and indistinct: an earring
gleamed.

'I adore your patience!'

'She seems to have had eleven children.'

'Who, dear?'

'Mrs. Kettler, Catherine, Kitty.'

'I wonder you don't get tired of going just on and on.'

'My dear, you're always wondering.'

'But now that Effie has begun her Tuesdays——'

'So often the mood only takes me as the gong sounds for dinner.'
Viola Neffal moved her lips as if she were counting.

'Well, that Mortlake tapestry,' she said, 'pierced with nails and
overhung by mirrors, is enough to make one weep!'

The Biographer clasped nervously her long, expressive hands.

'I sometimes think,' she ventured, 'that Modern things, rightly
chosen, accentuate the past.'

Through the open windows, a line of trees, leaning all one way,
receded across the garden like figures escaping from a ball.

'Who was that woman, dear, who put her lover's head into a pot
of basil?'

'You mean Isabel. But nothing shall ever dissuade me! Besides,
after Princess Orvi I need a change. Two Italian women . . .'

Miss Neffal sprayed herself liberally with 'Lethe Incarnate.'

'. . . Here's luck!' she wished.

'Somehow I feel it may be a failure. I saw the new moon with my
left eye.'

'You never told me quite what there is to admire in Mrs. Kettler. Why she attracts you.'

'It's hard to explain. . . . As a man of rare weight once remarked, she was like some radiant milkmaid.'

'Are milkmaids so radiant as a rule?'

'She was. And then she was so English! Even from her earliest utterance: "I would worship," she said, "to spend a summer in a hut in a hollow of Old Sarum." She was then barely two.'

'She appears to have been a gipsy.'

'After all, very little about her is known! There's not much material. Hers was one of those flickering shadow-lives. . . . You catch her in flashes. In her hey-day she is said to have grown weary of her world and gone to Ceylon.'

'*Ceylon?*'

'Well, if it wasn't Ceylon—— With these constant changes one is bound to get mixed. I'm not sure if it wasn't Greece. I've an idea it was Athens!'

'At any rate she was insular.'

'Soul is as rare as radium.'

Miss Neffal revealed her mind.

'The persons whom I should most have cared to meet were Walpole and Sappho,' she said.

'If you aren't contented now you never will be!'

'That's vain.'

'I was referring only to Hugh.'

'Hugh! I am marrying him, Geraldine, as you know, mainly for his conversation. And of course I shall be very glad to be married. . . .'

'My dear Viola.'

'When one is nearing the *end* of the twenties——'

'Nonsense!'

'Tell me more about the little milkmaid.'

'Oh, well, very soon, now, I hope to be setting out again on my travels. I intend making a fairly extensive trip in *her* footsteps.'

'You're off to Greece?'

'I'm going wherever she went.'

'Perhaps you'll wander round by Cannes!'

Geraldine O'Brookomore, the authoress of *Six Strange Sisters*, *Those Gonzagas,* etc., unlocked a sombre lacquer case: a work of art, in its way, with its many painted labels all on tinted pearl.

'Reminiscences. Anecdotes. Apologias. Crimes. Follies. Fabri tions. Nostalgia. Mysticism. Trivia. Human Documents. Love Letters. His to Me: Mine to Him,' she read.

'It's Nostalgia you need. . . .'

Miss O'Brookomore raised her eyes.

'I'm sure I'm willing to hope so.'

'Isn't it difficult often to be impartial?'

'It depends so much upon one's health. When one is tired a little or below par——'

'How I wish you were more sensible. *Is* it wise when the gong goes——'

'I know. But Effie spoils me. . . . Only a moment ago she sent me a peach that tasted like a dark carnation. . . .'

'Effie overdoes her hospitality I somehow think. Placing rouge in all the bedrooms. Even in Mr. Fairmile's room, poor boy!'

'Who is there downstairs?'

'Such gold-wigged Botticellis—playing bridge. They've sent me up to look for you.'

'For me?'

'To watch them.'

'I won't. Because where would be the good?'

'Then they'll come trooping here instead. After dinner it's usually Effie's way to take a candle and drag everybody to gaze at the children in bed and asleep.'

'Here comes someone now!'

'Were I to look in should I bother, weary, worry you?'

'It's Miss Collins.'

'Mabel!'

'I've been waiting for you ever so long. This is quite the dullest house——'

'You poor little dreary cat!'

Miss Collins, who had never gone out before, seemed to believe a soirée to be a succession of bons-mots, songs and bursts of laughter.

'One should try to be happy always!'

'I suppose you'll say it's silly, but I want so much to l-i-v-e! I want to go flitting about the world like you.'

Miss O'Brookomore became pensive.

'My work,' she said, 'lies largely among the dead.'

'Is it imperative?'

'The worst of modern biography, you understand, is, one is never quite sure to what one is entitled——'

'If only to avoid the pitiful consequences,' Miss Neffal theorised, 'we should go through the world neatly and compact.'

Miss Collins turned from her, oppressed.

'Effie sends a fresh supply of fruit. She is coming up very soon to look at the children.'

'Raspberries!'

'Are there raspberries in Chaldea?'

'You astonish me! Why do you ask?'

'For information. Naturally, living continually in the same place——'

'Do you never go away?'

'From home? Oh yes ... Sometimes, in winter, we go to Scotland.'

'Surely Scotland in winter would be a desolation! Stone, and slate, and asphalt, and the wrong red hair. . . .'

'You see, we cannot get rid of our house.'

'Indeed. And why not?'

'Because it stands in a valley. Although, of course, at times one gets some surprising effects of mist. . . .'

Miss Neffal leaned back in her chair with listless arms and fingers interlaced.

'Why attack the scenery?' she enquired.

Miss Collins shuddered.

'All that waving green,' she said, 'before the windows. . . . Why, the Chase looks haunted even in the sun.'

'Poor child!'

'You've no conception. . . . I assure you there isn't a creature in all the countryside to interest one except, perhaps, Madame La Chose, who's an actress, although she has nothing to do with the stage.'

'How can one be an actress without anything to do with the stage?' the Biographer wondered, drawing Miss Collins to her.

But Miss Collins did not seem to know.

'I love that ripple in your throat,' she said. 'It isn't a second chin. It's just a . . . ripple!'

'Mrs. Kettler had the same.'

'Are you perpetually pondering your great men?'

'Naturally, those in hand.'

'Often they must haunt you.'

Miss O'Brookomore smiled.

'Occasionally,' she said, 'they do. In my dream last night I seemed to hear all those whose lives I've lately written moaning and imploring me not. Let the editions die, one good woman said to me. Let them be cancelled!'

'Ingratitude!'

'Dreams, have you never heard, go by *contraries*.'

'Still, I'm sure you must need a change.'

'Am I getting cloddish?'

'Quite otherwise.'

'Once again in a *wagon-lit*——'

Miss Collins slipped to her knees.

'What would I not give,' she said, 'to go with you!'

Slightly startled, Miss O'Brookomore took from a cardboard box a cigarette.

'Supposing . . .'

'. . . supposing?'

'Supposing—I only say "supposing"—supposing you were to accompany me to Greece. . . .'

Sparkling, Miss Collins rose.

'Only at the thought,' she cried, 'I could clap my feet in the air.'

The Biographer considered her. Dark against the brilliance.

'My chief amusement,' she explained, 'has always been to exchange ideas with someone. And to receive new ones in return.'

'At Corinth! . . .'

'At Aulis!'

'At Athens!'

'At Epidauros!'

'At Mycenæ!'

'In Arcadia!'

'It would be like a fairy dream.'

'So long as you're good-humoured and sunny!'

'They say I'm rather silly sometimes at home.'

Miss O'Brookomore dropped a sigh.

'Few of us are born mellow,' she declared.

Miss Collins sank again to the floor.

'I suppose we should stifle all our emotions,' she said. 'And hide things. . . . But I never do. I just let my heart speak. And so——'

'I'm reading Lady Gray's *Travels*,' Miss Neffal broke in. ' "In the desert," she says, "once I tried to cook a partridge with a string, but the fire burnt the string and the partridge——" '

'Better to be foolish at home than——'

'Here's Effie!'

Candlestick in hand, and quite alone, their hostess appeared at the door.

'I knocked, but could get no answer!'

'I never heard you.'

'Wild, interesting woman! Have you been doing *much*?'

'Not a great deal. One's best work is always unwritten.'

'What she needs most,' Miss Neffal reflected, 'is the forsaken wing of a palace.'

'Are you coming, Viola, to look at the children?'

'Dare I, I wonder, in these shoes. . . .'

'Is there anything wrong with them?'

'They might wake little Phillis. . . .'

'In any case, Mrs. Orangeman, I fancy, is destined to do that.'

'. . . You hear her sad mind when she sings!'

Miss Collins looked shrewd.

'Her worries aren't enough,' she prophesied, 'to keep her going. . . .'

'Unless you are more careful,' Miss Neffal threatened, 'I will write you down in my *Book of Cats*.'

'Have you kept it long?'

'Since I became engaged.'

Their hostess tittered.

'Even we! . . .' she said. 'Usually now on a dull day Jack likes to touch up his will.'

'Doesn't it make you *nervous*?'

'Why should it?'

'I'd be afraid of his painting me out.'

'That's because you're over-highly strung. When people are pale and tired like you they need a rest.'

'Well, I've finished almost for to-night. Perhaps I may come down presently when the curate's gone. The last time we met he referred to poor Kettler as a Hospital Case. . . .'

'Have you no sketch of her at all that we could see?'

'Only a replica. The original, if I recollect, is in the Liechtenstein Gallery.'

And with her long and psychic fingers Miss O'Brookomore smoothed out a scroll.

'As a portrait,' she said, 'of course, it's a miracle of badness. But I think her face is so amusing and so alight.'

Miss Collins gazed at the likeness sadly.

'I've seen so few good pictures,' she lamented; 'although an artist did come one autumn to Bovonorsip. He took a room at the Wheat Sheaf and trespassed all day at the Chase.'

'Some artists can be very insinuating.'

'So was he! It was impossible not to share this man's joy when he said he had captured a whole mood with a little grey paint. . . . "Do not be too anxious to be like Corot, young ladies," he would say when we went sketching too. And before he left he gave me a little wood scene with naked peasants.'

Her hostess took up her torch.

'Poor Mr. Fairmile seems so miserable, Mabel, since you've disappeared!'

'How is he to show what he feels when——'

'When?'

'Oh, Effie, why did you tempt him? . . .' Miss Collins asked as she darted out.

'I wonder at anyone sitting down to pen the life of a woman so baggy about the eyes!' Miss Neffal exclaimed, returning the engraving.

'. . . Hark to Mrs. Orangeman. Well, Viola, will you come?'

Alone, Miss O'Brookomore wandered leisurely to the window and leaned out.

Beneath her a landscape all humming with little trees stretched away towards such delicate, merest hills.

'Was it solely Vampirism that made me ask her,' she queried, 'or is it that I'm simply bored?'

She looked up.

There was a suggestion of azalea in the afterglow that recalled to her the East.

'Either way,' she murmured, 'her mother most likely would never consent.'

And seating herself before her mirror she began an examination of her raspberries for fear of little worms.

'When people are pale and tired like you . . .' had not Effie said? She paused to dream.

How it tallied with Kate Kettler's description:

'Hair almost silver—incredibly fair: a startling pallor. . . .'

☙. II ☙.

ABEEHIVE in Brompton, a tray of gleaming fish, the way the wind blew—everything that morning seemed extraordinarily Greek.

As Miss O'Brookomore made her way towards Harrods she rejoiced.

Miss Collins actually was in town!

'Take her and keep her,' Mrs. Collins somewhat unexpectedly wrote. 'Who better than Miss O'Brookomore could break my child of her tomboy habits? Athens, I imagine, must be a sweet spot. Those glorious noses! Fancies fade, but a portrait of Byron on horseback,' etc.

And now, as Miss O'Brookomore strolled along, for some reason or other she screwed up her eyes and smiled.

All about her in heroic strips of green showed pastoral plots. Dark shrubberies. . . .

'Of course she will need a few new frocks,' she mused, pausing before a 'Robes—Artistic Equipments' at the corner of Ygdrasil Street, from whose folding doors at the same moment stepped the famous Mrs. Asp.

The veteran Biographer held out a hand.

'Your extensive acquaintance,' she said, 'I fear, has almost destroyed you for myself! They told me you had gone.'

'I shall be leaving town now in about a week.'

'Are you to be alone?'

'I shall have a maid—and a little Miss Collins, who is not yet fifteen.'

Mrs. Asp began to purr.

'Should you need a really reliable maid,' she said, 'I could tell you of an excellent woman. Nine weeks with a Mrs. Des Pond and two . . . A treasure! Or, should you be requiring a becoming blouse, or an eerie hat, or anything . . . Mrs. Manwood in there . . . It would be a charity! Silly thing . . . She put all her money on Quiet Queenie, or was it Shy Captain, and lost. . . .'

'For my journey,' Miss O'Brookomore said, with a glance of concern, 'I shall take with me only what is most serviceable and neat, and absolutely austere.'

'My dear, you will allow me, I hope, to know as much about

travelling as you do. I expect I have been abroad as many times as you have.'

'Rumours, no doubt, have reached you of my present choice?'

Mrs. Asp became faintly asthmatic.

'How hugely, purely, curiously and *entirely* reckless one's disciples are. . . .'

'Naturally, I shall suggest poor Kitty's cynicisms with fairy lightness . . . in fact——'

'To me,' Mrs. Asp said, 'Mrs. Kettler has always made her appeal. . . . And when you're in Athens you should go to Tanagra —not that there's very much there to see.'

Miss O'Brookomore held up an arm.

'If I'm late at all,' she observed, 'I shall miss Miss Collins . . . or keep her waiting, perhaps, about the street. One can hardly credit it, but she has never been away from home before!'

'Well, even when I was still seventeen I would take my skipping-rope into the Park. . . .'

'I should like to have seen you.'

'We have a wee box in the third tier at the opera for to-night if you would care to come!'

'This evening we are going to the Dream Theatre, and can't. . . . Besides, I've an aversion for Covent Garden, I fear. One sits in a blaze of light, looking eighty, or ninety, or a hundred—as the case may be.'

Mrs. Asp nodded.

'I shall expect to hear from you,' she said, 'at any rate, quite soon. An Athenian husband for you both . . . a villa each in Thrace . . . I could wish for nothing more! And now, as the Oratory is so near, I feel tempted almost to run in. Although, as a rule, I never care to go to Confession in anything that's *tight*.'

And there, in front of Harrods, teasing a leashed dog with a requirements-list, stood Miss Collins.

'Let us make haste,' Miss O'Brookomore said, saluting her somewhat nervously, 'to do our shopping. And afterwards, just to break the ice, I intend to take you to an Oriental restaurant in Soho. . . .'

🖉 *III* 🖉

'IT'S funny,' Miss Collins said, 'but even the most trivial things
amuse me now I'm away from home!'

'Your strong *joie de vivre*,' Miss O'Brookomore informed her,
'your youthfulness, already have done me good.'

'Tell me whom you see.'

'Hardly one's ideal. On the couch, half asleep, are Guarini and
Ozinda. Pirouetting round them, making their survey, is Lord
Horn and the Misses Cornhill, and on the dais there's January,
Duchess of Dublin, and her Doxy.'

'Which is Doxy?'

'In tears. At galleries she's quite dreadful. She will begin to weep
almost for the Spinario's "poor foot." '

'Once while beagling, accidentally——'

There came a murmur of voices.

'. . . terrifying nightmare women.'

'. . . One of his wild oats.'

'. . . fascinating, fiendish colours.'

'It's unmistakably *his*.'

'Pish!'

'Take me away!'

'And behind us,' Miss O'Brookomore chimed in, 'Lady Betty
Benson is being escorted by a tenth son and a real murderer, and in
ambush by the door, chatting to Miss Neffal's fiancé, is Mrs.
Elstree, the actress.'

'O-o-o-o-h!'

'You have the catalogue.'

'What should you say it was?'

'Dear old Mr. Winthrop! He's so vague always—"Sunrise
India." And I know for a fact it was painted in his street. Those
trees are in Portman Square.'

'Is not that Miss O'Brookomore? We heard that you had gone.'

Miss O'Brookomore turned slightly.

'We are in Ospovat's hands,' she murmured, 'still.'

'Have you chosen yet your route?'

'We go from Marseilles to the Piræus, and from there we take the
tram.'

'O-o-o-o-h!'

'You have the catalogue.'

'... know Mr. Hicky?' Mrs. Elstree was beginning to scream. 'Why, when I was playing in the *Widow of Wells* I died in his arms every night for over a year.'

'Hugh, where's Viola?'

'I'm afraid I must decline to tell you.'

'Indeed! ...'

'I left her burning *Zampironi* before a Guardi and invoking Venice.'

'Anything later than the eighteenth century I know how she dislikes.'

Mrs. Elstree addressed the Historian.

'Daring one,' she murmured, 'I admire you more than you're aware of! You're simply never trite.'

'You mean my Mrs. Kitty? ...'

'And even should you not discover much, failure makes one subtler!'

'All I hope to get's a little glamour.'

'Once—did I ever tell you?—I rented a house in Lower Thames Street, where the Oyster Merchants are.'

Miss O'Brookomore closed her eyes.

'When I was quite a child,' she said, 'I did not care for sweets ... but I liked Oysters. Bring me Oysters, I would say. I want Oysters.'

'Poet.'

Miss Collins folded herself together as though for a game of hide-and-seek.

'Really, Mabel! Noting you with dismay is Mrs. Felicity Carrot of *Style*.'

'A reporter!'

'One should be the spectator of oneself always, dear, a little.'

'Don't move—I am not sure but I see my aunt!'

'Your aunt?'

'Mrs. Hamilton-of-Hole.'

'... My husband's horizons are solely political ones,' Mrs. Hamilton was explaining as she elbowed by.

'And there is Mr. Winthrop, whose landscape——'

Mrs. Elstree moved away.

'Ozinda has fallen sound asleep in Guarini's arms! ...'

There came a confusion of voices.

'Babes-in-the-Wood.'

'We think of crossing over to witness the autumn at Versailles.'

'. . . goes to auctions.'

'The slim, crouching figure of the Magdalen is me.'

'Those break-neck brilliant purples.'

'Pish!'

'A scarlet song.'

' "Order what you please from Tanguay," he said—"a tiara, what you please." '

'——You'd think they'd been set by Bœhmer!'

'O-o-o-h!'

'You have the catalogue.'

'Mrs. Elstree took it with her.'

❧. IV ❧

'**L**ET us all cling together!'

Miss O'Brookomore blinked her eyes.

'Is it a station?'

'Tomorrow,' Miss Collins announced from behind her chronicle, ignoring the sleep-murmurings of the Historian's maid, 'six Cornish girls are to dance at the Lune Grise. What a pity to have missed them. Although I believe I mind more about Mona. When she discovers I've been in Paris without even trying to find her——'

'Who is that, dear?'

'Napier's sister—Mr. Fairmile's. Oh, Gerald!'

'What is it?'

'Mr. Fairmile and I once . . . Yes, dear! We're engaged. . . . And when he said good-bye he didn't kiss me. He just crushed me to his heart. . . .'

'Crushed you?'

'My frock a little. One of Miss Johnson's jokes.'

'That white one?'

'Of course Mona I've known always. She's just a dear. Tall, with a tiny head. And such beautiful, mystic hands. . . . She and I were at school together.'

'I didn't know you had ever been at school.'

'. . . a Term. She was quite my bosom-chum at York Hill. Once we exchanged a few drops of each other's blood. Oh, Gerald!'

'Really!'

'It was on a certain Sunday in June.'

Miss O'Brookomore dropped the fireproof curtain across her eyes. She glazed them.

'I think I shall tuck up my feet,' she said, 'and lie down.'

'Just as there's a sunset coming on?'

'I'm tired. My head aches. My mind has been going incessantly all day. . . .'

Miss Collins showed her sympathy.

'Reading in the train would upset anyone,' she observed. 'I'm sure it would me.'

'I was renewing my acquaintance with the classics.'

'Before I came away mum made me get by heart a passage from *The Queen of Tartary* to recite to you the instant we landed, as a surprise. You know the great tirade! The Queen has taken the poison and leaves the Marquee on her confidante's arm. Inside, the banquet is in full swing. Now and again you can hear their hearty laughter. . . . Ha, ha, ha! Ha, ha, ha, ha! And the Queen turns to Melissa—and mum declares she shall never forget the impression Madam Dolce Naldi made as the Queen, although Miss Faucet, as Melissa, was exquisite in her fragility as a foil—and says: "My hands are cold. It's as if my eyelids had weights upon them. . . . I hear a singing in my ears. I feel," etc. And so on through the greater part of the medical dictionary.'

'It's curious your mother did not select the triumphal speech. Act II, Scene 3: "Everybody crowded round me, . . ." ' Miss O'Brookomore remarked.

'I don't know. The only books I care for are those about Farms.'

'My dear, when one speaks of Farms one forgets the animals. Little piggy-wiggs. . . .'

'I don't think that *that* would matter.'

'Perhaps some day, when you marry a country squire, you will have a farm of your own.'

'It isn't likely. Before leaving town I consulted a clairvoyant. There are indications, she said, that something *very disgraceful* will come about between January and July.'

'Oh, Mabel!'

Miss Collins reached towards a bag of sweets.

'In the crystal she could see mum reading my letters . . . she could see her, she said, on all fours hunting about. . . .'

'Your poor mother.'

'What's the good of grieving?'

'Mab dear, you're always nibbling!'

'To beguile the time.'

'But so bad for you.'

'Beware of a dazzling fair man, the woman said. Beware of him. And in the end, after many petty obstructions, which you will overcome, she said, you'll marry a raven!'

Miss O'Brookomore became attentive to the scenery.

To watch the trees slip past in the dusk was entrancing quite. In a meadow a shepherdess with one white wether stood up and waved her crook.

'Poor Palmer seems completely worn out.'

The maid stirred slightly at her name.

'When Greek meets Greek, miss,' she asked informingly, 'can you tell me what they're supposed to do?'

'Since we're all English,' Miss O'Brookomore replied, 'I don't think it matters. . . .'

Miss Collins covered her face with a soiled *suède* glove.

'Another tunnel!'

'You should really rest, Mab. You'll arrive so tired.'

'I'm that already. But I won't lean back—for fear of contracting something . . . infectious.'

'Some day, dear, I may arrange your sayings in a wreath. . . .'

'Our coachman once——'

'No, please—I'm altogether incurious.'

'Although, even bolt upright, dear, I can sleep as easily as a *prima donna* upon a dais! Nothing wakes me.'

Palmer raised an eye towards the waning moon.

'The evenings,' she remarked, 'turn quite bleak. Had I known, I'd not have come away without my bit of fur.'

Ø. V Ø

'AND then we almost ran. Anybody would have said our husbands were behind . . . And perhaps they pitied us. But Miss O'Brookomore's so unpunctual always; it's a marvel we ever catch a train.'

He waved a hand.

'Those talents! That gift! Her mind!'

'At Marseilles we even missed the boat. Otherwise, very likely, we would have never met.'

'M-a-b-e-l,' Miss O'Brookomore called.

Miss Collins turned.

'Do you need me, dear?'

'Who is your handsome friend?'

'He's . . . Oh, Gerald!'

'Where did you pick him up?'

'He began by speaking of the tedium of water for a sailor, and then——'

'I see!'

'Oh, Gerald, it's Count Pastorelli. . . .'

Miss O'Brookomore leaned back a little in her deck-chair.

'Take my word for it,' she said, 'he's not so pastoral as he sounds.'

'And there's another!'

'You mean——?'

'A porpoise!'

Miss O'Brookomore crossed herself.

'I always do,' she said, 'when **anyone** points.'

'Shall we take a little prowl?'

'Voluntarily.'

'There's a person on board, someone perhaps should speak to her, who sits all day staring at the sea beneath a very vivid violet veil. And when the waves break over her she never even moves. . . .'

The Biographer watched sagaciously the sun touch the dark water into slow diamonds.

'One should blur,' she observed, 'the agony.'

Miss Collins became evidently intellectual.

'Which would you prefer,' she enquired, 'a wedding or a funeral out at sea?'

'I'd prefer there was no unpacking.'

'For the one emergency I've enough, of course, of white . . . and for the other, I dare say I could lean from the ship-side in a silver hat crowned with black Scotch roses.'

'Were it mine, I'd give that hat to Palmer.'

'Poor thing, every time the ship rolls she seems to hear something say: *The captain—his telescope.*'

'She will see the land very soon now with her naked eye.'

Miss Collins slipped an arm about her friend.

'I look forward first to eleven o'clock,' she said, 'when the ship-boy goes round with bananas.'

'Tell me, at Bovonorsip does everyone speak so loud?'

Miss Collins clicked her tongue.

'Shall we go down upon the lower-deck, Gerald, and look through the cabin windows? There's the Negress you called a *Gauguin*. ... All alone in her cabin it would be interesting to see what she does. ...'

'Somehow I'd sooner save that poor veiled thing from getting wet.'

But that 'poor veiled thing' was enjoying herself, it appeared.

'. . . I don't object to it, really,' she said. 'I rather like the sea! . . . I'm Miss Arne. Mary Arne—the actress. Some people call me their Mary Ann, others think of me as Marianne.'

'The tragedienne.'

'Comedy is my province. I often say I'm the only Lady Teazle!'

'Then of course you've met Lizzie Elstree?'

'. . . I can recall her running about the green-room of the Garden Theatre in I should be afraid to say quite what. . . .'

'Well, I always hate to hustle.'

Miss Collins nodded.

'There's the Count,' she exclaimed. 'He will keep bumping into me.'

'I wonder who he can be.'

'I believe he's a briefless barrister.'

Miss O'Brookomore looked wary.

'How is one to tell?' she murmured. 'He may *not* be so brief-less . . . !'

'I know nothing about the law,' Miss Arne said. 'Although when I played in *The Coronation of Lucy* there was a trial scene that lasted nearly forty minutes.'

'You must be delighted now to rest.'

'Rest! I'm on my way to Greece to study Lysistrata.'

'But couldn't you have done it at home?'

'Not with the same results. As I told the silly critics, I mean to treat her as a character-part.'

'I understand. When one traces a shadow it's mostly for the scenery.'

'At Cape Sunium,' Miss Collins said, 'I shall lie like a starfish all day upon the sand.'

'My dear, at Sunium there is no sand. It's all rocks.'

'How do you know there are rocks?'

'Do you think I haven't seen old engravings?'

'Perhaps I might paddle.'

' "Oh! joy, joy! no more helmet, no more cheese nor onions!" '
Miss Arne soliloquised.

'I adore Aristophanes.'

'Certainly, he has a flavour——'

Miss Arne stood up.

'What can that be over there?'

'Those slopes. . . .'

'These villas. . . .'

'And temples. . . .'

'It must be . . .'

'It is——'

Miss Collins commenced a feverish country dance.

'It's Athens!'

✑. VI ✑

'SO far I've not observed one!'

'Of what?'

'A nose! Athens and heavenly noses. . . . Mum said I should.'

Miss O'Brookomore threw upon her head a bewildering affair
with a vampire-bat's-wing slanting behind.

'Patience,' she murmured. 'We haven't been here long enough.'

'Quite long enough to find out the English chemist isn't
English!'

'Why, aren't you up to the mark?'

'I was attempting to ward off freckles.'

'Pretty Mrs. Wilna often used to say the utmost she ever did was
to apply a little cold-cream *just* as she got into bed.'

Miss Collins moved from one chair to another.

'Oh, come and look! Oh!'

'Whatever is it?'

'There's such a shocking dispute in the Square!'

Beneath a bruised blue, almost a violet, sky lay the town. Very
white and very clean.

On the pavement some youths, with arms entwined, seemed to be locked in the convulsions of a dance.

'Let us go down and sit in a café.'

Miss O'Brookomore became evasive.

'I want you to repress yourself a little for a few days. Be more discreet.'

'Because——'

'Professor and Mrs. Cowsend have the rooms next ours. . . .'

'Buz! Let them!'

'Also, the Arbanels are here on their honeymoon. . . . You never saw such ghosts on their rambles.'

'Who is Mr. Arbanel?'

'He's very blasé.'

Miss Collins clasped her hands.

'I'd give almost anything to be blasé.'

Miss O'Brookomore turned from her.

'Those Customs!' she lamented. 'Everything arrives so *crushed*.'

'Are you going out to see what you can find?'

'I dare say I may look in at the library of the University.'

Miss Collins became contemplative.

'Who knows, away in the Underworld she may be watching you. . . .'

'My poor puss, Athens must seem to you a trifle dull.'

'It isn't really. I could sit for hours on my balcony and watch the passers-by. So many of them don't pass. At least, not directly.'

'You mean they stop?'

'Sometimes. But what does it matter?—when one isn't a linguist.'

'Palmer should be with you more.'

'Palmer seems so squeamish.'

The Biographer fetched a sigh.

'Indeed, the way she sprinkles naphthaline has quite put out the violets.'

'All except her own!'

'Her own?'

'Oh, Gerald. . . . Every week there is a dance, dear, in the hotel.'

Miss O'Brookomore shrugged her shoulders.

'Don't expect me to attend any of them,' she said, 'that's all.'

'Oh, darling, how can you be so Spartan! How?'

'You forget, dear, my dancing days are nearly done.'

'Wait. . . . Wait. . . . *Wait* till you hear the throb-thrumb-throb of a string band. . . . Oh, Gerald!'

'I should be sound asleep.'

'Fiddlesticks! You'd fling a wrap about you and down you'd come.'

'It's true.'

'And you'd heighten your cheeks in such a hurry that everybody would suppose you'd been using jam.'

'Believe me, I'd deal with the manager without the least compunction.'

'You'd complain?'

'I'd demand to change my room.'

'S-s-s-h! Here's Palmer.'

'Ah, no more naphthaline, please.'

'There's a packet for Miss Hill. . . .'

'Take it away. It's not for us.'

'I expect it's for me! Collins, Colline, Collina *Hill*. I thought it was advisable not to give my own name at any of the shops. . . .'

'Collina! Have you been chatting with the Count?'

'As I went out he was stirring up the weatherglass in the front hall.'

'I fear he takes you to be an heiress.'

'But he's very well off as it is! Haven't you noticed? He doesn't tip. He *rewards*. Besides, dear, I could never marry a man who had corns on his feet, or who didn't say his prayers.'

'How do you know he has corns?'

'Because he told me. He couldn't get up to the Acropolis, he said, on account of his corns. . . .'

'Isn't that a blessing?'

'Look, Gerald, I bought these tags to keep off flies.'

'In Arcadia they will be just the thing.'

'The Count was saying how rash it was for two docile women to go alone into such inaccessible places. . . .'

With pursed lips the Historian tuned her veil.

'Pooh!' she fiddled.

☙ VII ❧

'AND when papa's reverse of fortune did come . . . why, then, of course, I thought of *everything* . . . to be a maid, I thought. . . . To look up at the moon through the palings. . . . But somehow, no! I couldn't. . . .'

'. . . Shall we have our coffee in the lounge?'

'The night is wonderful,' a woman with a thrilling voice declared. 'Evening here is really the nicest time!'

In an alcove, unable to contain her laughter, Miss Collins was teaching English versicles to the Count.

> 'The naked oak-tree in the deer-park stands
>   Mocking the brooding moose.'

'Dear?'

'*D-e-e-r!*'

'Oh, my dear!'

'*Hinds! . . . Deer!*'

'I adore you, dear.'

'*Harts!*'

'Our two hearts!'

'Mabel! Miss O'Brookomore called.'

'Oh, Gerald, what ever is it?'

'Come and thank Mrs. Cowsend. . . . She has consented to take you out occasionally when I'm engaged.'

'I shall be delighted,' Mrs. Cowsend said. 'To-morrow we intend to pass the morning in the royal gardens.'

'Unfortunately I'm not overfond of flowers. Gardening in the rain was one of our punishments at home.'

'But at the palace there are so few flowers. Scarcely any! It's bays a bit, and cypress a bit, and ilex a little, and laurel a lot, with here and there an oleander, perhaps, or a larch. . . . Nothing that could remind you!'

'The very sight of a wheelbarrow quite upsets me.'

'Personally, I'm inclined to worship a wheelbarrow. It makes a change with the temples.'

Miss O'Brookomore became introspective.

'To visit Greece with Professor Cowsend,' she said, 'would be *my* idea of happiness. . . .'

'My dear Miss O'Brookomore, I have found things in Somerset just as lovely as in the Vale of Tempe. And with none of the fatigue.'

The Historian held up a map.

'Where we are going,' she announced, 'is dotted white.'

'You must be very careful! . . . It's just the region——'

Miss O'Brookomore stiffened.

'Tell me everything,' she begged.

'I dare say you've not encountered a sheep-dog here before? Some of them are so fierce. More like wolves.'

'And dogs frequently fly at me!'

'Round Delphi they are quite dreadful. Parnassos, I assure you, is literally overrun. . . .'

'Dogs delight to lick me,' Miss Collins said, 'when they get the chance. . . .'

With a lorgnon Mrs. Cowsend drummed the map.

'At Megara,' she said, 'there is a calvary to commemorate one of the Seymoures. But of course Lady Maisie attracted attention by her peplum even in the town.'

'I'm told the measles in Athens just now is very bad.'

'Even so, I must say, I find the city dull. Mr. Cowsend, you see, is continually out gathering notes for lectures. Often he will leave the hotel as soon as it is light and pass the entire day poking about the Pnyx. . . . And the shops for me. . . . Well, on the whole, I don't think much of them.'

'I would take a camp-stool sometimes and sit on the Pnyx as well.'

'. . . When I did the other day he didn't seem to like it! And in any case, he never tells me much. I approach Greece by way of the Renaissance, and I don't pretend to know anything about either.'

Miss O'Brookomore bowed amicably.

'Mrs. Arbanel to-night is really an Eastern dream. . . .'

'Her husband, it seems, is incredibly inattentive to her, poor dear.'

'It seems a little soon.'

'There's a boy in the porch selling strings and strings of amber,' the lady murmured as she ambled by.

'Miss O'Brookomore has just been saying you could scarcely be more Zara or Turkish if you tried.'

'How suggestive that is of chains!'

Miss O'Brookomore protested.

'With you,' she said, 'I only see the beads.'

'We were wedded at St. Margaret's almost a month ago!'

'I read of your little adventure in the *Morning Post*.'

'I forget if you know Gilbert at all. . . .'

'I can hardly say I know him, but I think we sat together once upon the same settee.'

'Would it be lately?'

Mrs. Cowsend smiled urbanely.

'Absence or surfeit,' she observed, 'it seems there's nothing between.'

'Although it *is* my honeymoon I'm not at all exacting.'

Miss O'Brookomore used her fan.

'It's been such a heavenly day!'

'I spent most of it in a wood on the Marathon Road,' Mrs. Arbanel said, 'with *A Midsummer Night's Dream*. . . .'

'Hermia! Lysander! Oberon! Titania! Oh dear!'

Miss Collins showed her culture.

'Bottom,' she added.

' . . . I hate to sight-see. However, to-morrow, I'm told I must. Mr. Arbanel has engaged an open coach. . . . But, as I said to him, it would no longer be a coach. It would be a waggon. . . .'

'You should take a cab and drive to Eleusis. . . . On Sunday, I believe, it's the only thing to do.'

Mrs. Arbanel looked bored.

'I've seen nothing here quite as delicate,' she confessed, 'as the Little Trianon in a shower of April rain.'

Mrs. Cowsend twinkled.

'You should tell that to the Professor presently when he comes in.'

'Where do the men tide through the evening? They invariably disappear.'

'In the covered passage behind the hotel,' Miss Collins said, 'there's a Viennese beer hall and a picture palace. Oh, Gerald!'

'Mr. Cowsend after dinner usually goes to a café in the Rue d'Hermès and does dominoes.'

'All alone!'

'Or with Professor Pappas—who's apt, on the whole, to be dull. When he was introduced he started off about the county of Warwick. Or the Countess of Warwick. And then he referred to Shakespeare.'

Miss Arne turned.

'What is that about the stage?'

'Nothing,' Miss Collins said.

'One of these days, Marianne, you should arrange a Lysistrata *matinée* upon the Acropolis.'

'Boxes full. Stalls full. Gallery full. Pit full. *Standing-room only!*'

'Don't people stand at concerts? They promenade. . . .'

'I dare say.'

'There is a girl in the corner over there watching you who'd make a rare Lampito. . . .'

'She is an Australian, poor thing, seeking her parents.'

Miss O'Brookomore blinked.

'Well, she needn't start staring at me!'

'In certain lights,' Miss Collins murmured, 'she has a look of Edith Jackson, who was sacked from York Hill.'

'Why, what had she done?'

'Oh, nothing very much.'

'She must have done something.'

'. . . She gave a dance in her bedroom—the *houla-houla!* But that wasn't *really* all. . . . Oh, good gracious!'

'To-morrow we shall have one here I expect in the hotel.'

'Mr. Arbanel has composed a charming air expressly for it.'

'My dear, how can one dance to his brain pictures?'

'Oh, listen!'

'When the wind breaks this way you can hear distinctly what they're saying in the café.'

> 'Ta-lirra-lirra-lo-la-la.
> La-lirra-lirra-lo-la-la!
> Ta-lirra-lirra-lirra,
> La-lirra-lirra-lirra,
> Ta-lirra-lirra-lo-la-la!'

'It's politics!'

'It must be.'

'Such optimism!'

'One does hope that Mr. Cowsend——'

Miss Collins drifted over to the Count.

'Deer—have you forgotten? . . .'

'Oh, the "little dear"!'

'Mercy!'

'Another verse.'

'Not now; I mustn't!'

'When shall I see you again!'

'To-morrow, I dare say, at the siesta hour—when Miss O'Brooko-more goes to her room for a snooze. . . .'

He bent his head above her fingers.

'Good night, Miss Mabina. I kiss those charming hands.'

Miss Collins glanced at them.

'Mine?' she sighed.

∅. VIII ✇

SARDONIC, she stirred the salad: tumbling, jostling, pricking, poking it, parting the trembling leaves. Pursuing a rosy radish or . . .

'Oh, Gerald, everyone is watching you! . . .' unearthing the glaring eyes of eggs.

'Why begin throwing it about?'

Orchestrating olives and tomatoes, breaking the violet beet-root. . . .

'Oh, Gerald!'

. . . tracking provoking peas—scattering paprika, pouring tarragon, dashing *huile*.

'Yoicks, dear!'

'Athenæus, you know, maintains a lettuce is calming to Love!'

'Who ever mentioned love? I only said I liked him dreadfully.'

Miss O'Brookomore leaned her chin upon her hand: she rested.

'Where *is* this Pastorelli?' she asked. 'I mean the town.'

'It's a little way outside of Orvieto. Not very far from Rome.'

'Really? Rome. . . .'

'Avid thing! I believe you long to be there.'

'I see no reason to complain.'

'Think of the countless persons who've never come to Greece.'

Then finding Worcester Sauce—

'It doesn't seem fair!'

Miss Collins looked sage.

'Such,' she remarked, 'is life!'

'You haven't told me, Mab, about Pastorelli yet. . . . There's a cathedral with frescoes there, you say. Scuola di—*who*? A campo-santo. And what else?'

'There's the house, of course, where he was born. It stands beside such a wicked-looking lake, and the gardens sowed with statues. He showed me a photograph of his family seated in it. Oh, my gracious!'

'His family?'

'Just the natural blood ones. . . .'

'After *déjeuner* you should really write to your——'

'What's the good? . . . Mum's away in Edinburgh. She says she must try to content herself with *Modern Athens* as she doesn't suppose she shall ever see the other. So papa—poor old gentleman—is left all alone to look after my kiddy sister Daisy, who can neither read nor write. Mum won't let her be educated, she says, as it hasn't answered at all with me. And frequently, for a f-f-friend, she is asked to display her ignorance.'

'Her what?'

'How you said it: What! I love Napier *best*, dear, always when he says, "What." W-h-a-t! What! Oh, Gerald, I can't explain. . . . You'll never know——'

'I do know. It's like the crack of a cart-whip. Exactly.'

Miss Collins began eating crumbs at random.

'A whip? Oh, Gerald——'

'You seem to have entirely forgotten Napier since you've become interested in the Count.'

'After all, what is he but a Yorkshire pudding?'

'Still, he's your fiancé!'

'Do look at the man exactly opposite. Doesn't he give you the impression rather of something torn up by the roots?'

'He obviously has a little money, and she is spending it!'

Miss Collins whisked her eyes over the room.

Midway along Mrs. Arbanel appeared to be absorbed in a vivacious and seemingly vital conversation with the *maître d'hôtel*.

'I should love to seem so thoughtful!'

'I don't see Mrs. Cowsend, do you?'

'Breakfast was laid for four covers in her room.'

'For four!'

'Or perhaps it was only three.'

'Greece via the Renaissance would knock up most of us.'

'Why, even the Tartary tirade——'

'Remember you owe me that.'

'The library at Bovon, you know, is full of that sort of thing. . . .

Although mum detests all serious books. She likes them frothy. Whenever she goes into York she's sure to come back with something smart.'

'Hasn't the eccentricity of living near York ever occurred to your mother?'

'Oh, Gerald, it's dreadful for us all, dear, but what can we do if nobody takes the house?'

'There must be some way of getting rid of it.'

'Mum's in Edinburgh now to see what can be done. She thinks some person perhaps pining for the South——'

'One never knows!'

'I'll read you her letter, shall I? There's a message too for you.'

Miss O'Brookomore sipped listlessly her Château Décélée.

' "My adored angel," she says, "my darling child, Mab. . . . If you knew how wretched I am without you!" Oh! . . . "Couldn't you have got a *quieter* violet? . . ." She's interested too in Miss Arne! "As Juliet," she says, "she was astonishing! Though one can't help feeling she has danced at the Empire. Crossing Princes Street I let fall the Ethiopian skin that I got from Mrs. Mattocks." And she asks me to be photographed in your . . . something . . . "hat and Zouave jacket and a bunch of violets on one shoulder." (Then she says, as I told you:) "I must try to content myself with Modern Athens," she says, "as I don't suppose I shall ever see the Other. . . . Who should I come across at the Caledonian but Sukey and Booboo. They *were* so glad to find me here, and on Sunday we all went together to hear Father Brown. He spoke to us so simply, so eloquently, so touchingly that I quite . . . Never forget, my pet, that . . .

' "He reminds me just a little of St. Anthony of Padua. . . . What is all this about *an Italian*? Oh, Girlie. If ever we let the Chase we must persuade papa to travel. . . .

' "Listening lately to the Y.M.C.A. singing 'There is a Green Hill,' I felt I wanted to take a taxi and drive straight to it. Mum's picnic days are nearly over now. . . . Soon it's *she* who'll be the ruin. Those that care enough for her will toil to her bedside, perhaps, with their baskets, as they would to some decayed, romantic tower—the Lermers, poor Nell Flint, dear Mrs. Day—and they will sprawl upon her *causeuse* and trot out their ginger beer. Doctors will try to restore her, patch her up . . .

' "But mum won't let them. She will just roll over on one side and show them . . ." '

'And the message?'

'I'm coming.'

' ". . . and show them, as Dolce Naldi did, they arrive *too late*. The prospects of another damp winter——" '

'The message!'

' "Give my kind regards to Miss O'Brookomore." '

'She writes curiously in the style of one of my unknown correspondents.'

'She's full of trivial sadness.'

'Scotland should do her good.'

'What would you do, Gerald, if you were to look round and there was somebody in a kilt?'

Miss O'Brookomore blinked.

'I don't suppose I should do anything,' she said.

'Oh wouldn't you?'

'I *might* . . .'

'Try one. . . . I don't know what they are; at school we called them French Madonnas.'

'They look fairly rich, anyway.'

'Once I ate nineteen méringues. . . .'

'Pig!'

'You've to eat a peck of dirt before you die, Gerald.'

'Not if I know it.'

'Give me a bit of the brown.'

'What are your father's initials, in case I should write to him?'

'C. It's for Charles! . . . Poor old gentleman.'

'You should answer your mother yourself. Promise her a photograph.'

'On the night they draw the lottery there's to be a subscription ball at the opera.'

'What has that to do with it?'

'It's to be in fancy dress.'

'I understand.'

'I thought we could be photographed in our dresses.'

'I see.'

'Oh, Gerald, you could be a silver-tasselled Portia almost with what you have, and I a Maid of Orleans.'

'You!'

'Don't be tiresome, darling. It's not as if we were going in *boys'*
clothes!'

'Really, Mabel——'

'Of course, it's as you like!'

'So that's settled.'

'Oh, Gerald, for my sake subscribe.'

'I subscribe? I subscribe! I subscribe nothing.'

'When the Shire-Hall at home was blown away I helped to collect
for the restorations. . . .'

Miss O'Brookomore pinned up her veil.

'After the siesta what do you propose to do?'

'I'm going out to do some shopping. I should like to buy a small
piece of old pottery for Mrs. Elk, of York. You know she collects
jars. And then our head housemaid asked me to lay out a few
shillings on "some very Greek-looking thing," she said. And I
mustn't forget the footman. . . .'

'What did he want?'

'A knife.'

'You seem to have commissions for all the servants.'

'At home, you see, dear, I nearly always use the back stairs . . .
They're so much more interesting than the front ones . . . Once
Daisy saw a soldier on them . . . He was going up! And another
time——'

Miss O'Brookomore yawned.

'Mercy,' she said, 'the siesta-hour's upon us!'

❦. IX ❦

NO, there's really no resisting him. I'm sure there isn't. Who
could? There's no resisting him at all—none. No. . . .'

Demurely she shed a shoe.

'I shouldn't care to be more in love than I am at present. No,
indeed! Even if I could. . . .'

She sank slowly into bed.

'Oh, you silly creature!

'Love! O Lord!

'I shall never sleep. I don't see how I can. The die is cast! There's
no telling, child, how it will end! . . .

'... Via Tiber. ... Countess P-a-s-t-o-r-e-l-l-i. Via Tiber. ...
"O Tiber, Father Tiber, *to whom the Romans pray*." Impossible! ...
If they did, it was a perfect scandal.

'And suppose he made me too? Oh, good gracious!'

By the bedside, mellowing among a number of vellum volumes,
were the *Nine Prayers* of the Countess of Cochrane and Cray.

Who would do the burning?

That eighth one! What a clamour for a crown!

On the subject of jewels there wasn't much she didn't teach.

Two loose diamonds made a charming toc-toc sound.

At a dinner-party, now, who would walk in first? She or Lady
Cray? One would push past her probably, in any case—'the *Italian*
woman!' ... '*The Pasto* Countess thing!'

She played her eyes and flung out a hand towards a sugar-crystal-
rose.

No; one couldn't exactly tell how it would end. 'My dear, I
shouldn't care to say! ...'

There were those Beer-Hall voices. ... 'Fal de rol di do do,
di do do! Fal de rol——'

Miss Collins turned her pillow.

'I suppose I've to lie and listen! ... Oh, good gracious!'

Ø. X Ø

' "I AM sure I always found her to be most industrious, clever,
natty, and honest." That was Mrs. Vernigan's. This is Miss
Miser. And here is the Ex-Princess Thleeanouhee.'

'Why bother Miss Palmer any more about it? I always say it's a
lottery wherever one goes.'

'Once,' Mrs. Arbanel's maid declared, 'I took a situation with a
literary lady—the Scottish-Sappho. She wrote *Violet's Virtue*, or
it might have been *The Virtue of Violet*.'

'Anyway!'

'Oh, for the wings of a dove.'

'Come along, Miss Clint, now. It's not so far.'

Before them the Acropolis, half hidden by thin clouds, showed
like a broken toy.

'Naturally, one sees it has its old associations. ...'

'I dare say. But to my mind it doesn't look half the age of the Abbey church at home. Now, that does look worn if you like.'

'Worn, my dear, don't speak of being worn!'

Clint sighed.

'Whenever I'm lonely or depressed,' she said, 'or valeting anyone who's just a little wee bit . . . Well! I know there's only one thing for me to do. I take a taxi and go and sit in the church of St. Bartholomew the Great. It has a *je ne sais quoi* about it somehow that comforts me.'

'It would give some people the dismals, dear.'

'Well, I always leave when I'm annoyed!'

' "Quick with her needle, an early riser, I am sure——" '

'Give them back to me.'

' "I am sure no hours are too *long* for her." '

'It's what I should call the portrait of a slave.'

'Where is Elizabeth?'

'I'm here.'

'And Mademoiselle?'

'Lagging along behind.'

Miss Clint made a gesture towards the Erechtheum.

'Come along, girls!' she called.

'Oh! I never knew Lot had six wives. . . .'

'Can't you see she's always the same?'

'Our previous butler was a widower. He seemed inconsolable.'

'Sooner or later, we each of us bear our cross! . . . Where I lived last you might gather one of those downy-puffy things and, blowing, say: "First footman, second footman, third footman, fourth footman. . . ." And if there was any down over "Pantry-boy, page. . . ." '

'With the Jamjanets, of course, it was hotel-life half the time. Eating, drinking and dressing made up *their* day.'

'In Arcady, if you go, you'll find the food is vile.'

'What I look forward to most is the Cyclops Castle at Tiryns. We've a dwarf in our family, you see.'

'There's nothing more lucky, is there?'

'Oh well, my dear, perhaps it may come, some day.'

Clint turned.

'Come along, girls!'

'I shouldn't care to go with *them* on a walking tour. . . .'

'Mam'zelle Croizette, *chérie*, wherever have you been?'

'Looking for the Arbanel's bracelet.'

'I'd forgotten it! "The true-love-knot bangle he gave me when we became engaged." '

Clint stood still.

'I don't know,' she said, 'but I believe I smell a rat.'

'Fresh from the East, one is used to indelicate scents.'

'Of course it's not for me to say. . . .'

'In a strange land, Miss Clint, we women should stand together.'

'I noticed nothing until yesterday.'

'And what did you notice then?'

'There's more than one trap set for Miss Collins.'

'Lauk!'

'My gentleman's after her too.'

'Oh, my poor strained nerves!'

'I suppose the bride's a bore.'

'Of course she's neurasthenic and excitable and highly tuned. This morning, for instance, she sat and stormed at me because her white tennis shoes weren't white enough.'

'Most young married women are ashamed of anything pale. . . . The Honourable Hester Dish on her wedding tour wore black all the time.'

'Well, were there twenty traps laid for Miss Mabel she has too much gumption ever to go in.'

'You astonish me! I'd have said now she would be very easily *épris*.'

'Oh, mind the step!'

They had reached the Belvedere.

'I'd dearly like to carve my name on the leg of this seat.'

'Without a fiancé's entwined, Miss Palmer, it looks almost as if——'

'*My* boy is in the Guards.'

'Once I was engaged to a soldier.'

'And you broke it off?'

'How he did bore me with his battles!'

Croizette peered down.

'Such a sunset,' she remarked, 'would have scared the ancients.'

Palmer cleared her throat.

'I doubt it! . . .' she said. 'When I went out into the world my dear mother told me a little about *them*. . . . There was the adventure of Titia Clarges. . . . She was one of those smart girls like the Midianites in Paris. Believe me, senility takes some scaring.'

'Chatterbox!'

'What is the matter with Elizabeth?'

Elizabeth hid her face.

'There's a man,' she said, 'Miss Clint, carrying on in such a crazy way. . . . I think he means to draw us!'

'Let him ask permission.'

'All this note-taking out of doors in my opinion really isn't nice. I'd as soon start hair-dressing in the street.'

'It's on the cards you may. Professor Cowsend is to lecture in the Museum shortly from busts and coins and vases upon the Classic Coiffure. "I shall expect you to attend," Miss O'Brookomore said to me. "It is never too l-l-late to learn! Campstools, flowers, unguents, pins and *peignoirs* provided. And we just sit down and do each other's hair." '

'He'll not catch me there, I can promise him!'

'There'll be a prize.'

'So I should hope!'

'The winner will have her expenses to any one of the islands—a day off.'

'Who'd take an airing here from choice?'

'*Alone!*'

'Sprinkle ashes over me,' Elizabeth murmured, 'sooner!'

'Because Miss O'Brookomore's a bit of a blue-stocking it doesn't signify that Dorinda, Lady Gaiheart's that way! Ours is quite another story. We're here to be nearer to Colonel Sweetish, who's at Malta. . . .'

'In your place, I'd not own it.'

'How we do enjoy the saline breezes! "Where's the wind?" "Which way's the wind?" "I don't know, your ladyship," I reply, "but it's as keen as mustard!" '

Palmer examined her nails.

'My mistress isn't that sort,' she said.

'What do you mean?'

'When I tapped at her door one night she didn't seem earthly. She came out to me with her pen in her hand, looking quite deranged—and old! My word! More like a mummy!'

'Worn out in intellectual excesses I dare say.'

'*When she's with Miss Mabel she looks quite different.*'

'Were ever footsteps more out of tune!'

'An old dirge and a valse!'

Elizabeth giggled.

'Don't forget, Miss Palmer,' she said, 'you've promised to dance with me to-night when the band begins.'

'Surely; only bear it, please, in mind, I never will dance gentleman.'

'It doesn't matter. The chef said directly he'd finished he'd——'

'Finish me!'

'Whereabouts now were you born?'

'What makes you so inquisitive?'

'I could tell a London voice anywhere! Even in the dark.'

'Hammersmith's my home.'

'Hammersm——'

The Captive Women stared before them.

It was a bright and windy evening, with a mist that almost hid the sea. Now and then across Hymettos at a hint of sun swept a few pale shadows.

Miss Clint scanned the great groups of sailing clouds.

'Come along, girls,' she murmured. 'If it comes on to rain and we in our *derniers cris* . . . !'

✑. XI ✑

'NIGHT came with a big brown moon. . . . Ignatius knocked repeatedly on the door. At last a feeble voice—it was Haidée's —cried: "Come in! . . ." And I was led into the room by a Cowley Father. Oh, good gracious!'

'Go on. . . . His tired ecstasy makes me——'

'How's the poor head?'

'The dove did it good.'

'I shouldn't have thought you had held it long enough.'

'Quite long enough.'

'Soon it'll grow weary of flying about the room.'

'It sickens me so to watch it.'

Miss Collins got up stealthily.

'Coo!'

'Don't, Mabel.'

'It's looking at us both, dear, as much as to say . . .'

Miss O'Brookomore tittered.

'I believe all the time you're shamming.'

'Oh, very well!'

'I'd do anything for you, Gerald.'

'That's sweet. . . .'

'. . . It's exploring the ceiling now!'

'Open the window wide.'

'Oh, listen! What tune is it? It's a slow-step of some sort.'

The Biographer sat up slightly among her pillows.

'It sounds like the Incest-music,' she murmured, 'to some new opera.'

'Oh, Gerald. . . . You do look bad. Upon my word you do.'

'Really, Mabel, you have the tongue of a midwife, my dear.'

'I'd run over to the pharmacy willingly if you thought. . . . It was they who invented the "Eau de Parnasse." It's made mostly out of sunflower seed. It's really *violets*.'

'You'd stop to dance on the way!'

'Well? And if I did!'

'Just lately I've felt so nervous. I don't know why!'

'Accidents don't occur in a room full of people. Not often.'

'It depends.'

'Be good, Gerald. Now, there's a dear.'

Miss O'Brookomore seemed touched.

'Run, twirl, dance, spin!' she said, 'and come back in ten minutes.'

'You're an angel.'

'Carry me in your thoughts!'

'What good could *that* do you, Gerald?'

'Enjoy yourself—that's all.'

In a black gauze gown with glorious garnitures, her hair tied up behind in a very Greek way, Miss Collins walked out into the hall where Miss Arne, to her surprise, was drilling a huge recruit.

' "Good day, Lampito," ' she was saying, ' "dear friend from Lacedæmon. How well and handsome you look! What a rosy complexion! and how strong you seem; why, you could strangle a bull surely!" '

The Australian girl grew rigid.

' "Yes, indeed," ' she drawled, ' "I really think I could. 'Tis because I do gymnastics and practise the kick dance." '

'There, of course, I think Lampito should throw up a leg. We'd better begin again.'

Miss Collins paused.

'Haven't you got it pat by this time?' she enquired.

Miss Arne waved a fan with the names of some old adorers scribbled across the sticks.

'Art,' she remarked, 'doesn't like being jostled. How's your friend?'

'Gerald? She's pretty bad.'

'Health is like a revue. It comes and goes. Even I—in the morning when I rise I feel fit enough—at least! . . . But by lunchtime I'm exhausted . . . and then in the evening I'm myself again! . . .'

'Oh, good gracious!'

The Australian girl sat down.

'Phew! . . . It's warm acting!' she observed.

'We might have an ice.'

'Won't you have a Vermouth-Cobbler with me?'

'What's that?'

'It's just a drink.'

'Is it refreshing?'

'As a liqueur,' Miss Collins said, 'there's nothing like *mint sauce*. You can't fancy what it's like alone.'

The Colonial looked intriguing.

'Tell me about the stage,' she implored, 'or of the people on your fan.'

'I've forgotten! I forget!'

'Who's *Wellbridge*?'

'Ah! Dublin was a gay place when *he* was viceroy there. . . .'

'Silent Stanley!'

'At the Garden Theatre he was Bassanio. . . .'

'Freddy Fortune?'

'Oh, my dear, he was the lover in Lady Twyford's last play. He's the paramour in all her pieces.'

'Alice.'

Miss Arne took back her fan.

'I rang,' she said to the waiter. 'It's for an ice.'

Miss Collins turned towards the ball-room. People either were pushing their way in or struggling to get out.

The Count touched her arm.

'Could you spare me half-an-ear for half-a-minute?' he asked.

'I'd sooner dance, if you don't mind.'

'Are you fond of dancing?'

'I love it. Every winter nearly we give a ball. At least Mrs. Collins does. . . . It's really for me and Daisy. . . . We begin about half-past five and go on till about eight. After that there's a wizard.'

'Outside the snow would be falling. The land would be white.'

'Naturally *we* supply the rabbits.'

'Have you much shooting?'

'We get all Lord Linco's birds as they fly across.'

The Count sighed.

'With us,' he said, 'it's mostly hares and larks.'

'I suppose you mean the Opera.'

'Indeed no!'

'Are you in the country much?'

'Now and then. My mother, you see, is obliged to be a good deal in Orvieto. She has also an apartment in Rome.'

Miss Collins was mystified.

'*Apartments?*' she asked.

'An apartment, a flat, a floor—it is the first floor.'

'Oh, good gracious!'

'This is your very first season, isn't it?'

'I don't know. I shouldn't care to say!'

'Excuse me.'

'I live like a buried diamond half the year.'

'Enjoy yourself now.'

'Ah, that's . . . easier said than done. . . .'

'Your friend ought not to be too hard on you.'

'Gerald isn't really hard . . . You wouldn't say so if you knew her well . . . Once she bought a little calf for some special binding, but let it grow up . . . and now it's a cow!'

They swung slowly out into the throng.

'I know this dance well. It's *Lady Randolph and the Old Shepherd*!'

'The old shepherd part is charming.'

Miss Collins looked languid.

'Would you care to Cook me?' she asked.

'Cook you?'

'Show me round.'

'Certainly. I should be delighted.'

All Athens was responding to the dance. To Elizabeth, craning from the stairs, it seemed that the men resembled big black pearls while the women diamond drops—

'We might sit the rest out.'

'Of course it's just as you like. . . .'

'There's such a moon!'

'I've just been reading to Gerald about the moon—a big brown one!'

'Do you read a lot?'

'Lately, out of pure politeness, I've been dipping into some of Gerald's spawn. But I never open a book unless I'm obliged. And my sister's just the same. Poor mite, she can't! . . . Oh, she's such a pickle! She is really *too* obstreperous. . . . You never know what she's up to!'

Mrs. Arbanel approached.

'What weapons can you muster,' she asked, 'besides darts?'

'Darts?'

'Did you bring a gun?'

'Gerald has a gold revolver. "*Honour*" she calls it.'

'Well, to-morrow I and a few other women are going wild-duck shooting round Salamis, if you would care to come.'

'Oh, wouldn't I enjoy it!'

'We meet outside the church in the Rue d'Hermès at ten o'clock.'

'Gerald is very particular about whom she meets.'

'She can pick and choose. We're sure to be rather a band.'

'I don't know what Gerald will say. . . .'

'I noticed there was a tray outside her door.'

'We did all we could to tempt her. But she took her tea. And that was a mercy.'

'It's nothing, I hope, serious?'

'She gets these turns. . . . I think it's due to diet. Lately she has complained so much of her extraordinarily vivid dreams. . . .'

Mrs. Arbanel smiled darkly.

'When I dream,' she said, 'I'm watching most.'

'What—for instance?'

'How do I know?'

'Then don't expect me to say.'

Mrs. Arbanel addressed the 'Hippolytus Charioteer' upon the ceiling.

'At the Rotunda,' she murmured, as she moved away, 'please to turn. . . .'

'What could she mean?'

'I've not the least idea!'

'Be careful of her if you go!'

'She's a jealous fury. . . .'

'Her husband appears completely depressed.'

'I fancy he wants me to dance.'

'Don't! And never let him.'

'Why not?'

'Little miss, when love springs under your nose! . . .'

'Love? . . .'

'Only dance with me!'

'No. I'm going back to Gerald. Were anything to happen to her while I'm off duty I should never forgive myself.'

Miss O'Brookomore had lowered her lights.

'Is that you, Mabel?' she asked.

'How's the poor head?'

'I've been drowsing.'

'I'm glad you could manage that.'

'Isn't the band *awful*?'

'Boom, boom, boom. . . .'

'Did you have a nice time?'

'I've found out one or two things by going down.'

'What things?'

'Oh, Gerald, his mother keeps Apartments!'

'There. What did I tell you?'

'She has an Apartment in Rome. And I suppose it's a Boarding-house in the country. . . .'

'Well, to be sure!'

'After all, dear, Lady Frithelstock sells her fruit!'

'Even so!'

'And he has asked me, I think, to marry him.'

'He's proposed?'

'Of course it's purely verbal. . . .'

'What did he say?'

'First he asked to speak to me . . . and then he said, "Little miss," he said, "when Love springs under your nose! . . ." That was his expression.'

'A pretty one. But it has nothing to do with marriage. Oh, Mabel!'

'I long to be loved, Gerald.'

'My dear.'

'When he spoke of love it made me feel so important.'

Miss O'Brookomore looked grim.

'You've yet to learn, I find, what frivolous things men are. . . .'

'What has that got to do with it, Gerald?'

'Be patient. You are sure to find a better *parti*.'

'A party?'

'A girl like you.'

'And Mrs. Arbanel has invited us to join her at a shoot.'

'In town?'

'At Salamis.'

'It's so far off. . . .'

'Bring "Honour," she said.'

'Honour's no use. It won't go off!'

'Oh, good gracious!'

'Besides, if I went I would lie on the Plage and watch you all.'

'Gracious me, Gerald!'

'It's the dove again!'

'Unless I'm much mistaken, dear, that bird will stay in the room all night.'

⊘. XII ⬙

A WARM, miraculous morning made the Athenian pavements split.

Before an Ikon in the little dark building of the Kapnikaræa Miss O'Brookomore knelt. And if she stopped long upon her knees most likely it was more that she found herself comfortable than anything else.

Miss Collins touched her arm.

'Oh, Gerald, we're all waiting for you,' she said.

'I'm just coming.'

'I shouldn't over care to be troubled by a conscience like that!'

The Biographer drew on a glove.

'After all,' she enquired, 'isn't heaven a sort of snobbism? A looking-up, a preference for the best hotel?'

'It's no good asking me, Gerald. It's like that button-hook of yours. . . .'

'We won't discuss that now.'

'You don't imagine, do you, dear, I'd take your button-hook? I suppose you think I'd steal it!'

'Hush, Mabel!'

'I'm glad it isn't teaspoons. Although, of course, it's equally unpleasant.'

Outside all was confusion, chatter, cracking of whips.

'Βρεκεκεκέε κοάξ κοάξ!' Miss Arne harangued the mob.

'I don't suppose I shall knock down much,' the Australian girl declared. 'And, frankly, I don't much care. I'm one of those girls who wouldn't harm a fly. . . .'

'Dear Miss Dawkins. You'd think she was an auctioneer!'

With a sword-stick Mrs. Cowsend gave a sudden lunge into the air.

'In case the birds fly near,' she said, 'I shall simply prod them——'

'Mind the man.'

'. . . δεν ἔχω χρήματα.'

'What does he say?'

'He says he has no money.'

'Hasn't he any?'

'οὐχί!'

'Apparently not. . . .'

'Oh, isn't it dreadful, Gerald?'

'Some of these heads are really rather fine.'

'That looks like the English Consul!'

Miss Dawkins pressed her heart.

'Every time I see anyone——' she said.

'Is your father tall?'

'As we drive I shall give you all his measurements.'

Along a sympathetic, winding road skirting the Acropolis their carriages made their way.

'All these open-air theatres amuse me,' Miss Arne said. 'It is like old *café-chantant* days.'

Seated between Mrs. Arbanel and Dorinda, Lady Gaiheart, her personality struggled.

'Thank you, I never touch tobacco,' Lady Dorinda said. 'A cigarette with me would create a thirst. . . .'

'Fortunately Miss Dawkins has a flask.'

'At the Antiquarians in Priam Place just now they've some nice Phœnician bottles.'

Miss Collins nestled herself winningly against her neighbour.

'They showed me the smartest set of tea-things,' she said, 'that I ever saw. It belonged to Iphigenia—in Tauris. Oh, such little tiny

cups! Such little teeny spoons! Such a darling of a cream-jug ...
And such a sturdy little tea-pot! With the sweetest spout...
Pout. And a little sugar-basin! And a little slop-bowl. ...'

'I suppose all destined for America!'

Mrs. Arbanel turned and threw a few kisses to someone in the
brake behind.

'Who's the sun-helmet?'

'It's a Mrs. Lily Gordon Lawson—she has that big new villa on
the Olympian Road. You know.'

'They say Olympia for Love!'

'For love?'

'If people should come together there—it's all up with them.'

'My dear, to see Greece, it's what I came out for!'

'Well, somewhere in me, far down,' Miss Dawkins declared, 'I
don't mind admitting, there's a field with cows browsing.'

'Have you been seeking them long?'

'Almost always.'

'Just wandering!'

'Hotels, always hotels. *Yes!* And one does get so tired of tavern
life!'

'You must be very weary.'

'After this I propose to do the I's ... India, Italy, Ireland, Ice-
land. ...'

'When you've found them you'll be so bored.'

Miss Dawkins raised to her lips her flask.

'Whatever is in it?' Miss Collins asked.

Miss Dawkins fixed her.

'It's a digestive—cocktail,' she said at last. 'Or a *Blue Brazilian,* as
some people prefer to call it ... that is so.'

Mrs. Arbanel gave a cry.

'The *sea.*'

'Have you never seen it?'

'Mabel! ...'

'What emerald or sapphire!' Miss Arne asked. 'Aren't you
:avished?'

'I mean to bathe,' Miss Collins announced.

'My dear, how can you?'

'Oh, Gerald, just a dip!'

Dorinda, Lady Gaiheart, relaxed.

'Colonel Sweetish and Captain Muckmaisie, both old and very

dear friends of mine,' her attitude seemed to say, 'are somewhere across that light. . . .'

'How many guns are there?'

'Not so many as there seem. Neither Mrs. Cowsend nor Lady Dorinda will be shots. They're only going to pick up the birds.'

Mrs. Cowsend chuckled.

'Like good retrievers,' she said.

Mrs. Arbanel turned to throw an extra kiss.

'There's Mrs. Erso-Ennis and Mrs. Viviott,' she said.

'Those two!'

'And little Mrs. Lawson, who's really *très* sport. . . .'

'She says she's sure she shall shoot someone!'

'Oh, she's clever, she's fascinating.'

Miss Collins scowled.

'I should like her to start trying her tricks on me!'

'And then there're ourselves.'

'I've no gun,' Miss O'Brookomore said. 'At most I could throw a book. . . .'

'What have you brought with you?'

'I've my Wordsworth.'

'Is he your poet?'

'I'm told I should read *Le Charme d' Athènes*,' Mrs. Cowsend said. 'But I always disliked that series.'

'I fancy there's a new one: *Notes on the Tedium of Places*—comprising almost everywhere.'

Miss Collins glanced at her guardian.

'It's extraordinary Gerald doesn't go dotty,' she observed, 'writing as she does. . . .'

'Does the *Life* progress?'

'It's enough to say it assumes proportions.'

Lady Dorinda spread out her parasol.

'The Kettler cult seems the only shade we have to speak of!' she said. 'Since . . . Eleusis.'

Mrs. Cowsend freckled faintly.

'Were I to have a baby girl here,' she said at random, 'O'Brien would insist on calling her Athene; and it would be Olympia. Or Delphine. Or, if on the way there, Helen! . . .'

'I should have thought Violet, or *Violets*,' Mrs. Arbanel suggested as the carriage stopped.

Across a vivid, a perfectly pirate sea, Salamis showed shimmering in the sun.

Miss Arne held out arms towards it.

'It's like a happy ending!' she breathed.

Boats were in readiness.

'Where's the wind?' the Countess sniffed.

'There's almost an autumnal feel, isn't there?'

The wild apple-trees along the shore stood tipped with gold.

'Perhaps we shall see Pan!'

Mrs. Arbanel shouldered her gun.

'To avoid accidents,' she said, 'we should drift about in line.'

'My dear, I always fire sideways!'

Mrs. Viviott covered up her ears.

'Don't!' she said.

'Why not?'

'I never could bear the crack-of-a-gun business,' she confessed.

'Then whatever made you come?' Miss Collins queried.

'Mainly for Mrs. Erso-Ennis—to look after her.'

' "And the sun went down and the stars came out far over the summer sea!"—eh, Gerald?'

Miss O'Brookomore looked blank.

'I hope you know we're sweeping straight south-west!' she murmured presently. . . . 'I've an inkling there's Megara.'

'It was above Megara the Seymoures——'

Overhead the sky was purely blue.

Miss Arne scanned it.

'What is that large bird?' she enquired.

'Where?'

Miss Dawkins picked up an imaginary guitar.

> 'That which yonder flies [she sang]
>   Wild goose is it?—Swan is it?
>   Wild goose if it be—
>   Haréya tōtō,
>   Haréya tōtō,
>   Wild goose if it be,
>   It's name I soon shall say. . . .
>   Wild swan if it be—better still.
>   Tōtō! '

'Enchanting!'

'I learnt it in Japan—that is so.'

Miss Collins drooped.

'The water's so clear you can see everything that's going on.'

'Couldn't we moor ourselves somewhere and anchor?'

'I could fancy I hear turtle doves,' Lady Dorinda remarked.

'Oh, they're city!'

Miss Arne appeared to pray.

'I love Finsbury Circus for its Doves,' she said. 'And I adore the Aspens in Cadogan Square. . . .'

'Does the sea upset you?'

'Oh, Gerald! . . . She's certainly going to be queer.'

'I'm fond of that garden too, behind Farm Street, with those bow-windows staring out upon it. I could sit for ever huddled up in a black frock there exciting sympathy . . . listening to the priests' voices in the Farm.'

Miss Collins jumped up.

'Don't, Mabel! You'll capsize the boat.'

Mrs. Cowsend shuddered.

'I never could swim,' she said.

'I trust the gods would drop down strings—a sort of parachute affair—drawing us through the water.'

Mrs. Viviott addressed her friend.

'Were yours to give, Geneviève! . . .' she said.

'That's just *you*, Iris!'

Miss O'Brookomore fluttered her eyelids.

'Did you ever see such a rag of a sail?'

'It's black.'

'O-h, there went a fish with wings!'

'With——'

'Where?'

'Oh, my dear——!'

Mrs. Arbanel turned her gun about and—fired.

☞ *XIII* ☜

'I SHALL never forget the hideous moment!'
'They're driving her round the town.'
Lady Dorinda slowly wiped an eye.
'To the departed,' she said, 'short cuts are disrespectful.'
'I know Athens pretty well,' Mrs. Viviott declared. 'And they're going a statesman's way!'
Miss Collins threw herself into an easy seat.
'Oh, it's awful, awful, awful!' she said. 'It doesn't do to think. . . .'
The Room of the Minerva in the National Museum lay steeped in light.
'It's as though one held a Memorial service to her somehow,' Miss O'Brookomore commented, 'amidst all these busts and urns and friezes. . . .'
'For the Lysistrata that Nymph in the corner was to have inspired her gown. "I shall play her in lavender and helio," she said to me. And now, poor dear, where is she?'
'Oh, it's awful, it's hideous!' Miss Collins broke out . . . 'To-day I feel turned forty! This has made an old woman of me. Oh, good gracious!'
In her silver hat crowned with black Scotch roses drawn down close across the eyes she might perhaps have been taken for more.
'Mr. Arbanel, poor man, seems almost to be broken. Vina's vulgar violence, he said, disgusts me more than I can ever say—and when her maid went to her door she said, "Go away! I'm Proserpine." '
'Oh. . . . If anyone had *told* me, Gerald, that I'd become acquainted with a bride-murderess . . . I should never have believed it.'
'What do they intend to do?'
'Decamp—if they're wise.'
'When I saw her in a black dress, Gerald!'
'It was a pure accident—naturally, she said, when questioned.'
'One tries to believe it was.'
'She *would* wave her gun about so. I was in terrors all the time!'
'I suppose there was an inquest?' Miss Collins said.
'I really couldn't say. . . .'
'I should like to have been at it.'
'One longs for the country now—to get away.'

'We leave for Delphi directly,' Miss O'Brookomore said.

'Kettling?'

'Well ... more or less.... Poor Kitty, she went to Delphi to consult the Oracle and found it had gone. You can imagine her bitterness.'

'I dare say she consoled herself with the fruit.... There's a garden on the way to Itea.... You never *saw* such apples!'

'I dare say that's gone too.'

'Be careful in Olympia.'

'What *does* one do in Olympia? Tell me, please!'

Mrs. Viviott fetched a sigh.

'Oh, well,' she said, 'of course one sits, and sits, and sits, and *sits*, before the Praxiteles.... And then, if two people come together there I warn you they're sure to fall in love....'

Miss O'Brookomore bowed.

'Here're more mourners!' she exclaimed.

'Oh, isn't it gruesome, Gerald?'

'We turned in here, dear,' Mrs. Cowsend said, 'I didn't feel I wanted to go on....'

'That turquoise tinsel thing—*violet*, I should say—the pall!'

The Historian seemed to touch it.

'It was her doom, poor dear.... On the voyage out I've a recollection still of the way she sat on board while the waves burst over her.'

'At any rate she had the sad satisfaction of dying in Greece.'

'My dear, there was no time for reflections!'

Miss Collins covered her face.

'Was there no post-mortem?' she enquired.

Mrs. Cowsend showed distress.

'Have you been to look at the coiffures yet?' she asked. 'It's to-day my husband holds his classes, and they're all in the Vase Room now.'

'There's a room set aside somewhere for the "Obscene," ' Miss Collins said. 'Where is it?'

'My dear, how could one think of such a thing at such a minute!'

'Only to distract us.'

'The Professor's classes are more likely to do that.'

'In Arcadia,' Miss O'Brookomore declared, 'I intend to coil my hair like rams' horns.'

Mrs. Viviott vibrated.

'My dear,' she said, 'I never vary. I *couldn't*!'

'In Arcadia you'll find the continual singing of the cicadas require some excluding.'

Lady Dorinda raised a hand.

'Were I the wife of a gunner,' she protested, 'it would make no difference. I should always be high!'

Miss Collins slipped an arm about her companion's waist.

'Oh . . . It's the Dance of the Hours, Gerald!'

'Dance of the Drumerdairies, my dear.'

'Whose doing was it?'

Miss O'Brookomore appeared absorbed. . . . For a moment Time hovered, wobbled, swerved. Miss Collins aged for her.

'It's lovely, Mabel,' she said, 'when—— Oh, Mabel!' she said.

Miss Collins started.

'This caps everything!' she exclaimed.

'Is there anything wrong, dear?'

'Mrs. Arbanel's actually dressing. . . .'

Mrs. Viviott glided forward.

'Geneviève!' she implored—'Geneviève *Erso-En-n-is*!'

Miss Collins caught at the Historian.

'Let us go, Gerald,' she said, 'before it happens again.'

XIV

'IT'S nice to be in Delphi, Gerald!'

'After Athens,' Miss O'Brookomore said, 'it really is delightful.'

' . . . We never saw the king and queen, dear.'

'No more we did!'

'This morning I followed an empty river bed for miles and miles. . . .'

'To do justice to the walks,' Miss O'Brookomore observed, 'one would need to have legs as hard, pink and resisting as a ballerina.'

'Aren't you going round to look at the Auriga as usual?'

'I hardly know. Possibly I may take a turn presently in the direction of Parnassos. . . .'

'There's a shrub in the garden, Gerald, all covered in mauve rosettes!'

'It's perhaps a Delphinium.'

'Oh! I do think it sweet!'

'I wonder who's here beside ourselves.'

'I noticed the names of Cyril Cloudcap, and of Charlie Cumston in the Visitors' Book. . . .'

'That sounds English.'

'They left yesterday for Olympia, and there was a Mrs. Clacton, Gerald.'

'Has she gone too?'

'The Count said we weren't to be surprised if——'

'My dear, if Pastorelli turns up here we move on.'

'Fussy, fidgety thing!'

'When he makes that sort of *clearing* noise . . . No! Really——'

'That's nothing, Gerald. Why I do it myself.'

Miss O'Brookomore stared hard at the floor.

'I miss a carpet,' she said.

'In my bedroom at home, Gerald, the carpet has big blue tulips on a yellow ground.'

'Has the postman been?'

'He's been.'

'Wasn't there anything?'

'There was a letter from mum. And another from Daisy.'

'I thought she couldn't write.'

'She sets her mark.'

'Let me see.'

'It's only a smear.'

'Is the house disposed of—does your mother say?'

'I conclude it isn't. She says the greenfly this year has destroyed almost everything. Hardly anybody has been spared. At Patchpole Park the peaches just dried on the walls as though they were dates. And she's quite in despair about Daisy! She says she gets more hopeless hourly. She's taking her into York so as to have her ears pierced, poor mite. And papa, he's at Helstan with Napier—it's that new seaside——'

'Is the Count aware you're *fidanzata*?'

'I didn't tell him I wasn't quite free, and I don't think I will. I must write to Napier, I suppose, and break it off—I feel sorry for him, poor boy.'

Miss O'Brookomore wandered to the window.

'It's going to be hot to-day.'

'In the Gulf there's been rain in two places.'

'Here we've the sun.'

'Whatever would the vines do, Gerald, without the olives to hold them up?'

'I can't think.'

'They always say at home nothing can compare with the view from Mockbird Hill. On a clear day you can see to Ditchley.'

Miss O'Brookomore shaded her eyes.

'There's an arrival,' she said.

'Oh!'

'What is it?'

'He's here!'

'Oh! Mabel!'

'Oh! Gerald!'

'Oh! Mabel!'

'Oh! Gerald!'

Hand meeting hand, palm meeting palm (the vitality of the one rambling off into the other), they sought to find vent to their emotion.

⊘. XV ⊗

THE inn of the Pythian Apollo winked its lights.

Moving about the bare boards of her room, Miss O'Brookomore made her box. Now bending, now rising, now falling to her knees, it appeared from the road below as though she were imploring for forgiveness.

> 'For I am the old King's daughter,
> The *youngest*, sir, said she!
> The King he is my father,
> And my name is Marjorie. . . .
>
> Oh, my name is Marjorie, she said,
> My father he is the King,
> I am the youngest child he had,
> And what will to-morrow bring
>
> What will to-morrow bring, she said,
> Oh, what will to-morrow bring?

> The King he is my father,
> And what will to-morrow bring?'

'... Gerald, she always sings as she packs! Just making it up as she goes——'

'Why is she in such a hurry to be off?'

'I don't know. To-day she's been all veins and moods, whims and foibles.'

'Induce her to remain.'

'If only she would. . . . We haven't yet been up to the Cave of the Nymphs!'

'Ecco!'

'It's annoying to have to miss it.'

> 'One night I sat upon the stairs
> And heard him call my name!
> I crept into the darkness
> And covered my head for shame.
>
> I covered my head for shame, she said,
> Oh, I covered my head for shame!
> The King he is my father,
> And I covered my head for shame.'

'Sometimes when she starts to sing she'll keep it up for hours. It depends on what she's doing!'

> 'My sister Yoland she is dead,
> And Ygrind is no more. . . .
> They went away to Ireland,
> And nobody knows where they are!
>
> Nobody knows where they are at all,
> No one seems able to say——'

'Will you come for a little stroll?'

'Wherever to?'

'Anywhere.'

She raised her eyes towards Parnassos, whose cold white heights glimmered amid the stars.

'Oh, it gets grimmish!'

'You shouldn't be afraid.'

'Tell me,' she asked, 'would it be a Pension?'

'A Pension?'

'Those apartments of your mother's.'

'What does it matter now?'

'Oh! . . . Perhaps I ought to aid poor Gerald!'

'Aiding harms the hands.'

'Mine are spoilt already.'

'I can't believe it.'

'Mum pretends my hands are large because Time hangs heavy upon them.'

'Time in the country, they say, is apt to drag.'

'Not if there's a farm. Who could be bored by watching the manners of some old surly bull, or a dog on the scent of things, or a dove paying visits?'

'Very likely!'

'You're blasé.'

'Nothing of the sort.'

'Poor little Geraldine, her weariness exceeds most things. She says the world's an "8." '

'That's better than an "o." '

'The repetition palls.'

'There is always a nuance.'

'It's better to be an Indifferentist, she says. Not to care! But if anything ever goes wrong . . . It's impossible not to smile at her philosophy.'

'You must be her comfort.'

'I don't know what she'd do without me. Because the maid's a perfect fool. When we arrive anywhere usually it's I who improve the terms. . . . Gerald hates to bargain. She seems to think it sordid. So I do it for her. Oh, it's such fun! . . . Is it to be a back room or a front room, with a double bed or a single bed, or would the lady disdain a back bedroom without any balcony? Then Gerald asserts herself. "The lady requires a balcony with an unobstructed horizon"—and if there isn't such a thing, then we try elsewhere.'

He stooped a little.

'It's the case of a courier,' he said.

'I think we ought to turn.'

'We will,' he answered, 'when the road bends. Remember, the world's an " 8" !'

⊘. *XVI* ⊗

'WILL you talk to me about the Moon and Stars?... Would it amuse you?'

Miss O'Brookomore raised herself.... A young man whom she had never seen until now stood before her.

'I shall be delighted to talk to you about anything,' she replied.

'When did you arrive?'

'My dear, we only got here yesterday.'

There came a voice of protest.

'Oh, Gerald! It was the day before.'

'What are your impressions of Olympia?'

'I love it, I think it sweet.'

'Everybody says the same.'

Miss O'Brookomore breathed a sigh.

'I should like you to be my Literary Executor,' she said.

He knelt down and took her hand.

'No, my dear Thing!' he answered. 'I'm sorry—but I simply can't. Simply I should love to, my dear Thing! But it's impossible....'

Miss Collins rose discreetly.

'Gerald—I think I shall leave you,' she said.

⊘. *XVII* ⊗

'WHOEVER was it, Gerald?...

Seated before a mirror, her shoulders gilded by the evening sun, Miss O'Brookomore drew a net of sapphire stones across her hair.

'Some god of the woods—no doubt!'

'That's only for a diary.... It doesn't do for me....'

'Things do happen so quickly!'

'Very likely it was Cyril Cloudcap....'

'It may have been Charlie Cumston.'

'Mer-cy! Gerald.'

'How soon will you be ready?'

'I've no appetite, Gerald. While the Count's at Delphi I don't seem to care.'

'Foolish girl!'

'Oh! I do long to be married, Gerald. . . . It's what I long to be most. Just married, dear.'

'Not without your parents' consent.'

'Nonsense, Gerald!'

'It's a caprice that will pass.'

'Oh, Gerald, his love talk with me and what I reply—it's a real duet!'

Miss O'Brookomore tucked a few mauve satin flowers into her frock.

'Aren't they heavenly?' she enquired. 'Especially the purple ones. . . .'

'Oh, Gerald!'

'My poor puss——'

'People's lives, dearie, don't seem to be a bit their own once they're in love.'

'Love is a seed that needs watering from day to day. Otherwise it dies.'

'With me it all accumulates.'

'Don't let's miss the sunset—the later half.'

'It's a sunset and a sobset, Gerald. Oh, it's so sad. . . .'

'In the end everything has to be paid for.'

'Principally for that I'd sooner I didn't dine. It really isn't worth it, Gerald. . . .'

'No dinner?'

'Even gratis. Oh, Gerald!'

'We're sure to meet the Arbanels.'

'I tapped at their door as I came along.'

'I fear that was intrusive.'

'Directly it dawned upon her it was me she flew forward brandishing a powder-puff.'

'Her behaviour's getting Byzantine—more and more.'

Miss Collins folded an arm about her friend.

'Why do you think it's Byzantine, Gerald? Whatever makes you think it is?'

'On certain natures environment frequently reacts. I can recall the Queen of Snowland (when a guest at Windsor) frisking off one afternoon into the town in search of lodgings. She came to the very house where I was writing her life . . . and we met in the front hall.'

'Oh, good gracious!'

'Similarly, I feel inclined to believe that Mrs. Arbanel in Egypt would be less vivid and more *Athenian* in her ways.'

'Can a leopard change its spots, Gerald?'

'My dear, it can modify them.'

'I'm surprised you lend her Palmer.'

'I've only offered her, of course, until the faithless Clint can be replaced. Mrs. Arbanel hopes to secure someone locally.'

'I shouldn't think there were many maids to be found locally, Gerald. I shouldn't think there was one. Not in Olympia.'

'The deciphering of their characters, in any case, would require a skilful student,' Miss O'Brookomore observed as Palmer came in.

Miss Collins rolled her eyes.

'Thank heaven!' she exclaimed.

'It didn't take you long!'

'I was as quick with her, miss, as I could be.'

'We were prepared to hear some screams. . . .'

'Were I to be stabbed, Miss Mabel, I should endeavour to be considerate.'

'Violets!'

'I suppose, poor thing, she is still very dazed?'

'She seemed lost in reverie, miss.'

'I expect it's the air.'

'She intends to ride to Sparta almost immediately, since Olympia, she hears, is nothing but cliques and coteries.'

'It's their season now.'

'There's a good deal of entertaining, miss, to-night. Dorinda, Lady Gaiheart, is to have a party for the Irish Archæological School. And Mrs. L. G. Lawson is bringing over some of her friends from the Villa Sophonisba.'

Miss O'Brookomore began muffling a foot up in a silver-spangled shoe.

'Had I been told earlier I'd have gone into Corinth,' she said.

'No doubt you'd have found Miss Dawkins there.'

'My dear, she's in Olympia. She arrived this afternoon. I overheard her telling her father's chest-measurements to the boy that works the lift.'

'And I dare say half-seas-over?'

'Poor thing.'

'Oh, she's so common, Gerald!'

'I should like to be on a balcony, miss, for the Recognition.'

'I dare say she'll be made to display her birthmarks first.'

'There's no need, miss—if you'll pardon me—for birthmarks with a face like that.'

'Brute!... You've pricked me....'

The sound of the dinner-gong came dwindling up.

'Oh, the way they beat it!'

Miss O'Brookomore smothered a sigh.

'It might be the Ramadan!' she declared.

⌀ *XVIII* ⌀

O STARS! O perfumes! O night!

In the grey cedar crests, from the blue fir-trees of the Kronian hill, the owls flapped gabbling; among the fields of mournful olives the cicadas called; over the fragments of fallen marble, crushing the wild thyme, the fire-flies flashed; and on the veranda of the Hôtel de France, the scintillation of her diamonds harmonising equally with the heavens as with the earth, Dorinda, Lady Gaiheart was finishing a tale.

'He then walked off with her,' she said, 'in an appalling pair of old black slippers.'

'He didn't run!'

'Why should he? Men seldom run away with girls. Not in these days.'

Miss O'Brookomore looked relieved.

'I always think of Europa,' she said.

'That comes from chattering so much about farms.'

'With daughters of your own I was determined to consult you.'

'I never bothered. They were just a nest of sisters, until one by one, alas, without requiring my advice, they deserted the family tree.'

> 'Her hour of love,
> How soon it passed!
> It passed ere Mary knew.

And that is the worst of all these rash marriages.'

'I fear the Arbanels are already getting fidgety.'

'She was crying so much at dinner, poor thing.'

'He was telling me they propose to plant a bed of violets, big white single ones, on the Acropolis, to the glory of the delicate and individual artiste, *Arne*—the "only" Lady Teazle of our time—in the presence of the *corps diplomatique* and the king and queen.'

'Tears!'

'Toilettes!'

'Speeches!'

'I expect so!'

Miss Dawkins dropped a sigh.

'Where's Troy?' she said, wheeling round in her chair.

'You surely don't think they're there!'

Lady Dorinda looked reserved.

'I must rejoin my friends,' she murmured. 'In a few minutes we're all going over to the ruins.'

Miss O'Brookomore lifted up her eyes.

'I shall stay where I am for the new girl dancer,' she devoutly mumbled.

'Is she one of the Sophonisba set?'

'Mrs. Viviott found her ... whirling to herself among the Treasuries.'

'At Tanagra,' Miss Dawkins said, 'she was balancing herself, not long ago, in the village street. I was obliged to interrupt her to ask if a smart fair woman with an elderly, stoutish man had been seen that way: S-s-s-s-h! she said. In the evening when the peacocks dance ...'

'I should be afraid of her!'

'She is really wildly pretty.'

'Those deep wonder-rings about her eyes are quite unholy.'

'At dinner Mrs. Viviott sat like a player with an unsatisfactory hand at cards.'

'I hate all ingratitude,' Miss O'Brookomore observed. 'In Biography, of course, one sees so much of it. ...'

'Tell me! How is *it* getting on?'

'Gaps! Gaps! Gaps!!!'

'There are bound to be a few.'

'Did you ever meet Max Metal?' Miss Dawkins asked.

'No, never.'

'Or Nodo Vostry?'

'I don't remember him.'

'Or Harry Strai?'

'I'm sure I never did!'

'Why?...'

'In my opinion their books for girls are full of unsound advice.'

'I'm glad I can still sometimes drug my senses with a book,' Lady Dorinda exclaimed.

'Unluckily, racing round as I do, I very rarely find a chance.'

'You must have met with some adventures by the way.'

Miss Dawkins mixed herself a sombre liqueur.

'I had a good time in Smyrna,' she drowsily declared.

'Only there?'

'Oh, my dears, I'm weary of streets; so weary!'

'And have you never found any trace——?'

'At Palermo, once. . . . I was wandering in the Public Gardens before the hotel, amid blown bus tickets and autumn leaves, when I thought I saw them. Father, anyway. He was standing at an open window of an eau-de-Nil greenhouse. He looked very much younger—altered almost to be a boy. I stood and stared. He smiled. I believe I spoke. And then, before I was able to realise it, I was inside his dark front hall. . . .'

'Who was he?'

'I can only tell you he was a dear thing. I shall hope to meet him in heaven.'

Mrs. Arbanel swooped up lightly.

'I respond to the sound of the sea,' she said, 'and the tinkle of ice!'

'Let me make you a Cherry Cobbler.'

'After interviewing a temporary-maid there's nothing I'd like *more*!'

'Are you satisfied?'

'Is one ever——'

'Still, if she understands hair!'

'That is all she seemed to follow.'

'She'll do, I'm sure, for Sparta.'

Miss O'Brookomore unfurled her fan.

'Frankly, I rather shrink from Sparta,' she said.

'What is there to take one there?'

'I really forget—I believe there's a crouching Venus.'

'What does Mr. Arbanel say?'

'He doesn't say anything. He leaves me to go alone.'

'What? Isn't he going at all?'

'When the weather is milder he may.'

'A man will have his comforts,' Lady Dorinda affirmed.

'I long to hear about your new home.'

'. . . Oh well. . . . It's quite a clever little house. . . . Five bedrooms. . . .'

'Modest.'

'If you would care to see the plans——'

'My dear, there's no hurry,' Miss Dawkins said. 'Any-old-time will do.'

Miss O'Brookomore turned her head stiffly towards the stars.

On all sides through the dusk, intermingling with faint nocturnal noises, rose up a sound of kisses.

She shivered as she felt something touch her own exceedingly sensitive skin.

'Where have you been, Mabel?' she asked.

'Writing letters. I've been describing the Temples to mum.'

'Writing letters,' Mrs. Arbanel said. 'I think it must be an Olympic Game.'

'Why, what?'

'Do you ask me for the rules?'

'How should I know—the rules?'

'They're really very simple. . . . You sit two at a table. A young man, perhaps, and a chit of a girl. With a piece of plate-glass in between. And then, when you've drummed with your fingers and played with your pen, you shuffle with your feet, and you throw dying glances over the top.'

Miss Collins challenged.

'. . . Prove it!' she said.

'Wild girl! You surely don't suppose I'm going to prove it?'

'Why, I was sitting with a widow!'

Miss Dawkins speared herself a cherry.

'Oh, for a quiet corner!'

'First, Mrs. Lawson's guest is going to dance.'

'Who, exactly, is she?'

'She's a pupil of Tasajara, Gerald.'

Miss O'Brookomore's nose grew long.

'I never heard of her,' she said.

'Oh, she's a study, Gerald.'

'One sees so many artists here——'

'With a water-colour in the Academy. Some people seem to think it permissible to look a little mad and to behave as if they *really* were. . . .'

'I heard the flowers scream as I picked them!' Mrs. Erso-Ennis was saying as she scattered a shower of blossoms upon the floor.

'If it's to be Botticelli——' Miss O'Brookomore complained.

Mrs. Erso-Ennis looked indignant.

'Botticelli! . . . I invented the whole thing just now.'

'How could you!'

'It's the *Hesitation of Klytemnestra*. The poor Queen, you see, cannot quite bring herself to kill the King, and while he sleeps she performs a suite of interesting, *idyllic* poses over him with a knife.'

'Better wait, Gerald,' Miss Collins advised.

Mrs. Erso-Ennis flung a few last leaves of roses.

'Oh! Think of the earwigs!'

'In those old-fashioned places one should only wear short skirts.'

'At the summer sales in Athens,' Miss Dawkins seraphically said, 'I picked up a regular siren's gown. . . . Looped up upon one side to reveal the knee.'

'What you have now, if one may say so, is also very original.'

'It doesn't fit. But it isn't meant to,' Miss Dawkins replied.

Mrs. Erso-Ennis directed her eyes to the room.

On a couch, destined to be the royal bed, a young woman, evidently a prima donna, was caressing rapturously her little boy.

'My son,' she was saying, 'my opera . . . x! Opera . . . xx! My Johannes . . . !! My *bébé*! . . .'

'She must be removed, I fear.'

'And there're some horrid arrivals, too.'

For those with ears fine enough Miss Collins caused an innocent bud to wail.

'Oh, Gerald,' she said, 'who do you think is here?'

'Not——!'

'He's in the bus, dearie!'

'My poor puss . . . You've turned quite pale.'

'Oh, the shock to me, Gerald! . . .'

'You look so tired, dear . . . so sad and so worn out.'

'It's because I'm dead beat, Gerald.'

'Feel faint, at all?'

'No—but I've never felt like this before, Gerald. . . . You little know how I feel—I could not have believed it was possible.'

☞ *XIX* ☜

'SIXTEEN of them,' she counted, 'and a diamond drop!'
'*Au revoir*. Until to-night.'

'Oh, the rush!'

'You're ready? Packed——'

'All I dare. I could hardly bring away my big box—the one with the furs and flannels! . . .'

'You'll need your passport.'

'It's lost.'

'Lost!'

'Gerald must have burnt it, she says, among her papers. She's everlastingly burning things. She lights her fire in the evening just as she bolts her door. . . . And then she burns things, and dreams things, and pokes things, and mutters things—*l'heure exquise*, she calls it.'

'. . . Very likely.'

'I've an idea it's rheumatics, poor soul. . . .'

'M-a-b-e-l!' Miss O'Brookomore called again.

'I must go to her. . . .'

'One kiss!'

'O-o-o-o-h!'

'Another!'

'Not till we get in the train.'

'*Cara mia dolce!*'

'And thanks very much for the diamonds,' Miss Collins replied.

Loitering up and down the hall among the tubs of orange-trees—now in full flower—Miss O'Brookomore was growing ruffled.

'It's charming!' she said. 'It appears he's on our floor.'

'Oh no, he's not, Gerald . . . He's on the floor above. Right overhead, dearie.'

Miss O'Brookomore looked away.

'There are people, I find, who have no heads,' she ruefully remarked. 'They've lost them.'

'I don't know why you should dislike him, Gerald. Because he doesn't you. He calls you the pretty priestess. . . .'

The Biographer unbent a shade.

'Does he?' she enquired.

'Are you going for your walk?'

'I told Miss Dawkins we would help her to find her parents.'

'It's too late to go far, dearie.'

'Nonsense!'

'How can she expect to find them, Gerald, sitting all day with a Gin Daisy or a Brandy Flip! Tell me that now!'

'Anyway we might take a turn round the garden. .... If they're here at all I expect they're in the shrubbery.'

It was the hour when, to a subtle string band, the bustling waiters would be bringing tea.

'Oh, the Sophonisbas, Gerald!—some of them.'

Their tired, art-stained faces turned towards a little Saint with rose lips, eyes and crown, Mrs. Erso-Ennis and Mrs. Viviott were overwhelming with attentions the pupil of Tasajara.

'Mercy, Gerald!'

'*Hein!*'

'There's bound to be heart-burnings, Gerald.'

' . . . I shouldn't wonder.'

'And there's your God-of-the-Wood, dearie. . . .'

Miss O'Brookomore changed her course.

'*Not* before the windows!' she exclaimed.

'Olympia for love, Gerald.'

'Olympia for tattle.'

'Oh, Gerald! I mean to fling in my lot with a crowd of absolute strangers. . . .'

'What!'

'Love isn't logical, Gerald.'

'Alas!'

'Oh, Gerald!'

'What has your friend a year?'

'How should I know, dearie?'

'It's important to know.'

'It's better to be poor—I've often heard mum say—than to have a soft seat in hell.'

'An Italian is very easily enamoured.'

'I love his dark plastered hair, Gerald. I think it quite sweet.'

'It isn't enough. . . .'

'He's like somebody from Marathon, Gerald!'

'You're young yet.'

'Oh, Gerald, when he sang the Shepherd-Star-Song from *Tann-*

häuser and gave that shake! . . . You can't think how much I was moved . . . How I responded. . . .'

'His *catches from Butterfly* would get on my nerves!'

'Had I nerves like you I couldn't rest without a passport.'

'It's tiresome, I admit.'

'It's that, dearie. . . .'

'Don't despond!'

'Suppose they detained you, Gerald?'

'Why, we'd sing a duet together.'

'Wait till there's a warrant!'

'A warrant!'

'Sometimes I think of the prison we saw in Patras, with the prisoners all thrusting their heads out between the bars.'

'Don't, Mabel!'

'Oh, Gerald! It's a climax and a perfect semax, dear.'

'We're not helping Miss Dawkins at all!'

'You go one way, Gerald. And I'll go another. . . .'

Miss O'Brookomore glanced behind her.

Already the sun-topped hills were lost in lilac towards the ground. It would soon be night.

'Very well,' she murmured, letting fall a glove; 'we will meet again at dinner.'

✐. XX ✎

'MABEL! Mabel! Mabel! Mabel! Mabel! Mabel! Mabel! Mabel!'

⊘. *XXI* .⊘

HOTEL CENTRAL,
CONSTITUTIONAL PLACE,
ATHENS.

Saturday.

DEAR GERALD,—I was married this morning and we leave to-morrow early for Corfu don't worry about me dear I'm alright O darling I'm the happiest girl in Greece I wore my little amber tricorne satin cap dear and Oio gave me the violets I shall get my trousseau bit by bit I suppose as we go along I had wanted rather badly to be married in the Kapnikaraea but it was a Registry after all good-bye now Gerald and take care of yourself dear do in haste yrs always affectionately

MABINA PASTORELLI.

P.S.—I laughed the whole time the priest who married us would keep whisking his skirt.

Mrs. Cowsend is here still Old ox.

Oio says if I write another word he'll pour all my ink away.

Inclinations

PART II

❧. I ❧

THE sunlight passing through the glass candlestick by the bedside shot out its rays towards her threefold and woke her with a start.

—Bovon! Home!

—The Countess gaped.

There was the fine old carpet stained with tulips, and the familiar text upon the lightly figured walls, and the dress bust in the corner, behind the *causeuse* that cast its consoling outline so effectively at night, and the medicine chest above the rocking-chair, with the sage-chinoiseries on top, that would swing their heads in the affirmative almost for a glance—which responsiveness had been known to work like a spell upòn certain sensitive natures in more instances than one.

The Countess sat up.

'Bianca!' she called.

By the wide 'Elysium' bed stood a bassinet tricked in bows.

'Bianca, Borghese, Nancy, Sabina!'

From the doorway came a swirl of skirts—a croon—and Mrs. Collins entered.

'While the mother was asleep the granny came and stole the darling, and whipped down the corridor, out into the garden, and round and round the house.'

The Countess held out her arms.

'Oh, my honey bear!'

'Don't, Mabel. You'll kill it.'

'Oh, the interesting little pickle! Oh, the Roman rascal!... Poveretta! *Ah, Dio!*'

Mrs. Collins considered her daughter.

'... There's something I want to say to you,' she said.

'Yes, what is it?'

'Everyone's enquiring for the Count—all the Bovon busybodies.'

'Kra, kra, Mrs. Rook.'

'They're concerned he hasn't come!'

'It's the Vintage. Directly that's over he will.'

287

Mrs. Collins beamed affectionately.

'In any case,' she murmured, 'I mean to give a small dinner for you, and that, my dear, directly.'

'Oh, good gracious!'

'I shall take you the rounds.'

'Visits!'

'Rectory, Patchpole, Rising-Proudly.'

The Countess lay back.

'I wish to offend the Warristons,' she said, 'and Napier—and the gorgeous Mrs. Lampsacus. Oh, and a whole pack besides!'

'Napier has asked for you repeatedly—almost every day.'

The Countess averted her face.

'I dare say,' she said, 'when he first heard of my marriage he was frightfully, frightfully upset?'

'Not so very. For five minutes he seemed inconsolably unhappy—and then he smiled!'

'Providentially!'

'Oh, my dear, you can't think how I've prayed for you all this while.'

'Of course it's Catholicism now with both of us.'

'It must be so strange.'

'The child was baptised in Santa Maria in Cosmedin—she's been baptised twice, poor dear.'

'For sake of ceremony?'

'At Santa Maria, it was on account of *them*. It's their parish. But afterwards I took her round quietly and had it done in St. Peter's.'

'You obtained your audience?'

'At the very last minute.'

'Well!'

'Oh, well! I was prepared to do anything. Naturally! I'm sure! Oh, good gracious!'

'Was the child with you?'

'Oh, she waved her fat little wrinkled wrists—and smacked his Holiness—mother's Bianca did! My blessing!'

'As a family I gather you're inclined to be devout.'

'Of course the dowager's goody. She never goes out without a string of nuns!'

'Is there any reason for it!'

'I couldn't say. Often she'll kneel in the garden. Or on the stairs. Or in a shop. Or on a tram. Whenever she wants to she'll kneel!'

'She appears to be insatiable.'

'It doesn't affect me. . . . On Sunday, as a rule, I've a box at the Argentina or a sofa stall at the Alcaza.'

'Oio too?'

'Occasionally he comes.'

'And when he doesn't!'

'There's always someone.'

Mrs. Collins looked round.

'Wow! Here comes a big black doggie!'

'Daisy—my *dear*! . . .'

'Papa's waiting breakfast. He wants you to boil him an egg.'

'Tell him I'll come.'

'He's grumbling so. According to him, nobody cares at all whether he lives or dies. . . .'

Mrs. Collins raised a hand to her curls!

'Oh, poor granny!' she murmured as she withdrew.

Daisy subdued her ways.

'How did your little child sleep!' she asked.

'Well.'

'Do you regret Rome?'

'It's a joy to have no mosquitoes!'

'That's not so bad as snakes. Suppose you had married an Indian.'

'Thank goodness.'

'Tell me about the Marriage State. Is it what you expected it to be?'

The Countess threw up her eyes.

'I didn't expect anything,' she said.

'Let me look at your wedding-ring, Mabel, may I? Only for a minute.'

'What do you want it for?'

'I won't eat it.'

'There's nothing very novel in a wedding-ring. Wait till you see my pearls?'

'Where are they?'

'With my other jewels. . . .'

'I should like to borrow some.'

'I dare say.'

'Do you know of anyone likely to suit me?'

'A lover?'

'Nobody, Mab! . . .'

'I'm sorry.'

' . . . Mabsey?'

'Oh, have *patience*.'

'It's a pity the Bovon boys are so rabbity—they're for ever with their noses down a hole.'

The Countess fluttered her eyelids.

'How are the dear ferrets?' she asked.

'All right.'

'And the farm?'

'All right.'

'Any changes?'

'Only in the house. Olga and Minnie have gone. Olga said she was glad to go. She said nothing would induce her to stop.'

'Is Queen as queer as ever?'

'Queerer.'

'Impossible.'

'He and Mrs. Prixon don't get on. What Spicer endures at meals— talk about silence! And next week there'll be a fresh footman. It's funny the effect it always has upon me—it's something no one could explain!'

'In days gone by,' the Countess said, 'the pantry with a stranger in it was as dull as any drawing-room. . . .'

Daisy wriggled.

'Shall you ever forget the time Frank flew at you and clapped his hands? You were reaching for the pickled walnuts.'

'Mercy!'

'And I was steadying the table for you as you got on it. Suddenly he . . . sprang.'

The Countess looked vexed.

'Now you've scared the child.'

'Oh, the poor wee sweetie!'

'Zito! Zito! Ah, Madonna.'

'I'll take her a turn in her little pram if she likes. Just the Aunt and the Niece together.'

'Stay within call.'

'We'll peep in the larder, shall we, Babs? There may be a bare birdie dangling there, and perhaps a little white corpse.'

The Countess rang.

'Better wheel her under the yew-trees,' she said, 'out of the wind. And don't upset the pram!'

◈ II ◈

'WHEN the crow's-feet come
And twirl about my eyes,
And my lips turn pale . . .
And my cheeks sink in,
Oh, say, wilt thou love me then?'

Divorcing itself from the piano, the voice trailed magnificently
away, ignoring altogether the tragical scepticism of the accompaniment.

The listeners looked shrewd.

Above the little party rose the Chase, dark and eerie in the autumn
sun.

'Wilt thou love me truly when my hair has flown,
When my teeth have fallen
And my hands are wan?
Oh, say, wilt thou love me then?

I will love you (said he) for ever and ever,
For ever and ever and ever and ever,
Amen.'

'Bis. Bis.'

'It's the air from *Cunégonde*,' Mrs. Collins explained, coming to the
window.

'We were wondering what it was.'

'In the death scene she introduces parts of it again in her delirium.'

Mr. Collins frowned ferociously.

'Hag!' he muttered.

'By-and-by I will rattle you some of the ballet-music from *The
Judgment of Paris*,' the Countess said. 'Oh, the valse Paris sings—!
He and the Three Graces. —Da-da-da-di-da!'

'If only the Chase were rid of!' Mrs. Collins complained.

'Has anyone been to view it?'

'Madame La Chose had the impudence to come. . . . Queen came
to me one morning with the news that a lady with *an order* desired
to see over the house. I guessed by his tone there was something

extraordinary, and on going into the drawing-room there was Madame La Chose.'

'Did you show her round?'

'Oh, my dear . . . yes. We even went so far as to fix some of the rooms.'

'Mercy!'

'I must say I thought her rather charming.'

'Would she care to take it?'

'Without the meadow she might. . . .'

'It shows her sense. Land nowadays is much too impoverishing.'

'Her idea is to revive *Basset*. . . .'

'York being mainly a military town it would probably be a boon.'

'In any case the decision, it seems, does not rest with herself alone, and she has asked to come back again.'

'My dear, if she does . . . !' Mr. Collins said.

The Countess caressed her child.

'Mother, oh! . . . Poor mother, oh! Give a kiss to mother, oh! She says she *won't*! Oh, good gracious! . . .'

'I'm unhappy about her nurse,' Mrs. Collins said. 'A trustworthy person is everything.'

The Countess crossed herself dejectedly.

'Oh, when I think of her nurses! . . .' she said. 'At first I had a Roman one for the child. She was a regular contadina—La Marietta! La Mariuccia! But she was so dirty! . . . A regular slut she was . . . she wasn't even clean. And too *sans gêne,* by far. Bianca's most impressionable. Nothing escapes her little eyes. . . . So I sent her away and took a stranded Irishwoman instead. Oh she was a terror. "I always try to please everybody," she said, "and I'm sorry I can't you!" But it was the tone of her voice, dear, in which she said it more than the actual words. . . . *Sapristi!* However, one or two of them I liked. There was a Swiss. . . . If she hadn't been so vague. One night, my dear, she overturned the pram right in the middle of the Corso! It might have killed the child. . . .'

'Are there no nice gardens that she could play in?'

'There are. But it's a climb to get to them!'

'I'd an idea that Rome was flat. . . .'

Mr. Collins handled meditatively his cigar.

'What of the seven hills?'

'Ah, Charles!'

'Seven little hilly-willies!'

'I suppose the surrounding scenery is.'

'You'd love Frascati. The land falls and rises, falls and rises. Oh, it's ever so dear.'

'I've a letter of yours from there.'

'Did you keep the Greek ones?'

'I kept them all.'

'I should like you to show me Gerald's.'

Mrs. Collins looked away.

'Had I known the sort of woman she was! But living as we do one never hears a thing.'

'You had read her books.'

'Ah, don't Mabel.'

'You liked her style.'

'I'm told she's a noted Vampire.'

'Whoever said so?'

'Some friend of hers—in Chelsea.'

'What do Vampires do?'

'What don't they!'

'Of course she was always bizarre.'

'Who could have foreseen her secret schemes?'

The Countess grew wan.

'Some of her literary secrets,' she said, 'were simply disgusting.'

'Dissolute!'

'She'd force them from printers'-devils.'

'Mabel.'

'Was her last remarkable?'

' . . . The Londonisms! The Cockney! The Slang!'

'She was a little too fond of her freedoms. . . .'

'Boys with their tutors. Girls with their mothers.'

'According to you, Charles,' Mrs. Collins said with umbrage, 'I might be unwilling to chaperon the girls instead of fretting my life out in a hole like Bovon!'

Mr. Collins quelled the rising storm.

'There, Isabel,' he said, with a glance towards the house, 'if I thought we'd be here another summer I'd get new sun-blinds, dear . . . but what's the good? Just leaving them as fixtures.'

⊘. III ⊘

'Q UEEN,' Daisy said to him one day. 'If a fair young gentleman
with large blue eyes should call and ask for Mrs. Collins you're
to say she has gone out. . . . But he'll find the Sisters in.
The Aunt and the Niece will be in the Yew-tree walk. With the
Mother.'

'Very good, miss.'

'And, Queen——!'

'Fie, miss.'

'Bashful?'

'I'm surprised.'

The Yew-tree walk, the cause of so much gloom, ran ring-like
about the house, to meet again before the drawing-room windows
above the main road, where a marble nymph with a worn flat face
dispensed water, rather meanly, out of a cornucopia into a trough
full of green scum.

On a garden swing near by the Countess was swaying fitfully
to and fro.

'Units, tens, hundreds, thousands. . . . Tens of thousands. . . .
Hundreds of thousands! *Units*——' she was murmuring cryptically
to herself with half rapt looks.

'Shall I push you, Mabs?'

'No. Ta.'

'To prevent the perspiration? . . .'

The Countess sighed.

'I'd sell my soul for an ice.'

'A strawberry. . . .'

'Or vanilla.'

'I told Queen we'd be in.'

'Where's mum?'

'Upstairs. Trying on. It's the armpits again. . . .'

'Goodness!'

'Do you know the new snook, Mab?'

'Is there one?'

'A beauty.'

'Not before Bianca.'

'It's a pity the child's so young. . . .'

'Carissima!'

'Her little amours. Tell me about them. . . . Has she many?'

'She makes new conquests from day to day.'

'Tell me things, Mabel.'

'What things?'

'All sorts of things.'

'Really!'

'In Italy have they Brussels sprouts—like we have?'

'In Italy they've everything,' the Countess replied.

'Can *he* speak English?'

'Fluently. Oh! . . .'

'Swear?'

'Certainly.'

'A foreign husband wouldn't suit me—not if he stayed abroad.'

'No?'

'Mabsey!'

'What is it?'

'Nothing. In the afternoon the yew-trees turn quite blue.'

'The quietness. . . . You can almost hear the clouds go by.'

'Let's all lie down on the grass as if we were dead.'

'It's too hot for rough games.'

'I shouldn't wonder if it rained.'

'Pitter-patter!'

'Every now and then she turns her great beseeching eyes at me and whispers "Aunt." Aunt! she says, come back with me to Rome. Come! And let me have no nonsense now. Oh, Blanche, I reply . . . it's my poverty, dear. But what can one do on a penny a week?'

'Papa, poor-old-gentleman, was saying how you should be going to school.'

'To school?'

'That was what he said.'

'He can't force me to if I choose to remain unlettered.'

'It's for the companionship there'd be.'

'Never.'

'School isn't so dreadful, Daisy.'

'Nothing would induce me to go.'

The Countess rocked drowsily.

'At York Hill,' she said, 'looking back on it all, I seem to have enjoyed everything. Even the walks! Oh. . . . Often we'd go round the city walls . . . or along the Ouse perhaps out to Bishopthorpe

and there we'd take the ferry. All we screaming girls and governesse
in mid-river. . . . Oh, good gracious!'

'I remember the letters you sent from there. And the complaints
that were in them!'

'And in the evening of course there'd be Preparation. . . . Oh—!
That was always a time for mischief. . . . One of us, Annie Oldport
perhaps ("Any-Old-Port" we used to call her), would give her next
neighbour a squeeze, with orders to pass it on. How we did thrill
when little Evelyn Rise, one of the new kids, took hold of the
Principal herself. "What are you doing to me, Evelyn?" "I'm
pinching you, Mrs. Whewell." "Are you indeed! Well, then——"
And she dealt her a blow on the ears before us all. . . . Oh, Evelyn
Rise! She was a little silly. . . . She hadn't any brains at all.'

'No brains, Mabsey?'

'No,' the Countess crooned. 'She hadn't any.'

'There! Queen's beckoning. . . .'

'Imbecile.'

'It may be him.'

'Who, him?'

'Your husband.'

'Hardly.'

'Your Excellency. . . .'

'Here I am.'

'There's a person at the gate.'

'Open it then.'

'I fear it's a trouble.'

'Why, who is it?'

'A stranger.'

'It's perhaps the Count.'

'It looks to be like a woman.'

'The Sisters have gone away. Queen. . . .'

'Does she refuse her name?'

'Quite.'

'A foreigner?'

'And *so* suspicious.'

'The Aunt's away from home. . . .'

'I've often heard of the Black Hand, your Excellence, and lately
I've noticed chalk-marks on the gate.'

'*Ah, Dio!*'

'Is there no gentleman, Queen?'

'No, miss.'

'It may be Jocasta Gisman.'

'What Gisman?'

'The accomplice of Bessie Bleek that suffocated seven little boys and girls and was tried and executed for doing so. . . .'

'Oh, heavens!'

'Jocasta got herself off at the last Assizes—there were extenuating circumstances the judge said—and so he forgave her.'

'*Bô!*'

'Mercy!'

'My dear, it's me,' Miss Dawkins said, peering through the fence.

'That is so,' she added, with an impetuous bound.

'Oh, the child!'

'Her aversion—I should say it's a flea,' Miss Dawkins commented, subsiding upon the swing.

The Countess pushed it.

'Of all the surprises!' she said.

'I refused to give my name because it makes me cry to say it. I break down. . . .'

'You've not found them then?'

'No, dear.'

'I imagined you in the I's.'

'I sail for India within a week.'

'The cathedral cities bring you north?'

'York and—they rhyme together . . . the first few letters. And I cling to every straw.'

'Courage.'

'Call me Ola.'

'Ola.'

'When I was in the Holy City I saw you one day.'

'When was it?'

'During Passion Week.'

'Were you with friends?'

'I scarcely knew anybody. I had an introduction to Countess Roderigos Samurez Dalmatia, but as I didn't like the look of her I didn't make use of it.'

'I've heard of her often,' the Countess said, 'through the Grittis.'

'Besides a letter to Princess Anna di Portici. . . .'

'Her house is occupied at present by the Marquesa Refoscosca!'

Inclinations

'And a card for Monsignor Ferrol.'

'Old *débauché*.'

'Well . . . and how's the pleasant husband?'

'Oio? He's in Orvieto still. It's the Vintage. . . .'

Miss Dawkins looked devout.

'In my opinion,' she said, 'Orvieto wine is superior to the best Castelli.'

'You should have a dozen, dear, of our Old-Old-Old—the *Certosa*, if I knew where it would find you.'

'I'm at the "Wheat Sheaf."'

'What?'

'Yes. I thought I'd repose myself there until I start.'

'If you've made no other plans you'll just stay and rest with us until your ship sails.'

'It's kind of you to ask me, but what will your kindred say?'

'My dear, they'll love to have you. And mum will tell you so herself. She's with the tailor now.'

'It's the armpits! . . .'

'This is my little sister.'

'And is that your babe?'

'Isn't she a darling!'

'Tell me, Contessa—have I changed since Greece?'

'I should say you're a little stouter.'

'Ireland makes one sloppy.'

'And I? . . .'

'My dear, you don't look fifteen.'

'She's seventeen,' Daisy said, 'or thereabouts. And the child will soon be two.'

'Were *I* to have a child I should be just like a lunatic,' Miss Dawkins declared.

'With your tender heart I wonder you don't marry.'

'Marriages are made in heaven, you know.'

'Let me find you someone!'

'You, my dear. . . . I've a sprig of the real Chinduai charm-flower from the Malay. I've only to wear it!'

'Why don't you then?'

'Voyages lose their illusions somehow. . . . They lose them. . . .'

'Take off your hat and really rest!'

'Shall I?'

'Do.'

'It's pretty peaceful here anyway,' Miss Dawkins said, with a sigh, her eyes riveted upon the cornucopia of the niggardly nymph.

'Is it iron?' she enquired.

'What, the water? It's always rather brown. . . .'

Miss Dawkins pressed a hand to her hip.

'It looks like a stream of brandy,' she said, going off into a laugh.

✠. IV ✠

THE 'intimate' dinner arranged by Mrs. Collins in honour of her daughter proved to be large one.

A dinner of twenty at a table to hold eighteen.

As course succeeded course came the recurring pressure of a forward footman's knee.

Half asleep holding a shell-shaped spoon Miss Dawkins explored a sauce-boat as though it had been an Orient liner.

'Yes, Mr. Collins.'

'No Mr. Collins.'

'Aha Mr. Collins.'

(*Thanks!*)

'Yes, God is Love, Mr. Collins, and I'm sure they couldn't help it!' she said at last.

'*Già! Già!*' the Countess struck in, allegro, across a bank of flowers.

'Well, here's health, old girl. The very best!'

'And success to you . . . and may the gods permit you to find them!'

'If you ask me, I think it silly to find people,' the Countess's former inamorato declared. 'I don't want to find anybody! . . .'

'No doubt you've tried clairvoyance?' the Member for Bovon asked.

'Indeed. And palmistry, and phrenology, and cards, and sand. . . .'

'Well?'

'Oh well . . .' Miss Dawkins said, 'I was warned I'd marry a septuagenarian within the forbidden degrees and never know it! . . . Helios, Mene, Tetragrammaton!'

'Have you looked by the Rhine at all?'

'Where haven't I?'

'Courage!' the Countess crooned.

'I've a presentiment they're in India. Somehow I connect my mother's fair hair with Bombay. . . .'

Mr. Collins raised his glass.

'Then here's to Bombay!'

'Oh, nectar, Mr. Collins! Show me the cork—I always like to see the cork—! And my dear father was like me there. "The cork, Ola," he'd say. "A bottle of wine is nothing without the cork." '

'The Count!' Napier Fairmile with generosity proposed.

The Countess shrugged her shoulders.

'I'd a letter from Italy this morning,' she said. 'It appears in Rome all the roads are up.'

'Up?'

'There's no getting by the Corso at all. Persons going to the Villa Borghese have to pass by the Via Babuino. Oh, good gracious! And my friend says the heat! It's a grill. Everyone is away still, of course, in villeggiatura. But even so! At the Baths Lucca she says she hears they're burning. . . .'

'Well, it was pretty warm, dear, in Greece,' Miss Dawkins said. 'The day of the accident I shall never forget how very hot it was!'

'At Salamis. . . .'

'Ah, don't.'

'Was there ever such a misfortune?'

'There seems to have been some inexcusable carelessness.'

'There are certain things we shall never know,' the Countess murmured, 'but I've sometimes thought that shot was aimed at me!'

Mrs. Collins shook her fan.

'The crazy people Mabel met in Greece!'

'Both Dorinda, Lady Gaiheart and Mrs. Arbanel are parting from their husbands, so I understand.'

'Poor Lady Dorinda! I fear she has fallen between two stools,' the Member for Bovon said.

'And a piano. And a waste-paper basket, if reports are true,' the Countess replied.

'Did you meet the Viviotts at all?'

'There was a Mrs. Viviott,' Miss Dawkins said—'a nervy, pretty thing. She and a Mrs. Erso-Ennis. . . . Inseparable. And always quarrelling.'

'They're reconciled again. And are gone to live at Birdingbury—quite near us—because it sounds Saxon. . . .'

'Really, Viola?'

Mrs. Newhouse, *née* Neffal, nodded.

'Anything *fair!*' the Countess crooned. 'Even a dancer.'

'La Tasajara? I saw her one night. I believe it was at Astrea Fortri's house in Pall Mall. . . .'

'Such a little starved-soul ghost-face. Like a little thin-pale-pinched St. John,' the Countess critically said.

'In the end she became indispensable to Miss O'Brookomore,' Miss Dawkins stated.

'With Gerald?'

'Oh, that woman.' Mrs. Collins shuddered.

'They tell me she's to chaperon an Eton boy straight to Tibet.' Miss Dawkins became abstracted.

'She evidently likes them young and fresh!' she observed.

The Countess started.

'What is it?' she asked.

'Come quickly!' her sister said. 'The child's in her cups.'

'Bianca is?'

'What have you been giving her?'

'It's only the little hiccoughs. . . .'

'Remember you weren't to come in till dessert.'

'During the Stratford mulberries papa said I might. You've had them.'

'Just look at her waist!'

'Now I'm here, mayn't I stop?'

'If you like to display your natural gifts,' Mr. Collins murmured, 'you may.'

'You can't do much on an empty stomach.'

'You can recite, I suppose,' the Countess said.

'Recite? It's always an effort for me to recite. . . . I feel struck dumb in society.'

'Remember Rome!' the Countess warned. 'We've no use for shyness there.'

'On his tombstone in the grass,
Record of him he was an ass,
He stretched out his neck and he flicked up his ears
And bid farewell to this valley of tears.

He lay himself down on a bed to die,
Right in a flower-bed himself he lay,
He stiffened his back and he whisked round his tail
And bid farewell to this earthly vale.

—On his tombstone in the grass,
Record of him he was an *Ass*.'

'Charming!'
'How very, very, very, very vulgar!' the Countess frowned.
'Was it the devil, my dear?'
Mrs. Collins rose.
'Gentlemen,' she murmured, '*à tout à l'heure*!'
'Let's all go into the garden, Mabsey.'
'There's no moon.'
'There are stars.'
Miss Dawkins peered out.
'It's dark and like Gethsemane,' she said.

[Chapter IV appears here as it stood in the edition of 1916.]
[Another, dated 'Rome, April 1925,' is now printed for the first
time.]

⬙. IV ⬙

THE 'intimate' dinner arranged by Mrs. Collins in honour of her
elder daughter promised to be a large one. Covers for twenty
guests, at a table to hold eighteen, insured nevertheless a touch of
welcome snugness. In the crepuscular double drawing-room, commanding the eternal moors,* county society, as it assembled, exchanged cheery greetings. It was indeed to all intents the Doncaster
Meeting lot.

Discanting away from homely topics, Sir Harry Ortop had just
seen a fox, it seemed, crossing Cockaway Common, while Miss
Rosalba Roggers had passed a traction-engine in the Rectory Lane.
'Horrid thing; but the Scarboro' road is really a disgrace,' she

* 'Finely situated on the edge of the moors.'—*Vide* Estate Agents'
Announcements.

pronounced, turning her attention to an angular beauty clad in sugary pink and a crown of birds' feathers.

Holding forth in a quizzical, hoarse-sweet voice, she was arraigning her husband with indescribable archness: 'He always gets into his carriage first, and then half shuts the door on you!'

Momentous in his butlerhood, Queen, supported by an extra footman, announced each new advent with an air of serene detachment.

Mr. Napier Fairmile, Miss Nespole——

Entering on the heels of the former inamorato of the Countess sailed a mite of a woman enveloped fancifully in a fairy-hued cashmere shawl. The Cyclopean chatelaine of Cupingforth Castle, and one of the wealthiest women in the Riding, she was held, by local opinion, to be eccentric for preferring to live all alone, which may possibly have had its dangers for a person of her condition and sex; nevertheless, on occasion, to convince an intrusive stranger she had a male in the house, she would discharge a cartridge out of window, and knot her hair across her chin in front in a thick cascade to imitate *a beard*.

Lady Watercarriage, The Hon. Viola West-Wind, Captain Margaret-Baker——

Quite re-vitalised, performing her duties, Mrs. Collins circulated smilingly here and there. Throwing a veil of glamour upon each guest, she had introduced Miss Dawkins twice as 'The Great Traveller.'

'I ain't going back to Australia not yet awhile. That is so!' Miss Dawkins declared, recognising across the Rector's shoulder in the damp-stained mezzotints upon the walls some views of popular thoroughfares her foot had trodden—Trafalgar Square, the Place de la Concorde, the Piazza Colonna, the Puerta del Sol. 'If I don't just spit at them!' she commented, idly opening and closing her fan.

The Farquhar of Farquhar, Mrs. Lampsacus of Gisborough Park——

Already a full quarter-of-an-hour late, they were yet not the last.

Masticating, chewing the air, Mr. Collins appeared to have become involved against his will in the esoteric confidences of a pair of expansive matrons: 'In York I saw some very pretty . . . I enquired the price. . . . Would you believe . . . *Need* I say I bought them!'

Delivered from their effusive unbosoming by The Farquhar of Farquhar, Mr. Collins turned away.

Advancing like some marvellous automaton, The Farquhar, known as 'Lulu' to all frequenters of the Turf, brought with him an atmosphere of one who had supplied a daughter, or at least a filly, to a Prince of the Blood. Excusing his wife Serafima (a woman for whom undergraduates had shot themselves), he enquired, with a leer, for 'la petite Comtesse.'

She was looking summery and semi-Southern in an imaginative gown in every shade of white.

'Precious darling! She's only eight months; it's a critical age,' she was exclaiming; apropos, doubtless, of her child.

Chatting to a bottle-nosed dowager in garnets and goose-flesh, she appeared indeed even prettier than she was.

Descending on her, The Farquhar was circumvented by Miss Viola West-Wind, a young girl of the County with a little Tatler-tainted face. She was supplying blocks of tickets, it seemed, for *The League of Patriots* ball . . . '*Fancy dress! Everyone to go as animals.*'

Dr. Dee——

It was as much as to say dinner; but an announcement, breathed from Queen, was to fill Mrs. Collins with apprehension.

'There's been a little catastrophe, 'm.'

'What, not . . . ? . . . ! . . . ? ?'

'To a cinder, 'm.'

In the long low-ceiled dining-room, all in the robust mid-Victorian style, the failure of an *entrée* seemed a more or less trivial thing; in such an environment it is the haunch that matters, it is the loin that tells. . . .

'Even so,' Mrs. Collins heard herself murmuring (almost callously) as she gained a chair on The Farquhar's arm—'Even so. The mornings begin to be frosty.'

A random word wafting the talk naturally to the subject of foxes.

'Count Pastorelli is fond of hunting?'

But Mrs. Collins presumed a prudent deafness.

Adorned with foreign spring flowers, smart jonquils and early tulips, the table-arrangements left nothing to be desired.

'I could never go to Russia; I turn quite green in the snow,' Miss Dawkins was telling Sir Harry Ortop of her Odyssey.

'I take it you've tried clairvoyance?' he asked.

'Indeed. And palmistry, and phrenology, and cards, and sand. . . .'
'Well?'

'Oh well . . .' she replied, regarding a scar on his third blue chin;
I was warned I'd marry a septuagenarian within the forbidden
degrees and never know it. . . . Helios, Mene, Tetragrammaton!'

'According to my experience, it's a mistake to find people. I don't
want to find anybody. . . .'

Miss Dawkins used her fan.

'I've a presentiment they're in India,' she said. 'Somehow I
connect my mother's fair hair with Bombay. . . .'

Owing to the absence of a guest, it was agreeable to find the
Countess in juxtaposition. With the Member for Bovon on her
right, her tongue tripped heedlessly from Mussolini to Miss Anne:
'Poor soul, she was interred in her lace, with a coin of Greece in
her mouth, and a flask of Chalkis wine, and a tambourine.'

A version of the Salamis affair that was new to Miss Dawkins.

'——!' she cooed, lifting her eyes in protest to a painting of Mary
Marchioness of Jamaica and Miss Elizabeth Cockduck, of the
school of Sir Thomas Lawrence.

' . . . just as in the Golden Age; and the moon that night was
extra enormous,' the Countess broke off her tale, arrested by a wail
of distress from the direction of the nursery.

The notion that Daisy might be diverting herself at Bianca's
expense caused the Countess to rise.

'Precious darling! *C'est l'heure du berger* for the child,' she exclaimed
directing her steps towards the door.

Traversing the hall, she perceived Daisy in the morning-room
examining the visitors' wraps; lifting the fabrics to her nose (much
as might a savage), she appeared to be voluptuously revelling in the
human odours they exhaled.

'Fie, girl! What are you up to?' her sister asked.

'The Farquhar of Farquhar's muffler, Mabel, has such a funny
smell, something between honey and flowers and new goloshes.'

'Oh!'

'And Lady Watercarriage's cloak! I don't know what it is, but
it's almost overpowering.'

'*Santo dio*,' the Countess breathed, lending an ear to the uproar
above.

Daisy displayed indifference.

'She's overturned her little Tamara again, I suppose, that's all! ! !

In the shadowy nursery, bafflingly lit by the dancing stars, some romantic fancy, it seemed, had disquieted the child.

On beholding both Mother and Aunt with a radiant light, she crowed, she smiled.

'Bianca . . . Mother's heaven.' The Countess hovered.

'From the look in those endless eyes of hers I shouldn't wonder if she hadn't seen the Owl that lived in an Oak.

> There was an owl lived in an oak—
> Whiskey, waskey, weedle;
> And every word he ever spoke
> Was fiddle, faddle, feedle.'

'Don't, Daisy!'

'Oh, she loves her little Buen Retiro (when it's dry); her own private corner in Bedfordshire.'

'Let her be,' the Countess answered, availing herself of the opportunity to deck with fresh white and red her constantly piquant face.

'Has anyone cast a doubt on your union, Mab, being legal?' Daisy asked, surveying with the eyes of a retired bus-horse her sister's comfortable back.

'Don't ask silly questions, Daisy, if you don't want foolish answers,' the Countess returned, following in the mirror her infant's yearning glance towards a bespangled negro doll, Topolobampa, Queen of the Sunset Isles.

' 'Cos I s'pose you know that's what Spicer's been tellin' George. . . . '

'George?'

'The extra footman.'

'Oh, good gracious!'

'Naturally he'll repeat it. It seems he goes all over Yorkshire waiting, but his home-proper is the Capital. Hull, he says, is a dreadful place. No season, and with the morals of Sodom. And, fancy, Mabsey, his brother is the boy from Willinghorse and Wheelits. . . .'

'What!'

'He aspires to the concert hall, he says, on account of his voice. So we made him sing and I must say his rendering of "Early one morning before the sun was dawning," won all our hearts.'

The Countess shrugged.

'She wants, I think, to take Topolobampa to bed!' she irrelevantly exclaimed.

'She'd rather take her old Aunt—eh, chubby?'

'Madonna, what next!'

'Her little body, Mab . . . it's as soft as satin! Oh, it's terrible!'

'——— . . . ?'

'How arch the puss looks in her little nainsook!'

'Mind and don't tease her, Daisy,' the Countess enjoined as she frisked away.

An odour of meat, wine and flowers hung erotically upon the dining-room air.

'I want my life to be purple———Never less,' Miss Dawkins was assuring the Member for Bovon.

Curtailing their colloquy, the Countess resumed her place.

At a delicate advantage with her newly-geraniumed lips, she was in a mood to enjoy herself.

'Look two to your right; who is she, Countess?' Miss Dawkins asked.

'An immense heiress! Miss Nespole of Cupingforth.'

'My dear, she's the most extraordinarily-looking woman that I ever set eyes on!' Miss Dawkins serenely stated.

Taking umbrage from her stare, Miss Nespole (with the eccentricity permitted to wealth) put out her tongue at her and drew it slowly in again.

'Oh, good gracious!' the Countess exclaimed, shooting a glance towards her father.

Listening to a description of Gleneagles from Lady Watercarriage, he appeared almost to have grown into his chair.

'And from there we went on to a ghastly hotel where *all the bedclothes are grey*,' the peeress fluted, fingering the pearls on her forward-falling shoulders.

The Countess raised a discreet glass of Perrier to her lips.

But as course succeeded course The Farquhar was moved to beg his hostess to allow her younger daughter to join them for the sugared kickshaws at dessert.

A lover of young girls and with a cult for them, he was believed to harbour Satanesque inclinations towards the Age of Candour.

'Just for a prune!' he insidiously pressed, brushing a napkin to the spreading branches of his moustache.

Miss Dawkins, meanwhile, was becoming blandly Bacchic.

'Oh, thank you, Member for Bovon, sweetest of men to me,' she exclaimed, addressing him champagnishly across her friend.

It was towards the close of dessert, just as the ladies were about to withdraw, that Daisy, clasping Bianca, chose to present herself. 'I brought Niece, too; I thought it would widen her little sphere,' she chirruped, coming blithely forward into the room.

She had a coronet-brooch on a well trussed-out blouse, and a strip of deep green velvet tied sparkishly below the middle.

Cautioned by her sister's eye, she turned towards the Rector, who was engaging to loan a stallion to a parishioner. 'A thing I seldom do,' he murmured, bestowing a frigid smile on the infant papist.

Refusing to wet her lips in some curaçoa, Daisy approached The Farquhar. Appreciating notice, his jolly ogle was a welcome stimulus.

A blood-orange? Grapes?... Preserve-of-ginger? She answered him whimsically by a little leap of the tongue.

'She's an amusette, Mrs. Collins, your wee girl; a sweet piece; ah, these golden blondes!... these golden blondes!'

'But why is that?' Mrs. Collins inattentively answered, watching her grandchild circulate, as might a fruit, from guest to guest along the table.

Flattered by The Farquhar's interest, Daisy was demonstrating already her social acumen.

'I've seen statues... often. Oh it's terrible?' she rapported, shooting back her hair.

'Little deviless! Where?' The Farquhar queried, stealing a surreptitious arm about her middle.

'Often on lawns, and in gardens, too; oh it's terrible!'

'... Indeed,' he murmured, alarmed by an ear-piercing shriek, attesting to Bianca's aversion to the Rector.

It was a warning, it seemed, to adjourn. Laughing hectically as she rose, Miss Dawkins had lost her bearings.

'Wherever was I last old October?' she exclaimed, waving the long lyric feathers of her fan in Sir Harry Ortop's face. 'I'll own I forget. ...'

⌀. V ⌀

'YES, dear, and so I'm really off—! And there were so many
things I had wanted to say to you. But somehow I've not
found time.'

'Stay another week,' the Countess begged.

'Call me Ola.'

'Ola.'

'Your father's a regular rake, darling.'

'What are you looking for?'

Miss Dawkins gazed with lethargy about the room.

Above the mantelpiece were engravings of Salammbô in Matho's
tent and Monna Vanna in Prinzivalle's, known collectively as *The
Fair Trespassers,* and published by the Fine Art Society 'as the Act
directs.'

'The Isol,' she said.

'I love your box, Ola.'

'It's not distinguished.'

'The labels it has on it!'

'Driving to and from a place in carnival time the students take
it away.'

'I envy you your independence.'

'I'd rather roost.'

'Domesticity tires one so. Every time I enter the nursery now it's
a strain. To-day was the climax. I've had many years' experience,
Mrs. Occles said to me, as a nurse, and I'll have no meddling. Very
well, I said to her, you can go! Oh, good gracious! Then at the
door, dear, I turned back, and I added, Am I the child's mother
or are you? That, she said, is no affair of mine! But as a rule I'm
accustomed to see the father! ! What do you mean by the father?
I said. But she wouldn't say.'

Miss Dawkins passed her parasol beneath the bed.

'My button boots——!'

'A child has so many little wants, nurse, I said. . . . It should have
proper attention. . . . *I* know what a child wants, she said (so rudely),
and when it wants it. . . . And there was Bianca looking at her with
her little eyes. . . .'

'Still, I wish the Count would come!'

'I hope he's not false to me,' the Countess quavered.

'Foreigners usually are, dear. They deceive their wives . .

'If I thought he was unworthy . . . ?'

'You're sure, of course, it's binding?'

'Binding?'

'No loopholes?'

The Countess tittered.

'None,' she said.

'Knowing the world as I know it,' Miss Dawkins sighed. 'Ah, well. . . .'

'There . . . the carriage is at the door.'

'I'm ready.'

'Have you a magazine or anything for the train?'

'I've a novel only—*Three Lilies and a Moustache*.'

'I like a love story,' the Countess confessed, 'so long as it isn't drivel.'

'Here is Daisy to say good-bye.'

'Where's Niece?'

'In France!' the Countess crooned.

'Isn't the child here?'

'Come and kiss me,' Miss Dawkins invited.

'I've such news!'

'What is it?'

'The Chase is let at last.'

'Goodness!'

'Madame La Chose is in the library now with a professional witness.'

'Well?'

'And they've taken the house. I was listening. . . . Madame La Chose said she was prepared to put her hand to an agreement for a ninety-nine years' lease without the farm. And it's to be pulled down immediately. . . . Oh, the rats!'

'Who's the witness?'

'General Lover.'

'My dear father once struck me for listening at a door,' Miss Dawkins observed.

'And as a reference she gives La Belle Zula. She says her diamonds *alone* are worth the half of Yorkshire.'

'Mum must be overjoyed.'

'She is.'

'One place or another!' Miss Dawkins drawled. 'Once the glamour's gone.'

'Oh, Ola!'

'I maintain there's little in it.'

'I long to go about!' Daisy murmured, pirouetting vainly before the glass.

'Jesu!'

'What openings have I here?'

'There's time enough yet,' the Countess assured.

'One sister should help another.'

'When you're eligible we'll see.'

'If I'm not eligible now I don't know who is!'

Miss Dawkins drew on nervously a glove.

'You've my address in Australia, Viscountess, all right?'

'Belleview—isn't it? Lake George?...'

'That's it, old girl.'

'I shan't forget.'

'I hope the sea'll be level, dear. I can't endure it rough.'

'Write soon.'

Miss Dawkins nodded.

'It depends on the Master Potter now. But if I ever should find my beloved ones in the East I'll be sure to let you know.'

✑. VI ✑

'HOW would Phryne Street appeal to you, Isabel?' Mr. Collins asked his wife as they sat one morning at breakfast.

'H-m, Charles!...'

'Maxilla Gardens then?'

'H-m!...'

'Or Gardingore Gate?'

'I want to live in Lisbon,' Mrs. Collins said.

Mr. Collins cast aside the paper.

'Where to bend our footsteps to is a problem and a tragedy,' he muttered.

' 'Vieto,' Daisy suggested in an insinuating voice.

'What would one do dumped down in Orvieto?' Mrs. Collins asked. 'It would be as bad as Bovon.'

'At 'Vieto it's all arcades, and right on top of a hill! You've to take the lift to get to it. It's the funicular for all....'

'If it's to be Italy I'd sooner it was Rome.'

Daisy showed fervour.

'Mab was telling me of the preserves they sell there. All speared on little sticks. At the street corners, she says, the sugar-plums sparkle in the sun just as if they were jewels. . . . I should like to see them. . . . And to taste them too,' she added.

'Papa has written to Mrs. Whewell already, alas,' Mrs. Collins said, 'to enquire whether she has a vacancy at all at York Hill.'

'If I studied anywhere it would be abroad.'

'Master your native tongue at any rate to begin with,' Mr. Collins advised.

'I don't care a jot for distinctions!'

'At your age,' Mrs. Collins asserted, 'I had a diploma.'

'For what?'

'As a nurse.'

'Nursing's different.'

'I assure you it's very disagreeable. Often it's by no means pleasant.'

'Why?'

'What I never could bear about nursing,' Mrs. Collins reminiscently said, 'was sponging the paint off the face of a corpse.'

'I would leave it.'

'Even a hospital nurse can go too far. . . .'

'Where's Mabel?'

'I heard her romping with Bianca as I passed her door.'

'She doesn't bother herself much of a morning about the time,' Mr. Collins complained.

'It's on account of prayers, Charles. Until they're over she naturally doesn't care to come down.'

Daisy sipped her tea.

'She did her best to convert me the other day,' she said. 'With one of her hatpins.'

'What?'

'. . . An old bead affair. Such a common thing. Not worth sixpence.'

'Mab did?'

'And she has her eye on Queen!'

'I fear the tap-room at the Mitre is as near as *he'll* ever get to Rome,' Mr. Collins remarked.

'S-s-s-h, Charles. Here he is!'

'Is the Signora stirring yet, Queen?' Daisy asked.

'She has just received her letters.'

'Is there anything for me?'

'No, Miss Daisy. There is not.'

'I was only wondering——'

Mrs. Collins raised a hand.

'Hark!'

'O-o-o-o-o-o-h!'

'It's her ladyship's cry.'

'You'd think Great Pan was dead again—at least.'

'Very likely it's her husband's handwriting that affects her,' Daisy said. 'Or it may be only a parcel! She's expecting, on approval, I know, some fancywork pyjamas.'

'O-o-o-o-o-o-h!'

'Breakfast!' Mrs. Collins carolled.

'He's coming. He'll be here to-day,' the Countess announced, elated. 'Oio will!'

'Positively?'

'So he says. Oh. . . . And in the night I was dreaming so vividly of a runaway hearse. . . . As it galloped by me one of the mourners gave me *such* a look. I can see it now.'

'Was it anybody, Mabsey?'

'How anybody?'

'Likely to suit me.'

'A husband!'

'Mabsey!'

'It was a young woman. . . . Poor soul!' the Countess replied.

'What does he say?'

'I'll read you out some of his letter. But it isn't all for you.'

'Is it in Italian, Mabel?'

'It's half and half.'

'Well?'

' "My dear dearly," he begins—he always calls me *dearly*!—"My own, own, little wife. My Mabina——" And then he simply says he's coming. "*Spero di venire Sabato verso la sera.* . . ." And he sends his filial love, with a kiss, to the English mother—à la mamma Inglese. . . .'

'Ah?'

'Yes. . . . And he intends to take her back with him to Italy, where he has prepared for her benefit a violet and rose salotto. . . .'

'Bless the boy!'

'And then there's a piece of scandal. Oh, good gracious! . . . He says poor Citta Zocchia isn't to wait on the Queen any more! She's done it *this* time. . . . And Dona Formosa de Bergère is to be married in Naples—*Naples*! Oh! Mercy!—to a certain Signor Popi! . . .'

'At what o'clock will he be here?'

'*Verso la sera!*'

'What time would that be?'

'Towards night.'

'How vague these husbands are.'

'He'll be here for dinner, I dare say,' Daisy said.

'We must try to consult his tastes.'

'Simple, nourishing things,' the Countess said, 'he likes. He has a passion for curry.'

Mrs. Collins concealed her anxiety.

'In Rome, for example, Mab,' she asked, 'what do they have when they dine?'

'It depends.'

'Besides curry . . .'

'Oh, well, perhaps some little round, pink, sweet potatoes they'll have, and some plain stewed rice. Or, again, very likely it'll be a piece of cold pickled pork. With olive oil and onions. . . . Whatever's seasonable they'll have. . . . And on Friday, of course, it's *fish*.'

'You'll need to tell all this presently to Mrs. Prixon,' Mrs. Collins said. 'And don't forget one thing. . . . You've to replace that Mrs. Occles.'

The Countess sighed.

'If I can't be suited with a Bovon girl or a York young thing I shall have an ayah and get the baby used to things. . . .'

Daisy raised a finger.

'There's her little howl!'

'Poor mite. She can't bear to be left alone with a strange Scotch woman. When Bianca takes an aversion! . . . She's a peculiar child in many ways.'

'Let me dress her to-day, Mabsey, may I—just for once?'

'Whatever for?'

'Leave her to me. I'll turn her out what's what!'

'Goodness!'

'I've my secrets. . . .'

'I dare say.'

'I can build her quite a presence. . . .'

'Mercy!'

'With a proper projection you wouldn't know the child.'

'I must fly to her.'

'And do, dear, finish your toilet,' Mrs. Collins beseeched.

'I trust her husband will confiscate all her trailing, bedraggled negligeys,' Mr. Collins said. 'Slovenly, nasty things!'

Daisy rippled.

'I wouldn't build upon it,' she replied. 'Her husband often doesn't get up himself in the morning at all.'

'Not?'

'He lies a-bed until all hours. He's a regular sluggard. The shadows will be falling sometimes, she says, and daylight almost gone, and you'll find him still between the sheets.'

'Fortunately Madame La Chose will be routing us out of this before very long.'

'Eh, Is-a-bel!'

Mrs. Collins glowed.

'And what heavenly happiness,' she remarked, 'to have no house-keeping—ever any more!'

'Let's all dance to-night.'

'My madcap fairy!'

'Her husband dances quite wonderfully, she says.'

'Who would there be to play?'

'Victoria owns a concertina.'

'That's no good.'

'Andy William has a banjo . . . . According to him, the banjo is the king of instruments.'

'Nonsense. I shouldn't think it was.'

'Oh! Mumsey! . . .'

'We might perhaps call in the Bovon string quartet,' Mrs. Collins said. 'Just for a serenade.'

'Oh! whatever has happened to Niece?'

'If she's peevish, poor mite,' the Countess said, returning, 'it's on account of the little mulligrubs. . . .'

'You can't expect a child of her years to be reasonable,' Mrs. Collins commented. 'It wouldn't be natural.'

'Let me have her,' Daisy begged.

'Don't Daisy!'

'What the child likes best is a reel of cotton. She'll play with that when she wouldn't play with me. . . .'

'*Pucci! Pucci!*' Mrs. Collins ventured.

'*Ecco la nonna! La buona cara nonna. . . .* Ah, *santo Dio!*'

'When I say *cui* to her, somehow she doesn't seem to like it!'

Daisy wagged her tongue.

'Lat-lat!'

'How can you be so gross!'

'Let me lull her. Shall I?'

'She's never quiet for you.'

'Wait till she hears the story of Blowzalinda and the Fairy Bee.'

'Oh, it's beyond the child. . . . She wouldn't know. Buz-z-z!'

'Isabel!'

'Yes, dear?'

'Cook requires her orders.'

'Where is she?'

'Behind the screen.'

'Help me, Mabel,' Mrs. Collins said.

'*Gigi! Ribu!* Oh, the clim pickle!'

'Give her to me Mabsey.'

'Yum. Yum.'

'Give her to me.'

'She lifts her little hand up to her little nose and then she presses it.'

'It's one of her little sarcasms, I expect.'

'She finds the world *so* weird.'

'Still it's good to know she has such an aunt. A good aunt, she says, is an untold blessing.'

'Help me!' Mrs. Collins implored.

'How?'

'Curry—and then? . . .'

The Countess turned her head.

'He can't endure a rabbit,' she remarked.

'My dear, no one proposes it!'

'Once the child and I were driving on the Via Appia Nuova when we saw a bunny peeping out of a tomb. Oh, such a darling! So I stopped the carriage and told Luigi, the footman, to run and dispatch it if he possibly could. He brought it back to me. . . . And a few hours afterwards it was bubbling away into a fine chicken broth. Oio had it all . . . . But hardly had it passed his lips when he was seized with the most violent spasms. Whereupon he turned round and accused me of attempting to do what certain Renaissance wives are supposed to have sometimes done. Oh! He was so cross. He was as cross as cross. . . . So don't let's have rabbit.'

'Polpettino, perhaps?'

'In olive oil; garnished "Mussolini-wise." '

'And then?'

'Oh, then, what he really adores, what he simply can't resist, is a fritter.'

'Cheese?'

'Any kind. And he loves a savoury! Zuccata, he likes. Zuccata, Zuccatini. . . . And he's fond of a soufflé too, so long as it isn't *led.*'

'Not to anticipate, my dear. . . .'

'Then——'

'Olive oil!'

'And then——'

'Then,' Mrs. Collins' voice rose as if inspired, 'then Côtelettes— à la Milanaise. . . .'

Caprice

I

THE clangour of bells grew insistent. In uncontrollable hilarity pealed S. Mary, contrasting clearly with the subdued carillon of S. Mark. From all sides, seldom in unison, resounded bells. S. Elizabeth and S. Sebastian, in Flower Street, seemed in loud dispute, while S. Ann 'on the Hill,' all hollow, cracked, consumptive, fretful, did nothing but complain. Near by S. Nicaise, half paralysed and impotent, feebly shook. Then, triumphant, in a hurricane of sound, S. Irene hushed them all.

It was Sunday again.

Up and up, and still up, the winding ways of the city the straggling townsfolk toiled.

Now and again a pilgrim perhaps would pause in the narrow lane behind the Deanery to rest.

Opening a black lacquer fan and setting the window of her bed-room wide, Miss Sarah Sinquier peered out.

The lane, very frequently, would prove interesting of an afternoon.

Across it, the Cathedral rose up before her with wizardry against the evening sky.

Miss Sinquier raised her eyes towards the twin grey spires, threw up her arms, and yawned.

From a pinnacle a devil with limbs entwined about some struggling crowned-coiffed prey grimaced.

> 'For I yearn for those kisses you gave me once
> On the steps by Bakerloo!

Miss Sinquier crooned caressingly, craning further out.

Under the little old lime trees by the Cathedral door lounged Lady Caroline Dempsey's Catholic footman.

Miss Sinquier considered him.

In her mind's eye she saw the impression her own conversion would make in the parochial world.

'Canon Sinquier's only daughter has gone over to Rome....' Or, 'Canon Sinquier's daughter has taken the veil.' Or, 'Miss Sinquier, having suffered untold persecution at the hands of her family, has been received into the Convent of the Holy Dove.'

Her eyes strayed leisurely from the powdered head and weeping shoulder-knots of Lady Caroline Dempsey's Catholic footman. The lack of movement was oppressive.

Why was not Miss Worrall in her customary collapse being borne senseless to her Gate in the Sacristan's arms? And why to-night were they not chaunting the Psalms?

Darting out her tongue, Miss Sinquier withdrew her head and resumed her book.

'Pouf!'

She shook her fan.

The room would soon be dark.

From the grey-toned walls, scriptural, a *Sasso Sassi* frowned.

'In all these fruitful years,' she read, 'the only time he is recorded to have smiled was when a great rat ran in and out among some statues. . . . *He* was the Ideal Hamlet. Morose of countenance, and cynical by nature, his outbursts, at times, would completely freeze the company.'

Miss Sinquier passed her finger-tips lightly across her hair.

'Somehow it makes no difference,' she murmured, turning towards a glass. To feign Ophelia—no matter what!

She pulled about her a lace Mantilla shawl.

It was as though it were Andalusia whenever she wrapped it on.

'*Doña Rosarda!*'

'*Fernan Perez? What do you want?*'

'*Ravishing Rosarda, I need you.*'

'*I am the wife of Don José Cuchillo—the Moor.*'

'*Doña Rosarda Castilda Cuchillo, I love you.*'

'*Sh—! My husband will be back directly.*'

Stretched at ease before a pier-glass, Miss Sinquier grew enthralled.

An hour sped by.

The room was almost dark.

Don José would wish his revenge.

'*Rosarda.*'

'*Fernando?*'

'*Ah-h!*'

Miss Sinquier got up.

She must compose herself for dinner—wash off the blood.

Poor Fernan!

She glanced about her, a trifle Spanish still.

From a clothes-peg something hanging seemed to implore.

'To see me? Why, bless you. Yes!'

With an impetuous, pretty gesture she flung it upon a couch.

'How do I like America?'

'I adore it . . . You see . . . I've lost my heart here—! Tell them so—oh! especially to the men. . . . Whereabouts was I born? In Westmorland; yes. *In England, Sir!* Inquisitive? Why not at all. I was born in the sleepy peaceful town of Applethorp (three p's), in the inmost heart—right in the very middle,' Miss Sinquier murmured, tucking a few wild flowers under her chin, 'of the *Close*.'

II

'SALLY,' her father said, 'I could not make out where you sat at Vespers, child, to-night.'

In the old-world Deanery drawing-room, coffee and liqueurs—a Sunday indulgence—had been brought in.

Miss Sinquier set down her cup.

Behind her, through the open windows, a riot of light leaves and creepers was swaying restively to and fro.

'I imagine the *Font* hid me,' she answered with a little laugh.

Canon Sinquier considered with an absent air an abundant-looking moon, then turned towards his wife.

'To-morrow, Mary,' he said, 'there's poor Mrs. Cushman again.'

At her cylinder-desk, between two flickering candles, Mrs. Sinquier, while her coffee grew cold, was opening her heart to a friend.

'Do, Mike, keep still,' she begged.

'Still?'

'Don't fidget. Don't talk.'

'Or dare to breathe,' her daughter added, taking up a Sunday journal and approaching nearer the light.

' "At the Olive Theatre," ' she read, ' "Mrs. Starcross will produce a new comedy, in the coming autumn, which promises to be of the highest interest." '

Her eyes kindled.

'O God!'

' "At the Kehama, Yvonde Yalta will be seen shortly in a Japanese piece, with singing mandarins, geishas, and old samurai—" '

'Dear Lord!'

' "Mr. and Mrs. Mary are said to be contemplating management again." '

'Heavens above!'

' "For the revival of *She Stoops to*——" '

Crescendo, across the mist-clad Close broke a sorrowful, sated voice.

'You can fasten the window, Sarah,' Canon Sinquier said.

'It's Miss Biggs!'

'Who could have taught her? How?' the Canon wondered.

Mrs. Sinquier laid down her pen.

'I dread her intimate dinner!' she said.

'Is it to be intimate?'

'Isn't she always? "Come round and see me soon, Miss Sarah, *there's* a dear, and let's be intimate!" '

'Really, Sally!'

'Sally can take off anyone.'

'It's vulgar, dear, to mimic.'

'Vulgar?'

'It isn't nice.'

'Many people do.'

'Only mountebanks.'

'I'd bear a good deal to be on the stage.'

Canon Sinquier closed his eyes.

'Recite, dear, something; soothe me,' he said.

'Of course, if you wish it.'

'Soothe me, Sally!'

'Something to obliterate the sermon?'

Miss Sinquier looked down at her feet. She had on black babouches all over little pearls with filigree butterflies that trembled above her toes.

> 'Since first I beheld you, Adèle,
>   While dancing the celinda,
> I have remained faithful to the thought of you;
>   My freedom has departed from me,

I care no longer for all other negresses;
I have no heart left for them;—
You have such grace and cunning;—
You are like the Congo serpent.'

Miss Sinquier paused.
'You need the proper movements ...' she explained. 'One
ought *really* to shake one's shanks!'
'Being a day of rest, my dear, we will dispense with it.'

'I love you too much, my beautiful one—
I am not able to help it.
My heart has become just like a grasshopper,—
It does nothing but leap.
I have never met any woman
Who has so beautiful a form as yours.
Your eyes flash flame;
Your body has enchained me captive.

Ah, you are like the rattlesnake
Who knows how to charm the little bird,
And who has a mouth ever ready for it
To serve it for a tomb.
I have never known any negress
Who could walk with such grace as you can,
Or who could make such beautiful gestures;
Your body is a beautiful doll.

When I cannot see you, Adèle,
I feel myself ready to die;
My life becomes like a candle
Which has almost burned itself out.
I cannot then find anything in the world
Which is able to give me pleasure:
I could well go down to the river
And throw myself in so that I might cease to suffer.

Tell me if you have a man,
And I will make an ouanga charm for him;
I will make him turn into a phantom,
If you will only take me for your husband.

I will not go to see you when you are cross:
Other women are mere trash to me;
I will make you very happy
And I will give you a beautiful Madras handkerchief.'

'Thank you, thank you, Sally.'

'It is from *Ozias Midwinter*.'

Mrs. Sinquier shuddered.

'Those scandalous topsies that entrap our missionaries!' she said.

'In Oshkosh——'

'Don't, Mike. The horrors that go on in certain places, I'm sure no one would believe.'

Miss Sinquier caressed lightly the Canon's cheek.

'Soothed?' she asked.

'. . . Fairly.'

'When I think of those coloured coons,' Mrs. Sinquier went on, 'at the Palace fête last year! Roaming all night in the Close. . . . And when I went to look out next day there stood an old mulattress holding up the baker's boy in the lane.'

'There, Mary!'

'Tired, dear?'

'Sunday's always a strain.'

'For you, alas! it's bound to be.'

'There were the Catechetical Classes to-day.'

'Very soon now Sally will learn to relieve you.'

Miss Sinquier threw up her eyes.

'I?' she wondered.

'Next Sunday; it's time you should begin.'

'Between now and *that*,' Miss Sinquier reflected, shortly afterwards, on her way upstairs, 'I shall most certainly be in town.'

'O London—City of Love!' she warbled softly as she locked her door.

⟺ III ⟺

IN the gazebo at the extremity of the garden, by the new parterre, Miss Sinquier, in a morning wrapper, was waiting for the post.

Through the trellis chinks, semi-circular, showed the Close, with its plentiful, seasoned timber and sedate, tall house, a stimulating sequence, architecturally, of whitewash, stone and brick.

Miss Sinquier stirred impatiently.

Wretch!—to deliver at the Palace before the Deanery, when the Deanery was as near!

'Shower down over there, O Lord, ten thousand fearsome bills,' extemporaneously she prayed, 'and spare them not at all. Amen.'

Hierarchic hands shot upwards.

Dull skies.

She waited.

Through the Palace gates, at length, the fellow lurched, sorting as he came.

'Dolt!'

Her eyes devoured his bag.

Coiled round and round like some sleek snake her future slumbered in it.

Husband; lovers ... little lives, perhaps—yet to be ... besides voyages, bouquets, diamonds, chocolates, duels, casinos! ...

She shivered.

'Anything for me, Hodge, to-day,' she enquired, 'by chance?'

'A fine morning, miss.'

'Unusually.'

It had come ...

That large mauve envelope, with the wild hand-writing and the haunting scent was from *her*.

As she whisked away her heart throbbed fast. Through the light spring foliage she could see her father, with folded hands, pacing meditatively to and fro before the front of the house.

'Humbug!' she murmured, darting down a gravel path towards the tradesmen's door.

Regaining her room, she promptly undid the seal.

> 'Panvale Priory, Shaftesbury Avenue,
> 'London, W.

'Mrs. Albert Bromley presents her compliments to Miss S. Sinquier and will be pleased to offer her her experience and advice on Thursday morning next at the hour Miss Sinquier names.

'*P.S.* Mrs. Bromley already feels a parent's sympathetic interest in Miss Sinquier. Is she dark or fair? ... Does she shape for Lady Macbeth or is she a Lady Teazle?'

'Both!' Miss Sinquier gurgled, turning a deft somersault before the glass.

To keep the appointment, without being rushed, she would be obliged to set out, essentially baggageless, to-night—a few requisites merely, looped together and concealed beneath her dress, would be the utmost she could manage.

'A lump here and a lump there!' she breathed' 'and I can unburden myself in the train.'

'Okh!'

She peeped within her purse.

. . . And there was Godmother's chain that she would sell!

It should bring grist; perhaps close on a thousand pounds. Misericordia: to be compelled to part with it!

Opening a levant-covered box, she drew out a long flat tray.

Adorable pearls!

How clearly now they brought her Godmother to mind . . . a little old body . . . with improbable cherry-cheeks and excrescent upper lip, with always the miniatures of her three deceased husbands clinging about one arm. . . . 'Aren't they pleasant?' she would say proudly every now and then. . . . What talks they had had; and sometimes of an evening through the mauve moonlight they would strut together.

Ah! She had been almost ugly then; clumsy, gawky, *gauche* . . .

Now that she was leaving Applethorp, for ever perhaps, how dormant impressions revived!

The Saunders' Fifeshire bull, one New Year's night, ravaging the Close, driven frantic by the pealings of the bells. The time poor Dixon got drowned—at a Flower Show, a curate's eyes—a German governess's walk—a mould of calves'-foot jelly she had let fall in the Cathedral once, on her way somewhere——

She replaced ruefully her pearls.

What else?

Her artist fingers hovered.

Mere bridesmaid's rubbish; such frightful frippery.

She turned her thoughts to the room.

Over the bed, an antique bush-knife of barbaric shape, supposed to have been *Abraham's*, was quite a collector's piece.

It might be offered to some museum perhaps. The Nation ought to have it . . .

She sighed shortly.

And downstairs in the butler's room there were possessions of hers, besides. What of those Apostle spoons, and the two-pronged forks, and the chased tureen?

Leonard frequently had said it took the best part of a day to polish her plate alone.

And to go away and leave it all!

'O God, help me, Dear,' she prayed. 'This little once, O Lord! For Thou knowest my rights ...'

She waited.

Why did not an angel with a basket of silver appear?

'Oh, well ...'

Gripper, no doubt, would suspect something odd if she asked for her things 'to play with' for an hour. ...

A more satisfactory scheme would be to swoop into the pantry, on her way to the station, and to take them away for herself.

She had only to say, 'Make haste with them crevets,' for Gripper to go off in a huff, and Leonard, should he be there, would be almost sure to follow.

Men were so touchy.

Hush!

Her mother's voice came drifting from below.

'Kate! Kate! Kate! Kate!'

She listened.

'Have the chintz curtains in the white room folded,' she could hear her say, 'and remember what I said about the carpet ...'

Dear soul!

Miss Sinquier sniffed.

Was it a tear?

Dear soul! Dear souls! ...

'Never mind,' she murmured, 'they shall have *sofas* in their box on the night of my début ...'

She consoled herself with the thought.

 IV

'MAKE haste now with them crevets!'
'For shame, miss. I shall go straight to the Dean!'
'Cr-r-r-revets!' Miss Sinquier called.
Clad in full black, with a dark felt *chapeau de résistance* and

a long Lancastrian shawl, she felt herself no mean match for any man.

'C-r-r-r,' she growled, throwing back her shawl.

After all, were not the things her own?

She laughed gaily.

'If dear Mrs. Bromley could see me,' she beamed, tucking dexterously away an apostolic spoon.

'St. Matthew—St. Mark—St. Luke—St. John—
    These sprang into bed with their breeches on.'

At a friendly frolic once a Candidate for Orders had waltzed her about to that.

She recalled Fräulein's erudite query still:

'Pray, why did they not take off all like the others!'

And the young man's significant reasons and elaborate suppositions, and Fräulein's creamy tone as she said she *quite* understood.

Miss Sinquier turned a key.

S-s-s-st!

'Butter fingers.'

In a moment she must run.

Terrible to forgo her great tureen . . .

She poked it. What magnitude to be sure!

Impossible to tow it along.

Under the circumstances, why not take something less cumbersome instead?

There were the Caroline sauce-boats, or the best Anne teapot, hardly if ever in use.

Her ideas raced on.

And who could resist those gorgeous grapes, for the train?

Together with their dish . . .

'Tudor, "Harry"!' she breathed.

From the corridor came a hum of voices.

Flinging her wrap about her, Miss Sinquier slipped quietly out by way of a small room, where the Canon preserved his lawn.

Outside, the moon was already up—a full moon, high and white, a wisp of cloud stretched across it like a blindfold face.

Oh Fame, dear!

She put up her face.

Across the garden the Cathedral loomed out of a mist as white as milk.

The damp, she reasoned, alone would justify her flight!

She shivered.

How sombre it looked in the lane.

There were roughs there frequently too.

'Villains . . .'

She felt fearfully her pearls.

After all, the initial step in any career was usually reckoned the worst.

Some day, at the King's, or the Canary, or the Olive, in the warmth of a stage dressing-room, she would be amused, perhaps, and say:

'I left my father's roof, sir, one sweet spring night—without so much as a word!'

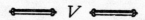

RAINDROPS were falling although the sky was visibly brightening as Miss Sinquier, tired, and a little uncertain, passed through the main exit of Euston terminus.

She wavered a moment upon the kerb.

On a hoarding, as if to welcome her, a dramatic poster of Fan Fisher unexpectedly warmed her heart; it was almost like being met . . .

There stood Fan, at concert pitch, as Masha Olgaruski in *The Spy*.

Miss Sinquier tingled.

A thing like that was enough to give one wings for a week.

She set off briskly, already largely braced.

Before meeting Mrs. Bromley on the morrow much would have to be done.

There was the difficulty of lodgment to consider.

Whenever she had been in the metropolis before she had stayed at *Millars* in Eric Street, overlooking Percy Place; because Mr. Millar had formerly been employed at the Deanery, and had, moreover, married their cook. . . .

But before going anywhere she must acquire a trunk.

Even Church dignitaries had been known to be refused accommodation on arriving at a strange hotel with nothing but themselves.

She threw a glance upwards towards a clock.

It was early yet!

All the wonderful day stretched before her, and in the evening she would take a ticket perhaps for some light vaudeville or new revue.

She studied the pleasure announcements on the motor-buses as they swayed along.

Stella Starcross—The Lady from the Sea—This evening, Betty Buttermilk and Co.—Rose Tournesol—Mr. and Mrs. Mary's Season: The Carmelite—The Shop Boy—Clemenza di Tito. To-night!

Miss Sinquier blinked.

Meanwhile the family teapot was becoming a bore.

Until the shops should open up it might be well to take a taxi and rest in the Park for an hour.

The weather was clearing fast; the day showed signs of heat.

She hailed a passing cab.

'Hyde Park,' she murmured, climbing slowly in.

She thrilled.

Upon the floor and over the cushions of the cab were sprinkled fresh confetti—turquoise, pink and violet, gold and green.

She took up some.

As a mascot, she reflected, it would be equivalent to a cinqfoil of clover, or a tuft of edelweiss, or a twist of hangman's rope.

⋈━━⟹ VI ⟸━━⋉

FROM the big hotel in the vicinity of the Marble Arch, to the consulting rooms in Shaftesbury Avenue of Mrs. Albert Bromley, it appeared, on enquiry, that the distance might easily be accomplished in less than forty minutes.

Miss Sinquier, nevertheless, decided to allow herself more.

Garmented charmingly in a cornflower-blue frock with a black gauze turban trimmed with a forest of tinted leaves, she lingered, uplifted by her appearance, before the glass.

The sober turban, no doubt, would suggest to Mrs. Bromley Macbeth—the forest-scene, and the blue, she murmured, 'might be anything.'

It occurred to her as she left her room that Mr. Bromley might quite conceivably be there to assist his wife.

'Odious if he is,' she decided, passing gaily out into the street.

It was just the morning for a walk. A pale silvery light spread over Oxford Street, while above the shop fronts the sun flashed down upon a sea of brass-tipped masts, from whence trade flags trembled in a vagrant breeze. Rejoicing in her independence, and in the exhilarating brightness of the day, Miss Sinquier sailed along. The ordeal of a first meeting with a distinguished dramatic expert diminished at every step. She could conjecture with assurance, almost, upon their ultimate mutual understanding. But before expressing any opinion, Mrs. Bromley, no doubt, would require to test her voice; perhaps, also, expect her to dance and declaim.

Miss Sinquier thrust out her lips.

'Not before Albert! Or at any rate not yet . . .' she muttered.

She wondered what she knew.

There was the thing from *Rizzio*. The Mistress of the Robes' lament upon her vanished youth, on discovering a mirror unexpectedly, one morning, at Holyrood, outside Queen Mary's door.

Diamond, Lady Drummond, bearing the Queen a cap, raps, smiles, listens . . . smiles, raps again, puts out her leg and rustles . . . giggles, ventures to drop a ring, effusive facial play and sundry tentative noises, when, catching sight of her reflection, she starts back with:

'O obnoxious old age! O hideous horror! O youthful years all gone! O childhood spent! Decrepitude at hand . . . Infirmities drawing near. . . .'

Interrupted by Mary's hearty laugh.

'Yes,' Miss Sinquier decided, crossing into Regent Street, 'should Mrs. Bromley bid me declaim, I'll do Diamond.'

Her eyes brightened.

How prettily the street swerved.

As a rule, great thoroughfares were free from tricks.

She sauntered.

'A picture-palace.'

And just beyond were the playhouses themselves.

Theatreland!

Shaftesbury Avenue with its slightly foreign aspect stretched before her.

With a springing foot she turned up it.

Oh, those fragile glass façades with the players' names suspended!

There was the new Merrymount Theatre with its roguish Amorini supporting torches and smiling down over gay flower-boxes on to the passers-by.

And beyond, where the burgeoning trees began, must be Panvale Priory itself.

Miss Sinquier surveyed it.

It looked to be public offices. . . .

On the mat, dressed in a violet riband, with its paw in the air, lay a great sly, black, joyous cat.

'Toms!'

She scratched it.

Could it be Mrs. Bromley's?

In the threshold, here and there, were small brass plates, that brought to mind somehow memorial tablets to departed virtue at home.

Miss Sinquier studied the inscriptions.

Ah, there showed hers!

'M-m-m!' she murmured, commencing to climb.

Under the skylight a caged bird was singing shrilly.

As much to listen as to brush something to her cheeks, Miss Sinquier paused.

If a microscopic mirror could be relied upon she had seldom looked so well.

Scrambling up the remaining stairs with alacrity, she knocked.

A maid with her head wreathed in curl-papers answered the door, surveying the visitor first through a muslin blind.

Miss Sinquier pulled out a card.

'Is Mrs. Bromley in?' she asked.

The woman gazed at her feet.

'Mrs. Bromley's gone!' she replied.

'I suppose she won't be long?'

'She's in Elysium.'

'At the——?'

'Poor Mrs. Bromley's dead.'

'Mrs. Bromley *dead* . . . ?'

'Poor Mrs. Bromley died last night.'

Miss Sinquier staggered.

'Impossible!'

'Perhaps you'd care to come in and sit down?'

Miss Sinquier hesitated.

'No, no, not if . . . *is*? Oh!' she stammered.

'She was taken quite of a sudden.'

'One can hardly yet believe it?'

'She'll be a loss to her world, alas, poor Betty Bromley will!'

Miss Sinquier swallowed.

'I should like to attend the funeral,' she said.

'There's no funeral.'

'No funeral?'

'No invitations, that is.'

Miss Sinquier turned away.

The very ground under her seemed to slide . . .

Mrs. Bromley dead!

Why, the ink of her friendly note seemed scarcely dry!

On the pavement once more she halted to collect herself.

Who was there left at all?

At Croydon there was a conservatoire, of course—

She felt a little guilty at the rapidity of the idea.

Wool-gathering, she breasted the traffic in St. Martin's Lane.

She would turn over the situation presently more easily in the Park.

Instinctively, she stopped to examine a portrait of Yvonde Yalta in the open vestibule of the Dream.

She devoured it: Really . . . ? Really? She resembled more some Girton guy than a great coquette.

All down the street indeed, at the theatre doors, were studies of artists, scenes from current plays.

By the time she found herself back in Piccadilly Circus again Miss Sinquier was nearly fainting from inanition.

She peered around.

In Regent Street, she reflected, almost certainly, there must be some nice tea-shop, some cool creamery . . .

How did this do?

'The Café Royal!'

Miss Sinquier fluttered in.

By the door, the tables all proved to be taken.

Such a noise!

Everyone seemed to be chattering, smoking, lunching, casting dice, or playing dominoes.

She advanced slowly through a veil of opal mist, feeling her way from side to side with her parasol.

It was like penetrating deeper and deeper into a bath.

She put out her hand in a swimming, groping gesture, twirling as she did so, accidentally, an old gentleman's moustache.

Thank heaven! There, by that pillar, was a vacant place.

She sank down on to the edge of a crowded couch, as in a dream.

The tall mirrors that graced the walls told her she was tired.

'Bring me some China tea,' she murmured to a passing waiter, 'and a bun with currants in it.'

She leaned back.

The realisation of her absolute loneliness overcame her suddenly.

Poor Mrs. Bromley, poor kindly little soul!

The tears sprang to her eyes.

It would have been a relief to have blotted her face against some neighbouring blouse or waistcoat and to have had a hearty cry.

'Excuse me, may I ask you to be so good——'

Just before her on the table was a stand for matches.

With a mournful glance she slid the apparatus from her in the direction of an adolescent of a sympathetic, somewhat sentimental, appearance, who, despite emphatic whiskers, had the air of a wildly pretty girl.

To have cherished such a one as a brother! Miss Sinquier reflected, as the waiter brought her tea.

While consuming it she studied the young man's chiselled profile from the corners of her eyes.

Supporting his chin upon the crook of a cane, he was listening, as if enthralled, to a large florid man, who, the centre of a small rapt group, was relating in a high-pitched, musical voice, how 'Poor dear Chaliapin one day had asked for Kvass and was given Bass. And that reminds me,' the speaker said, giving the table an impressive thump, 'of the time when Anna Held—let go.'

Miss Sinquier glowed.

Here were stage folk, artists, singers . . . that white thin girl in the shaggy hat opposite was without doubt a temperament akin.

She felt drawn to speak.

'Can you tell me how I should go to Croydon?' she asked.

The words came slowly, sadly almost . . .

'To Croydon?'

'You can't go to Croydon.'

'Why not?'

The young man of the whiskers looked amused.

'When we all go to Spain to visit Velasquez——'

'Goya——!'

'Velasquez!'

'Goya! Goya! Goya!'

'. . . We'll set you on your way.'

'Goose!'

'One goes to Croydon best by Underground,' the pale-looking girl remarked.

Miss Sinquier winced.

'Underground!'

Her lip quivered.

'Is there anything the matter?'

'Only——'

Folding her arms upon the table she sank despairingly forward and burst into tears.

'Poor Mrs. Bromley!' she sobbed.

'In the name of *Fortune* . . .' The pale young woman wondered.

'What has Serephine said? What has Mrs. Sixsmith done?'

'Monstrous tease!'

The stout man wagged a finger.

'Wicked!' he commented.

The lady addressed kindled.

'I merely advised her to go Underground. By tube.'

'O God.' Miss Sinquier shook.

'It's hysteria. Poor thing, you can see she's overwrought.'

'Give her a *fine*; *un bon petit cognac*.'

'Waiter!'

'Garçon.'

'Never mind, Precious,' the fat man crooned. 'You shall ride in a comfy taxi-cab with me.'

'No; indeed she shan't,' Mrs. Sixsmith snapped. 'You may rely on me, Ernest, for that!'

Rejecting the proffered spirits with a gesture, Miss Sinquier controlled her grief.

'It's not *often* I'm so silly,' she said.

'There, there!'

'Excuse this exhibition. . . .'

Mrs. Sixsmith squeezed her hand.

'My poor child,' she said, 'I fear you've had a shock.'

'It's over now.'

'I'm so glad.'

'You've been very good.'

'Not at all. You interest me.'

'Why?'

'Why? Why? . . . I'm sure I can't say *why*! But directly I saw you . . .'

'It's simply wonderful.'

'You marched in here for all the world like some great coquette.'

'You mean the Father Christmas at the door?'

'Tell me what had happened.'

In a few words Miss Sinquier recounted her tale.

'My dear,' Mrs. Sixsmith said, 'I shouldn't think of it again. I expect this Mrs. Bromley was nothing but an old procuress.'

'A procuress?'

'A stage procuress.'

'How dreadful it sounds.'

'Have you no artistic connections in town *at all*?'

'Not really . . .'

'Then here, close at hand . . . sitting with you and me,' she informally presented, 'is Mr. Ernest Stubbs, whose wild wanderings in the Gog-magog hills in sight of Cambridge, orchestrally described, recently thrilled us all. Next to him—tuning his locks and twisting his cane—you'll notice Mr. Harold Weathercock, an exponent of calf-love parts at the Dream. And, beyond, blackening her nose with a cigarette, sprawls the most resigned of women—Miss Whipsina Peters, a daughter of the famous flagellist—and a coryphée herself.'

Miss Peters nodded listlessly.

'Toodle-doo,' she murmured.

'As a coryphée, I suppose her diamonds are a sight?'

'A sight!' Mrs. Sixsmith closed her eyes. 'They're all laid up in lavender, I fear.'

'In lavender?'

'Pledged.'

'Oh, poor soul!'

'Just now you spoke of a necklace of your own . . . a pearl rope, or something, that you wish to sell.'

'Unhappily I'm obliged.'

'I've a notion I might be of service in the matter.'

'How?'

'Through an old banker-friend of mine—Sir Oliver Dawtry. Down Hatton Garden way and throughout the City he has enormous interests. And I should say *he* could place your pearls—if anyone could!'

'Do you think he'd be bothered?'

'That I'll undertake.'

'Does he live in town?'

'In a sense: he has a large house in the Poultry.'

'Of course I should be willing to show him my pearls.'

'Sir Oliver is offering me a little dinner to-night. And I should be happy for you to join us.'

'Oh? . . . I think I scarcely dare!'

'Rubbish! One must be bolder than that if one means to get on!'

'Tell me where you dine.'

'At Angrezini's. It's a little restaurant . . . with a nigger band. And we sing between the courses.'

'Will Mr. Sixsmith be there?'

'My dear, Mr. Sixsmith and I don't live together any more.'

'Forgive me.'

'That's all right. . . .'

Miss Sinquier's eyes grew dim.

'Used he to act?' she asked.

'*Act!*'

'I seem to have heard of him.'

Mrs. Sixsmith looked away.

'Are you coming, Serephine?' her neighbour asked.

'Are you all off?'

The florid man nodded impressively.

'Yes . . . we're going now . . .' he said.

'What are Whipsina's plans?'

Miss Peters leaned closely forward over several pairs of knees.

'I shall stay where I am,' she murmured, 'and perhaps take a nap. There's sure to be a tremendous exodus directly.'

Miss Sinquier rose. 'I've some shopping,' she said, 'to do.'

'Until this evening, then.'

'At what o'clock?'

'At eight.'

'On arrival, am I to ask for you?'

'Better ask for Sir Oliver—one never knows. . . . And I might perhaps happen to be late.'

'But you won't be? You mustn't. . . .'

'I will explain whatever's needful by telephone to Sir Oliver now. And during dinner,' Mrs. Sixsmith bubbled, 'while the old gentleman picks a quail, we will see what we can do!'

'How can I express my thanks . . . ?'

'The question of commission,' Mrs. Sixsmith murmured with a slight smile, 'we will discuss more fully later on.'

⇨ VII ⇦

SUBJECTIVE. On a rack in the loom. Powerless oneself to grasp the design. Operated on by others. At the mercy of chance fingers, unskilled fingers, tender fingers; nails of all sorts. Unable to progress alone. Finding fulfilment through friction and because of friction. Stung into sentiency gradually, bit by bit—a toe at a time.

After all there was a *zest* in it; and who should blame the raw material should an accident occur by the way. . . .

Careless of an intriguing world about her, Miss Sinquier left her hotel, just so as to arrive at Angrezini's last.

'For Thou knowest well my safety is in *Thee*,' she murmured to herself mazily as her taxi skirted the Park.

Having disposed of her Anne teapot for close on seventy pounds, she was looking more radiant than ever in a frail Byzantine tunic that had cost her fifty guineas.

'Thy Sally's safety,' she repeated, absently scanning the Park.

Through the shadowy palings it slipped away, abundantly dotted with lovers. Some were plighting themselves on little chairs, others preferred the green ground: and beyond them, behind the whispering trees, the sky gleamed pale and luminous as church glass.

Glory to have a lover too, she reflected, and to stroll leisurely-united through the evening streets, between an avenue of sparkling lamps. . . .

Her thoughts turned back to the young man in the Café Royal.

'Of all the bonny loves!' she breathed, as her taxi stopped.

'Angrezini!'

A sturdy negro helped her out.

'For Thou knowest very well——' her lips moved faintly.

The swinging doors whirled her in.

She found herself directly in a small bemirrored room with a hatch on one side of it, in which an old woman in a voluminous cap was serenely knitting.

Behind her dangled furs and wraps that scintillated or made pools of heavy shade as they caught or missed the light.

Relinquishing her own strip of tulle, Miss Sinquier turned about her.

Through a glass door she could make out Mrs. Sixsmith herself, seated in a cosy red-walled sitting-room beyond.

She was looking staid as a porcelain goddess in a garment of trailing white with a minute griffin-eared dog peeping out its sheeny paws and head wakefully from beneath her train.

At sight of her guest Mrs. Sixsmith smiled and rose.

'Sir Oliver hasn't yet come!' she said, imprinting on Miss Sinquier's youthful cheek a salute of *hospitality*.

'He hasn't? And I made sure I should be last.'

Mrs. Sixsmith consulted the time.

'From the Bank to the Poultry, and from the Poultry on . . . just consider," she calculated, subsiding leisurely with Miss Sinquier upon a spindle-legged settee.

'You telephoned?'

'I told him all your story.'

'Well?'

'He has promised me to do his utmost.'

'He will?'

'You should have heard us. This Mrs. Bromley, he pretends . . . Oh, well . . . one must not be too harsh on the dead.'

'Poor little woman.'

'Let me admire your frock.'

'You like it?'

'I never saw anything so waggish.'

'No, no, *please*——!'

'Tell me where they are!'

'What?'

'I'm looking for your pearls.'

'They're in my hair.'

'Show me.'

'I'll miss them terribly.'

'Incline!'

'How?'

'More.'

'I can't!'

'They're very nice. But bear in mind one thing——'

'Yes?'

Mrs. Sixsmith slipped an encircling arm about Miss Sinquier's waist.

'Always remember,' she said, 'to a City man, twelve hundred sounds less than a thousand. Just as a year, to you and me, sounds more than eighteen months!'

'I'll not forget.'

'Here is Sir Oliver now.'

Through the swing doors an elderly man with a ruddy, rather apoplectic face, and close-set opaque eyes, precipitantly advanced.

'Ladies!'

' "Ladies" indeed, Sir Oliver.'

'As if——'

'Monster.'

'Excuse me, Serephine.'

'Your pardon rests with Miss Sinquier,' Mrs. Sixsmith said with melodious inflections as she showed the way towards the restaurant. 'Address your petitions to her.'

In the crescent-shaped, cedar-walled, cedar-beamed room, a table at a confidential angle had been reserved.

'There's a big gathering here to-night,' Sir Oliver observed, glancing round him, a 'board-room' mask clinging to him still.

Miss Sinquier looked intellectual.

'I find it hot!' she said.

'You do.'

'I find London really very hot. . . . It's after the north, I suppose. In the north it's always much cooler.'

'Are you from the north?'

'Yes, indeed she is,' Mrs. Sixsmith chimed in. 'And so am *I*,' she said. 'Two north-country girls!' she added gaily.

Sir Oliver spread sentimentally his feet.

'The swans at Blenheim; the peacocks at Warwick!' he sighed.

'What do you mean, Sir Oliver?'

'Intimate souvenirs. . . .'

'I should say so. . . . Swans and peacocks! I wonder you're prepared to admit it.'

'Admit it?'

'Outside of *Confessions*, Sir Oliver.'

Miss Sinquier raised a hurried hand to her glass.

'No, no, no, no, no, no wine!' she exclaimed. 'Something milky . . .'

'Fiddlesticks! Our first little dinner.'

'Oh, Sir Oliver!'

'And not, I trust, our last!'

'I enjoy it so much—going out.'

Mrs. Sixsmith slapped her little dog smartly upon the eyes with her fan.

'Couche-toi,' she admonished.

'What can fret her?'

'She fancies she sees Paul.'

'Worthless fellow!' Sir Oliver snapped.

'I was his rib, Sir Oliver.'

'Forget it.'

'I can't forget it.'

'J-j-j——'

'Only this afternoon I ran right into him—it was just outside the Café Royal . . .'

'Scamp.'

'He looked superb. Oh, so smart; spats, speckled trousers, the rest all deep indigo. Rather Russian.'

'Who?'

'My actor-husband, Paul. There. One has only to speak his name for Juno to jerk her tail.'

'With whom is he at present?'

'With Sydney Iphis.'

'We went last night to see Mrs. Starcross,' Sir Oliver said.

'She's no draw.'

'I long to see her,' Miss Sinquier breathed.

'I understand, my dear young lady, you've an itch for the footlights yourself.'

Miss Sinquier began eating crumbs at random.

'God knows!' she declared.

'C'est une âme d'élite, Sir Oliver.'

'You've no experience at all?'

'None.'

Sir Oliver refused a dish.

'We old ones . . .' he lamented. 'Once upon a time, I was in closer touch with the stage.'

'Even so, Sir Oliver, you still retain your footing.'

'Footing, f-f-f——; among the whole demned lot, who persists still but, perhaps, the Marys?'

'Take the Marys. A word to them; just think what a boon!'

'Nothing so easy.'

Miss Sinquier clasped her hands.

'One has heard of them often, of course.'

'Mr. and Mrs. Mary have won repute throughout the realm,' Mrs. Sixsmith impressively said, wondering (as middlewoman) what commission she should ask.

'Mrs. Mary, I dare say, is no longer what she was!'

'Mrs. Mary, *aujourd'hui*, is a trifle, perhaps, full-blown, but she's most magnetic still. And a warmer, quicker heart never beat in any breast.'

'In her heyday, Sir Oliver—but you wouldn't have seen her, of course.'

The baronet's eyes grew extinct.

'In my younger days,' he said, 'she was comeliness itself . . . full of fun. I well recall her as the "wife" in *Macbeth*; I assure you she was positively roguish.'

'Being fairly on now in years,' Miss Sinquier reflected, 'she naturally wouldn't fill very juvenile parts—which would be a blessing.'

'She too often does.'

'She used to make Paul ill——' Mrs. Sixsmith began, but stopped discreetly. 'Oh, listen,' she murmured, glancing up towards the nigger band and insouciantly commencing to hum.

'What is it . . . ?'

'It's the *Belle of Benares*—

> 'My other females all yellow, fair or black,
> To thy charms shall prostrate fall,
> As every kind of elephant does
> To the white elephant Buitenack.
> And thou alone shalt have from me,
> Jimminy, Gomminy, whee, whee, whee,
> The Gomminy, Jimminy, whee.'

'Serephine, you're eating nothing at all.'

'I shall wait for the *pâtisserie*, Sir Oliver.'

'Disgraceful.'

'Father Francis forbids me meat; it's a little novena he makes me do.

> 'The great Jaw-waw that rules our land,
> And pearly Indian sea,
> Has now such *ab-solute* command
> As thou hast over me,
> With a Jimminy, Gomminy, Gomminy,
> Jimminy, Jimminy, Gomminy, whee.'

'Apropos of pearls . . .' Sir Oliver addressed Miss Sinquier, 'I look forward to the privilege before long of inspecting your own.'

'They're on her head, Sir Oliver!'

Sir Oliver started as a plate was passed unexpectedly over him from behind.

'Before approaching some City firm, it's possible Lady Dawtry might welcome an opportunity of acquiring this poor child's jewels for herself,' Mrs. Sixsmith said.

'Lady Dawtry!'

'Why not?'

'Lady Dawtry seldom wears ornaments; often I wish she would.'

'I wonder you don't *insist*.'

Sir Oliver fetched a sigh.

'Many's the time,' he said, 'I've asked her to be a little more spectacular—but she won't.'

'How women do vary!' Mrs. Sixsmith covertly smiled.

'To be sure.'

'My poor old friend . . . ?'

Sir Oliver turned away.

'I notice Miss Peters here to-night,' he said.

'Whipsina?'

'With two young men.'

'*Un trio n'excite pas de soupçons,* they say.'

'They do . . .'

'Have you a programme for presently, Sir Oliver?'

'I've a box at the Kehama.'

Miss Sinquier looked tragic

'It'll have begun!' she said.

'At a variety, the later the better as a rule.'

'I never like to miss *any* part.'

'My dear, you'll miss very little; besides it's too close to linger over dinner long.'

'Toc, toc; I don't find it so,' Sir Oliver demurred.

Mrs. Sixsmith plied her fan.

'I feel very much like sitting, *à la* Chaste Suzanne, in the nearest ice-pail!' she declared.

⟺ *VIII* ⟺

MARY LODGE, or Maryland, as it was more familiarly known, stood quite at the end of Gardingore Gate, facing the Park.

Half-way down the row, on the Knightsbridge side, you caught a glimpse of it set well back in its strip of garden with a curtain of rustling aspen-trees before the door.

Erected towards the close of the eighteenth century as a retreat for a fallen minister, it had, on his demise, become the residence of a minor member of the reigning Royal House, from whose executors, it had, in due course, passed into the hands of the first histrionic couple in the land.

A gravel sweep leading between a pair of grotesquely attenuated sphinxes conducted, via a fountain, to the plain, sober façade in the Grecian style.

Moving demurely up this approach some few minutes prior to the hour telegraphically specified by the mistress of the house, Miss Sinquier, clad in a light summer dress, with a bow like a great gold butterfly under her chin, pulled the bell of Mary Lodge.

Some day Others would be standing at her own front gate, their hearts a-hammer . . .

A trim manservant answered the door.

'Is Mrs. Mary . . . ?'

'Please to come this way.'

Miss Sinquier followed him in.

The entrance hall, bare but for a porphyry sarcophagus containing visiting cards, and a few stiff chairs, clung obviously to royal tradition still.

To right and left of the broad stairway two colossal battle-pictures, by Uccello, were narrowly divided by a pedestalled recess in which a frowning bust of Mrs. Mary as Medusa was enshrined.

Miss Sinquier, following closely, was shown into a compartment whose windows faced the Park.

'Mrs. Mary has not yet risen from lunch,' the man said as he went away. 'But she won't be many minutes.'

Selecting herself a chair with a back suited to the occasion, Miss Sinquier prepared to wait.

It was an irregularly planned, rather lofty room, connected by a wide arch with other rooms beyond. From the painted boiseries hung glowing Eastern carpets, on which warriors astride fleet-legged fantastic horses were seen to pursue wild animals, that fled helter-skelter through transparent thickets of may. A number of fragile French chairs formed a broken ring about a Louis XVI bed— all fretted, massive pillars of twisted, gilded wood—converted now to be a seat. Persian and Pesaro pottery conserving 'eternal' grasses, fans of feathers, strange sea-shells, bits of Blue-John, blocks of malachite, morsels of coral, images of jade littered the *guéridons* and *étagères*. A portrait of Mrs. Mary, by Watts, was suspended above the chimney-place, from whence came the momentous ticking of a clock.

'The old girl's lair, no doubt!' Miss Sinquier reflected, lifting her eyes towards a carved mythological ceiling describing the Zodiac and the Milky Way.

Tongue protruding, face upturned, it was something to mortify her for ever that Mrs. Mary, entering quietly, should so get her unawares.

'Look on your left.'

'Oh?'

'And you'll see it; in trine of Mars. The Seventh House. The House of *Marriage*. The House of Happiness.'

'Oh! Mrs. Mary!'

'You're fond of astrology?'

'I know very little about the heavenly bodies.'

'Ah! *Don't* be too impatient there.'

Miss Sinquier stared.

Mrs. Mary was large and robust, with commanding features and an upright carriage. She had a Redfern gown of 'navy' blue stuff infinitely laced. One white long hand, curved and jewelled, clung as if paralysed above her breast.

Seating herself majestically, with a glance of invitation to Miss Sinquier to do the same, the eminent actress appraised her visitor slowly with a cold dry eye.

'And so you're his "little mouse"! . . .'

'Whose?'

'Sir Oliver's "second Siddons." '

'Indeed——'

'Well, and what is your forte?'

'My forte, Mrs. Mary?'

'Comedy? Tragedy?'

'Either. Both come easy.'

'You've no bent?'

'So long as the part is good.'

' "Sarah"! Are you of Jewish stock?—Sarahs sometimes are!'

'Oh dear no.'

'Tell me something of the home circle. Have you brothers, sisters?'

'Neither.'

'Is your heart free?'

'Quite.'

'The Boards, I believe, are new to you?'

'Absolutely.'

'Kindly stand.'

'I'm five full feet.'

'Say, "Abyssinia." '

'Abyssinia!'

'As I guessed . . .'

'I was never there.'

'Now say "Joan." '

'Joan!'

'You're Comedy, my dear. Distinctly! And now sit down.'

Miss Sinquier gasped.

'You know with us it's Repertoire, I suppose?'

'Of course.'

'In parts such as one would cast Jane Jacks you should score.'

'Is she giving up?'

'Unfortunately she's obliged. She's just had another babelet, poor dear.'

'What were her parts?'

'In *Bashful Miss Bardine* the governess was one of them.'

'Oh!'

'And in *Lara* she was the orphan. That part should suit you well,' Mrs. Mary murmured, rising and taking from a cabinet a bundle of printed sheets.

'Is it rags?'

'Rags?'

'May she . . . is she allowed Evening dress?'

'Never mind about her dress. Let me hear how you'd deliver her lines,' Mrs. Mary tartly said, placing in Miss Sinquier's hands a brochure of the play.

'I should like to know my cue.'

'A twitter of birds is all. You are now in Lord and Lady Lara's garden—near Nice. Begin.'

'*How full the hedges are of roses!*'

'Speak up.'

'*How full the hedges are of roses! What perfume to be sure.*'

'And don't do that.'

'The directions are: "*she stoops.*" '

'Continue!'

'What's next?'

'A start.'

'*Oh! Sir Harry!*'

'Proceed.'

Miss Sinquier lodged a complaint.

'How can I when I don't know the plot?'

'What does it matter—the plot?'

'Besides, I feel up to something stronger.'

Mrs. Mary caressed the backs of her books.

'Then take the slave in *Arsinoe* and I'll read out the queen.'

'These little legs, Mrs. Mary, would look queerly in tights.'

'Think less of your costume, dear, do; and learn to do what you're told. Begin!'

'Arsinoe opens.'

'Arsi——? So she does. You should understand we're in Egypt, in the halls of Ptolemy Philadelphus, on the banks of the River Nile. I will begin.

'*Cease . . . Cease your song. Arisba! Lotos! THANKS.*
And for thy pains accept this ivory pin . . .
Shall it be said in many-gated Thebes

That Arsinoe's mean?
The desert wind . . .
Hark to't!
Methinks 'twill blow all night;
Lashing the lebbek trees anent Great Cheops' Pyre;
Tracing sombre shadows o'er its stony walls.
Within the wombats wail
Tearing the scarabs from Prince Kamphé's tomb.
His end was sudden . . . strangely so;
Osiris stalks our land. Kamphé and little Ti (his daughter—wife)
Both dead within a week. Ah me, I fear
Some priestly treachery; but see! What crouching shape is this? . . . Peace,
  fool!'
'*I did not speak . . . Oh, Queen.*'
'*ENOUGH. Thou weariest me.*'
'*I go!*'
'*Yet stay! Where is thy Lord?*'
'*Alas! I do not know.*'
'*Then get ye gone—from hence!*'
'*I shall obey.*'

'. . . Wail it!' Mrs. Mary rested.

'Wail what, Mrs. Mary?'

'Let me hear that *bey*: O-bey. Sound your menace.'

'I shall o-bey.'

'*O beating heart,*' Mrs. Mary paced stormily the room. '*Tumultuous throbbing breast. Alas! how art thou laden? . . .*'

She turned.

'Slave!'

'Me, Mrs. Mary?'

'Come on. Come on.'

'Slave's off.'

'Pst, girl. Then take *the Duke*!'

'*Fairest——*'

'*High Horus! . . . What! Back from Ethiopia and the Nubian Army! Is't indeed Ismenias . . . ?*'

'Listen.'

'*Hast deserted Ptolemy!*'

'*Fairest——*'

'*O Gods of Egypt——*'

'Someone wants you, Mrs. Mary.'

'Wants me?'

'Your chauffeur, I think.'

'The car, M'm,' a servant announced.

'Ah!' she broke off. 'An engagement, I fear. But come and see me again. Come one day to the theatre. Our stage-door is in Sloop Street, an *impasse* off the Strand.' And Mrs. Mary, gathering up her skirts, nodded and withdrew.

 IX

'BLACK her great boots! Not I,' Miss Sinquier said to herself as she turned her back on Mary Lodge to wend her way westward across the Park.

She was to meet Mrs. Sixsmith at a certain club on Hay Hill towards dusk to learn whether any tempting offer had been submitted Sir Oliver for her pearls.

'If I chose I suppose I could keep them,' she murmured incoherently to herself as she crossed the Row.

It was an airless afternoon.

Under the small formal trees sheltering the path she clapped her sunshade to, and slackened speed.

The rhododendrons, in vivid clumps of new and subtle colours brushing the ground, were in their pride. Above, the sky showed purely blue. She walked on a little way towards Stanhope Gate when, overcome by the odoriferous fragrance of heliotropes and zinnias, she sank serenely to a bench.

Far off by the Serpentine a woman was preaching from a tree to a small audience gathered beneath. How primeval she looked as her arms shot out in argument, a discarded cock's-feather boa looped to an upper bough dangling like some dark python in the air above.

Miss Sinquier sat on until the shadows fell.

She found her friend on reaching Hay Hill in the midst of muffins and tea.

'I gave you up. I thought you lost,' Mrs. Sixsmith exclaimed, hitching higher her veil with fingers super-manicured, covered in oxydised metal rings.

'I was dozing in the Park.'

'Dreamy kid.'

'On my back neck I've such a freckle.'

'Did you see Mammy Mary?'

'I did.'

'Well?'

'Nothing; she offered me Miss Jacks' leavings.'

'Not good enough.'

'What of Sir Oliver?'

'I hardly know how to tell you.'

'Has he——?'

Mrs. Sixsmith nodded.

'He has had an offer of two thousand pounds,' she triumphantly said, 'for the pearls alone.'

'Two thousand pounds!'

'Call it three o's.'

'Okh!'

'Consider what commercial credit that means. . . .'

'I shall play Juliet.'

'Juliet?'

'I shall have a season.'

'Let me take the theatre for you.'

'Is it a dream?'

'I will find you actors—great artists.'

'Oh, God!'

'And, moreover, I have hopes for the silver too. Sir Oliver is enchanted with the spoons—the Barnabas spoon especially. He said he had never seen a finer. Such a beautiful little Barny, such a rapture of a little sinner as it is, in every way.'

Miss Sinquier's eyes shone.

'I'll have that boy.'

'What—what boy?'

'Harold Weathercock.'

'You desire him?'

'To be my Romeo, of course.'

'It depends if the Dream will release him.'

'It must! It shall!'

'I'll peep in on him and sound him, if you like.'

'We'll go together.'

'Very well.'

'Do you know where he lives?'

'In Foreign-Colony Street. He and a friend of his, Noel Nice, share a studio there. Not to paint in, alas! It's to wash.'

'What?'

'They've made a little laundry of it. And when they're not acting actually, they wash. Oh! sometimes when Mr. Nice spits across his iron and says Pah! it makes one ill.'

'Have they any connection?'

Mrs. Sixsmith bent her eyes to her dress.

'Mr. Sixsmith often sent them things . . . little things,' she said. 'His linen was his pride. You might annex him, perhaps. He's played Mercutio before.'

'Is he handsome?'

'Paul? He's more interesting than handsome. *Unusual*, if you know . . .'

'What *did* you do to separate?'

'I believe I bit him.'

'You did!'

'He ran at me with the fire-dogs first.'

'I suppose you annoyed him?'

'The cur!'

'Something tells me you're fond of him still.'

From her reticule Mrs. Sixsmith took a small note-book and made an entry therein.

'. . . The divine Shakespeare!' she sighed.

'I mean to make a hit with him.'

'Listen to me.'

'Well?'

'My advice to you is, hire a playhouse—the Cobbler's End, for example—for three round months at a reasonable rent, with a right, should you wish, to sub-let.'

'It's so far off.'

'Define "far off."'

'Blackfriars Bridge.'

'I've no doubt by paying a fortune you could find a more central position if you care to wait. The Bolivar Theatre, possibly——; or the Cone . . . At the Cone there's a joy-plank from the auditorium to the stage, so that, should you want to ever, you can come right out into the stalls.'

'I want my season at once,' Miss Sinquier said.

Mrs. Sixsmith toyed with her rings.

'What do you say,' she asked, 'to making an informal début (before "royal" auspices!) at the Esmé Fisher "Farewell" coming off next week?'

'Why not!'

'Some of the stage's brightest ornaments have consented to appear.'

'I'd like particulars.'

'I'll send a note to the secretary, Miss Willinghorse, straight away,' Mrs. Sixsmith murmured, gathering up her constant Juno beneath her arm, and looking about her for some ink.

'Send it later, from the Café Royal.'

'I can't go any more to the Café Royal,' Mrs. Sixsmith said. 'I owe money there . . . To all the waiters.'

'Wait till after we've seen the Washingtons.'

'The Washingtons? Who are they?'

'Don't you know?'

'Besides, I've a small headache,' Mrs. Sixsmith said, selecting herself a quill.

'What can I do to relieve it?' Miss Sinquier wondered, taking up a newspaper as her friend commenced to write.

Heading the agony list some initials caught her eye.

'*S——h S——r*. Come back. All shall be forgiven,' she read.

'I can't epistolise while you make those *unearthly* noises,' Mrs. Sixsmith complained.

'I didn't mean to.'

'Where are we going to dine?'

'Where is there wonderful to go?'

'How about a grill?'

'I don't mind.'

'The Piccadilly? We're both about got up for it.'

Miss Sinquier rolled her eyes.

'The Grill-room at the Piccadilly isn't going to cure a headache,' she remarked.

 X

TO watch Diana rise blurred above a damp chemise from a fifth-floor laundry garden in Foreign-Colony Street, Soho, had brought all Chelsea (and part of Paris) to study illusive atmospherical effects from the dizzy drying-ground of those versatile young men Harold Weathercock and Noel Nice.

Like a necropolis at the Resurrection, or some moody vision of Blake, would it appear under the evanescent rays of the moon.

Nighties, as evening fell, would go off into proud Praxiteles-torsos of Nymphs or Muses: pants and ready-mades, at a hint of air, would piroutte and execute a phantom ballet from Don John.

Beyond the clothes-lines was a Pagoda, set up in an extravagant mood, containing a gilded Buddha—a thorn and a symbol of unrighteousness to a convent of Ursulines whose recreation yard was underneath.

Here, at a certain hour when the Mother Superior was wont to walk round and round her preserves, a young, bewhiskered man frequently would come bearing ceremonial offerings of rice or linen newly washed, and falling flat before the shrine would roll himself about and beat the ground as if in mortal anguish of his sins before her fascinated eye. Here, too, from time to time, festivities would take place—sauteries (to a piano-organ), or convivial *petits soupers* after the play.

An iron ladder connected the roof with the work-rooms and living-rooms below.

Ascending this by the light of the stars, Mrs. Sixsmith and the *New Juliet*, gay from a certain grill, audaciously advanced, their playful screams rendered inaudible by the sounds of a tricksome waltz wafted down to them from the piano-organ above.

Items of linen nestling close to a line overhead showed palely against the night like roosting doves.

'Help . . . Oh! she's falling,' Mrs. Sixsmith screamed. 'Are you there, Mr. Nice?'

'Give me your hand,' Miss Sinquier begged.

'Should she rick her spine . . .'

'Whew-ps!' Miss Sinquier exclaimed, scrambling to the top.

London, beyond the frail filigree cross on the Ursulines' bleached wall, blazed with light. From the Old Boar and Castle over the way came a perfect flood of it. And all along the curved river-line from Westminster to St. Paul's glittered lamps, lamps, lamps.

Folding an arm about her friend's 'wasp' waist, Mrs. Sixsmith whirled her deftly round to a wild street air:

'I like your ways,
   I like your style,
   You are my darling——'

she hummed as the organ stopped.

'Come to finish the evening?'

A small, thick-set, grizzled man with dark æsthetic eyes and a pinkish nose, the result maybe of continuously tinting it for music-hall purposes, addressed the breathless ladies in a broad, enquiring voice.

'Is that *you*, Mr. Smee?' Mrs. Sixsmith asked, surprised.

'Call me "Shawn."'

'We've only come on business.'

'Don't! You make me laf.'

'Then—do it,' Mrs. Sixsmith serenely said, resting her left knee against an empty beer keg.

'They're not back from the theatre yet.'

'Turn for us till they come.'

Mr. Smee dashed from a crimpled brow a wisp of drooping hair.

'By your leave, ladies,' he said, 'I'll just slip across to the Old Boar and Castle and sample a snack at the bar.'

'Don't run off, Mr. Smee. You really mustn't. On tiles, they say, one usually meets with *cats*.'

'Oh, my word.'

Mrs. Sixsmith placed a hand to her hip in the style of an early John.

'How long is it—say—since we met?' she enquired. 'Not since my wedding, I do believe.'

'What's become of those kiddy bridesmaids you had?' Mr. Smee warily asked.

'Gerty Gale and Joy Patterson?—I'm sure I don't know.'

'Oh, my word!'

'Well, how goes the world with *you*, Mr. Smee?'

'So-so. I've been away on tour. Mildred Milson and Co. Oh! my Lord—it was. No sooner did we get to Buxton—down in Derbyshire—than Miss Milson fell sick and had to be left behind.'

'What was wrong with her?'

'Exposure . . . On Bank Holiday some of the company hired a three-horse char-à-banc and drove from Buxton over to Castleton

Caves—my hat. What hills!—and from there we went to take a squint at Chatsworth, where Miss Milson came over queer.'

'And how does Mrs. Smee?'

'So-so.'

'One never sees her now.'

'There she sits all day, reading Russian novels. Talk of gloom!'

'Really?'

'Oh, it is!'

'Well . . . I'm fond of thoughtful, theosophical reading, too, Mr. Smee,' Mrs. Sixsmith said. 'Madame Blavatsky and Mrs. Annie Besant are both favourites with me.'

Mr. Smee jerked an eloquent thumb.

'Who have you brought along?'

'She's a special pal of mine.'

'Married?'

'Mon Dieu,' Mrs. Sixsmith doubtfully said. 'Je *crois* que c'est une Pucelle.'

'Never!' Mr. Smee, completely mystified, hazarded.

'Fie donc. Comme c'est *méchant*.'

'Wee, wee.'

Mrs. Sixsmith tittered.

'She's going into management very soon.'

'Swank?'

'We seek a Romeo, Mr. Smee.'

'Now, now! . . .'

'Don't look like that, Mr. Smee—nobody's asking you,' Mrs. Sixsmith murmured.

Mr. Smee scratched reflectively his head.

'Who is it you're after?' he asked.

'We fancied Mr. Weathercock, might suit.'

'God has given him looks, but no brains,' Mr. Smee emphatically declared. 'No more brains than a cow in a field.'

'His is indeed a charming face,' Mrs. Sixsmith sighed. 'And as to his brains, Mr. Smee—why, come!'

'Who's to create the countess?' he asked.

'Lady Capulet? It's not determined yet.'

'Why not canvass the wife?'

'Has she been in Shakespeare before?'

'From the time she could toddle; in *A Midsummer-Night's Dream*, when not quite two, she was the Bug with gilded wings.'

'Pet!'

'Sure . . .'

Mrs. Sixsmith clasped prayerfully her hands.

'And in Mr. Smee,' she said, 'I see the makings of a fine Friar Lawrence!'

'How's that?'

'With a few choice *concetti*.'

'Faith!'

'I see the lonely cell, the chianti-flask, the crucifix . . .'

'Gosh!'

'I see Verona . . . the torrid sky . . . the town ascending, up, up, up. I hear the panting nurse. She knocks. Your priest's eyes glisten. She enters, blouse-a-gape—a thorough coster. You raise your cowl . . . Chianti? She shakes her head. Benedictine? No! no! A little Chartreuse, then? Certainly not! Nothing . . . You squeeze her waist. Her cries "go through" Lady Capulet and her daughter in the distant city on their way to mass. Romeo enters. So!' Mrs. Sixsmith broke off as Mr. Weathercock and a curly-headed lad, followed by a swathed woman and a whey-faced child, showed themselves upon the stairs.

Mrs. Sixsmith sought Miss Sinquier's arm.

'Listen to me, my darling!' she said.

'Well?'

'Write.'

'What?'

'Write.'

'Why?'

'Because I fear we intrude.'

'Intrude?' Harold Weathercock exclaimed, coming up. 'I assure you it's a treat . . .'

Mrs. Sixsmith threw a sidelong, intriguing glance across her shoulder.

'Who's the cure in plaits?' she demanded.

'It's little Mary Mant—she's seeing her sister home.'

'Oh! . . . Is that Ita?' Mrs. Sixsmith murmured, stepping forward to embrace Miss 'Ita Iris' of the Dream.

Miss Sinquier swooped.

'I'm having a season,' she, without further preamble, began. 'And I want to persuade you to join——'

'Principal?'

'Yes.'

'I should like to play for you,' Mr. Weathercock said.

'Harold!'

Miss Mant addressed him softly.

'Well?'

'Honey husband . . .'

'Hook it!'

'Give me a cigarette.'

'Mary!' her sister called.

'Quick! 'cos of Ita.'

'Mary Mant.'

Miss Mant tossed disdainfully an ultra-large and pasty-faced head.

'Why must you insult me, Ita?' she bitterly asked. 'You *know* I'm Miss Iris.'

'I know you're Miss Mant.'

'No, I'm not.'

'Yes, you are.'

'No, I'm *not*.'

'I tell you, you are!'

'Liar!'

'M-A-N-T!'

'Oh, stow it,' Mr. Smee said. 'Put it by.'

'I'm Réné Iris.'

'Réné Rats.'

Mrs. Sixsmith looked detached.

'Is that a wash-tub?' she asked.

'Certainly.'

'What's that odd thing floating, like the ghost of a child unborn?'

'It belongs to Mrs. Mary.'

'There's a rumour—she refuses a fortune to show herself in Revue.'

'With her hearse-horse tread . . .'

'Sh—— Harold worships her.'

'Oh, no.'

'He sees things in her that we don't, perhaps.'

'To some ideas,' Mrs. Sixsmith said, 'I suppose she's very blooming still . . .'

'If it wasn't for her figure, which is really a disgrace.'

Miss Iris smiled.

She had a tired mouth, contrasting vividly with the artificial reshness of her teeth.

'When I reach my zenith,' she declared, 'it's Farewell.'

'Shall you assist at poor Esmé Fisher's?'

'A couple of songs—that's all.'

Mrs. Sixsmith looked away.

'Naturally,' Miss Sinquier was saying, 'one can't expect instantly to be a draw. More than—perhaps—just a little!'

'With a man who understands in the Box Office . . .'

'Someone with a big nose and a strong will, eh?'

Mr. Nice lifted a rusty iron and wiped it across his leg.

'In my opinion,' he said, 'to associate oneself with a sanctified classic is a huge mistake. And why start a season on the tragic tack?'

'Because——'

'Suppose it's a frost?'

'Oh!'

'Suppose your venture fails. Suppose the thing's a drizzle.'

'What then?'

'There's a light comedy of mine that should suit you.'

'Of yours!'

'Appelled *Sweet Maggie Maguire*.'

'Tell me why she was sweet, Mr. Nice,' Mrs. Sixsmith begged.

'Why she was sweet? I really don't know.'

'Was she sentimental? . . .'

'She was an invalid. A bed-ridden beauty . . . and, of course, the hero's a Doctor.'

'Oh! my word!'

'Is there anyone at home?' A tired voice came thrilling up from below.

'Who comes?'

Mrs. Sixsmith started.

'It sounds to me like my husband,' she said, with an involuntary nervous movement of the hands.

'I forgot,' Mr. Weathercock said. 'He mentioned he might blow in.'

'Oh!'

'I'd take to my heels!' Miss Iris advised.

Mrs. Sixsmith stood transfixed.

The moonlight fell full on her, making her features look drawn and haggard.

Caprice

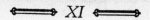 XI

LIKE wildfire the rumour ran. The King had knighted—he had knighted—by what accident?—Mr. Mary, in lieu of Mr. Fisher, at Mr. Fisher's own farewell. In the annals of the stage such an occurrence was unheard of, unique.

The excitement in the green-room was intense.

'M-m! He is not de first to zell 'is birs-r-rite for a mess of porridge!' Yvonde Yalta, the playgoers' darling, remarked as she poised with an extravagant play of arms, a black glittering bandeau on her short flaxen hair.

'A mess of pottage!' someone near her said.

'You correct me? Ah, sanx! I am so grateful, so—*so* grateful,' the charming creature murmured as she sailed away.

From the auditorium came a suppressed titter.

The curtain had risen some few minutes since on Mlle. Fanfette and Monsieur Coquelet de Chausse-pierre of the Théâtre Sans Rancune in the comedietta, *Sydney, or There's No Resisting Him*.

'It's extraordinary I've never seen a man knighted,' a show-girl twittered, 'and I've seen a good deal . . .'

'How do they do them?'

'Like this,' a sparkling brunette answered, bestowing a sly pat on the interlocutress with the back of a brush.

'Of all the common——!'

'Ladies! Ladies!'

'Who was in front at the time?'

'I was!' Mrs. Sixsmith said, who had just peeped in to exchange a few words with her friend.

'You were?'

'I was selling sweets in the vestibule and saw it all. Really! If I live to be an old woman I shan't forget it. Mr. Mary—*Sir Maurice*—was in the lobby chatting with Sylvester Fry of the *Dispatch*, when the Royal party arrived. The King instantly noticed him and sent one of his suite, quite unpremeditatedly, it seemed, to summon him, and in a trice . . . Oh! . . . and I *never* saw the Queen look so charming. She has a gold dress turning to white through the most exquisite gradations . . .'

Mrs. Sixsmith was overcome.

'A-wheel,' Miss Sinquier's dresser disrespectfully said, 'how

was the poor man to tell? Both the blighters—God forgive me—
are equally on their last legs.'

Miss Sinquier shivered.

'Is it a good house?' she enquired.

'Splendid! Outside they're flying five "full" boards . . . There's
not a single vacant place. Poor Sydney Iphis gave half a guinea
for seat in the slips.'

'Are you here all alone?'

'I'm with Sir Oliver Dawtry,' Mrs. Sixsmith replied, 'except
when I'm running about! . . . Can I sell anyone anything?' she
enquired, raising sonorously her voice. 'Vanilla! Caramel! Chocolate! . . . Comfits!' she warbled.

'What have you netted?'

'Eighteenpence only, so far;—from such an angel!'

'Comfits, did you say?' a round-faced, piquant little woman
asked.

'Despite disguise! If it isn't Arthurine Smee!'

The actress displayed astonishment.

Nature had thrown up upon her lip and cheek two big blonde
moles that procured for her physiognomy, somehow or other, an
unusual degree of expression.

'My husband has been waiting to hear from you,' she said, 'as
agent to this *Miss Sin*——, the new star with the naughty name,
and from all I could make out I understand it would be likely to be
a *Double Engagement*.'

'This is Miss Sinquier,' Mrs. Sixsmith exclaimed.

Miss Sinquier blinked.

'Have you done it much?' she asked.

'Often.'

'Where?'

'Everywhere.'

'For example?'

'I may say I've played Pauline and Portia and Puck . . .'

'Mother-to-Juliet I fear's the best I've to offer.'

Mrs. Smee consulted enigmatically the nearest mole in reach of
her tongue.

'Were I to play her in "good preservation," ' she enquired, 'I
suppose there'd be no objection!'

'Why, none!'

'Just a girlish touch . . .'

'Mrs. Smee defies time,' Mrs. Sixsmith remarked.

'My dear, I once was thought to be a very pretty woman. . . . . All I can do now is to urge my remains.'

Miss Sinquier raised a forefinger.

Voices shivering in altercation issued loudly from a private dressing-room next door.

'What's up?'

'Oh, dear! Oh, dear!' the wardrobe-mistress, entering, said. 'Sir Maurice and Mr. Fisher are passing sharp words with a couple of pitchforks.'

'What!'

'The "Farm-players" sent them over from the Bolivar for their Pig-sty scene—and now poor Mr. Mary, *Sir M'riss*, and Mr. Fisher are fighting it out, and Mrs. Mary, *her ladyship*, has joined the struggle.'

'Murder!' called a voice.

'Glory be to God.'

Mrs. Sixsmith rolled her eyes.

'Da!' she gasped, as Lady Mary, a trifle dazed but decked in smiles, came bustling in.

'Oh, Men! Men! Men!' she exclaimed, going off into a hearty laugh. 'Rough angelic brutes! . . .'

She was radiant.

She had a gown of shot brocade, a high lace ruff and a silver girdle of old German work that had an ivory missal falling from it.

'Quarrelsome, quarrelling kings,' she stuttered, drifting towards a toilet-table—the very one before which Miss Sinquier was making her face.

On all sides from every lip rose up a chorus of congratulations.

'Viva, Lady Mary!'

Touched, responsive, with a gesture springing immediately from the heart, the consummate Victorian extended impulsive happy hands.

'God bless you, dears,' she said.

'Three cheers for Lady Mary!'

The illustrious woman quashed a tear.

'Am I white behind?' she asked.

'Allow me, milady,' the wardrobe-mistress wheezed.

'I fancy I heard a rip! . . .'

'There must have been quite a scrimmage.'

Caprice

From the orchestra a melodious throb-thrum-throb told a 'curtain.'

'Lady Mary—*you*, Mum,' a call-boy chirped.

'Me?'

'Five minutes.'

Lady Mary showed distress.

'For goodness sake, my dear,' she addressed Miss Sinquier, 'do leave yourself alone. I want the glass.'

But Miss Sinquier seemed engrossed.

At her elbow a slip of a 'Joy-baby' was holding forth with animation to Mrs. Sixsmith and Mrs. Smee.

'That was one of my dreams,' she was saying, 'and last night again I had another—in spite of a night-light, too! It began by a ring formed of crags and boulders enclosing a troop of deer—oh, such a herd of them—delicate, distinguished animals with little pom-pom horns, and some had poodles' tails. Sitting behind a rhododendron bush was an old gentleman on a white horse; he never moved a muscle. Suddenly I became aware of a pack of dogs ... And then, before my very eyes, one of the dogs transformed itself into a giraffe ...'

'You must have been out to supper.'

'It's true I had. Oh, it was a merry meal.'

'Who gave it?'

'Dore Davis did; to meet her betrothed—Sir Francis Four.'

'What's he like?'

'Don't ask me. It makes one tired to look at him.'

'Was it a party?'

'Nothing but literary-people with their Beatrices ... My dear, *the scum*! Half-way through supper Dore got her revolver out and began shooting the glass drops off her chandelier.'

'I should like to see her trousseau,' Mrs. Sixsmith sighed.

'It isn't up to much. Anything good she sells—on account of bailiffs.'

'Pooh! She should treat them all *en reine*.'

Mrs. Smee looked wise.

'Always be civil with bailiffs,' she said; 'never ruffle them! If you queen a sheriff's officer remember there's no getting rid of him. He clings on—like a poor relation.'

'Oh, well,' Mrs. Sixsmith replied, 'I always treat the worms *en reine*; not,' she added wittily, 'that I ever have ...'

Miss Sinquier twirled herself finally about.

'There,' she murmured, 'I'm going out into the wings.'

'When's your call?'

'After Lady Mary.'

For her unofficial first appearance she was resolved to woo the world with a dance—a dance all fearless somersaults and quivering *battements*; a young Hungarian meanwhile recording her movements sensitively upon a violin.

She was looking well in an obedient little ballet skirt that made action a delight. Her hair, piled high in a towering toupee, had a white flower in it.

'Down a step and through an arch.' A pierrette who passed her in the corridor directed her to the stage.

It was Miss Ita Iris of the Dream.

Miss Sinquier tingled.

How often on the cold flags of the great church at home had she asked the way before!

'Oh Lord,' she prayed now, 'let me conquer. Let me! Amen.'

She was in the wings.

Above her, stars sparkled lavishly in a darkling sky, controlled by a bare-armed mechanic who was endeavouring, it seemed, to deliver himself of a moon; craning from a ladder at the risk of his life, he pushed it gently with a big soft hand.

Miss Sinquier turned her eyes to the stage.

The round of applause accorded Lady Mary on her entry was gradually dying away.

From her shelter Miss Sinquier could observe her, in opulent silhouette, perfectly at her ease.

She stood waiting for the last huzzas to subside with bowed head and folded hands—like some great sinner—looking reverently up through her eyelashes at the blue silk hangings of the Royal box.

By degrees all clatter ceased.

Approaching the footlights with a wistful smile, the favourite woman scanned the stalls.

'Now most of you here this afternoon,' she intimately began, 'I will venture to say, never heard of Judy Jacock. I grant you, certainly, there's nothing very singular in that; for her life, which was a strangely frail one, essentially was obscure. Judy herself was *obscure* ... And so that is why I say you can't have ever heard of her! ... Because she was totally unknown. ... Ah, poor wee waif!

alas, she's dead now. Judy's among the angels . . . and the beautiful little elegy which, with your consent, I intend forthwith to submit, is written around her, around little Judy, and around her old Father, her "*Da*"—James, who was a waiter. And while he was away waiting one day—he used to wipe the plates on the seat of his breeches!—his little Judy died. Ah, poor old James. Poor Sir James. But let the poet,' she broke off suddenly, confused, 'take up the tale himself, or, rather—to be more specific!—*herself*. For the lines that follow, which are *inédits*, are from the seductive and charming pen of Lady Violet Sleepwell.'

Lady Mary coughed, winked archly an eye, and began quite carelessly as if it were Swinburne:

> 'I never *knew* James Jacock's child . . .
> I knew he *had* a child!
> The daintiest little fairy that ever a father knew.
> She was all contentment . . .'

Miss Sinquier looked away.

To her surprise, lurking behind a property torso of 'a Faun,' her pigtails roped with beads of scarlet glass, was Miss May Mant.

'Tell me what you are up to!' she asked.

'Sh——! Don't warn Ita!'

'Why should I?'

'I dodged her. Beautifully.'

'What for?'

'If she thought I was going on the stage, she'd be simply wild.'

'Are you?'

'I intend tacking on in the Pope's Procession.'

'That won't be just yet.'

'Oh, isn't it wonderful?'

'What?'

'Being here.'

'It's rather pleasant.'

'Can you feel the boards?'

'A little.'

'They go *right* through me. Through my shoes, up my legs, and at my heart they sting.'

'Kiss me.'

'I love you.'

'Pet.'

'Do I look interesting?'

'Ever so.'

'Would you take me for a Cardinal's comfort?'

Lady Mary lifted up her voice:

> 'Come, Judy come, the angel said,
> And took her from her little bed,
> And through the air they quickly sped
> Until they reached God's throne;
> So, there, they dressed her all in white
> They say she was a perfect sight,
> Celestial was her mien!'

'Lady Violet Sleepwell admires Ita.'

'Indeed.'

'She's a victim to chloral.'

> 'Rose-coiffed stood J.
> Amid the choir,
> Celestial-singing!'

The august artiste glowed.

'Ita thinks she drinks.'

'I shouldn't wonder,' Miss Sinquier replied, covering her face with her hands.

Through her fingers she could contemplate her accompanist's lanky figure as he stood in the opposite wing busily powdering his nose.

The moment, it seemed, had come.

Yet not quite—the public, who loved tradition, was determined on obtaining an encore.

Lady Mary was prepared to acquiesce.

Curtseying from side to side and wafting kisses to the gods, she announced:

'The Death of Hortense; by *Desire*.'

XII

The Source Theatre.

DEAR MOTHER,—I saw your notice in a newspaper not very long ago, and this morning I came across it again in the *Dispatch*. Really I don't know what there can be to 'forgive' and as to 'coming back!'—I have undertaken the management of this theatre, where rehearsals of *Romeo and Juliet* have already begun. This is the house where Audrey Anderson made her début, and where Avize Mendoza made such a hit. You could imagine nothing cosier or more intimate if you tried. Father would be charmed (tell him, for, of course, he sometimes speaks of me in the long *triste* evenings as he smokes a pipe) with the foyer, which has a mural design in marquetry, showing Adam and Eve in the Garden of Eden, sunning themselves by the side of a well. They say the theatre contains a well *beneath the stage*, which is why it's known as the Source. I have left, I'm glad to say, the hotel, which was getting dreadfully on my nerves for a dressing-room here, where I pass the nights now: an arrangement that suits me, as I like to be on the spot. A sister of Ita Iris of the Dream Theatre keeps me company, so that I'm not a bit solitary. We understand each other to perfection, and I find her helpful to me in many ways. She is such an affectionate child, and I do not think I shall regret it. I've decided to have half my teeth taken out by a man in Knightsbridge—some trial to me, I fear; but, alas, we've all to carry our cross! I seem to have nothing but debts. Clothes, *as well* as scenery, would ruin anyone.

I'm allotting a little box to you and father for the opening night, unless you would prefer two stalls?

The other afternoon I 'offered my services' and obtained three curtains at a gala matinée; I wish you could have been at it!

Your devoted Daughter.

I went to the oratory on Sunday; it was nothing but a blaze of candles.

Remember me to Leonard and Gripper—also Kate.

◆══➤ *XIII* ◆══➤

AN absence of ventilation made the room an oven and discouraged sleep. Through the width of skylight, in inert recumbence, she could follow wonderingly the frail pristine tints of dawn. Flushed, rose-barred, it spread above her with fantastic drifting clouds masking the morning stars.

From a neighbouring church a clock struck five.

Miss Sinquier sighed; she had not closed her eyes the whole night through.

'One needs a blind,' she mused, 'and a pane——'

She looked about her for something to throw.

Cinquecento Italian things—a chest, a crucifix, a huge guitar, a grim carved catafalque all purple sticks and violet legs (Juliet's) crowded the floor.

'A mess of glass . . . and cut my feet . . .' she murmured, gathering about her a *négligé* of oxydised knitted stuff and sauntering out towards the footlights in quest of air.

Notwithstanding the thermometer, she could hear Miss May Mant breathing nasally from behind her door.

The stage was almost dark.

'Verona,' set in autumn trees, looked fast asleep. Here and there a campanile shot up, in high relief, backed by a scenic hill, or an umbrella-pine. On a column in the 'Market Place' crouched a brazen lion.

An acrobatic impulse took her at the sight of it.

> 'Sono pazza per te
> *Si!* Sono pazza, pazza, pazza, . . .
> Pazza per amore,'

she warbled, leaping lightly over the footlights into the stalls.

The auditorium, steeped in darkness, felt extinguished, chill.

Making a circuit of the boxes, she found her way up a stairway into the promenade.

Busts of players, busts of poets, busts of peris, interspersed by tall mirrors in gilt-bordered mouldings, smiled on her good-day.

Sinking to a low, sprucely-cushioned seat, she breathed a sigh of content.

Rid of the perpetual frictions of the inevitable *personnel,* she could possess the theatre, for a little while, in quietude to herself.

In the long window boxes, tufts of white daisies inclining to the air brought back to mind a certain meadow, known as *Basings,* a pet haunt with her at home.

At the pond end, in a small coppice, doves cried 'Coucoussou-coucoussou' all the day long.

Here, soon a year ago, while weaving herself a garland (she was playing at being Europa with the Saunders' Fifeshire bull; flourishing flowers at it; tempting it with waving poppies; defying it to bear her away from the surrounding stagnance), the realisation of her dramatic gift first discovered itself.

And then, her thoughts tripped on, *he* came, the Rev. George—'just as I was wondering to whom to apply'—and drew all Applethorp to St. Ann-on-the-Hill by the persuasive magnetism of his voice; largely due—so he said—to 'scientific production.' To the *Bromley Breath!* He never could adequately thank Elizabeth, Mrs. Albert Bromley, for all she had done. No; because words failed . . . Her Institute, for him, would be always 'top-o'-the-tree,' and when asked, by her, 'What tree?' he had answered with a cryptic look: 'She trains them for the stage.'

Dear heart! How much he seemed to love it. He had known by their green-room names all the leading stars, and could tell, on occasion, little anecdotes of each.

It was he who narrated how Mrs. Mary (as she was then), on the first night of *Gulnara, Queen of the Lattermonians,* got caught in the passenger-lift on the way from her dressing-room to the stage and was obliged to allow her understudy to replace her, which with the utmost *éclat* she did, while Mrs. Mary, who could overhear the salvos from her prison, was driven quite distraught at a triumph that, but for the irony of things, would most certainly have been hers.

Miss Sinquier sighed.

'Which reminds me,' she murmured, fixing her eyes upon the storied ceiling, 'that I've no one at all, should anything happen to me.'

She lay back and considered the inchoate imagery painted in gouache above her.

Hydropic loves with arms outstretched in invitation, ladies in

hectic hats and billowing silks, courtiers, lap-dogs, peacocks, etc.,
all intermingled in the pleasantest way.

As she gazed a great peace fell upon her. Her eyelids closed.

'Breakfast!'

Miss May Mant woke her with a start.

'Oh!'

'I laid it to-day in the stalls.'

'Extraordinary child.'

'Crumbs in the boxes, I've noticed, encourage mice. . . . They
must come from the spring, I think, under the stage.'

'One ought to set a trap!'

'Poor creatures . . . they enjoy a good play, I expect, as much
as we do,' Miss Mant murmured, setting down the kettle she was
holding and lowering her cheek graciously for a kiss.

'Well?'

'You were asleep.'

'Was I horrid?'

'You looked too perfectly orchidaceous.'

'Orchidaceous?'

'Like the little women of Outa-Maro.'

Miss Sinquier sat up.

'What is there for breakfast?' she asked.

'Do you like porridge?'

'Oh, René!'

Miss Mant raised a bare shoulder and crushed it to an ear.

'Really,' she remarked, 'I'm at a loss to know what to give you,
Sally; I sometimes ask myself what Juliet took . . .'

'Why, potions.'

'*Ita* takes tea luke with a lemon; and it makes her *so* cross.'

'Disgusting.'

'A la Russe.'

'Is she still away?'

'Yes . . . She writes from a toy bungalow, she says, with the sea
at the very door and a small shipwreck lying on the beach.'

'What of Paris?'

'I'm Page to him, you said so!'

'With her consent.'

'Oh, Ita hates the stage. She's only *on it* of course to make a
match . . . she could have been an Irish countess had she pleased,

only she said it wasn't smart enough, and it sounded too Sicilian.'

'Everyone can't be Roman.'

'. . . Oh, she's such a minx! In her letter she writes, "I don't doubt you'll soon grow tired of the Sally-Sin Theatre and of dancing attendance on the Fair Sink." '

'Cat.'

'And her Manting ways just to annoy. Mant, Mant, Mant! She does it to humiliate. Whenever the Tirds are in earshot she's sure to begin.'

'The Tirds?'

'Llewellyn and Lydia. Lydia Tird has an understanding with my big brother. Poor lad! Just before I left home he took the name of Isadore: Isadore Iris. Oh, when Ita heard! "Bill Mant", she said and made Llewellyn laugh.'

'Oh!'

'And now that Mrs. Sixsmith "Mants" me almost as much as Ita.'

'Why do you dislike her so much?'

'Cadging creature!'

'René?'

'Limpet.'

'René?'

'Parasite.'

'René——!'

'Scavanger.'

'*Basta!*'

'I know all about her.'

'What do you know?'

'If I tell you, I'll have to tell you in French.'

'Then tell me in French.'

'Elle fait les cornes à son mari!'

'What next?'

'She's *divorcée!*'

'Poor soul.'

'Out at *Bois St. Jean*—St. John's Wood—she has a villa.'

Miss Sinquier got up.

'Anyway,' she murmured.

'Oh, Sally . . .'

'Well?'

'You do love me?'

'Why, *of course*.'

'Let's go presently to a Turkish bath—after rehearsal.'

'Not to-day.'

'. . . Just for a "Liver-Pack"?'

'No.'

'Why not?'

'Because . . . and when you're out, don't, dear, forget a mouse-trap!'

◆══ XIV ══◆

TO bring together certain of the dramatic critics (such high arbiters of the stage as Sylvester Fry of the *Dispatch*, Lupin Petrol of *Now*, Amethyst Valer of *Fashion*, Berinthia of *Woodfalls*, the terrible, the embittered Berinthia who was also Angela) cards had been sent out from Foreign-Colony Street, in the comprehensive name of Sir Oliver Dawtry, the famous banker and financier, inviting them to meet the new lessee of the Source.

It was one of those sultry summer nights of electricity and tension, when nerves are apt to explode at almost nothing. Beyond the iron Calvary on the Ursulines' great wall, London flared with lights.

Perched upon a parapet in brilliant solitude, her identity unsuspected by the throng, Miss Sinquier, swathed in black mousseline and nursing a sheaf of calla lilies, surveyed the scene with inexpressive eyes.

'And there was the wind bellowing and we witches wailing: and no Macbeth!' a young man with a voice like cheap scent was saying to a sympathetic journalist for whatever it might be worth. . . .

Miss Sinquier craned her head.

Where were the two 'Washingtons'? or the little Iris girl?

By the Buddha shrine, festively decked with lamps, couples were pirouetting to a nigger band, while in the vicinity of the buffet a masked adept was holding a clairaudience of a nature only to be guessed at from afar. An agile negro melody, wild rag-time with passages of almost Wesleyan hymnishness—reminiscent of Georgia gospel-missions; the eighteenth century in the Dutch East Indies—charmed and soothed the ear.

Miss Sinquier jigged her foot.

At their cell windows, as if riveted by the lights and commotion, leaned a few pale nuns.

Poor things!

The call of the world could seldom wholly be quenched!

She started as a fan of seabirds' feathers skimmed her arm.

'Sylvester's come,' Mrs. Sixsmith in passing said.

'Oh!'

'Aren't you scared?'

'Scared?'

'You know, he always belittles people. Sylvester traduces everyone; he even crabs his daughter; he damns all he sees.'

'Boom!'

'How he got up those narrow stairs is a mystery to me.' Mrs. Sixsmith smiled.

Miss Sinquier raised her face towards the bustling stars. An elfish horse-shoe moon, felicitously bright, struck her as auspicious.

'One should bow to it,' she said.

'Idolatry!'

'There! look what nodding does.'

A blanche bacchante with a top-knot of leaves venturesomely approached.

'I'm Amethyst,' she murmured.

'Indeed?'

'Of *Fashion*. You are Miss Sinquier, I take it, whose costumes for Romeo—Renaissance, and ergo *à la mode*!—I so long to hear about.'

Miss Sinquier dimpled.

'The frocks,' she said, 'some of them, will be simply killing.'

'I want your first.'

'Loose white.'

'I suppose, *coiffé de sphinx avec un tortis de perles*?'

Miss Sinquier shook her head.

'No "Juliet-cap" of spurious pearls for me,' she said.

'You dare to abolish it?'

'I do.'

'You excite me.'

'Unless the bloom is off the peach, Juliet needs no nets.'

Miss Valer lowered discreetly her voice.

'And your Romeo?' she queried. 'He must make love angelically?'

'He does.'

'I admire enormously his friend.'

'Mr. Nice?'

'He has such perfect sloth. I love his lazarone-ness, his Riva-degli-Schiavone-ness ... He's very, very handsome. But, of course, it cannot last!'

'No?'

'Like an open rose. Have you no sympathy yourself?'

'None.'

'That's a pity. An actress ... she needs a lover: a sort of husbandina, as it were ... I always say Passion tells: *L'amour*!'

Miss Sinquier threw a glance towards Mrs. Sixsmith, who stood listlessly flirting her fan.

'I'm going to the buffet, child,' she said.

'Then I think I'll join you.'

And drawing her friend's arm within her own, Miss Sinquier moved away.

'She must belong to more than one weekly!' she reflected.

'You didn't mention your Old Mechlin scarf, or your fox-trimmed nightie,' Mrs. Sixsmith murmured, dexterously evading the psychic freedoms of the masked adept.

'Have you no shame, Paul?' she asked.

'Paul!'

Miss Sinquier wondered.

'Mephisto! I know his parlour tricks ... though it would only be just, perhaps, to say he did foresee our separation some time before it occurred.'

'Oh, how extraordinary.'

'Once as I was making ready to pay some calls, in order to frighten me, he caused the hare's foot on my toilet-table to leave its carton sheath and go skipping about the room.'

'Whatever did you do?'

'My dear, I was disgusted. It really seemed as if the whole of Womanhood was outraged. So, to *punish* him—for revenge—instead of going to a number of houses that day, I went to only one.'

'There wouldn't be time?'

'I shall always blame myself ...'

'Why?'

But a lanthorn falling in flames just then above them put an end to the conversation.

'That's the second I've seen drop,' Miss May Mant exclaimed, darting up.

'What have you been up to?'

'Having my bumps examined.'

'What!'

'By the masked professor . . . Oh, the things he said; only fancy, he told me I'd cause the death of one both near and dear? Ita's near . . . but she certainly isn't dear—odious cat.'

'He must have thought you curiously credulous,' Miss Sinquier murmured, turning her head aside.

To her annoyance she perceived the scholarly representative of the *Dispatch*—a man of prodigious size—leaning solidly on a gold-headed cane while appraising her to Sir Oliver Dawtry, from her bebandeaued head to her jewelly shoes.

'She reminds me just a little of someone *de l'Évangile*!' she could hear the great critic say.

'Sylvester!'

'Oh?'

'Should he speak,' Mrs. Sixsmith murmured, wincing at the summer lightning that flickered every now and then, 'don't forget the medieval nightie or the Mechlin lace! Five long yards—a cloud . . .'

Miss Sinquier buried her lips in her flowers.

Through the barred windows of the convent opposite certain novices appeared to be enjoying a small saltation among themselves.

Up and down the corridor to the yearning melody of the minstrel players they twirled, clinging to one another in an ecstasy of delight.

Her fine eyes looked beautiful as, raising them fraught with soul, they met the veteran critic's own.

XV

'O, DEAR God, help me. Hear me, Jesu. Hear me and forgive me and be offended not if what I ask is vain . . . soften all hostile hearts and let them love me—adore me!—O heaven, help me to please. Vouchsafe at each *finale* countless curtains; and in the "Potion Scene," O Lord, pull me through . . .'

Unwilling to genuflect in the presence of her maid, who would interpret any unwontedness of gesture as first-night symptoms of fear, Miss Sinquier lifted her face towards the bluish light of day that filtered obliquely through the long glass-plating above.

'There's a cat on the skylight, Smith,' was what she said as her maid with a telegram recalled her wandering gaze to earth.

It was a telegram from her father.

'Missed conveyance York,' she read. 'Bishopthorpe to-night archiepiscopal blessings.'

'Ah, well . . .' she professionally philosophised, 'there'll be *deadheads* besides, I've no doubt.'

'Any answer, miss?'

'Go, Smith, to the box office, and say G 2 and 3 (orchestra) have been returned; there's no answer,' she added, moving towards the brightly lit dressing-room beyond.

Ensconced in an easy chair, before a folding mirror that, rich in reflections, encompassed her screen-like about, sat Mrs. Sixsmith pensively polishing her nails.

Miss Sinquier bit her lip.

'I thought——' she began.

'Sh——! Be Juliet now. We're in Verona,' Mrs. Sixsmith exclaimed. '*Fuori* the doors.'

'Fancy finding *you*.'

'Me?'

'What are you doing in *my Italy*?'

Mrs. Sixsmith threw a glance at herself in the glass. 'I'm a girl friend,' she said; 'a Venetian acquaintance: someone *Julie* met while paddling in the Adriatic—in fact, *cara cuore*, I'm a daughter of the Doge. Yes; I'm one of the Dolfin-Trons.'

'Don't be ridiculous.'

'I'm Catarina Dolfin-Tron.'

'Kitty Tron!'

'Your own true Kate.'

'When are you going round?'

'Let me finish my hands. My manicurist has left me with such claws. . . . Poor little soul! When she came to my wedding-finger she just twiddled her rasp and broke out crying. "To be filing people's nails," she said, "while my husband is filing a petition!"'

'Wonderful that she could.'

'This city has its sadness. Your maid, Smith, while you were in the other room, said, "Oh, marm, what you must have endured; *one Smith* was enough for me."'

'Poor Kate!'

'Ah, Julie . . .' Mrs. Sixsmith sighed, when the opening of the door gently was followed by the entry of Mrs. Smee.

'Am I disturbing you?' she asked.

'No, come in.'

'I want to tell you my husband isn't himself.'

'He's ill?'

'He's not himself.'

'In what way?'

'It's a hard thing for a wife to confess. But for a première he's nearly always in wine.'

'Is he . . . *much*?'

'I never knew him like it!'

Mrs. Sixsmith examined her nails.

'So violent!' she ventured.

'He's more confused, dear, than violent,' Mrs. Smee explained. 'He seems to think we're doing *The Tempest*; Romeo's tanned breast he takes for Ferdinand's. "Mind, Ferdy boy," I heard him say, "and keep the —— out." Whereupon, his mind wandered to the Russian plays I love, and he ran through some of Irina's lines from *The Three Sisters*. "My soul," you know she says, "my soul is like an expensive piano which is locked and the key lost." Ah, there's for you; Shakespeare never wrote that. He couldn't. Even by making piano, spinet. O Russia! Russia! land of Tchekhov, land of Andreieff, of Solugub, of Korelenko, of Artzibashef—Maria Capulet salutes thee! And then my man was moved to sing. His love, she was in Otaheite . . . But as soon as he saw me he was back at *The Tempest* again, calling me Caliban, Countess, and I don't know what.'

'Oh, how disgraceful!'

'After the performance I'll pop home—Home!—in a drosky and shut him out.'

'Meanwhile?'

'He'll pass for a Friar. The Moujik!'

'Still . . .'

'He'll probably be priceless; the masses always love the man who can make them laugh.'

Miss Sinquier moved restlessly towards the door and looked out.

All was activity.

Plants for the balcony set, of a rambling, twining nature, together with a quantity of small wicker cages labelled 'Atmospherics,' and containing bats, owls, lizards, etc., were in course of being prepared.

The manageress knit her brows.

'Miss Marquis,' she called, 'instead of teasing the animals, I suggest you complete your toilet.'

'. . . She'd better look sharp!'

Mrs. Smee consulted her notes.

'She reminds me more of a nurse-maid than a nurse,' she murmured. 'Not what *I* should have chosen for Juliet at all.'

'Perhaps not.'

'Miss Marquis has no stage presence. And such a poor physique—she's too mean.'

'Anyway, Sally's got fine men. I never saw finer fellows. Even the Apothecary! Fancy taking the fatal dose from a lad like that; he makes me want to live.'

Mrs. Smee purred.

'To have interesting workmates is everything,' she said. 'Hughie Huntress, as Producer, seemed quite stunned at the subtle material at his disposal. . . . In fact, he realised from the first, he told me, he *couldn't* "produce" all of it.'

Mrs. Sixsmith lowered her voice.

'Where did Sally find her Balthasar?' she asked, 'and where did she secure her Tybalt?'

'My dear Mrs. Sixsmith, I'm not in the management's secrets, remember, so much as you!'

'Or who put her in the way of Sampson and Gregory? And *where* did she get her Benvolio?'

'Through an agent, I don't doubt.'

Mrs. Sixsmith threw a sidelong probing glance in the direction of the door. Already in her heart she felt herself losing her hold. Had the time inevitably come to make out the score?

Through the open door came a squeal.

'Sally, the owls!'

'Leave them, René,' Miss Sinquier ordered.

'*Dearest*, what diddlies; one has a look of old Sir Oliver!' Miss Mant declared, coming forward into the room.

Clad in a pair of striped 'culottes,' she had assumed, notwithstanding sororal remonstrance, the conspicuous livery of Paris.

'I just looked in to thank you, darling,' she began, 'for all your sweetness and goodness . . . Oh, Sally, when I saw the playbill with my name on it (right in among the gentlemen!) I thought I should have died. Who could have guessed ever it would be a breeches part?'

'Turn round.'

'Such jealous murmurings already as there are; a-citizen-of-Verona, an envious super without a line, whispered, as I went by, that my legs in these tissue tights had a look of forced asparagus.'

'Nonsense.'

'Of course: I knew that, Sally. But devil take me. How I'll hate going back into virginals again; these trousers spoil you for skirts.'

'Sprite.'

'And I'd a trifling triumph too, darling, which I chose to ignore; just as I was leaving my dressing-room, Jack Whorwood, all dressed up for Tybalt, accosted me with a fatuous, easy smile. "I want your picture, Miss Iris, with your name on it," he said. "*Do* you?" I said. "I do," he said. "Then I fear you'll have to," I said. Oh, he was cross! But all the while, Sally, he was speaking I could feel the wolf . . .'

'Better be careful,' Mrs. Sixsmith snapped.

'As if I'd cater to his blue besoins!'

'René, René!'

'Although I snubbed him,' Miss Iris murmured, stooping to examine upon the toilet-table a beribboned aeroplane filled with sweets, 'he looked *too* charming!'

Mrs. Smee chafed gently her hands.

'I must return to my Friar,' she said.

'He is saying the grossest, the wickedest things!'

'Mr. Smee's sallies at times are not for young ears,' Mrs. Smee loftily observed. 'His witticisms,' she added, 'aren't for everyone.'

'My friend, Miss Tird, who came to watch me dress, was quite upset by his cochonneries!'

'Although your little friend appears scarcely to be nine, she seems *dazed* by her sex and power,' Mrs. Smee unfavourably commented.

'I'll have to go, I suppose,' Miss Sinquier sighed, 'and see how matters stand.'

'Prenez garde: for when making up he mostly makes a palette of his hand,' Mrs. Sixsmith said. 'I happen to know—because one day he caught hold of me.'

Mrs. Smee protruded her tongue and drew it slowly in.

'Hist!' she exclaimed.

Along the corridor the call-boy was going his rounds.

'First act beginners,' chirped he.

Miss Sinquier quivered.

'... Soften all hostile hearts and let them love me ...' she prayed.

⬥═══➤ XVI ⬅═══⬥

THE sound of rain-drops falling vigorously upon the glass roof awoke her. A few wind-tossed, fan-shaped leaves tinged with hectic autumnal colours spotted marvellously the skylight without, half-screening the pale and monotonous sky beyond.

With a yawn she sat up amid her pillows, cushioning her chin on her knees.

After last night's proceedings the room was a bower of gardenia, heliotrope, and tuberose, whose allied odours during slumber had bewildered just a little her head.

Flinging back the bed-clothes, she discovered as she did so a note.

'Sally,' she read, 'should you be conscious before I return, I'm only gone to market, cordially yours R. Iris. Such mixed verdicts! I've arranged the early papers on your dressing-table. I could find no reference to me. This morning there were rat-marks again, and part of a mangled bat.'

'Oh, those "atmospherics"!' Miss Sinquier complained, finding somnolently her way into the inner room.

Here all was Italy—even the gauze-winged aeroplane filled with sweets had an air of a silvery water-fly from some serene trans-Alpine garden.

Dropping to a fine *cassone* she perused with contracted brows a small sheaf of notices, the gist of which bore faint pencilled lines below.

'Her acting is a revelation.'

'We found her very refreshing.'

'There has been nothing like it for years.'

'Go to the Source.'

'An unfeminine Juliet.'

'A decadent Juliet.'

'... The Romeo kiss—you take your broadest fan.'

'The kiss in Romeo takes only fifteen minutes ... "Some" kiss!'

'The Romeo kiss will be the talk of the town.'

'A distinctive revival.'

'I sat at the back of the pit-stalls and trembled.'

'Kiss——'

'The last word in kisses.'

'Tio, Tio, Io! Io! jug—jug!'

'Shakespeare as a Cloak.'

'A smart Juliet.'

'An immoral Juliet.'

'Before a house packed to suffocation——'

'Among those present at the Source last night were'—she looked —'were, Queen Henriette Marie, Duchess of Norwich, Dismalia Duchess of Meath-and-Mann, Lady Di Flattery, Lord and Lady Newblood, Mr. and Lady Caroline Crofts, Sir Gottlieb and Lady Gretel Teuton-Haven, ex-King Bomba, ex-King Kacatogan, ex-Queen of Snowland, ex-Prince Marphise, Hon. Mrs. Mordecai, Lady Wimbush, Lord and Lady Drumliemore, Sir John and Lady Journeyman, Lord and Lady Lonely, Lady Harrier, Feodorowna Lady Meadowbank, Lady Lucy Lacy, Duchess of Netherland and Lady Diana Haviours, Miss Azra, Miss Christine Cross, Sir Francis and Lady Four, Madame Kotzebue, Comtesse Yvonde de Tot, Mlle. de Tot, Duque de Quaranta, Marquesa Pitti-Riffa and Sir Siegfried Seitz.'

So ... she sneezed, all was well!

A success: undoubtedly.

'O God! How quite ... *delicious*!' she murmured, snatching up a cinquecento cope transformed to be a dressing-gown, and faring forth for an airing upon the stage.

At that hour there wasn't a soul.

The darkened auditorium looked wan and eerie, the boxes caves.

The churchyard scene with its unassuming crosses, accentuating the regal sepulchre of the Capulets (and there for that), showed grimly.

'Wisht!' she exclaimed, as a lizard ran over her foot.

Frisking along the footpaths, it disappeared down a dark trap-hole.

Had René been setting more traps? Upon a mysterious mound by a jam jar full of flowers was a hunk of cheese.

She stood a moment fascinated.

Then bracing herself, head level, hands on hips, she executed a few athletic figures to shake off sleep.

Suddenly there was a cry, a cry that was heard outside the theatre walls, blending half-harmoniously with the London streets.

⟸══ XVII ══⟹

THE rich trot of funeral horses died imperceptibly away.

Looking out somewhat furtively from beneath her veil, Mrs. Sixsmith could observe only a few farmers conversing together beneath the immemorial yews of S. Irene.

It was over.

There was nothing left to do but to throw a last glance at the wreaths.

'From the artists and staff of the Source Theatre as a trifling proof of their esteem'—such the large lyre crushing her own 'Resurgam.' And there also was the Marys' with their motto: 'All men and women are merely players. They have their exits and their entrances.' And the 'Heureuse!' tribute by the sexton's tools—she craned—was Yvonde de Yalta's, it appeared.

'Yvonde de Yalta!'

Mrs. Sixsmith gulped.

'You grieve?'

Canon Sinquier stood beside her.

'I——' she stammered.

'So many tributes,' he said.

'Indeed, sir, the flowers are extremely handsome.'

'So many crowns and crosses, harps and garlands.'

'One has to die for friends to rally!'

'Were you in her company?'

'I, Canon? . . . I never was on the stage in my life!'

'No?'

'My husband would never listen to it: he holds with Newman.'

'. . . I don't recollect.'

'Besides, I'm no use at acting at all.'

'You knew my poor daughter well?'

Caprice

'I was her protégée ... that is ... it was *I* who tried to protect her,' Mrs. Sixsmith replied.

'My dear madam.'

'Oh, Canon, why was her tomb not in Westminster where so many of her profession are? I was reading somewhere only the other day there are more *actresses* buried there than kings!'

'It may be so.'

'Here ... she is so isolated ... so lost. Sally loved town.'

'Tell me,' he begged, 'something of her end.'

'Indeed, sir——'

'You're too weary?'

'Oh, I *hate* a funeral, Canon! Listening to their Jeremiads.'

'You shall take my arm.'

'Her father was her cult, Canon. . . . In that she resembled much the irresistible Venetian—*Catarina Dolfin-Tron*.'

'Sally seldom wrote.'

'Her time, you should remember, was hardly her own.'

'Tell me something,' he insisted, 'of her broken brilliance.'

'Only by keening her could I hope to do that.'

'One would need to be a Bion. Or a Moschus . . .'

'We laid her, star-like, in the dress-circle—out on Juliet's bier . . . Mr. and Mrs. Smee and her dresser watched . . . Berinthia . . . Sylvester . . . came. I cannot lose from mind how one of the scene-shifters said to me, "How bonny she looked on the bloody balcony."'

'My poor darling.'

'On the evening of her dissolution, I regret to say, there was a most unseemly fracas in the foyer—some crazy wretch demanding back her money, having booked her place in advance; everyone of the staff in tears and too unstrung to heed her. Had it been a box, Canon; or even a stall! But she only paid four shillings.'

'Was there anything on my poor child's mind distressing her at all?'

'Not that I'm aware of.'

'No little affair ... ?'

'No ...'

'Nothing?'

'Your girl was never loose, Canon. She was straight. Sally was straight ... at least,' Mrs. Sixsmith added (with a slight shrug) ... 'to the best of my knowledge, she was!'

'In a life of opportunity ...'

'Ah, sh——, sir, sh——!'

'Had my daughter debts?'

'Indeed she had . . . she owed me money. Much money. But I won't refer to that . . . Sally owed me one thousand pounds.'

'She owed you a thousand pounds?'

'She was infinitely involved.'

'Upon what could she spend so much?'

'Her clothes,' Mrs. Sixsmith replied with a nervous titter, 'for one thing, were exquisite. All from the atelier of the divine Katinka King . . .'

'King?'

'She *knew*! Puss! The white mantilla for the balcony scene alone cost her close on three hundred pounds.'

'And where, may I ask, is it now?'

'It disappeared,' Mrs. Sixsmith answered, a quick red shooting over her face, 'in the general confusion. I hear,' she murmured with a little laugh, 'they even filched the till!'

'What of the little *ingénue* she took to live with her?'

'May Mant? Her sister is sending her to school—if (that is) she can get her to go!'

'It was her inadvertence, I take it, that caused my daughter's death'.

'Indeed, sir, yes. But for her—she had been setting traps! She and a girl called Tird! a charming couple!'

'Oh?'

'Your daughter and she used frequently to take their meals in the boxes, which made, of course, for mice. There was a well, you know, below the stage.'

'So she wrote her mother.'

Mrs. Sixsmith fumbled in the depths of a beaded pouch.

'There was a letter found in one of her jacket-pockets, Canon,' she said. 'Perhaps you might care to have it.'

'A letter? From whom?'

'A young coster of Covent Garden, who saw your daughter at a stage-farewell.'

'Be so good, dear lady, as to inform me of its contents.'

'It's quite illiterate,' Mrs. Sixsmith murmured, putting back her veil and glancing humorously towards the grave.

'DEAR MISS,

'I seed you at the Fisher Mat. on Friday last and you took my heart a treat. I'm only a young Gallery boy—wot's in the flower trade. But I knows wot I knows—And you're It. Oh Miss! I does want to see you act in Juliet in your own butey-ful ous, if only you ad a seat as you could spare just for me and a pal o' mine as is alright. I send you some red cars sweet and scenty fresh from Covent Market, your true-gone

'BILL.

'Hoping for tickets.'

'Poor lad. Sally would have obliged him, I feel sure,' Canon Sinquier said.

'Alas, what ephemeral creatures, Canon, we are!'

'We are in His hands.'

'She knew that. Sally's faith never forsook her ... Oh, Canon, some day perhaps I may come to you to direct me. I'm so soul-sick.'

'Is there no one in London to advise you?'

'Nobody at all.'

'Indeed? You astonish me.'

'I'm perfectly tired of London, Canon!'

'Your husband, no doubt, has his occupation there.'

'My husband and I are estranged ...'

'You've no child?'

'Alas, Canon! I often think ... sometimes ... I would like to adopt one. A little country buttercup! Really ... a dog, even the best of mannered—isn't very *comme il faut.*'

'You seek a boy?'

'Mer-cy *no*! Nothing of the sort ... You quite mistake my meaning.'

'Your meaning, madam, was obscure.'

'I imply a girl ... a blonde! And she'd share with me, sir, every facility, every advantage. Her education should be my care.'

'What is your age?'

'From thirteen——'

'An orphan?'

'Preferably.'

'I will discuss the affair presently with my wife,' Canon Sinquier said, turning in meditation his steps towards the wicket-gate.

'Before leaving your charming city, Canon, I should like beyond everything to visit the episcopal Palace: Sally used often to speak of the art treasures there.'

'Art-treasures?'

'Old pictures!'

'Are you an amateur of old pictures?'

'Indeed I am. My husband once—Paul—he paid a perfect fortune for a Dutch painting; and will you believe me, Canon! It was only of the back view of a horse.'

'A Cuyp?'

'A Circus—with straw-knots in its tail. It used to hang in Mr. Sixsmith's study; and there it always was! Frankly,' she added, brushing a black kid glove to her face, 'I used sometimes to wish it would kick.'

'If you're remaining here for any length of time, there are some portraits at the Deanery that are considered to be of interest, I believe.'

'Portraits!'

'Old ecclesiastical ones.'

'Oh, Canon?'

'Perhaps you would come quietly to dinner. At which of our inns are you?'

'I'm at the "Antelope."'

'I know that my girl would have wished our house to be open to you. You were her friend. Her champion. . . .'

'Dear Canon—don't . . . don't: you mustn't! She's at peace. Nothing can fret her. Nothing shall fret her . . . ever now. And, you know, as a manageress, she was liable to vast vexations.'

'My poor pet.'

'She's *hors de combat*: free from a calculating and dishonest world; ah, Canon!'

'We shall expect you, then, dear Sally's friend, to dinner this evening at eight,' Canon Sinquier murmured as he walked away.

Mrs. Sixsmith put up a large chiffon sunshade and hovered staccato before the dwindling spires and ogee dome of S. Irene.

It was one of the finest days imaginable. The sun shone triumphantly in the midst of a cloudless sky.

She would loiter awhile among the bougainvillæas and dark, spreading laurels of the Cathedral green, trespassing obtusely now and then into quiet gardens, through tall wrought-iron gates.

New visions and possibilities rare rose in her mind.

With Sally still, she could do a lot. Through her she would be received with honours into the courtly circles of the Close.

Those fine palatial houses, she reflected, must be full of wealth . . .

old Caroline plate and gorgeous green Limoges: Sally indeed had
proved it! The day she had opened her heart in the Café Royal she
had spoken of a massive tureen *too heavy even to hold*.

Mrs. Sixsmith's eyes grew big.

Her lost friend's father wished for anecdotes, anecdotes of her
'broken brilliance'; he should have them. She saw herself indulging
him with 'Salliana,' wrapped in a white mantilla of old Mechlin
lace.

An invitation from Canon and Mrs. Sinquier should be adroitly
played for to-night: 'And once in the house!...' she schemed,
starting, as a peacock, symbol of S. Irene, stretched from a bougain-
villæa-shrouded wall its sapphire neck at her as if to peck.

Her thoughts raced on.

On a near hill beyond the river reach the sombre little church of
S. Ann changed to a thing of fancy against a yellowing sky.

From all sides, seldom in unison, pealed forth bells. In fine
religious gaiety struck S. Mary, contrasting clearly with the bumble-
dumble of S. Mark, S. Elizabeth and S. Sebastian in Flower Street
seemed in high dispute, while across the sunset water S. Ann-on-the-
Hill did nothing but complain. Near by S. Nicaise, half-paralysed
and impotent, scarcely shook. Then triumphant, in a hurricane of
sound, S. Irene hushed the lot.

Mrs. Sixsmith fetched a long, calm breath.

It was already the hour he had said.

'And my experience tells me,' she murmured, as she took her
way towards the Deanery, 'that with opportunity and time he may
hope to succeed to Sir Oliver.'

Valmouth: A Romantic Novel

DAY was drooping on a fine evening in March as a brown barouche passed through the wrought-iron gates of Hare-Hatch House on to the open highway.

Beneath the crepuscular, tinted sky the countryside stretched away, interspersed with hamlets, meads and woods, towards low, loosely engirdling hills, that rose up against the far horizon with a fine monastic roll.

Although it was but the third month of the year, yet, from a singular softness of the air, already the trees were in full, fresh leaf. Along the hedgerows hawthorns were in bloom, while the many wild flowers by the roadside scented in fitful whiffs an invigorating, caressing breeze.

Seated immediately behind the coachman in the shell-like carriage was a lady no longer young. Her fragile features, long and pointed, were swathed, quasi-biblically, in a striped Damascus shawl that looked Byzantine, at either side of which escaped a wisp of red, crimped hair. Her big, wide eyes, full of innocent, child-like wonder, were set off by arched auburn brows that in the twilight seemed almost to be phosphorescent.

By her side reclined a plump, placidish person, whose face was half concealed beneath a white-lace coalscuttle hat.

'Some *suppose* . . . while *others*——; again, I'm told . . . And in *any case*, my dear!' The voice came droning in a monotonous, sing-song way.

Facing the ladies a biretta'd priest appeared to be perusing a little, fat, black, greasy book of prayers which he held aslant so as to catch the light. Every now and then he would raise a cold, hypnotic eye above the margin of his page towards the ladies *vis-à-vis*.

'Of whom are you so unkindly speaking, Mrs. Thoroughfare?' he enquired at length.

The head beneath the coalscuttle-shaped hat drooped confused.

'I? Oh, my dear Father——!'

'Yes? my dear child? . . .'

'I was only telling Mrs. Hurstpierpoint how——'

Mrs. Hurstpierpoint—the dowager of the gleaming brows—leaned forward all at once in the carriage and pulled the checkstring attached to her footman's arm.

'Benighted idiot!' she exclaimed.

The fellow turned towards his mistress a melancholy, dreamy face that had something of a *quia multum amavit* expression in its wizen whiteness, and raised stiffly to a frayed silk cockade a long, bare hand.

'Didn't I say, blunt-headed booby, to Valmouth?'

'To Valmouth?'

'By way of Fleet. *Pardon*, Thoroughfare,' the dowager murmured, 'you were saying——'

'Evil, evil, evil,' her companion returned. 'Nothing but slander, wickedness and lies. *N'est ce pas*, Father Colley?'

'What is your book, Father Colley-Mahoney?' Mrs. Hurstpierpoint asked.

'St. Stanislaus-Kostka, my child.'

'Kostka——! It sounds like one of those islands, those savage islands, where my big, handsome, strong—*and* delicate!—darling Dick stopped at once, just to write to his old mother,' Mrs. Thoroughfare declared.

'Where is he now, Eliza?'

'Off the coast of Jamaica. His *ship*——' she broke off as a voice full and flexible rose suddenly from behind a burgeoning quincunx of thorns:

'I heard the voice of Jesus say-y-y! Yahoo, to heel. Bad dog.'

'It's that crazy Corydon,' Mrs. Thoroughfare blinked.

'Which, dear, crazy?'

'David Tooke—the brother, you know, of that extraordinarily extraordinary girl.'

'Thoroughfare.'

'Father?'

'That tongue.'

'The last time Dick was at Hare, I thought——'

'*Meet me in glow-ry by the gate o' pearl*. Hi, Douce!' the voice irrelevantly veered, as, over a near meadow, barking lustily, sprang a shaggy sheep-dog. 'Hi, Douce boy? . . . Doucey! Douce!'

The Priest pulled the light merino carriage rug higher about his knees.

'How,' he addressed Mrs. Hurstpierpoint, whose chevelure in

the diminishing daylight was taking on almost the appearance of an aureole, 'how if the glorious Virgin required you to take this young fellow under your wing?'

Mrs. Hurstpierpoint bent thoughtfully her eyes to the somewhat 'phallic' passementerie upon her shawl.

'For the sake, I presume,' she queried, 'of his soul?'

'Precisely.'

'But is he ripe?' Mrs. Thoroughfare wondered.

'Ripe?'

'I *mean*——'

There was a busy silence.

Descending a narrow tree-lined lane the carriage passed into a leisurely winding road, bounded by market-gardens and the River Val. Through a belt of osier and alder Valmouth, with its ancient bridge and great stone church, that from the open country had the scheming look of an ex-cathedral, showed a few lit lamps.

Mrs. Thoroughfare twittered.

'I did require a ribbon, a roughish ribbon,' she announced, 'and to call as well at the music-shop for those Chopin sonatas.'

'A "roughish" ribbon?' Father Colley-Mahoney echoed in searching tones. 'And pray, might I ask, what is that?'

'It's—— Oh, Father.'

'Is it silk? Or satin? Or is it velvet? Is it,' he conscientiously pressed, 'something rose-leafy? Something lilac?... Eh? Or sky-blue, perhaps?... Insidious child!'

'Insidious, Father?'

'Prevaricating.'

'Pax, Father,' Mrs. Thoroughfare beseeched.

Father Colley-Mahoney gazed moodily above the floppy fabric of her hat at an electric two-seater that was endeavouring to forge by the barouche from behind.

As it came abreast of it the occupants, a spruce, middle-aged man, and a twinkling negress, who clasped in her arms a something that looked to be an india-rubber coil, respectfully bowed.

'Dr. Dee, and la Yajñavalkya!'

'Those appliances of hers——; that she flaunts!'

'In massaging her "cases," ' Mrs. Thoroughfare *sotto-voce* said, 'I'm told she has a trick of—um.'

'Oh?'

'And of—um!'

'Indeed?'

'So poor Marie Wilks' nurse told my maid . . .'

'When,' Father Colley-Mahoney murmured, '*was* Miss Wilks a hundred?'

'Only last week.'

'Nowadays,' Mrs. Hurtpierpoint commented, 'around Valmouth centenarians will be soon as common as peas!'

'The air,' Mrs. Thoroughfare sniffed, 'there's no air to compare to it.'

'For the sake of veracity, I should be tempted to qualify that.'

'I fancy I'm not the only one, Father, to swear by Valmouth air!'

'Valmouth air, Valmouth air.'

'At the Strangers' Hotel,' Mrs. Thoroughfare giddily went on, 'it seems there's not a single vacant bed. No; nor settle either. . . . Victor Vatt, the delicate *paysagiste*—the English Corot—came yesterday, and Lady Parvula de Panzoust was to arrive to-day.'

'I was her bridesmaid some sixty years ago—and she was no girl then,' Mrs. Hurstpierpoint smiled.

'She stands, I fear, poor thing, now, for something younger than she looks.'

'Fie, Thoroughfare!'

'Fie, Father?'

'*La jeunesse—hélas,*' Mrs. Hurstpierpoint softly said, '*n'a qu'un temps.*'

Father Colley-Mahoney looked absently away towards the distant hills whose outlines gleamed elusively beneath the rising moon.

Here and there, an orchard in silhouette, showed all in black blossom against an extravagant sky.

𝕸 *II* 𝕸

TROTTING before his master, the fire-flies singeing his tail, ran the watch-dog Douce. From the humid earth beneath his firm white paws the insects clamoured zing-zing-zing. Nuzzling intently the ground, sampling the pliant grasses, he would return from time to time to menace some lawless calf or cow.

Following a broken trackway through the deserted corn-land, the herd filed lazily towards the town in a long, close queue. Tookes's

Farm, or Abbot's Farm, as it indifferently was called, whither they now were bent, lay beneath the decayed walls of St. Veronica, the oldest church in the town. Prior to the Reformation the farm buildings (since rebuilt and considerably dwindled) had appertained, like much of the glebeland around Valmouth, to the Abbots of St. Veronica, when at the confiscation of the monasteries by the Crown one Thierry Monfaulcon Tooke, tennis-master to the Court of King Henry VIII, feinting to injure himself one day while playing with the royal princesses, had been offered by Henry, through their touching entreaties 'in consideration of his mishap,' the Abbey farm of St. Veronica's, then recently vacated by the monks; from which same Thierry (in the space of only six generations) the estate had passed to his descendants of the present time. Now in the bluey twilight as seen from the fields the barns and outhouses appeared really to be more capacious than the farm itself. With its whitewashed walls and small-paned latticed windows it showed poorly enough between the two sumptuous wheat-ricks that stood reared on either side. Making their way across the long cobble bridge that spanned the Val, the cattle turned into an elm-lined lane that conducted to the farmyard gates, where, pottering expectantly, was a tiny boy.

At a bark from Douce he swung wide a creaking cross-barred gate overspread by a thorn-tree all in flower.

With lethargic feet the animals stumbled through, proceeding in an automatic way to a strip of water at the far end of the yard into which they turned. By the side of it ran an open hanger upheld by a score of rough tarred posts. Against these precocious calves were wont as a rule to rub their crescent horns. Within showed a wagon or two, and a number of roosting doves.

Depositing his scrip in the outhouse the cowherd glanced around.

'Where's Thetis got?' he asked, addressing the small boy, who, brandishing a broken rhubarb-leaf, was flitting functionarily about.

'Thetis? . . . She's,' he hopped, 'standing in the river.'

'What's she standing there for?'

'Nothing.'

'. . . Must I thrash you, Bobby Jolly?'

'Oh, don't, David.'

'Then answer me quick.'

'When the tide flows up from Spadder Bay she pretends it binds her to the sea. Where her sweetheart is. Her b-betrothed. . . . Away in the glorious tropics.'

' 'Od! You're a simple one; you are!'

'Me?'

'Aye, you.'

'Don't be horrid, David, to me. . . . You mustn't be. It's bad enough quite without.'

' 'Od.'

'What with granny——'

'She'll not be here for long.'

'I don't think she'll die just yet.'

'It's a cruel climate,' the young man ruefully said, looking impatiently up through his eyelashes towards the stars.

It was one of the finest nights imaginable. The moon reigned full in the midst of a cloudless sky. From the thorn-tree by the gate the sound of a bird singing floated down exuberantly through the leaves.

'Aye, cruel,' he muttered, shouldering a pitchfork and going out into the yard. As he did so the church clock rang out loudly in the air above.

'Shall I find 'ee Thetis?'

'Nay. Maybe I'll go myself.'

Beyond the low yard wall gleamed the river, divided from the farm by a narrow garden parcelled out in vegetables and flowers.

A cindered pathway sloping between spring-lettuces and rows of early tulips whose swollen calyxes, milk-white, purple and red, probed superbly the moon-mist, led to the water's edge where, clinging to the branches of a pollard-willow, a girl was gently swaying with the tide. On her head, slightly thrown back, and slashed all over with the shadow of the willow leaves, was perched a small sailor's toque adorned with a spread gannet's wing that rose up venturesomely from the ribboned cord. Her light print frock, carelessly caught about her, revealed her bare legs below the knees.

The cowherd paused hesitant.

'Thetis—!' he called.

Self-absorbed, wrapped in enchanting fancies, she turned: 'H'lo?'

'Come in now.'

'I shan't.'

'Come in, Thetis.'

'I won't. I will not.'

'You'll catch your death!'

'What of it?'

'The-tis. . . .'

With a laugh, she whisked further out into the stream.

Through her parted fingers, in microscopic wavelets, it swept, all moon-plashed from the sea.

Laughing, she bent her lips to the briny water.

❧ *III* ❧

IN a little back sitting-room overlooking the churchyard Granny Tooke, in a high rush-chair, was sharing a basin of milk with the cat.

It was her 'Vibro day,' a day when a sound like wild-bees swarming made ghostly music through the long-familiar room. Above the good green trees the venerable wood dial of St. Veronica's great clock informed her that, in the normal course of things, Madam Yajñavalkya and her instruments should already be on their way.

'Was there ever a cat like ye for milk, Tom?' the old lady wondered, setting down the half-emptied bowl on the whatnot beside her, and following with a poulterer's discerning eye the careless movements of the farm pigeons as they preened themselves on the long gross gargoyles of the church.

Once, long ago, in that same building she had stood a round-cheeked bride. Alas for life's little scars! . . . Now, all wrapped up like a moulting canary, her dun, lean face was fuller of wrinkles than a withered russet. Nevertheless, it was good still to be alive! Old Mrs. Tooke sighed with self-complacence as her glance took in the grave-ground, in whose dark, doughy soil so many former cronies lay asleep. It was a rare treat for her to be able, without any effort, to witness from time to time a neighbour's last impressive pomps; to watch 'the gentlemen' in their tall town tiles 'bearing up poor fellows'; to join (unseen in her high rush-chair, herself in carpet-slippers) in the long, lugubrious hymn; to respire through the window chinks of her room the faint exotic perfume of aromatic flowers from a ground all white with wreaths.

But, to-day, there were no obsequies to observe at all.

Through the window glass she could see Maudie and Maidie Comedy, daughters of Q. Comedy, Esq., the local estate agent and auctioneer, amusing themselves by making daisy chains by the mortuary door, while within the church someone—evidently not the vicar's sister—was casting the stale contents of an altar-vase through a clerestory-window (sere sweet by sweet), quite callous of passers-by.

Mrs. Tooke blew pensively the filmy skin forming upon her milk. A long sunbeam lighting up the whatnot caused the great copper clasp of her Bible to emit a thousand playful sparks, bringing to her notice somewhat glaringly a work of fiction that assuredly wasn't hers. . . . Extending a horny hand towards it, she had hardly made out a line when her granddaughter looked languorously in.

'Your towels are nicely steaming,' she said, resting her prepossessing, well-formed face against the polished woodwork of the door.

Mrs. Tooke coughed drily.

'So far,' she murmured, 'Mrs. Yaj ha'n't come.'

'It's such a splendid morning.'

'Where's David?'

'He went out early with the barley-mow.'

'Any orders?'

'The hotel only—extra butter.'

'Be sure to say it's risen. Butter and eggs,' Mrs. Tooke dramatically declared, 'have gone up. And while you're at the Strangers' you might propose a pair of pigeons, or two, to the cook.'

Miss Tooke turned yearningly her head.

'You'd think,' she faltered, 'they were seagulls, poor darlings, up there so white.'

'If only I could get about the place,' Mrs. Tooke restively pursued, 'as once I did.'

'Maybe with the warmer weather here you will. This very night the old sweetbrier tree came out. The old sweetbrier! And none of us thought it could.'

'In heaven's name,' her grandmother peevishly snapped, 'don't let me hear you talk of thinking. A more feather-brained girl there never lived.'

'I often think, at any rate,' Miss Tooke replied, 'I was born for something *more brilliant* than waiting on you.'

'Impudent baggage! Here, take it—before I tear it.'

'My library book?'

'Pah to the library. I wish there was none.'

Miss Tooke shrugged slightly her shoulders.

'There's Douce barking,' she said, 'I expect it's Mrs. Yaj.'

And in effect a crisp rat-a-tat on the yard-door gate was followed by a majestical footfall on the stair.

'Devil dog, pariah! Let go of me,' a voice came loudly drifting from below; a voice, large, deep, buoyant, of a sonorous persuasiveness, issuing straight from the entrails of the owner.

Mrs. Tooke had a passing palpitation.

'Put the chain on Douce, and make ready the thingamies!' she commanded, as Mrs. Yajñavalkya, wreathed in smiles, sailed briskly into the room.

She had a sheeny handkerchief rolled round and round her head, a loud-dyed petticoat and a tartan shawl.

'Forgive me I dat late,' she began. 'But I just dropped off to sleep again—like a little chile—after de collation.'

'Howsomever!' Mrs. Tooke exclaimed.

'Ah! de clients, Mrs. Tooke!' The negress beamed. 'Will you believe it now, but I was on my legs this morning before four! . . . Hardly was there a light in the sky when an old gentleman he send for me to de Strangers' Hotel.'

Mrs. Tooke professed astonishment.

'I understood you never "took" a gentleman,' she said.

'No more do I, Mrs. Tooke. Only,' Mrs. Yajñavalkya comfortably sighed, 'I like to relieve my own sex.'

'Up at four!' Mrs. Tooke archly quavered.

'And how do you find yourself to-day, Mrs. Tooke? How is dat sciatica ob yours?'

'To be open with you, Mrs. Yaj, I feel to-day as if all my joints want oiling!'

'What you complain ob, Mrs. Tooke, is nothing but stiffness—due very largely from want ob par. Or (as we Eastern women sometimes say) from want ob vim. Often de libber you know it get sluggish. But it will pass. . . . I shall not let—you hear me?—I shall not let you slip through my fingers: Oh no, your life wif me is so precious.'

'I can't hope to last very much longer, Mrs. Yaj, anyway, I suppose.'

'That is for me to say, Mrs. Tooke,' the imperious woman murmured, beginning to remove, by way of preliminary, the numerous glittering rings with which her hands were laden.

'Heysey-ho!' the old lady self-solicitously sighed, 'she's getting on.'

'And so's de time, Mrs. Tooke! But have no fear. Waited for as I am by a peeress ob distinction, I would never rush my art, especially wif you. No; oh no. You, my dear, are my most beautiful triumph! Have I not seen your precious life fluttering away, spent? Den at a call . . . I . . . wif my science—wif dese two hand have I not restored you to all de world's delights?'

'Delights,' Mrs. Tooke murmured, going off into a mournful key. 'Since the day my daughter-in-law—Charlotte Carpster that was—died in child-bed, and my great, bonny wild-oat of a son destroyed himself in a fit of remorse, there's been nothing but trouble for me.'

'And how is your young grandchild's erot-o-maniah, Mrs. Tooke? Does it increase?'

'God knows, Mrs. Yaj, what it does.'

'We Eastern women,' Mrs. Yajñavalkya declared, drawing off what perhaps was once her union-ring, 'never take lub serious, And w'y is dis, Mrs. Tooke?—Because it is so serious!'

'Love in the East, Mrs. Yaj, I presume, is *only* feasible indoors?'

'Nobody bothers, Mrs. Tooke. Common couples wif no place else often go into de jungle.'

'Those cutting winds of yours must be a bar to courting.'

'Our cutting winds! It is you who have de cutting winds. . . . It is not us. . . . No; oh no. In de East it is joy, heat!'

'Then where do those wicked blasts come from?'

'Never you mind now, Mrs. Tooke, but just cross dose two dear knees ob yours, and do wot I bid you. . . . Dis incipient pass,' the beneficent woman explained, seating herself in the window-bench facing Mrs. Tooke's arm-chair, 'is a daisy. And dat is sure, O Allah la Ilaha,' she gurgled, 'but I shall have you soon out in de open air again, I hope, and den you shall visit *me*. . . . De white acacia-tree in my back garden is something so beautiful dis year; at dis season it even eclipse my holly. . . . Ah, Mrs. Tooke! Whenebber I look at a holly it put me in mind ob my poor Mustapha again. It has just de same playful prickle of a mastodon's moustache. Husband and wife ought to cling together, Mrs. Tooke; if only for de sake ob de maintenance; it's hard often, my dear, for one in de professional-way to make both ends meet; clients don't always pay; you may rub your arms off for some folk (and include all de best specifics), but never a dollar will you see!'

'Howsomever,' Mrs. Tooke exclaimed, eyeing mistrustfully her granddaughter, who had re-entered the room unobtrusively with the towels.

She had a sun-hat on, equipped to go out.

'Where are you off, so consequential?' the old lady interrogatively said.

'Nowhere in particular.'

'In that big picture-hat—? Don't tell me!'

'I shall be back again, I dare say, before you're ready,' Miss Tooke replied, withdrawing on tiptoe from the room.

'Dat enlarged heart should be seen to, Mrs. Tooke. Do persuade her now to try my sitz-baths. I sell ze twelve tickets ver cheap—von dozen only for five shillings,' the young girl could hear the mulattress murmur as she closed the door.

Taking advantage of her grandame's hour of treatment, it was her habit, whenever this should occur, to sally forth for a stroll. Often she would slip off to Spadder Bay and lie upon the beach there, her pale cheek pressed to the wet sea-shingle; oftener perhaps she would wander towards Hare-Hatch House in the hope of a miraculous return.

This morning her feet were attracted irresistibly towards Hare.

Crossing the churchyard into the Market Square, where, above booths and shops and the flowered façade of the Strangers' Hotel, towered the statue of John Baptist Daleman, *b.* 1698, *ob.* 1803, Valmouth's illustrious son, Miss Tooke sauntered slowly across the old brick bridge that spanned the Val. Here, beneath a cream canvas sunshade traced at the borders with narrow lines of blue, sat Victor Vatt, the landscape artist, a colour-box upon his knee. At either side of him crouched a pupil—young men who, as they watched the veteran painter's hand, grew quite hot and red and religious-looking.

Bearing on, Miss Tooke branched off into an unfrequented path that led along the river-reach, between briers and little old stunted pollard-willows, towards Hare. Kingfishers emeralder than the grass passed like dream-birds along the bank. Wrapped in fancy, walking in no great hurry, she would pause, from time to time, to stand and droop, and dream and die. Between the sodden, creaking bark of pollard-willows, weeping for sins not theirs, the sea, far off, showed pulsating in the sun.

> 'I loved a man
> And he sailed away,
> Ah hé, ah hé,'

she sang.

From Valmouth to Hare-Hatch House was reckoned a longish mile. Half buried in cedar woods, it stood on high ground above the valley of the Val, backed by the bluish hills of Spadder Tor. Ascending a zigzag track she entered a small fir plantation that was known by most people thereabouts as Jackdaw Wood; but, more momentously, for her it was '*the*' wood. How sweetly he had kissed her in its kindly gloom. . . . On those dead fir-needles hand in hand, his bright eyes bent to hers (those dear entrancing eyes that held the glamour of foreign seaports in them), he had told her of her goddess namesake of Greece, of the nereid Thetis, the sister of Calypso, and the mother of Achilles, the most paradoxical of all the Greeks. On these dead fir-needles he had told her of his ship— the *Sesostris*—and of his middy-chum, Jack Whorwood, who was not much over fifteen, and the youngest hand on board. 'That little lad,' he had said, with a peculiar smile that revealed his regular pointed teeth, 'that little lad, upon a cruise, is, to me, what Patroclus was to Achilles, and even more.'

Ruminating, she roamed along, brushing the rose-spiked self-heal and the red-thimbled fox-gloves with her dress. Upon a fitful breeze a wailing repeated cry of a peacock smote like music on her ear and drew her on. Striking the highway beyond the little copse she skirted the dark iron palings enclosing Hare. Through the armorial great gates—open as if expectant—the house lay before her across a stretch of drive.

Halting she stood, lost in amorous conjectures, surveying with hungry eyes the sun-bleached, mute façade.

Oh, which amongst those tiers of empty windows lit his room?

Above each tall window was a carved stone mask. Strange chiselled faces, singularly saturnine . . . that laughed and leered and frowned. His room perhaps faced the other way? Her eyes swept the long pseudo-classic pile. Above the gaunt grey slates showed the tops of the giant cryptomerias upon the lawn.

She had never penetrated there.

To one side of it on a wooded hillock rose a garden temple open to the winds, its four white columns uplifting each a bust.

Beneath the aerial cupola three people at present were seated, engaged in tranquil chat.

Transfixed, Miss Tooke considered them. She was there, in spirit, too, 'holding her own,' as her grandmother would have said, with those two patrician women and the priest.

♈ *IV* ♈

THEY were ringing the angelus. Across the darkling meadows, from the heights of Hare, the tintinnabulation sounded mournfully, penetrating the curl-wreathed tympanums of Lady Parvula de Panzoust.

'There's the dinner-bell, coachman!' her ladyship impatiently exclaimed, speaking through the ventilator of her cab. 'Please to get on.'

Whipping up his horse with an inventive expletive, the driver started forward at a trot.

Lady Parvula relaxed.

The invitation to dinner at Hare-Hatch House had included her daughter, the Hon. Gilda Vintage, as well; a fair girl whose vast fortune as sole heiress of the late Lord de Panzoust caused her to be considered one of the most tempting present *partis* in the land. Bring Gilda, Mrs. Hurstpierpoint had written to Lady Parvula, 'so that, not unlikely,' her ladyship blissfully mused, 'Captain Thoroughfare will be there!'

Captain Thoroughfare.

There were rumours, to be sure, he was above Love.

Lady Parvula studied dreamily her hands. (She had long, psychic, pallid, amorous fingers, much puffed at the tips and wrinkled.)

'Oh, how I wish *I* were!' she reflected. 'But that is something I never was. . . . Who was that I saw by the ditch just now? *Que, ioli garçon!* Quite—as Byron said of D'Orsay—a *"cupidon déchaîné."* . . . Such a build. And such a voice! Especially, when he called his horrid dog to heel. *I heard the voice of Jesus say, yahoo—yahoo, bad dog!*'

Lady Parvula threw a little palpitating smile towards the evening star.

'He must be mine,' she murmured, 'in my manner . . . in my way . . . I always told my dear late Lord I could love a shepherd—peace be to his soul!'

A grey-haired manservant, and a couple of underfootmen wearing the violet vestments of the House-basilica (and which for moral reasons they were requested of an evening to retain), were meanwhile awaiting the arrival of the Valmouth cab, while conversing in undertones among themselves as servants sometimes do.

'Dash their wigs!' the elderly man exclaimed.

'What's the thorn, Mr. ffines?' his colleague, a lad with a face gemmed lightly over with spots, pertly queried.

'The thorn, George?'

'Tell us.'

'I'd sooner go round my beads.'

'Mrs. Hurst cut compline, for a change, to-night.'

' . . . She's making a studied toilet, so I hear.'

'Gloria! Gloria! Gloria!'

'Dissenter.'

'What's wrong with Nit?'

The younger footman flushed.

'Father Mahoney sent for me to his room again,' he answered.

'What, *again?*'

'Catch me twice——'

'*Veni cum me in terra coelabus!*'

'S-s-s-s-s-s-sh.'

'*Et lingua . . . semper.*'

'On the whole,' the butler said, 'I preferred Père Ernest.'

'And so did half the maids.'

'Although his brilliance here was as you may say wasted.'

' 'Pon my word! It's a deadly awful place.'

'With the heir-presumptive so much away it's bound to be slow and quiet.'

'Why,' George gurgled, 'the Captain should be heir of Hare I never could make out!'

'Mr. Dick's dead father,' Mr. ffines replied, 'was a close relative of Mrs. Hurst.'

'The Admiral?'

'And it was as good as a combination . . .' he further explained, 'only he was too poor. And things fell out otherwise.'

'There'd be a different heir, I s'pose, if missis married ag'in?'

' 'Tisn't likely. Why she'll soon be a centenarian herself.'

'You've only to change her plate,' Nit, with acumen, said, 'to feel she's there.'

'So I should hope!'

'And as to Father Colley. My! How he do press!'

The servitors waxed silent, each lost in introspection, until the rattle of the Valmouth cab announced the expected guest.

Alighting like some graceful exotic bird from the captivity of a dingy cage, Lady Parvula de Panzoust hovered a moment before the portal as much to manipulate her draperies, it seemed, as to imbreathe the soft sweet air.

The sky was abloom with stars. . . .

In the faint elusive light flitter-mice were whirling about the mask-capped windows, hurtling the wind-sown wallflowers embedded in the fissure of each saturnine-hewn face.

'Come back for me again by ten o'clock, remember,' her ladyship commanded her coachman, prior to following the amaranthine skirts of the two footmen into the house.

Passing through the bleak penumbra of the hall and along a corridor bristling with horns of every description, she was shown into a deep, T-shaped, panelled room profusely hung with pictures.

There seemed at present to be no one in it.

'The mistress, I presume, is with the scourge,' the butler announced, peering impassably around.

Lady Parvula placed her fan to her train.

'Let her lash it!' she said. 'In this glorious room one is quite content to wait.'

And indeed there could not be the least doubt that the drawing-room at Hare-Hatch House was sufficently uplifting to be alone in without becoming dull.

Here were the precious Holbeins—the finest extant—and the Ozias Humphry in its original oval frame, while prominent above the great Jacobean fireplace, with a row of lamps shining footlight-wise beneath it, was the youthful portrait of the present mistress from the hand of Ingres.

Garbed in Greek draperies, she was seen leaning her head against a harpsichord, whose carved support rose perpendicularly from end to end of the canvas like some flower-wreathed capital.

Less redoubtable perhaps were an infinity of Morlands, fresh and fragrant, in their oblong, cross-ribboned frames, a Longhi or two—

a Piazza, a Punchinello in a little square, and a brilliant croquis signed *Carmontelle* of a Duchess trifling with a strawberry.

By a jaguar-skin couch far down the room an array of long-back chairs in the splendid upholstery of the seventeenth century suggested to Lady Parvula's mind an occasional 'public' correction. And everywhere ranged fortuitously about were *faïence* flower-tubs bearing large-leaved plants that formed tall canopies to the white, pensive statues grouped patiently beneath.

She was just passing a furtive hand over the promising feet and legs of a Discobolus, broken off, unfortunately, at the height of the loins, as Mrs. Thoroughfare entered.

All billowing silks and defenceless embroideries, she was looking to-night like a good-natured sphinx—her rather bulging, etiolated cheeks and vivid scarlet mouth expanded in a smile.

'I know of no joy,' she airily began, 'greater than a cool white dress after the sweetness of confession.'

Lady Parvula cast an evasive eye towards the supine form of a bronze hermaphrodite, whose long, tip-tilted, inquisitive nose protruded snugly above a smart Renaissance quilt.

'No! Really! Elizabeth!' she exclaimed.

Mrs. Thoroughfare breathed in a way that might have been called a sigh.

'And where is Gilda?' she asked.

'Gilda . . . Gilda's still at school!'

'Oh!'

'And Dick?'

'Dick . . . Dick's still at sea!'

'Wicked fellow.'

'A crate of some wonderful etherised flowers,' Mrs. Thoroughfare informed, pivoting with hands outspread, about a tripod surmounted by a small braziero, 'came from him only this afternoon, from Ceylon.'

Lady Parvula plied her fan.

'Even at Oomanton,' she murmured, 'certain of the new hybrids this year are quite too perfect.'

'Eulalia and I often speak of the wondrous orchids at Oomanton Towers.'

Lady Parvula expanded.

'We're very proud of a rose-lipped one,' she said, 'with a lilac beard.'

'A lilac . . . *what*?' It was Mrs. Hurstpierpoint's voice at the door.
'Eulalia!'

'Is it Sodom?' she enquired in her gruff, commanding way, coming forward into the room.

She had a loose, shapeless gown of hectically-contrasted colours—one of Zenobia Zooker's hardiest inspirations—draped from the head à l'Evangile.

Lady Parvula tittered.

'Goodness, no,' she said.

'Because Father Mahoney won't hear of it ever *before* dessert.'

'How right.'

'He seems to think it quite soon enough,' the mistress of Hare murmured, passing an intimate arm about her old friend's waist.

Lady Parvula cooed half-fluttered. In a time-corroded mirror she could see herself very frail, and small, and piquant in its silver-sheeted depth.

'To be continually beautiful, like *you*, dear,' her hostess said. 'How I wish I could. . . .'

'Yet I date my old age,' Lady Parvula replied, 'from the day I took the lift first at the Uffizi!'

'You dear angel.'

'One's envious, almost, of these country clowns, who live, and live, and live, and look so well!'

'Many find the climate here trying to begin with,' Mrs. Hurstpierpoint said, 'owing to the amount of cosmic activity there is; but the longevity of the Valmouthers attracts all kinds of visitors to the town.'

'At the Strangers' a Contessa di Torre Nuevas has the room next to me—and *oh*! how she snores!'

'Do they make you comfortable?'

'Most.'

'You must miss the society of your girl.'

'Dear child. She is training under Luboff Baltzer—in Milan.'

'To what end?'

'Music. And she is in such cruel despair. She says Luboff insists on endless counterpoint, and *she* only wants to play valses!'

'She hardly sounds to be ambitious.'

'It depends; measured by Scriabin's *Quasi-Valse,* or the *Valse in A flat major,* she may have quite intricate idylls. . . .'

Mrs. Thoroughfare simmered. 'I do so love his *Étrangeté*,' she said.

'Was it you, Betty,' Mrs. Hurstpierpoint demanded, 'before Office I heard amusing yourself in Our Lady?'

'I am sure, Eulalia, I forget.'

Lady Parvula's hand wandered vaguely towards the laurel-leaf fillet that encompassed irresponsibly her pale, liver-tinted hair.

'After the Sixtine Chapel,' she remarked, 'I somehow think your Nuestra Señora de la Pena is the one I prefer.'

'You *dear* you! You should have been with us Easter Day! Our little basilica was a veritable bower of love.'

'Have you any more new relics?'

'Only the tooth of St. Automona Meris, for which,' Mrs. Hurstpierpoint, in confidence, was moved to add, 'I've had my tiara-stones turned into a reliquary.'

'You funny animal!'

'If we go on as we go on,' Mrs. Thoroughfare commented as dinner was ceremoniously announced, 'we'll be almost *too* ornate!'

It was what they, each in their way, were ready for.

'I adore dining *en petit comité*,' Lady Parvula exclaimed, accepting gaily her hostess's propellent arm.

It was past blue, uncurtained windows to the dining-room, that remained, too, uncurtained to the night.

In the taper-lit, perhaps pre-sixteenth-century room—a piece of *Laughing and Triumphing* needlework in the style of Rubens completely hid the walls—the capacious oval of the dinner-table, crowned by a monteith bowl filled with slipper-orchids, showed agreeably enough.

'Where can Father be?' Mrs. Hurstpierpoint wondered, sinking to her chair with a slight grimace. Rumour had it that she wore a bag of holly-leaves pinned to the lining of her every gown; it even asserted that she sometimes assumed spiked garters.

'He went to the carpenter's shop, Eulalia,' Mrs. Thoroughfare replied, 'to give "a tap or two," as he said, to your new *prie-dieu*.'

'And so you've lost Père Ernest,' Lady Parvula murmured, humbling a mitred napkin with a dreamy hand.

'Alas! our stationariness soon bored him. He preferred flitting about the world like you.'

'I go about,' Lady Parvula admitted, 'as other fools, in quest of pleasure, and I usually find tedium.'

'If I recollect,' Mrs. Hurstpierpoint said, 'the Valmouth cattle-show was *our* last gaiety.'

'Your pathetic-eyed, curious oxen . . . it's a breed you don't see everywhere! My husband—my Haree-ee-ee' (either from coquetry or from some slight difficulty she experienced in pronouncing her y's, Lady Parvula pronounced 'Harry' long) 'tried them, in the park down at Oomanton Towers; but they didn't do.'

'No?'

'They got leaner and leaner and leaner and leaner in spite of cakes and cakes and cakes and cakes. . . . Poor Haree-ee-ee, my dearly beloved lord, even allowed them on to the lawn, where they used to look in at the ground-floor windows. One dreadful evening —we were taking tea—a great crimson head and two huge horns tossed the cup I was holding out of my hands, which sent me off— I'm just all over nerves!—into a state of *défaillance*; the last thing you may imagine I wanted, as it was Gilda's last night at home.'

'You should consult local advice.'

'It's what I intend doing.'

'We hear of several of our hidalgos having been immortalised lately, thanks to Victor Vatt.'

Mrs. Thoroughfare smiled indulgently.

'Those disciples of his,' she demurely said, 'oh; are they all they seem?'

'Lady Lucy Saunter swears not!'

'Is Lady Lucy at Valmouth?'

'Indeed she is. . . . And *so* poorly and *so* run-down. She says her blood is nothing but rose-water.'

'I suppose the town is full of imaginary invalids *comme toujours*?'

'My dear, one sees nothing else. So many horrid parliament-men come here apparently purely to bask.'

Mrs. Thoroughfare's face lit.

'Like our two whips!' she made chucklingly rejoinder. 'Last Epiphany in a fit of contrition we sent a tiny *enfant du chœur* (a dangerous, half-witted child . . . but pious: pious . . . ! And with the sweetest face; oh hadn't Charlie a witching face last Epiphany, Eulalia? His hair's good yet, and so are his taper hands, but his voice has gone, and so too have his beautiful roses) into town for a couple of whips. They duly appeared. But two such old vote-hunters. . . . "My God," Eulalia said, "we asked for whips and Thou sendest *scourges*." '

'Well! Quite a harum-scarum, one of the Vile-islands, sits for Oomanton, who pretends, I believe,' Lady Parvula breathed, 'to be an advocate for Gilda; but if *I* ever venture to propose an alliance to my ewe-lamb usually she answers: "I don't want to marry *any-one*, thank you, mama! I prefer to bc free." She has no real cognisance, dear lambkin, of anything at all.'

'Sooner or later she'll make her choice!'

'Men, men! . . . "They are always there," dear, aren't they, as the Russians say?'

Mrs. Hurstpierpoint repressed a grimace.

'Nowadays,' she murmured, 'a man . . . to me . . . somehow . . . oh! he is something so wildly *strange*.'

'Strange?'

'Unglimpsable.'

'Still, some men are ultra-womanly, and they're the kind I love!' Mrs. Thoroughfare chirruped.

'I suppose that none but those whose courage is unquestionable can venture to be effeminate?' Lady Parvula said, plunging a two-pronged fork into a 'made' dish of sugared-violets served in aspic.

'It may be so.'

'It was only in war-time, was it, that the Spartans were accustomed to put on perfumes, or to crimp their beards?'

'My dear, how your mind seems to dwell upon beards.'

'Upon *beards*?'

'It's perfectly disgusting.'

'In the old days do you remember "Twirly" Rogers?'

'Out with the Valmouth Drag,' Mrs. Thoroughfare sighed, 'how well he looked in his pink coat!'

Lady Parvula assented.

'Those meets,' she said, 'on the wintry cliffs above the world had a charm about them. One could count more alluring faces out with the Valmouth, my husband used to say, than with any other pack. The Baroness Elsassar—I can see her now on her great mauve mount with her profile of royalty in misfortune—never missed. Neither, bustless, hipless, chinless, did "Miss Bligh"! It was she who so sweetly hoisted me to my saddle, when I'd slid a-heap after the run of a "fairy" fox. We'd whiffed it—the baying of the dogs is something I shall never forget; dogs always know!—in a swede-field below your house from where it took us by break-neck, rapid stages—(oh! oh!)—to the sands. There, it hurried off along the sea's edge, with the harriers in full cry; all at once, near Pizon Point, it vanished. Mr. Rogers, who was a little ahead, drew his horse in with the queerest gape—like a lost huntsman (precisely) in the *Bibliothèque bleue.*'

'It's a wonder he didn't vomit.'

'I and Miss Bligh lay on the beach for hours——!'

'With a *dominus vobiscum,*' Mrs. Hurstpierpoint remarked, turning her head at the silken swish of her chaplain's gown.

Flecked with wood shavings, Saint Joseph-wise, it brought with it suggestions of Eastern men in intriguing, long burnooses; of sandalled feet; of shadûf singing boys; of creaking water-wheels and lucerne-laden camels.

Bowing her face before the stiff, proud thumb and crooked fore-finger raised to bless, Mrs. Hurstpierpoint remained a moment as if in transport, looking, with her figured veils and fuzzed hair-wreathings, like some Byzantine peacock searching for fleas.

'Lulu Veuve? Veaujolais? Clos Voukay? Or Château-Thierry!' the butler broke the silence.

Lady Parvula hesitated.

'If only not to be too like everyone else, *mon ami,*' she murmured, her perfervid, soul-tossed eyes wandering towards the priest, 'you shall give me some of each.'

Father Colley-Mahoney launched a dry, defensive cough, involuntarily starting Nit.

'How incomparable their livery is!' Lady Parvula commented.

'It has a seminary touch about it,' Mrs. Hurstpierpoint conceded, 'though at Headquarters it's regarded (I fear!) as inclining to modernism, somewhat.'

'Pray what's that?'

'Modernism? Ask any bishop.'

Lady Parvula rippled.

'I once,' she said (resolutely refusing a stirring salmis of cocks'-combs *saignant* with *Béchamel* sauce), 'I once peeped under a bishop's apron!'

'Oh . . . ?'

'And what ever did you see?' Mrs. Thoroughfare breathlessly asked.

'Well . . . I saw,' Lady Parvula replied (helping herself to a few *pointes d'asperges à la Laura Leslie*), 'I saw . . . the dear Bishop!'

Father Mahoney kindled.

'Apropos,' he said, 'his Eminence writes he is offering an ex-voto to Nuestra Señora of a silver heart.'

'In any particular intention?'

'No. Its consecration he leaves to our discretion.'

'He owes, they say,' Mrs. Thoroughfare murmured, consulting the menu with Spanish gravity, 'to women at least the half of his red hat. . . .'

Lady Parvula's glance explored the garden.

A hyacinthine darkness flooded the titanic cedars before the house above whose immemorial crests like a sad opal the moon was rising.

'Parvula,' her hostess evinced concern, 'you're tasting nothing.'

'I shall wait,' Lady Parvula made answer, 'Eulalia, for the *Madeleines en surprise*!'

'An abbess, and one of my earliest penitents,' Father Mahoney said, 'professed to find "delicious" small slips of paper traced thickly across with holy texts.'

'Really? . . . It sounds like parlour games!'

Mrs. Hurstpierpoint was moved to sigh.

'No one remembers cribbage now,' she lamented, 'or gleek, or bi-ri-bi.'

'No; or ombre. . . .'

'Or lansquenet. . . .'

'Or spadille. . . .'

'Or brelan. . . .'

'But for cards, country evenings would be too slow!'

'Indeed, when Father reads us Johnny Bunyan after dinner I fall asleep,' Mrs. Thoroughfare declared.

'Have you nothing brighter than that?'

'We read here,' Father Mahoney interpolated, 'books only of a theological trend. Not that,' he disconsolately added, 'the library upstairs doesn't contain a certain amount of Rabelaisian literature, I regret to say.'

'Rabelaisian, Father?' Mrs. Hurstpierpoint faintly shrieked.

'I don't choose, my child, to think of some of the "works" we harbour.'

'Those Jacobean dramatists, and the French erotic works of the eighteenth century, of course, would be free . . . but Père Ernest didn't reject them; many a stern metaphor have I heard him draw from *Dr. James's Powders* and *Mr. Foote's Tea*—and all the rest of it.'

Lady Parvula considered with a supercilious air the immaterial green of a lettuce-leaf.

'Oh, well,' she said, 'even at Oomanton, I dare say, there are some bad books too; in fact, I know there are! Once my ewe-lamb came to me with what appeared to be a medieval lutrin. "Oh, mama," she said, "I've found such a funny word." "What is it, my precious?" I said. "——, mama!" she answered with the most innocent lips in life . . . which sent me off—I'm just all over nerves! —into a fainting state; fairly scaring my lambkin out of her wits.'

Mrs. Hurstpierpoint extended towards her guest a hand that was not (as Lady Parvula confided afterwards to the Lady Lucy Saunter) too scrupulously clean.

'Those fainting-fits,' she said, motioning an order to Nit as he flitted by with an ingenuity of tartelettes, 'should be taken in time. For my sake, allow Dr. Dee of Valmouth to systematically overhaul you.'

'Overhaul me! What for?'

But Mrs. Thoroughfare uttered a cry.

'Oh poor wee mothlet!' she exclaimed, leaning forward to extricate a pale-winged moth, struggling tragically in one of the sconces of a candelabra. . . .

'If ffines to-night was not enough to infuriate an archangel!' Mrs. Hurstpierpoint commented, resplendently trailing (the last toothsome dish having been served) towards the holy-water stoup of old silver-work behind the door.

Lady Parvula joined her.

'After your superexcellent champagne,' she exclaimed, 'I feel one ought to go with bared feet in pilgrimage to Nuestra Señora and kindle a wax light or two.'

'My dear, I believe you've latent proclivities!'

'Eulalia!'

'Parvula!'

'Never.'

'Ah, don't say that.'

'Dearest,' Lady Parvula perversely marvelled, 'what a matchless lace berthe!'

'It was part of my corbeille——'

'Like *doubting Thomas*, I must touch with my hands.'

'Touch! Touch!'

Father Mahoney fidgeted.

'Beyond the vigil-lamp,' he objected, 'Nuestra Señora will be quite obscure.'

'Then all the more reason, Father, to illumine it!' Lady Parvula reasoned.

'Are you resolved, Parvula?'

'Of course. And I'm agog to see the tooth, too, of St. Automona Meris (Do you imagine she ever really ate with it horrid Castilian garlic *olla cocida*? Or purple *pistos insalada*? She and Teresa together, in some white *posada*, perhaps, journeying South), and your Ghirlandajo and the miracle-working effigy, and afterwards, until the fly comes round, you shall teach me gleek!'

'You dear angel . . . it's very simple!'

'Then let us play for modest points.'

Mrs. Hurstpierpoint crossed herself with her fan.

'As if,' she horror-struck said, 'I should consent to play for immodest ones! Are you coming, Elizabeth, too?' she asked.

'In one moment, Eulalia; I must speak to Father first,' Mrs. Thoroughfare replied, folding her arms lightly across the back of her chair.

'Don't, dear, desert us!' Mrs. Hurstpierpoint, withdrawing, enjoined.

There was a short pent silence.

'Do you think, Father,' Mrs. Thoroughfare broke in at last, 'she suspects?'

'Rest assured, my poor child,' Father Mahoney answered, 'your confession to me to-night exceeds belief.'

'Was there ever such a quandary!' Mrs. Thoroughfare jabbered.

'They obeyed the surge of their blood—what else?' Father Mahoney dispassionately said.

Mrs. Thoroughfare's full cheeks quivered.

'Oh, my darling boy,' she burst out, 'how *could* you!'

'My poor child, try not to fret.'

'It makes one belch, Father—belch.'

'They're joined irremediably, I understand?'

'From what he writes I conclude the worst.'

'Won't you show me what he says?'

'The card,' she murmured, drawing it from her dress, 'is covered, I fear, by the chemicals that were in the crate, gummed to the stem as it was of a nauseating lily.'

'Decipher the thing, then, to me—if you will.'

Mrs. Thoroughfare adjusted a lorgnon tearfully to her nose.

' "These are the native wild-flowers," he writes (what, I wonder, Father, must the others be!), "the native wild-flowers of my betrothed bride's country. Forgive us, and bless us, mother. Ten thousand loves to you all." '

'O, wretched boy.'

'O, Father.'

'That ever any Black woman should perform the honours at Hare!'

Mrs. Thoroughfare smiled mirthlessly.

'Well—if it comes to that—Eulalia, *herself*, to-night, is more than grubby,' she said.

ฦ *V* ฦ

THE installation of a negress at the 'Nook,' Mrs. Yajñavalkya's old-style dwelling in the Market Square, came to Valmouth, generally, as a surprise.

Almost from the outset of her arrival in the town, soft-muted music, the strange, heart-rending, mournful music of the East—suggestive of apes, and pearls, and bhang, and the colour blue—was to be heard, surging from the Nook in monotonous improvisation.

Madame Mimosa, the demi-mondaine, the only 'one' there was thereabouts, hearing it from the Villa Concha, next door, fancied she detected rivalry, competition—*the younger generation*—and took to her *bravura* (cerise chiffon, and a long, thick, black aigrette) before the clock told noon. Nurse Yates, hard by, heard 'zithers' too, and flattered herself the time was ripe to oust Mrs. Yajñavalkya from the town, 'automatically' capturing her clients as they dropped away. Mrs. Q. Comedy, *née* Le Giddy, ever alert to flare an auction, told her Quentin she supposed Mrs. Yajñavalkya would shortly be giving up her house and going off into Valopolis, or New-Valmouth, where she might conduct a *bagnio* with more facility, perhaps, than beneath the steeple of the church. While all the time, shining smiles, Mrs. Yajñavalkya herself went about affairs much in her usual way.

Of a morning early she would leave the Nook followed by a

little whey-faced English maid, to whom she allowed twelve pounds a year 'because she is so white,' to take her way towards the provision stalls encamped beneath John Baptist Daleman's virile, but rudimentary, statue in the square, where, flitting from light to shade, she would exchange perhaps a silver coin against a silver fish, or warm-leafed cauliflower, half dead on the market stones. Sometimes, quickly dismissing her little Gretchen, she would toddle off up Peace Street into Main Street, and enter, without knocking, the house of Dr. Dee, but more frequently mistress and maid would return to the Nook together, when almost immediately from her chimneys would be seen to rise a copious torrent of smoke.

From the Strangers' Hotel across the way Lady Parvula de Panzoust, like the local residents themselves, had been a puzzled spectator of the small particular coterie at the Nook, since, to her ever-deepening vexation, her shepherd-with-the-dog was a constant caller there.

Had he anything, then, the matter? His constitution, was it not the mighty thing it seemed? His agile figure (glowing through coduroys and hob-nailed boots; his *style d'amour*), was it nothing but a sham? Or had he an intrigue, perhaps, with one or other of the women of the house?

Now and then a dark face framed in unbound hair would look out through a turret window of the Nook, as if moved to homesickness at the cries of a beautiful cockatoo that hung all day in the window of Sir Victor Vatt's sitting-room at the hotel.

'Dear Vatt,' the bird would say with sonorous inflections, taking off some artist, or sitter perhaps, 'dear Vatt! He is splendid; so o-ri-gi-nal and exuberant; like an Italian Decorator.' Or, *vivo*: 'Now, Vatt! Do me a Poussin.' Or, the inflection changing *languido dolce*: 'Come, Vatt! Paint me in a greenhouse . . . in a st-oove; a little exotic; paint me (my little Victor!) like Madame Cézanne! They say,' *meno languido*, 'they say he gave her one hundred and fifteen sittings! Pretty Poll!'

Loiterers in the Market Square, observing the attentive negress trim the window, smiled and called her a caution, more cautious-like, said they in the local vernacular, than 'Old Mrs. Rub-me-down,' inferring Mrs. Yajñavalkya. Lady Parvula de Panzoust, alone, a sure connoisseur of all amative values, was disposed to allow the negress her dues, divining those ethnologic differences, those uneasy nothings, that again and again in the history of the world have tempted mankind to err. She descried, therefore, whenever the parrot's loquaciousness induced the negress to look out, a moon-faced girl with high-set, scornful eyes almost in her forehead and bow-curved pagan lips of the colour of rose-mauve stock. Her anatomy, singularly independent in every way, was, Lady Parvula surmised, that of a little *woman* of twelve. Was it, she asked herself, on this black Venus' account Adonis visited the Nook? Or was it for other reasons, graver, sadder ones . . . such as, for instance, dressing the gruesome injury of the boar?

One sunny May-day morning, full of unrest, Lady Parvula de Panzoust left the hotel for a turn on the Promenade. It was a morning of pure delight. Great clouds, breaking into dream, swept slowly across the sky, rolling down from the uplands behind Hare-Hatch House, above whose crumbling pleasances one single sable streak, in the guise of a coal-black negress, prognosticated rain.

'Life would be perfect,' she mused, 'if only I hadn't a corn!' But the Oriental masseuse was the sole proficient of the chiropodist's art at Valmouth, and Lady Parvula de Panzoust felt disinclined to bare her tender foot to the negress's perspicacious gaze. Yet after going a few painful yards this is what she realised she must do. 'After all,' she reflected, 'I may perhaps ascertain her pastoral client's condition, and so free my mind from doubt!'

She was looking charmingly matinal in a simple tweed costume, with a shapely if perhaps *invocative* hat, very curiously indented, and well cocked forward above one ear. She held a long ivory-handled sunshade in the form of a triple-headed serpent, and a book that bore the irreproachable Christian title *Embrassons Nous*.

'And who knows,' she sighed, lifting Mrs. Yajñavalkya's sun-fired knocker with a troubled hand, 'he may even be there himself!'

The little chalk-faced maid that answered the door said her mistress was in, and preceding the evident 'London lady' up a short flight of stairs, ushered her with a smile of triumph into a small but crowded cabinet whose windows faced the Square.

'Is it for a douche, m'm,' she asked, 'or ought I to start the steam?'

'Not on *my* account!' Lady Parvula murmured with dilated retinas, scanning the signed diplomas and framed credentials displayed upon the walls. A coloured 'Insurance' almanac, privately marked with initials and crosses—engagements no doubt of Mrs. Yajñavalkya's—gladdened gaily their midst.

'Chance me finding her,' she reflected, moving involuntarily towards a brilliant draped mirror above the chimney-place, where a tall piece of branched coral was stretched up half-forbiddingly against the glass.

Through its pink sticks she could see reflected in the room behind part of a calico-covered couch with the negress's bureau beyond, on which at present stood a half-eaten orange and a jar of white pinks.

A twitter of negro voices was shrilly audible through the wood partition of the wall.

'*Yahya!*'

'*Wazi jahm?*'

'*Ah didadidacti, didadidacti.*'

'*Kataka mukha?*'

'*Ah mawardi, mawardi.*'

'*Jelly.*'

'A breeze about their jelly!' Lady Parvula conjectured, complacently drawing nearer the window.

Before the Villa Concha, a little curtained carriage attached to an undocked colt with a bell at its ear signified that Madame Mimosa was contemplating shortly a drive.

Through what blue glebe or colza-planted plains would her rainbow axles turn?

Mrs. Yajñavalkya's ambling step disturbed her speculations.

'Have I not de satisfaction?' she ubiquitously began, 'ob addressing Milady Panzoust?'

Lady Parvula nodded.

'I believe you do chiropody?' she said.

'Dat is a speciality ob de house—de cultivation ob de toes. Vot is dair so important? O wen I consider de foot . . . de precious precious foot! For de foot support de body; it ber de burden ob ten thousand treasures! . . . *Kra*. And dat's vot I alvays say.'

'Undoubtedly,' Lady Parvula assented, 'whatever there *is*, it bears.'

'It gib gentle rise to ebberything,' Mrs. Yajñavalkya pursued.

'Perhaps—sometimes—it carries charms.'

'*Ukka-kukka!*' the negress broke off, dropping darkly to the floor. 'My niece, Niri-Esther, she fill de flower vases so full dat de water do all drip down and *ro-vine* de carpet.'

'Then of course she's in love?'

'Niri-Esther!'

'Now and then an interesting patient must wish to approach you.'

'I alvays,' Mrs. Yajñavalkya blandly yapped, 'decline a gentleman. Often ze old greybeards zey say, "Oh, Mrs. Yaj," zey say, "include our sex." And I laugh and I say, "I've enough to do wif my own!"'

Lady Parvula surrendered smilingly her shoes.

'Still, I sometimes see,' she said, 'call here a young tall man with his dog.'

'He call only to fetch de fowls dat flit across to my acacia-tree from de farm.'

'Is that all?'

'Being so near de church, de house is open to ebbery passing ghoul. De incubes and de succubes dat come in, and are so apt to molest . . . ob an evening especially, ven de sun fall and de sky turn all caprice, I will constantly dispatch my little maid to beg, to implore, and to beseech dat Dairyman Tooke will remove his roosters.'

'Dairyman Tooke?'

'Or his prize sow, maybe—a sow! Ah, dat is my abomination!'

'Probably the antipathy springs through the belief in reincarnation.'

'No doubt at all dat is one ob de causes.'

'The doctrine of Transubstantiation must often tell on your nerves.'

'When I die,' Mrs. Yajñavalkya said, her eyes disappearing expiringly in their sockets, 'I would not wish to be transubstantiated into a horse or a cow or a sheep or a cat. No; oh no! I will wish to be changed into a little bird, wid white, white feathers; treasuring,' she wistfully added, 'meantime de poet's words:

' "My mother bore me in the southern wild,
    And I am black, but O! my soul is white." '

'Your songsters, too,' Lady Parvula said, 'have also their poignance.'

'Ah! when Niri-Esther read Tagore,' Mrs. Yajñavalkya glowed, 'dat is something beautiful! Dat is something to make de tears descend.'

'To hear her render the love lyrics of her country, just the most typical things, would interest me immensely if it might some day be arranged.'

'But why not?'

'A *séance* in your garden amidst the acacia leaves——Mademoiselle Esther and I! And when the young man came to retrieve his birds, I vow he'd find no turkey!'

'Believe me,' Mrs. Yajñavalkya murmured, indrawing succulently her cheeks and circumspectly toying with her file, 'believe me, he's awfully choice.'

'He has youth.'

'He's awfully, awfully choice!' the negress murmured, admiring the intricate nerve-play of her patient's foot.

'It's just a Valmouth type,' Lady Parvula observed.

'Ah! It is more dan dat.'

'How?'

'Much more in ebbery way.' Mrs. Yajñavalkya looked insoluble.

'I don't I fear follow . . .' Lady Parvula gasped.

'I have known what love is, I!' The negress heaved. 'Dair are often days ven I can neither eat, nor drink, nor sleep, ven my fingers hab no strength at all (massage den is quite impossible)—I am able only to groan and groan and groan—ah, my darling!'

'A nigger?'

'A nigger! No. He was a little blond Londoner—all buttoned-and-braided, one ob de *chasseurs* at your hotel.'

'Thank you.' Lady Parvula looked detached.

'De dear toe,' the operatress raised a glinting, sooty face, 'is quite inflamed! De skin,' with unwitting cynicism she theorised, 'may vary, but de Creator ob de universe has cast us all in de same mould; and dat's vot I alvays say.'

'In what part, tell me, is your home?'

'Here!' the negress lisped.

'Geographically, I mean.'

'Geographically, we're all so scattered. Von ob my brother, Djali, he in Ujiji Land. *Kra*. He a Banana-Inspector. Official. He select de virgin combs from off de tree; dat his Pash-on, dat his Cult. Other brother, Boujaja, he in Taihaiti. He a lady-killer, well-to-do-ish; he three wives, *kra*; and dose three women are my sisters-in-law. . . . De Inspector, he no marry; I don't know why!'

'Then your niece,' Lady Parvula pressed, 'is from Taihaiti?'

But Mrs. Yajñavalkya was abstruse.

'Do you care to undergo a course ob me?' she asked. 'For de full course—I make you easy terms; and I alvays try,' she airily cozened, 'to end off wid a charming sensation.'

'Massage merely as sensation does not appeal to me:—and otherwise, thank you, I'm perfectly well.'

'I gib a massage lately to de widowed Duchess ob Valmouth for less! Yajñavalkya, she laugh and say after I had applied my court cream (half a crown; five shillings): "Yajñavalkya, your verve, it's infectious." "My what, your grace?" I say. "Your verve," she reply; "it's so *catching*." '

'I always admired her,' Lady Parvula remarked, 'you'd almost say she was a man.'

'Her testimonial is on my bureau dair.'

'You must be proud of your tributes.'

'Zey come from all sides. . . . Queen Quattah, she write again and again for my balsam ob mint, or my elixir ob prunes; but my greatest discovery, milady, my dear, was de use ob tiger-lily pollen for "superfluous hair." '

Lady Parvula moved uncomfortably in her chair. She was sufficiently alert to feel the animal magnetism from a persistent pair of eyes.

'*Wushi!*' Mrs. Yajñavalkya turned too.

'*Kataka?*' a voice came from the door.

'My relative Niri-Esther,' Mrs. Yajñavalkya explained, 'she ask me what I do.'

'She seems,' Lady Parvula commented, 'to have been crying.'

'She cry for a sting ob a wasp dat settle on her exposed bosom. I tell her—at de window—she shouldn't expose it!'

'Oh?'

'De wasps dis year dey are a plague.'

'*Kataka . . . ; kataka mukha?*'

Advancing with undulating hesitation, the young black girl brought with her a something of uttermost strangeness into the room.

Incontestably, she was of a superior caste to Mrs. Yajñavalkya, albeit her unorthodox values tended, perhaps, to obscure a little her fundamental merit.

She wore a dishabille of mignonette-green silk and a bead-diapered head-dress that added several inches to her height; her finger-slim ankles were stained with lac and there were rings of collyrium about her eyes.

With one hand clasped in the other behind her back, she stood considering Lady Parvula de Panzoust.

'*Chook*,' Mrs. Yajñavalkya grumbled.

'*Owesta wan?*'

'*Obaida.*'

'She has the exuberance of an orchid,' Lady Parvula cried. 'Could Sfax—he is my gardener down at Oomanton Towers—behold her now, he'd exclaim, "A Urania Alexis, your ladyship!" and pop her into a pot.'

'Niri-Esther's clothes, I sometimes venture to tink, are a little too vainglorious! ! ! At her age,' Mrs. Yajñavalkya retailed, 'and until I was past eighteen, I nebber had more in de course ob a year dan a bit ob cotton loincloth. You may wear it how you please, my poor mother would say, but dat is all you'll get! And so, dear me, I generally used to put it on my head.'

'She eyes one like a cannibal.'

'Are you quite well?' the young black woman waveringly asked.

Lady Parvula answered with a nod.

'Come here and show me,' she said.

'I drop de *mushrabiyas*—; so nobody den can see in!'

'Why O, why O,' Mrs. Yajñavalkya complained, 'will dat *betæra's* horrid coachman draw up always just opposite to my gate?'

'She is later dan usual to-day,' her relative rejoined.

'Wears her horse,' the elder negress demanded, 'a rose?'

'De poor unhappy thing; he wear both a favour and a strap.'

'The looser the mistress . . . the tighter the bearing-rein!' Lady Parvula remarked.

Mrs. Yajñavalkya languished.

'She dribe her chestnut for day work, and reserbe a white for evening use. Not dat,' she amplified, 'one move more rapidly dan de other; no, oh no; Madame Mimosa refuse to dribe her horses fleet! She seldom elect to aribe betimes; she say it "good" to keep de clients waiting. It's a question ob policy wif her dat "two hours late."'

'I suppose simply to engender suspense.'

'*C'est une femme qui sait enrager. Allez!*'

'You know French?'

'Like ebberything else!'

Lady Parvula expanded.

'I said to my maid this morning: "Oh, Louison!" I said, "what does the prommy place here remind you of?" "Of nothing, your lady-ship," replied she. "Oh, *doesn't* it?" I said; "well, it does me! It reminds me of the Promenade des Sept Heures at Spa." '

'Ah, de dear spot!'

'For brio, and for beauty and from the look of the trees, I said to her, it reminds me of the Promenade des Sept Heures at Spa.'

'You may go far before you will find a prettier place dan dis is.'

'True, I never go out but I see someone sketching.'

Mrs. Yajñavalkya was convulsed.

'A certain Valmouth widow, living yon side de church, found a Francis Fisher lately lying in her ditch (some small *plein-air* ob his, I suppose, he had thrown away), so she forwarded it to London just to ask what it would fetch, and sold it to a dealer for more dan fifty pounds.'

'Bravo. I must try to pick up a Vatt!'

'Curious how he faber de clodhopper type. Who would want to hang a beggar on his walls? Dair are enough in de world without. Believe me.'

'Indeed there are.'

'An artist I alvays admire, now,' the negress murmured, retying with coquetry her patient's shoe-string, 'is Mr. FitzGeorge! All his models are ladies ... daughters ob clergymen, daughters of colonels ... and even his male sitters are,' she twittered, 'sons ob good houses.'

'Someone should paint your niece!' Lady Parvula rose remarking.

'*Fanoui ah maha?*'

'*Tauroua ta.*'

'*Yahya.*'

'What's that she says?'

'That she will be glad to make music for you at any time.'

'That will be delightful.'

'And I, also,' the dark-skinned woman assumed her silkiest voice, 'will endeavour to have a few fugitive fowls over from de farm. De dogs shall bark, and de birds shall fly (de sky is full ob de whirring ob wings), but de lover and his beloved shall attain Nirvana.'

'Nirvana?'

'Leave it to me and you and he shall come together.'

'Oh, impossible.'

'Leave it to me.'

'I never run *any* risks,' Lady Parvula babbled.

'Risks! Vot risks? Risks?... O Allah la Ilaha! Shall I tell you vot de Yajñavalkya device is? Vot it has been dis thousand and thousand ob year? It is *bjopti. Bjopti!* And vot does *bjopti* mean? It means *discretion. S-s-s-s-s-s-s-s-s-s-s-s-s-s-s-s-s-s-s-s-s-s-s-s-sh!*'

Lady Parvula toyed reflectively with her rings.

'At balls in a quilted skirt and with diamonds in my hair I've often been hugely admired as a shepherdess,' she said. 'I well remember,' she tittered, 'the success I had one evening—it was at the British Embassy in Paris—as a shepherdess of Lely. I had a lamb (poor, innocent darling, but so heavy and so hot; worse than any child) with me, that sprang from my arms quite suddenly while I was using my powder-puff and darted bleating away beneath the legs of Lord Clanlubber (at that time ambassador) out into the Champs-Élysées, where it made off, I afterwards heard, towards the Etoile. And *I* never saw it again! So that you see,' she murmured, depositing her benefactress's fee vaguely upon the couch, 'I've a strong bond with shepherds, having myself, once, lost a lamb....'

'In a like rig-up you would stir de soul ob Krishna, as de milk-maid Rádhá did!'

'I'm quite content to "stir" my neighbour instead.'

'Believe me,' the dark-skinned woman murmured, following her visitor to the stairhead, with a sigh that shook the house, 'he's awfully, awfully choice!'

'—...'

'He has a wee mole—on de forehead.'

'Ah, and he has another: yes! in the deep pool above his upper-lip—; the channel affair....'

'He's *awfully* choice!'

'*C'est un assez beau garçon,*' Lady Parvula answered with a backward æsthetic glance.

Leaning from the hand-rail, like some adoring chimpanzee, Mrs. Yajñavalkya watched her recede, the wondrous crown of the vanishing hat suggesting forcibly the peculiar attributes of her own tribal gods.

The shadow upon the forewall of her little English maid descending the staircase with a chamber-pot from above recalled her to herself.

'Ah, *zoubé kareen phf!* Why weren't you in readiness, Carry, to open de door?' she enquired, returning thoughtfully towards her sanctum with the intent to sterilise her tools.

On a spread kerchief, pitcher-posture, upon the floor her relative was bleaching idly her teeth with a worn bit of bone, while turning round and round like a water-wheel in her henna-smeared fingers the glass hoop-clasp at her abdomen.

Mrs. Yajñavalkya gave way to a joyous chuckle.

'Mrs. Richard Thoroughfare, Mrs. Richard Thoroughfare!' she addressed the prostrate belle.

'*Chakrawaki—wa?*'

'Mrs. Dick, Mrs. Thorough-dick, Mrs. Niri fairy!'

'*Suwhee?*'

With an eloquent listening eye, Mrs. Yajñavalkya laid a hand to her ear.

'De bridal litter,' she playfully announced, 'from Hare-Hatch House, is already at de far corner ob de adjacent street!'

The water-wheel ceased as the mauve lips parted.

'Ah, Vishnu!' the young black girl yawned. 'Vot den can make it come so slow?'

ℜ VI ℜ

A CAMPAIGN of summer storms of a quasi-tropical nature was delaying the hay harvest that in Valmouth, as in the neighbouring Garden Isles, was usually celebrated before the last week in May.

Not since the year 17—, when milord Castlebrilliant's curricle was whirled to sea with her ladyship within, had there been such vehement weather.

At Hare-Hatch House, the finest hornbeam upon the lawn had succumbed, none too silently, while in the park several of the centennial cedars were fallen, giving to the grounds somehow a tragic, classic look.

And indeed, with her favourite hornbeam, Mrs. Hurstpierpoint's nerves had also given way.

One afternoon, just as the bell of Nuestra Señora was sounding Terce, the lament of the peacocks announced a return of the storm. Since mid-day their plangent, disquieting cries had foretold its approach. Moving rapidly to and fro in their agitation, their flowing fans sweeping rhythmically the ground, they traced fevered curves beneath the overarching trees, orchestrating, with barbarity, as they did so, their strident screech with the clangour of the chapel bell that seemed, as it rang, to attract towards it a bank of tawny gold, cognac-coloured cloud, ominously fusing to sable.

Sauntering up and down in the shadow of the chapel wing the mistress of the manor, this afternoon, was also mingling her voice, intermittently, as though a plaintive, recurring motif in a slightly trying musical score, with her birds and her bell. 'Eliza! Eliza!' she called.

Seated upon the fallen hornbeam, Mrs. Thoroughfare was regarding distraitly the sky.

Ever since the windy weather a large pink kite like a six-humped camel had made above the near wood its extraneous appearance. To whom, Mrs. Thoroughfare asked herself, bewildered, could such a monstrous toy belong? There was something about it that alarmed her, alarmed her more than all the storm-clouds put together.

'Elizabeth!'

As if cleft by passing lightning the name on the tense hot air writhed lugubriously away amid the trees.

'In, in,' Mrs. Thoroughfare beseeched.

But Mrs. Hurstpierpoint had already turned towards the house, where an under-footman was busily closing the ground-floor windows against the dark, shining spots of falling rain. And falling too, Mrs. Thoroughfare noted, came the bewildering kite, head-foremost, as though jerked smartly earthward in the flyer's hand. A burst of near thunder sent her perforce to join her friend, whose finer, more delicate nature was ever apt to be affected by a storm.

She found her in a corner of the vast drawing-room clasping a 'blessed' rosary while listening in a state of compressed hysterics to the storm.

'I'm an old woman now': she was telling her beads: 'and my only wish it to put my life in order—was that another flash?'

'Darling.'

'Is that you, my little Lizzie?'

'Tchut! Eulalia.'

'Oh-h-h-h! . . . Betty dear! The *awful* vividness of the lightning!' Mrs. Hurstpierpoint wailed.

Through the nine tall windows with their sun-warped, useless shutters, like violet-darting swallows, the lightning forked.

'Let us go,' Mrs. Thoroughfare said in a slightly unsteady voice, 'shall we both, and confess?'

'Confess!'

'Father's in Nuestra now.'

'My dear, in my opinion, the lightning's so much more ghastly through the stained-glass windows!'

Mrs. Thoroughfare pressed her hands lightly to her admired associate's humid brow.

'Dear mother was the same,' she cooed. 'Whenever it thundered she'd creep away under her bed, and make the servants come and lie down on top . . . (it was in the eighteenth century of course . . .) so that should the brimstone burst it must vent its pristine powers on them. Poor innocent! It was during a terrific thunderstorm at Brighton, or *Brighthelmstone* as they called it then, that several of the domestics fell above her head. . . . And the fruits of that storm, as I believe I've told you before, Eulalia, are in the world to-day.'

'My dear . . . every time the weather breaks you must needs hark back to it.'

Mrs. Thoroughfare showed pique.

'Well *I*,' she said, ambling undeterred towards the door, 'intend to pray.'

'Who knows but our prayers may meet?' Mrs. Hurstpierpoint murmured, returning to her beads, that in the sombre brilliance of the darkened room shed different pale and supernatural lights as they swung from side to side in her nerveless hands.

'Adorable Jesus,' her mouth moved faintly beneath the charcoal shadow of her moustache, 'love me even as I do Thee, and I,' she deeply breathed, 'will land Thee a fish! I will hook Thee a heretic; even though,' her tongue passed wistfully over her lips, 'to gain an open sinner I should be impelled to go to London, O Lord; for I will bend to Thy Sovereign Purpose (irrespective of my little kitchen-maid whom I most certainly mean to force) a thorough-going infidel; something very putrid . . . very lost. And so, O my Saviour Dear,' beatifically she raised her face, 'I will make Thee retribution for the follies of my youth.'

Her lips grew still.

From the adjacent chapel soft, insinuating voices assailed agreeably the ear.

'Victories . . .' 'Vanquish . . .' 'Virtue . . .' 'Virgin . . .'

Mrs. Hurstpierpoint's veiled glance dropped from her rafters, hovering with a certain troubled diffidence over the ruff and spade-beard of a dashing male portrait, until it dwelt on the face of the time-piece on the commode below, so placed as to exclude as far as possible the noble arch of her kinsman's shapely legs. The slow beat of the flower-wreathed pendulum usually filled the room.

Long ago, it was related, it had been consulted in an hour of most singular stress. And it was as if still some tragic pollen of anguish-staring eyes clung to the large portentous numerals of the Louis-Sixteenth dial. Two steel key-holes in the white full face loomed now like beauty patches in the flickering light.

'I feel I'm ready for my tea,' Mrs. Hurstpierpoint reflected, taking up an invalidish posture on the jaguar-skin couch.

The inebriating, slightly acrid perfume of a cobra lily, wilting in its vase, awoke solicitous thought within her of her distant heir.

Soon the dear lad would give up his junketings, she mused, and take to himself a wife.

Her eyes absorbed fondly the room.

'Ah! Ingres!' she sighed, 'your portrait of me is still indeed most like . . . more like and much more pleasing, I think, than the marble Dalou did. . . .' And fearful lest she should fall a victim to her own seductiveness, against the peevish precepts of the church, she averted her eyes towards the young naval officer in the carved Renaissance frame, into whose gold-wrapped, slim-wristed hands, with the long and lissom fingers swelling towards their tips like big drop pearls, Hare-Hatch House and all its many treasures would one day pass.

A flare of dazzling brightness on the wainscoting caused her to knit her brows, and like a tall reed, wrapped in silk, her maid, wheeling a light chaufferette, advanced towards her.

'Is the worst of the storm yet over, Fowler, do you consider?' Mrs. Hurstpierpoint gently groaned.

The maid's sallow-face, flame-lit, looked malign as she drooped her trim-coiffed head.

'Now that the wind has deprived the statues of their fig leaves, 'm,' she replied, 'I hardly can bear to look out.'

'Oh? *Has* it? What? Again?'

'All around the courtyard and in the drive you'd think it was October from the way they lie!'

'Sister Ecclesia will be distressed going home, I fear. Even *an altar-cupid——* She's so sensitive,' Mrs. Hurstpierpoint remarked.

'It's mostly dark 'm, before she's done.'

'Unless the summer quickly mends the Hundred Club's fête must be postponed!'

'It's odd, 'm,' the waiting woman answered, adding a pinch of incense to the fire, 'how many a centenarian seems more proof against exposure than others not yet in their prime. Only a short while since my Lady Parvula's maid—she's been spending the day here among us—got caught in the wet while taking a turn with Miss Fencer and Nit; and now there she is, sitting before the kitchen range, in borrowed hose, with a glass of hot toddy.'

'I dare say her licentious stories have brought on this storm!'

'She was very full to be sure at meal-time of a fraudulent marriage, saying how no one or nothing was inviolate or safe.'

'The sole dependable marriage is the Spiritual marriage! On that alone can we implicitly rely.'

'And she was very full, too, of her ladyship's jewelled pyjamas.'

'Holy Virgin!'

'The storm sounds almost above us.'

'Lift the lid of the long casket—and pick me a relic,' Mrs. Hurst-pierpoint enjoined, surveying apprehensively the dark clumps of wind-flogged trees upon the lawn.

'Any one in particular, 'm?' the maid enquired, slipping, with obedient alacrity, across the floor.

'No; but not a leg-bone, mind! A leg-bone relic somehow——' she broke off, searching with her great dead eye dreaming the sad camphor-hued hills for the crucifix and wayside oratory that surmounted the topmost peak.

'You used to say the toe, 'm, of the married sister of the Madonna, the one that was a restaurant proprietress (Look alive there with those devilled kidneys, and what is keeping Fritz with that sweet-omelette?), in any fracas was particularly potent.'

'Yes . . . bring the toe of the Madonna's married sister, and then come and read to me out of Père Pujol,' her mistress answered, it being one of her chosen modes of penance (as well as a convenient means of paving the way to papalism) to call from time to time on her servants to come and read to her aloud. How often afterwards, in the soundless watches of the night, must the tonic words of a Pujol, or a brother Humphrey Caton, recur to dull procrastinating minds linked, made earthly in souvenir, with her own kind encouraging looks! Indeed, as a certain exalted churchman had excellently expressed it once, Oral-punishment, the mortification of the sparkling ear, was more delightful to heaven inasmuch as frequently it was more far-reaching than a knot in a birch or a nail in a boot.

But with Fowler, one of the earliest converts of the house, there was no need any more to push to extremes.

'*Figlia mia*,' she jarringly began with a great thick 'G' fully equal, her mistress reckoned, to a plenary indulgence alone, '*figlia mia*, examine your conscience, ask your heart, invoke that inner voice which always tells the truth, and never, no, never, betrays us! For the spark will live through the rains, lighting up dead fires: fire which is still fire, but with purer flame. . . .'

'Lest your cap-pin kindles, *presto* there. Never,' Mrs. Hurstpierpoint intervened, 'read of bad weather during storm!'

'One day St. Automona di Meris, seeing a young novice yawning, suddenly spat into her mouth, and *that* without malice or thought of mischief. Some ninety hours afterwards the said young novice brought into the world the Blessed St. Elizabeth Bathilde, who, by dint of skipping, changed her sex at the age of forty and became a man.'

'A *man*—! Don't speak to me of *men*. Especially one of that description!' Mrs. Hurstpierpoint rapped. 'Inflict something else.'

'Something more poetical perhaps?'

'What is that thick, twine-coloured linen book I see the back of, beneath the young mistress's shawl?'

'Anthropology again, I expect, 'm,' Fowler answered.

'This craze for anthropology with her is something altogether new.'

'It frets her to form no idea of the tribes the Captain's been among.'

'It only makes her dream. She was talking so (being forced to fly to my little rosewood night-stool, I overheard her) in her sleep again.'

'Miss Fencer was saying so, too. Only this morning (in calling her) she heard her say: "I will *not* go in beads to the opera." (Or was it "berries" she said?) "Tell King Mbmonbminbon so!" Anyway, Miss Fencer was so completely seized she just emptied the early tea vessel on to the floor.'

Mrs. Hurstpierpoint exchanged with her maid a lingering, expressive glance.

'I *know* she's worried! I *know* she's keeping something from me! and I *know* she'll tell me in the end!' so the dependent, who was apt to read her mistress's face with greater accuracy than she did her books, interpreted the glance.

'The volume I find, 'm, beneath the shawl,' she said, 'is the *Tales from Casanova.*'

'Child that my soul's treasure is!' There was a second significant glance.

'Well, well; for St. Francis's sake,' Mrs. Hurstpierpoint said, steeling herself to listen, 'an Italian story is always permitted at Hare.'

'There was once upon a time two sisters,' Fowler falteringly began, 'named Manette and Marton, who lived with a widowed aunt, a certain Madame Orio, in the city of Venice. The disposition of these fair Venetians was such that——, such——,' she floundered.

'Their disposition? ... Yes? It was such?'

'Such——'

'That?'

'... Well, I declare!'

'How often, Fowler,' Mrs. Hurstpierpoint said with some asperity, 'must I beg you not to employ that ridiculous phrase in my hearing?'

'Very good, 'm, but it's all Portuguese to *me*! ... And wagged his Persian tail.'

'Go on.'

'One evening,' she went on, 'while Madame Orio was fast asleep in her little belvedere (it being the good old lady's habit to repair there to rest after a bottle or two of red Padua wine), Manette and Marton left the widow's house noiselessly in the Campo San Zobenigo, and made their way running towards the Piazza of St. Mark's. It was a radiant night in early April. All Venice was in the open air. The moon, which——'

Listening with detached attention lest her ears should be seduced and tickled rather than soundly chastened, Mrs. Hurstpierpoint's mind turned somewhat sombrely to her future connection with her heir's fiancée. Some opinionated, wrong-headed creature, *une femme mal pensante*, in the house, she mused, would be indeed tormenting. While on the other hand, of course, Dick's bride *might* add a new interest to the place; in which case Elizabeth's attitude too would be sure to change.

Mrs. Hurstpierpoint plied speculatively her beads, catching between her *Aves* just enough of the tale to be able to follow its drift.

Music, she heard. Those sisters ✠ a ripe and rich marquesa ✠ strong proclivities ✠ a white starry plant ✠ water ✠ lanterns ✠ little streets ✠ Il Redentore ✠ Pasqualino ✠ behind the Church of ✠ Giudecca ✠ gondola ✠ Lido ✠ Love ✠ lagoon ✠ Santa Orsola ✠ the Adriatic——

With a sigh at the mutability of things, she realised that with a young daughter-in-law of her own Elizabeth would no longer be towards her her same gracious self. With the advent of Dick's wife a potential disturbing force would enter Hare. New joy would bring new sorrow. Whoever he might choose to marry, intrigue, jealousy would seldom be far away. Should Gilda Vintage be the *partie*, the Lady Parvula de Panzoust with her irrelevant souvenirs would be a constant figure at Hare: she would 'come over' probably quite easily—sooner, even, than her daughter! 'And her *First* Confession,' Mrs. Hurstpierpoint ruminated with a crucial, fleeting smile, 'if (by some little harmless strategy) I could arrange it, I should dearly love to hear!'

Her cogitations were interrupted by the return of Mrs. Thoroughfare, leading by the hand a reluctant Poor Clare for a cup of tea.

Proscribed by her Order to Silence, and having nothing in her physiognomy to help her out, Sister Ecclesia's position at present was one of peculiar difficulty and constraint.

In the Convent of Arimathæa, at Sodbury hard by Hare whence she came, her indiscreet talkativeness had impelled a wise, if severe, Mother-Superior to impose upon her the *Torture* of Silence—which supplice had led her inevitably into tricks; Sister Ecclesia had contracted mannerisms therefrom. Though uttering no audible word her lips seldom were till. Strangers sometimes took her to be a saint, in touch with heaven. Bursting to speak she would frequently, when in society, shake clenched hands in the air impotently like a child. Sometimes, in order to find an outlet to her pent emotions, she would go as far as to kick and to pinch, and even to dance (her spirited hornpipes with Captain Thoroughfare were much admired at Hare), while with a broomstick she was invaluable—a very tigress—drawing blood directly. Indeed, as Mrs. Hurstpierpoint was wont to say, her arm seemed born for a birch. Thrice a year Sister Ecclesia was allowed the use of her tongue when instead of seeking intercourse among the nuns she would flit off quite alone towards the sea-shore and blend her voice with the errant gulls

until her unrestrained cries and screams frequently caused her to
faint.

With vacuous, half-closed lids, Mrs. Hurstpierpoint accepted her
generous shower-bath of Eau Bénite.

'Out? Already,' she murmured, simultaneously offering her hand
on one side while abandoning her lips on the other.

'And oh! Eulalia,' Mrs. Thoroughfare's voice shook with inflections, 'who should one find in Nuestra Señora ... (in the Capella
Love of the Salutation) but Lady Violet Logg? Lady Violet! Elegant
to tears, and with two such wisps of boys! Boys of about seventeen
—or eighteen, Eulalia! Like the mignons of Henry the Third.'

'I suppose ... no umbrella.'

'And I am sure that Edie's pricked.'

'I know of more than one in the house to be wobbling!' Fowler
averred as with rush-like gait at the view of the butler's crane-like
legs, harbinger of the tea-board (in the dark of his mind might he not
aspire to build with her? Swoop! Fly to church with her: make a
nest of her? Snatch at her? Bend her, break her—God knew how!—
to his passions' uses?), she flexibly withdrew.

'If anyone calls, ffines,' Mrs. Hurstpierpoint said, rousing herself
and running a hand to her half-falling hair, 'better simply say I'm
out.'

'Les-bia—ah-h ... !' Mrs. Thoroughfare struck a few chords
airily on the open piano.

'And, ffines ... an extra cup.'

'An extra, 'm?'

'Insensate!'

'Hitherto, 'm (and I've seen some choice service I am sure) I
always gave entire satisfaction.'

'You never saw choicer service (I am quite sure) than with *me*,
ffines,' Mrs. Hurstpierpoint said, complacently adjusting a pin.
'And I'd have you to remember it!'

'Julia, Duchess of Jutland thought the world of me.'

'And so do I, ffines. I think the world of you too—*this* world! ..."

'White Mit-y-lene ...' Mrs. Thoroughfare broke melodiously in,
'where the gir——'

'What was that song about lilacs, Lizzie?' Mrs. Hurstpierpoint,
turning to her, asked.

'*Lilacs*, Eulalia?'

'Something to do with lilacs: *lilas en fleur*; an old air of France.'

'Le temps des lilas et le temps des roses,
Ne reviendra plus à ce printemps ci.
Le temps de lilas et les temps des roses
Est passé, le temps des œillets aussi.

Le vent a changé les cieux sont moroses,
Et nous n'irons plus courir et cueillir
Les lilas en fleur et les belles roses;
Le printemps est triste et ne peut fleurir.

Oh, joyeux et doux printemps de l'année
Qui vint, l'an passé, nous ensoleiller,
Notre fleur d'amour est si bien fanée.
Las! que ton baiser ne peut l'eveiller.

Et toi, que fais-tu? pas de fleurs écloses,
Point de gai soleil ni d'ombrages frais;
Le temps des lilas et le temps des roses
Avec notre amour est mort à jamais.'

Mrs. Thoroughfare's voice ebbed.

'May a woman know, dear,' Mrs. Hurstpierpoint softly said, 'when she may receive her drubbing?'

'Oh I've no strength left in me to-day, Eulalia, I fear, for anything,' Mrs. Thoroughfare answered.

'Positively?'

'Ask Ecclesia!'

But with the French song over Sister Ecclesia had edged, with much wild grace, from the room.

'She's returned to her prayers, I suppose.'

'Or to Father.'

'Happily, quite in vain!'

'*Chè volete?*'

'I miss Père Ernest,' Mrs. Hurstpierpoint sighed, leisurely sipping her tea.

'Yes, dear, but he had too many ultramontane habits. . . . There was really no joy in pouring out one's sins while he sat assiduously picking his nose.'

'Which reminds me,' Mrs. Hurstpierpoint serenely said, 'to gather my nectarines. . . .'

'Your nectarines . . . ?'

'Sir Victor begs me for a few nectarine models. Nectarines meet to sit to him. Not *too* ripe.'

'I should think he only wanted them for himself,' Mrs. Thoroughfare cooed, opening wide a window that commanded an outlook of the lawns.

The atmosphere was clearer now. Before the house the mutilated statues and widowed urns showed palely white against a sky palely blue through which a rainbow was fast forming. By the little garden pergola open to the winds some fluttered peacocks were blotted nervelessly amid the dripping trees, their heads sunk back beneath their wings: while in the pergola itself, like a fallen storm-cloud, lolled a negress, her levelled, polecat eyes semi-veiled by the nebulous alchemy of the rainbow.

'What are you doing fiddle-faddling over there, Elizabeth?' Mrs. Hurstpierpoint asked.

'Look, Eulalia,' Mrs. Thoroughfare said, catching her breath, 'someone with a kite is on our lawn!'

Mrs. Hurstpierpoint was impelled to smile.

'In the old days,' she murmured, brushing a few crumbs from her gown, 'sailing a kite heavenward was my utmost felicity. No ball of string, I remember, was ever long enough!'

'This is no christian and her kite, Eulalia, or I'm much mistaken. . . .'

'No christian, Elizabeth?'

'It's a savage.'

Mrs. Hurstpierpoint sank humbly to her knees.

'*Gloria in Excelsis tibi Deo!*' she solemnly exclaimed.

๙ *VII* ๙

THE plaintive pizzicato of Madame Mimosa's Pom pup 'Plum Bun' aroused Mrs. Yajñavalkya one triumphal summer morning while lying in the voluminous feather-bed that since lately she shared with her niece.

'*Zbaffa pbf!*' she complained, addressing an ape-like image, cut in jade, that stood at the bed-end, its incensed arms and elongated eyes defensively alert. Beside her Niri-Esther, indiscreetly *enceinte*, was still asleep.

'O de worries!' the negress murmured, leaving indolently her bed and hitching higher the blind.

It was Market morning. . . . Beneath a mottled sky some score or so of little carts covered in frail tarpaulins of unnamable sun-scorched colours were mustered before the Daleman Memorial where already a certain amount of petty chicanery had begun.

'Dat is a scene now which somehow make me smile,' Mrs. Yajñavalkya commented. 'Ya Allah, but whenever I see a Market I no longer feel Abroad. . . . And w'y, I wonder, is de reason ob dis? . . . Because human nature is de same ebberywhere.'

'Any old flint glass or broken bottles for a poor woman to-day?' a barrow-hawker smote into her reflections from below.

Mrs. Yajñavalkya indrew her head.

It was one of her fullest mornings, being the eve of Mrs. Hurst-pierpoint's reunion in honour of the centenarians of the place, who together with their progeny assembled yearly in the closed drawing-rooms, or beneath the titanic cedars, of Hare.

And for these annual resuscitations Mrs. Yajñavalkya's invigorating touch was deemed almost indispensable.

Consulting her tablets, she found Tooke's Farm to be first on her list, when it might be that the dairyman himself would be about. Disheartening contretemps had followed hitherto her every intriguing effort. He had responded to her summons to 'take a look at the Vine' in the small grape-house at the extremity of the garden, politely, if unorthodoxly enough, bringing with him, with Mrs. Tooke's 'compliments,' a sumptuous barrowful of well-seasoned offal, whereat Lady Parvula de Panzoust, poised like a Bacchante amid the drooping grapes, had taken to fastidious heels in alarm.

'If I cannot throw dem both together,' she brooded, 'be it only out ob doors . . . I will be obliged to quench lub's fever wif a sedative.'

The venerable dial of St. Veronica's wood clock, and a glimpse of Nurse Yates' under-sized form crossing the Square, advised her not to dawdle, and soon she, too, was threading her way amid the arguing yokels and the little carts.

Beneath a strip of awning that shook slightly in the soft sea air a sailor with eyes like sad sapphires was showing a whale caught in the bay, to' view which he asked a penny. Partially hid within a fishing creel it brought back to Mrs. Yajñavalkya the unfaithful wives of her own native land who were cast as a rule to the sharks.

Refusing payment only to revive poignant memories of aunts and cousins, sisters and sisters-in-law, as well as a close escape of her own, Mrs. Yajñavalkya disdainfully moved away.

In a cottage garden at the corner of the market-place she could distinguish the sexton of St. Veronica's meandering round his beehives in a white paper mask. From his shuffling step and obvious air of preoccupation, it was as though in some instinctive way he was aware that the consequences of the Hare-Hatch rout would shortly drive him to 'resume' his spade.

Flitting fleetly by, Mrs. Yajñavalkya attained the weather-beaten farmyard gate where, grinning as he watched her approach, stood Bobby Jolly.

'Is your master in, you little giggling Valmouth goose?' she enquired.

'David? He won't be back till evenfall.'

'Oho?'

'He's felling trees in Wingley Woo,' the child replied, looking up quizzically into the negress's face.

Between his long curly lashes were blue eyes—not very deep: a slight down, nearly white, sprouted below a dainty little nose, just above the lip at the two corners.

'No matter. So long as the dear dowager has not gone with him,' Mrs. Yajñavalkya replied, jauntily entering the yard. On the dung-hill that rose against the church to the sill of the clerestory-windows lay Douce—treacherously asleep, his muzzle couched on a loose forepaw.

'He leave behind de dog?'

''Cos of pheasants.'

Mrs. Yajñavalkya shaded her brow from the sun with her hand. Through an open barn she could trace the River Val winding leisurely coastward through cornfields white with glory. A hum of bees from the flower plat by the garden wall filled the air with a ceaseless sound and raised the mind up to Allah.

She chanced on Mrs. Tooke essaying the effect of a youthful little cap before the glass.

'Charming,' the negress cried. 'Delicious!'

Decked with silk bandstrings and laces, the old lady's long bluish profile, calcined on the grave-ground without, recalled to Mrs.

Yajñavalkya one of the incomparable Dutch paintings assigned to
Franz Hals, in Evadne, Duchess of Valmouth's boudoir.

'Faith, my dear,' Mrs. Tooke exclaimed, 'but you frightened me.'

'And how do you find yourself, Mrs. Tooke, to-day?' the negress
archly asked.

Troubled at being surprised in an act of vanity, a thing she
professed to abhor, Mrs. Tooke was inclined to be captious.

'To-day I feel only passably well, Mrs. Yaj,' she replied.

'I've seen you worse, Mrs. Tooke.'

'I fear I shall soon become now a portion for foxes.'

'Dat is for me to say, Mrs. Tooke.'

'I ha'n't the constitution at all that I had.'

'De prospect ob a function may have occasioned a touch ob
fever; nothing but a little cerebral excitement, de outcome ob neuras-
thenia, which my methods, I hope, will remove.'

'I wish I hadn't a wen, Mrs. Yaj! A sad hash your methods made
of it.'

'De more you cauterise a wen, Mrs. Tooke ... Besides, wot's
de good ob worry? Not poppy, nor mandragora, nor all the drowsy
syrups of the world, shall ever soothe it or medicine it away.
Remember.'

Mrs. Tooke sighed submissively.

'Where did I put my Bible?' she plaintively asked, peering around
the long-familiar room.

'I wonder you're not tired ob your Bible, Mrs. Tooke.'

'Fie! Mrs. Yaj. You shouldn't speak so.'

'You should read de Talmud for a change.'

'It sounds a poor exchange.'

'Do you really believe now, Mrs. Tooke my dear, in de Apostolic
Succession? Can you look me in de eyes and say you do?'

'I ha'n't paid any heed lately to those chaps, Mrs. Yaj; I'm going
on to Habakkuk.'

'Was not he de companion ob de Prodigal son?'

'Maybe he was, my dear. He seems to have known a good many
people.'

'Dat is not de name now ob a man, Mrs. Tooke, to observe a
single wife, nor even a single sex. ... No! Oh no; a man wif a
name like dat would have his needs!'

'Heysey-ho! We most of us have our wants.'

'From all one hears, Mrs. Tooke, your grandson hasn't many.'

'Yoiks, Mrs. Yaj! He was at me just now for a Bull.'

'And do you tell me so, Mrs. Tooke?'

'A farm's no farm without a Bull, says he; and t'other day 'twas a shorthorn milcher he'd have had me buy.'

'He seems insensitive to women, Mrs. Tooke! I think, my dear, he never was truly enmeshed.'

'He's unimpressionable, I'm thankful to say.'

'I know ob one now, Mrs. Tooke, who would be glad to be on his two legs again to-morrow night—and who *will* be, my dear, I dare say, although I did refuse him.'

Mrs. Tooke evinced detachment.

'They tell me Doris Country's dress is being edged with ermine,' she observed, fastening her eye on a piece of old Valmouth ware representing a dog with a hen in its mouth, that occupied the dresser.

'You'll need your *boa* as de nights are chilly.'

' 'Od: I've no ermine skin myself!'

'Dair are furs besides ermine, Mrs. Tooke. Wot is dair smarter dan a monkey's tail trimmed in black lace?—wid no stint mind to de strings; dat is a combination dat always succeed.'

'Belike.'

'In my land ermine, you know, is exclusive to de khan or, as you would say, de king.'

'His Majesty, the Can!' the old lady shyly marvelled.

'He my beloved sovereign.'

'And your Queens (I presume) are Pitchers?'

'Never you mind now, Mrs. Tooke, never you mind! but just let me rub a little ob dis on de seat ob your ovaries; de same as I did once to a Muscovite princess. . . . "Your magic hand, my dear," she say, "it bring such joy and release. . . ." '

'I wish I had your brawn, Mrs. Yaj!'

'Noble, or ignoble, Mrs. Tooke, I treat my clients just de same!'

'You old black bogey, what should I do without you?'

'*Inshallah!*' The negress shrugged, glancing over her shoulder at a sudden sneeze from Miss Tooke behind her.

Bearing in her arms the sacrificial linen, she waded forward in a ray of dusty sunlight, as if fording in fancy the turbid Val that should transport her to Love's transcendent delights, in illimitable, jewelly seas.

'It's a hard thing, Mrs. Yaj,' Mrs. Tooke observed, 'to be dependent on a wench who spends half her life in the river! If *I* was a fish I'd snap at her legs.'

'I've no doubt you would, Mrs. Tooke, but joking, my dear, apart, unless as a finish to a douche cold water I always discommend. Dair (in moderation no doubt) it is good; otherwise in my opinion it is injurious to de circulation, impeding and clogging de natural channels and so hampering de course ob de blood, and often even gibbing excuse to de body's worst enemy ob all—I mean de gastric juices.'

Mrs. Tooke's brows knit together. She scowled.

'Let her keep her distance,' she exclaimed, 'with her contagious heavy cold!'

'I am sure I've no will to come near you,' Miss Tooke replied with a desolating sigh as she fell to earth.

She was looking restless and pale and strangely avid for love.

'You'll not die in an old skin if you fret it so, Thetis girl, ah, that ye won't.'

'What's the use of living then? Life is only acceptable on the condition that it is enjoyed.'

Mrs. Tooke blinked, eluded.

'Belike,' she said, 'by God's grace to-morrow night we'll both have a bit of a fling. Oh-ay, I do mind the nestful of field-mice we had in the spring-cart last year. I had been out all day among the clover, but, Lord! I never knew 'twas full of they mice, till a satyr, in livery, shoved his hand (like a sauce-box) into the cart, under pretext of helping me down, when pouf! out they all hopped from under my train, furnishing the tag-rag and bobtail there was standing about with all manner of *immund* remarks. . . .'

'And where was this, Mrs. Tooke?' the negress aloofly asked.

'Why at Hare, Mrs. Yaj, last year.'

Miss Tooke sighed again, and drawing a cut citron from her apron pocket she applied it gently (as directed by 'Susuva' in *The Woman's Friend*) to the roots of her nails.

> 'When I am dead
> Ah bring me flow-ers,
> Spread roses and forget-me-nots,'

she somewhat hectically hummed.

'You bits of raw shoots seldom hark to any sense, though 'twere better often to be a primrose in the wilderness than a polyanthus in a frame. And you'll remember, maybe, I said so, when I'm grassed down in the earth and gone,' Mrs. Tooke declared, riveting her attention on the tombstones below.

Several of the nearer epitaphs were distinctly legible through the farmstead windows, such as '*Josephine—first wife of Q. Comedy Esqre died of Jealousy, March 31st 1898: Remember her,*' while the rest, monotonously identical, for the most part betokened 'inconsolable widows' and were nothing, according to Mrs. Tooke (who had eyes for a wedding as well as for a funeral), but 'a "———" tangle of lies!' One gaunt, tall cross, however, half hidden by conifers, a little apart, almost isolated, solitary, alone, was, to the excellent English-woman, in its provocativeness, as a chalk egg is to a sensitive hen. Here lay Balty Vincent Wise, having lived and died—*unmarried*. Oh what a funny fellow! Oh what a curious man! . . . What did he mean by going off like that? Was no woman good enough for him then? Oh what a queer reflection to be sure; what a slur on all her sex! Oh but he should have settled; ranged himself as every bache-lor should! Improper naughty thing! He should be exorcised and whipped: or had he loved? Loved perchance *elsewhere* . . . ? The subject of many a fluttered reverie he gave, by his eccentric manes, just that touch of mystery, that piquant interest to the churchyard that inwardly she loved—Balty!

'There are times, Mrs. Yaj, when I find the look-out cheerless.'

'Still! Radder dan see "Marsh-lights" . . .'

'Ah . . . I shall never forget how Mr. Comedy (when he lost his first wife) passed the night in the graveyard, crying and singing and howling, with a magnum of Mumm. . . .'

With a wry little laugh Miss Tooke turned and moved away.

'Since you've all, then, you need,' she said, 'I'll take a pail of clams and yams, I think, to feed the pigs.'

'Let 'em farrow if they choose, and keep clear of the river, mind; don't let me hear of you in the Val again to-day.'

'The Val! You ought to see the Ganges, Mrs. Tooke! Ah, dat is some river indeed.'

'In what way, Mrs. Yaj?'

'A girl may loiter there with her amphora and show her ankles to de fleets of sailing sampans often to her advantage. . . . Many a match-making mother have I known, my dear, to send her daughter to stand below some eligible Villa with instructions to toy for an hour with her crock.'

'As I'm a decent widow, Mrs. Yaj, you negresses are a bad lot, I'm afraid.'

'O w'y?'

'I expect it's something to do with your climate.'

'We Eastern women love the sun ... ! When de thermometer rise to some two hundred or so, ah dat is de time to lie among de bees and canes.'

'I could never stand the stew——, it would take all *my* stamina.'

'My little maid, Carry, is de same as you. De least spell ob warmth prostrate her wid de vertigoes.'

'You've had her some time now, Mrs. Yaj.'

'So I have, Mrs. Tooke, so I have; dô I say often I've a mind to take a page; but a growing boy in de house, my dear—you *know* what dey are! However, Carry I soon shall have to dismiss. ... She dat otiose! She dat idle! She will read by de hour from my medical dictionary, dô I defend her eber to open it, because dair are tings she is perhaps better without de knowledge ob! *Kra.* And how she wreck my china! Before I came to dis place I had no stylish services; but I would go out and pick myself a plate ob a fresh green leaf, and den wen it had served its purpose, after each course, I would just throw it away; and like dat dair was no expense, and none ob dese breakages at all.'

'Well, there are plenty of pleasant trees round Valmouth, Mrs. Yaj, I'm sure; and you're welcome to flower-leaf or vegetable from these acres, my dear, at any time; you shall sup off Dock a-Monday, and Cabbage Tuesday, Violet-hearts on Wednesday, Ivy Thursday, Nettle Friday, King Solomon's seal Saturday, and Sunday, you old black caterpillar, you can range as you please through the grass.'

'I have my own little garden, Mrs. Tooke, my dear, you forget: but dat white calf now out yonder ... my niece beg me to say she'd buy it, as she desire to sacrifice it to a certain goddess for private family reasons.'

'For shame, Mrs. Yaj. It makes me sad to hear you talk like a heathen.'

'Such narrow prejudice; for I suppose it will only go to de butcher in de end?'

'Disgusting.'

'Butchers are so brutal, Mrs. Tooke ... ! Dair hearts must be so unkind ... men without mercy! And dat's wot I alvays say.'

'Ts!'

'And remember dis, my dear. It is for her deity and not for herself she seek the calf.'

'Be quiet.'

'Niri-Esther only relish roots, a dish ob white roots and fruits—unless dis last few day, when she express a fancy for water-melon jam! But where I say in Valmouth can you find water-melon jam? O de worries, Mrs. Tooke!'

'I ha'n't seen her kite so much lately, Mrs. Yaj.'

'Babies are so tender. . . . Little children are so frail . . .' the negress said to herself aloud.

'What's that, my dear?'

'I miss a mosque, Mrs. Tooke, and de consolation ob de church; but when I turn to Allah, I suppose de Holy Mihrab near to me and den,' the negress murmured, bestowing a parting pinch upon the aged dame, 'all is well.'

Her day indeed was but begun. In many a cloud-swept village bespattering the hills her presence was due anon.

Issuing from the farm-house she hovered to consider the itinerary ahead—culminating picturesquely (towards sunset) in a ruined stomach—some six miles from the town. Deliberatingly traversing the yard, where, here and there, fowl were pecking negligently at their shadows, she recognised in the penumbra of a cart-shed the arrowy form of Lady Parvula de Panzoust.

She wore a dress of becoming corduroy and a hat all rose-pink feathers, the little basket upon her arm signifying, evidently—*eggs*.

Following her (with more perhaps than his habitual suspicion) was churlish Douce.

'Poor, dear, beautiful, patient beast!' the negress could hear her say in tones of vivacious interest as she fondled the dog's supple back and long, soft, nervelessly drooping ears. Then suddenly stooping, she exclaimed vehemently, as if transported: 'Kiss me, Bushy!'

☙ VIII ☙

IT was the auspicious night when as to a Sabbat the centenarians of Valmouth, escorted by twittering troops of expectant heirs and toad-eating relatives, foregathered together, like so many warlocks and witches, in the generously loaned drawing-rooms and corridors of Hare.

Originating in the past with the corporation, as a subtle advertisement to the salubrity of the climate, these reunions were now in such high favour that the Valmouth Town Hall, a poor poky place, was no longer capable of holding so numerous an attendance, obliging the municipality to seek a more convenient rendezvous elsewhere; hence the cordial offer of the Hare ladies to 'throw open' their doors annually had been accepted officially with a thousand pleasant thanks; and by degrees, by dint of some acted *Mystery*, played to perfection by the Nuns of Sodbury and the Oblates of Up-More, these reunions had afforded full scope for the diplomatic furtherance of Rome.

Something of Limbo, perhaps, was felt by those at present gathered in the long salon, bafflingly lit by an old-fashioned chain-chandelier that threw all the light upwards, towards the ceiling, leaving the room below (to the untold relief of some) in semi-obscurity; but, the night being fine, many preferred to wander out attracted by the silken streamers of a vast marquee.

Leaning on the arm of a swathed tangerine figure, Mrs. Hurstpierpoint, decked in wonderful pearls like Titian's Queen of Cyprus, trailed about beneath the mounting moon, greeting here and there a contemporary with vague cognition. She seemed in charming spirits.

'Your ladyship dribbles!' she complacently commented, shaking from the curling folds of her dress a pious leaflet, *The —— of Mary*, audaciously scouting the Augustinian theory 'that the Blessed Virgin conceived our Lord through the Ears.'

Looking demurely up she saw wide azure spaces stabbed with stars like many Indian pinks.

The chimeric beauty of the night was exhilarating.

In the heavy blooming air the rolling, moon-lit lawns and great old toppling trees stretched away, interfusing far off into soft deeps of velvet, dark blue violet, void.

'The last time I went to the play,' the tangerine figure fluted, 'was with Charles the Second and Louise de Querouaille, to see Betterton play Shylock in *The Merchant of Venice*.'

'Was he so fine?' Mrs. Hurstpierpoint asked, her query drowned in a dramatic dissonance from the pergola—climax to a blood-stirring waltz.

On the lawn-sward couples were revolving beneath the festooned trees that twinkled convivially with fairy lamps, but the centre of attraction, perhaps, at present was the Mayor.

'Congratulations,' his voice pealed out, 'to Peggy Laughter, Ann and Zillah Bottom, Almeria Goatpath, Thisbe Brownjohn, Teresa Twistleton, Rebecca Bramblebrook, Junie Jones, Susannah Sneep, Peter Palafox, Flo Flook, Simon Toole, Molly Ark, Nellie Knight, Fanny Beard, May Thatcher, May Heaven, George Kissington, Tircis Tree, Gerry Bosboom, Gilbert Soham, Lily Quickstep, Doris Country, Anna Clootz, Mary Teeworthy, Dorothy Tooke, Patrick Flynn, Rosa Sweet, Laurette Venum, Violet Ebbing, Horace Hardly, Mary Wilks——'

'*In saeculum saeculi,* apparently!' Mrs. Hurstpierpoint shrugged.

On the fringe of the throng, by a marble shape of Priapus green with moss, Lady Parvula de Panzoust was listening, as if petrified at her thoughts, to the Mayor.

'I shall never forget her,' the tangerine bundle breathed, 'one evening at Salsomaggiore——!'

'For a fogy, she's not half bad, is she, still?'

'I consider her a charming, persuasive, still beautiful, and *always* licentious woman. . . .'

'And with the art . . . not of returning thistles for figs?'

'There are rumours—I dare say you know—of an affair here in the town.'

'Poor Parvula . . . ! a scandal, more or less, it will make no difference to her whatever,' Mrs. Hurstpierpoint answered lucidly, turning apprehensively at the sound of a jocose laugh from Mrs. Yajñavalkya.

Très affairée, equiped in silk of Broussa, she was figurable perhaps to nothing so much as something from below.

'That little black niece of hers, my dear, is extremely exciting. . . .'

'Divinely voluptuous.'

Mrs. Hurstpierpoint tossed a troubled leaflet.

'She is ravishing,' she declared, wafting a butterfly kiss to the Abbess of Sodbury—Mère Marie de Cœurbrisé. Née a Begby of 'Bloxworth,' Mère Marie's taste for society was innate, and her petits goûters in the convent parlour were amazing institutions, if Sister Ecclesia, before her lips were bound, was to be believed.

'It puts me in mind of Vauxhall when I was a girl,' she chuckled.

'Oh—oh!'

'Wunderschön! Bella, bella.'

Her old orchidised face, less spiritualised than orchidised by the convent walls, in the moonlight seemed quite blue.

'And my birch, the blessed broom. . . . Is it in Italy? Has His Holiness complied with the almond-twigs?' Mrs. Hurstpierpoint enquired, drawing her away just as Mrs. Yajñavalkya, believing the leaflet to be as fraught with meaning as a Sultan's handkerchief, dispatched her niece to pick it up.

Such an unorthodox mode of introduction could not but cause the heart a tremor.

'In de case ob future advance,' Mrs. Yajñavalkya enjoined her niece (smiling impenetrably at her thoughts), 'be sure to say de dear billet shall receive your prompt attention.'

'*Paia!*' Niri-Esther assented.

She was looking vanquishing in a transparent, sleeveless tunic over a pair of rose-mauve knickers of an extraordinary intensity of hue. In her arms she held a sheaf of long-stemmed, pearl-white roses—*Soif de Tendresse*.

'We shall enter de palace by de garden gate . . . by de gate ob de garden . . .' Mrs. Yajñavalkya reflected, her eyes embracing the long, semi-Grecian outline of the house.

Before the mask-capped windows, Lady Parvula de Panzoust pointed sharply the dusk with a shimmering fan.

'Your Diana,' the negress, approaching, coughed, 'we speak ob as Hina. But she is de same; she is de moon.'

'Ah?'

'She is de moon. . . .'

'Soon, again, she'll be dwindling.'

'May you enjoy ambrosia: a lover's tigerish kisses, ere she disappears.'

Lady Parvula braced nervously her shoulders.

'Who is the woman in the cerements?' she inconsequently wondered.

'Dat dair she some stranger.'

'It amuses one to watch their dying flutters. . . .'

'You should take notice ob de wife ob de Mayor. Dô she be a hundred and forty, and more, yet she hardly look de age ob "consent"!'

'Have you nothing else—more interesting—to tell me?' Lady Parvula asked, motioning to the shade of the nearest tree.

'Assuredly,' the negress answered, following towards the dark-spreading Spina-Christi over against the house.

I, I, I, I! A night-bird fled on startled wings.

'Like the cry of an injured man!' Lady Parvula murmured, sinking composedly to a garden chair.

'Like de cry ob a djinn!'

'Well; is one any nearer? does he seem in a coming-on stage?' her ladyship blithely asked.

The oriental woman swelled.

'De way he questioned me concerning you, milady,' she unctuously made reply, 'was enough to make a swan bury its head beneath de water.'

'Silly fellow and is he crazy about me, you say? Dear boy. Well.'

'He say he ready to eat you.'

'To—what?'

'Ah de rogue!'

'Eat me . . . and when does he wish to devour me?' Lady Parvula touched nervously the white plumes and emeralds in the edifice of her hair.

'Ah de wretch!'

'Doesn't he say?'

'Al-ways he is hungry, de ogre!'

'The great, big, endless fellow!'

'Al-ways he is clamouring for a meal.'

'Let him guard as he can those ambered freckles!'

'Dey would draw de mazy bees.'

'I so feared he was going to be shy.' With pensive psychic fingers the enamoured Englishwoman toyed with a talismanic bagatelle in New Zealand jade.

'Believe me, he only play de part ob de timid youth de better to surprise you.'

'Simple angel!'

'He resist.'

'I once made a grand resistance—and oh! don't I regret it now . . . the poor dear was of low birth: humble origin: no condition: my husband's amanuensis! But oh! oh! !'

'Dose villain valets. Dey are de very men wif dair fair hard hair and dair chiselled faces. . . .'

'This was a paid secretary. . . . But oh, oh! Even my Lord. He could hardly spell. . . .'

'His face was his fortune?'

'Possibly. But I never was careless of appearances, as I told you think once before. To my good name I cling. Mine, I congratulate myself, is entirely proof. No one has ever really been able to make a heroine out of me! The bordomette of circumlocution one submits to meekly perforce. In the Happy East you live untrammelled by the ghouls of our insular convention.'

Mrs. Yajñavalkya shook a stiff forefinger.

'Sho,' she muttered, allowing soft, discarnate voices to articulate and move on.

'Her great regret you know . . .' the murmur came, 'she is . . . God forgive her . . . the former Favourite of a king; although, as she herself declares, *only* for a few minutes. Poor darling! . . . Yes! My poor Love! She gave herself to an *earthly* crown. . . .'

'An ex-mistress of a king: she has the air.'

'It is Eulalia's *constant torment*!' The voices ebbed.

Lady Parvula looked down at the blue winter-violets in the front of her dress.

'Her sway was short!' she wondered.

She was all herself in a gown of pale brocade with a banana pattern in gold fibre breaking all over it.

'In an affair ob kismet—for it is kismet; what (I ask you to tell me) is reputation? What is it, reputation, in a case ob dis discription? Dis Smara. Dis Mektoub. Dis Destiny!'

'Sound him again. Put out final feelers,' Lady Parvula murmured, waving dismissal with a tap of her fan.

With a wise expressive nod the negress turned away.

Picking her way over the contorted roots of the trees she shaped her course towards the house, pausing to admire a universe of stars in a marble basin drip drop dripping, drip drip dropping, over with the clearest water.

'Væa, væa,' she mused, 'satufa lu-lu fiss.'

Looking up she perceived David Tooke, as if in ambush behind a statue of Meleager that resembled himself.

'Vot do you dair so unsocial?' she demanded in her softest gavroche speaking voice.

The young yeoman smiled slowly.

'Is it true,' he abstrusely answered, 'that in your country bulls consort with mares, and rams seek after cows, and the males of partridges do curious things among themselves?'

'Whoebber told you so told lies.'

'Told lies?'

'Dey told you only ob de few exceptions.'

'Ah.'

He seemed a trifle moonstruck.

'But ob vot importance is it? . . . Suppose *dey do*? Come on now, and hitch your wagon to a star.'

'I'll hitch my wagon where I choose.'

'Up wid dose dear shafts.'

'Tiddy-diddy-doll!' ungraciously he hummed.

'You marry her—and be a Lord!'

'Be off! Don't pester me.'

'Come on now.'

'Heart and belly: not I!'

'Must I *pull* you?'

'Pull me?'

'Drag you to milady.'

'Don't make me a scene, because my nerves can't stand it!'

'Vas dair ebber a eunuch like you?'

'Why does she want to come bothering me?'

'I have nebber heard of such contempt ob de peerage,' Mrs. Yajñavalkya fairly snorted.

'Here's Granny,' he breathed.

And indeed rounding a garden path on her grand-daughter's arm Mrs. Tooke was making a spirited progress of the grounds.

'Glad am I, my dear,' the negress cried, 'to see you're still so able . . .'

'Isht! My legs gae all tapsalteerie!'

'Dat is nothing but Nature's causes. What is wobblyness ever but de outcome simply ob disuse?'

'Just hark to my joints! I'm positively tumbling to bits!'

'And where are you off to, Mrs. Tooke?'

'To make a beau-pot, Mrs. Yaj.'

'What do you call a *beau-pot*, Mrs. Tooke?'

'A posy, Mrs. Yaj.'

'And vot's a posy, Mrs. Tooke?'

'A bunch of flowers, my dear.'

'In de East dair is a rose, deep and red, dat wen she open go off, pop, pop, pop—like de crack ob a gun!' and relinquishing her quarry, with a meaning glance, the negress strolled away.

'He is frigid. Dat I will admit: and bearish a little, too. But de boy is not such a fool,' she philosophised, gazing around her for a sign of her niece.

Through a yew-hedge, thinner at the bottom than at the top, she could see the feet of the dancers as they came and went.

A drowsy Tzigane air, intricate, caressing, vibrated sensuously to the night.

'May I have the pleasure . . . ?' a mild-faced youth, one of the Oblates of Up-More, addressed her.

'Delighted,' she answered, with equanimity, accepting his arm.

'Your countrywoman doesn't dance,' he observed, signalising Niri-Esther astride the seat-board of a garden swing, attached to the aerial branches of a silver fir.

She was clinging mysteriously to the ropes as though her instinct told her they had known the pressure of the palms of someone not altogether indifferent to her heart.

'Just at present . . .' the negress shrugged, submitting to be borne off by the will of a man.

'Ga—ga,' Niri-Esther gurgled, rubbing her cheek languorously against the cord.

'A push is it?' Mrs. Hurstpierpoint aborded her with a smile. 'Is it a push you wish for, dear child? Is that,' she dismantlingly ogled, 'what you're after?' and taking silence for assent, she resolutely clasped the black girl from behind below the middle.

Niri-Esther fetched a shout.

'Oh! Eulalia! ! !' Mrs. Thoroughfare approached *à pas de loup*. 'What are you up to, Eulalia? What are you doing?'

'Go away, Thoroughfare. Now, go away.'

'Oh, Eulalia.' Mrs. Thoroughfare shrank.

'Is not that *heavenly*, dear child?' the formidable woman queried, depositing a rich muff of Carrick-macross lace, bulging with propaganda, upon the ground.

'Stop!'

'Was not that divine, my dear? Didn't you like it?' The hieratic woman pressed, passing her tongue with quiet but evident relish along her upper lip.

Niri-Esther turned aside her head.

The constipated whiteness of a peacock in the penumbra of the tree was disquieting to her somewhat.

'Bird! !' Mrs. Hurstpierpoint chuckled.

'Ours at home are much bigger.'

'Are they, dear child?'

'Much.'

'I want us to be friends. Will you?'

'Why?'

'Ah, my dear ... "why"? Because,' Mrs. Hurstpierpoint quavered, leaning forward to inhale the singularly pungent perfume proceeding from the negress's person, 'because you're very lovable.'

'Eulalia!' Mrs. Thoroughfare reimportunated.

'Yes, Elizabeth!'

'I'm anxious to speak to you for a moment privately, Eulalia.'

'Well——'

'Oh, Eulalia!' Mrs. Thoroughfare faltered. 'Madame Mimosa is here ... exercising her calling ...'

'What?'

'Oh, Eulalia. ...'

'ffines! And turn her out.'

'At least, darling, she was arm-in-arm ... entwined, Eulalia.'

'Prude Elizabeth. Was that all you had to say?'

Mrs. Thoroughfare cast a grim glance towards Niri-Esther.

'Oh, she's a monstrous kid, Eulalia! ... Isn't she just?'

'I don't agree with you there, Elizabeth, at all.'

'Oh, she's a nutty girl; she's a bit of all right.'

'Why are you so down on her, Eliza?'

'I, Eulalia? I'm not down. I think her charming.'

'I'm glad you do.'

'She has her immaturity. I divine this and that.'

'Pho.'

'I guess a great deal.'

'How dear Richard would have admired her.'

'Dick would? How?'

Mrs. Hurstpierpoint lifted her shoulders slightly.

'Your son has a many-sided nature to him, Elizabeth,' she observed; 'which I suppose is not surprising when one thinks of you!'

'What do you mean, Eulalia?'

'What I say, darling. Dick's a man of several facets—no specialist! Thank the Lord!'

'Her habit of covering up her mouth with her hand when not speaking isn't exactly pretty.'

447

'She needs debarbarising, of course.'

'She'd still be black, Eulalia!'

'Black or no, she's certainly perfectly beautiful.'

'She may appeal to your epicurism, dear, although she mayn't to mine.'

'She was telling me—only fancy, Lizzie—that the peacocks in her land are much bigger——!'

'I should think they were, Eulalia. I should imagine they would be.'

'I found her so interesting.'

'I've no doubt of that, Eulalia.'

'But where is she?'

Apparently, like the majority of persons present, she had sauntered over to where a wordless passional play performed by mixed religious seemed to be scoring a hit.

On an overt stage ranged beneath the walls of *Nuestra Señora de la Pena* brilliantly lit within, two pretty probationers, Mystylia and Milka Morris, protégées of the ladies of the house, were revealing themselves to be decidedly promising artists, while gathered in a semi-circle about the stage the audience was finding occasion to exchange a thousand casuistries relative to itself or to the crops.

There uprose a jargon of voices:

'Heroin.'

'Adorable simplicity.'

'What could anyone find to admire in such a shelving profile?'

'We reckon a duck here of two or three and twenty not so old. And a spring chicken *anything to fourteen*.'

'My husband had no amorous energy whatsoever; which just suited me, of course.'

'I suppose when there's no more room for another crow's-foot, one attains a sort of peace?'

'I once said to Doctor Fothergill, a clergyman of Oxford and a great friend of mine, "Doctor," I said, "oh, if only you could see my——" '

'*Elle était jolie! Mais jolie! . . . C'était une si belle brune . . . !*'

'Cruelly lonely.'

'Leery. . . .'

'Vulpine.'

'Calumny.'

'People look like pearls, dear, beneath your wonderful trees.'

'. . . Milka, to-night—she is like a beautiful Cosway.'

'Above social littleness. . . .'

'Woman as I am!'

'Philanthropy.'

'. . . A Jewess in Lewisham who buys old clothes, old teeth, old plate, old paste, old lace. And gives very good prices indeed.'

' 'Er 'ealth I'm pleased to say is totally established.'

'If she pays her creditors *sixpence* in the *pound* it's the utmost they can expect.'

'Wonderful the Duchess of Valmouth's golden red hair, is it not?'

' "You lie to me," he said. "I'm not lying, and I *never* lie," I said. "It's *you* who tell the lies." Oh! I reproached him.'

'I'm tired, dear, but I'm *not* bored! . . .'

'What is a boy of twenty to me?'

'It's a little pain-racked face—not that she really suffers.'

Sister Ecclesia chafing at her Vows, martyred to find some outlet to expression, was like to have died, had not Nature inspired her to seek relief in her sweetest, most inconsequent way.

'I give her leave,' Mère Marie de Cœurbrisé said, 'to demand "the Assembly's pardon." '

Drawn by this little incident together, Lady Parvula de Panzoust and Mrs. Q. Comedy, a lady with white locks and face—the only creature present in a hat—had fallen into an animated colloquy

'These big show seats,' Lady Parvula sighed, 'are all alike: insanitary death-traps!'

The local land-agent's wife sent up her brows a little.

'Were you ever over Nosely?' she interjected.

'The Lauraguays'? Never!' Lady Parvula fluttered a painted fan of a bouquet of flowers by Diaz.

'My husband has the letting of it, you know.'

'Ah, hah—? Well, I always admire Richard the Third, who leased his house in Chelsea to the Duchess of Norfolk for the yearly rental of one red rose.'

Mrs. Comedy's mouth dropped.

'But that was hardly business!' she remarked.

'Who knows though? Perhaps it was,' Lady Parvula answered, appraising her Corydon through the eyelits of her fan.

'I've a sure flair for a figure,' she mused, 'and this one is prodigious.'

'Some say they find the country "warping." '

'Oh, but I feel I want to kiss you!' Lady Parvula ecstatically breathed.

'Madam?' Mrs. Comedy recoiled.

Just at this juncture, over the lawn-party, appeared the truant poll-parrot of Sir Victor Vatt. Wheeling round and round the chapel cross in crazy convolutions, the bird was like something demented.

'Dear Vatt,' it cried, 'he is splendid: so o-ri-gi-nal: and exuberant; like an Italian Decorator. Come, Vatt! Paint me in a greenhouse . . . in a st-oove; a little exotic! . . . Where's my bloody Brush?'

'I forget,' the Abbot of Up-More (a man like a sorrowful colossus) said, fingering fancifully the ring of red beard that draped his large ingenious face, 'if Vatt is for us or no.'

'He is to be had,' Mrs. Hurstpierpoint answered. 'In my private-list I have entered him as "Shakeable": Very: he will come for a touch . . .' she added, wincing at some shooting stars that slipped suddenly down behind the house.

'As Othniel prevailed over Chushanrishathaim so ought likewise we, by self-mortification and by abstinence, to proselytise all those who, themselves perhaps uncertain, vacillate ingloriously upon the brink,' the Abbot cogently commented.

With angelic humour Mrs. Hurstpierpoint swept skyward her heavy-lidded eyes.

'I thought last night, in my sleep,' she murmured, 'that Christ was my new gardener. I thought I saw Him in the Long Walk there, by the bed of Nelly Roche, tending a fallen flower with a wisp of bast. . . . "Oh, Seth," I said to Him . . . "remember the fresh lilies for the alter-vases. . . . Cut all the myosotis there is," I said, "and grub plenty of fine, feathery moss. . . ." And then, as He turned, I saw of course it was not Seth at all.'

'Is Seth leaving you?'

'He leaves us, yes, to be married,' Mrs. Hurstpierpoint replied, acknowledging a friendly little grimace from Niri-Esther, who appeared to be comporting herself altogether unceremoniously towards Thetis Tooke over the matter of a chair.

'Nowadays, the young people sit while their elders stand!' the Abbot succinctly said, riveting a curly-pated enfant de chœur lolling coxcombically beneath the nose of a doating Statilia.

Mrs. Hurstpierpoint kicked out the fatigued silver folds of her Court train with some annoyance.

'Charlie,' she beckoned.

'Here, 'm,' the child chirped, coming up.

'Where's your chivalry, Charlie? Your respect to the ladies?'

The lad looked down abashed.

'Come nearer, Charlie. (Quite close, Little-Voice!) Is that ink, on your head, I see?'

'Probably. . . . Father often wipes his pen in my hair,' the boy replied, darting off down a gravel path, where, having strayed away from the rest, Mrs. Tooke was dropping curtsies to the statues.

'She's loose.'

'Oh! At her time?'

'Very, very loose.'

The Abbot caressed his beard.

'Indeed, she looks a squilleon,' he raptly conjectured.

'She's *shakeable*, Abbot, I mean: in other words one could have her . . .' Mrs. Hurstpierpoint explained.

'Ah: I see.'

'My tongue is over-prone perhaps to metaphor. My cherished friend sometimes scolds me for it; only a fellow-mystic—some saint, would ever know, she says, what I'm driving at often. . . . Dear Lizzie. . . . If I could but influence her to make a Retreat; a change from Hare seems highly expedient for her; and at Arimathæa she would have still her Confessor! For something, I fear, is weighing on her mind; some sorrow she tells me nothing of; and it makes her so difficult. Just now we almost quarrelled. Yes. She grew jealous. And of a negress. Not the old one, "Dina-dina-do." I mean the girl in drawers. So I feel somehow Sodbury is the place for my poor angel. Just for a time. They have there, I believe, at present, Julie Bellojoso, and her sister, Lady Jane Trajane—also little Mrs. Lositer; Grouse Dubelly that was; she, of course, a fixture! . . . Thus my excellent, exquisite friend would have comradeship: and she would return here, I trust, softened, chastened, and with a less dingy outlook on life. For her talk, lately, Abbot, has been anything but bright. Indeed, she frightens me at times with her morose fits of gloom. Entre nous I lay the blame on the excellence of the garden as much as anything else! Our wall-fruit this year has been so very delicious; were not those dark Alphonsos perfection? Dear Father Notshort, though, forgets my wicker basket! But he was always a favourite of mine; and one hears he has great authority with the Duchess. I hope she will decide to make the plunge from

Hare. Her little starveling flower-face almost makes me want to cry.
I feel as if I wanted to give her straight to Jesus. She is here somewhere to-night. With her triste far look. I often say she has the
instinct for dress. Even a skirt of wool with her feels to shimmer. . . .
Lady Violet Logg also is somewhere about: my Poor Heart found
her the other day—the day, it was, of the appalling storm—in
Nuestra Señora, practically on her knees—and with *both* her boys.'
Mrs. Hurstpierpoint diffusely broke off, directing her glance towards
the municipal marquee.

Emerging from it amid a volley of laughter, came a puny, little
old, osseous man of uncertain age, brandishing wildly to the night
an empty bottle of Napoléon brandy.

'Ho! broder Teague,' his voice flew forth, 'dost hear de decree?

'Lilli burlero, bullen a-la.
Dat we shall have a new deputie,
Lilli burlero, bullen a-la.
Lero lero, lilli burlero, lero lero, bullen a-la,
Lero lero, lilli burlero, lero lero, bullen a-la.

Ara! but why does he stay behind?
Lilli burlero, bullen a-la.
Ho! by my shoul 'tis a protestant wind.
Lilli burlero, bullen a-la.
Lero lero, lilli burlero, lero lero, bullen a-la,
Lero lero, lilli burlero, lero lero, bullen a-la.

Now, now de heretics all go down,
Lilli burlero, bullen a-la.
By Chrish' and Shaint Patrick, de nation's our own—"

But with quick insight the maître d'orchestre had struck up a
capricious concert waltz, an enigmatic *au delà* laden air: Lord
Berners? Scriabin? Tschaikovski? On the wings of whose troubled
beat were borne some recent arrivals.

Entering the garden from the park, they would have reached the
house, perhaps, unheeded, but for a watchman upon his rounds.

'A fine night, Captain!' The armed protector Mrs. Hurstpierpoint
saw fit to employ against itinerant ravishers or thieves addressed
his master.

'A delicious night indeed!'

'A little rain before morning maybe . . .'

For Captain Thoroughfare had found his way home again, anxious yet diffident enough to introduce his bride to her new relations: while to lend a conciliatory hand Lieutenant Whorwood himself had submitted to pass a few days at Hare, his cajoling ways and prepossessing face having quite melted Mrs. Hurstpierpoint upon a previous visit.

And, indeed, as he lagged along in the faint boreal light behind his friend he resembled singularly some girl masquerading as a boy for reasons of romance.

He had a suit of summer mufti, and a broad-brimmed blue beaver hat looped with leaves broken from the hedgerows in the lanes, and a Leander scarf tucked full of flowers: loosestrife, meadowrue, orchis, ragged-robin.

But it was due to Thetis Tooke that their advent was first made known.

'Oh! Is it y-you, Dick?' she crooned, catching sight of her lover: 'dear, is it you? Oh, Dick, Dick, Dick, my life!' She fell forward with a shattering cry.

꘎ IX ꘎

IT was in the deserted precincts of a sort of Moorish palace in the purlieus of the town that Lady Parvula de Panzoust and David Tooke were to come together one afternoon some few days subsequent to the Hare-Hatch fête.

In the crazy sunlight the white embattled Kasbahs of the vast rambling villa (erected by a defunct director of the Valbay Oyster-beds, as a summer resort, towards the close of the eighteenth century) showed forcefully, albeit, perhaps, a little sullenly, above the frail giraffe-like trunks of the birch-trees, and the argent trembling leaves of the aspens, that periodically shaded the route.

'I know I should despise myself, but I don't!' Lady Parvula told herself, unrolling a bruised-blue, sick-turquoise, silk sunshade very small like a doll's. 'Such perfect cant, though, with four "honey-moons" in the hotel, to be forced oneself to take to the fields . . . ! Oh, Haree-ee-ee,' she flashed an œillade up into the electric-blue dome of her parasol, 'why did you leave me? Why did you leave your tender "Cowslip" by the wayside all alone? Do you hear me,

Haree-ee-ee? Why did you ever leave me? And Gilda too, my girl. Oh, my darling child . . . do you know the temptation your mother is passing through? Pray for her . . . excuse her if you can. . . . . We shall be like the little birds to-night. Just hark to that one: *tiara, tiara, tiara*. It wants a tiara!'

Her aphrodisiac emotions nicely titillated, Lady Parvula de Panzoust was in her element.

'The Roman bridge in Rimini, the *Long* bridge in Mantua . . .' she murmured to herself erotically, dreamily, as she crossed the Val.

She wore a dress of filmy white stuff, embroidered with bunches of pale mauve thistles, a full fichu, and a large mauve hat with wide mauve ribbons, tied in front in a large knot where the fichu was crossed on her bosom.

'Such red poppies, such blue hills and sea, I never saw!' she reflected, entering a luxurious lime alley leading to the house.

A sign-board bearing the words 'commodious residence,' with the name of Mr. Comedy subjoined, struck a passing chill.

Evidently he was not yet come.

'I shall scream if he turns up in a dreadful billycock, or plays stupid pranks,' she murmured, pursing forward her lips that showed like a ripe strawberry in a face as whitened as a mask of snow.

Beneath the high trees there was a charming freshness.

'Kennst du das Land, wo die Citronen blühen?' she vociferated lightly, glancing up at the sun-fired windows of the house.

'It might suit me, perhaps,' she sighed, sinking down on an old green garden-seat with the paint peeling off in scales.

But to one of her impatient character expectance usually makes substantial demands upon the vitality.

' "Oui, prince, je languis, je *brûle* pour Thésée—Je l'aime," ' she lyrically declaimed.

Mightn't he be, perhaps, lurking close somewhere out of sight?

' "Laissez-moi ma main . . ." ' she languidly hummed (affecting Carré in Manon).

After all there was no need, it seemed, to have put herself in quite such a hurry.

'I begin now to wish I'd worn my little bombasine,' she mused, 'notwithstanding the infernal quantities of hooks. It's too late to turn back for it, I suppose? I feel all of a-twitter. . . . These accidental affairs . . . I said I know I never would. I can't forget the caïquejee on the Golden Horn; since that escapade my nerve has gone completely. How quiet the rooks are to-day. I don't hear any. Why aren't they chanting their unkydoodleums? Swing high, swing low, swing to, swing fro, swing lal-lal-lal-la. What keeps him ever? Some horrid cow? I can't bear to think of the man I love under some cow's chidderkins. Oh, Haree-ee-ee, Haree-ee-ee! Why did you leave me, Henry, to this sort of thing?'

She peered about her.

In the shade of a tree, a book, forgotten, doubtless, by some potential tenant, was lying face downwards, open upon the grass.

With a belief in lovers' lightest omens, Lady Parvula de Panzoust was tempted to rise.

'*Un Document sur l'Impuissance d'Aimer*,' she pouted, pricking the brochure of Jean de Tinan with the point of her parasol.

'I seem to receive a special warning to take steps. . . . He may require inciting,' she deliberated, dropping very daintily to a grassy slope.

The turquoise tenderness of the sky drew from her heart a happy coo.

Overhead a wind-blown branch, upheld in its fall by another branch below, flecked precociously, with hectic tints, the heavy midsummer greenery.

Half sitting, half reclining, she settled herself reposefully against the tree-bole—limp, undefensive, expectant.

'I shall be down to-morrow with lumbago I dare say,' the latent thought flashed through her.

Nevertheless, the easy eloquence of the pose was worth while, perhaps, preserving.

A weasel, 'with a face like a little lion,' she told herself, skipped from behind a garden dial—paused, puzzled at the diaphanous whiteness of her gown,—turned tail, and disappeared briskly beneath a fissure in the plinth.

The words, '*Donec eris felix, multos numerabis amicos, Tempora si fuerint nubila, solus eris!*' traced thereon, irritated her somehow.

Pulling out a letter from her dorothy bag she beguiled the tediousness of waiting by perusing distraitly its contents.

'The *première* of Paphos,' she read. 'Castruccio . . . Delmé. The choruses made me weep. The Carmen Nuptiale was wholly divinely given. I fear these few months in Milan have been all in vain. My glory my voice. An old diva, a pupil of Tiejens . . . *Ah, fors' è lui!* Purity of my . . . No Patti, or Pasta . . . Signor Farsetti . . . thrilling

shake ... *Caro Nome*. Lessons. Liras. One of the pensionnaires. ...
From Warsaw ... worship ... Mademoiselle Lucie de Cleremont
Chatte. Lucie ... Lucie ... Lucie.'

Her head flopped forward beneath her heavy hat, her apathetic
eyelids closed. ...

When at length she looked up, the fretted shadow of the house
had sloped far toward the south.

Something broke the stillness.

An object that to her perplexity resolved itself into a large pink
kite was being dragged slowly past her over the grass. Preceding it,
the forms of Captain Thoroughfare and Niri-Esther were to be
descried retreating together into the dusk. Catching itself in the
garden weeds like a great maimed bird, the kite tore its way along
in the wake of an insouciant pair, followed discreetly a few yards
to the rear by the sorrowing figure of Thetis Tooke.

Lady Parvula was still meditating on what she had seen, when
Mrs. Yajñavalkya presented herself from beneath the shade of the
boskage.

Her downcast eyes and rapid respiration prepared Lady Parvula
to expect the worse.

'What brings you?' she faintly asked.

'Milady P.!' the negress clasped perfervidly beneath her chin her
white-gloved hands. 'It is a case ob *unrequited love* ... but dat does
not mean to say you shall not be satisfied. No; oh no. On my honour.'

'The affair then'—Lady Parvula de Panzoust broke a pale-veined
leaf, and bit it—'proves abortive?'

'He will offer no opposition. ... But on de other hand, he pretend
he cannot guarantee to make any advance!'

Her ladyship's lip curled.

'I fear he must be cold, or else he's decadent? ...' she said, 'for
I have known men, Mrs. Yajñavalkya—yes, and *many men* too!—
who have found us little women the most engrossing thing in
life——'

'He has abjured, he says, de female sex.'

'Abjured us? Oh impossible!'

'However! he will content your caprice on one condition.'

'Let me hear it.'

'Marriage.'

'Marriage ! ! ! ! !'

Lady Parvula wrapped herself in her dignity.

'He seems to *me* to be an unpublished type,' she said severely.

'De great, sweet slighter.'

'I try to follow his train of feeling—but I can't.'

'He is inhuman, milady, and dat is sure.'

Lady Parvula followed absently with her glance a huge clock-beetle, exploring restively the handle to her parasol.

'At once. Where is he?' she demanded.

'I left him yonder at de gate.'

'You got him to the gate!'

'And dair we just parted. "Come along, now," I said, "for wif-out you I refuse to budge." '

'Well, what made you leave him then?'

'*Kra.*'

'As he is a shy, mistrustful misanthrope . . . an inverted flower . . .'

' "Why won't you come?" I say to him. "Do I ask de impossible?" *Kra!*'

'Oh . . . I want to spank the white-walls of his cottage!'

'Vot is von misadventure.'

'Do you really believe candidly there's *any* chance?'

'Dis but a hitch!'

'A disappointment, Mrs. Yajñavalkya——'

'Take what you can get, milady . . . Half a loaf is better dan no bread! Remember; and dat's vot I alvays say.'

'Nonsense—; he must trot out—; I want more than crumbs.'

'I get you both de crust *and* de crumb. I obtain you all you desire: only give me de time,' the negress wheezed.

Lady Parvula looked malicious.

'Of course he's *stable*,' she remarked.

'*Inshallah!*'

'Since seeing him in his shirt-sleeves with the peak of his cap turned over his neck, and redolent, upon the whole, of anything but *flowers* . . . he no longer thrills me,' she alleged, 'to the former extent.'

'I could get you de cousin.'

'What cousin?'

'De Bobby Jolly boy.'

' . . . Too young!'

'He twelve.'

'Go on! He's not eight.'

'Dat child is a king's morsel.'

Lady Parvula had a headshake.

'In the depths of the wilds you'd think young folk were bound to be more or less pent up,' she reflected, in tearful tones.

Mrs. Yajñavalkya smiled beneficently.

'It is not right, my dear,' she declared, 'you should be bilked. . . . Vot do you say to de captain ob a ketch? Beyond de Point out dair I have in mind de very goods.'

'As a rule that class is much too Esau. You understand what I mean.'

'Or; have you ever looked attentively at de local school-master?'

'No; I can't say I have.'

'Den you certainly should!'

'A schoolmaster—there's something so very *dredged*——'

'I sometimes say to Doctor Dee he put me in mind ob Dai-Cok.'

'Dai-Cok?'

'De Japanese God ob Wealth.'

'Well—; I dare say he would do as a poor *pis aller*,' Lady Parvula tittered, retouching her cheeks lightly with a powder-ball.

Not a breath of wind was stirring the trees. High up in the incandescent blue the whitest of moons was riding.

'Hina has lit her lamp. Hina here.'

'Damnation! ! ! !'

'Come with me now, my beautiful darling. Come. Come. Be brave. Be patient,' the negress begged.

Lady Parvula rose stiffly to her feet.

'I'll come perhaps a short way with you,' she said, regarding speculatively the interchanging fires of the lighthouse, that revealed, far off, their illusive radiance round the Point.

'How I wish, my dear, I could bow to your wishes!'

'You?'

'Supply de need.'

'I have reconsidered——' Lady Parvula breathed. 'Tell me . . . This captain of a ketch . . . Has he . . . (There are one or two petty questions I would like to put to you quietly as we go along . . . !)'

ℜ X ℜ

THE sky was empurpled towards the west, and the long, desolate, road, winding seaward, was wrapped in shadow; and desolate equally, was her heart.

'I loved you, Dick—: I asked for nothing better, Dear, than to be the wool of your vest . . .' Thetis softly wailed.

Her pale lips quivered.

'I would have done it yesterday,' she moaned, 'only the sea was as smooth as a plate!'

Yet now that it was slashed with little phantom horses it affrighted her. To be enveloped utterly by that cold stampede! Recalling the foolishness they had talked of her naiad namesake, she spat.

A fleet white pony and a little basket-wagon, with Maudie and Maidie, the charming children of Mrs. Q. Comedy, rattled by, returning from a picnic on the beach.

'I'd have blacked myself, Dick, for you. All over every day. There would have been such delight, Dear, in my aversion. . . . But you never told me your tastes. You concealed what you cared for from me. And I never guessed. . . . No; you never trusted me, Dick. . . . Besides! Everything's useless now,' she soliloquised, inclining to decipher the torn particles of a letter, littering the high road beneath her feet.

Willows near Pavia——

Weeping-willows near Pavia——

Pavia University——

Pavia——

Her bruised mind sought comfort . . . (vainly) . . . amid the bits——

'Yes. Everything's useless now. For very soon, Dick, I'll be dead!'

From a bank of yellowing bracken, a beautiful cock-pheasant flew over her with a plaintive shriek.

'Dead. . . . I suppose they'll put out the Stella Maris and dredge the Bay. But the tide will bear me beyond the Point; fortunately; I'm so lightsome! Seven stone. If that . . . oh dear, oh dear. When Nellie Nackman did the same she never left the rocks. It's a matter of build purely.'

Two bare-footed men—Up-Moreites—passed her with a 'famished' stare.

'I have a lovely figure. Totally superior to hers. He doesn't know what I am .... Poor Dear. How should he? My honey-angel .... Oh, Dick, Dick, Dick, Dick. ... I ought to curse you, my darling.'

A labourer striding fugitively along in front of her, a young spruce-fir on his back (its bobbing boughs brushing the ground), perplexed her briefly.

'But I can't, I can't curse you, Dick. ... Dear one, I can't. Neither, I find, can I forgive you. ... I hope your brats may resemble their mother—that's all.'

As in a stupor, forging headlong forward she was overtaken in the vicinity of Valopolis by the evening voiture of Madame Mimosa, the lady's monogram, 'Kiki,' wreathed in true-love-knots, emblazoning triply the doors and rear. Presumably the enchantress was returning from the parsonage there—her penchant for Canon Wertnose being well known.

Canon Wertnose, Thetis's thoughts ran on, would bury her were she to be cast ashore. The beach was considered as his 'domain.' ... Canon Wertnose would call at the Farm. Her grandmother would put on her cap to receive his visit with the whiskerage appended. Canon Wertnose would caress the cat. There would be talk of Habakkuk. ...

She started.

Seated on a mileage-stone near the road's end was Carry, the little slavey of Mrs. Yajñavalkya, her head sunk low over a book.

She had in her hands a huge bright bouquet of Chinese asters, sunflowers, chrysanthemums and dahlias, which she inhaled, or twisted with fabulous nonchalance in the air as she read. ... She appeared to be very much amused.

'What are you laughing for, Carry Smith?' Thetis made question.

'Me?' the negress's little apprentice tittered. ... 'Oh, Miss! ... I know at last. ...'

'What futility have you discovered now?'

'I know *at last*—about the gentlemen.'

'About what gentlemen?'

'I know all about them.'

'So do I—traitors.'

'Oh, miss!'

'Don't be a fool, Carry Smith.'

'I know, miss, about them.'

'You may think you do.'

'Ah, but I *know*.' The child kissed her two frail hands to the first white star.

'Pick up your flowers, Carry Smith, and don't be a dilly,' Thetis advised, turning from her.

Day was waning.

The retreating tide exposed to view the low long rocks, encrusting sombrely the shore. Towards the horizon a flotilla of fishing-boats showed immutable, pink-lacquered by the evening sun.

'I shall remove my hat I think,' she cogitated. 'It would be a sin indeed to spoil such expensive plumes. . . . It's not perhaps a head-piece that would become everyone;—and I can't say I'm sorry!'

Her gaze swept glassily the deserted strand.

'It exasperates me though to think of the trouble I gave myself over maquillage. Blanching my face and fingers (and often my neck and arms . . .) surreptitiously in the cream-cans, before their con-signment to Market, when all the while,' she mumbled, fumbling convulsively amid the intricacies of her veil, 'he'd sooner have had me black!'

A little sob escaped her.

'Yes, he'd sooner I'd have been black,' she pursued, approaching determinedly the water's brink, when, from the shade of a cruciform stone, stepped Ecclesia, the Nun.

It was her 'Day.'

Mingling her voice with the planing gulls, winding her way dolorously amid the harsh bare rocks, she approached Thetis Tooke as if divinely impelled.

From the grey headland, where the stone Pharos cast through the gloom its range of shimmering light, a coastguard was surprised to see two women wrestling on the beach below, their outlines dim against the western sky.

৯ XI ৯

CLAD in a Persian-Renaissance gown and a widow's tiara of white batiste, Mrs. Thoroughfare, in all the ferment of a *Marriage Christening,* left her chamber one vapoury autumn day and descending a few stairs, and climbing a few others, knocked a trifle brusquely at her son's wife's door.

Through the open passage windows scent-exhaling Peruvian roses filled the long corridors with unutterable unrest, their live oppressive odour quickening oddly the polished assagais and spears upon the walls.

'Yahya?'

'It's me, dear.'

'Safi?'

'May Mother come in?'

'N . . . o.'

'Hurry up, then, Esther—won't you?' Mrs. Thoroughfare made reply, continuing resourcefully her course towards the lower regions of the house.

A tapestry curtain depicting *The Birth of Tact*, in which *Taste* was seen lying on a flower-decked couch amid ultra-classic surroundings, divided the stairway from the hall.

'Her eye was again at the keyhole,' Mrs. Thoroughfare reflected, pausing to glare at ffines, who was imparting technicalities relative to the Bridal-breakfast to his subordinates.

All was hurry and verve, making the habitual meditation in *Nuestra Señora* a particular effort to-day.

Yet, *oremus*—there being, indeed, the need.

Beyond a perpetual vigil-lamp or two the Basilica was unlit.

Glancing nervously at the unostentatious (essentially unostentatious) font, Mrs. Thoroughfare swept softly over a milky-blue porcelain floor (slightly slithery to the feet) to where her pet prie-dieu, laden with pious provender like some good mountain mule, stood waiting, ready for her to mount, which with a short sigh she did.

'Teach me to know myself, O Lord. Show me my heart. Help me to endure,' she prayed, addressing a figurine in purple and white faience by Maurice Denis below the *quête*.

Through the interstices of the be-pillared nave (brilliant with a series of Gothic banners) the sunlight teemed, illuminating the numerous *ex-votos*, and an esoteric little altar-piece of the 'School' of Sodoma.

'O grant me force!' she murmured, unbending a shade at sight of the gala altar-cloth where, crumpled up amid paschal lilies and *fleurs-de-luce*, basked an elaborate frizzed lamb of her own devoted working, the smart sophisticated crown displayed by the creature ablaze with Mrs. Hurstpierpoint's unset precious stones.

'Our nuptial bouquets (hers and mine) I like to think are conserved below,' she mused, laying her cheek to her hands and smiling a little wistfully towards a statue of the Virgin—*Nuestra Señora de la Pena*—standing solitary under the canopy of the apse, her heart a very pin-cushion of silver darts.

'Hail, Mary . . . !' she breathed, ignoring a decanter of sherry and a plate of herring-sandwiches—a contrivance akin to genius in drawing attention to an offertory-box near by.

From the sacristy the refined roulades of a footman (these 'satanic' matches!) reached her faintly:

> 'Oh I'm his gala-gairle . . .
> I'm his gala child,
> Yes,' etc.

Useless, under the circumstances, to attempt a *station*! 'Besides,' Mrs. Thoroughfare speculated, trailing her Ispahanish flounces over to the dapper, flower-filled chapel of the Salute, 'I bear my own cross, God knows. . . .'

The mystic windows, revealing the astonishing Life of Saint Automona Meris, smouldered brightly.

Automona by way of prelude lolling at a mirror plein de chic, her toes on a hassock, reading a billet-doux. Automona with a purple heartsease, pursuing a nail-pink youth. Automona with four male rakes (like the little brown men of Egypt)—her hair down, holding an ostrich-fan. Automona, in marvellous mourning and with Nile-green hair, seated like a mummy bolt upright. Automona meeting Queen Maud of Cassiopia:—'You look like some rare plant, dear!' Her growing mysticism. She meets Mother Maïa: 'I'm not the woman I was!' Her moods. Her austerities. Her increasing dowdiness. Her indifference to dress. She repulses her couturier: 'Send her away!' Her founding of Sodbury. Her end.

'Dear ardent soul!' Mrs. Thoroughfare commented, her spirit rejoicing in the soft neurotic light.

Seldom had the Basilica shown itself as seductive.

From a pulpit festooned fancifully in prelatial purple the benediction of Cardinal Doppio-Mignoni would shortly fall.

The last time the Cardinal had preached at Hare had been for the harvest festival, when a pyre of wondrous 'wurzels' had been heaped so high on the pulpit-ledge that he had been almost hidden from sight. Whereupon, dislodging a layer, His Eminence had deplaced the lot—the entire structure, Mrs. Thoroughfare remembered well, rattling down like cannon-balls on to the heads of those below.

Glancing round, her eyes encountered a taper-lighting acolyte—Charlie, revolving with an air of half-cynical inquiry before a *Madeleine Lisante,* attributed to the 'Master of the Passion,' usually kept veiled, but to-day exposed to view.

Dipping a grimly sardonic finger in the vase of holy water by the door, Mrs. Thoroughfare withdrew, halting mechnically just outside to lend a listening ear to a confused discursive sound—the eternal *she she she* of servants' voices.

' . . . She . . . she . . .'

Through a service hatch ajar the chatter came.

'She . . .'

'There's the Blue-Room bell!'

'Confound it.'

' . . . Well, dear . . . as I was saying . . . Never before was I so insulted or outraged! Just catch me taking any more topsy freedoms from her.'

'I should keep my breath to cool my porridge. In your shoes, Sweetie.'

'Sweetie? Who's your sweetie? . . . I'm not your sweetie.'

'No? I shouldn't think you was.'

'In your shoes . . . I'd put-myself-out to school, I would, and be taught some grammar!'

'Hurry up, please. . . . Come on now with the samovar—and make haste sorting the letter-bag.'

'His Eminence. His Eminence: didn't someone say Cardinal Mignoni's correspondence passed first through Monsignor Girling? . . . Lord Laggard . . . Lady Laggard. Her Ladyship. Her ladyship. . . . Mademoiselle Carmen Colonnade—; *do, re, mi, fa.* . . . Signora Pinpipi. The Mrs. The Mrs. . . .'

'I always know instinctive when the Mrs. has on her spiked garters.'

'Do you, dear? . . . And *so* do I.'

'You could hear her a-tanning herself before cock-crow this morning in her room. Frtt! but she can swipe.'

'Those holly-bags, too, must tickle one's hams.'

'Now her sister's visiting Valmouth, you'd have thought it was Penance enough!'

'Who are the sponsors beside Lady Laggard?'

'What's that, my dear, to you?'

'There's the Blue-Room bell again!...'

> 'I'll be your little blue-bell
> If you'll be my little bee.'

'And *don't* forget Mrs. Thoroughfare.'

'... What Mrs. Thoroughfare? Which Mrs. Thoroughfare?... the white Mrs. Thoroughfare? The black Mrs. Thoroughfare?'

'I've seen a mort o' queer things in my day' (the voice was ffines's), 'but a *negress*; oh deary me!'

'Give me strength, my God, to bear this cross. Uphold me, Holy Mary, or I fail,' Mrs. Thoroughfare inwardly breathed, retreating softly towards the drawing-room door.

The renowned room was completely bathed in sun, revealing equally the qualities and defects of the numerous baptismal or bridal gifts set out to be admired.

Bending over a charming little mirror of composite precious woods, Mrs. Thoroughfare detected Lieutenant Whorwood grooming assiduously his romantical curls.

Embarrassed at being taken thus unawares, the young man blushed up to the *rose-mauve* of his lips.

'I realise,' said he, 'I'm one of those who, at the last Trump, would run their hand across their hair!'

'Ah? Really—; would you? Why?'

'Probably,' he replied, 'because I'm naturally vain.'

'I adore your hair:—and so does Dick.'

'Did he say so?'

'My boy is very fond of you.'

'And I'm very attached to him.'

'I know you are—and that *is why* I can talk to you about my son,' Mrs. Thoroughfare said, keeping the lieutenant's hand captive in her own a moment longer, perhaps, than was actually required.

'After the ceremony, I trust you'll all at length be easy.'

'Their re-union in my opinion,' Mrs. Thoroughfare declared, 'is nothing but nonsense, but Eulalia seemed so fidgety and nervous —oh! she's so particular now about the least flaw or hitch——! And we thought it best, perhaps, to humour her.'

'Those black weddings are rarely *en règle*.'

'I would give the whole world willingly for the poor fellow to repudiate the affair altogether—; *get out of it*! Such a marvellous opportunity . . . But no; he's utterly infatuated by his wife, it seems;—too much, alas, I fear . . .'

'Dear Mrs. Thoroughfare,' the lieutenant sympathetically said, 'don't think I can't understand. I do . . . absolutely.'

Mrs. Thoroughfare looked appreciative.

'I wish I was more stoic, Lieutenant Whorwood,' she replied, 'I wish I had less heart. . . . But I'm super-sensitive. So I suffer like a fool!'

'It isn't my business of course,' he said, 'to meddle in souls. But Father Colley-Mahoney should be skilled to advise.'

'I've an inkling that Father very soon may be resigning his post,' Mrs. Thoroughfare returned. 'Such a pity! None of the chaplains ever stay long. . . . They seem to dislike Eulalia hauling them out of bed o' nights to say Midnight Masses for her.'

'But *does* she?' the lieutenant murmured, ensconcing himself in an easy-chair.

'Oh, my dear, she's merciless. . . . Eulalia's inexorable. . . . Dom Jonquil, Père Ernest des Martelles, she wore them *out*. You're aware of course about THE KING . . .'

'The old story?'

'For Eulalia with her glowing artist mind—she is a born artist—she reminds me often of Delysia—it is anything but "old." Her poor spirit, I fear, is everlastingly in the back of the Royal Box that ghastly evening of Pastor Fido: or was it in a corner of it she was? She is so liable to get mixed.'

'I understand at any rate she projects presenting Mrs. Richard herself at one of the coming courts.'

'Oh, she's very full of plans—although she tells *me* none of them now.'

'She has been consulting me instead!'

'You remind her of a pet *cicisbeo* she had on her wedding tour—so she pretends.'

'She designs a trip to Paris, and to Vienna too, and Rome; and she has a wild delicious scheme even of visiting *Taormina*.'

'She'll be all over the place now I suppose. I shouldn't wonder if she didn't marry again.'

'It's for little Mrs. Richard presumably that she goes.'

'It's ridiculous how she spoils her. But it's useless to remonstrate. One would have thought she'd have shaved her head and put on mourning. One would have thought she would have received her death-blow. I've known her to take to her bed for a mere black-beetle. Yes, oh, I have . . . blubbering and lamenting like a great frightened silly. But for a hulking *black* savage! not a bit of it! She enjoys all the kudos of a heathen's conversion (a "double conversion," as she says, on account of the child) and forgets altogether the discreditable connection.'

'It's really not such a discreditable one after all.'

'I'll refuse to believe this little madcap negress was ever born a Tahaitian princess. No, Lieutenant Whorwood, or that Mrs. Yajñavalkya of Valmouth is only her nurse.'

'At Tarooa we knew quite well the brother—the banana man . . . employed on King Jotifa's estate.'

'Beuh!'

'The bride's credentials anyway will probably be examined; as Mrs. Hurstpierpoint declares she shall know "no rest" until she has secured for her *the precedence of the daughter of an earl*.'

'Through the Laggard's wire pulling, I wonder.'

'He's vastly struck by her.'

'She provokes him. . . . He finds her piquant.'

'If only she wouldn't run at one quite so much and rumple one's hair!'

'Last night after dinner when *we* all withdrew she amused herself by smacking the hermaphrodite. . . . So Eulalia's full of hopes, she says, that she will sometimes take a hand with the broom. . . .'

'She made a sudden dash for my b-t-m. Greatly to my amazement.'

'Oh, she's a regular puss; my word she is! A regular *civet* if ever there was,' Mrs. Thoroughfare wickedly commented.

'She's perhaps a little too playful.'

'Having torn to piecemeal Eulalia's copy of *Les Chansons de Bilitis* and "mis-used" my set of dear Dumas the Elder, one might say in truth—she was destructive.'

'A book is anathema to her.'

'Even a *papier poudré* one; for when I gave her my little precious volume, my little inseparable of *blanc de perle* in order to rub her nose, she started grating her teeth at me—to my utter terror! Rolling her eyes; lolling out her tongue——'

'One has to feel one's way with her.'

'I'm sure I meant it kindly!'

'A negress never powders.'

'Why not?'

'Because she *knows* it's useless,' the lieutenant lucidly explained.

'Her chief pleasure she seems to find in digging about among the coco-nut fibre in the conservatory with her hands.'

'She's very fond of gardening.'

'And she is also very fond, I fear, of betel. Yes, I fear my boy is married to a betel-chewer. But of course *that* is nothing. . . . "De worst ob dis place," she said to us last night, "is dat dair is no betel! No betel at all;—not ob any discription!" "Are you a betel-chewer, then, my dear?" I asked, *aghast*. "Oh yes," she answered without winking. "How I do crave for some." '

'It's likely to be injurious to her babe at present.'

'*Which?* She's expecting a second enfantement, you know, immediately . . . Oh she's such a quick puss.'

'A prettier, more câline mite than Marigold I never saw.'

Mrs. Thoroughfare exchanged a quick glance with heaven.

'It's a pity the servants don't think so,' she said, 'for none of them will go near her! Baby has had three nurses in one fortnight; not that she perhaps is altogether to blame. The new woman, Mrs. Kent, that came only yesterday (I got her too through the columns of "Femina") Eulalia seems all against. She can't "abide" her, in fact, as they say in Papiete.'

'So soon?'

'Oh Eulalia's so difficult. And she goes far too much to the Nursery. . . ! And unfortunately she isn't *mealy-mouthed*. . . . Eulalia says what she thinks,' Mrs. Thoroughfare murmured, her voice discreetly sinking as an old maid-servant of the house peered into the room—ostensibly only to sneeze twice—and out again.

'It disturbs her,' the young man ventured, 'that you don't get on better with Mrs. Dick!'

Mrs. Thoroughfare's eyes wandered ruefully to a superlatively sensitive miniature—one of the numerous wedding-gifts—portraying Niri-Esther, radiant with wax-white cheeks, as seen through the temperament of a great artist.

'There'd be more affection, perhaps, between us,' she returned sadly, 'if she resembled that.'

'It's rather a gem— Who did it?'

'Sir Victor . . .'

'It's quite inspired!'

With pensive precision Mrs. Thoroughfare drew on a pair of long, primrose-tinted gloves.

'To surprise Eulalia,' she murmured, 'I've commissioned him—only don't let it go further—to compose a Temptation of Saint Anthony for *Nuestra Señora*, a subject she has ever been fond of, it being so full of scope. He proposes inducing the local Laïs, Madame Mimosa, to pose as the Temptation; but I say, she isn't seductive enough. . . . No "Temptation": at least, *I* shouldn't find her one.'

'But why be dull and conventional; why be banal; why should you have a female model?'

'Why, what else, Lieutenant,' Mrs. Thoroughfare shifted a cameo bangle dubiously from one of her arms to the other, 'would you suggest?'

'Oh! A thousand things . . .' the lieutenant was unprecise.

'No; if he can't find a real temptation, a proper temptation, an irresistible temptation—I shall put him "off" with a little flower-piece, some arrangement, perhaps, of *flame-coloured roses* and tell Eulalia it's the "Burning Bush." '

'The Nation should prevent his old Mother from leaving the country.'

'Oh . . . why? What has she done?'

'Nothing—His masterpiece, I meant.'

'I understood him, once, I think, to say that *that* was the *Madame Georges Goujon with Arlette and Ary*. . . .'

'Oh he has so many. His drawing of a Valmouther getting over a stile is something I could covet.'

'They say his study of the drawer of the Bawd's Head Hostelry here is worthy of Franz Hals,' Mrs. Thoroughfare related.

But the entry of Mrs. Hurstpierpoint bearing a long-clothes baby put an end to the colloquy.

Out of courtesy to the bride, and perhaps from some motive of private thanksgiving, her face was completely covered by a jet-black visard. Big beaded wings rose from her back with a certain moth-like effect.

'Tell me, Elizabeth,' she asked, 'will I do?'

'Do! ! Eulalia—I never saw anything like you.'

'I hope the dear Cardinal won't tell me I'm unorthodox; or do you think he will?'

'Take it off, Eulalia,' Mrs. Thoroughfare begged.

'I shall not, Elizabeth!'

'Take it off!'

'No.'

'But why should you conceal yourself behind that odious mask?'

'I wear it, dear, only because a white face seems to frighten baby,'
Mrs. Hurstpierpoint explained.

'Eulalia, Eulalia.'

'Mind, Elizabeth. . . . Be careful of my wings.'

'You're beyond anything, Eulalia.'

Mrs. Hurstpierpoint sat down.

'Sister Ecclesia has just been giving me an account, in dumb show,
of the young woman whom she saved from drowning. . . . But for
her the sea would have absorbed her. . . . However, she is now
comfortably installed in the Convent of Arimathæa, and already
shows, it seems, signs of a budding vocation! So peradventure
she will become a Bride of the Church.'

'Let us hope so, anyway. But talking of "brides," Eulalia, *where's
Esther*?'

'She was outside, dear, a moment ago. . . .'

'In *toilette de noce*?'

'And so excited! She's just floating in happiness—floating,
swimming, sailing, soaring, flying. The darling! She is happy. So
hap-py! Oh——'

'Really, dear, it's you that seem elated.'

'Your boy has my condemnation, Bessy; but he has also my
forgiveness,' Mrs. Hurstpierpoint blandly declared.

'Oh! Eulalia, you're too subtle for me.'

'Call her in, darling, do, or she may perhaps take cold, and a bride
ought not to do that. I had such a cold on *my* honeymoon I remember, I never really ceased sneezing.'

'Oh, she'll come in I dare say when she wants to, Eulalia.'

'You amuse me, Eliza. . . . What makes you so unaccommodat-
ing?'

'It's odd you should ask, Eulalia!'

'Our friendship is unalterable, my little Lizzie, nothing has
changed, or come between.'

'Mind Marigold, Eulalia.'

'What is it she wants? I expect it's her bobo!'

'No she doesn't, Eulalia. She doesn't want it at all.'

'Esther has no notion yet of managing a child. . . . Although
she appears to have any number of quixoticisms.'

'I fear we shall find she has her own little black ideas about everything, Eulalia.'

'Well, well; if she has, she must drop them.'

'Naturally,' the lieutenant interposed, 'her intellectual baggage is nil—simply nil,' he added, lighting complacently a cigarette.

'Father wouldn't agree with you there at all; and he has had her, remember, daily, for pious Instruction.'

'I fear, Eulalia, she was won as much as anything by our wardrobe of stoles.'

'Father seems half in awe of her. . . . "Is an *egregious* sin a *mortal* sin?" she asked him quite suddenly the other day.'

'Oh! Eulalia!'

'She's devoted, though disrespectful, he tells me,' Mrs. Hurstpierpoint murmured, blowing a kiss to the bride who was passing the windows just then.

'Rain fell steadily in the night; the grass must be drenched.'

'Oh, Esther—your feet.'

'When the Spina-Christi sheds its leaves my God what sorrow and stagnance,' Mrs. Thoroughfare sighed oppressed.

'Shall you want the horses, do you think, this evening, Elizabeth?'

'I don't want them, Eulalia.'

'Are you sure, Elizabeth?'

'Perfectly, Eulalia.'

'The evening drive is almost an institution of the past. . . .'

Mrs. Thoroughfare assented.

'Here we are too with winter upon us,' she observed.

'Yes; and this is not the Tropics, my mignonne Niri!' Mrs. Hurstpierpoint reminded her convert as she came forward into the room.

'In de winter,' the negress lisped, 'our trees are green wif parrots.'

'Are they, my dear?'

'Green!'

'Think of that now, dear child.'

'Green wif dem.'

'Did you hear, Elizabeth, what she said?'

'No, Eulalia.'

'It appears their trees are never bare. Always something.'

'Her salvation, in my estimate, Eulalia, should be equivalent quite to a Plenary-perpetual-Indulgence.'

'And so *I* think too.'

'Had she been more accomplished: wives should second their husbands; if not, perhaps, actually lead them. . . .'

'She does not want abilities, I can assure you, Eliza. She knows how to weave grasses. She can make little mats. She's going to teach me some day: aren't you, Esther? She and I are going to make a mat together. And when we've made it, we'll spread it out, and kneel down on it, *side by side*; won't we, Esther!'

'Yaas!' the negress answered, fondling playfully the Hare hermaphrodite.

'You may look, dear, but don't touch. Esther! Pho pet. My *dear*, what next?'

'There's a mean in all things . . . really.'

'Giddy.'

'Incorrigible.'

'You must learn to recollect yourself, dear child, or else I shall return the Lord Chamberlain our Cards.' Mrs. Hurstpierpoint made show of rising.

'Oh, she'd better be presented in Ireland, Eulalia. Dublin Castle to *begin* with—afterwards we'll see——! !'

'Ireland?'

'What do you say, Lieutenant Whorwood?'

The lieutenant laid whimsically his face to a long cylindrical pillow of cloth of silver garnished with beaded-flowers.

'What do *I* say?' he echoed, half closing his eyes and flicking the cigarette-end from his knees, when a discharge of bells from *Nuestra Señora*, and the arrival of the vanguard of the bridal guests, prevented further discussion.

'Her Grace, the Duchess of Valmouth; the Honourable Mrs. Manborough of Castle Malling"—ffines' voice filled the room.

'You shall hold Baby, Lieutenant, while I——' Mrs. Hurstpierpoint flapped expressively her loose-winged sleeves.

'Sir William West-Wind, Mr. Peter Caroon, Mrs. Trotter-Stormer, Sir Wroth and Lady Cleobulina Summer-Leyton, Sir Victor Vatt, Master Xavier Tanoski, Lady Lucy Saunter, Miss à Duarté, Miss Roxall, Lady Jane Congress, Lady Constance Cadence-Stewart, Mrs. Q. Comedy, Lady Lauraguay, Lady Lukin de Lukin, Mrs. Lumlun, Mr. Argrove, Mrs. Lositer, General George Obliveon, Lady Parvula de Panzoust.'

Exhaling indescribably the esoteric gentillezze of Love, she was looking almost girlish beneath a white beret de Picador, enwreathed with multifarious clusters of silken balls, falling behind her far below the waist. Wearing a light décolleté day-dress, her figure since her previous visit to Hare had perceptibly grown stouter.

She was eyeing her hostess with wonder unrestrained when a dowager with a fine film of rouge wrapped in many shawls sailing up to her said:

'Persuade my sister do to take off her mask. Can't you persuade her to doff it?'

Lady Parvula dimpled.

'If you, Arabella, can't—why how,' she returned, 'should I?'

Lady Laggard shook censoriously her shawls.

'I fear,' she observed, 'my poor sister will be soon a *déclassée*. She has been a sore grief to us—a sad trial! But when she begged me to be a godmother to the little Aida, I could hardly say no.'

'Cela va sans dire.'

'Her escapade with King Edred was perfectly disgraceful! She got nothing out of him, you know, for anyone—like the fool that she was. And to see her to-day going about be-winged, be-masked . . .'

'Sad, isn't it, how the old Hare days seem completely gone: vanished.'

'She conceals her upper-lip, one must allow,' Lady Laggard commented. 'But there was no—or *next* to no—was there—to *speak* of—about the eyes? . . . And nothing, nothing to excuse all that long fall of dreary lace.'

'Really she looks so quaint I can hardly help laughing,' Lady Parvula declared.

'She must be bitterly mortified, I imagine, by this marriage.'

'It shows though, I think, her savoir faire, to put the best construction on it.'

'The old Noblesse—where is it now?'

'Ah! I wonder.'

'With a woman like that his career is closed.'

'You may be sure they'll soon be separated!'

Lady Laggard removed an eyelash.

'They're not really married yet, you know,' she alleged.

'N . . . o?'

'The ceremony before I gather was quite null and void.'

'In . . . deed?'

'Their own rites, so it seems, are far simpler. All they do is *simply*

to place each a hand to the torso of the Beloved. And that's as far—
will you *believe it*, dear?—as we are at present!'

'Your sister spoke of "special licence." '

'She would; she has the tongue of a Jesuit.'

'I didn't of course realise . . .'

'We were pumping the bride, Lord Laggard and I, and she told
us, poor innocent, she was not married yet,' Lady Laggard averred,
shaking long tremulous earrings of the time of Seti II of Egypt.

'I notice she likes lights and commotion, which goes to show she
has social instincts!'

'Well, it's some time I suppose since there's been a negress——'

'All the fair men—the blondes, she will take from us. . . .'

'I wish I'd a tithe of your charms, dear.'

'But I don't really mind! . . . So long as *I* get the gypsies. . . .'

'They should forbid her from repeating a horrid equivocal
epigram of old Dr. Dee's—on the Masseuse, La Yajñavalkya.'

'What was it, Arabella?'

'*Her brains are in her arms.*'

'And are they?'

'I don't know, dear, where they are. Such a pity *hers* aren't
anywhere. Her incessant "Wot for dis?" gets so on my nerves.'

'I don't wonder. It would on mine. I'm such a nervous woman!
Now I've no Haree-ee-ee to look after me I get so fluttered. . . .'

'All these priests in the house I find myself a strain. The old
Cardinal, with his monstrous triple-mitre, one goes in terrors of.
He was in the passage just now as I came through waiting for some-
one. And last night—there's only a panel door between our rooms—
I heard him try the handle.'

'Their last chaplain—Père Ernest—I remember was a danger. A
perfect danger! He could have done anything with me, Arabella,
had he willed. I was plastic wax with him.'

'With their faggots of candles (and their incense) they seek to
render imbecile our poor sex. Coming by Nuestra, I assure you, I
was almost *poisoned*. Or, to use a juster metaphor, perhaps,' Lady
Laggard corrected herself, 'suffocated,' she added, 'by the fumes.'

'Monsignor Vanhove, Father O'Donoghue, Frater Galfrith,
Brother Drithelm, Père Porfirio'—ffines insistently continued in his
office until, in sweeping purple and scarlet biretta, Cardinal Doppio-
Mignoni himself passed valedictionally through the rooms.

In the extravagant hush, following on his transit, a prolonged peacock's wail sounded electrifying from the park: *Nijny-Novgorod, Nijny-Novgorod*—creating among the younger bridesmaids an impression of 'foreboding.'

Only Mrs. Hurstpierpoint, to judge by her rich enveloping laugh, seemed really happy or serene.

'I always intended to visit *Walt Whitman,* didn't I, Lizzie? Poor old Walt! . . . I wrote: "Expect me and my maid. . . . I'm coming!" I said. . . . It was the very spring he died.'

Involving some interesting, intellectual trips, she was descanting lightly to right and left.

'I remember you intended once to visit me,' the Bolshevik member for Valmouth, Sir William West-Wind, softly remarked.

'You, Sir William? And when did I ever intend to visit you, I wonder?'

'There was a time,' Sir William murmured, 'when I confess I expected you.'

'Have you any intention, Eulalia,' a *douairière* enquired, 'of visiting the present châtelaine of Nosely?'

'You dear angel—I wasn't aware even it was let.'

'To a field-marshal's widow.'

'My brother,' one of the bridesmaids giggled, 'was his favourite *aide-de-camp.*'

'And what is *she* like?'

'He describes her as lissom as a glove, lively as a kid, and as fond of tippling as a Grenadier-Guard.'

'She sounds a treasure,' Mrs. Hurstpierpoint declared, with a glance backward over her wings.

'Go to Vivi Vanderstart—and say I sent you!' the Duchess of Valmouth was saying.

'Very well, dear, I will.'

'Her boast is, she makes only "Hats for Happy Women." '

'I always pin my faith in Pauline Virot. . . .'

'One should pin one's faith only in God,' Mrs. Hurstpierpoint commented blithely.

'Only where, Eulalia?'

'Only with Him.'

'I remember,' Mrs. Thoroughfare dryly laughed, ' when Eulalia's God was *Gambetta.*'

'Gambetta, Betty—what next will you say, naughty, naughty angel?'

But what Mrs. Thoroughfare subsequently would have said was lost amid Church canticles.

It was the call to the altar.

Oscillating freely a long chain incense swinger, a youthful server, magnificent in white silk stockings and Neapolitan-violet maroquin shoes, presented himself on the threshold in a fragrant veil of smoke.

Venite.

Followed by Charlie with the Holy Pyx and by Father Colley-Mahoney and various officiating priests, he traversed from end to end, amid much show of reverence (crossing and crouching), the vast salon.

'Grant she shall find,'

(Pinpipi with her great male voice from 'Nuestra' was waking the echoes beyond)

'On Yniswitrins altars pale,
The gleaming vision of the Holy Grail.'

'Yes; grant Lord her *soul* shall find,' Mademoiselle Carmen Colonnade, the beloved of the Orpheum, Scala, San Carlo, Costanzi, simultaneously (more or less) struck in, her soft vocal flourishes and pimpant variations soaring, baby-like, high above the strong soprano voice of the severe Pinpipi.

    ''*Es, gwant 'Ord 'er 'oul*—
    Grant it shall find—
    On Ynis-wi-trins walters—
    Altars—
    WALTERS PALER!
    The gleaming vision—
    —*dazzling*—
    Of—
    The Holy Grail-a!'

'Come, Esther,' Mrs. Hurstpierpoint murmured, dashing a tear from her mask.

'Yield the *pas* to a negress! *Never!*' Lady Laggard looked determined.

'Oh, Eulalia!' Mrs. Thoroughfare touched her arm.

'You dear queen.'

'Have you seen my boy, Eulalia?'

'No, Elizabeth—; not to-day.'

'No one can find him.'

'Ah les oiseaux amoureux,' Mrs. Hurstpierpoint began a series of seraphic giggles, 'chers oiseaux . . . paradise uccellinis . . . delicious vogels. . . .'

'I feel half-worn-out.'

'Come, Esther child, to church!'

But Niri-Esther had run out of the house (old, grey, grim, satanic Hare) into the garden, where, with her bride's bouquet of malmaisons and vanessa-violets, she was waywardly in pursuit of—a butterfly.

FAREWELL

Santal

USUALLY it was to the brown-and-silver rug he went, to the brown-and-silver rug at the East angle of the Mosque. He had come to look upon it almost as his own. From it he could contemplate the holy mihrab at his ease, gathered up in his long gandourah that was draggled at the ends. Here he was able to forget for a while the difficulties of his existence, for the boy had no parents. His father, Biskri ben Aissa, had died while carving a sunflower upon a door of a mosque, and his mother had not long survived him; and so he lived at present with an uncle and aunt, who were petty commerçants, and performed their various errands. But always, when he could, it was to the Mosque of Sidi-Yossef he came. Gazing up into the vast cupola of blue-mother-of-pearl he would be transported to Allah in the realms of beauty and bliss: 'Allah, show compassion to thy child Cherif,' he would daily entreat.

Cherif had a tiny head like the proudest of camels, and forlorn, profound eyes that had vision in them. Many long hours had he passed in consideration of the Koran, the larger number of whose inspired precepts he could repeat by heart.

But somehow or other to-day he was unable to think of the Koran. Perhaps it was the first touch of summer that left him so inert. It was pleasant to watch the swaying shadow of the vine-leaves that climbed without on the flower-tiled walls, or to note the wandering butterflies that would pass, from time to time, through the heavy, open jalousies. Sometimes they would cross the Mosque and lose themselves among the rows of old lanterns in the roof, though oftener they would play around the bowed heads of the elders as they nodded over the Suras.

Beneath the holy mihrab, Cherif recognised now the travelling marabout from Sfa, his gaunt etiolated faced half hidden in a white peaked hood, while dragging over the many prayer rugs his babouched feet came Ibn Ibrahim. At sight of him Cherif shrank. It was whispered throughout the Souk that he was daily expecting a cargo of very young boys from Tunis. He had amassed vast wealth, rumour had it, in the traffic of handsome youths. With hands locked in prayer, he stood a moment before Cherif, then trailed away to where a few perfervid persons seemed lost in adoration. The faint swish-sweep, sweep-swish of the haiks, as they rose and fell, charmed all the noonday stillness. . . .

Cherif closed his eyes in a fabulous contentment. Near him some burning incense diffused through the air its fragrant smoke, causing him, after a little while, to sink asleep. And in his sleep he fancied himself journeying towards high hills that as he advanced seemed ever to recede, and presently the vision changed and he saw, seated by a pool of clear shining water, an old man, marvellously majestic. A great melancholy was in his face, and in his hands he held a book. And Cherif, in his dream, seemed to hear him say:

I swear by the Fig and by the Olive,
By Mount Sinai,
And by this inviolate soil!
That of goodliest fabric we created man,
Then brought him down to the lowest of the lowly;
Save who believe and do the things that are right,
For theirs shall be the reward that faileth not.

When he awoke it was getting late, and the Mosque was all but empty. The glint of the minbar, tipped with pearl, told that in the East the sun must already be setting. Wrapped up in his haik like no thing living, the travelling marabout appeared wholly earth-detached, or Cherif, as he glided by, would have asked him for an explanation of his dream.

It was cooler now outside.

All about, high palms threw their plume-like branches to the golden air. The house of his kinsfolk was situated at the corner of the street Bab-Azoun; a street that could boast more beggars, perhaps, than any other street in the town. But Cherif had no desire to hurry home; he liked to linger in the courtyard of the Mosque, by the vine-shaded fountain that murmured sonorously in its midst. Green ferns, of a freshness indescribable, fringed its brink. From all sides pilgrims came to taste its waters which were considered sovereign in consumptive complaints. But the wonder of the Mosque was a golden dove that lived all alone in the minaret. Occasionally the Guardian would leave ajar the door of the tower, when Cherif rarely failed to ascend. It was good to peer out over the city rooftops towards the distant desert, especially in the early mornings when the sun would break through the white dews of dawn, or to lie and watch the slow floating clouds that would evoke strange thoughts of Mecca. Sometimes, at noon, a brilliant blue mirage would form upon the horizon, offering an illusion of the sea.

After waiting some time for the marabout to emerge, Cherif disappointedly left the Mosque. Turning into a street of somewhat perilous narrowness, he was obliged to stand aside to allow a quadruped laden with boughs of eucalyptus-leaves to pass.

To reach the street Bab-Azoun it was necessary to cross the Souk. Already it was thronged. Advancing warily, lest by chance he should meet his Uncle Mahmoud or his Aunt Amoucha, Cherif made his way beneath the bulging, coloured balconies that, piled one above another, overhung the multifarious merchants' stalls. Before Achouri ben Brahim the butcher's (where blue meat, like putrid satin, dangled above the door), a half-naked negro was dragging a reluctant ram by the horns. Cherif turned his head aside to avoid witnessing its writhings: the sight of all suffering to him was intensely terrible. 'Allah will make amends some day to all sad animals,' he reflected, passing quickly on. A faint twitter-twitter of pipes, concerted with the insistent hammering of the copper-smiths, assailed his ears at every step. Continuing, he found himself soon in the vast open square that formed the centre of the Souk. Here were the workshops of the Shoemakers, the Weavers, the Silversmiths, the Saddlers. He stood a moment watching a young apprentice nailing black pom-poms to a violet holster. To employ one's whole life so—'Allah forbid!' he devoutly murmured. The shrill cry of a passing fruit-vendor resounded briefly above the clatter: 'Pomegranates all red, pomegranates all red.' Cherif moved away.

A round moon, like an amber ball, hung low above the town. It was enchanting to breathe the cool evening breeze after the sultry day. Climbing leisurely the steep arcaded stairs that led from the Souk towards the quarter in which he lived, he encountered the suave perfumes from countless thankful gardens.

It was almost dusk as he entered the street Bab-Azoun. An arched doorway that scarcely would allow one to pass upright gave access to his kinsfolk's dwelling.

A lamb, on a truss of hay, seemed attentively minding the little dark shop: at sight of Cherif it gave a friendly bleat.

He found his Aunt Amoucha seated in the principal room of the house, with the widow Embarka (who was of negro extraction), and the widow Mabrouka.

'Believe me,' she was saying, 'my last couscous, before Ramadan-Eve, was a ravishment to the sense.'

Evidently one of her sociable moods was upon her, and Cherif, coming in unheeded, inwardly groaned.

He liked his aunt best when she was cross and sulky, and upon terms of silence with his uncle, which she very often was. Once she had refused to utter a syllable for four whole consecutive weeks, her silence being occasioned by her husband refusing to better his calling, for it was her misfortune to be married to a man whose profession it was to hawk live chickens by the legs about the streets.

'Yes, you've a hand for a couscous, my dear, that you may well be proud of!' the widow Mabrouka replied, caressing with the knob of her fly-whisk a lame pigeon that was hobbling about the room.

It was a large, low-ceilinged room, lit by deep grated windows opening on the town. Against the walls, which were chalked here and there with imagery—a gazelle, a sailing-ship, a lotus-flower, a star—were carved Moorish chests that sometimes served as seats.

'In order to make couscous,' the widow Embarka observed, with a sigh, 'there must first be rice.'

Having squandered her husband's meagre fortune upon the purchase of a gramophone, she was dependent now for all necessities upon her friends.

'Aye, in order to make a couscous,' the widow Mabrouka murmured, with a sardonic sidelong smile, 'it is requisite, in effect, to strew some rice.'

Being advanced now in years, she no longer veiled her face, which was hot and an expense.

'Because I'm poor, I suppose you think you can insult me!' the widow Embarka flared.

Amoucha displayed her tactfulness. 'I hear,' she said, 'Amar ben Sadak had left for Sfa, for wonder without his Ayesha darling!'

'Can it be true?'

'Perfectly,' Amoucha assured, looking round and perceiving Cherif. 'Ah, there he is,' she broke out, 'and with *the Koran* as usual.'

'I find, myself, the Koran,' Mabrouka confessed, 'just a wee bit bewildering.'

'There is nothing to absorb a woman much in the Koran,' Amoucha agreed. ' "Given in at Mecca"; "Handed in at Mecca"; it reminds one, doesn't it, of the Post Office?'

'I've noticed,' Embarka remarked, 'that Mecca born men are nearly always naughty.'

'You veiled women notice more than others,' Mabrouka murmured shaking her thin black shawl, which was crawling all over with flies.

'Better a bad Mussulman than a good Christian! as the adage goes.'

'Oh, my dear—a Christian!' Mabrouka shuddered.

'To me, they all look just like white tired parakeets,' Amoucha said.

'Muhammad himself knows what they resemble,' Mabrouka returned, as her granddaughter, the little Yamina, who had been amusing herself on the roof-top, came into the room.

'Give me a tender kiss, dear,' Amoucha entreated.

But with matrimonial expectations in the wind, the little Yamina was first impelled to veil her face scrupulously from the eyes of Cherif.

'Come and clap!' she murmured.

'Come and *what*, my precious sweet?'

'Jemila and Nejma are upstairs dancing, and Mama and I are clapping our hands.'

Mabrouka looked displeased: 'My daughter ought to know better,' she declared, 'than to clap her hands for a couple of Ouled Nails!'

'What of it?' Amoucha said.

'Since my dear husband's death,' the widow replied, 'I fear we no longer keep the company we did!'

Amoucha stiffened.

'I shall never forget,' she said, 'I was *née* an Abdelhafid.'

In the awed hush which filled the room Cherif was allowed to peruse in welcome quietness the printed page:

> *By the glorious Koran!*
> *Now know we that the earth is charged with warnings.*
> *Oh ye infidels!*

> *Look to the skies above you, and consider*
> *how we have decked them forth. And as*
> *to the earth we have spread it out, and*
> *have thrown the mountains upon it, and*
> *have caused an upgrowth upon it of all*
> *beauteous kinds of plants, for insight*
> *and admonition to every servant who*
> *loveth to turn to God.*

'An *Abdelhafid*,' Amoucha repeated again.

Embarka tittered: 'I thought you were a spirit!' she exclaimed, addressing herself to the lamb that had entered pleasantly from the shop.

Yamina gave vent to a gleeful whoop. She enjoyed a romp with the lamb, and managing, to her grandmother's extreme vexation, to scramble to its back, she commenced to ride it round and round the room at a rapid rate, summoning from the roof-top, by her piercing screams, her mother and the breathless Ouled Naïls.

'Oh, Ourida! Ourida!' Mabrouka rebuked her daughter. But Ourida only rolled her large, idle eyes and laughed.

'A little glass of *Kebir*,' Amoucha suggested, 'might not be disagreeable to us all,' indicating the wine-jar which reposed against the wall.

'Indeed just the reverse,' Nejma gratefully answered, giving an arranging touch to the knot of white Seljem flowers above her ear. 'Quite,' she murmured, undulating her shapely arms, 'the contrary!' As an exponent of the *Handkerchief Dance* there was not to be found, perhaps, her equal. Her wrigglings, her writhings, her facial play—these were things not to be forgot.

Mabrouka plied her fan.

'How is it possible,' she wondered, 'to run about in this close weather?'

'Ah yes—these summer heats do try one,' Nejma nonchalantly owned.

'One is better off in the country.'

'Oh, I hate the country. The grasshoppers fly up into your face, and the gnats bite you.'

Embarka sighed. 'Before my great loss,' she said, brushing a fly from her face, 'we used to live there, and oh, how often now, I long to return!'

'I should miss the bazaars,' Ourida protested.

'But there are other diversions besides.'

'No doubt.'

'Ah, how content we were!'

'Men in the country,' Ourida said, 'are too often a burden. . . .'

'My dearest never was.'

'What used he to do?'

'He would often walk a mile to watch two amorous camels!'

'And then?'

But what he would do then was never made known, as with a brisk *volte-face* the lamb flung the little Yamina to the floor.

'Serve her right,' Mabrouka chuckled.

'O Allah la Ilaha!' the little Yamina wept.

'She has torn her veil,' Ourida lamented, 'and what, by the hand of Fatma,' she upbraided, 'looks worse than a veil that is torn?'

'A rent veil,' Amoucha assented, 'is anathema to the sense!'

Embarka glanced guiltily towards her feet. She had deep holes in her stockings, which, however, scarcely showed on a negress. . . .

'In the name of the Prophet,' Jemila implored, 'cease weeping, and have done.' Seated in a corner of the room, she was making her face with some result. She was fond of sauntering at night beneath the blue arcades.

Amoucha fetched forth refreshment.

'For once, I haven't set foot in the Souk all day!' she averred, lighting the little lamp, used by her upon occasions of festivity, and which was hanging from a hook in the wall; a number of glass balls in brilliant colours were dangling from it, to the delight of all crawling flies.

'I saw such a sumptuous white shawl as I was coming through, with a golden finish,' Jemila chirruped, busy still with her face.

'Did you resist it?'

'I shall think it over.'

Ourida considered whimsically her hennaed nails. 'Whenever I've to decide anything of importance at all,' she declared, 'I usually take a Hammam!'

'The Hammam! It is so weakening.' Marouka shook her head.

'I often say,' Amoucha murmured, 'it's a pleasure to see her at the Bath with nothing on.'

'One might,' Mabrouka politely returned, 'say the same of *most* here present.'

All rose from their seats and curtsied.

'Safia, the lately repudiated wife of Abou Zazâa, takes a Hammam every day!'

'She is growing so exotic.'

'They say she's in love with a peacock's feather.'

'Give me a black moustache,' Amoucha sighed, 'and two passionate legs!'

'Unless,' Nejma murmured, going off into little shivers of laughter, 'unless it be a beard.'

'Ah, dear heart,' Amoucha breathed.

'Fettah, the negress from Sidi-bel-Abbès, was saying she has but a pond to bathe in—and which, in summer, is mostly always dry.'

'I noticed her in the street this evening looking as weak, poor soul, as a cut flower out of water,' Embarka said.

'Since the corn was green she has been ailing.'

'It is the divine wish of Allah, doubtless, if she is so,' Cherif was tempted to observe.

'Fiddlededee!' Jemila replied, seizing a pale-winged moth, known as Love-Flits-By, that was revolving about the lamp.

> 'Love seldom comes my way,
> Seldom my way comes Love,'

she trolled.

> 'And only yesterday——!'

she broke off.

'She's wearing a comb,' Ourida slyly observed, 'I don't remember seeing before.'

Nejma raised a glass to her lips.

'I would not give a date stone for it,' she declared.

'Oh, she's so jealous,' Jemila laughed.

'Was it from the Cadi?' Amoucha archly asked.

'No—who but Salahine again.'

'Before the lilac ceases flowering, I hear he will be wed.'

'Ah?'

'They say *she* has forty chins.'

'Oh!'

'And a waist that would take one a week to go round.'

Mabrouka blinked.

'I think I hear someone in the shop, dear!' she murmured, not without a touch of malice. It pleased her to remember Fate had placed her above the *mesquin* necessities of trade.

Amoucha made no movement. 'It's Mahmoud,' she replied, 'I daresay.'

'It may be a thief, dear.' Mabrouka looked sententious. 'Not, perhaps,' she gently added, 'that there's a great deal to attract them.'

But the poignant cluck of a hen appraised Amoucha that her surmise was correct.

'Is't thou, dear love?' she exclaimed as her husband entered the room with a pair of almost lifeless chickens.

'Salaam!' he made reply, raising a hand to a turban of frayed *crêpe* jauntily wreathed with jasmine.

'What wouldst, pearl of husbands?' Amoucha questioned.

'A glass of fresh Kebir.'

'A glass of sweet Kebir—what is more welcome to the sense?' Amoucha beamed.

'Hah,' Mahmoud wiped his brow, ''twas hot enough in the Souk.'

'Are you going out with the fowl, my dear, again to-night?' Mahmoud slowly spat.

'Not for a thousand camels!' he declared.

'From the sharp eye of the yellow hen,' Amoucha observed, 'I fancy we may expect before morning an egg!'

'May Allah grant it so!'

'Her last was laid on our conjugal couch nigh a moon gone by, so 'tis time she produced again.'

'Is it,' Mahmoud demanded, 'duly recorded *in the Book*?'

'No, dear heart,' Amoucha confessed, glancing apprehensively towards some old soiled ledgers upon which at present was reclining the lamb.

Mabrouka sighed.

'I can recall a time when a wife frequently would be repudiated,' she murmured, 'for disobedience to her husband.'

'I should like to meet the man,' Amoucha menaced, 'who'd repudiate me!'

'In the days of Ahmed the Traitor a wife was often dismissed for much less.'

'Hah, in the age of Ahmed,' Mahmoud exclaimed, 'a husband's scimitar was seldom far from his side.'

'How long ago,' the little Yamina wondered, nibbling with relish a cake of pomegranate grains, 'was that?'

'I fear she wants to know more than is good for her!' Mabrouka commented.

'She has the refinement of a mimosa-leaf,' Amoucha declared.

'Well, dear,' Nejma rose remarking, 'I suppose I must say good night!'

'So soon?'

'Taalith, down the road, is giving a party in honour of the circumcision of her little son. And I've promised to dance.'

'I dare say,' Embarka said, 'I may look in myself, dear, later.'

'About supper-time, *eh*?' Mabrouka sardonically murmured.

But Embarka tied a scarf across her mouth, as though she no longer wished to speak.

'Hah, for a feast of the Rejoicing,' Mahmoud reflectively said, 'there is seldom stint of choice fare!'

'Dost recollect, dear heart,' Amoucha asked, 'of the couscous I made thee last Ramadan Eve?'

'Hah.'

'Was't not, my dear, to thy liking?'

'Hah.'

'And during Ramadan, even, didst not enjoy still my endeavours?'

'Hah, in Ramadan, a delicate bunch of watercress is not disagreeable to the sense.'

'Such as my kinsfolk, the Abdelhafids, find on their domain at Sââda!'

'Hah,' Mahmoud absently assented, glancing round towards Jemila who, elated by the Kebir wine, was executing the lascivious movements of the *Buckle Dance*, serenely oblivious of Mabrouka's disparaging eye.

Unheeded, as he had entered, Cherif slipped away. He slept in the storeroom adjoining the shop, and thither he repaired. It was sweet to be alone. Through the slender grated windows, coloured blue, the cupola of the Mosque appeared, far off, like a great white egg against the night.

It was too dark to read, but he could recite at least the suras as he lay on his pallet-bed.

In a small wicker cage above him (breast almost touching breast) four tiny love-birds were twittering among themselves. How often had he longed to set them free! And it pleased his mind to fancy them spreading their wings towards the palm-trees that grew near by in the gardens of ben Chemoun.

A fitful murmur, rising from the town below, blended drowsily with his thoughts.

He fell asleep at length, lulled by the distant drum and tambourine of a snake-charmer.

୭୭ *II* ୭୭

A STRETCH of sand, the colour of ripe corn, lay close behind the house, and here each morning he would go, on rising, to make his prayer at daybreak, his face turned towards the brightening East.

Up before the last star had scarcely faded from the sky, he would noiselessly steal forth lest by mischance his uncle should detain him to tend the fowl.

To begin God's day by tending cocks and hens was altogether contrary to Cherif's nature.

Some little way off, amid the sand, was a shrine composed of bricks as white as ivory, and towards this place of veneration he liked most to shape his course.

Cherif made his way towards it, to-day, half enveloped still in the thrall of sleep. It was not yet fully light. Leaving the Town-gate, where a little mournful child, in a long black shawl, was toying with a ram's skull in the dust, he found himself soon in the open steppe. A flock of sheep and goats nourished sparsely by the pallid, sun-outraged vegetation of the plains, were seeking eagerly the tussocks of burnt grass that appeared on all sides amid the stones, while minding them, a bronze-limbed boy was playing forlornly to himself with a pipe. His piping followed Cherif yearningly.

By the time his prayer had ended the sun had wooed and won the copper Crescent that surmounted the low domed roof of the shrine.

Cherif peeped inside.

Upon the tomb that reposed within, a long sunbeam played, revealing, as his eyes became accustomed to the light, the delicate tracery upon the walls beyond, and disclosing also the drooping form of the travelling Marabout from Sfa. Beside him, in a bowl of livid pottery, daubed with black, burned sticks of Santal; the air was aromatic with its resinous sweet scent.

Perceiving a shadow stirring at his feet, the marabout was moved to turn.

'What would you, boy, with me?' he said.

'Nothing.'

'Then go away.'

'I would like,' Cherif ventured, 'above everything, to accompany you.'

'And to what end?'

'To travel throughout the land with you—from shrine to shrine!'

'Very soon I shall enter into eternal felicity.'

'But—until then!' Cherif pleaded.

'What would you see?'

'The divine Mosque of Djema Djedid!'

The marabout raised beautiful half-blind eyes.

'Thou wouldst visit *Mecca*?' Soft as the sound of rain upon high palm-leaves were the tones of his voice.

'It is my desire.'

'There are more worthy to go with than I,' the marabout declared.

'I know of none.'

'Far away across the Sahara there is one.'

'His name?'

'Some said his name was even as the Most Merciful's. . . .' And the old man told of a hermit dwelling in the high hills across the plains, thought by some even to be the Prophet himself. And as he spoke Cherif recalled his dream.

If indeed it were so. . . . A thousand questions came starting to his lips.

'Would it be possible to go to him?'

'All things, my child, are possible.'

'But would I find him?'

'Heaven grant thy soul Eyes, my child.'

And as though to close the conversation the old man pulled the hood of his haik down low across his eyes.

As the boy re-entered the Town-gate, from the summit of the minaret rose the clear, sustained cry of the muezzin summoning men to prayer.

ᗰᗰ *III* ᗰᗰ

IT was soon after his aunt had killed the lamb that he finally
determined to go. Coming back one day, he found her in the
kitchen with Mabrouka holding the very knife, while on the Moorish chest in a stream of gushing blood, lay the lamb.

'I think *cutlets*!' Amoucha was saying.

'But be guided by me, dear, now won't you,' Mabrouka replied,
'about the leg?'

Cherif retreated wrathfully to the shop.

The smell of hot custard and flies pervading it made him gasp
for air. Through a tattered awning without, the sunrays entered,
assisting a pet white cock (Habibi by name) that was looking about
for grain.

'She'll have *you* next, I shouldn't wonder!' Cherif murmured to
himself aloud, passing out into the street.

It was mid-day.

Lounging like sprawling flowers before their doors men were
arguing drowsily over small shell-shaped cups of Kahoua. The
clamour of the Souk had ceased. Along white walls receptive to
every shadow, Cherif meditatively advanced. In the streets of the
Courtesans, behind a doorway mysteriously ajar, a woman with
myrtle-leaves in her hair was waiting for a lover flattened listlessly
against the wall. But it was not for the courtesans, but rather for
the unfrequented garden of ben Chemoun, that at present his spirit
craved. Wide sweeping steps that time had worn all away led up to it
from the street. It was quite a beautiful garden, where often he had
experienced before the heart serenity that comes with solitude.
Entering the great gate (where an old, old negro sat all day long
vending musk-melons and sugared fruits in light boxes tipped with
tin), Cherif passed down a pathway overhung by low leaning trees
that brought him to a post of observation giving on the town.
Through the summer vernery it spread before him, its cupolas and
minarets calcined vividly upon the far horizon. There, beyond the
Souk, was the Mosque of Sidi-Yossef, while hard by the Mosque
of Vesoul-Vialar was visible, its five golden domes ablaze in the
noonday sun. And so clear was it that looking towards Tattaouine,
the tomb of a marabout could be distinguished many leagues away
across the tawny wastes of sand.

'Please, Muhammad, I, too, will be a marabout!' Cherif murmured, clasping in ardour his hands.

But first, indeed, it would be fitting to entreat a blessing of the
Prophet, deemed by some to be even the Most-Merciful himself.
He raised deliriously his face.

Overhead a palm let fall a thousand drooping fans. The day was
so still that in all the garden there was not one moving leaf.

Yes, he would seek the Saint among the remotest places of the
hills and hear the sound of his voice.

Following a sunny curving path he strolled along until he came to
where a ring of spreading ilex towered above a marble basin,
containing water, that reflected back the branches of the trees.
Bright humming birds flew in and out among the boughs on rapid
wings like notes of joy.

'But how to reach him—how?' Cherif paused to consider: Were
there not speedy horses grazing in the plains, and would not Allah
pardon him for taking one?

Self-absorbed he wandered on.

By a parterre he passed a gardener watering lilies, his face veiled
by a handkerchief to conceal a terrible complaint.

Yes ... he would capture one of the horses from the plain, and
Allah (who was all-powerful) would find a way to return it perhaps!

A sound of voices arrested him. Seated beneath a little rustic
temple, he perceived Ibn Ibrahim and a slim Tunisian boy. 'My
lazy, drowsy darling,' Cherif heard him sigh.

Stealing by unremarked, he threw himself down at some length
off upon the grass. Here and there strange sinuous roots broke
irregularly the ground. Glancing upward, he beheld against the
glittering fronds of the palms, trees all heavy with pomegranates.
He had had no refreshment that day and a pomegranate just then
was precisely what he needed. Stretching out his hand, he plucked
one from its tree. Sampling the sweet-grained fruit, he fell to thinking of the course best adapted for him to pursue. He must return
once more at any rate to his uncle's house to fetch his cherished
Koran, together with a volume of songs by Antar that he adored.

The drone of bees about him filled all the air with harmony, and
leaning against a tree-bole he watched them, sunk in distant speculation as they came and went. They seemed to hive within an old
sarcophagus partially hidden beneath the soft deep-blue of clinging
convolvuli.

And what ecstasy, he mused, to see the world!

At Mecca, it was said, there was a mosque with carpets more radiant than a summer dream.

From behind a wall of green leaves, the occasional clip-clip of a gardener's shears charmed agreeably his thoughts, anon inviting sleep.

And in his sleep again he saw the high hills that as he advanced seemed ever to recede.

When at length he opened his eyes the sun had disappeared below the trees. Great was the tranquillity. So calm was it, he could hear a watch-dog wailing several leagues away. A fitful breeze had arisen, but the lifeless green of the palms saddened him a little now that the sun was gone.

Cherif lay still inhaling all the sweet perfumes of the gathering night. From an adjacent thicket, a little black bat started up against the twinkling primrose of the twilight, followed by a second and then a third.

A tremulous trill broke the stillness. It fell sorrowfully from somewhere among the hardly moving trees, growing intenser and still intenser, until whiter than snow in the spring of the year, or the lilies that are found near the lake-side of Mornag, arose the moon.

He entered the town at dusk through a street of shadows.

🐚 *IV* 🐚

NOTHING more beautiful in the way of days can have ever dawned than on the morning he set out. Mounted on a fleet-trotting little horse, that assuredly the All-Knowing One would forgive him for taking, he galloped away from his native place beneath a sky of purest blueness.

The wave of emotion experienced on becoming first a marabout— who shall faithfully describe? As Cherif rode he sang. He knew that the Sage he sought had withdrawn to the hills beyond Mount Matmata, many miles to the East, and Eastward, therefore, he turned his face.

Racing the skimming swallows over the hard, sparkling sand was rapture quite. He anticipated to reach by noon the Oasis of El-Oued, where, out of the sun's rays, he would repose himself and his horse.

He had not gone far before he came to a village located pleasantly by the side of a stream. A leaning palm spanned the green-gliding water, where women were kneeling washing wool. Beyond the village he turned to throw a backward final look towards his native town. Old walls, like dead white Queens, encircling it about—the mosques of Sidi-Yossef, and Vesoul-Vialar, rising proudly through the pearl-hued haze. He thought of his Aunt Amoucha enclosed within those ample walls, 'preparing a couscous, perhaps, or killing a hen,' he reflected, resuming his journey on. The Oasis of El-Oued lay further ahead than he had expected, and quite a long time seemed to pass before it came into view. As the day matured the sun increased in strength, and beneath its fierce fire the sand glowed red as with a wealth of poppies. Noon was well advanced when he reached the Pasis and, joyfully dismounting, he gave praise to heaven for having led him thus far without mischance and to such a delectable place. After the heat of the way it was good to rest a while beneath the spreading fans of the palms. Divided every here and there by *seguias* of water they were more beautiful than any he had ever seen before. Lying at ease upon the ground, he untied the ends of a knotted kerchief, that served as baggage, to make sure that all was as it should be! The Koran, a lead amulet, the Antar, six pomegranates, and a few loose sticks of Santal to burn at passing shrines were what it contained, and through the Compassionate One's grace, the pomegranates had not split and stained his books as he half feared they might. It seemed imprudent, though, when water and wild figs abounded, to draw upon these, that might be welcome later, and observing a well among the brushwood hard by, he got up and went towards it. Lavender-blue, pansy-blue was the water of the well and with a song as charming and melodious as a bird's. When he had satisfied his thirst enough he lay down once more upon the ground, and almost instantly he sank into entire forget-fulness. Towards Moghreb, the hour of sunset, the hour of prayer, he awoke, and capturing his grazing steed, he soon was in the saddle again. Not far beyond the Oasis was the town of In-Salah (famous in the world of Islam for the beauty of its roses), and beneath whose walls he proposed that night to sleep. Although he would scarcely admit it, he disliked the idea of the jackals that might come in quest of prey to the Oasis after it grew dark. He recalled the wretched end of the negress Embarka's husband, who had perished beneath the tooth of a famished lioness, and he could not help wondering to himself how the black woman had become informed of the sex of the wild animal that had dealt her her bereavement. As likely as not it was a lion, since there was nobody there to see; and in any case, one would be too terrified, in all probability, to pay much attention to minor details of that sort, he reasoned, as he rode along. And certainly, as the sun went down, it seemed a happy plan to pass the first night, at least, beneath the walls of a town, although, on drawing nearer to In-Salah, it looked cheerless enough with its dark doorless portals agape upon the night. At his approach wild dogs ran out along the roof-tops barking, and all the night through ceaselessly they barked, barked, barked, making him think that at In-Salah there were more dogs indeed than roses. Aroused by the cold marvel of the sunrise, he was off directly, galloping away into the iris East beneath a sky of purest blueness.

He made the halt of noon, this time, beneath a solitary palm-tree on a billowy dune, perusing with diligence the suras until close on the hour of Moghreb, when, arising, he prostrated his face repeatedly to the ground whose touch as it met his brow was warm yet with the heat of the day. And after a time riding on, appeared far off the low walls and gold-peaked domes of Tadekka. Here without the walls of the town he resolved to stop that night. Aroused by the first rays of Allah, he determined to visit the main mosque, the Mosque of Amor-Ali, and shortly after sunrise he entered the great gate, the gate of Lallah-Rehana, beneath a sky of purest blueness. Early though it was, already a certain number of mendicants had taken up their station (for the day) upon the steps of the Mosque, and Cherif looked around for one with whom he could conveniently leave his horse. A cripple, whose yellow eyelids drooped as though weighed down by the sun, was prepared to oblige in return for a coin; but this, alas! was more than Cherif could spare. Nevertheless, in the end, since so by Fate it was written, the cripple consented 'out of love of Muhammad' to mind the horse, and Cherif thus was free to enter the Mosque. Treading delicately over the many glistening mats, he approached the mystic Mihrab in an ecstasy of delight. Wrought with pink and peacock pearl it was a miracle to behold. 'Allah be merciful to thy child, and grant that his pilgrimage may be fruitful,' he begged.

Casting his eyes about, he wondered that hand of men could contrive the slender windows, gemmed in painted glass, or fashion the long-chained tiers of lights that came tumbling from the roof.

Outside, once more, he was soon remounted, and galloping away into the effulgent East.

He passed the ardent hours of noon among a grove of gum-trees and strelitzias, and towards evening came to Gardaia, a town of evil repute, and the birthplace of Khadidja ben Izza, the Sorceress. There being no suitable place to pass the night on the side of his approach (fragments of broken water-jars and refuse of all kinds littered the ground), he was compelled to cross the town. Riding through the street of the courtesans, decked like a street of dreams with hanging carpets, he was soon on the other side, and with the dawn he was galloping away again into the beckoning East beneath a sky of purest blueness.

And as the days went by the country grew wilder and the towns fewer and the sun more and more insistent. Once he recognised a clump of silver senbel, little flowers that responded only to the extremes of light. Thorny dust-white bushes with foliage sensitive as seaweed thrived everywhere in the drifts of sand, that rose like Royal Tumuli against the skyline. Sometimes he caught sight of a gazelle running away among the dunes, reminding him of the gazelle upon his uncle's wall at home—'Not a bit like!' was his brief comment. Sometimes, though more rarely, a nomad shepherd driving his herd of little blue-shadowed goats would pass, and from love of Allah, or the look in Cherif's face, would offer a bowl of milk.

And at last one day Mount Matmata appeared in far-off solitude, trembling through a haze of heat.

Leaping from his horse his heart went up in adoration, offering to heaven homage for its many bounties.

It was the season of early autumn when the caravans most abounded, and as he rode on he met before long a troop of camels bearing saddle-bags packed with dates. At the head of the caravan rode a veiled woman on a camel all caparisoned in black. It was good in these wild places to pass at times one's kind, and Cherif was glad to exchange a salute; but none could tell him of the prophet's where-abouts when he made the demand.

He rode forward that day with his eyes fixed upon the distant mountain, and in the blue of evening halted for the night in the open plain. There was light enough still to read his Koran (which seemed to hold new meanings among altered surroundings), but the delight of beholding Mount Matmata before him made it difficult to concentrate the mind entirely upon it now. Coiffered with clouds, it had the air of some fabulous mosque as it soared amid the sky, and Cherif was moved to untold gladness when he thought that he whom he was seeking might possibly be contemplating the same grandeur also from afar.

A more serene evening was impossible to imagine. Straining his ears, he could hear nothing anywhere; a profound calm ruled over all. As though drunk with silence the fireflies turned and turned in the twilight, then sank among the long *chigh* grass half muffled in the sand. Following them absently as they rose and fell, his eyes were attracted to an object close beside him in the grass. He had seen the skull of an animal before, but never that of a man, and wonderi g a little, he raised it in his hand. It was not a perfect skull for it had been broken, and as he examined it a passing disquietude seized his heart. The reflection of the afterglow seemed to linger in its bleached and brittle surface, that recalled the polished stones along the sides of the *oueds,* and holding it up, maskwise, he contemplated through the empty eye-sockets the deepening night. There was no moon, only the white track of the Milky Way strewn with stars that spanned the clear sky projecting a gentle light. One star, throbbing more brightly, appeared nearer to the earth than all the rest. A star so brilliant, such a brilliant star, could be but Venus.

There was something both strange and charming in gazing up into the starry clearness through the empty eye-sockets of the skull, and only towards the return of morning did he fall asleep.

🙶 *V* 🙶

AND after riding many a day (sometimes sideways, to vary, however slightly, the tedium of his saddle), he entered the wished-for region of the hills. Their slopes were overgrown at first with aloes and little sandy shrubs that sparkled in the sun, but soon they were more fertile and he perceived familiar flowers—lilac harebells, and purple pansies, and orchids of the palest sort. Date-bearing palms too mingled their branches with tall trees of strange solemnity, whose names he did not know. Then riding on and on, and leaving these behind, he came to a country less clement. It was a country all

of rock, a land of crags and boulders, over whose riven steeps circled
restless flocks of birds. Looking up it was a delightful thing to
follow the waltzing flight of an eagle, or to watch the violet vultures
as they soared and soared, as though suspended in the air. Occasionally a venturesome ibis would fly a little before him, and wait
until he had almost reached it, and then fly on. But as the country
grew more, and still more, desolate, these birds, as well, he left
behind. Beneath the pitiless sun all signs of life had vanished,
and in the deep of noon the hills looked to ache with light. The
leathern water-bottle at his side was empty, and as the hours went
by the want of water was acute. 'Allah show compassion to thy
child Cherif,' he implored. And there came a time when hope quite
left him. Nevertheless, to keep his courage a little, he tried to sing.
He sang a song addressed by Antar long ago to a Queen of a land
called Egypt. Her name was Turquia, and she lived at Thebes, on
the banks of the River Nile. And he sang a song the Pilgrims sing
as they journey towards Mecca—one day, as he stumbled on and on,
beneath a sky pale with heat. The day had been hotter than any yet
he could remember, and for many hours now he was without water
at all. He had come, as evening drew in, to a valley that seemed less
hostile, maybe, among the rocks. But search as he would there was
no water, or any trace, anywhere, of the one whom he sought. White
beneath the glory of the moon the hills rolled away as though
eternally; elusive hills, recalling to mind his dream. Alas, was the
world all illusion then?

In the early light he re-opened, once again, the Koran. He read:

In the name of God, the Compassionate, the Merciful,
By the noon-day BRIGHTNESS,
And by the night when it darkeneth!
The Lord hath not forsaken thee, neither hath he been displeased.
And surely the Future shall be better for thee than the Past,
And in the end shall thy Lord be bounteous to thee and thou be satisfied.

A great resignation filled his heart. And standing, his face turned
towards the kindling East, he prayed: 'Lord Allah! Show compassion to thy child Cherif.'

Algiers, Tunis.

The Flower Beneath the Foot

❦ I ❦

NEITHER her Gaudiness the Mistress of the Robes nor her Dreaminess the Queen were feeling quite themselves. In the Palace all was speculation. Would they be able to attend the *Fêtes* in honour of King Jotifa, and Queen Thleeanouhee of the Land of Dates?—Court opinion seemed largely divided. Countess Medusa Rappa, a woman easily disturbable, was prepared to wager what the Countess of Tolga 'liked' (she knew), that another week would find the Court shivering beneath the vaulted domes of the Summer Palace.

'I fear I've no time (or desire) now, Medusa,' the Countess answered, moving towards the Royal apartments, 'for making bets'; though, turning before the ante-room door, she nodded: 'Done!'

She found her sovereign supine on a couch piled with long Tunisian cushions, while a maid of honour sat reading to her aloud:

'*Live with an aim, and let that aim be high!*' the girl was saying as the Countess approached.

'Is that you, Violet?' her Dreaminess enquired without looking round.

'How is your condition, Madam?' the Countess anxiously murmured.

'Tell me do, of a place that soothes and lulls one . . .'

The Countess of Tolga considered.

'Paris,' she hazarded.

'Ah! Impossible.'

'The Summer Palace, then,' the Countess ejaculated, examining her long slender fingers that were like the tendrils of a plant.

'Dr. Cuncliffe Babcock flatly forbids it,' the Royal woman declared, starting slightly at the sound of a gun. 'That must be *the Dates*!' she said. And in effect, a vague reverberation, as of individuals cheering, resounded fitfully from afar. 'Give me my diamond anemones,' the Queen commanded, and motioning to her Maid: 'Pray conclude, mademoiselle, those lofty lines.'

With a slight sigh, the lectress took up the posture of a Dying Intellectual.

'*Live with an aim, and let that aim be high!*' she reiterated in tones tinged perceptibly with emotion.

'But not *too* high, remember, Mademoiselle de Nazianzi . . .'

There was a short pause. And then——

'Ah, Madam! What a dearest he is!'

'I think you forget yourself,' the Queen murmured with a quelling glance. 'You had better withdraw.'

'He has such strength! One could niche an idol in his dear, dinted chin.'

'Enough!'

And a moment later the enflamed girl left the room warbling softly: *Depuis le Jour*.

'Holy Virgin,' the Countess said, addressing herself to the ceiling. 'Should his Weariness, the Prince, yield himself to this caprice . . .'

The Queen shifted a diamond bangle from one of her arms to the other.

'She reads at such a pace,' she complained, 'and when I asked her *where* she had learnt to read so quickly she replied "On the screens at Cinemas." '

'I do not consider her at all distinguished,' the Countess commented, turning her eyes away towards the room.

It was a carved-ceiled and rather lofty room, connected by tall glass doors with other rooms beyond. Peering into one of these the Countess could see reflected the 'throne,' and a little piece of broken Chippendale brought from England, that served as a stand for a telephone, wrought in ormolu and rock-crystal, which the sun's rays at present were causing to emit a thousand playful sparks. Tapestry panels depicting the Loves of *Mejnoun and Leileh* half concealed the silver *boiseries* of the walls, while far down the room, across old rugs from Shirvan that were a marvellous wonder, showed fortuitous jardinières filled with every kind of flowering plant. Between the windows were canopied recesses, denuded of their statues by the Queen's desire, 'in order that they might appear suggestive,' while through the windows themselves the Countess could catch, across the forecourt of the castle, a panorama of the town below, with the State Theatre and the Garrisons, and the Houses of Parliament, and the Hospital, and the low white dome, crowned by turquoise-tinted tiles, of the Cathedral, which was known to all churchgoers as *the Blue Jesus*.

'It would be a fatal connexion,' the Queen continued, 'and it must never, never be!'

By way of response the Countess exchanged with her sovereign a glance that was known in Court circles as her *tortured-animal* look. 'Their Oriental majesties,' she observed, 'to judge from the din, appear to have already endeared themselves with the mob!'

The Queen stirred slightly amid her cushions.

'For the aggrandisement of the country's trade, an alliance with Dateland is by no means to be depreciated,' she replied, closing her eyes as though in some way or other this bullion to the State would allow her to gratify her own wildest whims, the dearest, perhaps, of which was to form a party to excavate (for objects of art) among the ruins of Chedorlahomor, a *faubourg* of Sodom.

'Am I right, Madam, in assuming it's Bananas? . . . ' the Countess queried.

But at that moment the door opened, and his Weariness the Prince entered the room in all his tinted Orders.

Handsome to tears, his face, even when he had been a child, lacked innocence. His was of that *magnolia* order of colouring, set off by pleasantly untamed eyes, and teeth like flawless pearls.

'You've seen them? What are they like . . . ? Tell Mother, darling!' the Queen exclaimed.

'They're merely dreadful,' his Weariness, who had been to the railway-station to welcome the Royal travellers, murmured in a voice extinct with boredom.

'They're in European dress, dear?' his mother questioned.

'The King had on a frock coat and a cap. . . .'

'And she?'

'A tartan skirt, and checked wool stockings.'

'She has great individuality, so I hear, marm,' the Countess ventured.

'Individuality be——! No one can doubt she's a terrible woman.' The Queen gently groaned.

'I see life to-day,' she declared, 'in the colour of mould.'

The Prince protruded a shade the purple violet of his tongue.

'Well, it's depressing,' he said, 'for us all, with the Castle full of blacks.'

'That is the least of my worries,' the Queen observed. 'Oh, Yousef, Yousef,' she added, 'do you wish to break my heart?'

The young man protruded some few degrees further his tongue.

'I gather you're alluding to Laura!' he remarked.

'But what can you *see* in her?' his mother mourned.

'She suits my feelings,' the Prince simply said.

'Peuh!'

'She meets my needs.'

'She's so housemaid. . . . I hardly know . . . !' The Queen raised beautiful hands, bewildered.

'Très gutter, ma'am,' the Countess murmured, dropping her voice to a half-whisper.

'She saves us from *cliché*,' the Prince indignantly said.

'She saves us from nothing,' his mother returned. 'Oh, Yousef, Yousef. And what *cerné* eyes, my son. I suppose you were gambling all night at the Château des Fleurs!'

'Just hark to the crowds!' the Prince evasively said. And never too weary to receive an ovation, he skipped across the room towards the nearest window, where he began blowing kisses to the throng.

'Give them the Smile Extending, darling,' his mother beseeched.

'Won't you rise and place your arm about him, Madam?' the Countess suggested.

'I'm not feeling at all up to the mark,' her Dreaminess demurred, passing her fingers over her hair.

'There is sunshine, ma'am . . . and you have your *anemones* on . . .' the Countess cajoled, 'and to please the people, you ought indeed to squeeze him.' And she was begging and persuading the Queen to rise as the King entered the room preceded by a shapely page (of sixteen) with cheeks fresher than milk.

'Go to the window, Willie,' the Queen exhorted her Consort, fixing an eye on the last trouser button that adorned his long, straggling legs.

The King, who had the air of a tired pastry-cook, sat down.

'We feel,' he said, 'to-day, we've had our fill of stares!'

'One little bow, Willie,' the Queen entreated, 'that wouldn't kill you.'

'We'd give perfect worlds,' the King went on, 'to go, by Ourselves, to bed.'

'Get rid of the noise for me. *Quiet them*. Or I'll be too ill,' the Queen declared, 'to leave my room to-night!'

'Should I summon Whisky, Marm?' the Countess asked, but before there was time to reply the Court physician, Dr. Cuncliffe Babcock, was announced.

'I feel I've had a relapse, doctor,' her Dreaminess declared.

Dr. Babcock beamed: he had one blind eye—though this did not prevent him at all from seeing all that was going on with the other.

'Leave it to me, Madam!' he assured, 'and I shall pick you up in *no* time!'

'Not Johnnie, doctor?' the Queen murmured with a grimace. For a glass of *Johnnie Walker* at bedtime was the great doctor's favourite receipt.

'No; something a little stronger, I think.'

'We need expert attention, too,' the King intervened.

'You certainly are somewhat pale, sir.'

'Whenever I go out,' the King complained, 'I get an impression of raised hats.'

It was seldom King William of Pisuerga spoke in the singular tense, and Doctor Babcock looked perturbed.

'Raised hats, sir?' he murmured in impressive tones.

'Nude heads, doctor.'

The Queen commenced to fidget. She disliked that the King should appear more interesting than herself.

'These earrings tire me,' she said, 'take them out.'

But the Prince, who seemed to be thoroughly enjoying the success of his appearance with the crowd, had already begun tossing the contents of the flower vases into the street.

'Willie . . . prevent him! Yousef . . . I forbid you!' her Dreaminess faintly shrieked. And to stay her son's despoiling hand she skimmed towards him, when the populace, catching sight of her, redoubled their cheers.

Meanwhile Mademoiselle de Nazianzi had regained her composure. As a niece of her Gaudiness the Mistress of the Robes (the Duchess of Cavaljos), she had made her recent début at Court under the brightest conceivable of conditions.

Laura Lita Carmen Etoile de Nazianzi was more piquant perhaps then pretty. A dozen tiny moles were scattered about her face, while on either side of her delicate nose a large grey eye surveyed the world with a pensive critical glance.

'Scenes like that make one sob with laughter,' she reflected, turning into the corridor where two of the Maids of Honour, like strutting idols, were passing up and down.

'Is she really very ill? Is she *really* dying?' they breathlessly enquired.

Mademoiselle de Nazianzi disengaged herself from their solicitously entwining arms.

'She is not!' she answered, in a voice full of eloquent inflections.

But beguiled by the sound of marching feet, one of the girls had darted forward towards a window.

'Oh, Blanche, Blanche, Blanchie love!' she exclaimed, 'I could dance to the click of your brother's spurs.'

'You'd not be the first to, dear darling!' Mademoiselle de Lambèse replied, adjusting her short shock of hair before a glass.

Mademoiselle de Lambèse believed herself to be a very valuable piece of goods, and seemed to think she had only to smile to stir up an ocean of passion.

'Poor Ann-Jules,' she said: 'I fear he's in the clutches of that awful woman.'

'Kalpurnia?'

'Every night he's at the Opera.'

'I hear she wears the costume of a shoeblack in the new ballet,' Mademoiselle de Nazianzi said, 'and is too strangely extraordinary!'

'Have you decided, Rara,* yet, what you'll wear for the ball?'

'A black gown and three blue flowers on my tummy.'

'After a shrimp-tea with the Archduchess, I feel I *want* no dinner,' Mademoiselle Olga Blumenghast, a girl with slightly hunched shoulders, said, returning from the window.

'Oh? Had she a party?'

'A curé or two, and the Countess Yvorra.'

'Her black-bordered envelopes make one shiver!'

'I thought I should have died it was so dull,' Mademoiselle Olga Blumenghast averred, standing aside to allow his Naughtiness Prince Olaf (a little boy racked by all the troubles of spring) and Mrs. Montgomery, the Royal Governess, to pass. They had been out evidently among the crowd, and both were laughing heartily at the asides they had overheard.

' 'Ow can you be so frivolous, your royal 'ighness?' Mrs. Montgomery was expostulating: 'for shame, wicked boy! For shame!' And her cheery British laugh echoed gaily down the corridors.

'Well, *I* took tea at the Ritz,' Mademoiselle de Lambèse related.

'Anybody?'

'Quite a few!'

* The name by which the future saint was sometimes called among her friends.

'There's a rumour that Prince Yousef is entertaining there to-night.'

Mademoiselle Blumenghast tittered.

'Did you hear what he called the lanterns for the *Fête*?' she asked.

'No.'

'A lot of "bloody bladders"!'

'What, what a dearest!' Mademoiselle de Nazianzi sighed beneath her breath. And all along the almost countless corridors as far as her bedroom door she repeated again and again: 'What, *what* a dearest!'

❧ II ❧

BENEATH a wide golden ceiling people were dancing. A capricious concert waltz, drowsy, intricate, caressing, reached fitfully the supper-room, where a few privileged guests were already assembled to meet King Jotifa and Queen Thleeanouhee of the Land of Dates.

It was one of the regulations of the Court that those commanded to the King's board should assemble some few minutes earlier than the Sovereigns themselves, and the guests at present were mostly leaning stiffly upon the chair-backs, staring vacuously at the olives and salted almonds upon the table-cloth before them. Several of the ladies indeed had taken the liberty to seat themselves, and were beguiling the time by studying the menu or disarranging the smilax, while one dame went as far as to take, and even to nibble, a salted almond. A conversation of a non-private kind (carried on between the thin, authoritative legs of a Court Chamberlain) by Countess Medusa Rappa and the English Ambassadress was being listened to by some with mingled signs of interest.

'Ah! How clever Shakespeare!' the Countess was saying. 'How gorgeous! How glowing! I once knew a speech from "Julia Sees Her!..." perhaps his greatest *œuvre* of all. Yes! "Julia *Sees* Her" is what I like best of that great, great master.'

The English Ambassadress plied her fan.

'Friends, Comrades, Countrymen,' she murmured, 'I used to know it myself!'

But the lady nibbling almonds was exciting a certain amount of comment. This was the Duchess of Varna, voted by many to be one of the handsomest women of the Court. Living in economical obscurity nearly half the year round, her appearances at the palace were becoming more and more infrequent.

'I knew the Varnas were very hard up, but I did not know they were *starving*,' the Countess Yvorra, a woman with a would-be indulgent face that was something less hard than rock, remarked to her neighbour the Count of Tolga, and dropping her glance from the Count's weak chin she threw a fleeting smile towards his wife, who was looking 'Eastern' swathed in the skin of a blue panther.

'Yes, their affairs it seems are almost desperate,' the Count returned, directing his gaze towards the Duchess.

Well-favoured beyond measure she certainly was, with her immense placid eyes, and bundles of loose, blonde hair. She had a gown the green of Nile water, that enhanced to perfection the swan-like fairness of her throat and arms.

'I'm thinking of building myself a Villa in the Land of Dates!' she was confiding to the British Ambassador, who was standing beside her on her right. 'Ah, yes! I shall end my days in a country strewn with flowers.'

'You would find it I should say too hot, Duchess.'

'My soul has need of the sun, Sir Somebody!' the Duchess replied, opening with equanimity a great black ostrich fan, and smiling up at him through the sticks.

Sir Somebody Something was a person whose nationality was written all over him. Nevertheless, he had, despite a bluff and somewhat rugged manner, a certain degree of feminine sensitiveness, and any reference to the *soul* at all (outside the Embassy Chapel) invariably made him fidget.

'In moderation, Duchess,' he murmured, fixing his eyes upon the golden head of a champagne bottle.

'They say it is a land of love!' the Duchess related, raising indolently an almond to her sinuously chiselled lips.

'And even, so it's said, too,' his Excellency returned, 'of licence!' when just at this turn of things the Royal cortège entered the supper-room to the exhilarating strains of King Goahead's War-March.

Those who had witnessed the arrival of King Jotifa and his Queen earlier in the afternoon were amazed at the alteration of their aspect now. Both had discarded their European attire for the loosely-flowing vestments of their native land, and for a brief while there was some slight confusion among those present as to which was the gentleman and which the lady of the two. The King's beard, long and blonde, should have determined the matter outright, but on the other hand the Queen's necklet of reeds and plumes was so very misleading. . . . Nobody in Pisuerga had seen anything to compare with it before. 'Marvellous, though terrifying,' the Court passed verdict.

Attended by their various suites, the Royal party gained their places amid the usual manifestation of loyal respect.

But one of the Royal ladies, as it soon became evident, was not yet come.

'Where's Lizzie, Lois?' King William asked, riveting the Archduchess's empty chair.

'We'd better begin without her, Willie,' the Queen exclaimed, 'you know she never minds.'

And hardly had the company seated themselves when, dogged by a lady-in-waiting and a maid-of-honour, the Archduchess Elizabeth of Pisuerga rustled in.

Very old and very bent, and (even) very beautiful, she was looking, as the grammar-books say, 'meet' to be robbed, beneath a formidable tiara, and wearing a dozen long strands of pearls.

'Forgive me, Willie,' she murmured, with a little high, shrill, tinkling laugh: 'but it was so fine that, after tea, I and a Lady went paddling in the Basin of the Nymphs.'

'How was the water?' the King enquired.

The Archduchess repressed a sneeze. 'Fresh,' she replied, 'but not too . . .'

'After sunset beware, dear Aunt, of chills.'

'But for a frog I believe nothing would have got me out!' the august lady confessed as she fluttered bird-like to her chair.

Forbidden in youth by parents and tutors alike the joys of paddling under pain of chastisement, the Archduchess Elizabeth appeared to find a zest in doing so now. Attended by a chosen lady-in-waiting (as a rule the dowager Marchioness of Lallah Miranda), she liked to slip off to one of the numerous basins or natural grottos in the castle gardens, where she would pass whole hours in wading blissfully about. Whilst paddling, it was her wont to run over those refrains from the vaudevilles and operas (with their many shakes and rippling *cadenze*) in favour in her day, interspersed at intervals by such cries as: 'Pull up your skirt, Marquise, it's dragging a little, my friend, below the knees . . .' or, 'A shark, a shark!' which was her way of designating anything that had fins, from a carp to a minnow.

'I fear our Archduchess has contracted a slight catarrh,' the Mistress of the Robes, a woman like a sleepy cow, observed, addressing herself to the Duke of Varna upon her left.

'Unless she is more careful, she'll go paddling once too often,' the Duke replied, contemplating with interest, above the moonlight-coloured daffodils upon the table board, one of the button-nosed belles of Queen Thleeanouhee's suite. The young creature, referred to cryptically among the subordinates of the castle as 'Tropical Molly,' was finding fault already, it seemed, with the food.

'Take it away,' she was protesting in animated tones: 'I'd as soon touch a foot-squashed mango!'

'No *mayonnaise,* miss?' a court-official asked, dropping his face prevailingly to within an inch of her own.

'Take it right away . . . And if you should *dare,* sir, to come any closer . . . !'

The Mistress of the Robes fingered nervously the various Orders of Merit on her sumptuous bosom.

'I trust there will be no contretemps,' she murmured, glancing uneasily towards the Queen of the Land of Dates, who seemed to be lost in admiration of the Royal dinner-service of scarlet plates, that looked like pools of blood upon the cloth.

'What pleases me in your land,' she was expansively telling her host, 'is less your food than the china you serve it on; for with us you know there's none. And now,' she added, marvellously wafting a fork, 'I'm for ever spoilt for shells.'

King William was incredulous.

'With you no china?' he gasped.

'None, sir, none!'

'I could not be more astonished,' the King declared, 'if you told me there were fleas at the Ritz,' a part of which assertion Lady Something, who was blandly listening, imperfectly chanced to hear.

'Who would credit it!' she breathed, turning to an attaché, a young man all white and penseroso, at her elbow.

'Credit what?'

'Did you not hear what the dear King said?'

'No.'

'It's almost *too* appalling . . .' Lady Something replied, passing a small, nerveless hand across her brow.

'Won't you tell me though?' the young man murmured gently, with his nose in his plate.

Lady Something raised a glass of frozen lemonade to her lips.

'Fleas,' she murmured, 'have been found at the Ritz.'

'. . . . . . ! . . . . ? . . . ! !'

'Oh and *poor* Lady Bertha! And poor good old Mrs. Hunter!' And Lady Something looked away in the direction of Sir Somebody, as though anxious to catch his eye.

But the British Ambassador and the Duchess of Varna were weighing the chances of a Grant being allowed by Parliament for the excavation of Chedorlahomor.

'Dear little Chedor,' the Duchess kept on saying, 'I'm sure one would find the most enthralling things there. Aren't *you*, Sir Somebody?'

And they were still absorbed in their colloquy when the King gave the signal to rise.

Although King William had bidden several distinguished Divas from the Opera House to give an account of themselves for the entertainment of his guests, both King Jotifa and Queen Thleeanouhee with disarming candour declared that, to their ears, the music of the West was hardly to be borne.

'Well, I'm not very fond of it either,' her Dreaminess admitted, surrendering her skirts to a couple of rosy boys, and leading the way with airy grace towards an adjacent salon, 'although,' she wistfully added across her shoulder to a high dignitary of the Church, 'I'm trying, it's true, to coax the dear Archbishop to give the first act of *La Tosca* in the Blue Jesus. . . . Such a perfect setting, and with Desiré Erlinger and Maggie Mellon . . . !'

And as the Court now pressed after her the rules of etiquette became considerably relaxed. Mingling freely with his guests, King William had a hand-squeeze and a fleeting word for each.

'In England,' he paused to enquire of Lady Something, who was warning a dowager, with impressive earnestness, against the Ritz, 'have you ever seen two cooks in a kitchen-garden?'

'No, never, sir!' Lady Something simpered.

'Neither,' the King replied, moving on, 'have *we*.'

The Ambassadress beamed.

'My dear,' she told Sir Somebody, a moment afterwards, 'my

dear, the King was simply charming. Really I may say he was more than gracious! He asked me if I had ever seen two cooks in a kitchen-garden, and I said no, never! And he said that neither, either, had he! And oh isn't it so strange how few of us ever have?'

But in the salon one of Queen Thleeanouhee's ladies had been desired by her Dreaminess to sing.

'It seems so long,' she declared, 'since I heard an Eastern voice, and it would be such a relief.'

'By all means,' Queen Thleeanouhee said, 'and let a *darbouka* or two be brought! For what charms the heart more, what touches it more,' she asked, considering meditatively her babouched feet, 'than a *darbouka*?'

It was told that, in the past, her life had been a gallant one, although her adventures, it was believed, had been mostly with men. Those, however, who had observed her conduct closely had not failed to remark how often her eyes had been attracted in the course of the evening towards the dimpled cheeks of the British Ambassadress.

Perceiving her ample form not far away, Queen Thleeanouhee signalled to her amiably to approach.

Née Rosa Bark (and a daughter of the Poet) Lady Something was perhaps not sufficiently tactful to meet all the difficulties of the rôle in which it had pleased life to call her. But still, she tried, and did do her best, which often went far to retrieve her lack of *savoir faire*. 'Life is like that dear,' she would sometimes say to Sir Somebody, but she would never say what it was that life was like; '*That*,' it seemed. . . .

'I was just looking for my daughter,' she declared.

'And is she as sympathetic,' Queen Thleeanouhee softly asked, 'as her mamma?'

'She's shy—of the Violet persuasion, but that's not a bad thing in a young girl.'

'Where *I* reign shyness is a quality which is entirely un-known . . . !'

'It must be astonishing, ma'am,' Lady Something replied, caressing a parure of false jewels, intended, indeed, to deceive no one, 'to be a Queen of a sun-steeped country like yours.'

Queen Thleeanouhee fetched a sigh.

'Dateland—my dear, it's a scorch!' she averred.

'I conclude, ma'am, it's what *we* should call "conservatory" scenery?' Lady Something murmured.

'It is the land of the jessamine-flower, the little amorous jessamine-flower,' the Queen gently cooed, with a sidelong smiling glance, 'that twines itself sometimes to the right hand, at others to the left, just according to its caprices!'

'It sounds, I fear, to be unhealthy, ma'am.'

'And it is the land, also, of romance, my dear, where *shyness* is a quality which is entirely unknown,' the Queen broke off, as one of her ladies, bearing a *darbouka*, advanced with an air of purposefulness towards her.

The hum of voices which filled the room might well have tended to dismay a vocalist of modest powers, but the young matron known to the Court as 'Tropical Molly,' and whom her mistress addressed as Timzra, soon showed herself to be equal to the occasion.

> 'Under the blue gum-tree
> I am sitting waiting,
> Under the blue gum-tree
> I am waiting all alone!'

Her voice reached the ears of the fresh-faced ensigns and the beardless subalterns in the Guard Room far beyond, and startled the pages in the distant dormitories, as they lay smoking on their beds.

And then, the theme changing, and with an ever-increasing passion, fervour and force:

> 'I heard a watch-dog in the night ...
> Wailing, wailing ...
> Why is the watch-dog wailing?
> He is wailing for the Moon!'

'That is one of the very saddest songs,' the King remarked, 'that I have ever heard. "Why is the watch-dog wailing? He is wailing for the Moon!"' And the ambitions and mortifications of kingship for a moment weighed visibly upon him.

'Something merrier, Timzra!' Queen Thleeanouhee said.

And throwing back her long love-lilac sleeves, Timzra sang:

> 'A negress with a margaret once lolled frousting in the sun
> Thinking of all the little things that she had left undone ...
> With a hey, hey, hey, hey, hi, hey ho!'

'She has the air of a cannibal!' the Archduchess murmured behind her fan to his Weariness, who had scarcely opened his lips except to yawn throughout the whole of the evening.

'She has the air of a ——' he replied laconically turning away.

Since the conversation with his mother earlier in the day his thoughts had revolved incessantly around Laura. What had they been saying to the poor wee witch, and whereabouts was she to be found?

Leaving the salon, in the wake of a pair of venerable politicians, who were helping each other along with little touches and pats, he made his way towards the ball-room, where a new dance known as the Pisgah Pas was causing some excitement, and gaining a post of vantage, it was not long before he caught a glimpse of the agile, boyish figure of his betrothed. She passed him, without apparently noticing he was there, in a whirlwind of black tulle, her little hand pressed to the breast of a man like a sulky eagle; and he could not help rejoicing inwardly that, *once* his wife, it would no longer be possible for her to enjoy herself exactly with whom she pleased. As she swept by again he succeeded in capturing her attention, and, nodding meaningly towards a deserted picture-gallery, wandered away towards it. It was but seldom he set foot there, and he amused himself by examining some of the pictures to be seen upon the walls. An old shrew with a rose ... a drawing of a man alone in the last extremes ... a pink-robed Christ ... a seascape, painted probably in winter, with cold, hard colouring ...

'Yousef?'

'Rara!'

'Let us go outside, dear.'

A night so absolutely soft and calm was delicious after the glare and noise within.

'With whom,' he asked, 'sweetheart, were you last dancing?'

'Only the brother of one of the Queen's Maids, dear,' Mademoiselle de Nazianzi replied. 'After dinner, though', she tittered, 'when he gets Arabian-Nighty, it's apt to annoy one a scrap!'

'*Arabian-Nighty?*'

'Oh, never mind!'

'But (pardon me, dear) I do.'

'Don't be tiresome, Yousef! The night is too fine,' she murmured, glancing absently away towards the hardly moving trees, from whose branches a thousand drooping necklets of silver lamps palely burned.

Were *those* the 'bladders' then?

Strolling on down hoops of white wistaria in the moon they came to the pillared circle of a rustic temple, commanding a prospect on the town.

'There,' she murmured, smiling elfishly and designating something, far below them, through the moon mist, with her fan, 'is the column of Justice and,' she laughed a little, 'of *Liberty*!'

'And there,' he pointed inconsequently, 'is *the Automobile Club*!'

'And beyond it . . . the Convent of the Flaming-Hood. . . .'

'And those blue revolving lights; can you see them, Rara?'

'Yes, dear . . . what are *they*, Yousef?'

'Those,' he told her, contemplating her beautiful white face against the dusky gloom, 'are the lights of the Café Cleopatra!'

'And what,' she questioned, as they sauntered on, pursued by all the sweet perfumes of the night, 'are those berried-shrubs that smell so passionately?'

'I don't know,' he said. 'Kiss me, Rara!'

'No, no.'

'Why not?'

'Not now!'

'Put your arm about me, dear.'

'What a boy he is!' she murmured, gazing up into the starry clearness.

Overhead a full moon, a moon of circumstance, rode high in the sky, defining phantasmally, far off, the violet-farded hills beyond the town.

'To be out there among the silver bean-fields!' he said.

'Yes, Yousef,' she sighed, starting at a Triton's face among the trailing ivy on the castle wall. Beneath it, half concealed by water-flags, lay a miniature lake: as a rule, nobody now went near the lake at all, since the Queen had called it '*appallingly smelly*,' so that for rendezvous it was quite ideal.

'Tell me, Yousef,' she presently said, pausing to admire the beautiful shadow of an orange-tree on the path before them: 'tell me, dear, when Life goes like that to one—what does one do?'

He shrugged. 'Usually nothing,' he replied, the tip of his tongue (like the point of a blade) peeping out between his teeth.

'Ah, but isn't that being strong?' she said half audibly, fixing her eyes as though fascinated upon his lips.

'Why,' he demanded, with an engaging smile that brought half-moons to his hollow cheeks, 'what has the world been doing to Rara?'

'At this instant, Yousef,' she declared, 'it brings her nothing but Joy!'

'You're happy, my sweet, with me?'

'No one knows, dearest, how much I love you.'

'Kiss me, Rara,' he said again.

'Bend, then,' she answered, as the four quarters of the twelve strokes of midnight rang out leisurely from the castle clock.

'I've to go to the Ritz!' he announced.

'And *I* should be going in.'

Retracing reluctantly their steps they were soon in earshot of the ball, and their close farewells were made accompanied by selections from *The Blue Banana*.

She remained a few moments gazing as though entranced at his retreating figure, and would have, perhaps, run after him with some little capricious message, when she became aware of someone watching her from beneath the shadow of a garden vase.

Advancing steadily and with an air of nonchalance, she recognised the delicate, sexless silhouette and slightly hunched shoulders of Olga Blumenghast, whose exotic attraction had aroused not a few heart-burnings (and even feuds) among several of the grandes dames about the court.

Poised flatly against the vase's sculptured plinth, she would have scarcely been discernible but for the silver glitter of her gown.

'Olga? Are you faint?'

'No; only my slippers are *torture*.'

'I'd advise you to change them, then!'

'It's not altogether my feet, dear, that ache. . . .'

'Ah, I see,' Mademoiselle de Nazianzi said, stooping enough to scan the stormy, soul-tossed eyes of her friend: 'you're suffering, I suppose, on account of Ann-Jules?'

'He's such a gold-fish, Rara . . . any fingers that will throw him bread. . . .'

'And there's no doubt, I'm afraid, that lots do!' Mademoiselle de Nazianzi answered lucidly, sinking down by her side.

'I would give all my soul to him, Rara . . . my chances of heaven!'

'Your chances, Olga——' Mademoiselle de Nazianzi murmured, avoiding some bird-droppings with her skirt.

'How I envy *the men*, Rara, in his platoon!'

'Take away his uniform, Olga, and what does he become?'

'Ah *what*——!'

'No. . . . Believe me, my dear, he's not worth the trouble!'

Mademoiselle Blumenghast clasped her hands brilliantly across the nape of her neck.

'I want to possess him at dawn, at dawn,' she broke out: 'beneath a sky striped with green. . . .'

'Oh, Olga!'

'And I shall never rest,' she declared, turning away on a languid heel, 'until I *do*.'

Meditating upon the fever of love, Mademoiselle de Nazianzi directed her course slowly towards her room. She lodged in that part of the palace known as 'The Bachelors' Wing,' where she had a delicious little suite just below the roof.

'If she loved him absolutely,' she told herself, as she turned the handle of her door, 'she would not care about the colour of the sky; even if it snowed or hailed!'

Depositing her fan upon the lid of an old wedding-chest that formed a couch, she smiled contentedly about her. It would be a wrench abandoning this little apartment that she had identified already with herself, when the day should come to leave it for others more spacious in the Keep. Although scarcely the size of a ship's cabin, it was amazing how many people one could receive together at a time merely by pushing the piano back against the wall and wheeling the wedding-chest on to the stairs; and once no fewer than seventeen persons had sat down to a birthday *fête* without being made too much to feel like herrings. In the so-called salon, divided from her bedroom by a folding lacquer screen, hung a few studies in oils executed by herself, which, except to the initiated, or the naturally instinctive, looked sufficiently enigmatic against a wall-paper with a stealthy design.

Yes, it would be a wrench to quit the little place, she reflected, as she began setting about her toilet for the night. It was agreeable going to bed late without anybody's aid, when one could pirouette interestingly before the mirror in the last stages of déshabillé, and do a thousand (and one) things besides* that one might otherwise

*Always a humiliating recollection with her in after years. *Vide* 'Confessions',

lack the courage for. But this evening, being in no frivolous mood, she changed her ball dress swiftly for a robe-de-chambre bordered deeply with ermines, that made her feel nearer somehow to Yousef, and helped her to realise her position in its various facets as future Queen.

'Queen!' she breathed, trailing her fur flounces towards the window.

Already the blue revolving lights of the Café Cleopatra were growing paler with the dawn, and the moon had veered a little towards the Convent of the Flaming-Hood. Ah ... how often as a lay boarder there had she gazed up towards the palace wondering half-shrinkingly what life 'in the world' was like; for there had been a period, indeed, when the impulse to take the veil had been strong with her—more, perhaps, to be near one of the nuns whom she had *idolised* than from any more immediate vocation.

She remained immersed in thoughts, her introspectiveness fanned insensibly by the floating zephyrs that spring with morning. The slight sway-sway of the trees, the awakening birds in the castle eaves, the green-veined bougainvillæas that fringed her sill—these thrilled her heart with joy. All virginal in the early dawn what magic the world possessed! Slow speeding clouds like knots of pink roses came blowing across the sky, sailing away in titanic bouquets above the town.

Just such a morning should be their wedding-day! she mused, beginning lightly to apply the contents of a jar of milk of almonds to her breast and arms. Ah, before that Spina Christi lost its leaves, or that swallow should migrate ... that historic day would come!

Troops ... hysteria ... throngs. ... The Blue Jesus packed to suffocation. ... She could envisage it all.

And there would be a whole holiday in the Convent, she reflected, falling drowsily at her bedside to her knees.

'Oh! help me, heaven,' she prayed, 'to be decorative and to do right! Let me always look young, never more than sixteen or seventeen—at the *very* outside, and let Yousef love me—as much as I do him. And I thank you for creating such a darling, God (for he's a perfect dear), and I can't tell you how much I love him; especially when he wags it! I mean his tongue. ... Bless all the sisters at the Flaming-Hood—above all Sister Ursula ... and be sweet, besides, to old Jane. ... Show me the straight path! And keep me ever free from the malicious scandal of the Court. Amen.'

And her orisons (ending in a brief self-examination) over, Mademoiselle de Nazianzi climbed into bed.

III

IN the Salle de Prince or Cabinet d'Antoine, above the Café Cleopatra, Madame Wetme, the wife of the proprietor, sat perusing the Court gazettes.

It was not often that a *cabinet particulier* like Antoine was disengaged at luncheon time, being as a rule reserved many days in advance, but it had been a 'funny' season, as the saying went, and there was the possibility that a party of late-risers might look in yet (officers, or artistes from the Halls), who had been passing a night 'on the tiles.' But Madame Wetme trusted not. It was pleasant to escape every now and again from her lugubrious back-drawing-room that only faced a wall, or to peruse the early newspapers without having first to wait for them. And to-day precisely was the day for the hebdomadal *causerie* in the *Jaw-Waw's Journal* on matters appertaining to society, signed by that ever popular diarist 'Eva Schnerb.'

'Never,' Madame Wetme read, 'was a gathering more brilliant than that which I witnessed last night! I stood in a corner of the Great ball-room and literally *gasped* at the wealth of jewels. . . . Beauty and bravery abounded, but no one, *I* thought, looked better than our most gracious Queen, etc. . . . Among the supper-guests I saw their Excellencies Prince and Princess Paul de Pismiche—the Princess impressed me as being *just* a trifle pale: she is by no means strong, and unhappily our nefarious climate does not agree with everybody!—their Excellencies Sir Somebody and Lady Somebody (Miss Ivy Something charming in cornflower *charmeuse* danced indefatigably all the evening, as did also one of the de Lambèse girls); the Count and Countess of Tolga—she all in blue furs and literally *ablaze* with gorgeous gems (I hear on excellent authority she is shortly relinquishing her post of Woman of the Bedchamber which she finds is really too arduous for her); the Duchess of Varna, looking veritably radiant (by the way where has she been?) in the palest of pistachio-green mashlaks, which are all the rage at present.

'*Have you a Mashlak?*

'Owing to the visit of King Jotifa and Queen Thleeanouhee, the Eastern mashlak is being worn by many of the smart women about the Court. I saw an example at the Opera the other night in silver and gold *lamé* that I thought too——' Madame Wetme broke off to look up, as a waiter entered the room.

'Did Madame ring?'

'No! . . .'

'Then it must have been "Ptolemy"!' the young man murmured, bustling out.

'I dare say. When will you know your bells?' Madame Wetme retorted, returning with a headshake to the gazette: her beloved Eva was full of information this week and breathlessly she read on:

'I saw Minnie, Lady Violetrock (whose daughter Sonia is being educated here), at the garden *fête* the other day at the Château des Fleurs, looking chic as she *always* does, in a combination of petunia and purple ninon raffling a donkey.

'I hear on the best authority that before the Court goes to the Summer Palace later on there will be at least *one* more Drawing-room. Applications, from those entitled to attend, should be made to the Lord Chamberlain as *soon* as possible.'

One more Drawing-room—! The journal fell from Madame Wetme's hand.

'I'm getting on now,' she reflected, 'and if I'm not presented soon I never will be. . . .'

She raised imploring eyes to the mural imagery—to the 'Cleopatra couchant,' to the 'Arrival of Anthony,' to the 'Sphinx,' to the 'Temple of Ra,' as though seeking inspiration. 'Ah my God!' she groaned.

But Madame Wetme's religion, her cruel God, was the *Chic*: the God Chic.

The sound of music from below reached her faintly. There was not a better orchestra (even at the Palace) than that which discoursed at the Café Cleopatra—and they played, the thought had sometimes pleased her, the same identical tunes!

'Does it say when?' she murmured, re-opening the gazette. No: but it would be 'before the Court left.' . . . And when would that be?

'I have good grounds for believing,' she continued to read, 'that in order to meet his creditors the Duke of Varna is selling a large portion of his country estate.'

If it were true ... Madame Wetme's eyes rested in speculation on the oleanders in the great flower-tubs before the Café; if it were true, why the Varnas must be desperate, and the Duchess ready to do anything. 'Anything—for remuneration,' she murmured, rising and going towards a table usually used for correspondence. And seating herself with a look of decision, she opened a leather writing-pad, full of crab-coloured, ink-marked blotting-paper.

In the fan-shaped mirror above the writing-table she could see herself in fancy, all veils and aigrettes, as she would be on 'the day' when coiffed by Ernst.

'Among a bevy of charming débutantes, no one looked more striking than Madame Wetme, who was presented by the Duchess of Varna.' Being a client of the house (with an unpaid bill) she could *dictate* to Eva. ... But first, of course, she must secure the Duchess. And taking up her pen she wrote: 'Madame Wetme would give the Duchess of Varna fifty thousand crowns to introduce her at Court.' A trifle terse perhaps? Madame Wetme considered. How if the Duchess should take offence. ... It was just conceivable! And besides, by specifying no fixed sum, she might be got for less.

'Something more mysterious, more delicate in style ...' Madame Wetme murmured with a sigh, beginning the letter anew:

'If the Duchess of Varna will call on Madame Wetme this afternoon, about five, and partake of a cup of tea, she will hear of something *to her advantage*.'

Madame Wetme smiled. 'That should get her!' she reflected, and selecting an envelope, she directed it boldly to the Ritz. 'Being hard up, she is sure to be there!' she reasoned, as she left the room in quest of a page.

The French maid of the Duchess of Varna was just putting on her mistress's shoes, in a private sitting-room at the Ritz, when Madame Wetme's letter arrived.

The pleasure of being in the capital once more, after a long spell of the country, had given her an appetite for her lunch and she was feeling braced after an excellent meal.

'I shall not be back, I expect, till late, Louison,' she said to her maid, 'and should anyone enquire where I am, I shall either be at the Palace, or at the Skating Rink.'

'Madame la Duchesse will not be going to her corsetier's?'

'It depends if there's time. What did I do with my shopping-list?' the Duchess replied, gathering up abstractedly a large, becoroneted vanity-case and a parasol. She had a gown of khaki and daffodil and a black tricorne hat trimmed with green. 'Give me my other sunshade, the jade—and don't forget—On me trouvera, soit au Palais Royal, soit au Palais de Glace!' she enjoined, sailing quickly out.

Leaving the Ritz by a side door, she found herself in a quiet shady street bordering the Regina Gardens. Above, a sky so blue, so clear, so luminous seemed to cry out: 'Nothing matters! Why worry? Be sanguine! Amuse yourself! ! Nothing matters!'

Traversing the gardens, her mind preoccupied by Madame Wetme's note, the Duchess branched off into a busy thoroughfare leading towards the Opera, in whose vicinity lay the city's principal shops. To learn of anything to one's advantage was, of course, always welcome, but there were various other claims upon her besides that afternoon, which she was unable, or loath, to ignore— the palace, a *thé dansant* or two, and then her favourite rink . . . although the unfortunate part was that most of the rink instructors were still unpaid, and on the last occasion she had hired one to waltz with her he had taken advantage of the fact by pressing her waist with greater freedom than she felt he need have done.

Turning into the Opera Square with its fine arcades, she paused, half furtively, before a florist's shop. Only her solicitors and a few in the secret were aware that the premises known as *Haboubet of Egypt* were her own; for, fearful lest they might be occupied one day by sheriffs' officers, she had kept the little business venture the closest mystery. Lilies 'from Karnak,' Roses 'from the Land of Punt' (all grown in the gardens of her country house, in the purlieus of the capital) found immediate and daily favour among amateurs of the choice. Indeed, as her gardener frequently said, the demand for Roses from the Land of Punt was more than he could possibly cope with without an extra man.

'I may as well run in and take whatever there's in the till,' she reflected—'not that, I fear, there's much. . . .'

The superintendent, a slim Tunisian boy, was crouching pitcher-posture upon the floor, chanting languidly to himself, his head supported by an osier pannier lately arrived from 'Punt.'

'Up, Bachir!' the Duchess upbraided. 'Remember the fresh consignments perish while you dream there and sing.'

The young Tunisian smiled.

He worshipped the Duchess, and the song he was improvising

as she entered had been inspired by her. In it (had she known) he had led her by devious tender stages to his father's fonduk at Tifilalet 'on the blue Lake of Fetzara,' where he was about to present her to the Sheik and the whole assembled village as his chosen bride.

The Duchess considered him. He had a beautiful face spoiled by a bad complexion, which doubtless (the period of puberty passed) he would outgrow.

'Consignment him come not two minute,' the youth replied.

'Ah, Bachir? Bachir!'

'By the glorious Koran, I will swear it.'

'Be careful not to shake those *Alexandrian Balls*,' the Duchess peremptorily enjoined, pointing towards some Guelder-roses—'or they'll fall before they're sold!'

'No matter at all. They sold already! An American lady this morning she purchase all my Alexandrian-balls; two heavy bunch.'

'Let me see your takings. . . .'

With a smile of triumph, Bachir turned towards the till. He had the welfare of the establishment at heart as well as his own, and of an evening often he would flit, garbed in his long gandourah, through the chief Cafés and Dancings of the city, a vast pannier upon his head heaped high with flowers, which he would dispose of to dazzled clients for an often exorbitant sum. But for these excursions of his (which ended on occasion in adventure) he had received no authority at all.

'Not so bad,' the Duchess commented. 'And, as there's to be a Court again soon, many orders for bouquets are sure to come in!'

'I call in outside hands to assist me: I summon Ouardi! He an Armenian boy. Sympathetic. My friend. More attached to him am I than a branch of jessamine is about a vine.'

'I suppose he's capable?' the Duchess murmured, pinning a green-ribbed orchid to her dress.

'The garlands of Ouardi would make even a jackal look bewitching!'

'Ah: he has taste?'

'I engage my friend. Much work always in the month of Redjeb!'

'Engage nobody,' the Duchess answered as she left the shop, 'until I come again.'

Hailing in the square one of the little shuttered cabs of the city, she directed the driver to drop her at the palace gates, and pursued by an obstreperous newsboy with an evening paper, yelling 'Chedorlahomor! Sodom! Extra Special!' the cab clattered off at a languid trot. Under the plane-trees, near the Houses of Parliament, she was overtaken by the large easy-stepping horses of the Ambassadress of England and acknowledged with a winning movement of the wrist Lady Something's passing accueil. It was not yet quite the correct hour for the Promenade, where beneath the great acacias Society liked best to ride or drive, but, notwithstanding, that zealous reporter of social deeds, the irrepressible Eva Schnerb, was already on the prowl and able with satisfaction to note: 'I saw the Duchess of Varna early driving in the Park, all alone in a little one-horse shay, that really looked more elegant than any Delaunay-Belleville!'

Arriving before the palace gates, the Duchess perceived an array of empty carriages waiting in the drive, which made her apprehensive of a function. She had anticipated an intimate chat with the Queen alone, but this it seemed was not to be.

Following a youthful page with a *resigned* face down a long black rug woven with green and violet flowers, who left her with a sigh (as if disappointed of a tip) in charge of a couple of giggling colleagues, who, in turn, propelled her towards a band of sophisticated-looking footmen and grim officials, she was shown at last into a vast white drawing-room whose ceiling formed a dome.

Knowing the Queen's interest in the Chedorlahomor Excavation Bill, a number of representative folk, such as the wives of certain Politicians or Diplomats, as well as a few of her own more immediate circle, had called to felicitate her upon its success. Parliament had declared itself willing to do the unlimited graceful by all those concerned, and this in a great measure was due to the brilliant wire-pulling of the Queen.

She was looking singularly French in a gold helmet and a violet Vortniansky gown, and wore a rope of faultless pearls, clasped very high beneath the chin.

'I hope the Archbishop will bless the excavators' tools!' she was saying to the wife of the Premier as the Duchess entered. 'The *picks* at any rate. . . .'

That lady made no reply. In presence of Royalty she would usually sit and smile at her knees, raising her eyes from time to time to throw, beneath her lashes, an ineffable expiring glance.

'God speed them safe home again!' the Archduchess Elizabeth, who was busy knitting, said. An ardent philanthropist, she had begun already making 'comforts' for the men, as the nights in the East are cold. The most philanthropic perhaps of all the Royal Family, her hobby was designing, for the use of the public, sanitary, but artistic, places of necessity on a novel system of ventilation. The King had consented to open (and it was expected appropriately) one of these in course of construction in the Opera Square.

'Amen,' the Queen answered, signalling amiably to the Duchess of Varna, whose infrequent visits to court disposed her always to make a fuss of her.

But no fuss the Queen could make of the Duchess of Varna could exceed that being made by Queen Thleeanouhee, in a far-off corner, of her Excellency Lady Something. The sympathy, the *entente* indeed that had arisen between these two ladies, was exercising considerably the minds of certain members of the diplomatic corps, although, had anyone wished to eavesdrop, their conversation upon the whole must have been found to be anything but esoteric.

'What I want,' Queen Thleeanouhee was saying, resting her hand confidentially on her Excellency's knee, 'what I want is an English maid with Frenchified fingers—— Is there such a thing to be had?'

'But surely——' Lady Something smiled: for the servant-topic was one she felt at home on.

'In Dateland, my dear, servant girls are nothing but sluts.'

'Life is like *that*, ma'am, I regret, indeed, to have to say: I once had a housemaid who had lived with Sarah Bernhardt, and oh, wasn't she a terror!' Lady Something declared, warding off a little black bat-eared dog who was endeavouring to scramble on to her lap.

'Teddywegs, Teddywegs!' the Archduchess exclaimed, jumping up and advancing to capture her pet. 'He arrived from London not later than this morning,' she said; 'from the Princess Elsie of England.'

'He looks like some special litter,' Lady Something remarked.

'How the dear girl loves animals!'

'The rumour of her betrothal it seems is quite without foundation?'

'To my nephew: ah alas. . . .'

'Prince Yousef and she are of an equal age!'

'She is interested in Yousef I'm inclined to believe; but the worst of life is, nearly everyone marches to a different tune,' the Archduchess replied.

'One hears of her nothing that isn't agreeable.'

'Like her good mother, Queen Glory,' the Archduchess said, 'one feels, of course, she's all she should be.'

Lady Something sighed.

'Yes . . . and even *more*!' she murmured, letting fall a curtsey to King William who had entered. He had been lunching at the Headquarters of the Girl Guides and wore the uniform of a general.

'What is the acme of nastiness?' he paused of the English Ambassadress to enquire.

Lady Something turned paler than the white candytuft that is found on ruins. 'Oh *la*, sir,' she stammered, 'how should I know!'

The King looked the shrinking matron slowly up and down. 'The supreme disgust——'

'Oh *la*, sir!' Lady Something stammered again.

But the King took pity on her evident confusion. 'Tepid potatoes,' he answered, 'on a stone-cold plate.'

The Ambassadress beamed.

'I trust the warmth of the girls, sir, compensated you for the coldness of the plates?' she ventured.

'The inspection, in the main, was satisfactory! Although I noticed that one or two of the guides seemed inclined to lead astray,' the King replied, regarding Teddywegs, who was inquisitively sniffing his spurs.

'He's strange yet to everything,' the Archduchess commented.

'What's this—a new dog?'

'From Princess Elsie. . . .'

'They say she's stupid, but I do not know that intellect is always a blessing!' the King declared, drooping his eyes to his abdomen with an air of pensive modesty.

'Poor child, she writes she is tied to the shore, so that I suppose she is unable to leave dear England.'

'Tied to it?'

'And bound till goodness knows.'

'As was Andromeda!' the King sententiously exclaimed. . . . 'She would have little, or maybe nothing, to wear,' he clairvoyantly went on. 'I see her standing shivering, waiting for Yousef. . . . Chained by the leg, perhaps, exposed to the howling winds.'*

* *Winds*, pronounced as we're told 'in poetry.'

'Nonsense. She means to say she can't get away yet on account of her engagements; that's all.'

'After Cowes-week,' Lady Something put in, 'she is due to pay a round of visits before joining her parents in the North.'

'How I envy her' the Archduchess sighed, 'amid that entrancing scene. . . .'

Lady Something looked *attendrie*.

'Your Royal Highness is attached to England?' she asked.

'I fear I was never there. . . . But I shall always remember I put my hair up when I was twelve years old because of the Prince of Wales.'

'Oh? And . . . which of the Georges?' Lady Something gasped.

'It's so long ago now that I really forget.'

'And pray, ma'am, what was the point of it?'

The Archduchess chuckled.

'Why, so as to look eligible of course!' she replied, returning to her knitting.

Amid the general flutter following the King's appearance it was easy enough for the Duchess of Varna to slip away. Knowing the palace inside out it was unnecessary to make any fuss. Passing through a long room, where a hundred holland-covered chairs stood grouped, Congresswise, around a vast table, she attained the Orangery, that gave access to the drive. The mellay of vehicles had considerably increased, and the Duchess paused a moment to consider which she should borrow when, recollecting she wished to question one of the royal gardeners on a little matter of mixing manure, she decided to return through the castle grounds instead. Taking a path that descended between rhododendrons and grim old cannons towards the town, she was comparing the capriciousness of certain bulbs to that of certain people when she heard her name called from behind and, glancing round, perceived the charming silhouette of the Countess of Tolga.

'I couldn't stand it inside. Could you?'

'My *dear*, what a honeymoon hat!'

'It was made by me!'

'Oh, Violet . . .' the Duchess murmured, her face taking on a look of wonder.

'Don't forget, dear, Sunday.'

'Is it a party?'

'I've asked Grim-lips and Ladybird, Hairy and Fluffy, Hardylegs and Bluewings, Spindleshanks and Our Lady of Furs.'

'Not Nanny-goat?'

'Luckily . . .' the Countess replied, raising to her nose the heliotropes in her hand.

'Is he no better?'

'You little know, dear, what it is to be all alone with him chez soi when he thinks and sneers into the woodwork.'

'*Into the woodwork?*'

'He addresses the ceiling, the walls, the floor—me never!'

'Dear dove.'

'All I can I'm plastic.'

'Can one be plastic ever enough, dear?'

'Often but for Olga . . .' the Countess murmured, considering a little rosy ladybird on her arm.

'I consider her ever so compelling, ever so wistful——' the Duchess of Varna averred.

'Sweet girl—! She's just my consolation.'

'She reminds me, does she you? of that *Miss Hobart* in de Grammont's *Memoirs*.'

'C'est une âme exquise!'

'Well, au revoir, dear: we shall meet again at the Princess Leucippe's later on,' the Duchess said, detecting her gardener in the offing.

By the time she had obtained her recipe and cajoled a few special shoots from various exotic plants, the sun had begun to decline. Emerging from the palace by a postern-gate, where lounged a sentry, she found herself almost directly beneath the great acacias on the Promenade. Under the lofty leafage of the trees, as usual towards this hour, society in its varying grades had congregated to be gazed upon. Mounted on an eager-headed little horse, his Weariness (who loved being seen) was plying up and down, while in his wake a '*screen artiste*,' on an Arabian mare with powdered withers and eyes made up with kohl, was creating a sensation. Every time she used her whip the powder rose in clouds. Wending her way through the throng the duchess recognised the rose-harnessed horses of Countess Medusa Rappa—the Countess bolt upright, her head carried stiffly, staring with a pathetic expression of dead *joie-de-vie* between her coachman's and footman's waists. But the intention of calling at the Café Cleopatra caused the duchess to hasten. The possibility of learning something beneficial to herself was a lure not to be resisted. Pausing to allow the marvellous blue automobile of Count Ann-Jules to pass (with the dancer Kalpurnia inside), she crossed the Avenue, where there seemed, on the whole, to be fewer people. Here she remarked a little ahead of her the masculine form of the Countess Yvorra, taking a quiet stroll before *Salut* in the company of her Confessor. In the street she usually walked with her hands clasped behind her back, huddled up like a statesman. '*Des choses abominables! . . . Des choses hors nature!*' she was saying, in tones of evident relish, as the duchess passed.

Meanwhile Madame Wetme was seated anxiously by the samovar in her drawing-room. To receive the duchess, she had assumed a mashlak à la mode, whitened her face and rouged her ears, and set a small but costly aigrette at an insinuating angle in the edifice of her hair. As the hour of Angelus approached the tension of waiting grew more and more acute, and beneath the strain of expectation even the little iced sugar cakes upon the tea-table looked green with worry.

Suppose, after all, she shouldn't come? Suppose she had already left? Suppose she were in prison? Only the other day a woman of the highest fashion, a leader of 'society' with an *A*, had served six months as a consequence of her extravagance. . . .

In agitation Madame Wetme helped herself to a small glassful of *Cointreau* (her favourite liqueur), when, feeling calmer for the consommation, she was moved to take a peep out of Antoine.

But nobody chic at all met her eye.

Between the oleanders upon the kerb, that rose up darkly against a flame-pink sky, two young men dressed 'as poets' were arguing and gesticulating freely over a bottle of beer. Near them, a sailor with a blue drooping collar and dusty boots (had he walked, poor wretch, to see his mother?) was gazing stupidly at the large evening gnats that revolved like things bewitched about the café lamps, while below the window a lean soul in glasses, evidently an impresario, was loudly exclaiming: 'London has robbed me of my throat, sir! ! It has deprived me of my voice.'

No, an 'off' night certainly!

Through a slow, sun-flower of a door (that kept on revolving long after it had been pushed) a few military men bent on a game of billiards, or an early *fille de joie* (only the discreetest *des filles 'serieuses'* were supposed to be admitted), came and went.

'To-night they're fit for church,' Madame Wetme complacently smiled as the door swung round again. 'Navy-blue and silver-fox looks the goods,' she reflected, 'upon any occasion! It suggests something sly—like a nurse's uniform.'

'A lady in the drawing-room, Madame, desires to speak to you,' a chasseur tunefully announced, and fingering nervously her aigrette Madame Wetme followed.

The Duchess of Varna was inspecting a portrait with her back to the door as her hostess entered.

'I see you're looking at my Murillo!' Madame Wetme began.

'Oh. . . . Is it o-ri-gi-nal?' the Duchess drawled.

'No.'

'I *thought* not.'

'To judge by the bankruptcy-sales of late (and it's curious how many there've been . . .), it would seem, from the indifferent figure he makes, that he is no longer accounted chic,' Madame Wetme observed as she drew towards the Duchess a chair.

'I consider the chic to be such a very false religion! . . .' the Duchess said, accepting the seat which was offered her.

'Well, I come of an old Huguenot family myself!'

'—— . . . ?'

'Ah, my early home. . . . Now, I hear, it's nothing but a weed-crowned ruin.'

The Duchess considered the ivory cat handle of her parasol. 'You wrote to me?' she asked.

'Yes: about the coming court.'

'About it?'

'Every woman has her dream, Duchess! And mine's to be presented.'

'The odd ambition!' the Duchess crooned.

'I admit we live in the valley. Although *I* have a great sense of the hills!' Madame Wetme declared demurely.

'Indeed?'

'My husband, you see . . .'

'. . . . .'

'Ah! well!'

'Of course.'

'If I'm not asked this time, I shall die of grief.'

'Have you made the request before?'

'I have attempted!'

'Well?'

'When the Lord Chamberlain refused me, I shed tears of blood,' Madame Wetme wanly retailed.

'It would have been easier, no doubt, in the late king's time!'

Madame Wetme took a long sighing breath.

'I only once saw him in my life,' she said, 'and then he was standing against a tree, in an attitude offensive to modesty.'

'Tell me . . . as a public man, what has your husband done——'

'His money helped to avert, I always contend, the noisy misery of a War!'

'He's open-handed?'

'Ah . . . as you would find. . . .'

The Duchess considered. 'I *might*,' she said, 'get you cards for a State concert. . . .'

'A State concert, Duchess? That's no good to me!'

'A drawing-room you know is a very dull affair.'

'I will liven it!'

'Or an invitation perhaps to begin with to one of the Embassies—the English for instance might lead. . . .'

'Nowhere . . . ! You can't depend on that: people have asked me to lunch, and left me to pay for them . . . ! There is so much trickery in Society. . . .' Madame Wetme laughed.

The Duchess smiled quizzically. 'I forget if you know the Tolgas,' she said.

'By "name"!'

'The Countess is more about the throne at present than I.'

'Possibly—but oh *you* who do *everything*, Duchess?' Madame Wetme entreated.

'I suppose there are things still one wouldn't do however——!' the Duchess took offence.

'The Tolgas are so hard.'

'You want a misfortune and they're sweet to you. Successful persons they're positively hateful to!'

'These women of the bedchamber are all alike so glorified. You would never credit they were chambermaids at all! I often smile to myself when I see one of them at a *première* at the Opera, gorged with pickings, and think that, most likely, but an hour before she was stumbling along a corridor with a pailful of slops!'

'You're fond of music, Madame?' the Duchess asked.

'It's my joy: I could go again and again to *The Blue Banana*!'

'I've not been.'

'Pom-pom, pompity-pom! We might go one night, perhaps, together.'

'...'

'Doudja Degdeg is always a draw, although naturally now she is getting on!'

'And I fear so must I'—the Duchess rose remarking.

'So soon?'

'I'm only sorry I can't stay longer——!'

'Then it's all decided,' Madame Wetme murmured archly as she pressed the bell.

'Oh, I'd not say that.'

'If I'm not asked, remember, this time, I shall die with grief.'

'To-night the duke and I are dining with the Leucippes, and possibly ...' the Duchess broke off to listen to the orchestra in the café below, which was playing the waltz-air from *Der Rosenkavalier*.

'They play well!' she commented.

'People often tell me so.'

'It must make one restless, dissatisfied, that yearning, yearning music continually at the door!'

Madame Wetme sighed.

'It makes you often long,' she said, 'to begin your life again!'

'Again?'

'Really it's queer I came to yoke myself with a man so little fine. ...'

'Still——! If he's open-handed,' the Duchess murmured as she left the room.

IV

ONE grey, unsettled morning (it was the first of June) the English Colony of Kairoulla* awoke in arms. It usually did when the Embassy entertained. But the omissions of the Ambassador were, as old Mr. Ladboyson, the longest-established member of the colony, declared, 'not to be fathomed,' and many of those overlooked declared they should go all the same. Why should Mrs. Montgomery (who, when all was said and done, was nothing but a governess) be

* The Capital of Pisuerga.

invited and not Mrs. Barleymoon who was 'nothing' (in the most distinguished sense of the word) at all? Mrs. Barleymoon's position, as a captain's widow with means, unquestionably came before Mrs. Montgomery's, who drew a salary and hadn't often an h.

Miss Grizel Hopkins, too—the cousin of an Earl, and Mrs. Bedley, the 'Mother' of the English Colony, both had been ignored. It was true Ann Bedley kept a circulating library and a tea-room combined and gave 'Information' to tourists as well (a thing she had done these forty years), but was that a sufficient reason why she should be totally taboo? *No*; in old Lord Clanlubber's time all had been made welcome and there had been none of these heartburnings at all. Even the Irish coachman of the Archduchess was known to have been received—although it had been outside of course upon the lawn. Only gross carelessness, it was felt, on the part of those attachés could account for the extraordinary present neglect.

'I don't myself mind much,' Mrs. Bedley said, who was seated over a glass of morning milk and 'a plate of fingers' in the *Circulating* end of the shop: 'going out at night upsets me. And the last time Dr. Babcock was in he warned me not.'

'What is the Embassy there for but to be hospitable?' Mrs. Barleymoon demanded from the summit of a ladder, where she was choosing herself a book.

'You're showing your petticoat, dear—excuse me telling you,' Mrs. Bedley observed.

'When will you have something new, Mrs. Bedley?'

'Soon, dear . . . soon.'

'It's always "soon," ' Mrs. Barleymoon complained.

'Are you looking for anything, Bessie, in particular?' a girl, with loose blue eyes that did not seem quite firm in her head, and a literary face, enquired.

'No, only something,' Mrs. Barleymoon replied, 'I've not had before and before and before.'

'By the way, Miss Hopkins,' Mrs. Bedley said, 'I've to fine you for pouring tea over *My Stormy Past*.'

'It was coffee, Mrs. Bedley—not tea.'

'Never mind, dear, what it was, the charge for a stain is the same as you know,' Mrs. Bedley remarked, turning to attend to Mrs. Montgomery who, with his Naughtiness, Prince Olaf, had entered the Library.

'Is it in?' Mrs. Montgomery mysteriously asked.

Mrs. Bedley assumed her glasses.

'*Mmnops*,' she replied, peering with an air of secretiveness in her private drawer where she would sometimes reserve or 'hold back' a volume for a subscriber who happened to be in her special good graces.

'I've often said,' Mrs. Barleymoon from her ladder sarcastically let fall, 'that Mrs. Bedley has her pets!'

'You are all my pets, my dear,' Mrs. Bedley softly cooed.

'Have you read *Men—My Delight*, Bessie?' Miss Hopkins asked, 'by Cora Velasquez.'

'No!'

'It's not perhaps a very . . . It's about two dark, and three fair, men,' she added vaguely.

'Most women's novels seem to run off the rails before they reach the end, and I'm not very fond of them,' Mrs. Barleymoon said.

'And anyway, dear, it's out,' Mrs. Bedley asserted.

'*The Passing of Rose* I read the other day,' Mrs. Montgomery said, 'and *so* enjoyed it.'

'Isn't that one of Ronald Firbank's books?'

'No, dear, I don't think it is. But I never remember an author's name and I don't think it matters!'

'I suppose I'm getting squeamish! But this Ronald Firbank I can't take to at all. *Valmouth!* Was there ever a novel more coarse? I assure you I hadn't gone very far when I had to put it down.'

'It's *out*,' Mrs. Bedley suavely said, 'as well,' she added, 'as the rest of them.'

'I once met him,' Miss Hopkins said, dilating slightly the *retinae* of her eyes. 'He told me writing books was by no means easy!'

Mrs. Barleymoon shrugged.

'Have you nothing more enthralling, Mrs. Bedley,' she persuasively asked, 'tucked away?'

'Try *The Call of the Stage*, dear,' Mrs. Bedley suggested.

'You forget, Mrs. Bedley,' Mrs. Barleymoon replied, regarding solemnly her *crêpe*.

'Or *Mary of the Manse*, dear.'

'I've read *Mary of the Manse* twice, Mrs. Bedley—and I don't propose to read it again.'

'. . . . . ?'

'. . . . . !'

Mrs. Bedley became abstruse.

'It's dreadful how many poets take to drink,' she reflected.

A sentiment to which her subscribers unanimously assented.

'I'm taking *Men are Animals*, by the Hon. Mrs. Victor Smythe, and *What Every Soldier Ought to Know*, Mrs. Bedley,' Miss Hopkins breathed.

'And I *The East is Whispering*,' Mrs. Barleymoon in hopeless tones affirmed.

'Robert Hitchinson! He's a good author.'

'Do you think so? I feel his books are all written in hotels with the bed unmade at the back of the chair.'

'And I dare say you're right, my dear.'

'Well, Mrs. Bedley, I must go—if I want to walk to my husband's grave,' Mrs. Barleymoon declared.

'Poor Bessie Barleymoon,' Mrs. Bedley sighed, after Mrs. Barleymoon and Miss Hopkins had gone: 'I fear she frets!'

'We all have our trials, Mrs. Bedley.'

'And some more than others.'

'Court life, Mrs. Bedley, it's a funny thing.'

'It looks as though we may have an English Queen, Mrs. Montgomery.'

'I don't believe it!'

'Most of the daily prints I see are devoting leaders to the little dog the Princess Elsie sent out the other day.'

'Odious, ill-mannered, horrid little beast. . . .'

'It seems, dear, he ran from room to room looking for her until he came to the prince's door, where he just lay down and whined.'

'And what does that prove, Mrs. Bedley?'

'I really don't know, Mrs. Montgomery. But the press seemed to find it "significant," ' Mrs. Bedley replied as a Nun of the Flaming-Hood with a jolly face all gold with freckles entered the shop.

'Have you *Valmouth* by Ronald Firbank or *Inclinations* by the same author?' she asked.

'Neither, I'm sorry—both are out!'

'Maladetta ✠ ✠✠ ✠ ! But I'll be passing soon again,' the Sister answered as she twinklingly withdrew.

'You'd not think now by the look of her she had been at Girton!' Mrs. Bedley remarked.

'Once a Girton girl always a Girton girl, Mrs. Bedley.'

'It seems a curate drove her to it. . . .'

'I'm scarcely astonished. Looking back, I remember the average curate at home as something between a eunuch and a snigger.'

'Still, dear, I could never renounce my religion. As I said to the dear Chaplain only the other day (while he was having some tea), Oh, if only I were a man, I said! Wouldn't I like to *denounce* the disgraceful goings-on every Sabbath down the street at the church of the Blue Jesus.'

'And I assure you it's positively *nothing*, Mrs. Bedley, at the Jesus, to what it is at the church of St. Mary the Fair! I was at the wedding of one of the equerries lately, and never saw anything like it.'

'It's about time there was an English wedding, in *my* opinion, Mrs. Montgomery!'

'There's not been one in the Colony indeed for some time.'

Mrs. Bedley smiled undaunted.

'I trust I may be spared to dance before long at Dr. and Mrs. Babcock's!' she exclaimed.

'Kindly leave Cunnie out of it, Mrs. Bedley,' Mrs. Montgomery begged.

'So it's Cunnie already you call him!'

'Dr. Cuncliffe and I scarcely meet.'

'People talk of the immense sameness of marriage, Mrs. Montgomery; but all the same, my dear, a widow's not much to be envied.'

'There are times, it's true, Mrs. Bedley, when a woman feels she needs fostering; but it's a feeling she should try to fight against.'

'Ah, my dear, I never could resist *a mon*!' Mrs. Bedley exclaimed.

Mrs. Montgomery sighed.

'Once,' she murmured meditatively, 'men (those procurers of delights) engaged me utterly.... I was their *slave*.... Now ... One does not burn one's fingers twice, Mrs. Bedley.'

Mrs. Bedley grew introspective.

'My poor husband sometimes would be a little frightening, a little fierce ... at night, my dear, especially. Yet how often now I miss him!'

'You're better off as you are, Mrs. Bedley, believe me,' Mrs. Montgomery declared, looking round for his Naughtiness, who was amusing himself on the library-steps.

'You must find him a handful to educate, my dear.'

'It will be a relief *indeed*, Mrs. Bedley, when he goes to Eton!'

'I'm told so long as a boy is grounded ...'

'His English accent is excellent, Mrs. Bedley, and he shows quite a talent for languages,' Mrs. Montgomery assured.

'I'm delighted, I'm sure, to hear it!'

'Well, Mrs. Bedley. I mustn't stand dawdling: I've to 'ave my 'air shampooed and waved for the Embassy party to-night you know!' And taking his Naughtiness by the hand, the royal governess withdrew.

V

AMONG those attached to the Chedorlahomor expedition was a young—if thirty-five be young—eccentric Englishman from Wales, the Hon. 'Eddy' Monteith, a son of Lord Intriguer. Attached first to one thing and then another, without ever being attached to any, his life had been a gentle series of attachments all along. But this new attachment was surely something better than a temporary secretaryship to a minister, or 'aiding' an ungrateful general, or waiting in through draughts (so affecting to the constitution) in the ante-rooms of hard-worked royalty, in the purlieus of Pall Mall. Secured by the courtesy of his ex-chief, Sir Somebody Something, an old varsity friend of his father, the billet of 'surveyor and occasional help' to the Chedorlahomorian excavation party had been waywardly accepted by the Hon. 'Eddy' just as he had been upon the point of attaching himself, to the terror of his relatives and the amusement of his friends, to a monastery of the Jesuit Order as a likely candidate for the cowl.

Indeed he had already gone so far as to sit to an artist for his portrait in the habit of a monk, gazing ardently at what looked to be the Escurial itself, but in reality was nothing other than an 'impression' from the kitchen garden of Intriguer Park. And now this sudden change, this call to the East instead. There had been no time, unfortunately, before setting out to sit again in the picturesque 'sombrero' of an explorer, but a ready camera had performed miracles, and the relatives of the Hon. 'Eddy' were relieved to behold his smiling countenance in the illustrated weeklies, pick in hand, or with one foot resting on his spade while examining a broken jar, with just below the various editors' comments: *To join the Expedition to Chedorlahomor—the Hon. 'Eddy' Monteith, only son of Lord Intriguer*; or, *Off to Chedorlahomor!* or, *Bon Voyage . . . !*

Yes, the temptation of the expedition was not to be withstood, and for vows and renunciations there was always time! . . . And now leaning idly on his window ledge in a spare room of the Embassy, while his man unpacked, he felt, as he surveyed the distant dome of the Blue Jesus above the dwarf-palm trees before the house, half-way to the East already. He was suffering a little in his dignity from the contretemps of his reception; for, having arrived at the Embassy among a jobbed troop of serfs engaged for the night, he had at first been mistaken by Lady Something for one of them. 'The cloak-room will be in the smoking-room!' she had said, and in spite of her laughing excuses and ample apologies he could not easily forget it. What was there in his appearance that could conceivably recall a cloak-room attendant—? *He* who had been assured he had the profile of a 'Rameses' ! And going to a mirror he scanned, with less perhaps than his habitual contentment, the light, liver-tinted hair, grey narrow eyes, hollow cheeks, and pale mouth like a broken moon. He was looking just a little fatigued, he fancied, from his journey, and, really, it was all his hostess deserved, if he didn't go down.

'I have a headache, Mario,' he told his man (a Neapolitan who had been attached to almost as many professions as his master). 'I shall not leave my room! Give me a kimono: I will take a bath.'

Undressing slowly, he felt, as the garments dropped away, he was acting properly in refraining from attending the soirée, and only hoped the lesson would not be 'lost' on Lady Something, who, he feared, must be incurably dense.

Lying amid the dissolving bath crystals while his man-servant deftly bathed him, he fell into a sort of coma, sweet as a religious trance. Beneath the rhythmic sponge, perfumed with *Kiki,* he was St. Sebastian, and as the water became cloudier, and the crystals evaporated amid the steam, he was Teresa . . . and he would have been, most likely, the Blessed Virgin herself but that the bath grew gradually cold.

'You're looking a little pale, sir, about the gills!' the valet, solicitously observed, as he gently dried him.

The Hon. 'Eddy' winced. 'I forbid you ever to employ the word gill, Mario,' he exclaimed. 'It is inharmonious, and in English it jars; whatever it may do in Italian.'

'Overtired, sir, was what I meant to say.'

'Basta!' his master replied, with all the brilliant glibness of the Berlitz-school.

Swathed in towels, it was delicious to relax his powder-blanched limbs upon a comfy couch, while Mario went for dinner: 'I don't care what it is! So long as it isn't—' (naming several dishes that he particularly abhorred, or might be 'better,' perhaps, without)—'And be sure, fool, not to come back without champagne.'

He could not choose but pray that the Ambassadress had nothing whatever to do with the Embassy cellar, for from what he had seen of her already he had only a slight opinion of her discernment.

Really he might have been excused had he taken her to be the cook instead of the social representative of the Court of St. James, and he was unable to repress a caustic smile on recollecting her appearance that afternoon, with her hat awry, crammed with *Maréchal Niel* roses, hot, and decoiffed, flourishing a pair of garden-gauntlets, as she issued her commands. What a contrast to his own Mamma—'so different,' . . . and his thoughts, returned to Intriguer —'dear Intriguer, . . .' that, if only to vex his father's ghost, he would one day turn into a Jesuit college! The Confessional should be fitted in the paternal study, and engravings of the Inquisition, or the sweet faces of Lippi and Fra Angelico, replace the Agrarian certificates and tiresome trophies of the chase; while the crack of the discipline in Lent would echo throughout the house! How 'useful' his friend Robbie Renard would have been. But alas poor Robbie; he had passed through life at a rapid canter, having died at nineteen. . . .

Musingly he lit a cigarette. Through the open window a bee droned in on the blue air of evening. Closing his eyes he fell to considering whether the bee of one country would understand the remarks of that of another. The effect of the soil of a nation, had it consequences upon its flora? Were plants influenced at their roots? People sometimes spoke (and especially ladies) of the language of flowers . . . the pollen therefore of an English rose would probably vary, not inconsiderably, from that of a French, and a bee born and bred at home (at *Intriguer,* for instance) would be at a loss to understand (it clearly followed) the conversation of one born and bred, here, abroad. A bee's idiom varied then, as did man's! And he wondered, this being proved the case, where the best bees' accents were generally acquired. . . .

Opening his eyes, he perceived his former school chum, Lionel

Limpness—Lord Tiredstock's third (and perhaps most gifted) son, who was an honorary attaché at the Embassy—standing over him, his spare figure already arrayed in an evening suit.

'Sorry to hear you're off colour, Old Dear!' he exclaimed, sinking down upon the couch beside his friend.

'I'm only a little shaken, Lionel . . . : have a cigarette.'

'And so you're off to Chedorlahomor, Old Darling?' Lord Tiredstock's third son said.

'I suppose so . . .' the only son of Lord Intriguer replied.

'Well, I wish I was going too!'

'It would be charming, Lionel, of course to have you: but they might appoint you Vice-Consul at Sodom, or something?'

'Why *Vice*? Besides . . . ! There's no consulate there yet,' Lord Tiredstock's third son said, examining the objects upon the portable altar, draped in prelatial purple, of his friend.

'Turn over, Old Dear, while I chastise you!' he exclaimed, waving what looked to be a tortoiseshell lorgnon to which had been attached three threads of 'cerulean' floss silk.

'Put it down, Lionel, and don't be absurd.'

'Over we go. Come on.'

'Really, Lionel.'

'Penitence! To thy knees, Sir!'

And just as it seemed that the only son of Lord Intriguer was to be deprived of all his towels, the Ambassadress mercifully entered.

'*Poor* Mr. Monteith!' she exclaimed in tones of concern, bustling forward with a tablespoon and a bottle containing physic, '*so* unfortunate. . . . Taken ill at the moment you arrive! But Life is like that!'

Clad in the flowing circumstance of an oyster satin ball-dress, and all a-glitter like a Christmas tree (with jewels), her arrival perhaps saved her guest a 'whipping.'

'Had I known, Lady Something, I was going to be ill, I would have gone to the Ritz!' the Hon. 'Eddy' gasped.

'And you'd have been bitten all over!' Lady Something replied.

'Bitten all over?'

'The other evening we were dining at the Palace, and I heard the dear King say—but I oughtn't to talk and excite you——'

'By the way, Lady Something,' Lord Tiredstock's third son asked: 'what is the etiquette for the Queen of Dateland's eunuch?'

'It's all according; but you had better ask Sir Somebody, Mr.

Limpness,' Lady Something replied, glancing with interest at the portable altar.

'I've done so, and he declared he'd be jiggered!'

'I recollect in Pera when we occupied the Porte, they seemed (those of the old Grand Vizier—oh what a good-looking man he was—! such eyes—! and such a *way* with him—! *Despot!* !) only too thankful to crouch in corners.'

'Attention with that castor-oil . . . !'

'It's not castor-oil; it's a little decoction of my own,—aloes, gregory, a dash of liquorice. And the rest is buckthorn!'

'Euh!'

'It's not so bad, though it mayn't be very nice. . . . Toss it off like a brave man, Mr. Monteith (nip his nostrils, Mr. Limpness), and while he takes it, I'll offer a silent prayer for him at that duck of an altar,' and, as good as her word, the Ambassadress made towards it.

'You're altogether too kind,' the Hon. 'Eddy' murmured, seeking refuge in a book—a volume of *Juvenilia* published for him by 'Blackwood of Oxford,' and becoming absorbed in its contents: 'Ah Doris'—'Lines to Doris'—'Lines to Doris: written under the influence of wine, sun and fever'—'Ode to Swinburne'—'Sad Tamarisks'—'Rejection'—'Doigts Obscènes'—'They Call me *Lily* !!' —'Land of Titian! Land of Verdi! O Italy!'—'I Heard the Clock:

> 'I heard the clock strike seven,
> Seven strokes I heard it strike!
> His Lordship's gone to London
> And won't be back to-night.'

He had written it at Intriguer, after a poignant domestic disagreement; his Papa,—the 'his lordship' of the poem—had stayed away, however, considerably longer. . . . And here was a sweet thing suggested by an old Nursery Rhyme, 'Loves, have you Heard?'

> 'Loves, have you heard about the rabbits? ?
> They have such odd fantastic habits. . . .
> Oh, Children . . . ! I daren't disclose to You
> The licentious things *some* rabbits do.'

It had 'come to him' quite suddenly out ferreting one day with the footman. . . .

But a loud crash as the portable altar collapsed beneath the weight of the Ambassadress roused him unpleasantly from his thoughts.

'Horrid dangerous thing!' she exclaimed as Lord Tiredstock's third son assisted her to rise from her 'Silent' prayer: 'I had no idea it wasn't solid! But Life is like that . . .' she added somewhat wildly.

'Pity O my God! Deliver me!' the Hon. 'Eddy' breathed, but the hour of *deliverance* it seemed was not just yet; for at that instant the Hon. Mrs. Chilleywater, the 'literary' wife of the first attaché, thrust her head in at the door.

'How are you?' she asked, 'I thought perhaps I might find *Harold*. . . .'

'He's with Sir Somebody.'

'Such mysteries!' Lady Something said.

'This betrothal of Princess Elsie's is simply wearing him out,' Mrs. Chilleywater declared, sweeping the room with half-closed, expressionless eyes.

'It's a pity you can't pull the strings for us,' Lady Something ventured: 'I was saying so lately to Sir Somebody.'

'I wish I could, dear Lady Something: I wouldn't mind wagering I'd soon bring it off!'

'Have you fixed up Grace Gillstow yet, Mrs. Chilleywater?' Lord Tiredstock's third son asked.

'She shall marry Baldwin: but not before she has been seduced first by Barnaby. . . .'

'What are you talking about?' the Hon. 'Eddy' queried.

'Of Mrs. Chilleywater's forthcoming book.'

'Why should Barnaby get Grace—? Why not Tex?'

But Mrs. Chilleywater refused to enter into reasons.

'She is looking for cowslips,' she said, 'and oh I've such a wonderful description of a field of cowslips. . . . They make quite a darling setting for a powerful scene of lust.'

'So Grace loses her virtue!' Lord Tiredstock's third son exclaimed.

'Even so she's far too good for Baldwin; after the underhand shabby way he behaved to Charlotte, Kate, and Millicent!'

'Life is like that, dear,' the Ambassadress blandly observed.

'It ought not to be, Lady Something!' Mrs. Chilleywater looked vindictive.

Née Victoria Gellybore-Frinton, and the sole heir of Lord Seafairer of Sevenelms, Kent, Mrs. Harold Chilleywater, since her marriage 'for Love,' had developed a disconcerting taste for fiction

—a taste that was regarded at the Foreign Office with disapproving forbearance. . . . So far her efforts (written under her maiden name in full with her husband's as well appended) had been confined to lurid studies of low life (of which she knew nothing at all); but the Hon. Harold Chilleywater had been gently warned that if he was not to remain at Kairoulla until the close of his career the style of his wife must really grow less *virile*.

'I agree with V. G. F.,' the Hon. Lionel Limpness murmured, fondling meditatively his 'Charlie Chaplin' moustache—'Life ought not to be.'

'It's a mistake to bother oneself over matters that can't be remedied.'

Mrs. Chilleywater acquiesced. 'You're right indeed, Lady Something,' she said, 'but I'm so sensitive. . . . I seem to *know* when I talk to a man the colour of his braces . . . I I say to myself: "Yours are violet. . . ." "Yours are blue. . . ." "His are red. . . ." '

'I'll bet you anything, Mrs. Chilleywater, you like, you won't guess what mine are,' the Hon. Lionel Limpness said.

'I should say, Mr. Limpness, that they were *multi-hued*—like Jacob's,' Mrs. Chilleywater replied, as she withdrew her head.

The Ambassadress prepared to follow.

'Come, Mr. Limpness,' she exclaimed, 'we've exhausted the poor fellow quite enough—and besides, here comes his dinner.'

'Open the champagne, Mario,' his master commanded immediately they were alone.

' "Small " beer is all the butler would allow, sir.'

'Damn the b . . . butler!'

'What he calls a *demi-brune*, sir. In Naples we say *spumanti*!'

'To —— with it.'

'Non è tanto amaro, sir, it's more sharp, as you'd say, than bitter. . . .'

' . . . . . . ! ! ! ! ! ! '

And language *unmonastic* far into the night reigned supreme.

Standing beneath the portraits of King Geo and Queen Glory, Lady Something, behind a large sheaf of mauve malmaisons, was growing stiff. Already, for the most part, the guests were welcomed, and it was only the Archduchess now, who as usual was late, that kept their Excellencies lingering at the head of the stairs. Her Majesty Queen Thleeanouhee of the Land of Dates had just arrived, but seemed loath to leave the stairs, while her hostess, whom she addressed affectionately as her *dear gazelle*, remained upon them—

'Let us go away by and by, my dear gazelle,' she exclaimed with a primitive smile, 'and remove our corsets and talk.'

'Unhappily Pisuerga is not the East, ma'am!' Lady Something replied.

'Never mind, my dear; we will introduce this innovation. . . .'

But the arrival of the Archduchess Elizabeth spared the Ambassadress from what might too easily have become an 'incident.'

In the beautiful chandeliered apartments several young couples were pirouetting to the inevitable waltz from the Blue Banana, but most of the guests seemed to prefer exploring the conservatories and winter garden, or elbowing their way into a little room where a new portrait of Princess Elsie had been discreetly placed. . . .

'One feels, of course, there *was* a sitting—; but still, it isn't like her!' those that had seen her said.

'The artist has attributed to her at least the pale spent eyes of her father!' the Duchess of Cavaljos remarked to her niece, who was standing quite silent against a rose-red curtain.

Mademoiselle de Nazianzi made no reply. Attaching not the faintest importance to the rumours afloat, still, she could not but feel, at times, a little heart-shaken. . . .

The duchess plied her fan.

'She will become florid in time like her mother!' she cheerfully predicted, turning away just as the Archduchess herself approached to inspect the painting.

Swathed in furs, on account of a troublesome cough contracted paddling, she seemed nevertheless in charming spirits.

'Have you been to my new *Pipi*?' she asked.

'Not yet——'

'Oh but you must!'

'I'm told it's even finer than the one at the railway station. Ah, from musing too long on that Hellenic frieze, how often I've missed my train!' the Duchess of Cavaljos murmured, with a little fat deep laugh.

'I have a heavenly idea for another—yellow tiles with thistles. . . .'

'Your Royal Highness never repeats herself!'

'Nothing will satisfy me this time,' the Archduchess declared, 'but files of state-documents in all the dear little boxes: in secret, secrets!' she added archly, fixing her eyes on the assembly.

'It's positively pitiable,' the Duchess of Cavaljos commented,

'how the Countess of Tolga is losing her good looks; she has the
air to-night of a tired business-woman!'

'She looks at other women as though she would inhale them,' the
Archduchess answered, throwing back her furs with a gesture
of superb grace, in order to allow her robe to be admired by a lady
who was scribbling busily away behind a door, with little nervous
lifts of the head. For *noblesse oblige*, and the correspondent of the
Jaw-Waw, the illustrious Eva Schnerb, was not to be denied.

'Among the many balls of a brilliant season,' the diarist, with her
accustomed fluency wrote, 'none surpassed that which I witnessed
at the English Embassy last night. I sat in a corner of the Winter
Garden and literally gorged myself upon the display of dazzling
uniforms and jewels. The Ambassadress Lady Something was
looking really regal in dawn-white draperies, holding a bouquet
of the new mauve malmaisons (which are all the vogue just now),
but no one, *I* thought, looked better than the *Archduchess*, etc. . . .
Helping the hostess, I noticed Mrs. Harold Chilleywater, in an
"æsthetic" gown of flame-hued Kanitra silk edged with Armousky
fur (to possess a dear woolly Armousk as a pet as considered *chic*
this season), while over her brain—an intellectual caprice, I wonder?—I saw a tinsel bow. . . . She is a daughter of the fortieth
Lord Seafairer of Sevenelms Park (so famous for its treasures)
and is very artistic and literary, having written several novels of
English life under her maiden name of Victoria Gellybore-Frinton:
—she inherits considerable cleverness *also* from her Mother. Dancing
indefatigably (as she always does!), Miss Ivy Something seemed
to be thoroughly enjoying her Father's ball: I hear on *excellent
authority* there is no foundation in the story of her engagement to a
certain young Englishman, said to be bound ere long for the ruins of
Sodom and Gomorrah. Among the late arrivals were the Duke
and Duchess of Varna—*she* all in golden tissues: they came together
with Madame Wetme, who is one of the new hostesses of the season,
you know, and they say has bought the Duke of Varna's palatial
town-house in Samaden Square——'

'There,' the Archduchess murmured, drawing her wraps about
her with a sneeze: 'she has said quite enough now I think about
my *toilette*!'

But the illustrious Eva was in unusual fettle, and only closed
her notebook towards Dawn, when the nib of her pen caught fire.

VI

AND suddenly the Angel of Death passed by and the brilliant season waned. In the Archduchess's bed-chamber, watching the antics of priests and doctors, he sat there unmoved. Propped high by many bolsters, in a vast blue canopied bed, the Archduchess lay staring laconically at a diminutive model of a flight of steps, leading to what appeared to be intended, perhaps, as a hall of Attent, off which opened quite a lot of little doors, most of which bore the word: 'Engaged.' A doll, with ruddy face, in charge, smiled indolently as she sat feigning knitting, suggesting vague 'fleshly thoughts,' whenever he looked up, in the Archduchess's spiritual adviser.

And the mind of the sinking woman, as her thoughts wandered, appeared to be tinged with 'matter' too: 'I recollect the first time I heard the *Blue Danube* played!' she broke out: 'it was at Schön-brunn—schönes Schönbrunn—My cousin Ludwig of Bavaria came—I wore—the Emperor said——'

'If your imperial highness would swallow this!' Dr. Cuncliffe Babcock started forward with a glass.

'Trinquons, trinquons et vive l'amour! Schneider sang that——'

'If your imperial highness——'

'Ah my dear Vienna. Where's Teddywegs?'

At the Archduchess's little escritoire at the foot of the bed her Dreaminess was making ready a few private telegrams, breaking without undue harshness the melancholy news, 'Poor Lizzie has ceased articulating,' she did not think she could improve on that, and indeed had written it several times in her most temperamental hand, when the Archduchess had started suddenly cackling about Vienna.

'*Ssssh*, Lizzie—I never can write when people talk!'

'I want Teddywegs.'

'The Countess Yvorra took him for a run round the courtyard.'

'I think I must undertake a convenience next for dogs. . . . It is disgraceful they have not got one already, poor creatures,' the Arch-duchess crooned, accepting the proffered glass.

'Yes, yes, dear,' the Queen exclaimed, rising and crossing to the window.

The bitter odour of the oleander flowers outside oppressed the breathless air and filled the room as with a faint funereal music. So still a day. Tending the drooping sun-saturated flowers, a gardener with long ivory arms alone seemed animate.

'Pull up your skirt, Marquise! Pull it up. . . . It's dragging, a little, in the water.'

'*Judica me, Deus,*' in imperious tones the priest by the bedside besought: '*et discerne causam meam de gente non sancta. Parce, Domine. Parce populo tuo. Ne in aeternum irasceris nobis.*'

'A whale! A whale!'

'*Sustinuit anima mea in verbo ejus, speravit anima mea in Domino.*'

'Elsie?' A look of wondrous happiness overspread the Archduchess's face—She was wading—wading again among the irises and rushes; wading, her hand in Princess Elsie's hand, through a glittering golden sea, towards the wide horizon.

The plangent cry of a peacock rose disquietingly from the garden.

'I'm nothing but nerves, doctor,' her Dreaminess lamented, fidgeting with the crucifix that dangled at her neck upon a chain. *Ultra* feminine, she disliked that another—even *in extremis*—should absorb *all* the limelight.

'A change of scene, ma'am, would be probably beneficial,' Dr. Cuncliffe Babcock replied, eyeing askance the Countess of Tolga who unobtrusively entered.

'The couturiers attend your pleasure, ma'am,' in impassive undertones she said, 'to fit your mourning.'

'Oh, tell them the Queen is too tired to try on now,' her Dreaminess answered, repairing in agitation towards a glass.

'They would come here, ma'am,' the Countess said, pointing persuasively to the little ante-room of the Archduchess, where two nuns of the Flaming-Hood were industriously telling their beads.

'—— I don't know why, but this glass refuses to flatter me!'

'*Benedicamus Domino! Ostende nobis Domine misericordiam tuam. Et salutare tuum da nobis!*'

'Well, just a toque,' the Queen sadly assented.

'*Indulgentiam absolutionem et remissionem peccatorum nostrorum tribuat nobis omnipotens et misericors Dominus.*'

'Guess who is at the Ritz, ma'am, this week!' the Countess demurely murmured.

'Who is at the Ritz this week, I can't,' the Queen replied.

'*Nobody!*'

'Why, how so?'

'The Ambassadress of England, it seems, has alarmed the world away. I gather they mean to prosecute!'

The Archduchess sighed.

'I want mauve sweet-peas,' she listlessly said.

'Her spirit soars; her thoughts are in the *Champs-Elysées*,' the Countess exclaimed, withdrawing noiselessly to warn the milliners.

'Or in the garden,' the Queen reflected, returning to the window. And she was standing there, her eyes fixed half wistfully upon the long ivory arms of the kneeling gardener, when the Angel of Death (who had sat unmoved throughout the day) arose.

It was decided to fix a period of mourning of fourteen days for the late Archduchess.

❧ *VII* ❧

SWANS and sunlight. A little fishing-boat with coral sails. A lake all grey and green. Beatitude intense. Consummate calm. It was nice to be at the Summer Palace after all.

'The way the air will catch your cheek and make a rose of it,' the Countess of Tolga breathed. And as none of the company heeded her: 'How sweetly the air takes one's cheek,' she sighed again.

The post-prandial exercise of the members of the Court through the palace grounds was almost an institution.

The first half of the mourning prescribed had as yet not run its course, but the tongues of the Queen's ladies had long since made an end of it.

'I hate dancing with a fat man,' Mademoiselle de Nazianzi was saying: 'for if you dance at all near him, his stomach hits you, while if you pull away, you catch either the scent of his breath or the hair of his beard.'

'But, you innocent baby, *all* big men haven't beards,' Countess Medusa Rappa remarked.

'Haven't they? Never mind. Everything's so beautiful,' the young girl inconsequently exclaimed. 'Look at that Thistle! and that Bee! Oh, you darling!'

'Ah, how one's face unbends in gardens!' the Countess of Tolga said, regarding the scene before her with a far-away pensive glance.

Along the lake's shore, sheltered from the winds by a ring of wooded hills, showed many a proud retreat, mirroring its marble terraces to the waveless waters of the lake.

Beneath a twin-peaked crag (known locally as the White Mountain, whose slopes frequently would burst forth into patches of garlic that from the valley resembled snow) nestled the Villa Clement, rented each season by the Ambassador of the Court of St. James, while half screened by conifers and rhododendrons, and in the lake itself, was St. Helena—the home and place of retirement of a 'fallen' minister of the Crown.

Countess Medusa Rappa cocked her sunshade. 'Whose boat is that,' she asked, 'with the azure oars?'

'It looks nothing but a pea-pod!' the Countess of Tolga declared.

'It belongs to a darling, with delicious lips and eyes like brown chestnuts,' Mademoiselle de Lambèse informed.

'Ah!... Ah!... Ah!... Ah!...' her colleagues crooned.

'A sailor?'

The Queen's maid nodded. 'There's a partner, though,' she added, 'a blue-eyed, gashed-cheeked angel....'

Mademoiselle de Nazianzi looked away.

'I love the lake with the white wandering ships,' she sentimentally stated, descrying in the distance the prince.

It was usually towards this time, the hour of the siesta, that the lovers would meet and taste their happiness, but to-day it seemed ordained otherwise.

Before the heir apparent had determined whether to advance or retreat, his father and mother were upon him, attended by two dowagers newly launched.

'The song of the pilgrim women, how it haunts me,' one of the dowagers was holding forth: 'I could never tire of that beautiful, beautiful music! Never tire of it. Ne-ver....'

'Ta, ta, ta, ta,' the Queen vociferated girlishly, slipping her arm affectionately through that of her son.

'How spent you look, my boy.... Those eyes....'

His Weariness grimaced.

'They've just been rubbing in Elsie!' he said.

'Who?'

'"Vaseline" and "Nanny-goat"!'

'Well?'

'Nothing will shake me.'

'What are your objections?'

'She's so extraordinarily uninteresting!'

'Oh, Yousef!' his mother faltered: '*do you wish to break my heart?*'

'We had always thought you too lacking in initiative,' King William said (tucking a few long hairs back into his nose), 'to marry against our wishes.'

'They say she walks too wonderfully,' the Queen courageously pursued.

'What? Well?'

'Yes.'

'Thank God for it.'

'And can handle a horse as few others can!'

Prince Yousef closed his eyes.

He had not forgotten how as an undergraduate in England he had come upon the princess once while out with the hounds. And it was only by a consummate effort that he was able to efface the sinister impression she had made—her lank hair falling beneath a man's felt-hat, her habit skirt torn to tatters, her full cheeks smeared in blood—the blood, so it seemed, of her 'first' fox.

A shudder seized him.

'No, nothing can possibly shake me,' he murmured again.

With a detached, cold face, the Queen paused to inhale a rose.

(Oh, you gardens of Palaces . . . ! How often have you witnessed agitation and disappointment? You smooth, adorned paths . . . ! How often have you known the extremes of care . . . ?)

'It would be better to do away I think next year with that bed of cinerarias altogether,' the Queen of Pisuerga remarked, 'since persons won't go round it.'

Traversing the flower plat now, with the air of a black-beetle with a purpose, was the Countess Yvorra.

'We had supposed you higher-principled, Countess,' her sovereign admonished.

The Countess slightly flushed.

'I'm looking for groundsel for my birds, Sire,' she said—'for my little dickies!'

'We understand your boudoir is a sort of menagerie,' His Majesty affirmed.

The Countess tittered.

'Animals love me,' she archly professed. 'Birds perch on my breast if only I wave. . . . The other day a sweet red robin came and stayed for hours . . . !'

'The Court looks to you to set a high example,' the Queen declared, focusing quizzically a marble shape of Leda green with moss, for whose time-corroded plinth the late Archduchess's toy-terrier was just then showing a certain contempt.

The Countess's long, slightly pulpy fingers strayed nervously towards the rosary at her thigh.

'With your majesty's consent,' she said, 'I propose a campaign to the Island.'

'What? And beard the Count?'

'The salvation of one so fallen, in my estimation should be worth hereafter (at the present rate of exchange, but the values vary) . . . a Plenary perpetual-indulgence: I therefore,' the Countess said, with an upward fleeting glance (and doubtless guileless of intention of irony), 'feel it my *duty* to do what I can.'

'I trust you will take a bodyguard when you go to St. Helena?'

'And pray tell Count Cabinet from us,' the King looked implacable, 'we forbid him to serenade the Court this year! or to throw himself into the Lake again or to make himself a nuisance!'

'He was over early this morning, Willie,' the Queen retailed: 'I saw him from a window. Fishing, or feigning to! And with white kid gloves, and a red carnation.'

'Let us catch him stepping ashore!' The King displayed displeasure.

'And as usual the same mignon youth had charge of the tiller.'

'I could tell a singular story of that young man,' the Countess said: 'for he was once a choir-boy at the Blue Jesus. But perhaps I would do better to spare your ears. . . .'

'You would do better, a good deal, to spare my cinerarias,' her Dreaminess murmured, sauntering slowly on.

Sun so bright, trees so green, it was a perfect day. Through the glittering fronds of the palms shone the lake like a floor of silver glass strewn with white sails.

'It's odd,' the King observed, giving the dog Teddywegs a sly prod with his cane, 'how he follows Yousef.'

'He seems to know!' the Queen replied.

A remark which so annoyed the Prince that he curtly left the garden.

✿ VIII ✿

B}UT this melancholy period of *crêpe,* a time of idle secrets and
unbosomings, was to prove fatal to the happiness of Mademoiselle de Nazianzi. She now heard she was not the first in the
Prince's life, and that most of the Queen's maids, indeed, had had
identical experiences with her own. She furthermore learned, amid
ripples of laughter, of her lover's relations with the Marquesa Pizzi-
Parma and of his light dealings with the dancer April Flowers, a
negress (to what depths??), at a time when he was enjoying the
waxen favours of the wife of his Magnificence the Master of the
Horse.

Chilled to the point of numbness, the mortified girl had scarcely
winced, and when, on repairing to her room a little later, she had
found his Weariness wandering in the corridor on the chance of a
surreptitious kiss, she had bolted past him without look or word and
sharply closed her door.

The Court had returned to colours when she opened it again, and
such had been the trend of her meditations that her initial steps
were directed, with deliberate austerity, towards the basilica of the
Palace.

Except for the Countess Yvorra, with an *écharpe de décence* drawn
over her hair, there was no one in it.

'I thank Thee God for this *escape,*' she murmured, falling to her
knees before the silver branches of a cross. 'It is terrible; for I did
so love him. . . . .
. . . .
. . . .
. . . . .and oh how could he ever, with *a
negress?* . . . .
. . . .
. . . . Pho . . . .
. . . . I fear this complete upset has
considerably aged me. . . . .
. . . . .But to Thee I cling . . . .
. . . .
. . . .
Preserve me at all times from the toils of the wicked, and forgive
him, as *I* hope to forgive him soon.' Then kindling several candles,

with a lingering hand, she shaped her course towards the Kennels, called Teddywegs to her, and started, with an aching heart, for a walk.

It was a day of heavy somnolence. Skirting the Rosery, where gardeners with their slowly moving rakes were tending the sandy paths, she chose a neglected footway that descended towards the lake. Indifferent to the vivacity of Teddywegs, who would race on a little before her, then wait with leonine accouchments of head until she had almost reached him, when he would prick an ear and spring forward with a yap of exhortation, she proceeded leisurely and with many a pause, wrapped in her own mournful thoughts.

Alack! Among the court circle there was no one to whom in her disillusion she could look for solace, and her spirit yearned for Sister Ursula and the Convent of the Flaming-Hood.

Wending her way amid the tall trees, she felt she had never cared for Yousef as she had for Ursula ... and broodingly, in order to ease her heart, she began comparing the two together as she walked along.

After all, what had he ever said that was not either commonplace or foolish? Whereas Sister Ursula's talk was invariably pointed, and often indeed so delicately that words seemed almost too crude a medium to convey her ethereal meanings, and she would move her evocative hands, and flash her aura, and it was no fault of hers if you hadn't a peep of the beyond. And the infinite tenderness of her last caress! Yousef's lips had seldom conveyed to hers the spell of Ursula's; and once indeed lately, when he had kissed her, there had been an unsavoury aroma of tobacco and *charcuterie*, which, to deal with, had required both tact and courage. ... Ah dear Hood! What harmony life had held within. Unscrupulous and deceiving men might lurk around its doors (they often did) coveting the chaste, but Old Jane, the porteress, would open to no man beyond the merest crack. And how right were the nuns in their mistrust of man! Sister Ursula one day had declared, in uplifted mood, that 'marriage was obscene.' Was it—? ... ? ? ... Perhaps it might be—! How appalling if it was!

She had reached the lake.

Beneath a sky as white as platinum it lay, pearly, dove-like, scintillating capriciously where a heat-shrouded sun kindled its torpid waters into fleeting diamonds. A convulsive breeze strayed gratefully from the opposite shore, descending from the hills that rose up all veiled, and without detail, against the brilliant whiteness of the morning.

Sinking down upon the shingle by an upturned boat, she heaved a brief sigh, and drawing from her vanity-case the last epistles of the Prince, began methodically to arrange them in their proper sequence.

(1) 'What is the matter with my Dearest Girl?'
(2) 'My own tender little Lita, I do not understand—'
(3) 'Darling, what's this—?'
(4) 'Beloved one, I swear—'
(5) 'Your cruel silence—'

If published in a dainty brochure format about the time of his Coronation they ought to realise no contemptible sum and the proceeds might go to charity, she reflected, thrusting them back again carefully into the bag.

Then, finding the shingle too hard through her thin gown to remain seated long, she got up, and ran a mournful race with Teddywegs along the shore.

Not far along the lake was the 'village,' with the Hôtel d'Angleterre et du Lac, its stucco, belettered walls professing: 'Garages, Afternoon Tea, Modern Comfort!' Flitting by this and the unpretentious pier (where long, blonde fishing-nets lay drying in the sun), it was a relief to reach the remoter plage beyond.

Along the banks stretched vast brown carpets of corn and rye, broken by an occasional olive-garth, beneath whose sparse shade the heavy-eyed oxen blinked and whisked their tails, under the attacks of the water-gnats that were swarming around.

Musing on Negresses—and Can-Can dancers in particular—she strolled along a strand all littered with shells and little jewel-like stones.

The sun shone down more fiercely now, and soon, for freshness sake, she was obliged to take to the fields.

Passing among the silver drooping olives, relieved here and there by a stone-pine, or slender cypress-tree eternally green, she sauntered on, often lured aside to pluck the radiant wild-flowers by the way. On the banks the pinkest cyclamens were in bloom, and cornflowers of the hue of paradise, and fine-stemmed poppies flecked with pink.

'Pho! A Negress . . .' she murmured, following the flight of some waterfowl towards the opposite shore.

The mists had fallen from the hills, revealing old woods wrapped in the blue doom of summer.

Beyond those glowing heights, towards this hour, the nuns, each in her cool, shuttered cell, would be immersed in noontide prayer.

'Ursula—for thee!' she sighed, proffering her bouquet in the direction of the town.

A loud splash . . . the sight of a pair of delicate legs (mocking the Law's requirements under the Modesty Act as relating to bathers). . . . Mademoiselle de Nazianzi turned and fled. She had recognised *the Prince.**

❦ IX ❦

AND in this difficult time of spiritual distress, made more trying perhaps because of the blazing midsummer days and long, pent feverish nights, Mademoiselle de Nazianzi turned in her tribulation towards religion.

The Ecclesiastical set at Court, composed of some six, or so, ex-Circes, under the command of the Countess Yvorra, were only too ready to welcome her, and invitations to meet Monsignor this or 'Father' that, who constantly were being *coaxed* from their musty sacristies and wan-faced acolytes in the capital, in order that they might officiate at Masses, Confessions and Breakfast-parties *à la fourchette*, were lavished daily upon the bewildered girl.

Messages, and hasty informal lightly-pencilled notes, too, would frequently reach her; such as: 'I shall be pouring out cocoa after dinner in bed. Bring your biscuits and join me!' . . . or a rat-a-tat from a round-eyed page and: 'The Countess's comp'ts and she'd take it a Favour if you can make a "Station" with her in chapel later on,' or: 'The Marchioness will be birched to-morrow, and *not* to-day.'

Oh, the charm, the flavour of the religious world! Where match it for interest or variety!

An emotion approaching sympathy had arisen, perhaps a trifle incongruously, between the injured girl and the Countess Yvorra, and before long, to the amusement of the sceptical element of the Court, the Countess and her Confessor, Father Nostradamus, might often be observed in her society.

* The recollection of this was never quite forgotten.

'I need a cage-companion, Father, for my little bird,' the Countess one evening said, as they were ambling, all the three of them, before Office up and down the perfectly tended paths: 'ought it to be of the same species and sex, or does it matter? For as I said to myself just now (while listening to a thrush), *All* birds are His creatures.'

The priest discreetly coughed.

'Your question requires reflection,' he said. 'What is the bird?'

'A hen canary!—and with a voice, Father! Talk of soul! !'

'H—m . . . a thrush and a canary, I would not myself advise.'

Mademoiselle de Nazianzi tittered.

'Why not let it go?' she asked, turning her eyes towards the window-panes of the palace, that glanced like rows of beaten-gold in the evening sun.

'A hawk might peck it!' the Countess returned, looking up as if for one into a sky as imaginative and as dazzling as Shelley's poetry.

'Even the Court,' Father Nostradamus ejaculated wryly, 'will peck at times.'

The Countess's shoulder-blades stiffened.

'After over thirty years,' she said, 'I find Court-life *pathetic*. . . .'

'Pathetic?'

'Tragically pathetic. . . .'

Mademoiselle de Nazianzi considered wistfully the wayward outline of the hills.

'I would like to escape from it all for a while,' she said, 'and travel.'

'I must hunt you out a pamphlet, by and by, dear child, on the "Dangers of Wanderlust." '

'The Great Wall of China and the Bay of Naples! It seems so frightful never to have seen them!'

'I have never seen the Great Wall, either,' the Countess said, 'and I don't suppose, my dear, I ever shall; though I once did spend a fortnight in Italy.'

'Tell me about it.'

The Countess became reminiscent.

'In Venice,' she said, 'the indecent movements of the gondolieri quite affected my health, and, in consequence, I fell a prey to a sharp nervous fever. My temperature rose and it rose, ah, yes . . . until I became quite ill. At last I said to my maid (she was an English girl from Wales, and almost equally as sensitive as me): "Pack. . . . Away!" And we left in haste for Florence. Ah, and Florence, too, I regret to

say I found very far from what it ought to have been! ! ! I had
a window giving on the Arno, and so I could *observe*. . . . I used to
see some curious sights! I would not care to scathe your ears, my
Innocent, by an inventory of one half of the wantonness that went
on; enough to say the tone of the place forced me to fly to Rome,
where beneath the shadow of dear St. Peter's I grew gradually less
distressed.'

'Still, I should like, all the same, to travel!' Mademoiselle de
Nazianzi exclaimed, with a sad little snatch of a smile.

'We will ask the opinion of Father Geordie Picpus when he comes
again.'

'It would be more fitting,' Father Nostradamus murmured
(professional rivalry leaping to his eye), 'if Father Picpus kept himself free of the limelight a trifle more!'

'Often I fear our committees would be corvés without him. . . .'

'Tchut.'

'He is very popular . . . too popular, perhaps . . .' the Countess
admitted. 'I remember on one occasion, in the Blue Jesus, witnessing
the Duchess of Quaranta and Madame Ferdinand Fishbacher fight
like wild cats as to which should gain his ear ·· (any girl might envy
Father Geordie his ear)—at Confession next. The odds seemed fairly
equal until the Duchess gave the Fishbacher-woman such a violent
push—(well down from behind, in the crick of the joints)—that
she overturned the confessional box, with Father Picpus within:
and when we scared ladies, standing by, had succeeded in dragging
him out, he was too shaken, naturally as you can gather, to absolve
anyone else *that* day.'

'He has been the object of so many unseemly incidents that one
can scarcely recall them all,' Father Nostradamus exclaimed,
stooping to pick up a dropped pocket-handkerchief with 'remem-
brance' knots tied to three of the corners.

'Alas. . . . Court life is not uplifting,' the Countess said again,
contemplating her muff of *self-made* lace, with a half-vexed forehead.
What that muff contained was a constant problem for conjecture;
but it was believed by more than one of the maids-in-waiting to
harbour 'goody' books and martyrs' bones.

'By generous deeds and Brotherly love,' Father Nostradamus
exclaimed, 'we should endeavour to rise above it!'

With the deftness of a virtuoso, the Countess seized, and crushed
with her muff, a pale-winged passing gnat.

'Before Life,' she murmured, 'that saddest thing of all, was thrust upon us, I believe I was an angel. . . .'

Father Nostradamus passed a musing hand across his brow.

'It may be,' he replied; 'and it very well may be,' he went on, 'that our ante-nativity was a little more brilliant, a little more *h—m* . . .; and there is nothing unorthodox in thinking so.'

'Oh what did I do then to lose my wings? ? What did I ever say to Them? ! Father, Father. How did I annoy God? Why did He put me here?'

'My dear child, you ask me things I do not know; but it may be you were the instrument appointed above to lead back to Him our neighbour yonder,' Father Nostradamus answered, pointing with his breviary in the direction of St. Helena.

'Never speak to me of that wretched old man.'

For despite the ablest tactics, the most diplomatic angling, Count Cabinet had refused to rally.

'We followed the sails of your skiff to-day,' Mademoiselle de Nazianzi sighed, 'until the hazes hid them!'

'I had a lilac passage.'

'You delivered the books?'

The Countess shrugged.

'I shall never forget this afternoon,' she said. 'He was sitting in the window over a decanter of wine when I floated down upon him; but no sooner did he see me than he gave a sound like a bleat of a goat, and disappeared: I was determined however to call! There is no bell to the villa, but two bronze door-knockers, well out of reach, are attached to the front-door. These with the ferrule of my parasol I tossed and I rattled, until an adolescent, with bougainvillæa at his ear, came and looked out with an insolent grin, and I recognised Peter Passer from the Blue Jesus grown quite fat.'

'Eh mon Dieu!' Father Nostradamus half audibly sighed.

'Eh mon Dieu . . .' Mademoiselle de Nazianzi echoed, her gaze roving over the palace, whose long window-panes in the setting sun gleamed like sumptuous tissues.

'So that,' the Countess added, 'I hardly propose to venture again.'

'What a site for a Calvary!' Father Nostradamus replied, indicating with a detached and pensive air the cleft in the White Mountain's distant peaks.

'I adore the light the hills take on when the sun drops down,' Mademoiselle de Nazianzi declared.

'It must be close on *Salut*. . . .'

It was beneath the dark colonnades by the Court Chapel door that they received the news from the lips of a pair of vivacious dowagers that the Prince was to leave the Summer Palace on the morrow to attend 'the Manœuvres,' after which it was expected his Royal Highness would proceed '*to England*.'

❧ X ❧

AND meanwhile the representatives of the Court of St. James were enjoying the revivifying country air and outdoor life of the Villa Clement. It was almost exquisite how rapidly the casual mode of existence adopted during the summer villeggiatura by their Excellencies drew themselves and their personnel together, until soon they were as united and as *sans gêne* as the proverbial family party. No mother, in the 'acclimatisation' period, could have dosed her offspring more assiduously than did her Excellency the attachés in her charge; flavouring her little inventions frequently with rum or gin until they resembled cocktails. But it was Sir Somebody himself if anyone that required a tonic. Lady Something's pending litigation, involving as it did the crown, was fretting the Ambassador more than he cared to admit, and the Hon. Mrs. Chilleywater, ever alert, told 'Harold' that the injudicious chatter of the Ambassadress (who even now, notwithstanding her writ, would say to every other visitor that came to the villa: 'Have you heard about the Ritz? The other night we were dining at the Palace, and I heard the King,' *etc*.) was wearing their old Chief out.

And so through the agreeable vacation life there twitched the grim vein of tension.

Disturbed one day by her daughter's persistent trilling of the latest coster song *When I sees 'im I topple giddy*, Lady Something gathered up her morning letters and stepped out upon the lawn.

Oh so formal, oh so slender towered the cypress-trees against the rose-farded hills and diamantine waters of the lake. The first hint of autumn was in the air; and over the gravel paths, and in the basins of the fountains, a few shed leaves lay hectically strewn already.

Besides an under-stamped missive, with a foreign postmark, from Her Majesty the Queen of the Land of Dates beginning 'My dear Gazel,' there was a line from the eloquent and moderately victorious young barrister, engaged in the approaching suit with the Ritz: He had spared himself no pains, he assured his client, in preparing the defence, which was, he said, to be *the respectability of Claridge's*.

'Why bring in Claridge's? . . . ?' the Ambassadress murmured, prodding with the tip of her shoe a decaying tortoiseshell leaf; 'but anyway,' she reflected, 'I'm glad the proceedings fall in winter, as I always look well in furs.'

And mentally she was wrapped in leopard-skins and gazing round the crowded court saluting with a bunch of violets an acquaintance here and there, when her eyes fell on Mrs. Chilleywater seated in the act of composition beneath a cedar-tree.

Mrs. Chilleywater extended a painful smile of welcome which revealed her pointed teeth and pale-hued gums, repressing, simultaneously, an almost irresistible inclination to murder.

'What! . . . Another writ?' she suavely asked.

'No, dear; but these legal men *will* write. . . .'

'I love your defender. He has an air of d'Alembert, sympathetic soul.'

'He proposes pleading Claridge's.'

'Claridge's?'

'Its respectability.'

'Are hotels ever respectable?—I ask you. Though, possibly, the horridest are.'

'Aren't they all horrid!'

'*Natürlich:* but do you know those cheap hotels where the guests are treated like naughty children?'

'No. I must confess I don't,' the Ambassadress laughed.

'Ah, there you are. . . .'

Lady Something considered a moment a distant gardener employed in tying chrysanthemum blooms to little sticks.

'I'm bothered about a cook,' she said.

'And I, about a maid! I dismissed ffoliott this morning—well I simply *had* to—for a figure salient.'

'So awkward out here to replace anyone; I'm sure I don't know . . .' the Ambassadress replied, her eyes hovering tragically over the pantaloons strained to splitting point of the stooping gardener.

'It's a pretty prospect. . . .'

'Life is a compound!' Lady Something defined it at last.

Mrs. Chilleywater turned surprised. 'Not even Socrates,' she declared, 'said anything truer than that.'

'A compound!' Lady Something twittered again.

'I should like to put that into the lips of Delitsiosa.'

'Who's Delitsiosa?' the Ambassadress asked as a smothered laugh broke out beside her.

Mrs. Chilleywater looked up.

'I'd forgotten you were there. Strange thing among the cedar-boughs,' she said.

The Hon. Lionel Limpness tossed a slippered foot flexibly from his hammock.

'You may well ask "who's Delitsiosa"!' he exclaimed.

'She is my new heroine,' Mrs. Chilleywater replied, after a few quick little clutches at her hair.

'I trust you won't treat her, dear, quite so shamefully as your last.'

The Authoress tittered.

'Delitsiosa is the wife of Marsden Didcote,' she said, 'the manager of a pawnshop in the district of Maida Vale, and in the novel he seduces an innocent seamstress, Iris Drummond, who comes in one day to redeem her petticoat (and really I don't know how I did succeed in drawing the portrait of a little fool!) . . . and when Delitsiosa, her suspicions aroused, can no longer doubt or ignore her husband's intimacy with Iris, already engaged to a lusty young farmer in Kent (some boy)—she decides to yield herself to the entreaties of her brother-in-law Percy, a junior partner in the firm, which brings about the great tussle between the two brothers on the edge of the Kentish cliffs. Iris and Delitsiosa—Iris is anticipating a babelet soon—are watching them from a cornfield, where they're boiling a kettle for afternoon tea; and oh, I've such a darling description of a cornfield. I make you *feel* England!'

'No, really, my dear,' Lady Something exclaimed.

'Harold pretends it would be wonderful arranged as an Opera . . . with duos and things and a *Liebestod* for Delitzi towards the close.'

'No, no,' Mr. Limpness protested. 'What would become of our modern fiction at all if Victoria Gellybore-Frinton gave herself up to the stage?'

'That's quite true, strange thing among the cedar-boughs,' Mrs.

Chilleywater returned, fingering the floating strings of the bandelette at her brow. 'It's lamentable; yet who is there doing anything at present for English Letters . . . ? Who among us to-day,' she went on, peering up at him, 'is carrying on the tradition of Fielding? Who really cares? I know *I* do what I can . . . and there's Madam Adrian Bloater, of course. But I can think of no one else;—we two.'

Mr. Limpness rocked, critically.

'I can't bear Bloater's books,' he demurred.

'To be frank, neither can I. I'm very fond of Lilian Bloater, I adore her *weltbürgerliche* nature, but I feel like you about her books; I *cannot* read them. If only she would forget Adrian; but she will thrust him headlong into all her work. Have *I* ever drawn Harold? No. (Although many of the public seem to think so!) And please heaven, however *great* my provocation at times may be, I never shall!'

'And there I think you're right,' the Ambassadress answered, frowning a little as the refrain that her daughter was singing caught her ear.

> 'And when I sees 'im
> My heart goes BOOM! . . .
> And I topple over;
> I topple over, over, over,
> All for Love!'

'I dreamt last night my child was on the Halls.'

'There's no doubt she'd dearly like to be.'

'Her Father would never hear of it!'

> 'And when she sees me,
> Oh when she sees me—
> (*The voice slightly false was Harold's*)
> Her heart goes BOOM! . . .
> And she topples over;
> She topples over, over, over,
> All for Love!'

'There; they've routed Sir Somebody. . . .'

'And when anything vexes him,' Lady Something murmured, appraising the Ambassador's approaching form with a glassy eye, 'he always, you know, blames me!'

Shorn of the sombre, betailed attire, so indispensable for the town-duties of a functionary, Sir Somebody, while rusticating, usually wore a white twill jacket and black multi-pleated pantaloons; while for headgear he would favour a Mexican sugar-loaf, or green-draped puggaree. 'He looks half-Irish,' Lady Something would sometimes say.

'Infernal Bedlam,' he broke out: 'the house is sheer pande-monium.'

'I found it so too, dear,' Lady Something agreed; 'and so,' she added, removing a fallen tree-bug tranquilly from her hair, 'I've been digesting my letters out here upon the lawn.'

'And no doubt,' Sir Somebody murmured, fixing the placid person of his wife with a keen psychological glance, 'you succeed my dear, in digesting them?'

'Why shouldn't I?'

'. . .' the Ambassador displayed discretion.

'We're asked to a Lion hunt in the Land of Dates; quite an *entreating* invitation from the dear Queen,—really most pressing and affectionate,—but Princess Elsie's nuptial negotiations and this pending Procès with the Ritz may tie us here for some time.'

'Ah, Rosa.'

'Why these constant moans? . . . ? A clairvoyant once told me I'd "the bump of Litigation"—a *cause célèbre* unmistakably defined; so it's as well, on the whole, to have it over.'

'And quite probably; had your statement been correct——'

The Ambassadress gently glowed.

'I'm told it's simply swarming!' she impenitently said.

'Oh, Rosa, Rosa. . . .'

'And if you doubt it at all, here is an account direct from the Ritz itself,' her Excellency replied, singling out a letter from among the rest. 'It is from dear old General Sir Trotter-Stormer. He says: "I am the only guest here. I must say, however, the attendance is beyond all praise, more *soigné* and better than I've ever known it to be, but after what you told me, dear friend, I feel *distinctly uncomfortable* when the hour for bye-bye comes!"'

'Pish; what evidence, pray, is that?'

'I regard it as of the very first importance! Sir Trotter admits—a distinguished soldier admits, his uneasiness; and who knows—he is so brave about concealing his woes—his two wives left him!—what he may not have patiently and stoically endured?'

'Less I am sure, my dear, than I of late in listening sometimes to you.'

'I will write, I think, and press him for a more detailed report. . . .' The Ambassador turned away.

'She should no more be trusted with ink than a child with fire-arms!' he declared, addressing himself with studious indirectness to a garden-snail.

Lady Something blinked.

'Life is a compound,' she murmured again.

'Particularly with women!' the Authoress agreed.

'Ah, well,' the Ambassadress majestically rose, 'I must be off and issue household orders; although I derive hardly my usual amount of enjoyment at present, I regret to say, from my morning consultations with the cook. . . .'

XI

IT had been once the whim and was now the felicitous habit of the Countess of Tolga to present Count Cabinet annually with a bouquet of flowers. It was as if Venus Anadyomene herself, standing* on a shell and wafted by all the piquant whispers of the town and court, would intrude upon the flattered exile (with her well-wired orchids, and malicious, soulless laughter), to awaken delicate, pagan images of a trecento, Tuscan Greece.

But upon this occasion desirous of introducing some few features, the Countess decided on presenting the fallen senator with a pannier of well-grown, early pears, a small 'heath' and the Erotic Poems, bound in half calf with tasteful tooling, of a Schoolboy Poet, cherishable chiefly perhaps for the vignette frontispiece of the author. Moreover, acting on an impulse she was never able afterwards to explain, she had invited Mademoiselle Olga Blumenghast to accompany her.

Never had summer shown a day more propitiously clement than the afternoon in mid-autumn they prepared to set out.

Fond of a compliment, when not too frankly racy,† and knowing

---

* *Vide* Botticelli.

† In Pisuerga compliments are apt to rival in this respect those of the ardent South.

how susceptible the exile was to clothes, the Countess had arrayed herself in a winter gown of kingfisher-tinted silk turning to turquoise, and stencilled in purple at the arms and neck with a crisp Greek-key design; while a voluminous violet veil, depending behind her to a point, half concealed a tricorne turquoise toque from which arose a shaded lilac aigrette branching several ways.

'I shall probably die with heat, and of course it's most unsuitable; but poor old man, he likes to recall the Capital!' the Countess panted, as, nursing heath, poems and pears, she followed Mademoiselle Olga Blumenghast blindly towards the shore.

Oars, and swaying drying nets, a skyline lost in sun, a few moored craft beneath the little rickety wooden pier awaiting choice:—'The boatmen, to-day, darling, seem all so ugly; let's take a sailing-boat and go alone!'

'I suppose there's no danger, darling?' the Countess replied, and scarcely had she time to make any slight objection when the owner of a steady wide-bottomed boat—the *Calypso*—was helping them to embark.

The Island of St. Helena, situated towards the lake's bourne, lay distant some two miles or more, and within a short way of the open sea.

With sails distended to a languid breeze the shore eventually was left behind; and the demoiselle cranes, in mid-lake, were able to observe there were two court dames among them.

'Although he's dark, Vi,' Mademoiselle Olga Blumenghast presently exclaimed, dropping her cheek to a frail hand upon the tiller, 'although he's dark, it's odd how he gives one the impression somehow of perfect fairness!'

'Who's that, darling?' the Countess murmured, appraising with fine eyes, faintly weary, the orchid-like style of beauty of her friend.

'Ann-Jules, of course.'

'I begin to wish, do you know, I'd brought pomegranates, and worn something else!'

'What are those big burley-worleys?'

'Pears. . . .'

'Give me one.'

'Catch, then.'

'Not that I could bear to be married; especially like *you*, Vi!'

'A marriage like ours, dear, was so utterly unworthwhile. . . .'

'I'm not sure, dear, that I comprehend altogether?'

'Seagulls' wings as they fan one's face. . . .'

'It's vile and wrong to shoot them: but oh! how I wish your happiness depended, even ever so little, on me.'

The Countess averted her eyes.

Waterfowl, like sadness passing, hovered and soared overhead, casting their dark, fleeting shadows to the white, drowned clouds, in the receptive waters of the lake.

'I begin to wish I'd brought grapes,' she breathed.

'Heavy stodgy pears. So do I.'

'Or a few special peaches,' the Countess murmured, taking up the volume of verse beside her, with a little, mirthless, half-hysterical laugh.

To a Faithless Friend.

To V.O.I. and S.C.P.

For Stephen.

When the Dormitory Lamp burns Low.

Her gaze travelled over the Index.

'Read something, dear,' Mademoiselle Blumenghast begged, toying with the red-shaded flower in her burnished curls.

'Gladly; but oh, Olga!' the Countess crooned.

'What!'

'Where's the wind?'

It had gone.

'We must row.'

There was nothing for it.

To gain the long, white breakwater, with the immemorial willow-tree at its end, that was the most salient feature of the island's approach, required, nevertheless, resolution.

'It's so far, dear,' the Countess kept on saying. 'I had no idea how far it was! Had you any conception at all it was so far?'

'Let us await the wind, then. It's bound to rally.'

But no air swelled the sun-bleached sails, or disturbed the pearly patine of the paralysed waters.

'I shall never get this peace, I only realise it *exists* . . .' the Countess murmured with dream-glazed eyes.

'It's astonishing . . . the stillness,' Mademoiselle Blumenghast murmured, with a faint tremor, peering round towards the shore.

On the banks young censia-trees raised their boughs like strong white whips towards the mountains, upon whose loftier heights lay, here and there, a little stray patch of snow.

'Come hither, ye winds, come hither!' she softly called.

'Oh, Olga! Do we really want it?' the Countess in agitation asked, discarding her hat and veil with a long, sighing breath.

'I don't know, dear; no; not, not much.'

'Nor I,—at all.'

'Let us be patient then.'

'It's all so beautiful it makes one want to cry.'

'Yes; it makes one want to cry,' Mademoiselle Blumenghast murmured, with a laugh that in brilliance vied with the October sun.

'Olga!'

'So,' as the *Calypso* lurched: 'lend me your hanky, dearest.'

'*Olga*—?—? Thou fragile, and exquisite thing!'

Meanwhile Count Cabinet was seated with rod-and-line at an open window, idly ogling a swan. Owing to the reluctance of tradespeople to call for orders, the banished statesman was often obliged to supplement the larder himself. But hardly had he been angling ten minutes to-day when lo! a distinguished mauvish fish with vivid scarlet spots. Pondering on the mysteries of the deep, and of the subtle variety there is in Nature, the veteran ex-minister lit a cigar. Among the more orthodox types that stocked the lake, such as carp, cod, tench, eels, sprats, shrimps, etc., this exceptional fish must have known its trials and persecutions, its hours of superior difficulty ... and the Count with a stoic smile recalled his own. Musing on the advantages and disadvantages of personality, of 'party' viewpoints, and of morals in general, the Count was soon too self-absorbed to observe the approach of his 'useful' secretary and amanuensis, Peter Passer.

More valet perhaps than secretary, and more errand-boy than either, the former chorister of the Blue Jesus had followed the fallen statesman into exile at a moment when the Authorities of Pisuerga were making minute enquiries for sundry missing articles,* from the *Trésor* of the Cathedral, and since the strain of constant choir-practice is apt to be injurious for a youngster suffering from a delicate chest, the adolescent had been willing enough to accept, for a time at least, a situation in the country.

---

* The missing articles were:

    5 chasubles.

    A relic-casket in lapis and diamonds, containing the Tongue of St. Thelma.

    4¾ yards of black lace, said to have 'belonged to' the Madonna.

'Oh, sir,' he exclaimed, and almost in his excitement forgetting altogether the insidious, lisping tones he preferred as a rule to employ: 'oh, sir, here comes that old piece of rubbish again with a fresh pack of tracts.'

'Collect yourself, Peter, pray do: what, lose our heads for a visit?' the Count said, getting up and going to a glass.

'I've noticed, sir, it's impossible to live on an island long without feeling its effects; you *can't* escape being insular!'

'Or insolent.'

'Insular, sir!'

'No matter much, but if it's the Countess Yvorra you might show her round the garden this time, perhaps, for a change,' the Count replied, adjusting a demure-looking fly, of indeterminate sex, to his line.

And brooding on life and baits, and what *A* will come for while *B* won't, the Count's thoughts grew almost humorous as the afternoon wore on.

Evening was approaching when, weary of the airs of a common carp, he drew in, at length, his tackle.

Like a shawl of turquoise silk the lake seemed to vie, in serenity and radiance, with the bluest day in June, and it was no surprise, on descending presently for a restricted ramble—(the island, in all, amounted to scarcely one acre)—to descry the invaluable Peter enjoying a pleasant swim.

When not boating or reading or feeding his swans, to watch Peter's fancy-diving off the terrace end was perhaps the favourite pastime of the veteran *viveur*: to behold the lad trip along the riven breakwater, as naked as a statue, shoot out his arms and spring, the *Flying-head-leap* or the *Backsadilla*, was a beautiful sight, looking up now and again—but more often now—from a volume of old Greek verse; while to hear him warbling in the water with his clear alto voice—of Kyries and Anthems he knew no end—would often stir the old man to the point of tears. Frequently the swans themselves would paddle up to listen, expressing by the charmed or rapturous motions of their necks (recalling to the exile the ecstasies of certain musical or 'artistic' dames at Concert-halls, or the Opera House, long ago) their mute appreciation, their touched delight. . . .

'Old goody Two-shoes never came, sir,' Peter archly lisped, admiring his adventurous shadow upon the breakwater wall.

'How is that?'

'Becalmed, sir,' Peter answered, culling languidly a small, nodding rose that was clinging to the wall.

> 'Oh becalmed is my soul,
> I rejoice in the Lord!'

At one extremity of the garden stood the Observatory, and after duly appraising various of Peter's neatest feats the Count strolled away towards it. But before he could reach the Observatory he had first to pass his swans.

They lived, with an ancient water-wheel, beneath a cupola of sun-glazed tiles, sheltered, partially, from the lake by a hedge of towering red geraniums, and the Count seldom wearied of watching these strangely gorgeous creatures as they sailed out and in through the sanguine-hued flowers. A few, with their heads sunk back beneath their wings, had retired for the night already; nevertheless, the Count paused to shake a finger at one somnolent bird, in disfavour for pecking Peter. 'Jealous, doubtless of the lad's grace,' he mused, fumbling with the key of the Observatory door.

The unrivalled instrument that the Observatory contained, whose intricate lenses were capable of drawing even the remote Summer Palace to within an appreciable range, was, like most instruments of merit, sensitive to the manner of its manipulation; and fearing lest the inexpert tampering of a homesick housekeeper (her native village was visible in clear weather, with the aid of a glass) should break or injure the delicate lenses, the Count kept the Observatory usually under key.

But the inclination to focus the mundane and embittered features of the fanatic Countess, as she lectured her boatmen for forgetting their oars, or, being considerably superstitious, to count the moles on their united faces as an esoteric clue to the Autumn Lottery, waned a little before the mystery of the descending night.

Beneath a changing tide of deepening shadow, the lifeless valleys were mirroring to the lake the sombreness of dusk. Across the blue forlornness of the water, a swan, here and there, appeared quite violet, while coiffed in swift, clinging, golden clouds the loftiest hills alone retained the sun.

A faint nocturnal breeze, arising simultaneously with the Angelus-bell, seemed likely to relieve, at the moon's advent, the trials to her patience of the Countess Yvorra: 'who must be cursing,' the Count reflected, turning the telescope about with a sigh, to suit her sail.

Ah poignant moments when the heart stops still! Not since the hour of his exile had the Count's been so arrested.

From the garden Peter's voice rose questingly; but the Count was too wonderstruck, far, to heed it.

Caught in the scarlet radiance of the afterglow, the becalmed boat, for one brief and most memorable second, was his to gaze on.

In certain lands with what diplomacy falls the night, and how discreetly is the daylight gone. Those dimmer-and-dimmer, darker-and-lighter twilights of the North, so disconcerting in their playfulness, were unknown altogether in Pisuerga. There, Night pursued Day as though she meant it. No lingering or arctic sentiment! No concertina-ishness. . . . Hard on the sun's heels pressed Night. And the wherefore of her haste; Sun-attraction? Impatience to inherit? An answer to such riddles as these may doubtless be found by turning to the scientist's theories on Time and Relativity.

Effaced in the blue air of evening became everything, and with the darkness returned the wind.

'Sir, sir? . . . Ho, Hi, hiiiiiiiiiiii!!' Peter's voice came again.

But transfixed, and loath just then for company, the Count made no reply.

A green-lanterned barge passed slowly, coming from the sea, and on the mountain-side a village light winked wanly here and there.

'Oh, why was I not *sooner*?' he murmured distractedly aloud.

'Oh, Olga!'
'Oh, Vi!'
' . . . I hope you've enough money for the boat, dear? . . . ?'
' . . . ! ! ?'
'Tell me, Olga: Is my hat all sideways?'
' . . . . '

The long windows of the Summer Palace were staring white to the moon as the Countess of Tolga, hugging still her heath, her aigrettes casting *heroic* shadows, re-entered the Court's precincts on the arm of her friend.

❧❧ XII ❧❧

ONE evening, as Mrs. Montgomery was reading *Vanity Fair* for the fifteenth time, there came a tap at the door. It was not the first interruption since opening the cherished green-bound book, and Mrs. Montgomery seemed disinclined to stir. With the Court about to return to winter quarters, and the Summer Palace upside down, the royal governess was still able to command her habitual British phlegm. It had been decided, moreover, that she should remain behind in the forsaken palace with his Naughtiness, the better to 'prepare' him for his forthcoming Eton exam.

Still, with disputes as to the precedence of trunks and dress-baskets simmering in the corridors without, it was easier to enjoy the barley-sugar stick in one's mouth than the novel in one's hand.

'Thank God I'm not touchy!' Mrs. Montgomery reflected, rolling her eyes lazily about the little white-wainscoted room.

It was as if something of her native land had crept in through the doorway with her, so successfully had she inculcated its tendencies, or spiritual Ideals, upon everything around.

A solitary teapot, on a bracket, above the door, two *Jubilee* plates, some peacocks' feathers, an image of a little fisher-boy in bathing-drawers with a broken hand,—'a work of delicate beauty!' —a mezzotint, *The Coiffing of Maria*—these were some of the treasures which the room contained.

'A blessing to be sure when the Court has gone!' she reflected, half rising to drop a curtsey to Prince Olaf who had entered.

'Word from your country,' sententiously he broke out. 'My brother's betrothed! So need I go on with my preparation?'

'Put your tie straight! And just look at your socks all tumbling down. Such great jambons of knees!... What will become of you, I ask myself, when you're a lower boy at Eton.'

'How can I be a lower boy when I'm a Prince?'

'Probably the Rev. Ruggles-White, when you enter his House, will be able to explain.'

'I won't be a lower boy! I will *not*!'

'Cs, Cs.'

'Damn the democracy.'

'Fie, sir.'

'Down with it.'

'For shame.'

'Revenge.'

'That will do: and now, let me hear your lessons: I should like,' Mrs. Montgomery murmured, her eyes set in detachment upon the floor, 'the present-indicative tense of the Verb *To be*! Adding the words, Political h-Hostess;—more for the sake of the pronunciation than for anything else.'

And after considerable persuasion, prompting, and 'bribing' with various sorts of sweets:

> 'I am a Political Hostess,
> Thou art a Political Hostess,
> He is a Political Hostess,
> We are Political Hostesses,
> Ye are Political Hostesses,
> They are Political Hostesses.'

'Very good, dear, and only one mistake. *He* is a Political h-Hostess: can you correct yourself? The error is so slight. . . . '

But alas the Prince was in no mood for study; and Mrs. Montgomery very soon afterwards was obliged to let him go.

Moving a little anxiously about the room, her meditations turned upon the future.

With the advent of Elsie a new régime would be established: increasing Britishers would wish to visit Pisuerga; and it seemed a propitious moment to abandon teaching, and to inaugurate in Kairoulla an English hotel.

'I have no more rooms. I am quite full up!' she smiled, addressing the silver andirons in the grate.

And what a deliverance to have done with instructing unruly children, she reflected, going towards the glass mail-box attached to her vestibule door. Sometimes about this hour there would be a letter in it, but this evening, there was only a picture postcard of a field mouse in a bonnet, from her old friend Mrs. Bedley.

'We have *Valmouth* at last,' she read, 'and was it you, my dear, who asked for *The Beard Throughout the Ages*? It is in much demand, but I am keeping it back anticipating a *reply*. Several of the plates are missing I see, among them those of the late King Edward and of Assur Bani Pal; I only mention it that you may know I shan't blame you! We are having wonderful weather, and I am keeping pretty well, although poor Mrs. Barleymoon, I fear, will not see through another winter. Trusting you are benefiting by the beautiful country air: your obedient servant to command,   Ann Bedley.

'P.S.—*Man, and All About Him,* is rebinding. Ready I expect soon.'

'Ah! Cunnie, Cunnie . . . ?' Mrs. Montgomery murmured, laying the card down near a photograph of the Court-physician with a sigh. 'Ah! Arthur Amos Cuncliffe Babcock . . . ?' she invoked his name dulcetly in full: and, as though in telepathic response, there came a tap at the door, and the doctor himself looked in.

He had been attending, it seemed, the young wife of the Comp-troller of the Household at the extremity of the corridor, a creature who, after two brief weeks of marriage, imagined herself to be in an interesting state. '*I believe baby's coming!*' she would cry out every few hours.

'Do I intrude?' he demanded, in his forceful, virile voice, that ladies knew and liked: 'pray say so if I do.'

'Does he intrude!' Mrs. Montgomery flashed an arch glance towards the cornice.

'Well, and how are you keeping?' the doctor asked, dropping on to a rep causeuse that stood before the fire.

'I'm only semi-well, doctor, thanks!'

'Why, what's the trouble?'

'You know my organism is not a very strong one, Dr. Cun-cliffe . . .' Mrs. Montgomery replied, drawing up a chair, and settling a cushion with a sigh of resignation at her back.

'Imagination!'

'If only it were!'

'Imagination,' he repeated, fixing a steady eye on the short train of her black brocaded robe that all but brushed his feet.

'If that's your explanation for continuous broken sleep . . .' she gently snapped.

'Try mescal.'

'I'm trying Dr. Fritz Millar's treatment,' the lady stated, desiring to deal a slight *scratch* to his masculine *amour propre*.

'Millar's an Ass.'

'I don't agree at all!' she incisively returned, smiling covertly at his touch of pique.

'What is it?'

'Oh it's horrid. You first of all lie down; and then you drink cold water in the sun.'

'Cold what? I never *heard* of such a thing: it's enough to kill you.'

Mrs. Montgomery took a deep-drawn breath of languor.

'And would you care, doctor, so *very* much if it did?' she asked, as a page made his appearance wth an ice-bucket and champagne.

'To toast our young Princess!'

'Oh, oh, Dr. Cuncliffe? What a wicked man you are.' And for a solemn moment their thoughts went out in unison to the sea-girt land of their birth—Barkers', Selfridge's, Brighton Pier, the Zoological Gardens on a Sunday afternoon.

'Here's to the good old country!' the doctor quaffed.

'The Bride, and,' Mrs. Montgomery raised her glass, 'the Old Folks at h-home.'

'The Old Folks at home!' he vaguely echoed.

'Bollinger, you naughty man,' the lady murmured, amiably seating herself on the causeuse at his side.

'You'll find it dull here all alone after the Court has gone,' he observed, smiling down, a little despotically, on to her bright, abundant hair.

Mrs. Montgomery sipped her wine.

'When the wind goes whistling up and down under the colonnades: oh, then!' she shivered.

'You'll wish for a fine, bold Pisuergian husband; shan't you?' he answered, his foot drawing closer to hers.

'Often of an evening I feel I need fostering,' she owned, glancing up yearningly into his face.

'Fostering, eh?' he chuckled, refilling with exuberance her glass.

'Why is it that wine always makes me feel *so good*?'

'Probably because it fills you with affection for your neighbour!'

'It's true; I feel I could be very affectionate: I'm what they call an "amoureuse" I suppose, and there it is. . . .'

There fell a busy silence between them.

'It's almost too warm for a fire,' she murmured, repairing towards the window; 'but I like to hear the crackle!'

'Company, eh?' he returned, following her (a trifle unsteadily) across the room.

'The night is so clear the moon looks to be almost transparent,' she languorously observed, with a long tugging sigh.

'And so it does,' he absently agreed.

'I adore the pigeons in my wee court towards night, when they sink down like living sapphires upon the stones,' she sentimentally said, sighing languorously again.

'Ours,' he assured her; 'since the surgery looks on to it, too. . . .'

'Did you ever see anything so ducky-wucky, so completely twee!' she inconsequently chirruped.

'Allow me to fill this empty glass.'

'I want to go out on all that gold floating water!' she murmured listlessly, pointing towards the lake.

'Alone?'

'Drive me towards the sweet seaside,' she begged, taking appealingly his hand.

'Aggie?'

'Arthur—Arthur, for God's sake!' she shrilled, as with something between a snarl and a roar he impulsively whipped out the light.

'H-Help! Oh, Arth——'

Thus did they celebrate the 'Royal engagement.'

XIII

BEHIND the heavy moucharaby in the little dark shop of Habou-bet of Egypt all was song, *fête* and preparation. Additional work had brought additional hands, and be-tarbouched boys, in burn-ouses, and baskets of blossoms lay strewn all over the floor.

'Sweet is the musk-rose of the Land of Punt!
Sweet are the dates from Khorassân . . .
But bring *me* (O wandering Djinns) the English rose,
    the English apple!
O sweet is the land of the Princess Elsie,
Sweet indeed is England——'

Bachir's voice soared, in improvisation, to a long-drawn, strident wail.

'Pass me the scissors, O Bachir bed Ahmed, for the love of Allah,' a young man with large lucent eyes and an untroubled face, like a flower, exclaimed, extending a slender, keef-stained hand.

'Sidi took them,' the superintendent of the Duchess of Varna replied, turning towards an olive-skinned Armenian youth, who, seated on an empty hamper, was reading to a small, rapt group the *Kairoulla Intelligence* aloud.

' "Attended by Lady Canon-on-Noon and by Lady Bertha Chamberlayne (she is a daughter of Lord Frollo's*) the Princess was seen to alight from her saloon, in a *chic* toque of primrose paille, stabbed with the quill of a nasturtium-coloured bird, and, darting forward, like the Bird of Paradise that she *is,* embraced her future parents-in-law with considerable affection. . . ." '

'Scissors, for the love of Allah!'

' "And soon I heard the roll of drums! And saw the bobbing plumes in the jangling browbands of the horses: it was a moment I shall never forget. She passed . . . and as our Future Sovereign turned smiling to bow her acknowledgments to the crowd I saw a happy tear . . . !'

'Ah Allah.'

'Pass me two purple pinks.'

' "Visibly gratified at the cordial ovation to her Virgin Daughter was Queen Glory, a striking and impressive figure, all a-glitter in a splendid dark dress of nacre and nigger tissue, her many Orders of Merit almost bearing her down." '

'Thy scissors, O Sidi, for the love of Muhammed!'

' "It seemed as if Kairoulla had gone wild with joy. Led by the first Life-Guards and a corps of ladies of great fashion disguised as peasants, the cortège proceeded amid the whole-hearted plaudits of the people towards Constitutional Square, where, with the sweetest of smiles and thanks, the Princess received an exquisite sheaf of Deflas (they are the hybrids of slipper-orchids crossed with maidens-rue, and are all the mode at present), tendered her by little Paula Exelmans, the Lord Mayor's tiny daughter. Driving on, amid showers of confetti, the procession passed up the Chausée, which presented a scene of rare animation: boys and even quite elderly dames swarming up the trees to obtain a better view of their new Princess. But it was not until Lilianthal Street and the Cathedral Square were reached that the climax reached its height! Here a short standstill was called and, after an appropriate address from the Archbishop of Pisuerga, the stirring strains of the National Anthem, superbly rendered by Madame Marguerite Astorra of the State Theatre (she

---

* Although the account of Princess Elsie's arrival in Kairoulla is signed 'Green Jersey,' it seems not unlikely that 'Eva Schnerb' herself was the reporter on this eventful occasion.

is in perfect voice this season), arose on the air. At that moment a black cat and its kitties rushed across the road, and I saw the Princess smile." '

'Thy scissors, O Sidi, in the Name of the Prophet!'

' "A touching incident," ' Sidi with equanimity pursued, ' "was just before the English Tea Rooms, where the English Colony had mustered together in force. . . ." '

But alack for those interested. Owing to the clamour about him much of the recital was lost: ' "Cheers and tears. . . . Life's benison . . . Honiton lace. . . . If I live to be *forty*, it was a moment I shall never forget. . . . Panic . . . congestion. . . . Police." '

But it was scarcely needful to peruse the paper, when on the boulevards outside the festivities were everywhere in full swing. The arrival of the princess for her wedding had brought to Kairoulla unprecedented crowds from all parts of the kingdom, as much eager to see the princess as to catch a glimpse of the fine pack of beagles that it was said had been brought over with her, and which had taken an half-eerie hold of the public mind. Gilderoy, Beausire, Audrey, many of the hounds' names were known pleasantly to the crowd already; and anecdotes of Audrey, picture-postcards of Audrey, were sold as rapidly almost as those even of the princess. Indeed mothers among the people had begun to threaten their disobedient offspring with Audrey, whose silky, thickset frame was supported, it appeared, daily on troublesome little boys and tiresome little girls. . . .

'Erri, erri, get on with thy bouquet, oh Lazari Demitraki!' Bachir exclaimed in plaintive tones, addressing a blond boy with a skin of amber, who was 'charming' an earwig with a reed of grass.

'She dance the *Boussadilla* just like in the street of Halfaouine in Gardaïa, my town, any Ouled Naïl!' he rapturously gurgled.

'Get on with thy work, oh Lazari Demitraki,' Bachir besought him, 'and leave the earwigs alone for the clients to find.'

'What with the heat, the smell of the flowers, the noise of you boys, and with filthy earwigs Boussadillaing all over one, I feel I could *swoon*.' The voice, cracked yet cloying, was Peter Passer's.

He had come to Kairoulla for the 'celebrations,' and also, perhaps, aspiring to advance his fortunes, in ways known best to himself. With Bachir his connection dated from long ago, when as a Cathedral choir-boy it had been his habit to pin a shoulder- or bosom-blossom to his surplice, destroying it with coquettish, ring-laden fingers in the course of an anthem, and scattering the petals from the choir-loft, leaf by leaf, on to the grey heads of the monsignori below.

'Itchiata wa?' Bachir grumbled, playing his eyes distractedly around the shop. And it might have been better for the numerous orders there were to attend to had he called fewer of his acquaintance to assist him. Sunk in torpor, a cigarette smouldering at his ear, a Levantine Greek, known as 'Effendi darling' was listening to a dark-cheeked Tunisian engaged at the Count of Tolga's private Hammam Baths—a young man, who, as he spoke, would make mazy gestures of the hands as though his master's ribs, or those of some illustrious guest, lay under him. But by no means all of those assembled in the little shop bore the seal of Islam. An American, who had grown too splendid for the copper 'Ganymede' or Soda-fountain of a Café bar and had taken to teaching the hectic dance-steps of his native land in the night-halls where Bachir sold, was achieving wonders with some wires and Eucharist lilies, while discussing with a shy-mannered youth the many difficulties that beset the foreigner in Kairoulla.

'Young chaps that come out here don't know what they're coming to,' he sapiently remarked, using his incomparable teeth in place of scissors. 'Gosh! Talk of advancement,' he growled.

'There's few can mix as I can, yet I don't never get no rise!' the shy youth exclaimed, producing a card that was engraved: *Harry Cummings, Salad-Dresser to the King.* 'I expect I've arrived,' he murmured, turning to hide a modest blush towards a pale young man who looked on life through heavy horn glasses.

'Salad dressing? I'd sooner it was hair! You do get tips there anyway,' the Yankee reasoned.

'I wish *I* were—arrived,' the young man with the glasses, by name Guy Thin, declared. He had come out but recently from England to establish a 'British Grocery,' and was the owner of what is sometimes called an expensive voice, his sedulously clear articulation missing out no syllable or letter of anything he might happen to be saying, as though he were tasting each word, like the Pure tea, or the Pure marmalade, or any other of the so very Pure goods he proposed so exclusively to sell.

'If Allah wish it then you arrive,' Lazari Demitraki assured him with a dazzling smile, catching his hand in order to construe the nes.

'Finish thy bouquet, O Lazari Demitraki,' Bachir faintly moaned.

'It finished—arranged: it with Abou!' he announced, pointing to an aged negro with haunted sin-sick eyes who appeared to be making strange grimaces at the wall. A straw hat of splendid dimensions was on his head, flaunting bravely the insignia of the Firm.

But the old man seemed resolved to run no more errands:

'Nsa, nsa,' he mumbled. 'Me walk enough for one day! Me no go out any more. Old Abou too tired to take another single step! as soon would me cross the street again dis night as the Sahara! . . .'

And it was only after the promise of a small gift of Opium that he consented to leave a débutante's bouquet at the Théâtre Diana.*

'In future,' Bachir rose, remarking, 'I only employ the women; I keep only girls,' he repeated, for the benefit of 'Effendi darling' who appeared to be attaining Nirvana.

'And next I suppose you keep a Harem?' 'Effendi darling' somnolently returned.

Most of the city shops had closed their shutters for the day when Bachir, shouldering a pannier bright with blooms, stepped with his companions forth into the street.

Along the Boulevards thousands were pressing towards the Regina Gardens to view the Fireworks, all agog to witness the pack of beagles wrought in brilliant lights due to course a stag across the sky, and which would change, if newspaper reports might be believed, at the critical moment, into ' something of the nature of a surprise. '

Pausing before a plate-glass window that adjoined the shop to adjust the flowing folds of his gandourah, and to hoist his flower tray to his small scornful head, Bachir allowed his auxiliaries to drift, mostly two by two, away among the crowd. Only the royal salad-dresser, Harry Cummings, expressed a demure inclination (when the pushing young grocer caressed his arm) to 'be alone'; but Guy Thin, who had private designs upon him, was loath to hear of it! He wished to persuade him to buy a bottle of Vinegar from his Store, when he would print on his paper-bags *As supplied to his Majesty the King.*

'Grant us, O Allah, each good Fortunes,' Bachir beseeched, looking up through his eyelashes towards the moon, that drooped like a silver amulet in the firmament above: in the blue nocturnal

* The Théâtre Diana: a Music Hall dedicated to Spanish Zarzuelas and Operettes. It enjoyed a somewhat doubtful reputation.

air he looked like a purple poppy. 'A toute à l'heure mes amis!' he murmured as he moved away.

And in the little closed shop behind the heavy moucharaby now that they had all gone, the exhalations of the *flowers* arose; pungent, concerted odours, expressive of natural antipathies and feuds, suave alliances, suffering, pride, and joy. . . . Only the shining moon through the moucharaby, illumining here a lily, there a leaf, may have guessed what they were saying:

'My wires are hurting me: my wires are hurting me.'

'I have no water. I cannot reach the water.'

'They have pushed me head down into the bottom of the bowl.'

'I'm glad I'm in a Basket! No one will hurl *me* from a window to be bruised underfoot by the callous crowd.'

'It's uncomfy, isn't it, without one's roots?'

'You Weed you! You, you, you . . . *buttercup*! How dare you to *an Orchid*!'

'I shouldn't object to sharing the same water with him, dear . . . ordinary as he is! If *only* he wouldn't smell. . . .'

'She's nothing but a piece of common grass and so I tell her!'

Upon the tense pent atmosphere surged a breath of cooler air, and through the street-door slipped the Duchess of Varna.

Overturning a jar of great heavy-headed gladioli with a crash, she sailed, with a purposeful step, towards the till.

Garbed in black and sleepy citrons, she seemed, indeed, to be equipped for a long, long Voyage, and was clutching, in her arms, a pet Poodle dog, and a levant-covered case, in which, doubtless, reposed her jewels.

Since her rupture with Madame Wetme (both the King and Queen had refused to receive her), the money *ennuis* of the Duchess had become increasingly acute. Tormented by tradespeople, dunned and bullied by creditors, menaced, mortified, insulted—an offer to 'star' in the *rôle* of *A Society Thief* for the cinematograph had particularly shocked her—the inevitable hour to quit the Court, so long foreseen, had come. And now with her departure definitely determined upon, the Duchess experienced an insouciance of heart unknown to her assuredly for many a year. Replenishing her reticule with quite a welcome sheaf of the elegant little bank-notes of Pisuerga, one thing only remained to do, and taking pen and paper she addressed to the Editor of the *Intelligence* the supreme announcement:—'*The Duchess of Varna has left for Dateland.*'

Eight light words! But enough to set *tout* Kairoulla in a rustle.

'I only regret I didn't go sooner,' she murmured to herself aloud, breaking herself a rose to match her gown from an arrangement in the window.

Many of the flowers had been newly christened, 'Elsie,' 'Audrey,' 'London-Madonnas' (black Arums these), while the roses from the 'Land of Punt' had been renamed 'Mrs. Lloyd George'—and priced accordingly. A basket of odontoglossums eked out with gypsophila seemed to anticipate the end, when supplies from Punt must necessarily cease. However, bright boys, like Bachir, seldom lacked patrons, and the duchess recalled glimpsing him one evening, from her private sitting-room at the Ritz Hotel, seated on a garden bench in the Regina Gardens beside the Prime Minister himself; both, to all seeming, on the most cordial terms, and having reached a perfect understanding as regards the Eastern Question. Ah, the Eastern Question! It was said that, in the Land of Dates, one might study it well. In Djezira, the chief town, beneath the great golden sun, people, they said, might grow wise. In the simoon that scatters the silver sand, in the words of the nomads, in the fairy mornings beneath the palms, society with its foolish *cliché* ... the duchess smiled.

'But for that poisonous woman, I should have gone last year,' she told herself, interrupted in her cogitations by the appearance of her maid.

'The train, your Grace, we shall miss it. ...'

'Nonsense!' the duchess answered, following, leaving the flowers alone again to their subtle exhalations.

'I'm glad *I'm* in a Basket!'

'I have no water. I cannot reach the water.'

'Life's bound to be uncertain when you haven't got your roots!'

XIV

ON a long-chair, with tired, closed eyes, lay the Queen. Although spared from henceforth the anxiety of her son's morganatic marriage, yet, now that his destiny was sealed, she could not help feeling perhaps he might have done better. The bride's lineage was nothing to boast of—of her great-great-grandparents, indeed, in the year 17—, it were gentler to draw a veil—while, for the rest, disingenuous, undistinguished, more at home in the stables than in a drawing-room, the Queen much feared that she and her future daughter-in-law would scarcely get on.

Yes, the little princess was none too engaging, she reflected, and her poor sacrificed child if not actually trapped . . .

The silken swish of a fan, breaking the silence, induced the Queen to look up.

In waiting at present was the Countess Olivia d'Omptyda, a person of both excellent principles and birth, if lacking, somewhat, in social boldness. Whenever she entered the royal presence she would begin visibly to tremble, which considerably flattered the Queen. Her father, Count 'Freddie' d'Omptyda, an infantile and charming old man, appointed in a moment of unusual vagary Pisuergan Ambassador to the Court of St. James', had lately married a child wife scarcely turned thirteen, whose frivolity and numerous pranks on the high dames of London were already the scandal of the *Corps Diplomatique.*

'Sssh! Noise is the last vulgarity,' the Queen commented, raising a cushion embroidered with raging lions and white uncanny unicorns behind her head.

Unstrung from the numerous *fêtes,* she had retired to a distant boudoir to relax, and, having partly disrobed, was feeling remotely Venus of Miloey with her arms half hidden in a plain white cape.

The Countess d'Omptyda furled her fan.

'In this Age of push and shriek . . .' she said and sighed.

'It seems that neither King Geo, nor Queen Glory, *ever* lie down of a day!' her Dreaminess declared.

'Since his last appointment, neither does Papa.'

'The affair of your step-mother, and Lady Diana Duff Semour,' the Queen remarked, 'appears to be assuming the proportions of an Incident!'

The Countess dismally smiled. The subject of her step-mother, mistaken frequently for her grand-daughter, was a painful one. 'I hear she's like a colt broke loose!' she murmured, dropping her eyes fearfully to her costume.

She was wearing an apron of Parma-violets, and the Order of the Holy Ghost.

'It's a little a pity she can't be more sensible,' the Queen returned, fingering listlessly some papers at her side. Among them was the

Archæological Society's initial report relating to the recent finds among the Ruins of Sodom and Gomorrah. From Chedorlahomor came the good news that an *amphora* had been found, from which it seemed that men, in those days, rode sideways, and women straddle-legs, with their heads to the horses' tails, while a dainty cup, rav-ished from a rock-tomb in the Vale of Akko, ornamented with naked boys and goblets of flowers, encouraged a yet more extensive research.

'You may advance, Countess, with the Archæologists' report,' the Queen commanded. 'Omitting (skipping, I say) the death of the son of Lord Intriguer.'*

' "It was in the Vale of Akko, about two miles from Saada," ' the Countess tremblingly began, ' "that we laid bare a superb tear-bottle, a unique specimen in *grisaille,* severely adorned with a matron's head. From the inscription there can be no doubt whatever that we have here an authentic portrait of Lot's disobedient, though unfortunate, wife. Ample and statuesque (as the salten image she was afterwards to become), the shawl-draped, masklike features are by no means beautiful. It is a face that you may often see to-day, in down-town 'Dancings,' or in the bars of the dockyards or wharves of our own modern cities—Tilbury, 'Frisco, Vera Cruz—a sodden, gin-soaked face that helps to vindicate, if not, perhaps, excuse, the conduct of Lot. . . . With this highly interesting example of the Potters' Art was found a novel object, of an unknown nature, likely to arouse, in scientific circles, considerable controversy. . . ." '

And just as the lectrice was growing hesitant and embarrassed, the Countess of Tolga, who had the *entrée,* unobtrusively entered the room.

She was looking particularly well in one of the new standing-out skirts ruched with rosebuds, and was showing more of her stockings than she usually did.

'You bring the sun with you!' the Queen graciously exclaimed.

'Indeed,' the Countess answered, 'I ought to apologise for the interruption, but the *poor little thing* is leaving now.'

'What? has the Abbess come?'

'She has sent Sister Irene of the Incarnation instead. . . .'

'I had forgotten it was to-day.'

---

* The Hon. 'Eddy' Monteith had succumbed: the shock received by meeting a jackal while composing a sonnet had been too much for him. His tomb is in the Vale of Akko, beside the River Dis. Alas, for the *triste* obscurity of his end!

With an innate aversion for all farewells, yet the Queen was accustomed to perform a score of irksome acts daily that she cordially disliked, and when, shortly afterwards, Mademoiselle de Nazianzi accompanied by a Sister from the Flaming-Hood were announced, they found her quite prepared.

Touched, and reassured at the ex-maid's appearance, the Queen judged, at last, it was safe to unbend. Already very remote and unworldly in her novice's dress, she had ceased, indeed, to be a being there was need any more to either circumvent, humour, or suppress; and now that the threatened danger was gone, her Majesty glanced, half-lachrymosely, about among her personal belongings for some slight token of 'esteem' or *souvenir*. Skimming from cabinet to cabinet, in a sort of hectic dance, she began to fear, as she passed her bibelots in review, that beyond a Chinese Buddha that she believed to be ill-omened, and which for a nun seemed hardly suitable, she could spare nothing about her after all, and in some dilemma she raised her eyes, as though for a crucifix, towards the wall. Above the long-chair a sombre study of a strangled negress in a ditch by Gauguin conjured up to-day with poignant force a vivid vision of the Tropics.

'The poor Duchess!' she involuntarily sighed, going off into a train of speculation of her own.

Too tongue-tied, or, perhaps, too discreet, to inform the Queen that anything she might select would immediately be confiscated by the Abbess, Sister Irene, while professing her rosary, appraised her surroundings with furtive eyes, crossing herself frequently with a speed and facility due to practice, whenever her glance chanced to alight on some nude shape in stone. Keen, meagre, and perhaps slightly malicious, hers was a curiously pinched face—like a cold violet.

'The Abbess is still in retreat; but sends her duty,' she ventured as the Queen approached a guéridon near which she was standing.

'Indeed? How I envy her,' the Queen wistfully said, selecting as suited to the requirements of the occasion, a little volume of a mystic trend, the *Cries of Love* of Father Surin,* bound in grey velvet, which she pressed upon the reluctant novice, with a brief, but cordial, kiss of farewell.

'She looked quite pretty!' she exclaimed, sinking to the long-chair as soon as the nuns had gone.

* Author of *In the Dusk of the Dawn.*

'So like the Cimabue in the long corridor . . .' the Countess of Tolga murmured chillily. It was her present policy that her adored ally, Olga Blumenghast, should benefit by Mademoiselle de Nazianzi's retirement from Court, by becoming nearer to the Queen, when they would work all the wires between them.

'I'd have willingly followed her,' the Queen weariedly declared, 'at any rate, until after the wedding.'

'It seems that I and Lord Derbyfield are to share the same closed carriage in the wake of the bridal coach,' the Countess of Tolga said, considering with a supercilious air her rose *suède* slipper on the dark carpet.

'He's like some great Bull. What do you suppose he talks about?'

The Countess d'Omptyda repressed a giggle.

'They tell me Don Juan was nothing *nothing* to him. . . . He cannot see, he cannot be, oh every hour. It seems he can't help it, and that he simply *has* to!'

'Fortunately Lady Lavinia Lee-Strange will be in the landau as well!'

The Queen laid her cheeks to her hands.

'I all but died, dear Violet,' she crooned, 'listening to an account of her Ancestor, who fell, fighting Scotland, at the battle of Pinkie Cleugh.'

'These well-bred, but detestably insular women, how they bore one.'

'They are not to be appraised by any ordinary standards. Crossing the state saloon while coming here what should I see, ma'am, but Lady Canon of Noon on her hands and knees (all fours!) peeping below the loose-covers of the chairs in order to examine the Gobelins-tapestries beneath. . . .'

'Oh——'

' "Absolutely authentic," I said, as I passed on, leaving her looking like a pickpocket caught in the act.'

'I suppose she was told to make a quiet survey. . . .'

'Like their beagles and deer-hounds, that their Landseer so loved o paint, I fear the British character is, at bottom, *nothing* if not rapacious!'

'It's said, I believe, that to behold the Englishman at his *best* one should watch him play tip-and-run.'

'You mean of course cricket?'

The Queen looked doubtful: she had retained of a cricket-match at Lord's a memory of hatless giants waving wooden sticks.

'I only wish it could have been a long engagement,' she abstrusely murmured, fastening her attention on the fountains whitely spurting in the gardens below.

Valets in cotton jackets and light blue aprons, bearing baskets of crockery and *argenterie*, were making ready beneath the tall Tuba trees a supper *buffet* for the evening's Ball.

> 'Flap your wings, little bird,
> Oh flap your wings——'

A lad's fresh voice, sweet as a robin's, came piping up.

'These wretched workpeople——! There's not a peaceful corner,' the Queen complained, as her husband's shape appeared at the door. He was followed by his first secretary—a simple commoner, yet with the air and manner peculiar to the husband of a Countess.

'Yes, Willie? I've a hundred headaches. What is it?'

'Both King Geo and Queen Glory are wondering where you are.'

'Oh, really, Willie?'

'And dear Elsie's asking after you too.'

'Very likely,' the Queen returned with quiet complaisance, 'but unfortunately, I have neither her energy nor,' she murmured with a slightly sardonic laugh, 'her appetite!'

The Countess of Tolga tittered.

'She called for fried-eggs and butcher's-meat, this morning, about the quarter before eight,' she averred.

'An excellent augury for our dynasty,' the King declared, reposing the eyes of an adoring grandparent upon an alabaster head of a Boy attributed to Donatello.

'She's terribly foreign, Willie . . . ! Imagine ham and eggs . . .' The Queen dropped her face to her hand.

'So long as the Royal-House——' The King broke off, turning gallantly to raise the Countess d'Omptyda, who had sunk with a gesture of exquisite allegiance to the floor.

'Sir . . . Sir!' she faltered in confusion, seeking with fervent lips her Sovereign's hand.

'What is she doing, Willie!'

'Begging for Strawberry-leaves!' the Countess of Tolga brilliantly commented.

'Apropos of Honours . . . it appears King Geo has signified

his intention of raising his present representative in Pisuerga to the peerage.'

'After her recent *Cause*, Lady Something should be not a little consoled.'

'She was at the début of the new diva, little Miss Helvellyn (the foreign invasion has indeed begun!), at the Opera-House last night, so radiant.'

'When she cranes forward out of her own box to smile at someone into the next, I can't explain . . . but one feels she ought to hatch,' the Queen murmured, repairing capriciously from one couch to another.

'We neglect our guests, my dear,' the King expostulatingly exclaimed, bending over his consort anxiously from behind.

'Tell me, Willie,' she cooed, caressing the medals upon his breast. and drawing him gently down: 'tell me. Didst thou enjoy thy cigar, dear, with King Geo?'

'I can recall in my time, Child, a suaver flavour. . . .'

'Thy little chat, though, dearest, was well enough?'

'I would not call him crafty, but I should say he was a man of considerable subtlety . . .' the King evasively replied.

'One does not need, my dearest nectarine, a prodigy of intelligence, however, to take him in!'

'Before the proposed Loan, Love, can be brought about, he may wish to question thee as to thy political opinions.'

The Queen gave a little light laugh.

'No one knows what my political opinions are; I don't myself!'

'And I'm quite confident of it: But, indeed, my dear, we neglect our functions.'

'I only wish it could have been a *long* engagement, Willie. . . .'

❧ XV ❧

IN the cloister eaves the birds were just awakening, and all the spider scales, in the gargoyled gables, glanced fresh with dew. Above the Pietà on the porter's gate, slow-speeding clouds, like knots of pink roses, came blowing across the sky, sailing away in titanic bouquets towards the clear horizon. All virginal in the early sunrise, what enchantment the world possessed! The rhythmic sway-sway of the trees, the exhalations of the flowers, the ethereal candour of this early hour,—these raised the heart up to their Creator.

Kneeling at the casement of a postulant's cell, Laura de Nazianzi recalled that serene, and just thus, had she often planned must dawn her bridal day!

Beyond the cruciform flower-beds and the cloister wall soared the Blue Jesus, the storied windows of its lofty galleries aglow with light.

'Most gracious Jesus. Help me to forget. For my heart aches. Uphold me now.'

But to forget to-day was well-nigh, she knew, impossible. . . .

Once it seemed she caught the sound of splendid music from the direction of the Park, but it was too early for music yet. Away in the palace the Princess Elsie must be already astir . . . in her peignoir, perhaps? The bridal-garment unfolded upon the bed: but no: it was said the bed indeed was where usually her Royal-Highness's dogs . . .

With a long and very involuntary sigh, she began to sweep, and put in some order, her room.

How forlorn her cornette looked upon her *prie-Dieu*! And, oh, how stern, and 'old'!

Would an impulse to bend it slightly, but only so, *so* slightly, to an angle to suit her face, be attended, later, by remorse?

'Confiteor Deo omnipotenti, beatae Mariae semper virgini, beato Michaeli Archangelo (et *tibi* Pater), quia peccavi nimis cogitatione, verbo et opere,' she entreated, reposing her chin in meditation upon the handle of her broom.

The bluish shadow of a cypress-tree on the empty wall fascinated her as few pictures had.

'Grant my soul eyes,' she prayed, cheerfully completing her task.

It being a general holiday, all was yet quite still in the corridor. A sound as of gentle snoring came indeed from behind more than one closed door, and the new *pensionnaire* was preparing to beat a retreat when she perceived, in the cloister, the dumpish form of Old Jane.

Seated in the sun by the convent wall, the Porteress was sharing a scrap of breakfast with the birds.

'You're soonish for Mass, love,' she broke out, her large archaic features surcharged with smiles.

'It's such a perfect morning, I felt I must come down.'

'I've seen many a more promising sunrise before now, my dear, turn to storm and blast! An orange sky overhead brings back to me the morning that I was received; ah, I shall never forget, as I was taking my Vows, a flash of forked lightning, and a clap of Thunder (Glory be to God!), followed by a waterspout (Mercy save us!) bursting all over my Frinch lace veil. . . .'

'What is your book, Old Jane?'

'Something light, love, as it's a holiday.'

'*Pascal* . . .'

'Though it's mostly a *Fête* day I've extra to do!' the Porteress averred, dropping her eyes to the great, glistening spits upon the Cloister flags. It was her boast she could distinguish Monsignor Potts's round splash from Father Geordie Picpus's more dapper fine one, and again the Abbess's from Mother Martinez de la Rosa's—although these indeed shared a certain opaque sameness.

'Of course it's a day for private visits.'

'Since the affair of Sister Dorothea and Brother Bernard Soult, private visits are no longer allowed,' the Porteress returned, reproving modestly, with the cord of her discipline, a pert little lizard, that seemed to be proposing to penetrate between the nude toes of her sandalled foot.

But on such a radiant morning it was preposterous to hint at 'Rules.'

Beneath the clement sun a thousand cicadas were insouciantly chirping, while birds, skimming about without thoughts of money, floated lightly from tree to tree.

'Jesus—Mary—Joseph!' the Porteress purred, as a nun, with her face all muffled up in wool, crossed the Cloister, glancing neither to right nor left, and sharply slammed a door: for, already, the Convent was beginning to give signs of animation. Deep in a book of Our Lady's Hours, a biretta'd priest was slowly rounding a garden path, while repairing from a *Grotto-sepulchre*, to which was attached a handsome indulgence, Mother Martinez de la Rosa appeared, all heavily leaning on her stick.

Simultaneously the matin-bell rang out, calling all to prayer.

The Convent Chapel, founded by the tender enthusiasm of a wealthy widow, the Countess d'Acunha, to perpetuate her earthly comradeship with the beautiful Andalusian, the Doña Dolores Baatz, was still but thinly peopled some few minutes later, although the warning bell had stopped.

Peering around, Laura was disappointed not to remark Sister Ursula in her habitual place, between the veiled fresco of the 'Circumcision' and the stoup of holy-water by the door.

Beyond an offer to 'exchange whippings' there had been a certain coolness in the greeting with her friend that had both surprised and pained her.

'When those we rely on wound and betray us, to whom should we turn but Thee?' she breathed, addressing a crucifix, in ivory, contrived by love, that was a miracle of wonder.

Finished Mass, there was a general rush for the Refectory!

Preceded by Sister Clothilde, and followed, helter-skelter, by an exuberant bevy of nuns, even Mother Martinez, who, being short-sighted, would go feeling the ground with her cane, was propelled to the measure of a hop-and-skip.

Passing beneath an archway labelled 'Silence' (the injunction to-day being undoubtedly ignored), the company was welcomed by the mingled odours of tea, *consommé,* and fruit. It was a custom of the Convent for one of the Sisters during meal-time to read aloud from some standard work of fideism, and these edifying recitations, interspersed by such whispered questions as: 'Tea, or *Consommé*?' 'A Banana, or a Pomegranate?' gave to those at all foolishly or hysterically inclined a painful desire to giggle. Mounting the pulpit-lectern, a nun with an aristocratic though gourmand little face was about to resume the arid life of the Byzantine monk, Basilius Saturninus, when Mother Martinez de la Rosa took it upon herself, in a few patriotic words, to relax all rules for that day.

'We understand in the world now,' a little faded woman murmured to Laura upon her right, 'that the latest craze among ladies is to gild their tongues; but I should be afraid,' she added diffidently, dipping her banana into her tea, 'of poison, myself!'

Unhappy at her friend's absence from the Refectory, Laura, however, was in no mood to entertain the nuns with stories of the present pagan tendencies of society.

Through the bare, blindless windows, framing a sky so bluely luminous, came the swelling clamour of the assembling crowds, tinging the languid air as with some sultry fever. From the *Chausée,* music of an extraordinary intention—heated music, crude music, played with passionate élan to perfect time, conjured up, with vivid, heartrending prosaicness, the seething Boulevards beyond the high old creeper-covered walls.

'I forget now, Mother, which of the Queens it is that will wear a velvet train of a beautiful orchid shade; but one of them will!' Sister Irene of the Incarnation was holding forth.

'I must confess,' Mother Martinez remarked, who was peeling herself a peach, with an air of far attention, 'I must confess, I should have liked to have cast my eye upon the *lingerie* . . .'

'I would rather have seen the ball-wraps, Mother, or the shoes, and evening slippers!'

'Yes, or the fabulous jewels . . .'

'Of course Sister Laura saw the *trousseau*?'

But Laura made feint not to hear.

Discipline relaxed, a number of nuns had collected provisions and were picnicking in the window, where Sister Innez (an ex-Repertoire actress) was giving some spirited renderings of her chief successful parts—*Jane de Simerose, Frou-Frou, Sappho, Cigarette*. . . .

'My darling child! I always sleep all day and only revive when there's *a Man*,' she was saying with an impudent look, sending the scandalised Sisters into delighted convulsions.

Unable to endure it any longer, Laura crept away.

A desire for air and solitude led her towards the Recreation ground. After the hot refectory, sauntering in the silken shade of the old astounding cedars was delightful quite. In the deserted alleys, the golden blossoms of the censia-trees, unable to resist the sun, littered in perfumed piles the ground, overcoming her before long with a sensation akin to *vertige*. Anxious to find her friend, Laura turned towards her cell.

She found Sister Ursula leaning on her window-ledge all crouched up—like a Duchess on 'a First Night.'

'My dear, my dear, the *crowds*!'

'Ursula?'

'Yes, what is it?'

'Perhaps I'll go, since I'm in the way.'

'Touchy Goose,' Sister Ursula murmured, wheeling round with a glance of complex sweetness.

'Ah, Ursula,' Laura sighed, smiling reproachfully at her friend.

She had long almond eyes, one longer and larger than the other, that gave to her narrow, etiolated face an exalted, mystic air. Her hair, wholly concealed by her full coif, would be inclined to rich copper or chestnut: indeed, below the pinched and sensitive nostrils, a moustache (so slight as to be scarcely discernible) proved this beyond all controversy to be so. But perhaps the quality and beauty of her hands were her chief distinction.

'Do you believe it would cause an earthquake if we climbed out, dear little one, upon the leads?' she asked.

'I had forgotten you overlooked the street by leaning out,' Laura answered, sinking fatigued to a little cane armchair.

'Listen, Laura . . . !'

'This cheering racks my heart. . . .'

'Ah, Astaroth! There went a very "swell" carriage.'

'Perhaps I'll come back later: it's less noisy in my cell.'

'Now you're here, I shall ask you, I think, to whip me.'

'Oh, no. . . .'

'Bad dear Little-One. Dear meek soul!' Sister Ursula softly laughed.

'This maddening cheering,' Laura breathed, rolling tormented eyes about her.

A crucifix, a text, *I would lay Pansies at Jesus' Feet*, two fresh eggs in a blue paper bag, some ends of string, a breviary, and a birch were the chamber's individual if meagre contents.

'You used *not* to have that text, Ursula,' Laura observed, her attention arrested by the preparation of a Cinematograph Company on the parapet of the Cathedral.

The Church had much need indeed of Reformation! The Times were incredibly low. A new crusade . . . she ruminated, revolted at the sight of an old man holding dizzily to a stone-winged angel, with a wine-flask at his lips.

'Come, dear, won't you assist me now to mortify my senses?' Sister Ursula cajoled.

'No, really, no—!—!—!'

'Quite lightly. For I was scourged, by Sister Agnes, but yesterday with a heavy bunch of keys, head downwards, hanging from a bar.'

'Oh . . .'

'This morning she sent me those pullets' eggs. I perfectly was touched by her delicate sweet sympathy.'

Laura gasped.

'It must have hurt you?'

'I assure you I felt nothing—my spirit had travelled so far,' Sister Ursula replied, turning to throw an interested glance at the street.

It was close now upon the crucial hour, and the plaudits of the crowd were becoming more and more uproarious, as 'favourites' in Public life and 'celebrities' of all sorts began to arrive in brisk succession at the allotted door of the Cathedral.

'I could almost envy the fleas in the Cardinal's vestments,' Sister Ursula declared, overcome by the venial desire to see.

Gazing at the friend upon whom she had counted in some disillusion, Laura quietly left her.

The impulse to witness something of the spectacle outside was, nevertheless, infectious, and recollecting that from the grotto-sepulchre in the garden it was not impossible to attain the convent wall, she determined, moved by some wayward instinct, to do so. Frequently, as a child, had she scaled it, to survey the doings of the city streets beyond—the streets named by the nuns often 'Sinward ho.' Crossing the cloisters, and through old gates crowned by vast fruit-baskets in stone, she followed, feverishly, the ivy-masked bricks of the sheltering wall, and was relieved to reach the grotto without encountering anyone. Surrounded by heavy boskage, it marked a spot where once long ago one of the Sisters, it was said, had received the mystic stigmata. . . . With a feline effort (her feet supported by the grotto boulders), it needed but a bound to attain an incomparable post of vantage.

Beneath a blaze of bunting, the street seemed paved with heads. 'Madonna,' she breathed, as an official on a white horse, its mane stained black, began authoritatively backing his steed into the patient faces of the mob below, startling an infant in arms to a frantic fit of squalls.

'Just so we shall stand on the Day of Judgment,' she reflected, blinking at the glare.

Street boys vending programmes, 'lucky' horseshoes, Saturnalian emblems (these for gentlemen only), offering postcards of 'Geo and Glory,' etc., wedged their way, however, where it might have been deemed indeed impossible for anyone to pass.

And *he*, she wondered, her eyes following the wheeling pigeons, alarmed by the recurrent salutes of the signal guns, he must be there already: under the dome! restive a little beneath the busy scrutiny, his tongue like the point of a blade. . . .

A burst of cheering seemed to announce the Queen. But no, it was only a lady with a parasol sewn with diamonds that was exciting the rah-rahs of the crowd. Followed by mingled cries of 'Shame!' 'Waste!' and sighs of envy, Madame Wetme was enjoying a belated triumph. And now a brief lull, as a brake containing various delegates and 'representatives of English Culture,' rolled by at a stately trot—Lady Alexander, E. V. Lucas, Robert Hichens, Clutton Brock, etc.—the ensemble the very apotheosis of worn-out *cliché*.

'There's someone there wot's got enough heron plumes on her head!' a young girl in the crowd remarked.

And nobody contradicted her.

Then troops and outriders, and at last the Queen.

She was looking charming in a Corinthian chlamyde, in a carriage lined in deep delphinium blue, behind six restive blue roan horses.

Finally, the bride and her father, bowing this way and that . . .

Cheers.

'Huzzas . . .'

A hushed suspense.

Below the wall the voice of a beggar arose, persistent, haunting: 'For the Love of God . . . In the Name of Pity . . . of Pity.'

'Of Pity,' she echoed, addressing a frail, wind-sown harebell, blue as the sky: and leaning upon the shattered glass ends, that crowned the wall, she fell to considering the future—obedience—solitude—death.

The troubling *valse* theme from *Dante in Paris* interrupted her meditations.

How often had they valsed it together, he and she . . . sometimes as a two-step . . . ! What souvenirs. . . . Yousef, Yousef. . . . Above the Cathedral, the crumbling clouds had eclipsed the sun. In the intense meridian glare the thronged street seemed even as though half-hypnotised; occasionally only the angle of a parasol would change, or some bored soldier's legs would give a little. When brusquely, from the belfry, burst a triumphant clash of bells.

Laura caught her breath.

Already?

A shaking of countless handkerchiefs in wild ovation: from roof-tops, and balconies, the air was thick with falling flowers—the bridal pair!

But only for the bridegroom had she eyes.

Oblivious of what she did, she began to beat her hands, until they streamed with blood, against the broken glass ends upon the wall: 'Yousef, Yousef, Yousef. . . .'

July 1921, May 1922.
Versailles, Montreux, Florence.

Prancing Nigger

LOOKING gloriously bored, Miss Miami Mouth gaped up into the boughs of a giant silk-cotton-tree. In the lethargic noontide nothing stirred: all was so still, indeed, that the sound of someone snoring was clearly audible among the cane-fields far away.

'After dose yams an' pods an' de white falernum, I dats way sleepy too,' she murmured, fixing heavy, somnolent eyes upon the prospect that lay before her.

Through the sun-tinged greenery shone the sea, like a floor of silver glass strewn with white sails.

Somewhere out there, fishing, must be her boy, Bamboo!

And, inconsequently, her thoughts wandered from the numerous shark-casualties of late to the mundane proclivities of her mother; for to quit the little village of Mediavilla for the capital was that dame's fixed obsession.

Leave Mediavilla, leave Bamboo! The young negress fetched a sigh.

In what way, she reflected, would the family gain by *entering Society*, and how did one enter it at all? There would be a gathering, doubtless, of the elect (probably armed), since the best Society is exclusive and difficult to enter. And then? Did one burrow? Or charge? She had sometimes heard it said that people 'pushed' . . . and closing her eyes, Miss Miami Mouth sought to picture her parents, assisted by her small sister, Edna, and her brother, Charlie, forcing their way, perspiring but triumphant, into the highest social circles of the city of Cuna-Cuna.

Across the dark savannah country the city lay, one of the chief alluring cities of the world: the Celestial city of Cuna-Cuna, Cuna, city of Mimosa, Cuna, city of Arches, Queen of the Tropics, Paradise—almost invariably travellers referred to it like that.

Oh, everything must be fantastic there, where even the very pickneys put on clothes! And Miss Miami Mouth glanced fondly down at her own plump little person, nude but for a girdle of creepers that she would gather freshly twice a day.

'It would be a shame, sh'o, to cover it,' she murmured drowsily, caressing her body; and moved to a sudden spasm of laughter, she tittered: 'No! really. De ideah!'

∾ *II* ∾

'SILVER bean-stalks, silver bean-stalks, oh hé, oh hé,' down the long village street from door to door the cry repeatedly came, until the vendor's voice was lost on the evening air.

In a rocking-chair, before the threshold of a palm-thatched cabin, a matron with broad, bland features and a big, untidy figure surveyed the scene with a nonchalant eye.

Beneath some tall trees, bearing flowers like flaming bells, a few staid villagers sat enjoying the rosy dusk, while, strolling towards the sea, two young men passed by with fingers intermingled.

With a slight shrug, the lady plied her fan.

As the Mother of a pair of oncoming girls, the number of ineligible young men or confirmed bachelors around the neighbourhood was a constant source of irritation to her.

'Sh'o, dis remoteness bore an' weary me to death,' she exclaimed, addressing someone through the window behind; and receiving no audible answer, she presently rose and went within.

It was the hour when, fortified by a siesta, Mrs. Ahmadou Mouth was wont to approach her husband on general household affairs, and to discuss, in particular, the question of their removal to the town; for, with the celebration of their pearl wedding close at hand, the opportunity to make the announcement of a change of residence to their guests ought not, she believed, to be missed.

'We leave Mediavilla for de education ob my daughters,' she would say; or, perhaps: 'We go to Cuna-Cuna for de finishing ob *mes filles!*'

But, unfortunately, the reluctance of Mr. Mouth to forsake his Home seemed to increase from day to day.

She found him asleep, bolt upright, his head gently nodding, beneath a straw hat beautifully browned.

'Say, nigger, lub,' she murmured, brushing her hand featheringly along his knee, 'say, nigger, lub, I gotta go!'

It was the tender prelude to the storm.

Evasive (and but half awake), he warned her. 'Let me alone; Ah'm thinkin'.'

'Prancing Nigger, now come on!'

'Ah'm thinkin'.'

'Tell me what for dis procrastination?' Exasperated, she gripped his arm.

But for all reply Mr. Mouth drew a volume of revival hymns towards him, and turned on his wife his back.

'You ought to shame o' you-self, sh'o,' she caustically commented, crossing to the window.

The wafted odours of the cotton-trees without oppressed the air. In the deepening twilight the rising moonmist already obscured the street.

'Dis place not healthy. Dat damp! Should my daughters go off into a decline . . .' she apprehensively murmured, as her husband started softly to sing.

> ' "For ebber wid de Lord!"
> Amen; so let it be;
> Life from de dead is in dat word,
> 'Tis immortality.'

'If it's de meeting-house dats de obstruction, dair are odders too, in Cuna-Cuna,' she observed.

'How often hab I bid you nebba to mention dat modern Sodom in de hearing ob my presence!'

'De debil frequent de village, fo' dat matter, besides de town.'

'Sh'o nuff.'

'But yestiddy, dat po' silly negress Ottalie was seduced again in a Mango track—; an' dats de third time!'

> 'Heah in de body pent,
> Absent from Him I roam,
> Yet nightly pitch my movin' tent
> A day's march nearer home.'

'Prancing Nigger, from dis indifference to your fambly, be careful lest you do arouse de vials ob de Lord's wrath!'

'Yet nightly pitch—' he was beginning again, in a more subdued key, but the tones of his wife arrested him.

'Prancing Nigger, lemme say sumptin' more!' Mrs. Mouth took

a long sighing breath. 'In dis dark jungle my lil jewel Edna, I feah, will wilt away. . . .'

'Wha' gib you cause to speak like dat?'

'I was tellin' my fortune lately wid de cards,' she reticently made reply, insinuating, by her half-turned eyes, that more disclosures of an ominous nature concerning others besides her daughter had been revealed to her as well.

'Lordey Lord; what is it den you want?'

'I want a Villa with a watercloset—' Flinging wiles to the winds, it was a cry from the heart.

'De Lord hab pity on dese vanities an' innovations!'

'In town, you must rememba, often de houses are far away from de parks;—de city, in dat respect, not like heah.'

'Say nothin' more! De widow ob my po' brudder Willie, across de glen, she warn me I ought nebba to listen to you.'

'Who care for a common woman, dat only read de *Negro World*, an' nebba see anyt'ing else!' she swelled.

Mr. Mouth turned conciliatingly.

'To-morrow me arrange for de victuals for our ebenin' at Home!'

'Good, bery fine,' she murmured, acknowledging through the window the cordial 'good-night' of a few late labourers, returning from the fields, each with a bundle of sugar-cane poised upon the head.

'As soon as marnin' dawn me take dis biznis in hand.'

'Only pramas, nigger darlin',' she cajoled, 'dat durin' de course of de reception you make a lil speech to inform de neighbours ob our gwine away bery soon, for de sake of de education ob our girls.'

'Ah sha'n' pramas nothin'.'

'I could do wid a change too, honey, after my last miscarriage.'

'Change come wid our dissolution,' he assured her, 'quite soon enuff!'

'Bah,' she murmured, rubbing her cheek to his: 'we set out on our journey sh'o in de season ob Novemba.'

To which with asperity he replied: '*Not for two Revolutions!*' and rising brusquely, strode solemnly from the room.

'Hey-ho-day,' she yawned, starting a wheezy gramophone, and sinking down upon his empty chair; and she was lost in ball-room fancies (whirling in the arms of some blond young foreigner) when she caught sight of her daughter's reflection in the glass.

Having broken or discarded her girdle of leaves, Miss Miami Mouth, attracted by the gramophone, appeared to be teaching a hectic two-step to the cat.

'Fie, fie, my lass. Why you be so *Indian*?' her mother exclaimed, bestowing, with the full force of a carpet slipper, a well-aimed spank from behind.

'*Aïe, aïe!*'

'Sh'o: you nohow select!'

'*Aïe.* . . .'

'De low exhibition!'

'I had to take off my apron, 'cos it seemed to draw de bees,' Miami tearfully explained, catching up the cat in her arms.

'Ob course, if you choose to wear roses. . . .'

'It was but ivy!'

'De berries ob de ivy entice de same,' Mrs. Mouth replied, nodding graciously, from the window, to Papy Paul, the next-door neighbour, who appeared to be taking a lonely stroll with a lanthorn and a pineapple.

'I dats way wondering why Bamboo no pass dis evenin', too; as a rule, it is seldom he stop so late out upon de sea,' the young girl ventured.

'After I shall introduce you to de world (de advantage ob a good marriage; when I t'ink ob mine!), you will be ashamed, sh'o, to recall dis infatuation.'

'De young men ob Cuna-Cuna (tell me, Mammee), are dey den so nice?'

'Ah, Chile! If I was your age again . . .'

'Sh'o, dair's nothin' so much in dat.'

'As a young girl of eight (Tee-hee!), I was distracting to all the gentlemen,' Mrs. Mouth asserted, confiding a smile to a small, long-billed bird, in a cage, of the variety known as Bequia-Sweet.

'How I wish i'd been born, like you, in August-Town, across de Isthmus!'

'It gib me dis taste fo' S'ciety, Chile.'

'In S'ciety, don' dey dress wid clothes on ebery day?'

'Sh'o; surtainly.'

'An' don't dey nebba tickle?'

'In August-Town, de aristocracy conceal de best part ob deir bodies; not like heah!'

'An' tell me, Mammee . . . ? De first lover you eber had . . . was he half as handsome as Bamboo?'

'De first dude, Chile, I eber had, was a lil, lil buoy, . . . wid no hair (whatsoeber at all), bal' like a calabash!' Mrs. Mouth replied, as her daughter Edna entered with the lamp.

'Frtt!' the wild thing tittered, setting it down with a bang: with her cincture of leaves and flowers, she had the éclat of a butterfly.

'Better fetch de shade,' Mrs. Mouth exclaimed, staring squeamishly at Miami's shadow on the wall.

'Already it grow dark; no one about now at dis hour ob night at all.'

'Except thieves an' ghouls,' Mrs. Mouth replied, her glance straying towards the window.

But only the little blue-winged bats were passing beneath a fairyland of stars.

'When I do dis, or dis, my shadow appear as formed as Mimi's!'

'Sh'o, Edna, she dat provocative to-day.'

'Be off at once, Chile, an' lay de table for de ebenin' meal; an' be careful not to knock de shine off de new tin teacups,' Mrs. Mouth commanded, taking up an Estate-Agent's catalgoue and seating herself comfortably beneath the lamp.

' "City of Cuna-Cuna," ' she read, ' *"in the Heart of a Brainy District* (within easy reach of University, shops, etc.). A charming Freehold Villa. Main drainage. Extensive views. Electric light. Every convenience." '

'Dat sound just de sort ob lil shack for me.'

～ III ～

THE strange sadness of the evening, the *détresse* of the Evening Sky! Cry, cry, white Rain Birds out of the West, cry . . . !

'An' so, Miami, you no come back no more?'

'No, no come back.'

Flaunting her boredom by the edge of the sea one close of day, she had chanced to fall in with Bamboo, who, stretched at length upon the beach, was engaged in mending a broken net.

'An' I dats way glad,' she half resentfully pouted, jealous a little of his toil.

But, presuming deafness, the young man laboured on, since, to support an aged mother, and to attain one's desires, perforce necessitates work; and his fondest wish, by dint of saving, was to wear on his wedding-day a pink, starched, cotton shirt—a starched, pink cotton shirt, stiff as a boat's-sail when the North winds caught it! But a pink shirt would mean trousers . . . and trousers would lead to shoes . . . 'Extravagant nigger, don't you dare!' he would exclaim, in dizzy panic, from time to time, aloud.

'Forgib me, honey,' he begged, 'but me obliged to finish while de daylight last.'

'Sh'o,' she sulked, following the amazing strategy of the sunset-clouds.

'Miami angel, you look so sweet: I dat amorous ob you, Mimi!'

A light laugh tripped over her lips.

'Say, buoy, how you getting on?' she queried, sinking down on her knees beside him.

'I dat amorous ob you!'

'Oh, ki,' she tittered, with a swift mocking glance at his crimson loincloth. She had often longed to snatch it away.

'Say you lub me, just a lil, too, deah?'

'Sh'o,' she answered softly, sliding over on to her stomach, and laying her cheek to the flats of her hands.

Boats with crimson spouts, to wit, steamers, dotted the skyline far away, and barques, with sails like the wings of butterflies, borne by an idle breeze, were bringing more than one ineligible young mariner back to the prose of shore.

'Ob wha' you t'inking?'

'Nothin',' she sighed, contemplating laconically a little transparent shell of violet pearl, full of seawater and grains of sand, that the wind ruffled as it blew.

'Not ob *any* sort ob lil t'ing?' he caressingly insisted, breaking an open dark flower from her belt of wild Pansy.

'I should be gwine home,' she breathed, recollecting the undoing of the negress Ottalie.

'Oh, I dat amorous ob you, Mimi.'

'If you want to finish dat net while de daylight last.'

For oceanward, in a glowing ball, the sun had dropped already.

'Sho', nigger, I only wish to be kind,' she murmured, getting up and sauntering a few paces along the strand.

Lured, perhaps, by the nocturnal phosphorescence from its lair, a water-scorpion, disquieted at her approach, turned and vanished amid the sheltering cover of the rocks. 'Isht, isht,' she squealed, wading after it into the surf, but to find it, look as she would, was impossible. Dark, curious and anxious, in the fast failing light, the sea disquieted her too, and it was consoling to hear close behind her the solicitous voice of Bamboo.

'Us had best be movin', befo' de murk ob night.'

The few thatched cabins that comprised the village of Mediavilla lay not half a mile from the shore. Situated between the savannah and the sea, on the southern side of the island known as Tacarigua (the 'burning Tacarigua' of the Poets), its inhabitants were obliged, from lack of communication with the larger island centres, to rely to a considerable extent for a livelihood among themselves. Local Market days, held, alternatively, at Valley Village or Broken Hill (the nearest approach to industrial towns in the district around Mediavilla), were the chief source of rural trade, when such merchandise as fish, coral, beads, bananas and loincloths would exchange hands amid much animation, social gossip and pleasant fun.

'Wha' you say to dis?' she queried as they turned inland through the cane-fields, holding up a fetish known as a 'luck-ball,' attached to her throat by a chain.

'Who gib it you?' he shortly demanded, with a quick suspicious glance.

'Mammee, she bring it from Valley Village, an' she bring another for my lil sister, too.'

'Folks say she attend de Market only to meet de Obi man, who cast a spell so dat your Dada move to Cuna-Cuna.'

'Dat so!'

'Your Mammee no seek ebber de influence ob Obeah?'

'Not dat I know ob!' she replied; nevertheless, she could not but recall her mother's peculiar behaviour of late, especially upon Market days, when, instead of conversing with her friends, she would take herself off with a mysterious air, saying she was going to the Baptist Chapel.

'Mammee, she hab no faith in de Witch-Doctor at all,' she murmured, halting to lend an ear to the liquid note of a peadove among the canes.

'I no care; me follow after wherebber you go,' he said, stealing an arm about her.

'True?' she breathed, looking up languidly towards the white mounting moon.

'I dat amorous ob you, Mimi.'

~ *IV* ~

IT was the Feast night. In the grey spleen of evening, through the dusty lanes towards Mediavilla county society flocked.

Peering round a cow-shed door, Primrose and Phœbe, procured as waitresses for the occasion, felt their valour ooze as they surveyed the arriving guests, and dropping prostrate amid the straw, declared, in each other's arms, that never, never would they find the courage to appear.

In the road, before a tall tamarind-tree, a well-spread supper board exhaled a pungent odour of fried cascadura fish, exciting the plaintive ravings of the wan pariah dogs, and the cries of a few little stark naked children engaged as guardians to keep them away. Defying an ancient and inelegant custom by which the hosts welcomed their guests by the side of the road, Mrs. Mouth had elected to remain within the precincts of the house, where, according to tradition, the bridal trophies—cowrie-shells, feathers, and a bouquet of faded orange blossom—were being displayed.

'It seem no more dan yestidday,' she was holding forth gaily over a goblet of Sangaree wine, 'it seem no more dan yestidday dat I put on me maiden wreath ob arange blastams to walk wid me nigger to church.'

Clad in rich-hued creepers, she was both looking and feeling her best.

'Sh'o,' a woman with blonde-dyed hair and Buddery eyes exclaimed, 'it seem no more dan just like yestidday; dat not so, Papy Paul?' she queried, turning to an old man in a raspberry-pink kerchief, who displayed (as he sat) more of his person than he seemed to be aware of.

But Papy Paul was confiding a receipt for pickling yuccas to Mamma Luna, the mother of Bamboo, and made as if not to hear.

Offering a light, lilac wine, sweet and heady, Miami circled here and there. She had a cincture of white rose-oleanders, and a bandeau of blue convolvuli. She held a fan.

'Or do you care for anyt'ing else?' she was enquiring, automatic-ally, of Mr. Musket (the Father of three very common girls), as a melodious tinkle of strings announced the advent of the minstrels from Broken Hill.

Following the exodus roadward, it was agreeable to reach the outer air.

Under the high trees by the yard-door gate, the array of vehicles and browsing quadrupeds was almost as numerous as upon a market day. The quiet village road was agog, with bustling folk as perhaps never before, coming and going between the little Café of the 'Forty Parrots,' with its Bar, spelled *Biar* in twinkling lights. All iris in the dusk, a few loosely-loinclothed young men had commenced dancing aloofly among themselves, bringing down some light (if bitter) banter from the belles.

Pirouetting with these, Miami recognised the twinkling feet of her brother Charlie, a lad who preferred roaming the wide savannah country after butterflies with his net to the ever-increasing etiquette of his home.

'Sh'o, S'ciety no longer what it wa',' the mother of two spare lean girls, like young giraffes, was lamenting, when a clamorous song summoned the assembly to the festal board.

In the glow of blazing palm logs, stoked by capering pickneys, the company, with some considerable jostling, became seated by degrees.

'Fo' what we gwine to recebe de Lord make us to be truly t'ankful.' Mr. Mouth's low voice was lost amid the din. Bending to the decree of Providence, and trusting in God for the welfare of his house, he was resigned to follow the call of duty, by allowing his offspring such educational advantages and worldly polish that only a city can give.

'An' so I heah you gwine to leab us!' the lady at his elbow exclaimed, helping herself to a claw of a crab.

'Fo' de sake ob de chillen's schoolin',' Mr. Mouth made reply, blinking at the brisk lightning play through the foliage of the trees.

'Dey tell me de amount of licence dat go on ober dah—' she murmured, indicating with her claw the chequered horizon; 'but de whole world needs revising, as de Missionary truly say!'

'Indeed, an' dat's de trute.'

'It made me cry,' a plump little woman declared, 'when de Minister speak so serious on de scandal ob close dancing. . . .'

'Fo' one t'ing lead sh'o to be nex'!' Mr. Mouth obstrusely assented, turning his attention upon an old negress answering to the name of Mamma May, who was retailing how she had obtained the sunshade beneath which, since noon, she had walked all the way to the party.

'Ah could not afford a parasol, so Ah just cut miself a lil green bush, an' held it up ober my head,' she was crooning in gleeful triumph.

'It's a wonder, indeed, no one gib you a lif'!' several voices observed, but the discussion was drowned by an esoteric song of remote tribal times from the lips of Papy Paul:

> '*I am King Elephant-bag,*
> *Ob de rose-pink Mountains!*
> *Tatou, tatouay, tatou . . .*'

provoking from Miss Stella Spooner, the marvellous daughter of an elderly father, a giggle in which she was joined by the youngest Miss Mouth.

Incontestably a budding Princess, the playful mite was enjoying, with airy nonchalance, her initial experience of Society.

'Ob course she is very *jeune*,' Mrs. Mouth murmured archly, behind her hand, into the ear of Mr. Musket.

'It's de Lord's will,' he cautiously replied, rolling a mystified eye towards his wife (a sable negress out of Africa), continually vaunting her foreign extraction. 'I'm Irish,' she would say: 'I'm Irish, deah. . . .'

'Sh'o she de born image ob her elder sister!'

'De world all say she to marry de son ob ole Mamma Luna, dat keep de lil shop.'

'Suz! Wha' nex'?' Mrs. Mouth returned, breaking off to focus Papy Paul, apparently, already, far from sober. 'I hav' saw God, an' I hav' spoke wid de President, too!' he was announcing impressively to Mamma Luna, a little old woman in whose veins ran the blood of many races.

'Dair's no trute at all in *dat* report,' Mrs. Mouth quietly added, signalling directions to a sturdy, round-bottomed little lad, who had undertaken to fill the gap caused by Primrose and Phœbe.

Bearing a pannier piled with fruit, he had not got far before the minstrels called forth several couples to their feet.

The latest jazz, bewildering, glittering, exuberant as the soil, a jazz, throbbing, pulsating, with a zim, zim, zim, a jazz all abandon and verve that had drifted over the glowing savannah and the waving cane-fields from Cuna-Cuna by the Violet Sea, invited, irresestibly, to motion every boy and girl.

'Prancing Nigger, hab a dance?' his wife, transported, shrilled: but Mr. Mouth was predicting a banana slump to Mrs. Walker, the local midwife, and paid no heed.

Torso-to-torso, the youngsters twirled, while even a pair of majestic matrons, Mrs. Friendship and Mrs. Mother, went whirling away (together) into the brave summer dusk. Accepting the invitation of Bamboo, Miami rose, but before dancing long complained of the heat.

'Sh'o, it cooler in de Plantation,' he suggested, pointing along the road.

'Oh, I too much afraid!'

'What for you afraid?'

But Miami only laughed, and tossed her hand as if she were scattering dewdrops.

Following the roving fireflies and adventurous flittermice, they strolled along in silence. By the roadside, two young men, friends, walking with fingers intermingled, saluted them softly. An admirable evening for a promenade! Indescribably sweet, the floating field-scents enticed them witchingly on.

'Shi!' she exclaimed as a bird skimmed swiftly past with a chattering cry.

'It noddin', deah, but a lil wee owl.'

'An' it to make my heart go so,' she murmured, with a sidelong smiling glance.

He had a new crimson loincloth, and a blood-pink carnation at his ear.

'What for you afraid?' he tenderly pressed.

'It much cooler heah, doh it still very hot,' she inconsequently answered, pausing to listen to the fretting of the hammer tree-frogs in the dusk.

'Dey hold a concert, honey lub, all for us.'

Rig a jig jig, rig a jig jig. . . .

'Just hark to de noise!' she murmured, starting a little at the silver lightning behind the palms.

'Just hark,' he repeated, troubled.

Rig a jig jig, rig a jig jig. . . .

LITTLE jingley trot-trot-trot, over the Savannah, hey—!
Joggling along towards Cuna-Cuna the creaking caravan
shaped its course. Seated in a hooded chariot, berced by mule-bells,
and nibbling a shoot of ripe cane, Mrs. Mouth appeared to have
attained the heights of bliss. Disregarding or insensitive to the incessant groans of her husband (wedged in between a case of pineapples
and a box marked 'lingerie'), she abandoned herself voluptuously
to her thoughts. It was droll to contemplate meeting an old acquaintance, Nini Snagg, who had gone to reside in Cuna-Cuna long ago.
'Fancy seein' you!' she would say, and how they both would laugh.

Replying tersely to the innumerable 'what would you do ifs' of
her sister, supposing attacks from masked bandits or ferocious wild
animals, Miami moped.

All her whole heart yearned back behind her, and never had she
loved Bamboo so much as now.

' —if a big, shaggy buffalo, wid two sharp horns, dat long, were
to rush right at you!' Edna was plaguing her, when a sudden jolt of
the van set up a loud cackling from a dozen scared cocks and hens.

'Drat dose fowl; as if dair were none in Cuna-Cuna!' Mrs. Mouth
addressed her husband.

'Not birds ob dat brood,' he retorted, plaintively starting to sing.

'I t'ink when I read dat sweet story ob old,
  When Jesus was here among men,
How He called lil chillens as lambs to His fold,
  I should like to hab been wid dem den!
I wish dat His hands had been placed ahn my head,
  Dat His arms had been thrown aroun' me,
An' dat I might hab seen His kind look when He said,
"Let de lil ones come unto Me!"'

'Mind de dress-basket don't drop down, deah, an' spoil our clo','
Mrs. Mouth exclaimed, indicating a cowskin trunk that seemed to be
in peril of falling; for, from motives of economy and ease, it had
been decided that not before Cuna-Cuna should rear her queenly
towers above them would they change their floral garlands for the
more artificial fabrics of the town, and Edna, vastly to her importance, go into a pair of frilled 'invisibles' and a petticoat for the first

amazing time; nor, indeed, would Mr. Mouth himself 'take to de pants' until his wife and daughters should have assumed their skirts. But this, from the languid pace at which their vehicle proceeded, was unlikely to be just yet. In the torrid tropic noontime, haste, however, was quite out of the question. Bordered by hills, long, yellow and low, the wooded savannah rolled away beneath a blaze of trembling heat.

'I don't t'ink much ob dis part of de country,' Mrs. Mouth commented. 'All dese common palms ... de cedar-wood tree, dat my tree. Dat is de timber I prefer.'

'An' some,' Edna pertly smiled, 'dey like best de bamboo....'

A remark that was rewarded by a blow on the ear.

'Now she set up a hullabaloo like de time when de scorpion bit her botty,' Mrs. Mouth lamented, and indeed the uproar made alarmed from the boskage a cloud of winsome soldier-birds and inquisitive paroquets.

'Oh my God,' Mr. Mouth exclaimed. 'What for you make all dat dere noise?' But his daughter paid no attention, and soon sobbed herself to sleep.

Advancing through tracks of acacia-shrub or groves of nutmeg-trees, they jolted along in the gay, exalting sunlight. Flowers brighter than love, wafting the odour of spices, strewed in profusion the long guinea-grass on either side of the way.

'All dose sweet aprons, if it weren't fo' de flies!' Mrs. Mouth murmured, regarding some heavy, ambered, Trumpet flowers with a covetous eye.

'I trust Charlie get bit by no snake!'

'Prancing Nigger! It a lil too late now to t'ink ob dat.'

Since, to avoid overcrowding the family party, Charlie was to follow with his butterfly net and arrive as he could. And never were butterflies (seen in nigger-boys' dreams) as brilliant or frolicsome as were those of mid-savannah. Azure Soledads, and radiant Conquistadors with frail flamboyant wings, wove about the labouring mules perpetual fresh rosettes.

'De Lord protect de lad,' Mr. Mouth remarked, relapsing into silence.

Onward through the cloudless noontide, beneath the ardent sun, the caravan drowsily crawled. As the afternoon advanced, Mrs. Mouth produced a pack of well-thumbed cards, and cutting, casually, twice, began interrogating Destiny with these. Reposing as best she might, Miami gave herself up to her reflections. The familiar aspect of the wayside palms, the tattered pennons of the bananas, the big silk-cottons (known, to children, as 'Mammee-trees'), all brought to her mind Bamboo.

'Dair's somet'in' dat look like a death dah, dat's troublin' me,' Mrs. Mouth remarked, moodily fingering a greasy ace.

'De Almighty forgib dese foolish games!' Mr. Mouth protestingly said.

'An' from de lie ob de cards . . . it seem as ef de corpse were ob de masculine species.'

'Wha' gib you de notion ob dat?'

'Sh'o, a sheep puts his wool on his favourite places,' Mrs. Mouth returned, reshuffling slowly her pack.

Awakened by her Father's psalms, Edna's 'What would you do's' had commenced with volubility anew, growing more eerie with the gathering night.

' . . . if a Wood-Spirit wid two heads an' six arms were to take hold ob you, Mimi, from behind?'

'I no do nothin' at all,' Miami answered briefly.

'Talk not so much ob de jumbies, Chile, as de chickens go to roost!' Mrs. Mouth admonished.

'Or, if de debil himself should?' Edna insisted, allowing Snowball, the cat, to climb on to her knee.

'Nothin', sh'o,' Miami murmured, regarding dreamily the sun's sinking dusk, that was illuminating all the Western sky with incarnadine and flamingo-rose. Ominous in the falling dusk, the savannah rolled away, its radiant hues effaced beneath a rapid tide of deepening shadow.

'Start de gramophone gwine, girls, an' gib us somet'in' bright!' Mrs. Mouth exclaimed, depressed by the forlorn note of the Twa-oo-Twa-oo bird, that mingled its lament with a thousand night cries from the grass.

'When de saucy female sing "My Ice Cream Girl," fo' sh'o she scare de elves.'

And as though by force of magic the nasal soprano of an invisible songstress rattled forth with tinkling gusto a music-hall air with a sparkling refrain.

> 'And the boys shout Girlie, hi!
> Bring me soda, soda, soda,

(Aside, spoken) (Stop your fooling there and let me alone!)
     For I'm an Ice Cream Soda Girl.'

'It put me in mind ob de last sugar-factory explosion. It was de same day dat Snowball crack de Tezzrazine record. Drat de cat!'

'O Lordey Lord! Wha' for you make dat din?' Mr. Mouth complained, knotting a cotton handkerchief over his head.

'I hope you not gwine to be billeous, honey, afore we get to Lucia?'

'Lemme alone. Ah'm thinkin'.'

Pressing on by the light of a large clear moon, the hamlet of Lucia, the halting-place proposed for the night, lay still far ahead.

Stars, like many Indian pinks, flecked with pale brightness the sky above; towards the horizon shone the Southern Cross, while the Pole Star, through the palm-fronds, came and went.

     '*And the men cry Girlie, hi!*
     Bring me—'

'Silence, dah! Ah'm thinkin'. . . .'

❧ VI ❧

CUNA, full of charming roses, full of violet shadows, full of music, full of Love, Cuna . . . !

Leaning from a balcony of the Grand Savannah hotel, their instincts all aroused, Miami and Edna gazed out across the Alemeda, a place all foliage, lamplight, and flowers. It was the hour when Society, in slowly parading carriages, would congregate to take the air beneath the pale mimosas that adorned the favourite promenade. All but recumbent, as though agreeably fatigued by their recent emotions (what wild follies were not committed in shuttered-villas during the throbbing hours of noon?), the Cunans, in their elegant equipages, made, for anyone fresh from the provinces, an interesting and absorbing sight. The liquid-eyed loveliness of the women, and the handsomeness of the men, with their black moustaches and their treacherous smiles—these, indeed, were things to gaze on.

'Oh ki!' Miami laughed delightedly, indicating a foppish, pretty youth, holding in a restive little horse dancing away with him.

Rubbing herself repeatedly, as yet embarrassed by the novelty of her clothes, Edna could only gasp.

'. . .,' she jabbered, pointing at some flaunting belles in great evening hats and falling hair.

'All dat fine,' Miami murmured, staring in wonderment around.

Dominating the city soared the Opera House, uplifting a big, naked man, all gilt, who was being bitten, or mauled, so it seemed, by a pack of wild animals carved of stone; while near by were the University, and the Cathedral with its low white dome crowned by moss-green tiles.

Making towards it, encouraged by the Vesper bell, some young girls, in muslin masks, followed by a retinue of bustling nuns, were running the gauntlet of the profligates that clustered on the kerb.

'Oh, Jesus honey!' Edna cooed, scratching herself in an ecstasy of delight.

'Fo' shame, Chile, to act so unladylike; if any gen'leman look up he t'ink you make a wicked sign,' Mrs. Mouth cautioned, stepping out upon the balcony from the sitting-room behind.

Inhaling a bottle of sal volatile, to dispel *de megrims,* she was looking dignified in a *décolleté* of smoke-blue tulle.

'Nebba do *dat* in S'ciety,' she added, placing a protecting arm around each of her girls.

Seduced, not less than they, by the animation of the town, the fatigue of the journey seemed to her amply rewarded. It was amusing to watch the crowd before the Ciné Lara, across the way, where many were flocking attracted by the hectic posters of 'A Wife's Revenge.'

'I keep t'inking I see Nini Snagg,' Mrs. Mouth observed, regarding a negress in emerald-tinted silk, seated on a public bench beneath the glittering greenery.

'Cunan folk dat fine,' Edna twittered, turning about at her Father's voice:

> 'W'en de day ob toil is done,
> W'en de race ob life is run,
> Heaven send thy weary one
> Rest for evermore!'

'Prancing Nigger! Is it worth while to wear dose grimaces?'

'Sh'o, dis no good place to be.'

'Why, what dair wrong wid it?'

'Ah set out to look fo' de Meetin'-House, but no sooner am Ah in de street dan a female wid her hair droopin' loose down ober her back an' into her eyes, she tell me to Come along.'

'Some of dose bold women, dey ought to be shot through dair bottoms!' Mrs. Mouth indignantly said.

'But I nebba answer nothin'.'

'May our daughters respect dair virtue same as you!' Mrs. Mouth returned, focusing wistfully the vast flowery parterre of the Café McDhu'l.

Little city of cocktails, Cuna! The surpassing excellence of thy Barmen, who shall sing?

'See how dey spell "Biar," Mammee,' Miami tittered: 'dey forget de *i*!'

'Sh'o, Chile, an' so dey do. . . .'

'Honey Jesus!' Edna broadly grinned: 'imagine de ignorance ob dat.'

∼ *VII* ∼

NOW, beyond the Alemeda, in the modish faubourg of Faran-anka, there lived a lady of both influence and wealth—the widow of the Inventor of Sunflower Piquant. The *veto* of Madame Ruis, arbitress absolute of Cunan society, and owner, moreover, of a considerable portion of the town, had caused the suicide indeed of more than one social climber. Unhappy, nostalgic, disdainful, selfish, ever about to abandon Cuna-Cuna to return to it no more, yet never budging, adoring her fairy villa far too well, Madame Ruiz, while craving for the International-world, consoled herself by watching from afar European Society going speedily to the dogs. Art-loving, and considerably musical (many a dizzy venture at the Opera-house had owed its audition to her), she had, despite the self-centredness of her nature, done not a little to render more brilliant the charming city it amused her with such vehemence to abuse.

One softly gloomy morning, preceding Madame Ruiz's first *cotillon* of the Season, the lodge-keeper of the Villa Alba, a negress, like some great, violet bug, was surprised, while tending the brightly hanging grape-fruit in the drive, by an imperative knocking on the gate. At such a matutinal hour only trashy errand-boys

shouldering baskets might be expected to call, and giving the summons no heed the mulatress continued her work.

The Villa Alba, half buried in spreading awnings, and surrounded
by many noble trees, stood but a short distance off the main road, its
pleasaunces enclosed by flower-enshrouded walls, all a-zig-zag, like
the folds of a screen. Beloved of lizards and velvet-backed humming-
birds, the shaded gardens led on one side to the sea.

'To make such a noise at dis hour,' the negress murmured, going
grumblingly at length to the gate, disclosing, upon opening, a
gentleman in middle life, with a tooth-brush moustache and a sapphire ring.

'De mist'ess still in bed, sah.'

'In bed?'

'She out bery late, sah, but you find Miss Edwards up.'

With a nod of thanks the visitor directed his footsteps discreetly
towards the house.

Although not, precisely, *in* her bed, when the caller, shortly afterwards, was announced, Madame Ruiz was nevertheless as yet in
dishabille.

'Tiresome man, what does he want to see me about?' she exclaimed, gathering around her a brocaded wrap formed of a priestly
cope.

'He referred to a lease, ma'am,' the maid replied.

'A lease!' Madame Ruiz raised eyes dark with spleen.

The visit of her agent, or man of affairs, was apt to ruffle her
composure for the day. 'Tell him to leave it and go,' she commanded,
selecting a nectarine from a basket of iced fruits beside her.

Removing reflectively the sensitive skin, her mind evoked, in
ironic review, the chief salient events of society, scheduled to take
place on the face of the map in the course of the day.

The marriage of the Count de Nozhel, in Touraine, to Mrs.
Exelmans of Cincinnati, the divorce of poor Lady Luckcock in
London (it seemed quite certain that one of the five co-respondents
was the little carrot-haired Lord Dubelly again), the last 'pomps,'
at Vienna, of Princess de Seeyohl *née* Mitchening-Meyong (Peace
to her soul! She had led her life). . . . The christening in Madrid
of the girl-twins of the Queen of Spain. . . .

'At her time, I really *don't* understand it,' Madame Ruiz murmured
to herself aloud, glancing, as though for an explanation, about the
room.

Through the flowing folds of the mosquito curtains of the bed, that swept a cool, flagged floor spread with skins, showed the oratory, with its waxen flowers, and pendent flickering lights, that burned, night and day, before a Leonardo saint with a treacherous smile. Beyond the little recess came a lacquer commode, bearing a masterly marble group, depicting a pair of amorous hermaphrodites amusing themselves; while above, suspended against the spacious wainscoting of the wall, a painting of a man, elegantly corseted, with a violet in his moustache, 'Study of a Parisian,' and its pendant, 'Portrait of a Lady,' signed Van Dongen, were the chief outstanding objects that the room contained.

'One would have thought that at forty she would have given up having babies,' Madame Ruiz mused, choosing a glossy cherry from the basket at her side.

Through the open window a sound of distant music caught her ear.

'Ah! If only he were less weak,' she sighed, her thoughts turning towards the player, who seemed to be enamoured of the opening movement (rapturously repeated) of *L'Après-midi d'un Faune*.

The venetorial habits of Vittorio Ruiz had been from his earliest years the source of his mother's constant chagrin and despair. At the age of five he had assaulted his Nurse, and, steadily onward, his passions had grown and grown. . . .

'It's the fault of the wicked climate,' Madame Ruiz reflected, as her companion, Miss Edwards, came in with the post.

'Thanks, Eurydice,' she murmured, smilingly exchanging a butterfly kiss.

'It's going to be oh so hot to-day!'

'Is it, dear?'

'Intense,' Miss Edwards predicted, fluttering a gay-daubed paper fan.

Sprite-like, with a little strained ghost-face beneath a silver shock of hair, it seemed as if her long blue eyes had absorbed the Cunan sea.

'Do you remember the giant with the beard?' she asked, 'at the Presidency fête?'

'Do I?'

'And we wondered who he could be!'

'Well?'

'He's the painter of Women's Backs, my dear!'

'The painter of women's *what*?'

'An artist.'

'Oh.'

'I wanted to know if you'd advise me to sit.'

'Your back is charming, dear, *c'est un dos d'élite.*'

'I doubt, though, it's classic,' Miss Edwards murmured, pirou-etting slowly before the glass.

But Madame Ruiz was perusing her correspondence and seemed to be absorbed.

'They're to be married, in Munich, on the fifth, 'she chirruped.

'Who?'

'Elsie and Baron Sitmar.'

'Ah, Ta-ra, dear! In those far worlds . . .' Miss Edwards impatiently exclaimed, opening wide a window and leaning out.

Beneath the flame-trees, with their spreading tops a mass of crimson flower, cooly white-garbed gardeners, with naked feet and big bell-shaped hats of straw, were sweeping slowly, as in some rhythmic dance, the flamboyant blossoms that had fallen to the ground.

'Wasn't little Madame Haase, dear, born Kattie von Guggen-heim?'

'I really don't know,' Miss Edwards returned, flapping away a fly with her fan.

'This villainous climate! My memory's going. . . .'

'I wish I cared for Cuna less, that's all!' Miss Edwards said, her glance following a humming bird, poised in air, above the sparkling turquoise of a fountain.

'Captain Moonlight . . . duty . . . (tedious word) . . . can't come!'

'Oh?'

'Such a dull post,' Madame Ruiz murmured, pausing to listen to the persuasive tenor voice of her son.

> 'Little mauve nigger boy,
> I t'ink you break my heart!'

'My poor Vitti! Bless him.'

'He was out last night with some Chinese she.'

'I understood him to be going to *Pelléas and Mélisande.*'

'He came to the Opera-house, but only for a minute.'

'Dios!'

'And, oh, dearest.' Miss Edwards dropped her cheek to her hand.

'Was Hatso as ever delicious?' Madame Ruiz asked, changing the topic as her woman returned, followed by a pomeranian of parts, 'Snob'; a dog beautiful as a child.

'We had Gebhardt instead.'

'In Mélisande she's so huge,' Madame Ruiz commented, eyeing severely the legal-looking packet which her maid had brought her.

'Business, Camilla; *how* I pity you!'

Madame Ruiz sighed.

'It seems,' she said, 'that for the next nine-and-ninety-years I have let a Villa to a Mr. and Mrs. Ahmadou Mouth.'

∾ *VIII* ∾

FLOOR of copper, floor of gold. . . . Beyond the custom-house door, ajar, the street at sunrise seemed aflame.

'Have you nothing, young man, to declare?'

' . . . Butterflies!'

'Exempt of duty. Pass.'

Floor of silver, floor of pearl. . . .

Trailing a muslin net, and laughing for happiness, Charlie Mouth marched into the town.

Oh, Cuna-Cuna! Little city of Lies and Peril! How many careless young nigger boys have gone thus to seal their Doom!

Although the Sun-god was scarcely risen, already the radiant street teemed with life.

Veiled dames, flirting fans, bent on church or market, were issuing everywhere from their doors, and the air was vibrant with the sweet voice of bells.

To rejoin his parents promptly at their hotel was a promise he was tempted to forget.

Along streets all fresh and blue in the shade of falling awnings, it was fine, indeed, to loiter. Beneath the portico of a church a running fountain drew his steps aside. Too shy to strip and squat in the basin, he was glad to bathe freely his head, feet and chest: then, stirred by curiosity to throw a glance at the building, he lifted the long yellow nets that veiled the door.

It was the fashionable church of La Favavoa, and the extemporary address of the Archibishop of Cuna was in full and impassioned swing.

'Imagine the world, my friends, had Christ been born a girl!' he was saying in tones of tender dismay as Charlie entered.

Subsiding bashfully to a bench, Charlie gazed around.

So many sparkling fans. One, a delicate light mauve one: 'Shucks! If only you wa' butterflies!' he breathed, contemplating with avidity the nonchalant throng; then perceiving a richer specimen splashed with silver of the same amative tint: 'Oh you lil beauty!' And, clutching his itching net to his heart, he regretfully withdrew.

Sauntering leisurely through the cool, mimosa-shaded streets, he approached, as he guessed, the Presidency. A score of shoeblacks lolled at cards and gossip before its gilded pales. Amazed at their audacity (for the President had threatened more than once to 'wring the Public's neck'), Charlie hastened by. Public gardens, brilliant with sarracenias, lay just beyond the palace, where a music-pavilion, surrounded by palms and rocking-chairs, appeared a favourite, and much-frequented, resort; from here he observed the Cunan bay strewn with sloops and white-sailed yachts asleep upon the tide. Strolling on, he found himself in the busy vicinity of the Market. Although larger and more varied, it resembled in other respects the village one at home.

'Say, honey, say'—crouching in the dust before a little pyre of mangoes, a lean-armed woman besought him to buy.

Pursued by a confusion of voices, he threaded his way deftly down an alley dressed with booths. Pomegranates, some open with their crimson seeds displayed, banana-combs, and big, veined water-melons, lay heaped on every side.

'I could do wid a slice ob watteh-million,' he reflected: 'but to lick an ice-cream dat tempt me more!' Nor would the noble fruit of the baobab, the paw-paw, or the pine turn him from his fancy.

But no ice-cream stand met his eye, and presently he resigned himself to sit down upon his heels, in the shade of a potter's stall, and consider the passing crowd.

Missionaries with freckled hands and hairy, care-worn faces, followed by pale girls wielding tambourines of the Army of the Soul, foppish nigger bucks in panamas and palm-beach suits so cocky, Chinamen with osier baskets, their nostalgic eyes aswoon, heavily straw-hatted nuns trailing their dust-coloured rags, and suddenly, oh, could it be?—but there was no mistaking that golden waddle: 'Mamma!'

Mamma, Mammee, Mrs. Ahmadou Mouth. All in white, with snow-white shoes and hose so fine, he hardly dare.

'Mammee, Mammee, oh, Mammee. . . .'

'Sonny mine! My lil boy!'

'Mammee.'

'Just to say!'

And, oh, honies! Close behind, behold Miami, and Edna too: the Miss Lips, the fair Lips, the smiling Lips. How spry each looked. The elder (grown a trifle thinner), sweet *à ravir* in tomato-red, while her sister, plump as a corn-fattened partridge, and very perceptibly powdered, seemed like the flower of the prairie sugar-cane when it breaks into bloom.

'We've been to a Music-hall, an' a pahty, an' Snowball has dropped black kittens.' Forestalling Miami, Edna rapped it out.

'Oh shucks!'

'An' since we go into S'ciety, we keep a boy in buttons!'

Mrs. Mouth turned about.

'Where is dat idjit coon?'

'He stay behind to bargain for de pee-wee birds, Mammee, fo' to make de taht.'

'De swindling tortoise.'

'An' dair are no vacancies at de University: not fo' any ob us!' Edna further retailed, going off into a spasm of giggles.

She was swinging a wicker basket, from which there dangled the silver forked tail of a fish.

'Fo' goodness' sake gib dat sea-porcupine to Ibum, Chile,' Mrs. Mouth commanded, as a perspiring niggerling in livery presented himself.

'Ibum, his arms are full already.'

'Just come along all to de Villa now! It dat mignon an' all so nice. An' after de collation,' Mrs. Mouth (shocked on the servant's account at her son's nude neck) raised her voice, 'we go to de habadasher in Palmbranch Avenue an' I buy you an Eton colleh!'

∽ IX ∽

'PRANCING NIGGER, I t'ink it bery strange dat Madame Ruiz she nebba call.'

'Sh'o.'

'In August-Town, S'ciety less stuck-up dan heah!'

Ensconced in rocking-chairs, in the shade of the ample porch of the Villa Vista Hermosa, Mr. and Mrs. Mouth had been holding a desultory *tête-à-tête*.

It was a Sabbath evening, and a sound of reedy pipes and bafalons, from a neighbouring café, filled with a feverish sadness the brilliantly lamp-lit street.

'De airs ob de neighbehs, dat dair affair; what matter mo' am de chillen's schoolin'.'

'Prancing Nigger, I hope your Son an' Daughters will yet take dair Degrees, an' if not from de University, den from Home. From heah.'

'Hey-ho-day, an' dat would be a miracle!' Mr. Mouth mirthlessly laughed.

'Dose chillens hab learnt quite a lot already.'

' 'Bout de shops an' cinemas!'

Mrs. Mouth disdained a reply.

She had taken the girls to the gallery at the Opera one night to hear 'Louise,' but they had come out, by tacit agreement, in the middle of it: the plainness of Louise's blouse, and the lack of tunes . . . the suffocation of the gallery . . . Once bit twice shy, they had not gone back again.

'All your fambly need, Prancing Nigger, is social opportunity! But what is de good ob de Babtist parson?'

Mr. Mouth sketched a gesture.

'Sh'o, Edna, she some young yet. . . . But Miami dat *distinguée*; an', doh I her mother, b'lieb me dat is one ob de choicest girls I see; an' dat's de trute.'

'It queer,' Mr. Mouth abstrusely murmured, 'how many skeeter-bugs dair are 'bout dis ebenin'!'

'De begonias in de window-boxes most lik'ly draw dem. But as I was saying, Prancing Nigger, I t'ink it bery strange dat Madame Ruiz nebba call.'

'P'r'aps she out ob town.'

'Accordin' to de paper, she bin habing her back painted, but what dat fo' I dunno.'

'Ah shouldn't wonder ef she hab some trouble ob a dorsal kind; same as me gramma mumma long agone.'

'Dair'd be no harm in sendin' one ob de chillens to enquire. Wha' you t'ink, sah?' Mrs. Mouth demanded, plucking from off the porch a pale hanging flower with a languorous scent.

Mr. Mouth glanced apprehensively skyward.

The mutters of thunder and intermittent lightning of the finest nights.

'It's a misfortnit we eber left Mediavilla,' he exclaimed uneasily, as a falling star, known as a thief star, sped swiftly down the sky.

'Prancing Nigger,' Mrs. Mouth rose, remarking, 'befo' you start to grummle, I leab you alone to your Jereymiads!'

'A misfortnit sho' nuff,' he mused, and regret for the savannah country and the tall palm-trees of his village oppressed his heart. Moreover, his means (derived from the cultivation of the *Musa paradisica,* or Banana) seemed likely to prove ere long inadequate to support the whims of his wife, who after a lifetime of contented nudity appeared to be now almost insatiable for dress.

A discordant noise from above interrupted the trend of his thoughts.

'Sh'o, she plays wid it like a toy,' he sighed, as the sound occurred again.

'Prancing Nigger, de water-supply cut off!'

'It's de Lord's will.'

'Dair's not a drop, my lub, in de privy.'

' 'Cos it always in use!'

'I b'lieb dat lil half-caste, Ibum, 'cos I threaten to gib him notice, do somet'in' out ob malice to de chain.'

'Whom de Lord loveth He chasteneth!' Mr. Mouth observed, 'an dose bery words (ef you look) you will find in de twelfth chapter an' de sixth berse ob de Book ob Hebrews.'

'Prancing Nigger, you datways selfish! Always t'inkin' ob your soul, instead ob your obligations towards de fambly.'

'Why, wha' mo' can I do dan I've done?'

Mrs. Mouth faintly shrugged.

'I had hoped,' she said, 'dat Nini would hab bin ob use to de girls, but dat seem now impossible!' For Mrs. Snagg had been traced to a house of ill-fame, where, it appeared, she was an exponent of the Hodeidah—a lascive Cunan dance.

'Understand dat any sort ob intimacy 'tween de Villa an' de *Closerie des Lilas* Ah must flatly forbid.'

'Prancing Nigger, as ef I should take your innocent chillens to call on po' Nini; not dat eberyt'ing about her at de *Closerie* is not elegant an' nice. Sh'o, some ob de inmates ob dat establishment possess mo' diamonds dan dair betters do outside! You'd be surprised ef you could see what two ob de girls dair, Dinah an' Lew. . . .'

'Enuf!'

'It isn't always Virtue, Prancing Nigger, dat come off best!' And Mrs. Mouth might have offered further observations on the matter of ethics had not her husband left her.

∾ X ∾

PAST the Presidency and the public park, the Theatres Maxine Bush, Eden-Garden and Apollo, along the Avenida and the Jazz Halls by the wharf, past little suburban shops, and old, deserted churchyards where bloom geraniums, through streets of squalid houses, and onward skirting pleasure lawns and orchards, bibbitty-bobbitty, beneath the sovereign brightness of the sky, crawled the Farananka tram.

Surveying the landscape listlessly through the sticks of her fan, Miss Edna Mouth grew slightly bored—alas, poor child; couldst thou have guessed the blazing brightness of thy Star, thou wouldst doubtless have been more alert!

'Sh'o, it dat far an' tejus,' she observed to the conductor, lifting upon him the sharp-soft eyes of a paroquet.

She was looking bewitching in a frock of silverish *mousseline* and a violet tallyho cap, and dangled upon her knees an intoxicating sheaf of the blossoms known as Marvel of Peru.

'Hab patience, lil Missey, an' we soon be dah.'

'He tells me, dear child, he tells me,' Madame Ruiz was rounding a garden path, upon the arm of her son, 'he tells me, Vitti, that the systole and diastole of my heart's muscles are slightly inflamed; and that I ought, darling, to be *very* careful. . . .'

Followed by a handsome borzoi and the pomeranian 'Snob,' the pair were taking their usual post-prandial exercise beneath the trees.

'Let me come, Mother dear,' he murmured without interrupting, 'over the other side of you; I always like to be on the right side of my profile!'

'And, really, since the affair of Madame de Bazvalon, my health has hardly been what it was.'

'That foolish little woman,' he uncomfortably laughed.

'He tells me my nerves need rest,' she declared, looking pathetically up at him.

He had the nose of an actress, and ink-black hair streaked with gold, his eyes seemed to be covered with the freshest of fresh dark pollen, while nothing could exceed the vivid pallor of his cheeks or the bright sanguine of his mouth.

'You go out so much, Mother.'

'Not so much!'

'So very much.'

'And he forbids me my opera-box for the rest of the week! So last night I sat at home, dear child, reading the Life of Lazarillo de Tormes.'

'I don't give a damn,' he said, 'for any of your doctors.'

'So vexing, though; and apparently Lady Bird has been at death's door, and poor Peggy Povey too. It seems she got wet on the way to the Races; and really I was *sorry* for her when I saw her in the paddock; for the oats and the corn, and the wheat and the tares, and the barley and the rye, and all the rest of the reeds and grasses in her pretty Lancret hat, looked like nothing so much as manure.'

'I adore to folly her schoolboy's moustache!'

'My dear, Age is the one disaster,' Madame Ruiz remarked, raising the rosy dome of her sunshade a degree higher above her head.

They were pacing a walk radiant with trees and flowers as some magician's garden, that commanded a sweeping prospect of long, livid sands, against a white-green sea.

'There would seem to be several new yachts, darling,' Madame Ruiz observed.

'The Duke of Wellclose with his duchess (on their wedding-tour) arrived with the tide.'

'Poor man; I'm told that he only drove to the church after thirty brandies!'

'And the *Sea-Thistle*, with Lady Violet Valesbridge, and, *oh*, such a crowd.'

'She used to be known as "The Cat of Curzon Street," but I hear she is still quite incredibly pretty,' Madame Ruiz murmured, turning to admire a somnolent peacock, with moping fan, poised upon the curved still arm of a marble mænad.

'How sweet something smells.'

'It's the China lilies.'

'I believe it's my handkerchief . . .' he said.

'Vain wicked boy; ah, if you would but decide, and marry some nice, intelligent girl.'

'I'm too young yet.'

'You're *twenty-six*!'

'And past the age of folly-o,' he made airy answer, drawing from his breast-pocket a flat, jewel-encrusted case, and lighting a cigarette.

'Think of the many men, darling, of twenty-six . . .' Madame Ruiz broke off, focusing the fruit-bearing summit of a slender areca palm.

'Foll-foll-folly-o!' he laughed.

'I think I'm going in.'

'Oh, why?'

'Because,' Madame Ruiz repressed a yawn, 'because, dear, I feel armchairish.'

With a kiss of the finger-tips (decidedly distinguished hands had Vittorio Ruiz), he turned away.

Joying frankly in excess, the fiery noontide hour had a special charm for him.

It was the hour, to be sure, of 'the Faun!'

'Aho, Ahi, Aha!' he carolled, descending half trippingly a few white winding stairs that brought him upon a fountain. Palms, with their floating fronds radiating light, stood all around.

It was here 'the creative mood' would sometimes take him, for he possessed no small measure of talent of his own.

His *Three Hodeidahs,* and *Five Phallic Dances for Pianoforte and Orchestra,* otherwise known as 'Suite in Green,' had taken the whole concert world by storm, and, now, growing more audacious, he was engaged upon an opera to be known, by and by, as *Sumaïa.*

'Ah Atthis, it was Sappho who told me—' tentatively he sought an air.

A touch of banter there.

'*Ah Atthis*—' One must make the girl feel that her little secret is out . . . ; quiz her, but let her know, and pretty plainly, that the Poetess had been talking. . . .

'Ah Atthis—'

But somehow or other the lyric mood to-day was obdurate and not to be persuaded.

'I blame the oysters! After oysters—' he murmured, turning about to ascertain what was exciting the dogs.

She was coming up the drive with her face to the sun, her body shielded behind a spreading bouquet of circumstance.

'It's all right; they'll not hurt you.'

'Sh'o, I not afraid!'

'Tell me who it is you wish to see.'

'Mammee send me wid dese flowehs. . . .'

'Oh! But how scrumptious.'

'It strange how dey call de bees; honey-bees, sweat-bees, bumble-bees an' all!' she murmured, shaking the blossoms into the air.

'That's only natural,' he returned, his hand falling lightly to her arm. 'Madame Ruiz is in?'

'She is: but she is resting; and something tells me,' he suavely added, indicating a grassy bank, 'you might care to repose yourself too.'

And indeed after such a long and rambling course she was glad to accept.

'De groung's as soft as a cushom,' she purred, sinking with nonchalance to the grass.

'You'll find it,' he said, 'even softer, if you'll try it nearer me.'

'Dis a mighty pretty place!'

'And you—' but he checked his tongue.

'Fo' a villa so grand, dair must be mo' dan one privy?'

'Some six or seven!'

'Ours is broke.'

'You should get it mended.'

'De aggervatiness'!' she wriggled.

'Tell me about them.'

And so, not without digressions, she unfolded her life.

'Then you, Charlie, and Mimi are here, dear, to study?'

'As soon as de University is able to receibe us; but dair's a waiting list already dat long.'

'And what do you do with all your spare time?'

'Goin' round de shops takes up some ob it. An' den, ob course, dair's de Cinés. Oh, I love de Lara. We went last night to see *Souls in Hell*.'

'I've not been.'

'Oh it was choice.'

'Was it? Why?'

'De scene ob dat story,' she told him, 'happen foreign; 'way crost de big watteh, on de odder side ob de world . . . an' de principal gal, she married to a man who neglect her (ebery ebenin' he go to pahtys an' biars), while all de time his wife she sit at home wid her lil pickney at her breas'. But dair anodder gemplum (a friend ob de fambly) an' he afiah to woe her; but she only shake de head, slowly, from side to side, an' send dat man away. Den de hubsom lose his fortune, an', oh, she dat 'stracted, she dat crazed . . . at last she take to gamblin', but dat only make t'ings worse. Den de friend ob de fambly come back, an' offer to pay all de expenses ef only she unbend: so she cry, an' she cry, 'cos it grieb her to leab her pickney to de neglect ob de serbants (dair was three ob dem, an old buckler, a boy, an' a cook), but, in de end, she do, an' frtt! away she go in de fambly carriage. An' den, bimeby, you see dem in de bedroom doin' a bit ob funning.'

'What?'

'Oh ki; it put me in de gigglemints. . . .'

'Exquisite kid.'

'Sh'o, de coffee-concerts an' de pictchures, I don't nebba tiah ob dem.'

'Bad baby.'

'I turned thirteen.'

'You are?'

'By de Law ob de Island, I a spinster ob age!'

'I might have guessed it was the Bar! These Law-students,' he murmured, addressing the birds.

'Sh'o, it's de trute,' she pouted, with a languishing glance through the sticks of her fan.

'I don't doubt it,' he answered, taking lightly her hand.

'Mercy,' she marvelled: 'is dat a watch dah, on your arm?'

'Dark, bright baby!'

'Oh, an' de lil "V.R." all in precious stones so blue.' Her frail fingers caressed his wrist.

'Exquisite kid.' She was in his arms.

'Vitti, Vitti!—' It was the voice of Eurydice Edwards. Her face was strained and quivering. She seemed about to faint.

❦ *XI* ❦

EVER so lovely are the young men of Cuna-Cuna—Juarez, Jotifa, Enid—(these, from many, to distinguish but a few)—but none so delicate, charming, and squeamish as Charlie Mouth.

'Attractive little Rose . . .' 'What a devil of a dream . . .' the avid belles would exclaim when he walked abroad, while impassioned widows would whisper 'Peach!'

One evening, towards sundown, just as the city lifts its awnings, and the deserted streets start seething with delight, he left his home to enjoy the grateful air. It had been a day of singular oppressiveness and, not expecting overmuch of the vesperal breezes, he had borrowed his mother's small Pompadour fan.

Ah, little did that nigger boy know as he strolled along what novel emotions that promenade held in store!

Disrelishing the dust of the Avenida, he directed his steps towards the Park.

He had formed already an acquaintanceship with several young men, members, it seemed, of the University, and these he would sometimes join, about this hour, beneath the Calabash-trees in the Marcella Gardens.

There was Abe, a lad of fifteen, whose father ran a Jazz Hall on the harbour-beach, and Ramon, who was destined to enter the Church, and the intriguing Esmé, whose dream was the Stage, and who was supposed to be 'in touch' with Miss Maxine Bush, and there was Pedro, Pedro ardent and obese, who seemed to imagine that to be a dress-designer to foreign Princesses would yield his several talents a thrice-blessed harvest.

Brooding on these and other matters, Charlie found himself in Liberty Square.

Here, the Cunan Poet, Samba Marcella's effigy arose—that 'sable singer of Revolt.'

Aloft, on a pedestal, soared the Poet, laurel-crowned, thick-lipped, woolly, a large weeping Genius, with a bold taste for draperies, hovering just beneath; her one eye closed, the other open, giving her an air of winking confidentially at the passers-by.

' "Up, Cunans, up! To arms, to arms!" ' he quoted, lingering to watch the playful swallows wheeling among the tubs of rose-oleanders that stood around.

And a thirst, less for bloodshed than for a sherbet, seized him.

It was a square noted for the frequency of its bars, and many of their names, in flickering lights, showed palely forth already.

Cuna! City of Moonstones; how faerie art thou in the blue blur of dusk!

Costa Rica. Chile Bar. To the Island of June. . . .

Red roses against tall mirrors, reflecting the falling night.

Seated before a cloudy cocktail, a girl with gold cheeks like the flesh of peaches addressed him softly from behind: 'Listen, lion!'

But he merely smiled on himself in the polished mirrors, displaying moist-gleaming teeth and coral gums.

A fragrance of aromatic cloves . . . a mystic murmur of ice. . . .

A little dazed after a Ron Bacardi, he moved away. 'Shine, sah?' The inveigling squeak of a shoeblack followed him.

Sauntering by the dusty benches along the pavement-side, where white-robed negresses sat communing in twos and threes, he attained the Avenue Messalina with its spreading palms, whose fronds hung nerveless in the windless air.

Tinkling mandolins from restaurant gardens, light laughter, and shifting lights.

Passing before the Café de Cuna, and a people's 'Dancing,' he roamed leisurely along. Incipient Cyprians, led by vigilant, blanched-faced queens, youths of a certain life, known as bwam-wam bwam-wams, gaunt pariah dogs, with questing eyes, all equally were on the prowl. Beneath the Pharaohic pilasters of the Theatre Maxine Bush a street crowd had formed before a notice described 'Important,' which informed the Public that, owing to a 'temporary hoarseness,' the rôle of Miss Maxine Bush would be taken, on that occasion, by Miss Pauline Collier.

The Marcella Gardens lay towards the end of the Avenue, in the animated vicinity of the Opera. Pursuing the glittering thoroughfare, it was interesting to observe the pleasure announcements of the various theatres, picked out in signs of fire: *Aïda: The Jewels of the Madonna: Clara Novotny and Lily Lima's Season.*

Vending bags of roasted peanuts, or sapodillas and avocado pears, insistent small boys were importuning the throng.

'Go away; I can't be bodder,' Charlie was saying, when he seemed to slip; it was as though the pavement were a carpet snatched from under him, and, looking round, he was surprised to see, in a confectioner's window, a couple of marble-topped tables start merrily waltzing together.

Driven onward by those behind, he began stumblingly to run towards the Park. It was the general goal. Footing it a little ahead, two loose women and a gay young man (pursued by a waiter with a napkin and a bill), together with the horrified, half-crazed crowd; all, helter-skelter, were intent upon the Park.

Above the Calabash-trees, bronze, demoniac, the moon gleamed sourly from a starless sky, and although not a breath of air was stirring, the crests of the loftiest palms were set arustling by the vibration at their roots.

'Oh, will nobody *stop* it?' a terror-struck lady implored.

Feeling quite white and clasping a fetish, Charlie sank all panting to the ground.

Safe from falling chimney-pots and sign-boards (that for 'Pure Vaseline,' for instance, had all but caught him), he had much to be thankful for.

'Sh'o nuff, dat was a close shave,' he gasped, gazing dazed about him.

Clustered back to back near by upon the grass, three stolid matrons, matrons of hoary England, evidently not without previous earthquake experience, were ignoring resolutely the repeated shocks.

'I always follow the Fashions, dear, at a distance!' one was saying: 'this little gingham gown I'm wearing I had made for me after a design I found in a newspaper at my hotel.'

'It must have been a pretty old one, dear—I mean the paper, of course.'

'New things are only those you know that have been forgotten.'

'Mary . . . there's a sharp pin, sweet, at the back of your . . . *Oh!*'

Venturing upon his legs, Charlie turned away.

By the Park palings a few 'Salvationists' were holding forth, while, in the sweep before the bandstand, the artists from the Opera, in their costumes of Aïda, were causing almost a greater panic among the ignorant than the earthquake itself. A crowd, promiscuous rather than representative, composed variously of chauffeurs (making a wretched pretence, poor chaps, of seeking out their masters), Cyprians, patricians (these in opera cloaks and sparkling diamonds), tourists, for whom the Hodeidah girls would *not* dance that night, and bwam-wam bwam-wams, whose equivocal behaviour, indeed, was perhaps more shocking even than the shocks, set the pent Park ahum. Yet, notwithstanding the upheavals of Nature, certain persons there were bravely making new plans.

'How I wish I could, dear! But I shall be having a houseful of women over Sunday—that's to say.'

'Then come the week after.'

'Thanks, then, I *will.*'

Hoping to meet with Abe, Charlie took a pathway flanked with rows of tangled roses, whose leaves shook down at every step.

And it occurred to him with alarming force that perhaps he was an orphan.

Papee, Mammee, Mimi and lil Edna—the villa drawing-room on the floor. . . .

His heart stopped still.

'An' dey in de spirrit world—in heaven hereafter!' He glanced with awe at the moon's dark disk.

'All in dair cotton shrouds. . . .'

What if he should die and go to the Bad Place below?

'I mizzable sinneh, Lord. You heah, Sah? You heah me say dat? Oh, Jesus, Jesus, Jesus,' and weeping, he threw himself down among a bed of flowers.

When he raised his face it was towards a sky all primrose and silver pink. Sunk deep in his dew-laved bower, it was sweet to behold the light. Above him great spikes of blossom were stirring in the idle wind, while birds were chaunting voluntaries among the palms. And in thanksgiving, too, arose the matin bells. From Our Lady of the Pillar, from the church of La Favavoa in the West, from Saint Sebastian, from Our Lady of the Sea, from Our Lady of Mount Carmel, from Santa Theresa, from Saint Francis of the Poor.

❧ *XII* ❧

BUT although by the grace of Providence the city of Cuna-Cuna had been spared, other parts of the island had sustained irremediable loss. In the Province of Casuby, beyond the May Day Mountains, many a fair banana or sugar estate had been pitifully wrecked, yet what caused perhaps the widest regret among the Cunan public was the destruction of the famous convent of Sasabonsam. One of the beauties of the island, one of the gems of tropic architecture, celebrated, made immortal (in *The Picnic*) by the Poet Marcella, had disappeared. A Relief Fund for those afflicted had at once been started, and, as if this were not enough, the doors of the Villa Alba were about to be thrown open for 'An Evening of Song and Gala' in the causes of charity.

'Prancing Nigger, dis an event to take exvantage ob; dis not a lil t'ing, love, to be sneezed at at all,' Mrs. Mouth eagerly said upon hearing the news, and she had gone about ever since, reciting the names in the list of Patronesses, including that of the Cunan Archbishop.

It was the auspicious evening.

In their commodious, jointly shared bedroom, the Miss Lips, the fair Lips, the smiling Lips were maiding one another in what they both considered to be the 'Parisian Way'; a way, it appeared, that involved much nudging, arch laughter, and, even, some prodding.

'In love? Up to my ankles! Oh, yes.' Edna blithely chuckled.

'Up to your topknot!' her sister returned, making as if to pull it. But with the butt end of the curling-tongs Edna waved her away.

Since her visit to the Villa Alba 'me an' Misteh Ruiz' was all her talk, and to be his reigning mistress the summit of her dreams.

'Come on, man, wid dose tongs; 'cos I want 'em myself,' Miami murmured, pinning a knot of the sweet night jasmine deftly above her ear.

Its aroma evoked Bamboo.

Oh, why had he not joined her? Why did he delay? Had he forgotten their delight among the trees, the giant silk-cotton-trees, with the hammer-tree-frogs chanting in the dark: Rig-a-jig-jig, rig-a-jig-jig?

'Which you like de best, man, dis lil necklash or de odder?'

Edna asked, essaying a strand of orchid-tinted beads about her throat. 'I'd wear dem both,' her sister advised.

'I t'ink, on de whole, I wear de odder; de one he gib me de time he take exvantage ob my innocence.'

'Since dose imitation pearls, honey,—he gib you anyt'ing else?'

'No; but he dat generous! He say he mean to make me a lil pickney gal darter: an', oh, won't dat be a day,' Edna fluted, breaking off at the sound of her mother's voice in the corridor.

'. . . and tell de cabman to take de fly-bonnets off de horses,' she was instructing Ibum as she entered the room.

She had a gown of the new mignonette satin, with 'episcopal' sleeves lined with red.

'Come, girls, de cab is waiting; but perhaps you no savey dat.'

They didn't; and, for some time, dire was the confusion.

In the Peacock drawing-room of the Villa Alba the stirring ballet music from *Isfahan* filled the vast room with its thrilling madness. Upon a raised estrade, a corps of dancing boys, from Sankor, glided amid a murmur of applause.

The combination of charity and amusement had brought together a crowded and cosmopolitan assembly and, early though it was, it was evident already that with many more new advents there would be a shortage of chairs. From their yachts had come several distinguished birds of passage, exhaling an atmosphere of Paris and Park Lane.

Wielding a heavy bouquet of black feathers, Madame Ruiz, robed in a gown of malmaison cloth-of-silver, watched the dancers from an alcove by the door.

Their swaying torsos, and weaving gliding feet, fettered with chains of orchids and hung with bells, held a fascination for her.

'My dear, they beat the Hodeidahs! I'm sure I never saw anything like it,' the Duchess of Wellclose remarked admiringly: 'that little one, Fred,' she murmured, turning towards the Duke.

A piece of praise a staid small body in a demure lace cap chanced to hear.

This was 'the incomparable' Miss McAdam, the veteran ballet mistress of the Opera-house, and inventrix of the dance. Born in the frigid High Street of Aberdeen, 'Alice', as she was universally known among enthusiastic patrons of the ballet, had come originally to the tropics as companion to a widowed clergyman, when, as she would relate (in her picturesque, native brogue), at the sight of

Nature her soul had awoke. Self-expression had come with a rush; and now that she was ballet mistress of the Cunan Opera, some of the daring *ensembles* of the Scottish spinster would embarrass even the good Cunans themselves.

'I've warned the lads,' she whispered to Madame Ruiz, 'to cut their final figure on account of the Archbishop. But young boys are so excitable, and I expect they'll forget!'

Gazing on their perfect backs, Madame Ruiz could not but mourn the fate of the Painter, who, like Dalou, had specialised almost exclusively on this aspect of the human form; for, alas, that admirable Artist had been claimed by the Quake; and although his portrait of Madame Ruiz remained unfinished . . . there was still a mole . . . nevertheless, in gratitude, and as a mark of respect, she had sent her Rolls car to the Mass in honour of his obsequies, with the *crêpe* off an old black dinner-dress tied across the lamps.

'I see they're going to,' Miss McAdam murmured, craning a little to focus the Archbishop, then descanting to two ladies with deep purple fans.

'Ah, well! It's what they do in *Isfahan*,' Madame Ruiz commented, turning to greet her neighbour Lady Bird.

'Am I late for Gebhardt?' she asked, as if Life itself hinged upon the reply.

A quietly silly woman, Madame Ruiz was often obliged to lament the absence of intellect at her door: accounting for it as the consequence of a weakness for negroes, combined with a hopeless passion for the Regius Professor of Greek at Oxford.

But the strident cries of the dancers and the increasing volume of the music discouraged all talk, though ladies with collection-boxes (biding their time) were beginning furtively to select their next quarry.

Countess Katty Taosay, *née* Soderini, a little woman and sure of the giants, could feel in her psychic veins which men were most likely to empty their pockets: English Consul . . . pale and interesting, he would not refuse to stoop and fumble, nor Follinsbe 'Peter,' the slender husband of a fashionable wife, nor Charlie Campfire, a young boy like an injured camel, heir to vast banana estates, the darling, and six foot high if an inch.

'Why do big men like little women?' she wondered, waving a fan powdered with blue *paillettes*: and she was still casting about for a reason when the hectic music stopped.

And now the room echoed briefly with applause, while admiration was divided between the super-excellence of the dancers and the living beauty of the rugs which their feet had trod—rare rugs from Bokhara-i-Shareef, and Kairouan-city-of-Prayer, lent by the mistress of the house.

Entering on the last hand-clap, Mr. and Mrs. Mouth, followed by their daughters, felt, each in their several ways, they might expect to enjoy themselves.

'Prancing Nigger, what a *furore*!' Mrs. Mouth exclaimed. 'You b'lieb, I hope, now, dat our tickets was worth de money.'

Plucking at the swallow-tails of an evening 'West End,' Mr. Mouth was disinclined to re-open a threadbare topic.

'It queah how few neegah dair be,' he observed, scanning the brilliant audience, many of whom, taking advantage of an interval, were flocking towards a buffet in an adjoining conservatory.

'Prancing Nigger, I feel I could do wid a glass ob champagne.'

Passing across a corridor, it would have been interesting to have explored the spacious vistas that loomed beyond. 'Dat must be one ob de priveys,' Edna murmured, pointing to a distant door.

'Seben, Chile, did you say?'

'If not more!'

'She seem fond ob flowehs,' Mr. Mouth commented, pausing to notice the various plants that lined the way: from the roof swung showery azure flowers that commingled with the theatrically-hued cañas, set out in crude, bold, colour-schemes below, that looked best at night. But in their malignant splendour the orchids were the thing. Mrs. Abanathy, Ronald Firbank (a dingy lilac blossom of rarity untold), Prince Palairet, a heavy blue-spotted flower, and rosy Olive Moonlight, were those that claimed the greatest respect from a few discerning connoisseurs.

'Prancing Nigger, you got a chalk mark on your "West-End." Come heah, sah, an' let me brush it.'

Hopeful of glimpsing Vittorio, Miami and Edna sauntered on. With arms loosely entwined about each other's hips, they made, in their complete insouciance, a conspicuous couple.

'I'd give sumpin' to see de bedrooms, man, 'cos dair are chapels, an' barf-rooms, beside odder conveniences off dem,' Edna related, returning a virulent glance from Miss Eurydice Edwards with a contemptuous, pitying smile.

Traversing a throng, sampling sorbets and ices, the sisters strolled out upon the lawn.

The big silver stars, how clear they shone—infinitudes, infinitudes.

'Adieu, hydrangeas, adieu, blue, burning South!'

The concert, it seemed, had begun.

'Come chillens, come!'

In the vast drawing-room, the first novelty of the evening—an aria from *Sumaïa*—had stilled all chatter. Deep-sweet, poignant, the singer's voice was conjuring Sumaïa's farewell to the Greek isle of Mitylene, bidding farewell to its gracious women, and to the trees of white or turquoise in the gardens of Lesbos.

'Adieu, hydrangeas——'

Hardly a suitable moment, perhaps, to dispute a chair. But neither the Duchess of Wellclose nor Mrs. Mouth were creatures easily abashed.

'I pay, an' I mean to hab it.'

'You can't; it's taken!' the duchess returned, nodding meaningly towards the buffet, where the duke could be seen swizzling whisky at the back of the bar.

'Sh'o! Dese white women seem to t'ink dey can hab ebberyt'ing.'

'Taken,' the duchess repeated, who disliked what she called the *parfum d'Afrique* of the 'sooties,' and, as though to intimidate Mrs. Mouth, she gave her a look that would have made many a Peeress in London quail.

Nevertheless, in the stir that followed the song chairs were forthcoming.

'From de complexion dat female hab, she look as doh she bin boiling bananas!' Mrs. Mouth commented comfortably, loud enough for the duchess to hear.

'Such a large congregation should su'tinly assist de fund!' Mr. Mouth resourcefully said, envisaging with interest the audience; it was not every day that one could feast the gaze on the noble baldness of the Archbishop, or on the subtle *silhouette* of Miss Maxine Bush, swathed like an idol in an Egyptian tissue woven with magical eyes.

'De woman in de window dah,' Mrs. Mouth remarked, indicating a dowager who had the hard but resigned look of the mother of six daughters in immediate succession, 'hab a look, Prancing Nigger, ob your favourite statesman.'

'De immortal Wilberforce!'

'I' s'poge it's de whiskers,' Mrs. Mouth replied, ruffling gently her 'Borgia' sleeves for the benefit of the Archbishop. Rumour had it he was fond of negresses, and that the black private secretary he employed was his own natural son, while some suspected indeed a less natural connexion.

But Madame Hatso (of Blue Brazil, the Argentine; those nights in Venezuela and Buenos Ayres, 'bis' and 'bravas'! How the public had roared) was curtseying right and left, and Mrs. Mouth, glancing round to address her daughters, perceived with vexation that Edna had vanished.

In the garden he caught her to him.

'Flower of the Sugar Cane!'

'Misteh Ruiz. . . .'

'Exquisite kid.'

'I saw you thu de window-glass all de time, an' dair was I! laughing so silent-ly . . . .'

'My little honey.'

'. . . no; 'cos ob de neighbehs,' she fluted, drawing him beneath the great flamboyants that stood like temples of darkness all around.

'Sweetheart.'

'I 'clar to grashis!' she delightedly crooned as he gathered her up in his arms.

'My little Edna . . .? . . .? . . .?'

'Where you goin' wid me to?'

'There,' and he nodded towards the white sea sand.

A yawning butler, an insolent footman, a snoring coachman, a drooping horse. . . .

The last conveyance had driven away, and only a party of 'b—d—y niggers,' supposed to be waiting for a daughter, was keeping the domestics from their beds.

Ernest, the bepowdered footman, believed them to be thieves, and could have sworn he saw a tablespoon in the old coon's pocket.

Hardly able to restrain his tears, Mr. Mouth sat gazing vacuously at the floor.

'Wh' can keep de chile? . . . O Lord . . . I hope dair noddin' wrong.'

'On such a lovely ebenin' what is time?' Mrs. Mouth exclaimed, taking up an attitude of night-enchantment by the open door.

A remark that caused the butler and his subordinate to cough.

'It not often I see de cosmos look so special!'

'Ef she not heah soon, we better go widout her,' Miami murmured, who was examining the visitors' cards on the hall table undismayed by the eye of Ernest.

'It's odd she should so procrastinate; but la jeunesse, c'est le temps où l'on s'amuse,' Mrs. Mouth blandly declared, seating herself tranquilly by her husband's side.

'Dair noddin', I hope, de matteh. . . .'

'Eh, suz, my deah! Eh, suz.' Reassuringly, she tapped his arm.

'Sir Victor Virtue, Lady Bird, Princess Altamisal,' Miami tossed their cards.

'Sh'o it was a charming ebenin'! Doh I was sorry for de duchess, wid de duke, an' he all nasty drunk wid spirits.'

'I s'poge she use to it.'

'It was a perfect skangle! Howebber, on de whole, it was quite an enjoyable pahty—doh dat music ob Wagner, it gib me de retches.'

'It bore me, too,' Miami confessed, as a couple of underfootmen made their appearance and, joining their fidgeting colleagues by the door, waited for the last guests to depart, in a mocking, whispering group.

'Ef she not here bery soon,' Miami murmured, vexed by the servants' impertinent smiles.

'Sh'o, she be here directly,' Mrs. Mouth returned, appraising through her fan-sticks the footmen's calves.

'It daybreak already!' Miami yawned, moved to elfish mirth by the over-emphasis of rouge on her mother's round cheeks.

But under the domestics' mocking stare their talk at length was chilled to silence.

From the garden came the plaintive wheepling of a bird (intermingled with the coachman's spasmodic snores), while above the awning of the door the stars were wanly paling.

'Prancing Nigger, sah, heah de day. Dair no good waitin' any more.'

It was on their return from the Villa Alba that they found a letter signed 'Mamma Luna,' announcing the death of Bamboo.

∾ XIII ∾

HE had gone out, it seemed, upon the sea to avoid the earth-quake (leaving his mother at home to take care of the shop), but the boat had overturned, and the evil sharks . . .

In a room darkened against the sun, Miami, distracted, wept. Crunched by the maw of a great blue shark: 'Oh honey.'

Face downward, with one limp arm dangling to the floor, she bemoaned her loss: such love-blank, and aching void! Like some desolate, empty cave, filled with clouds, so her heart.

'An' to t'ink dat I eber teased you!' she moaned, reproaching herself for the heedless past; and as day passed over day still she wept.

One mid-afternoon, some two weeks later, she was reclining lifelessly across the bed, gazing at the sun-blots on the floor. There had been a mild disturbance of a seismic nature that morning, and indeed slight though unmistakable shocks had been sensed repeatedly of late.

'Intercession' services, fully choral—the latest craze of society—filled the churches at present, sadly at the expense of other places of amusement, many of which had been obliged to close down. A religious revival was in the air, and in the Parks and streets elegant dames would stop one another in their passing carriages and pour out the stories of their iniquitous lives.

Disturbed by the tolling of a neighbouring bell, Miami reluctantly rose.

'Lord! What a din; it gib a po' soul de grabe-yahd creeps,' she murmured, lifting the jalousie of a sun-shutter and peering idly out.

Standing in the street was a Chinese laundrymaid, chatting with two Chinamen with osier baskets, while a gaunt pariah dog was rummaging among some egg-shells and banana-skins in the dust before the gate.

'Dat lil-fool-fool Ibum, he throw ebberyt'ing out ob de window an' nebba t'ink ob de stink,' she commented, as an odour of decay was wafted in on a gust of the hot trade wind. The trade winds! How pleasantly they used to blow in the village of Mediavilla. The blue trade wind, the gold trade wind caressing the bending canes. . . . City life, what had it done for any of them, after all? Edna nothing else than a harlot (since she had left them there was no other word), and Charlie fast going to pieces, having joined the Promenade of a notorious Bar with its bright particular galaxy of boys.

'Sh'o, ebberyt'ing happier back dah,' she mused, following the slow gait across the street of some bare-footed nuns; soon they would be returning, with many converts and pilgrims, to Sasabonsam, beyond the May Day Mountains, where remained a miraculous image of Our Lady of the Sorrows still intact. How if she joined them, too? A desire to express her grief, and thereby ease it, possessed her. In the old times there had been many ways: tribal dances and wild austerities. . . .

She was still musing, self-absorbed, when her mother, much later, came in from the street.

There had been a great Intercessional, it seemed, at the Cathedral, with hired singers from the Opera-house and society women as thick as thieves, '*gnats*,' she had meant to say (Tee-hee!), about a corpse. Arturo Arrivabene . . . a voice like a bull . . . and she had caught a glimpse of Edna driving on the Avenue Amada, looking almost Spanish in a bandeau beneath a beautiful grey tilt hat.

But Miami's abstraction discouraged confidences.

'Why you so triste, Chile? Dair no good at all in frettin'.'

'Sh'o nuff.'

'Dat death was on de cards, my deah, an' dair is no mistakin' de fac'; an' as de shark is a rapid feeder it all ober sooner dan wid de crocodile, which is some consolation for dose dat remain to mourn.'

'Sh'o, it bring not an atom to me!'

' 'Cos de process ob de crocodile bein' sloweh dan dat ob de shark—'

'Ah, say no more,' Miami moaned, throwing herself in a storm of grief across the bed. And as all efforts to appease made matters only worse, Mrs. Mouth prudently left her.

'Prancing Nigger, she seem dat sollumcholly an' depressed,' Mrs. Mouth remarked at dinner, helping herself to some guava-jelly that had partly dissolved through lack of ice.

'Since de disgrace ob Edna dat scarcely s'prisin',' Mr. Mouth made answer, easing a little the napkin at his neck.

'She is her own woman, me deah sah, an' *I* cannot prevent it!'

In the convivial ground-floor dining-room of an imprecise style, it was hard, at times, to endure such second-rate company as that of a querulous husband.

Yes, marriage had its dull side, and its drawbacks; still, where would society be (and where morality!) without the married women?

Mrs. Mouth fetched a sigh.

Just at her husband's back, above the ebony sideboard, hung a Biblical engraving, after Rembrandt, of the *Woman Taken in Adultery*, the conception of which seemed to her exaggerated and overdone, knowing full well, from previous experience, that there need not, really, be so much fuss. . . . Indeed, there need not be any: but to be *Taken* like that! A couple of idiots.

'W'en I look at our chillen's chairs, an' all ob dem empty, in my opinion we both betteh deaded,' Mr. Mouth brokenly said.

'I dare say dair are dose dat may t'ink so,' Mrs. Mouth returned, refilling her glass; 'but, Prancing Nigger, I am not like dat: no, sah!'

'Where's Charlie?'

'I s'poge he choose to dine at de lil Cantonese restaurant on de quay,' she murmured, setting down her glass with a slight grimace: how *ordinaire* this cheap red wine! Doubtless Edna was lapping the wines of paradise! Respectability had its trials. . . .

'Dis jelly mo' like lemon squash,' Mr. Mouth commented.

''Cos dat lil liard Ibum, he again forget de ice! Howebber, I hope soon to get rid ob him: for de insolence ob his bombax is more dan I can stand,' Mrs. Mouth declared, lifting her voice on account of a piano-organ in the street just outside.

'I s'poge to-day Chuesdy'? It was a-Chuesd'y—God forgib dat po' frail chile.'

'Prancing Nigger, I allow Edna some young yet for dat position; I allow dat to be de matteh ob de case but, me good sah! bery likely she marry him later.'

'Pah.'

'An' why not?'

'Chooh, nebba!'

'Prancing Nigger, you seem to forget dat your elder daughter was a babe ob four w'en I put on me nuptial arrange blastams to go to de Church.'

'Sh'o, I wonder you care to talk ob it!'

'An', to-day, honey, as I sat in de Cathedral, lis'nin' to de Archbishop, I seemed to see Edna, an' she all in *dentelles* so *chic*, comin' up de aisle, followed by twelve maids, all ob good blood, holdin' flowehs an' wid hats kimpoged ob feddehs—worn raddeh to de side, an' I heah a stranger say: "Excuse me, sah, but who dis fine marriage?" an' a voice make reply: "Why, dat Mr. Ruiz de million'r-

'r-'r," an' as he speak, one ob dese Italians from de Opera-house commence to sing "De voice dat brieved o'er Eden," an' Edna she blow a kiss at me an' laugh dat arch.'

'Nebba!'

'Prancing Nigger, "wait an' see"!' Mrs. Mouth waved prophetically her fan.

'No, nebba,' he repeated, his head sunk low in chagrin.

'How you know, sah?' she queried, rising to throw a crust of loaf to the organ man outside.

The wind with the night had risen, and a cloud of blown dust was circling before the gate.

'See de raindrops, deah; here come at last de big rain.'

'. . .'

'Prancing Nigger!'

'Ah'm thinkin'.'

❦ *XIV* ❦

IMPROVISING at the piano, Piltzenhoffer, kiddy-grand, he was contented, happy. The creative fertility, bursting from a radiant heart, more than ordinarily surprised him. 'My most quickening affair since—' he groped, smiling a little at several particular wraiths, more or less bizarre, that, in their time, had especially disturbed him. 'Yes; probably!' he murmured enigmatically, striking an intricate, virile chord.

'Forgib me, dearest! I was wid de manicu' of de fingeh-nails.'

'Divine one.'

She stood before him.

Hovering there between self-importance and madcapery, she was exquisite quite.

'All temperament . . . !' he murmured, capturing her deftly between his knees.

She was wearing a toilette of white *crêpe de chine*, and a large favour of bright purple Costa-Rica roses.

'Soon as de sun drop, dey set out, deah: so de manicu' say.'

'What shall we do till then?'

'. . . or, de pistols!' she fluted, encircling an arm about his neck.

'Destructive kitten,' he murmured, kissing, one by one, her red, polished nails.

'Honey! Come on.'

He frowned.

It seemed a treason almost to his last mistress, an exotic English girl, perpetually shivering, even in the sun, this revolver practice on the empty quinine-bottles she had left behind. Poor Meraude! It was touching what faith she had in a dose of quinine! Unquestionably she had been faithful to *that*. And dull enough, too, it had made her. With her albums of photographs, nearly all of midshipmen, how insufferably had she bored him:—'This one, darling, tell me, isn't he—I, really—he makes me—and this one, darling! An Athenian viking, with hair like mimosa, and what ravishing hands!—oh my God!—I declare—he makes me—' Poor Meraude; she had been extravagant as well!

'Come on, an' break some bokkles!'

'There's not a cartridge left,' he told her, setting her on his knee.

> 'Ha-ha! Oh, hi-hi!
> Not a light:
> Not a bite!
> What a Saturday Night!'

she trilled, taking off a comedian from the Eden Garden.

Like all other negresses she possessed a natural bent for mimicry and a voice of that lisping quality that would find complete expression in songs such as: 'Have you seen my sweet garden ob Flowehs?', 'Sst! Come closer, Listen heah,' 'Lead me to the Altar, Dearest,' and 'His Little Pink, proud, Spitting-lips are Mine.'

'What is that you're wearing?'

'A souvenir ob to-day; I buy it fo' luck,' she rippled, displaying a black briar cross pinned to her breast.

'I hope it's blessed?'

'De nun dat sold it, didn't say. Sho'o, it's dreadful to t'ink ob po' Mimi, an' she soon a pilgrim all in blistehs an' rags,' she commented, as a page-boy with bejasmined ears appeared at the door.

'Me excuse. . . .'

'How dare you come in, lil saucebox, widdout knockin'?'

'Excuse, missey, but . . .'

'What?'

Ibum hung his head.

'I only thoughted, it bein' Crucifix day, I would like to follow in de procession thu de town.'

'Bery well: but be back in time fo' dinner.'

'T'ank you, missey.'

'An' mind fo' once you are!'

'Yes, missey,' the niggerling acquiesced, bestowing a slow smile on Snob and Snowball, who had accompanied him into the room. Easy of habit, as tropical animals are apt to be, it was apparent that the aristocratic pomeranian was paying sentimental court to the skittish mouser, who, since her περιπέτεια of black kittens, looked ready for anything.

'Sh'o, but she hab a way wid her!' Ibum remarked, impressed.

'Lil monster, take dem both, an' den get out ob my sight,' his mistress directed him.

Fingering a battered volume that bore the book-plate of Meraude, Vittorio appeared absorbed.

'Honey.'

'Well?'

'Noddin'.'

In the silence of the room a restless bluebottle, attracted by the wicked leer of a chandelier, tied up incredibly in a bright green net, blended its hum with the awakening murmur of the streets.

'Po' Mimi. I hope she look up as she go by.'

'Yes, by Jove.'

'Doh after de rude t'ings she say to me—' she broke off, blinking a little at the sunlight through the thrilling shutters.

'If I remember, beloved, you were both equally candid,' he remarked, wandering out upon the balcony.

It was on the palm-grown Messalina, an avenue that comprised a solid portion of the Ruiz estate, that he had installed her, in a many-storied building, let out in offices and flats.

Little gold, blue, lazy and romantic Cuna, what chastened mood broods over thy life to-day!

'Have you your Crucifix? Won't you buy a cross?' persuasive, feminine voices rose up from the pavement below. Active again with the waning sun, 'workers,' with replenished wares, were emerging forth from their respective depots nursing small lugubrious baskets.

'Have you bought your cross?' The demand, when softly cooed by some solicitous patrician, almost compelled an answer; and most of the social world of Cuna appeared to be vending crosses, or 'Pilgrims' medals' in imitation 'bronze,' this afternoon, upon the kerb. At the corner of Valdez Street, across the way, Countess Katty Taosay (*née* Soderini), austere in black with Parma violets, was presiding over a depot festooned with nothing but rosaries, that 'professed' themselves, as they hung, to the suave trade wind.

> 'Not a light:
> Not a bite!
> What a——'

Edna softly hummed, shading her eyes with a big feather fan.

It was an evening of cloudless radiance; sweet and mellow as is frequent at the close of summer.

'Oh, ki, honey! It so cleah I can see de lil iluns ob yalleh sands far away b'yond de Point!

'Dearest!' he inattentively murmured, recognising on the Avenue the elegant cobweb wheels of his mother's Bolivian buggy.

Accompanied by Eurydice Edwards, she was driving her favourite mules.

'An' de shipwreck off de coral reef, oh, ki!'

'Let me find you the long-glass, dear,' he said, glad for an instant to step inside.

Leaning with one foot thrust nimbly out through the balcony-rails towards the street, she gazed absorbed.

Delegates of agricultural guilds bearing banners, making for the Cathedral square (the pilgrims' starting-point), were advancing along the avenue amidst applause: fruit-growers, rubber-growers, sugar-growers, opium-growers, all doubtless wishful of placating Nature that redoubtable Goddess by showing a little honour to the Church. 'Oh Lord, *not* as Sodom,' she murmured, deciphering a text attached to the windscreen of a luxurious automobile.

'Divine one, here they are.'

'T'anks, honey, I see best widdout,' she replied, following the Bacchic progress of two girls in soldiers' forage-caps, who were exciting the gaiety of the throng.

'Be careful, kid; don't lean too far. . . .'

'Oh, ki, if dey don't exchange kisses!'

But the appearance of the Cunan Constabulary, handsome youngsters, looking the apotheosis themselves of earthly lawlessness, in their feathered sun-hats and bouncing kilts, created a diversion.

'De way dey stare up; I goin' to put on a tiara!'

'Wait, do, till supper,' he entreated, manipulating the long-glass to suit his eye.

Driving or on foot, were the usual faces.

Seated on a doorstep, Miss Maxine Bush, the famous actress, appeared to be rehearsing a smart society rôle, as she flapped the air with a sheet of street-foul paper, while, rattling a money-box, her tame monkey, 'Jutland-ho,' came as prompt for a coin as any demned Duchess.

'Ha-ha, Oh, hi-hi!' Edna's blasted catches. 'Bless her,' he exclaimed, re-levelling the glass. Perfect, Good lenses these; one could even read a physician's doorplate across the way: 'Hours 2-4, Agony guaranteed'—obviously, a dentist; and the window-card, too, above, 'Miss—? Miss—? Speciality: Men past thirty.'

Four years to wait. Patience.

Ooof! There went 'Alice' and one of her boys. Bad days for the ballet! People afraid of the Opera-house . . . that chandelier . . . and the pictures on the roof. . . . And wasn't that little Lady Bird? running at all the trousers: '*have* you your crucifix! . . . ? ?'

'Honey. . . .'

She had set a crown of moonstones on her head, and had moonstone bracelets on her arms.

'My queen.'

'I hope Mimi look up at me!'

'Vain one.'

Over the glistering city the shadows were falling, staining the white-walled houses here and there as with some purple pigment.

'Accordin' to de lates' 'ticklers, de Procession follow de Paseo only as far as de fountain.'

'Oh. . . .'

'Where it turn up thu Carmen Street, into de Avenue Messalina.'

Upon the metallic sheen of the evening sky she sketched the itinerary lightly with her fan.

And smiling down on her uplifted face, he asked himself whimsically how long he would love her. She had not the brains, poor child, of course, to keep a man for ever. Heigho. Life indeed was often hard. . . .

'Honey, here dey come!'

A growing murmur of distant voices, jointly singing, filled liturgically the air, just as the warning salute, fired at sundown from the heights of the fort above the town, reverberated sadly.

'Oh, la, la,' she laughed, following the wheeling flight of some birds that rose startled from the palms.

'The Angelus. . . .'

'Hark, honey: what is dat dey singin'?'

> *A thousand ages in Thy sight*
> *Are like an evening gone;*
> *Short as the watch that ends the night*
> *Before the rising sun.*

Led by an old negress leaning on her hickory staff, the procession came.

Banners, banners, banners.

'I hope Mimi wave!'

Floating banners against the dusk. . . .

'Oh, honey! See dat lil pilgrim-boy?'

> *Time like an ever-rolling stream,*
> *Bears all its sons away;*
> *They fly forgotten, as a dream*
> *Dies at the opening day.*

'Mimi, Mimi!' She had flung the roses from her dress. 'Look up, my deah, look up.'

But her cry escaped unheard.

> *They fly forgotten, as a dream*
> *Dies——*

The echoing voices of those behind lingered a little.

'Edna.'

She was crying.

'It noddin'; noddin' at all! But it plain she refuse to forgib me!'

'Never.'

'Perspirin', an' her skirt draggin', sh'o, she looked a fright.'

He smiled: for indeed already the world was perceptibly moulding her. . . .

'Enuff to scare ebbery crow off de savannah!'

'And wouldn't the farmers bless her.'

'Oh, honey!' Her glance embraced the long, lamp-lit avenue with supressed delight.

'Well.'

'Dair's a new dancer at de Apollo to-night. Suppose we go?'

Havana—Bordighera.

Concerning the Eccentricities
of Cardinal Pirelli

❈ *I* ❈

HUDDLED up in a cope of gold wrought silk he peered around. Society had rallied in force. A christening—and not a child's.

Rarely had he witnessed, before the font, so many brilliant people. Were it an heir to the DunEden acres (instead of what it *was*) the ceremony could have hardly drawn together a more distinguished throng.

Monsignor Silex moved a finger from forehead to chin, and from ear to ear. The Duquesa DunEden's escapades, if continued, would certainly cost the Cardinal his hat.

'And ease my heart by splashing fountains.'

From the choir-loft a boy's young voice was evoking Heaven.

'His hat!' Monsignor Silex exclaimed aloud, blinking a little at the immemorial font of black Macæl marble that had provoked the screams of pale numberless babies.

Here Saints and Kings had been baptised, and royal Infantas, and sweet Poets, whose high names thrilled the heart.

Monsignor Silex crossed his breast. He must gather force to look about him. Frame a close report. The Pontiff, in far-off Italy, would expect precision.

Beneath the state baldequin, or Grand Xaymaca, his Eminence sat enthroned, ogled by the wives of a dozen grandees. The Altamissals, the Villarasas (their grandee-ships' approving glances, indeed, almost eclipsed their wives'), and Catherine, Countess of Constantine, the most talked-off beauty in the realm, looking like some wild limb of Astaroth in a little crushed 'toreador' hat round as an athlete's coif with hanging silken balls, while beside her a stout, dumpish dame, of enormous persuasion, was joggling, solicitously, an object that was of the liveliest interest to all.

Head archly bent, her fine arms divined through darkling laces, the Duquesa stood, clasping closely a week-old police-dog in the ripple of her gown.

'Mother's pet!' she cooed, as the imperious creature passed his tongue across the splendid uncertainty of her chin.

Monsignor Silex's large, livid face grew grim.

What,—disquieting doubt,—if it were her Grace's offspring after all? Praise heaven, he was ignorant enough regarding the schemes of nature, but in an old lutrin once he had read of a young woman engendering a missel-thrush through the channel of her nose. It had created a good deal of scandal to be sure at the time: the Holy Inquisition, indeed, had condemned the impudent baggage, in consequence, to the stake.

'That was the style to treat them,' he murmured, appraising the assembly with no kindly eye. The presence of Madame San Seymour surprised him; one habitually so set apart and devout! And Madame La Urench, too, gurgling away freely to the four-legged Father: 'No, my naughty Blessing; no, not now! . . . By and by, a *bone*.'

Words which brought the warm saliva to the expectant parent's mouth.

Tail away, sex apparent (to the affected slight confusion of the Infanta Eulalia-Irene), he crouched, his eyes fixed wistfully upon the nozzle of his son.

Ah, happy delirium of first parenthood! Adoring pride! Since times primæval by what masonry does it knit together those that have succeeded in establishing here, on earth, the vital bonds of a family's claim? Even the modest sacristan, at attention by the font, felt himself to be superior of parts to a certain unproductive chieftain of a princely House, who had lately undergone a course of asses' milk in the surrounding mountains—all in vain!

But, supported by the Prior of the Cartuja, the Cardinal had arisen for the act of Immersion.

Of unusual elegance, and with the remains, moreover, of perfect looks, he was as wooed and run after by the ladies as any *matador*.

'And thus being cleansed and purified, I do call thee "Crack"!' he addressed the Duquesa's captive burden.

Tail sheathed with legs 'in master's drawers,' ears cocked, tongue pendent. . . .

'Mother's mascot!'

'Oh, take care, dear; he's removing all your rouge!'

'*What?*'

'He's spoilt, I fear, your roses.' The Countess of Constantine tittered.

The Duquesa's grasp relaxed. To be seen by all the world at this disadvantage.

'Both?' she asked, distressed, disregarding the culprit, who sprang from her breast with a sharp, sportive bark.

What rapture, what freedom!

'Misericordia!' Monsignor Silex exclaimed, staring aghast at a leg poised, inconsequently, against the mural-tablet of the widowed duchess of Charona—a woman who, in her lifetime, had given over thirty million pezos to the poor!

Ave Maria purissima! What challenging snarls and measured mystery marked the elaborate recognition of father and son, and would no one then forbid their incestuous frolics?

In agitation Monsignor Silex sought fortitude from the storied windows overhead, aglow in the ambered light as some radiant missal.

It was Saint Eufraxia's Eve, she of Egypt, a frail unit numbered above among the train of the Eleven Thousand Virgins: an imma-turish schoolgirl of a saint, unskilled, inexperienced in handling a prayer, lacking the vim and native astuteness of the incomparable Theresa.

Yes; divine interference, 'twixt father and son, was hardly to be looked for, and Eufraxia (she of Egypt) had failed too often before. . . .

Monsignor Silex started slightly, as, from the estrade beneath the dome, a choir-boy let fall a little white spit.

Dear child, as though *that* would part them!

'Things must be allowed to take their "natural" course,' he concluded, following the esoteric antics of the reunited pair.

Out into the open, over the Lapis Lazuli of the floor, they flashed, with stifled yelps, like things possessed.

'He'll tear my husband's drawers!' the Duquesa lamented.

'The duque's legs. Poor Decima.' The Infanta fell quietly to her knees.

'Fortify . . . asses . . .' the royal lips moved.

'Brave darling,' she murmured, gently rising.

But the Duquesa had withdrawn, it seemed, to repair her ravaged roses, and from the obscurity of an adjacent confessional-box was calling to order Crack.

'Come, Crack!'

And to the Mauro-Hispanic rafters the echo rose.

'Crack, Crack, Crack, Crack. . . .'

❆ *II* ❆

FROM the Calle de la Pasion, beneath the blue-tiled mirador of the garden wall, came the soft brooding sound of a seguidilla. It was a twilight planned for wooing, unbending, consent; many, before now, had come to grief on an evening such. 'It was the moon.'

Pacing a cloistered walk, laden with the odour of sun-tired flowers, the Cardinal could not but feel the insidious influences astir. The bells of the institutions of the *Encarnacion* and the Immaculate Conception, joined in confirming Angelus, had put on tones half-bridal, enough to create vague longings, or sudden tears, among the young patrician boarders.

'Their parents' daughters—convent-bred,' the Cardinal sighed.

At the Immaculate Conception, dubbed by the Queen, in irony, once 'The school for harlots,' the little Infanta Maria-Paz must be lusting for her Mamma and the Court, and the lilac carnage of the ring, while chafing also in the same loose captivity would be the roguish *niñas* of the pleasure-loving duchess of Sarmento, girls whose Hellenic ethics had given the good Abbess more than one attack of fullness.

Morality. Poise! For without temperance and equilibrium—— The Cardinal halted.

But in the shifting underlight about him the flushed camellias and the sweet night-jasmines suggested none; neither did the shape of a garden-Eros pointing radiantly the dusk.

'For unless we have balance——' the Cardinal murmured, distraught, admiring against the elusive nuances of the afterglow the cupid's voluptuous hams.

It was against these, once, in a tempestuous mood that his mistress had smashed her fan-sticks.

'Would that all liaisons would break as easily!' his Eminence framed the prayer: and musing on the appalling constancy of a certain type, he sauntered leisurely on. Yes, enveloping women like Luna Sainz, with their lachrymose, tactless 'mys,' how shake them off? 'My' Saviour, 'my' lover, 'my' parasol—and, even, 'my' virtue. . . .

'Poor dearie.'

The Cardinal smiled.

Yet once in a way, perhaps, he was not averse to being favoured by a glimpse of her: 'A little visit on a night like this.' Don Alvaro Narciso Hernando Pirelli, Cardinal-Archbishop of Clemenza, smiled again.

In the gloom there, among the high thickets of bay and flowering myrtle. . . . For, after all, bless her, one could not well deny she possessed the chief essentials: 'such, poor soul, as they are!' he reflected, turning about at the sound as of the neigh of a horse.

'Monseigneur. . . .'

Bearing a biretta and a silver shawl, Madame Poco, the venerable Superintendent-of-the-palace, looking, in the blue moonlight, like some whiskered skull, emerged, after inconceivable peepings, from among the leafy limbo of the trees.

'Ah, Don Alvaro, sir! Come here.'

'Pest!' His Eminence evinced a touch of asperity.

'Ah, Don, Don, . . .' and skimming forward with the grace of a Torero lassooing a bull, she slipped the scintillating fabric about the prelate's neck.

'Such nights breed fever, Don Alvaro, and there is mischief in the air.'

'Mischief?'

'In certain quarters of the city you would take it almost for some sortilege.'

'What next?'

'At the *Encarnacion* there's nothing, of late, but seediness. Sister Engracia with the chicken-pox, and Mother Claridad with the itch, while at the College of Noble Damosels, in the Calle Santa Fé, I hear a daughter of Don José Illescas, in a fit of caprice, has set a match to her coronet.'

'A match to her what?'

'And how explain, Don Alvaro of my heart, these constant shots in the Córtes? Ah, *sangre mio*, in what times we live!'

Ambling a few steps pensively side by side, they moved through the brilliant moonlight. It was the hour when the awakening fireflies are first seen like atoms of rosy flame floating from flower to flower.

'Singular times, sure enough,' the Cardinal answered, pausing to enjoy the transparent beauty of the white dripping water of a flowing fountain.

'And ease my heart by splashing—tum-tiddly-um-tum,' he hummed. 'I trust the choir-boys, Dame, are all in health?'

'Ah, Don Alvaro, no, sir!'

'Eh?'

'No, sir,' Madame Poco murmured, taking up a thousand golden poses.

'Why, how's that?'

'But few now seem keen on Leapfrog, or Bossage, and when a boy shows no wish for a game of Leap, sir, or Bossage——'

'Exactly,' his Eminence nodded.

'I'm told it's some time, young cubs, since they've played pranks on Tourists! Though only this afternoon little Ramón Ragatta came over queazy while demonstrating before foreigners the Dance of the Arc, which should teach him in future not to be so profane: and as to the acolytes, Don Alvaro, at least half of them are absent, confined to their cots, in the wards of the pistache Fathers!'

'To-morrow, all well, I'll take them some melons.'

'Ah, Don, Don!!'

'And, perhaps, a cucumber,' the Cardinal added, turning valedictionally away.

The tones of the seguidilla had deepened and from the remote recesses of the garden arose a bedlam of nightingales and frogs.

It was certainly incredible how he felt immured.

Yet to forsake the Palace for the Plaza he was obliged to stoop to creep.

With the Pirelli pride, with resourceful intimacy he communed with his heart: deception is a humiliation; but humiliation is a Virtue—a Cardinal, like myself, and one of the delicate violets of our Lady's crown. . . . Incontestably, too,—he had a flash of inconsequent insight, many a prod to a discourse, many a sapient thrust, delivered ex cathedrâ, amid the broken sobs of either sex, had been inspired, before now, by what prurient persons might term, perhaps, a 'frolic.' But away with all scruples! Once in the street in mufti, how foolish they became.

The dear street. The adorable Avenidas. The quickening stimulus of the crowd: truly it was exhilarating to mingle freely with the throng!

Disguised as a cabellero from the provinces or as a matron (disliking to forgo altogether the militant bravoura of a skirt), it became possible to combine philosophy, equally, with pleasure.

The promenade at the Trinidades seldom failed to be diverting, especially when the brown Bettita or the Ortiz danced! *Olé*, he swayed his shawl. The Argentina with Blanca Sanchez was amusing too; her ear-tickling little song 'Madrid is on the Manzanares,' trailing the ' 'ares' indefinitely, was sure, in due course, to reach the Cloisters.

Deliberating critically on the numerous actresses of his diocese, he traversed lightly a path all enclosed by pots of bergamot.

And how entrancing to perch on a bar-stool, over a glass of old golden sherry!

'Ah Jesus-Maria,' he addressed the dancing lightning in the sky.

Purring to himself, and frequently pausing, he made his way, by ecstatic degrees, towards the mirador on the garden wall.

Although a mortification, it was imperative to bear in mind the consequences of cutting a too dashing figure. Beware display. Vanity once had proved all but fatal: 'I remember it was the night I wore ringlets and was called "my queen." '

And with a fleeting smile, Don Alvaro Pirelli recalled the persistent officer who had had the effrontery to attempt to molest him: 'Stalked me the whole length of the Avenue Isadora!' It had been a lesson. 'Better to be on the drab side,' he reflected, turning the key of the garden tower.

Dating from the period of the Reformation of the Nunneries, it commanded the privacy of many a drowsy patio.

'I see the Infanta has begun her Tuesdays!' he serenely noted, sweeping the panorama with a glance.

It was a delightful prospect.

Like some great guitar the city lay engirdled ethereally by the snowy Sierras.

'Foolish featherhead,' he murmured, his glance falling upon a sunshade of sapphire chiffon, left by Luna: ' "my" parasol!' he twirled the crystal hilt.

'Everything she forgets, bless her,' he breathed, lifting his gaze towards the magnolia blossom cups that overtopped the tower, stained by the eternal treachery of the night to the azure of the Saint Virgin. Suspended in the miracle of the moonlight their elfin globes were at their zenith.

'Madrid is on the Manzan-ares,' he intoned.

But 'Clemenza,' of course, is in white Andalucia.

⊞ *III* ⊞

AFTER the tobacco-factory and the railway-station, quite the liveliest spot in all the city was the cathedral-sacristia. In the interim of an Office it would be besieged by the laity, often to the point of scrimmage: aristocrats and mendicants, relatives of acolytes —each had some truck or other in the long lofty room. Here the secretary of the chapter, a burly little man, a sound judge of women and bulls, might be consulted gratis, preferably before the supreme heat of day. Seated beneath a sombre study of the Magdalen way-laying our Lord (a work of wistful interest ascribed to Valdés Leal), he was, with tactful courtesy, at the disposal of anyone solicit-ing information as to 'vacant dates,' or 'hours available,' for some impromptu function. Indulgences, novenas, terms for special masses—with flowers and music? Or, just plain; the expense, it varied! Bookings for baptisms, it was certainly advisable to book well ahead; some mothers booked before the birth—; ah-hah, the little Juans and Juanas; the angelic babies! And arrangements for a corpse's lying-in-state: 'Leave it to me.' These, and such things, were in his province.

But the secretarial bureau was but merely a speck in the vast shuttered room. As a rule, it was by the old pagan sarcophaguses, outside the vestry-door, 'waiting for Father,' that *aficianados* of the cult liked best to foregather.

It was the morning of the Feast of San Antolin of Panticosa, a morning so sweet, and blue and luminous, and many were waiting.

'It's queer the time a man takes to slip on a frilly!' the laundress of the Basilica, Doña Consolacion, observed, through her fansticks, to Tomás the beadle.

'Got up as you get them. . . .'

'It's true, indeed, I've a knack with a rochet!'

'Temperament will out, Doña Consolacion; it cannot be hid.'

The laundress beamed.

'Mine's the French.'

'It's God's will *whatever* it is.'

'It's the French,' she lisped, considering the silver rings on her honey-brown hands. Of distinguished presence, with dark matted curls at either ear, she was the apotheosis of flesh triumphant.

But the entry from the vestry of a file of monsignori imposed a transient silence—a silence which was broken only by the murmur of passing mule bells along the street.

Tingaling, tingaling: evocative of grain and harvest the sylvan sound of mule bells came and went.

Doña Consolacion flapped her fan.

There was to be question directly of a Maiden Mass.

With his family all about him, the celebrant, a youth of the People, looking childishly happy in his first broidered cope, had bent, more than once, his good-natured head, to allow some small brothers and sisters to inspect his tonsure.

'Like a little, little star!'

'No. Like a *perra gorda*.'

'No, like a little star,' they fluted, while an irrepressible grandmother, moved to tears and laughter, insisted on planting a kiss on the old 'Christian' symbol. 'He'll be a Pope some day, if he's spared!' she sobbed, transported.

'Not he, the big burly bull.' Mother Garcia of the Company of Jesus addressed Doña Consolacion with a mellifluent chuckle.

Holding a bouquet of sunflowers and a basket of eggs she had just looked in from Market.

'Who knows, my dear?' Doña Consolacion returned, fixing her gaze upon an Epitaph on a vault beneath her feet. ' "He was a boy and she dazzled him." Heigh-ho! Heysey-ho . . . ! Yes, as I was saying.'

'Pho: I'd like to see him in a Papal tiara.'

'It's mostly luck. I well recall his Eminence when he was nothing but a trumpery curate,' Doña Consolacion declared, turning to admire the jewelled studs in the ears of the President of the College of Noble Damosels.

'Faugh!' Mother Garcia spat.

'It's all luck.'

'There's luck and luck,' the beadle put in. Once he had confined by accident a lady in the souterrains of the cathedral, and only many days later had her bones and a diary, a diary documenting the most delicate phases of solitude and loneliness, *a woman's contribution to Science*, come to light; a piece of carelessness that had gone against the old man in his preferment.

'Some careers are less fortunate than others,' Mother Garcia exclaimed, appraising the sleek silhouette of Monsignor Silex, then precipitantly issuing from the Muniment-Room.

It was known he was not averse to a little stimulant in the bright middle of the morning.

'He has the evil Eye, dear, he has the evil Eye,' Doña Consolacion murmured, averting her head. Above her hung a sombre Ribera, in a frame of elaborate, blackened gilding.

'Ah, well, I do not fear it,' the Companion of Jesus answered, making way for a dark, heavy belle in a handkerchief and shawl.

'Has anyone seen Jositto, my little José?'

Mother Garcia waved with her bouquet towards an adjacent portal, surmounted, with cool sobriety, by a long, lavender marble cross. 'I expect he's through there.'

'In the cathedral?'

'How pretty you look, dear, and what a very gay shawl!'

'Pure silk.'

'I don't *doubt* it!'

Few women, however, are indifferent to the seduction of a Maiden Mass, and all in a second there was scarcely one to be found in the whole sacristia.

The secretary at his bureau looked about him: without the presence of *las mujares* the atmosphere seemed to weigh a little; still, being a Holiday of Obligation, a fair sprinkling of boys, youthful chapter hands whom he would sometimes designate as the 'lesser delights,' relieved the place of its austerity.

Through the heraldic windows, swathed in straw-mats to shut out the heat, the sun-rays entered, tattooing with piquant freckles the pampered faces of the choir.

A request for a permit to view the fabled Orangery in the cloisters interrupted his siestose fancies.

Like luxurious cygnets in their cloudy lawn, a score of young singing-boys were awaiting their cue: Low-masses, cheapness, and economy, how they despised them, and how they would laugh at 'Old Ends' who snuffed out the candles.

'Why should the Church charge *higher* for a short *Magnificat* than for a long *Miserere*?'

The question had just been put by the owner of a dawning moustache and a snub, though expressive, nose.

'Because happiness makes people generous, stupid, and often as not they'll squander, boom, but unhappiness makes them calculate. People grudge spending much on a snivel—even if it lasts an hour.'

'It's the choir that suffers.'

'This profiteering . . . The Chapter . . .' there was a confusion of voices.

'Order!' A slim lad, of an ambered paleness, raised a protesting hand. Indulged, and made-much-of by the hierarchy, he was Felix Ganay, known as Chief-dancing-choir-boy to the cathedral of Clemenza.

'Aren't they awful?' he addressed a child with a very finished small head. Fingering a score of music he had been taking lead in a mass of Palestrina, and had the vaguely distraught air of a kitten that had seen visions.

'After that, I've not a dry stitch on me,' he murmured, with a glance towards the secretary, who was making lost grimaces at the Magdalen's portrait.

A lively controversy (becoming increasingly more shrill) was dividing the acolytes and choir.

'Tiny and Tibi! Enough.' The intervention came from the full-voiced Christobal, a youngster of fifteen, with soft, peach-textured cheeks, and a tongue never far away. Considered an opportunist, he was one of the privileged six dancing-boys of the cathedral.

'Order!' Felix enjoined anew. Finely sensitive as to his prerogatives, the interference of his colleague was apt to vex him. He would be trying to clip an altar pose next. Indeed, it was a matter of scandal already, how he was attempting to attract attention, in influential places, by the unnecessary undulation of his loins, and by affecting strong scents and attars, such as Egyptian Tahetant, or Long flirt through the violet Hours. Himself, Felix, he was faithful to Royal Florida, or even to plain *eau-de-Cologne*, and to those slow Mozarabic movements which alone are seemly to the Church.

'You may mind your business, young Christobal,' Felix murmured, turning towards a big, serious, melancholy boy, who was describing a cigarette-case he had received as fee for singing 'Say it with Edelweiss' at a society wedding.

'Say it with what?' the cry came from an oncoming-looking child, with caressing liquid eyes, and a little tongue the colour of raspberry-cream—*so bright*. Friend of all sweets and dainties, he held San Antolin's day chiefly notable for the Saint's sweet biscuits, made of sugar and white-of-egg.

'And you, too, Chicklet. Mind your business, can't you?' Felix exclaimed, appraising in some dismay a big, bland woman, then descending upon the secretary at his desk, with a slow, but determined, waddle.

Amalia Bermudez, the fashionable Actress-manageress of the Teatro Victoria Eugenia, was becoming a source of terror to the chapter of Clemenza. Every morning, with fatal persistence, she would aboard the half-hypnotised secretary with the request that the Church should make 'a little christian' of her blue chow, for unless it could be done it seemed the poor thing wasn't *chic*. To be *chic* and among the foremost vanward; this, apart from the Theatre, meant all to her in life, and since the unorthodox affair of 'the Dun-Edens,' she had been quite upset by the chapter's evasive refusals.

'If a police-dog, then why not a chow?' she would ask. 'Why not my little Whisky? Little devil. Ah, believe me, Father, she has need of it; for she's supposed to have had a snake by my old dog Conqueror! . . . And yet you won't receive her? Oh, it's heartless. Men are cruel. . . .'

'There she is! Amalia—the Bermudez': the whisper spread, arresting the story of the black Bishop of Bechuanaland, just begun by the roguish Ramón.

And in the passing silence the treble voice of Tiny was left talking all alone.

'. . . frightened me like Father did, when he kissed me in the dark like a lion':—a remark that was greeted by an explosion of coughs.

But this morning the clear, light laugh of the comedienne rang out merrily. 'No, no, *hombre*,' she exclaimed (tapping the secretary upon the cheek archly with her fan), 'now don't, don't stare at me, and intimidate me like that! I desire only to offer a "Mass of Intention," fully choral, *that the Church may change her mind.*'

And when the cannon that told of Noon was fired from the white fortress by the river far away she was still considering programmes of music by Rossini and Cimarosa, and the colour of the chasubles which the clergy should wear.

⊞⊞ *IV* ⊞⊞

AT the season when the oleanders are in their full perfection, their choicest bloom, it was the Pontiff's innovation to install his American type-writing apparatus in the long Loggie of the Apostolic Palace that had been in disuse since the demise of Innocent XVI. Out-of-doorish, as Neapolitans usually are, Pope Tertius II was no exception to the rule, preferring blue skies to golden ceilings —a taste for which indeed many were inclined to blame him. A compromise between the state-saloons and the modest suite occupied by his Holiness from choice, these open Loggie, adorned with the radiant frescoes of Luca Signorelli, would be frequently the scene of some particular Audience, granted after the exacting press of official routine.

Late one afternoon the Pontiff after an eventful and arduous day was walking thoughtfully here alone. Participating no longer in the joys of the world, it was, however, charming to catch, from time to time, the distant sound of Rome—the fitful clamour of trams and cabs, and the plash of the great twin-fountains in the court of Saint Damascus.

Wrapped in grave absorption, with level gaze, the lips slightly pinched, Pope Tertius II paced to and fro, occasionally raising a well-formed (though hairy) hand, as though to dismiss his thoughts with a benediction. The nomination of two Vacant Hats, the marriage annulment of an ex-hereditary Grand Duchess, and the 'scandals of Clemenza,' were equally claiming his attention and ruffling his serenity.

He had the head of an elderly lady's-maid, and an expression concealed by layers of tactful caution.

'Why can't they all behave?' he asked himself plaintively, descrying Lucrezia, his prized white squirrel, sidling shyly towards him.

She was the gift of the Archbishop of Trebizond, who had found her in the region of the Coelian hill.

'Slyboots, slyboots,' Pope Tertius exclaimed, as she skipped from reach. It was incredible with what playful zest she would spring from statue to statue; and it would have amused the Vicar of Christ to watch her slip and slide, had it not suggested many a profound moral metaphor applicable to the Church. 'Gently, gently,' he enjoined; for once, in her struggles, she had robbed a fig-leaf off a 'Moses.'

'Yes, why can't they all behave?' he murmured, gazing up into the far pale-blueness.

He stood a brief moment transfixed, as if in prayer, oblivious of two whispering Chamberlains.

It was the turn-in-waiting of Baron Oschatz, a man of engaging exquisite manners, and of Count Cuenca, an individual who seemed to be in perpetual consternation.

Depositing a few of the most recent camera portraits of the Pontiff requiring autograph in a spot where he could not fail but see them, they formally withdrew.

It had been a day distinguished by innumerable Audiences, several not uninteresting to recall. . . .

Certainly the increasing numbers of English were decidedly promising, and bore out the sibylline predictions of their late great and sagacious ruler—Queen Victoria.

'The dear *santissima* woman,' the Pontiff sighed, for he entertained a sincere, if brackish, enthusiasm for the lady who for so many years had corresponded with the Holy See under the signature of *the Countess of Lostwaters*.

'Anglicans . . . ? Heliolaters and sun-worshippers,' she had written in her most masterful hand, 'and your Holiness may believe us,' she had added, 'when we say especially our beloved Scotch.'

'I shouldn't wonder enormously if it were true,' the Pope exclaimed, catching through a half-shut door a glimpse of violet stockings.

Such a display of old, out-at-heel hose could but belong to Cardinal Robin.

There had been a meeting of the Board for Extraordinary Ecclesiastical Affairs, and when, shortly afterwards, the Cardinal was admitted he bore still about him some remote trace of faction.

He had the air of a cuttle-fish, and an enquiring voice. Inclined to gesture, how many miles must his hands have moved in the course of the sermons that he had preached!

Saluting the sovereign Pontiff with a deep obeisance, the Cardinal came directly to the point.

'These schisms in Spain . . .'

'They are ever before me,' His Holiness confessed.

'With priests like Pirelli, the Church is in peril!' the Cardinal declared, with a short, abysmal laugh.

'Does he suppose we are in the times of Baal and Moloch?' the Pope asked, pressing a harassed hand to his head. A Neapolitan of Naples (O Bay of Napoli! See Vesuvius, *and die*), he had curly hair that seemed to grow visibly; every few hours his tonsure would threaten to disappear.

The Cardinal sent up his brows a little.

'If I may tender the advice of the secret Consistory,' he said, 'your Holiness should Listen-in.'

'To what end?'

'A snarl, a growl, a bark, a yelp, coming from the font, would be quite enough to condemn...'

'Per Bacco. I should take it for a baby.'

'... condemn,' the Cardinal pursued, 'this Pirelli for a *maleficus pastor*. In which case, the earlier, the better, the unfrocking....'

The Pontiff sighed.

The excellent Cardinal was as fatiguing as a mission from Salt Lake City.

'Evidently,' he murmured, detecting traces of rats among the papyrus plants in the long walk below.

'They come up from the Tiber!' he exclaimed, piloting the Cardinal dexterously towards a flight of footworn steps leading to the Court of Bramante.

'It's a bore there being no lift!' he commented (the remark was a Vatican cliché), dismissing the Cardinal with a benediction.

'A painful interview,' the Holy Father reflected, regarding the Western sky. An evening rose and radiant altogether....

Turning sadly, he perceived Count Cuenca.

A nephew of the Dean of the Sacred College, it was rumoured that he was addicted, in his 'home' above Frascati, to the last excesses of the pre-Adamite Sultans.

'A dozen blessings, for a dozen Hymens—but only eleven were sent,' he was babbling distractedly to himself. He had been unstrung all day, 'just a mass of foolish nerves,' owing to a woman, an American, it seemed, coming for her Audience in a hat edged with white and yellow water-lilies. She had been repulsed successfully by the Papal Guard, but it had left an unpleasant impression.

'How's that?' the Vicar of Christ exclaimed: he enjoyed to tease his Chamberlains—especially Count Cuenca.

The Count turned pale.

'——,' he replied inaudibly, rolling eyes at Lucrezia.

Baron Oschatz had 'deserted' him; and what is one Chamberlain, alas, without another?

'The photographs of your Holiness are beside the bust of Bernini!' he stammered out, beating a diplomatic retreat.

Pope Tertius II addressed his squirrel.

'Little slyboots,' he said, 'I often laugh when I'm alone.'

BEFORE the white façade of the DunEden Palace, commanding the long, palm-shaded Paseo del Violón, an array of carriages and limousines was waiting; while, passing in brisk succession beneath the portico, like a swarm of brilliant butterflies, each instant was bringing more. Dating from the period of Don Pedro *el cruel*, the palace had been once the residence of the famous Princesse des Ursins, who had left behind something of her conviviality and glamour. But it is unlikely that the soirées of the exuberant and fanciful Princesse eclipsed those of the no less exuberant Duquesa DunEden. It was to be an evening (flavoured with rich heroics) in honour of the convalescence of several great ladies, from an attack of 'Boheara,' the new and fashionable epidemic, diagnosed by the medical faculty as 'hyperæsthesia with complications'; a welcoming back to the world in fact of several despotic dowagers, not one perhaps of whom, had she departed this life, would have been really much missed or mourned! And thus, in deference to the intimate nature of the occasion, it was felt by the solicitous hostess that a Tertúlia (that mutual exchange of familiar or intellectual ideas) would make less demand on arms and legs than would a ball; just the mind and lips . . . a skilful rounding-off here, developing there, chiselling, and putting-out feelers; an evening dedicated to the furtherance of intrigue, scandal, love, beneath the eager eyes of a few young girls, still at school, to whom a quiet party was permitted now and then.

Fingering a knotted scapular beneath a windy arch, Mother Saint-Mary-of-the-Angels was asking God His will. Should she wait for Gloria and Clyte (they might be some time) or return to the convent and come back again at twelve? 'The dear girls are with their mother,' she informed her Maker, inclining respectfully before the Princess Aurora of the Asturias, who had just arrived attended by two bearded gentlemen with tummies.

Hopeful of glimpsing perhaps a colleague, Mother Saint-Mary moved a few steps impulsively in their wake. It was known that Monseigneur the Cardinal-Archbishop himself was expected, and not infrequently one ecclesiastic will beget another.

The crimson saloon, with its scattered group of chairs, was waxing cheery.

Being the day it was, and the social round never but slightly varying, most of the guests had flocked earlier in the evening to the self-same place, i.e. the Circus, or *Arena Amanda,* where it was subscription night, and where, at present, there was an irresistibly comic clown.

'One has only to think of him to——!' the wife of the Minister of Public Instruction exclaimed, going off into a fit of wheezy laughter.

'What power, what genius, what——!' The young wife of the Inspector of Rivers and Forests was at a loss. Wedded to one of the handsomest though dullest of men, Marvilla de las Espinafre's perfervid and exalted nature kept her little circle in constant awe, and she would often be jealous of the Forests (chiefly scrub) which her husband, in his official capacity, was called upon to survey. 'Don't lie to me. I know it! You've been to the woods.' And after his inspection of the aromatic groves of Lograno, Phædra in full fury tearing her pillow with her teeth was nothing to Marvilla. 'Why, dear? Because you've been *among the Myrtles,*' was the explanation she chose to give for severing conjugal relations.

'Vittorio forbids the circus on account of germs,' the wife of the President of the National Society of Public Morals murmured momentously.

'Really, with this ghastly Boheara, I shall not be grieved when the time comes to set out for dear Santander!' a woman with dog-rose cheeks, and puffed, wrinkled eyes, exclaimed, focusing languishingly the Cardinal.

'He is delicious in handsomeness to-night!'

'A shade battered. But a lover's none the worse in my opinion for acquiring technique,' the Duchess of Sarmento declared.

'A lover; what? His Eminence . . . ? ?'

The duchess tittered.

'Why not? I expect he has a little woman to whom he takes off his clothes,' she murmured, turning to admire the wondrous *Madonna of the Mule-mill* attributed to Murillo.

On a wall-sofa just beneath, crowned with flowers and aigrettes, sat Conca, Marchioness of Macarnudo.

'*Que tal?*'

'My joie de vivre is finished; still, it's amazing how I go on!' the Marchioness answered, making a corner for the duchess. She had known her 'dearest Luiza' since the summer the sun melted the church bells and their rakish, pleasure-loving, affectionate hearts had dissolved together. But this had not been yesterday; no; for the Marchioness was a *grandmother* now.

'Conca, Conca: one sees you're in love.'

'He's from *Avila*, dear—the footman.'

'What!'

'Nothing *classic*—but, *oh*!'

'Fresh and blond? I've seen him.'

'Such sep . . .'

'Santiago be praised!'

The Marchioness of Macarnudo plied her fan.

'Our hands first met at table . . . yes, dear; but what I always say is, one spark explodes the mine!' And with a sigh she glanced rhapsodically at her fingers, powdered and manicured and encrusted with rings. 'Our hands met first at table,' she repeated.

'And . . . and the rest?' the duchess gasped.

'I sometimes wish, though, I resembled my sister more, who cares only for amorous, "delicate" men—the Claudes, so to speak. But there it is! And, anyway, dear,' the Marchioness dropped her voice, 'he keeps me from thinking (ah perhaps more than I should) of my little grandson. Imagine, Luiza . . . Fifteen, white and vivid rose, and ink-black hair. . . .' And the Marchioness cast a long, pencilled eye towards the world-famous Pietà above her head. 'Queen of Heaven, defend a weak woman from *that*!' she besought.

Surprised, and considerably edified, by the sight of the dowager in prayer, Mother Saint-Mary-of-the-Angels was emboldened to advance: The lovely, self-willed donkey (or was it a mule?) that Our Lady was prodding, one could almost stroke it, hear it bray. . . .

Mother Saint-Mary-of-the-Angels could have almost laughed.

But the recollection of the presence of royalty steadied her.

Behind pink lowered portières it had retired, escorted by the mistress of the house. She wore a gown of ivory-black with heavy golden roses and a few of her large diamonds of ceremony.

'I love your Englishy-Moorishy cosy comfort, Decima, and I love——' the Princess Aurora had started to rave.

'An hyperæsthesia injection? . . . a beaten egg?' her hostess solicitously asked.

'*Per caridad!*' the Princess fluted, stooping to examine a voluptuous small *terre cuite*, depicting a pair of hermaphrodites amusing themselves.

She was looking like the ghost in the Ballet of Ghislaine, after an unusually sharp touch of Boheara; eight-and-forty hours in bed, and, scandal declared, not alone.

'A Cognac? . . . a crême de Chile? . . .'

'Nothing, nothing,' the Princess negligently answered, sweeping her long, primrose trailing skirts across the floor.

It was the boudoir of the Winterhalters and Isabeys, once the bright glory of the Radziwollowna collection, which, after several decades of disesteem, were returning to fashion and favour.

'And I love——' she broke off, nearly stumbling over an old blind spaniel, that resided in a basket behind the 'supposed original' of the *Lesbia of Lysippus*.

'Clapsey, Clapsey!' her mistress admonished. The gift of a dear and once intimate friend, the dog seemed inclined to outlive itself and become a nuisance.

Alas, poor, fawning Clapsey! Fond, toothless bitch. Return to your broken doze, and dream again of leafy days in leafy Parks, and comfy drives and escapades long ago. What sights you saw when you could see; fountains, and kneeling kings, and grim beggars at Church doors (those at San Eusebio were the worst). And sheltered spas by glittering seas: Santander! And dark adulteries and dim woods at night.

'And I love your Winterhalters!'

Beneath one of these, like a red geranium, was Cardinal Pirelli.

'Oh, your Eminence, the utter forlornness of Society! . . . Besides, (oh, my God!) to be the *one* Intellectual of a Town . . .' a wizened little woman, mistaken, not infrequently, for 'Bob Foy,' the jockey, was exclaiming plaintively.

'I suppose?' Monseigneur nodded. He was looking rather like Richelieu, draped in ermines and some old lace of a beautiful fineness.

'It's pathetic how entertaining is done now. Each year meaner. There was a time when the DunEdens gave balls, and one could count, as a rule, on supper. To-night, there's nothing but a miserable Buffet, with flies trimming themselves on the food; and the champagne that I tasted, well, I can assure your Eminence it was more like foul flower-water than Mumm.'

'Disgraceful,' the Cardinal murmured, surrendering with suave dignity his hand to the lips of a pale youth all mouchoir and waist.

These kisses of young men, ravished from greedy Royalty, had a delicate savour.

The One Intellectual smiled obliquely.

'Your eminence I notice has several devout salve-stains already,' she murmured, defending her face with her fan.

'Believe me, not all these imprints were left by men!'

The One Intellectual glanced away.

'The poor Princess! I ask you, has one the right to look *so* dying?'

'Probably not,' the Cardinal answered, following her ethereal transit.

It was the turn of the tide, and soon admittance to the boudoir had ceased causing 'heartburnings.'

Nevertheless some few late sirens were only arriving.

Conspicuous among these was Catherine (the ideal-questing, God-groping and insouciant), Countess of Constantine, the aristocratic heroine of the capital, looking half-charmed to be naked and alive. Possessing but indifferent powers of conversation—at Tertulias and dinners she seldom shone—it was yet she who had coined that felicitous phrase: *Some men's eyes are sweet to rest in.*

Limping a little, since she had sprained her foot, alas, while turning backward somersaults to a negro band in the black ballroom of the Infanta Eulalia-Irene, her reappearance after the misadventure was a triumph.

'Poor Kitty: it's a shame to ask her, if it's not a ball!' the Inspector of Rivers and Forests exclaimed, fondling the silvery branches of his moustache.

But, at least, a Muse, if not musicians, was at hand.

Clasping a large bouquet of American Beauty-roses, the Poetess Diana Beira Baixa was being besieged by admirers, to 'give them something; just something! *Anything* of her own.' Wedded, and proclaiming (*in vers libres*) her lawful love, it was whispered she had written a pæan to her husband's '. . . .' beginning *Thou glorious wonder!* which was altogether too conjugal and intimate for recitation in society.

'They say I utter the cry of sex throughout the Ages,' she murmured, resting her free hand idly on a table of gold and lilac lacquer beside her.

The Duchess-Dowager of Vizeu spread prudishly her fan.

'Since me maid set me muskito net afire, I'm just a bunch, me dear, of hysterics," she declared.

But requests for 'something; just something!' were becoming insistent, and indeed the Muse seemed about to comply when, overtaken by the first alarming symptoms of 'Boheara,' she fell with a long-drawn sigh to the floor.

❈❈ *VI* ❈❈

REPAIRING the vast armholes of a chasuble, Madame Poco, the venerable Superintendent-of-the-Palace, considered, as she worked, the social status of a Spy. It was not without a fleeting qualm that she had crossed the borderland that divides mere curiosity from professional vigilance, but having succumbed to the profitable proposals of certain monsignori, she had grown as keen on her quarry as a tigress on the track.

'It's a wearing life you're leading me, Don Alvaro; but I'll have you,' she murmured, singling out a thread.

For indeed the Higher-curiosity is inexorably exacting, encroaching, all too often, on the hours of slumber and rest.

'It's not the door-listening,' she decided, 'so much as the garden, and, when he goes awenching, the Calle Nabuchodonosor.'

She was seated by an open window, commanding the patio and the gate.

'*Vamos, vamos!*' Madame Poco sighed, her thoughts straying to the pontifical supremacy of Tertius II, for already she was the Pope's Poco, his devoted Phœbe, his own true girl: 'I'm true blue, dear. True blue.'

Forgetful of her needle, she peered interestedly on her image in a mirror on the neighbouring wall. It was a sensation of pleasant novelty to feel between her skull and her mantilla the notes of the first instalment of her bribe.

'Earned, every *perra gorda*, earned!' she exclaimed, rising and pirouetting in elation before the glass.

Since becoming the courted favourite of the chapter, she had taken to strutting-and-languishing in private before her mirror, improvising occult dance-steps, semi-sacred in character, modelled on those of Felix Ganay at White Easter, all in the flowery Spring. Ceremonial poses such as may be observed in storied-windows and olden *pietas* in churches (Dalilaesque, or Shulamitish, as the case might be) were her especial delight, and from these had been evolved an eerie 'Dance of Indictment.'

Finger rigid, she would advance ominously with slow, Salomé-like liftings of the knees upon a phantom Cardinal: 'And thus I accuse thee!' or 'I denounce thee, Don Alvaro, for,' etc.

'*Dalila!* You old sly gooseberry,' she chuckled, gloating on herself in the greenish-spotted depth of a tall, time-corroded glass.

Punch and late hours had left their mark.

'All this Porto and stuff to keep awake make a woman liverish,' she commented, examining critically her tongue.

It was a Sunday evening of *corrida*, towards the Feast of Corpus, and through the wide-open window came the near sound of bells.

Madame Poco crossed and recrossed her breast.

They were ringing 'Paula,' a bell which, tradition said, had fused into its metal one of the thirty pieces of silver received by the Iscariot for the betrayal of Christ.

'They seem to have asked small fees in those days,' she reflected, continuing her work.

It was her resolution to divide her reward between masses for herself and the repose and 'release' (from Purgatory) of her husband's soul, while anything over should be laid out on finery for a favourite niece, the little Leonora, away in the far Americas.

Madame Poco plied pensively her needle.

She was growing increasingly conscious of the physical demands made by the Higher-curiosity upon a constitution already considerably far-through, and the need of an auxiliary caused her to regret her niece. More than once, indeed, she had been near the point of asking Charlotte Chiemsee, the maid of the Duchess of Vizeu, to assist her. It was Charlotte who had set the duchess's bed-veils on fire while attempting to nip a romance.

But alone and unaided it was astonishing the evidence Madame Poco had gained, and she smiled, as she sewed, at the recollection of her latest capture—the handkerchief of Luna Sainz.

'These hennaed heifers that come to confess! . . .' she scoffed sceptically. For Madame Poco had some experience of men—those brown humbugs (so delicious in tenderness)—in her time. 'Poor soul! He had the prettiest teeth . . .' she murmured, visualising forlornly her husband's face. He had been coachman for many years to the sainted Countess of Triana, and he would tell the story of the pious countess and the vermin she had turned to flowers of flame while foraging one day among some sacks before a second-hand-clothes shop. It was she, too, who, on another occasion, had changed a handful of marsh-slush into fine slabs of chocolate, each slab engraved with the insignia of a Countess and the sign of the Cross.

'Still, she didn't change *him*, though!' Madame Poco reflected dryly, lifting the lid to her work-box.

Concealed among its contents was a copy of the gay and curious *Memoirs of Mlle. Emma Crunch,* so famous as 'Cora Pearl';—a confiscated bedside-book once belonging to the Cardinal-Archbishop.

'Ps! ps!' she purred, feeling amorously for her scissors beneath the sumptuous oddments of old church velvet and brocade that she loved to ruffle and ruck.

'Ps.'

She had been freshening a little the chasuble worn last by his Eminence at the baptism of the blue-eyed police-pup of the Duquesa DunEden, which bore still the primrose trace of an innocent insult.

'A disgraceful business altogether,' Madame Poco sighed.

Not everyone knew the dog was christened in *white menthe.* . . .

'Sticky stuff,' she brooded: 'and a liqueur I never cared for! It takes a lot to beat aniseed brandy; when it's old. Manzanilla runs it close; but it's odd how a glass or two turns me muzzy.'

She remained a moment lost in idle reverie before the brilliant embroideries in her basket. Bits of choice beflowered brocade, multi-tinted, inimitably faded silks of the epoca of Theresa de Ahumada, exquisite tatters, telling of the Basilica's noble past, it gladdened the eyes to gaze on. What garden of Granada could show a pink to match that rose, or what sky show a blue as tenderly serene as that azure of the Saint Virgin?

'*Vamos*,' she exclaimed, rising: 'it's time I took a toddle to know what he's about.'

She had last seen the Cardinal coming from the orange orchard with a dancing-boy and Father Fadrique, who had a mark on his cheek left by a woman's fan.

Her mind still dwelling on men (those divine humbugs), Madame Poco stepped outside.

Traversing a white-walled corridor, with the chasuble on her arm, her silhouette, illumined by the splendour of the evening sun, all but caused her to start.

It was in a wing built in the troublous reign of Alfonso the Androgyne that the vestments were kept. Whisking by a decayed and ancient painting, representing 'Beelzebub' at Home, she passed slowly through a little closet supposed to be frequented by the ghosts of evil persons long since dead. Just off it was the vestry, gay with blue azulejos tiles of an admirable lustre.

They were sounding Matteo now, a little bell with a passionate voice.

'The pet!' Madame Poco paused to listen. She had her 'favourites' among the bells, and Matteo was one of them. Passiaflora, too—but Anna, a light slithery bell, 'like a housemaid in hysterics,' offended her ear by lack of tone; Sebastian, a complaining, excitable bell, was scarcely better,—'a fretful lover!' She preferred old 'Wanda' the Death-bell, a trifle monotonous, and fanatical perhaps, but 'interesting,' and opening up vistas to varied thought and speculation.

Lifting a rosary from a linen-chest, Madame Poco laid the chasuble within. It was towards this season she would usually renew the bags of bergamot among the Primate's robes.

'This espionage sets a woman all behindhand,' she commented to Tobit, the vestry cat.

Black as the Evil One, perched upon a Confessional's ledge, cleansing its belly, the sleek thing sat.

It was the 'ledge of forgotten fans,' where privileged Penitents would bring their tales of vanity, infidelity and uncharitableness to the Cardinal once a week.

'Directing half-a-dozen duchesses must be frequently a strain!' Madame Poco deliberated, picking up a discarded mitre and trying it absently on.

With a plume at the side or a cluster of balls, it would make quite a striking toque, she decided, casting a fluttered glance on the male effigy of a pale-faced member of the Quesada family, hewn in marble by the door.

"*Caramba!* I thought it was the Cardinal; it gave me quite a turn,' she murmured, pursuing lightly her way.

Being a Sunday evening of corrida, it was probable the Cardinal had mounted to his aerie, to enjoy the glimpse of Beauty returning from the fight.

Oh, mandolines of the South, warm throats, and winged songs, winging . . .

Following a darkened corridor with lofty windows closely barred, Madame Poco gained an ambulatory, terminated by a fresco of Our Lady, ascending to heaven in a fury of paint.

'These damp flags'll be the death of me,' she complained, talking with herself, turning towards the garden.

Already the blue pushing shadows were beguiling from the shelter of the cloister eaves the rueful owls. A few flittermice, too, were revolving around the long apricot chimneys of the Palace, that, towards sunset, looked like the enchanted castle of some sleeping Princess.

'Bits of pests,' she crooned, taking a neglected alley of old bay-tree laurels, presided over by a plashing fountain comprised of a Cupid sneezing. Wary of mole-hills and treacherous roots, she roamed along, preceded by the floating whiteness of a Persian peacock, mistrustful of the intentions of a Goat-sucker owl. Rounding a sequestered garden seat, beneath an aged cypress, the bark all scented knots, Madame Poco halted.

Kneeling before an altar raised to the cult of Our Lady of Dew, Cardinal Pirelli was plunged in prayer.

'Salve. Salve Regina. . . .' Above the tree-tops a bird was singing.

⊞ *VII* ⊞

THE College of Noble Damosels in the Calle Santa Fé was in a whirl. It was 'Foundation' day, an event annually celebrated with considerable fanfaronade and social éclat. Founded during the internecine wars of the Middle Age, the College, according to early records, had suffered rapine on the first day of term. Hardly, it seemed, had the last scholar's box been carried upstairs than a troop of military had made its appearance at the Pension gate demanding, with 'male peremptoriness,' a billet. 'I, alone,' the Abbess ingenuously states, in relating the poignant affair in her unpublished diary: 'I alone did all I was able to keep them from them, for which they (the scholars) called me "greedy."' Adding, not without a touch of modern socialism in disdain for titles, that she had preferred 'the staff-officers to the Field-Marshal,' while as to ensigns, in her estimation, why, 'one was worth the lot.'

Polishing urbanely her delicate nails, the actual President, a staid, pale woman with a peacock nose, recalled the chequered past. She hoped his Eminence when he addressed the girls, on handing them their prizes, would refer to the occasion with all the tactfulness required.

'When I think of the horrid jokes the old Marqués of Illescas made last year,' she murmured, bestowing a harrowed smile on a passing pupil.

She was ensconced in a ponderous fauteuil of figured velvet (intended for the plump posterior of Royalty) beneath the incomparable 'azulejos' ceiling of the Concert-room, awaiting the return of Madame Always Alemtejo, the English governess, from the printers, in the Plaza de Jesus, with the little silver-printed programmes (so like the paste-board cards of brides!), which, as usual, were late.

'Another year we'll type them,' she determined, awed by the ardent tones of a young girl rehearsing an aria from the new opera, *Leda*—'Gaze not on Swans.'

'Ah, gaze not so on Swan-zzz! . . .'

'Crisper, child. Distinction. Don't exaggerate,' the President enjoined, raising a hand to the diamonds on her heavy, lead-white cheeks.

Née an Arroyolo, and allied by marriage with the noble house of Salvaterra, the headmistress in private life was the Dowager-Marchioness of Pennisflores.

'*Nosotros,* you know, are not candidates for the stage! Bear in mind your moral,' she begged, with a lingering glance at her robe of grey georgette.

The word 'moral,' never long from the President's lips, seemed, with her, to take on an intimate tinge, a sensitiveness of its own. She would invest the word at times with an organic significance, a mysterious dignity, that resembled an avowal made usually only in solemn confidence to a doctor or a priest.

The severity of my moral. The prestige of my moral. The perfection of my moral. She has no dignity of moral. I fear a person of no positive moral. Nothing to injure the freshness of her moral. A difficulty of moral. The etiquette of my moral. The majesty of my moral, etc., etc.—as uttered by the President, became, psychologically, interesting *data*.

'Beware of a facile moral!' she added, for the benefit of the singer's accompanist, a young nun with a face like some strange white rock, who was inclined to give herself married airs, since she had been debauched, one otiose noon, by a demon.

'Ah, Madame Always.' The President swam to meet her.

British born, hailing from fairy Lisbon, Madame Always Alemtejo seemed resigned to live and die in a land of hitches.

'The delay is owing to the Printers' strike,' she announced. 'The Plaza's thronged: the Cigar factory girls, and all the rag-tag and bobtail, from the Alcazaba to the Puerta del Mar, are going out in sympathy, and——'

'The tarts?'

'The t's from Chamont are on the way.'

It was the President's custom to lay all vexations before Nostra Señora de los Remedios, the college's divine Protectress, with whose gracious image she was on the closest footing.

Consulting her now as to the concert-programmes, the President recalled that no remedy yet had been found for Señorita Violeta de las Cubas, who had thrown her engagement ring into a place of less dignity than convenience and refused to draw it out.

'Sapphires, my favourite stones,' the President reflected, wondering if she should ask 'la Inglese' to recover it with the asparagustongs.

But already a few *novios,* eager to behold their *novias* again, were in the Patio beneath the 'Heiresses' Wing,' exciting the connoisseurship of a bevy of early freshness.

'You can tell *that* by his eyebrows!' a girl of thirteen, and just beginning as a woman, remarked.

'*Que barbaridad.*'

'Last summer at Santander Maria-Manuela and I bathed with him, and one morning there was a tremendous sea, with *terrific* waves, and we noticed unmistakably.'

'I can't explain; but I adore all that mauvishness about him!'

'I prefer Manolito to Gonzalito, though neither thrill me like the Toreador Tancos.'

Assisted by Fräulein Pappenheim and Muley, the President's negress maid, they were putting the final touches to their vestal frocks.

'Men are my raging disgust,' a florid girl of stupendous beauty declared, saturating with a flacon of *Parfum cruel* her prematurely formed silhouette.

'Nsa, nsa, señorita,' Muley mumbled. 'Some know better dan dat!'

'To hell with them!'

'*Adios*, Carlo. *Adios*, Juan. Join you down dah in one minute.' The negress chuckled jauntily.

'Muley, Muley,' Fräulein chided.

'What wonder next I 'bout to hear?'

Delighting in the tender ferocities of Aphrodite, she was ever ready to unite the *novio* to the *novia*. For window-vigils (where all is hand play) few could contrive more ingeniously than she those fans of fresh decapitated flowers, tuberose punctuated with inebriating jasmine, so beloved in the East by the dark children of the sun. Beyond Cadiz the blue, the beautiful, in palm-girt Marrakesh, across the sea, she had learnt other arts besides. . . .

'Since seeing Peter Prettylips on the screen the Spanish type means nothing to me,' Señorita Soledad, a daughter of the first Marqués of Belluga, the greatest orange-king in the Peninsula, remarked.

'How low. She is not noble.'

'I *am* noble.'

'Oh no; you're not.'

'Cease wrangling,' Fräulein exclaimed, 'and enough of that,' she added sharply, addressing a *novio*less little girl looking altogether bewitching of naughtiness as she tried her ablest to seduce by her crude manœuvres the fiancé of a friend. Endowed with the lively temperament of her grandmother, Conca, Marchioness of Macarnudo, the impressionable, highly amative nature of the little Obdulia gave her governesses some grounds for alarm. At the Post Office one day she had watched a young man lick a stamp. His rosy tongue had vanquished her. In fact, at present, she and a class-chum, Milagros, were 'collecting petals' together—and much to the bewilderment of those about them, they might be heard on occasion to exclaim, at Mass, or in the street: 'Quick, did you see it?' 'No.' 'Santissima! *I* did!'

'Shrimp. As if Gerardo would look at her!' his *novia* scoffed. 'But let me tell you, young woman,' she turned upon the shrinking Obdulia, 'that social ostracism, and even, in certain cases' (she slapped and pinched her), '*assassination* attends those that thieve or tamper with another's lover! And Fräulein will correct me if I exaggerate.'

Fräulein Pappenheim was a little woman already drifting towards the sad far shores of forty, with no experience of the pains of Aphrodite caused by men; only at times she would complain of stomach aches in the head.

'Dat is so,' Muley struck in sententiously for her. 'Dair was once a young lady ob Fez——'

But from the Patio the college chaplain, Father Damien Forment, known as 'Shiny-nose,' was beckoning to the heiresses to join their relatives in the reception-hall below.

Since that sanguinary period of Christianity, synchronising with the foundation of the institution of learning in the Calle Santa Fé, what changes in skirts and trousers the world has seen. Alone unchanging are women's ambitions and men's desires.

'Dear child. . . . She accepts him . . . but a little à contre-cœur,' the President was saying to the Marchioness of las Cubas, an impoverished society belle, who went often without bread in order to buy lip-sticks and rouge.

'With Violeta off my hands . . . Ah, President, if only Cecilio could be suitably *casada*.'

'In my little garden I sometimes work a brother. The heiresses' windows are all opening to the flowers and trees. . . . The boy should be in polo kit. A uniform interests girls,' the President murmured, turning with an urbane smile to welcome the Duquesa DunEden.

She had a frock of black kasha, signed Paul Orna, with a cluster of brown-and-pink orchids, like sheep's-kidneys, and a huge feather hat.

'I'm here for my God-girl, Gloria,' she murmured, glancing mildly round.

Incongruous that this robust, rich woman should have brought to the light of heaven no heir, while the unfortunate Marchioness, needy, and frail of physique, a wraith, did not know what to do with them!

The President dropped a sigh.

She was prepared to take a dog of the daughterless Duquesa. A bitch, of course. . . . But let it be Police, or Poodle! It would lodge with the girls. A cubicle to itself in the heiresses' wing; and since there would be no extra class-charge for dancing or drawing, no course *in belli arti*, some reduction of fees might be arranged. . . .

'We would turn her out a creature of breeding. . . . An eloquent tail-wave, a disciplined moral, and with a reverence moreover for house-mats and carpets.' The President decided to draw up the particulars of the prospectus by and by.

'Your Goddaughter is quite one of our most promising exhibitioners,' she exclaimed, indicating with her fan some water-colour studies exposed upon the walls.

'She comes of a mother with a mania for painting,' the Duquesa declared, raising a lorgnon, critically, before the portrait of a Lesbian, with dying, fabulous eyes.

'Really?'

'A positive passion,' the Duquesa answered, with a swift, discerning glance at an evasive 'nude,' showing the posterior poudrederizé of a Saint.

'I had no idea,' the President purred, drawing attention to a silvery streetscape.

'It's the Rambla from the back of Our Lady of the Pillar! It was rare fun doing it, on account of the *pirapos* of the passers-by,' the artist, joining them, explained.

'Dear child, I predict for her a great deal of admiration very soon,' the President murmured, with a look of reproach at a youthful pupil as she plied her boy-Father with embarrassing questions: 'Who are the chief society women in the moon? What are their names? Have they got motor-cars there? Is there an Opera-House? Are there bulls?'

The leering aspect of a lady in a costume of blonde Guadalmedina lace and a hat wreathed with clipped black cocks' feathers arrested her.

Illusion-proof, with a long and undismayed service in Love's House (sorry brutes, all the same, though, these men, with their selfishness, fickleness and lies!) the Marchioness of Macarnudo with her mysterious 'legend' (unscrupulous minxes, all the same, though, these women, with their pettiness, vanity and ... !), was too temperamentally intriguing a type to be ignored.

'Isn't that little Marie Dorothy with the rosebuds stuck all over her?' she asked her granddaughter, who was teasing her brother on his moustache.

'To improve the growth, the massage of a *novia's* hand,' she fluted, provoking the marchioness to an involuntary nervous gesture. Exasperated by resistance, struggling against an impossible infatuation, her Spanish ladyship was becoming increasingly subject to passing starts. Indeed only in excitement and dissipation could her unsatisfied longings find relief. Sometimes she would run out in her car to where the men bathe at Ponte Delgado, and one morning, after a ball, she had been seen standing on the main road to Cadiz in a cabochon tiara, watching the antics of some nude muleteers: *Black as young Indians*—she had described them later.

'My sweet butterfly! What next?' she exclaimed, ogling Obdulia, whose elusive resemblance to her brother was really curiously disturbing.

Averting a filmy eye, she recognised Marvilla de las Espinafre, airing anti-patriotic views on birth control, her arms about an adopted daughter. 'Certainly not; most decidedly *no*! I should scream!' she was saying as from the Concert-room the overture began thinning the crowd.

'It's nothing else than a national disaster,' the marchioness declared to her grandson, 'how many women nowadays seem to shirk their duty!'

'Well, the de las Cubas hasn't, anyway,' he demurred.

'Poor thing. They say she jobs her mules,' the marchioness murmured, exchanging a nod with the passing President.

Something, manifestly, had occurred to disturb the equilibrium of her moral.

'Such a disappointment, *Nostra Señora*!' she exclaimed. 'Monseigneur, it seems, has thrown me over.'

'Indeed; how awkward!'

'I fear though even more so for his chapter.'

'He is not ill?'

'*Cardinal Pirelli has fled the capital!*'

⊠ *VIII* ⊠

STANDING amid gardens made for suffering and delight is the disestablished and, *sic transit,* slowly decaying monastery of the Desierto. Lovely as Paradise, oppressive perhaps as Eden, it had been since the days of the mystic Luigi of Granada a site well suited to meditation and retreat. Here, in the stilly cypress-court, beneath the snowy sierras of Santa Maria la Blanca, Theresa of Avila, worn and ill, though sublime in laughter, exquisite in beatitude, had composed a part of the *Way of Perfection*, and, here, in these same realms of peace, dominating the distant city of Clemenza and the fertile plains of Andalucia, Cardinal Pirelli, one blue mid-day towards the close of summer, was idly considering his Defence. '*Apologia,* no; merely a defence,' he mused: 'merely,' he flicked the ash-tip of a cigar, 'a defence! I defend myself, that's all! . . . '

A sigh escaped him.

Divided by tranquil vineyards and orange-gardens from the malice and vindictiveness of men it was difficult to experience emotions other than of forgiveness and love.

'Come, dears, and kiss me,' he murmured, closing consentingly his eyes.

It was the forgetful hour of noon, when Hesperus from his heavens confers on his pet Peninsula the boon of sleep.

'A nice nap he's having, poor old gentleman.' Madame Poco surveyed her master.

Ill at ease and lonely in the austere dismantled house, she would keep an eye on him at present almost as much for company as for gain.

As handsome and as elegant as ever, his physiognomy in repose revealed a thousand strange fine lines, suggestive subtleties, intermingled with less ambiguous signs, denoting stress and care.

'He's growing almost huntedish,' she observed, casting a brief glance at the literature beside him—The Trial of Don Fernando de la Cerde, Bishop of Barcelona, defrocked for putting young men to improper uses; a treatise on The Value of Smiles; an old volume of Songs, by Sà de Miranda; The Lives of Five Negro Saints, from which escaped a bookmark of a dancer in a manton.

'Everything but his Breviary,' she commented, perceiving a soutané form through the old flowered ironwork of the courtyard gateway.

Regretting her better gown of hooped watered-silk, set aside while in retreat (for economy's sake), Madame Poco fled to put it on, leaving the visitor to announce himself.

The padre of Our Lady of the Valley, the poor padre of Our Lady, would the Primate know? Oh, every bird, every rose, could have told him that: the padre of Our Lady bringing a blue trout for his Eminence's supper from the limpid waters of Lake Orense.

Respecting the Primate's rest Father Felicitas, for so, also, was he named, sat down discreetly to await his awakening.

It was a rare sweetness to have the Cardinal to himself thus intimately. Mostly, in the city, he would be closely surrounded. Not that Father Felicitas went very much to town; no; he disliked the confusion of the streets, and even the glories of the blessed basilicas made him scarcely amends for the quiet shelter of his hills.

The blessed basilicas, you could see them well from here. The giralda of Saint Xarifa, and the august twin towers of the cathedral, and the azulejos dome of Saint Eusebio, that was once a pagan mosque; while of Santissima Marias, Maria del Carmen, Maria del Rosario, Maria de la Soledad, Maria del Dolores, Maria de las Nieves, few cities in all the wide world could show as many.

'To be sure, to be sure,' he exclaimed absently, lifting his eyes to a cloudlet leisurely pointing above the lofty spur of the Pico del Mediodia. 'To be sure,' he added, seeking to descry the flower-like bellcot of Our Lady of the Valley just beneath.

But before he had discovered it, half concealed by trees, he was reminded by the sound of a long-drawn, love-sick wail, issuing out of the very entrails of the singer, of the lad left in charge of his rod by the gate.

'On the Bridge to Alcantara.'

With its protracted cadences and doleful, vain-yearning reaches, the voice, submerged in all the anguish of a Malagueña, troubled, nostalgically, the stillness.

God's will be done. It was enough to awaken the Primate. Not everyone relished a Malagueña, a dirgeful form of melody introduced, tradition said, and made popular in the land, long, long ago, beneath the occupation of the Moors.

Father Felicitas could almost feel the sin of envy as he thought of the flawless choir and noble triumphal organ of the cathedral yonder.

Possessed of no other instrument, Our Lady of the Valley depended at present on a humble guitar. Not that the blessed guitar, with its capacity for emotion, is unworthy to please God's listening ear, but Pepe, the lad appointed to play it, would fall all too easily into those Jotas, Tangos, and Cuban Habaneiras, learnt in wayside fondas and fairs. Some day, Father Felicitas did not doubt, Our Lady would have an organ, an organ with pipes. He had prayed for it so often; oh, so often; and once, quite in the late of twilight while coming through the church, he had seen her, it seemed, standing just where it should be. It had been as though a blinding whiteness.

'A blinding whiteness,' he murmured, trembling a little at the recollection of the radiant vision.

Across the tranquil court a rose-red butterfly pursued a blue. 'I believe the world is all love, only no one understands,' he meditated, contemplating the resplendent harvest plains steeped in the warm sweet sunlight.

'My infinite contrition!' The Cardinal spoke.

A rare occurrence in these days was a visitor, and now with authority ebbing, or in the balance at least, it was singular how he felt a new interest in the concerns of the diocese. The birth-rate and the death-rate and the super-rate, which it was to be feared that the Córtes——

Sailing down the courtyard in her watered-silken gown, Madame Poco approached with Xeres and Manzanilla, fresh from the shuttered snowery or nieveria.

'And I've just buried a bottle of champagne, in case your Emience should want it,' she announced as she inviolably withdrew.

'As devoted a soul as ever there was, and loyal to all my interests,' the Primate exclaimed, touched.

'God be praised!'

'An excellent creature,' the Cardinal added, focusing on the grey high road beyond the gate two youths on assback, seated close.

'Andalucians, though of another parish.'

'I should like much to visit my diocese again; it's some while since I did,' the Cardinal observed, filling the Padre's glass.

'You'd find up at Sodré a good many changes.'

'Have they still the same little maid at the Posada de la Melodia?'

'Carmencita?'

'A dainty thing.'

'She went Therewards about the month of Mary.'

'America? It's where they all go.'

'She made a ravishing corpse.'

'Ahi.'

And Doña Beatriz too had died; either in March or May. It was she who would bake the old Greek Sun-bread, and although her heirs had sought high and low no one could find the receipt.

The Cardinal expressed satisfaction.

'Bestemmia,' he breathed; 'and I trust they never may; for on the Feast of the Circumcision she invariably caused to be laid before the high-altar of the cathedral a peculiarly shaped loaf to the confusion of all who saw it.'

And the Alcalde of Ayamonte, Don Deniz, had died on the eve

of the bachelors' party he usually gave when he took off his winter beard.

'Ahi; this death . . .'

Ah, yes, and since the delicacies ordered by the corpse could rot. well be countermanded they had been divided among Christ's poon

Left to himself once more Cardinal Pirelli returned reluctantly to his Defence.

Half the diocese it seemed had gone 'Therewards,' while the rest were at Biarritz or Santander. . . .

'A nice cheery time this is!' he murmured, oppressed by the silent cypress-court. Among the blue, pointing shadows, a few frail oleanders in their blood-rose ruby invoked warm brief life and earth's desires.

'A nice cheery time,' he repeated, rising and going within.

The forsaken splendour of the vast closed cloisters seemed almost to augur the waning of a cult. Likewise the decline of Apollo, Diana, Isis, with the gradual downfall of their temples, had been heralded, in past times, by the dispersal of their priests. It looked as though Mother Church, like Venus or Diana, was making way in due turn for the beliefs that should follow: 'and we shall begin again with intolerance, martyrdom and converts,' the Cardinal ruminated, pausing before an ancient fresco depicting the eleven thousand virgins, or as many as there was room for.

Playing a lonely ball game against them was the disrespectful Chicklet.

'Young vandal,' the Cardinal chided, caressing the little acolyte's lustrous locks.

'Monseigneur? . . .'

'There: run along; and say a fragrant prayer for me, Child.'

Flinging back a shutter drawn fast against the sun, the boundless prospect from the balcony of his cell recalled the royal Escorial. The white scattered terraces of villas set in dark deeps of trees, tall palms, and parasol-pines so shady, and, almost indistinguishable, the white outline of the sea, made insensibly for company.

Changing into a creation of dull scarlet crêpe, a cobweb dubbed 'summer-exile,' Cardinal Pirelli felt decidedly less oppressed. 'Madrid is on the Manzanares,' he vociferated, catching sight of the diligence from Sodré. Frequently it would bring Frasquito, the postman—a big tawny boy, overgiven to passing the day in the woods with his gun and his guitar.

'The mail bag is most irregular,' he complained, fastening a few dark red, almost black, roses to his cincture. It was Cardinal Pirelli's fancy while in retreat to assume his triple-Abraham, or mitre, and with staff in hand to roam abroad as in the militant Springtide of the Church.

'When kings were cardinals,' he murmured quietly as he left the room.

It was around the Moorish water-garden towards shut of day he liked most to wander, seeking like some Adept to interpret in the still deep pools the mirrored music of the sky.

All, was it vanity? These pointing stars and spectral leaning towers, this mitre, this jewelled ring, these trembling hands, these sweet reflected colours, white of daffodil and golden rose. All, was it vanity?

Circling the tortuous paths like some hectic wingless bird, he was called to the refectory by the tintinnabulation of a bell.

In the deep gloominous room despoiled of all splendour but for a dozen old Zurbarans flapping in their frames, a board, set out with manifest care, was prepared for the evening meal.

Serving both at Mass and table, it was the impish Chicklet who, with a zealous napkin-flick (modelled on the *mozos* of the little café-cum-restaurant 'As in Ancient Andalucia' patronised by rising toreadors and *aficianados* of the Ring), showed the Primate to his chair.

Having promised José the chef a handsome indulgence, absolved him from bigamy, and raised his wages, Cardinal Pirelli, in gastronomy nothing if not fastidious, had succeeded in inducing him to brave the ghostly basements of the monastery on the mount.

Perhaps of the many charges brought against the Primate by his traducers, that of making the sign of the cross with his left foot at meals was the most utterly unfounded—looking for a foot-cushion would have been nearer the truth.

Addressing the table briefly in the harmonious Latin tongue, his Eminence sat down with an impenetrable sigh.

With vine-sprays clinging languorously to the candle-stands, rising from a bed of nespoles, tulips, and a species of wild orchid known as Devil's-balls, the Chicklet, to judge from his floral caprices, possessed a little brain of some ambition, not incapable of excess.

'I thought you were tired of jasmine, sir, and th'orange bloom's getting on,' he chirruped, coming forward with a cup of cold, clear consommé, containing hearts, coronets and most of the alphabet in vermicelli.

'I'm tired, true, child; but not of jasmine,' the Primate returned, following the little contretemps of a marqués' crown, sinking amid a frolicsome bevy of *O*'s.

'I hope it's right, sir?'

'Particularly excellent, child—tell José so.'

'Will I bring the trout, sir?'

'Go, boy,' the Cardinal bade him, opening a volume by the menu-stand formed of a satyr sentimentalising over a wood-nymph's breasts.

While in retreat it was his fancy, while supping, to pursue some standard work of devotion, such as Orthodoxy so often encourages or allows: it was with just such a golden fairy-tale as this that he had once won a convert: Poor woman. What had become of her? Her enthusiasm, had it lasted? She had been very ardent. Perfervid! 'Instruction' would quite wear it out of them. Saint Xarifa's at fall of day; . . . an Autumn affair! Chrysanthemums; big bronze frizzlies. A Mrs. Mandarin Dove. American. Ninety million sterling. Social pride and religious humility, how can I reconcile? The women in Chicago. My God! ! ! My little step-daughter. . . . Her Father, fortunately. . . . Yes, your Eminence, he's dead. And, oh, I'm *glad*. Is it naughty? And then her photograph à la Mary of Magdala, her hair unbound, décolletée, with a dozen long strands of pearls. 'Ever penitently yours, Stella Mandarin Dove.'

'I'd rather have had the blonde Ambassadress to the Court of St. James', he reflected, toying with the fine table-glass of an old rich glamour. A fluted bell cup sadly chipped provoked a criticism and a citation from Cassiodorus on the 'rude' ways of boys.

Revolving around an austere piece of furniture that resembled a Coffin-upon-six-legs, the Chicklet appeared absorbed.

'I hear it's the Hebrew in heaven, sir. Spanish is seldom spoken,' he exclaimed seraphically.

'Tut, dear child. Who says so?' the Primate wondered, his eyes wandering in melancholy towards the whitest of moons illumining elusively the room—illumining a long, sexless face with large, mauve, heroic lips in a falling frame, and an 'apachey,' blue-cheeked Christ, the Cardinal noticed.

'Who, sir? Why, a gentleman I was guide to once!'

The Cardinal chuckled comprehensively.

'I should surmise, dear child, there was little to show.'

'What, not the crypt, sir? Or the tomb of the beautiful Princess Eboli, the beloved of Philip the Second, sir?'

'Jewel boy. Yum-yum.' The Cardinal raised his glass.

'And the bells, sir? Last night, I'll tell you, sir, I thought I heard old "Wanda" on the wind.'

'Old Wanda, boy?'

'She rings for deaths, sir.'

'Nonsense, child; your little ears could never hear as far,' the Cardinal answered, deliberating if a lad of such alertness and perception might be entrusted to give him a henna shampoo: it was easy enough to remove the towels before it got too red. The difficulty was to apply the henna; evenly everywhere; fair play all round; no favouring the right side more than the left, but golden Justice for each grey hair. Impartiality: proportion! 'Fatal, otherwise,' the Primate reasoned.

'Are you ready for your Quail, sir?'

'Quail, quail? Bring on the *dulces*, boy,' his Eminence murmured, regarding absently through the window the flickering arc-lights of Clemenza far away. Dear beckoning lamps, dear calling lamps; lamps of theatres, cinemas, cabarets, bars and dancings; lamps of railway-termini, and excessively lit hotels, *olé* to you, enchantress lights!

'And, after all, dears, if I did,' the Cardinal breathed, tracing a caricature of his Holiness upon the table-cloth lightly with a dessert-fork. ('Which I certainly deny' . . .), he brooded, disregarding the dissolving Orange ice *à la* Marchioness of Macarnudo.

'Had you anything in the Lottery, sir?'

'Mind your business, boy, and remove this ballroom nastiness,' the Primate snapped.

It was while lingering, after dinner, over some choice vintage, that he oftenest would develop the outline of his Defence. To escape the irate horns of the Pontiff's bull (Die, dull beast) he proposed pressing the 'Pauline Privilege,' unassailable, and confirmed *A.D.* *1590* by Pope Sixtus V, home to the battered beauty of the Renaissance hilt. 'With the elegance and science,' he murmured, 'of a *matador*.'

'I have the honour to wish you, sir, a good and pleasant night.'

'Thanks, boy.'

'And if you should want me, sir' . . . the youthful acolyte possessed the power to convey the unuttered.

'If?? . . . And say a fragrant prayer for me, child,' the Cardinal enjoined.

Resting an elbow among the nespoles and tulips (dawn-pink and scarlet, awakening sensitively in the candle-glow), he refilled reflectively his glass.

'God's providence is over all,' he told himself, considering dreamfully a cornucopia heaped with fruit. Being just then the gracious Autumn, a sweet golden-plum called 'Don Jaime of Castile' was in great perfection. It had been for the Southern orchards a singularly fertile year. Never were seen such gaily rouged peaches, such sleek, violet cherries, such immensest white grapes. Nestling delectably amid its long, deeply-lobed leaves, a pomegranate (fruit of joy) attracted the Cardinal's hand.

Its seeds, round and firm as castanets, evoked the Ortiz. 'Ah, Jesus-Maria. The evening she waved her breasts at me!' he sighed, attempting to locate the distant lights of the Teatro Trinidades. Interpreting God's world, with her roguish limbs and voice, how witching the child had been but lately in *The Cestus of Venus*. Her valse-refrain 'Green Fairy Absinthe' (with a full chorus in tights) had been certainly, theatrically (if, perhaps, not socially), the hit of the season.

'The oleanders come between us,' he deliberated, oppressed by the amative complaint of some sweet-throated, summer night-bird.

'It's queer, dears, how I'm lonely!' he exclaimed, addressing the ancient Zurbarans flapping austerely in their frames.

The Archbishop of Archidona, for all his air of pomposity, looked not unsympathetic, neither, indeed, did a little lady with a nimbus, casting melting glances through the spokes of a mystic wheel.

'It's queer—; you'd be surprised!' he murmured, rising and setting an oval moon-backed chair beside his own.

As usual the fanciful watch-dogs in the hills had begun their disquieting barking.

'The evenings are suicide,' he ruminated, idly replenishing his glass.

Sometimes, after the fifth or sixth bumper, the great Theresa herself would flit in from the garden. Long had her radiant spirit 'walked' the Desierto, seeking, it was supposed, a lost sheet of the manuscript of her *Way of Perfection*. It may have been following on the seventh or even the eighth bumper that the Primate remarked he was not alone.

She was standing by the window in the fluttered moonshine, holding a knot of whitish heliotropes.

'Mother?'

Saint John of the Cross could scarcely have pronounced the name with more wistful ecstasy.

Worn and ill, though sublime in laughter, exquisite in tenderness she came towards him.

' . . . Child?'

'Teach me, oh, teach me, dear Mother, the Way of Perfection.'

⊠ IX ⊠

VERIFYING private dates, revising here and there the cathedral list of charges, Don Moscosco, the secretary of the chapter, seated before his usual bureau, was at the disposal of the public. A ministerial crisis had brought scattered Fashion home to town with a rush, and the pressure of work was enormous. 'Business' indeed had seldom been livelier, and chapels for Masses of special intention were being booked in advance as eagerly as opera-boxes for a première, or seaside-villas in the season.

'If the boys are brisk we might work in Joseph,' he mused, consulting with closely buttoned lips his Tarifa and plan; 'although I'd rather not risk a clash.'

Unknown to double-let like his compères on occasion outside, the swarthy little man was a master organiser, never forgetting that the chapter's welfare and prestige were inseparable from his own. Before allotting a chapel for a mass of Intent, it was his rule to analyse and classify the 'purity' of the intention (adding five per cent. where it seemed not altogether to be chaste, or where the purpose was 'obscure').

'I see no inconvenience,' he murmured, gauging delicately the motif of a couple of great ladies of the bluest blood in Spain who were commissioning masses for the safety of a favourite toreador in an approaching *corrida*.

'Five hundred flambeaux, at least, between them,' the secretary, negligently, spat.

It was the twenty-first day of September (which is the Feast of Saint Firmin), and the sacrista, thronged with mantons and monsignori, resembled some vast shifting parterre of garden-flowers. Having a little altercation together, Mother Mary of the Holy Face and Mother Garcia of the Company of Jesus, alone, seemed stable. In honour of Saint Firmin the door of Pardon (closed half the year) had just been thrown open, bringing from the basilica an odour of burning incense and the strains of a nuptial march.

How many of the bridal guests knew of the coffin installed in the next chapel but one? the little man wondered, rising gallantly to receive a client.

She wore no hat, but a loose veil of gold and purple enveloped her hair and face.

'I fear for him!'

'There, there. What is it?'

'I fear for him'—a man and the stars, nights of sweet love, oleander flowers were in her voice.

By her immense hooped earrings, as large as armlets, he knew her for the Adonira, the mistress of the toreador Tancos.

'Come to me after the Friday miserere,' the official objected: 'let me entreat an appointment.'

'No. Now.'

'Well.'

'I want a Mass.'

'The intention being ... ?' The secretary sent up his brows a little.

'His safety.'

'Whose?'

'My lover's.'

'But, señorita, it's all done! It's all *done,* dear lady,' the words were on Don Moscosco's lips. Still, being the pink of chivalry with *las mujares* and a man of business, he murmured: 'With what quantity of lights?'

'Two. Just for him and me.'

'Tell me how you would prefer them,' he exclaimed, glancing whimsically towards the canvas of the Magdalen waylaying our Lord.

'How I would——' she stammered, opening and closing the fansticks in her painted, love-tired hands.

'You would like them long and, I dare say, gross?'

'The best,' she breathed, almost fainting as though from some fleeting delicious vision in the air.

'Leave it to me,' Don Moscosco said, and dropping expressively his voice he added: 'Come, señorita; won't you make a date with me?'

'A date with you?'

'Ah-hah, the little Juans and Juanas; the charming cherubs!' the secretary archly laughed.

Returning however no answer, she moved distractedly away.

'Two tapers! *Two*. As many only as the animal's horns. It's amazing how some women stint,' he reflected, faintly nettled.

The marriage ceremony was over. From the summit of the giralda, volley on volley, the vibrant bells proclaimed the consummation.

'It was all so quick; I hope it's valid?' Madame la Horra, the mother of the 'Bride,' looked in to say. With a rose mole here and a strawberry mole there, men (those adorable monsters) accounted her entirely attractive.

'As *though* we should hurry, as *though* we should clip!'

'Ah?'

'As though we were San Eusebio, or the Pilar!'

'Forgive me, I came only to—I, . . . I, . . . I, . . . I think I cried. The first spring flowers looked so beautiful.'

A mother's love, and contrition, perhaps, for her own short-comings, the secretary brooded. 'I shall knock her off five per cent.'

Lost in bland speculation Don Moscosco considered the assembly collected outside the curtained *camarin* of the Virgin, where the gowns of the Image were dusted and changed.

For Firmin she usually wore an osprey or two and perfumed ball-gloves of Cordoba, and carried a spread fan of gold Guadalmedina lace. Among devotees of the sacrista it was a perpetual wonder to observe how her costumes altered her. Sometimes she would appear quite small, dainty and French, at others she would recall the sumptuous women of the Argentine and the New World, and aficianados would lament their fairy isle of Cuba in the far-off Caribbean Sea.

Traversing imperiously the throng, Don Moscosco beheld the Duquesa DunEden.

Despite the optimism of the gazettes it looked as though the Government must indeed be tottering, since the Duquesa too was up from her country quinta.

'I have a request to make,' she began, sinking gratefully to a chair.

'And charmed, in advance, to grant it.'

'I suppose you will have forgotten my old spaniel, Clapsey?'

'Ah, no more dogs!'

'She is passing-out, poor darling; and if the Church could spare her some trifling favour——'

'Impossible.'

'She is the first toy tail for my little cemetery!'

'Quite impossible.'

'Poor pet,' the Duquesa exclaimed undaunted: 'she has shared in her time my most intimate secrets: she stands for early memories; what rambles we'd go together, she and I, at Santander long ago! I remember Santander, Don Moscosco (imagine), when there was not even an hotel! A little fishing-village, so quiet, so quiet; ah, it was nicer, far, and more exclusive then. . . .'

'I dare say.'

'You know my old, blind and devoted friend was a gift from the king; and this morning I said to her: "Clapsey! Clapsey!" I said: "where's Carlos? Car-los . . . ?" And I'll take my oath she rallied.'

Don Moscosco unbent a shade: 'A token, is she, of royalty?'

'He also gave me "Flirt"!'

'Perhaps a brief mass . . .'

'Poor dearest: you'll keep it quiet and black?'

'We say all but the Black.'

'Oh?'

'One must draw the line somewhere!' Don Moscosco declared, his eye roving towards a sacristan piloting a party of travel-stained tourists, anxious to inspect the casket containing a feather from the Archangel Gabriel's wing.

'I know your creative taste! I rely on you,' the Duquesa rose remarking.

Nevertheless, beneath the routine of the sacristia the air was surcharged with tension. Rival groups, pro- or anti-Pirellian, formed almost irreconcilable camps, and partisanship ran high. Not a few among the cathedral staff had remained true to his Eminence, and Mother Sunlight, a charwoman (who sometimes performed odd jobs at the Palace), had taught her infant in arms to cry: 'Long live Spain and Cardinal Pirelli!'

Enough, according to some extreme anti-Pirellians, to be detrimental to her milk.

'I'm told the Pope has sent for him at last,' the laundress of the Basilica, Doña Consolacion, remarked to Sister June of the Way Dolorous.

'Indeed, indeed; it scarcely does to think!'

'Does anyone call to mind a bit of a girl (from Bilbao she was) that came once to stop as his niece?'

'Inclined to a moustache! Perfectly.'

'Phœbe Poco protests she wasn't.'

'Ah, well; a little *Don Juanism* is good,' the laundress said, and sighed.

'She declares . . .'

'She tells the truest lies, dear, of anyone I know!'

'Be that as it may it's certain he's getting increasingly eccentric. But Sunday last, entertaining his solicitor, it seems he ordered coffee after the merienda to be served in two chamber-pots.'

'Shameful—and he in his sunset years!' Mother Mary of the Holy Face commented, coming up with Tomás the beadle.

'It wouldn't surprise me,' he declared, drowsily shaking a heavy bouquet of keys, 'if the thread of his life was about to break.'

'*Hombre* . . .' The laundress expressed alarm.

'Often now, towards Angelus, as I climb the tower, I hear the bell Herod talking with old Wanda in the loft. Eeeeeee! Eeeeeee! Horrible things they keep saying. Horrible things they keep saying.'

'Nonsense,' Doña Consolacion exclaimed, bestowing a smile on Monsignor Cuxa. Old, and did-did-doddery, how frail he seemed beside Father Fadrique, the splendid swagger of whose chasuble every woman must admire.

'Sent for to Rome; ah, *sangre mio*, I wish someone would send for me,' a girl, with a rose in the hair beautifully placed, sighed romantically.

'Be satisfied with Spain, my dear, and remember that no other country can compare with it!' Doña Generosa, an Aunt of one of the cathedral dancing-boys (who drew a small pension as the widow of the late Leader of applause at the Opera-house), remonstrated.

'I've never travelled,' Doña Consolacion blandly confessed: 'but I dare say, dear, you can't judge of Egypt by *Aïda*.'

'Oh, can't I, though?' Doña Generosa sniffed, as the Father of an acolyte raised his voice.

'Spain!' he exclaimed, exalted, throwing a lover's kiss to the air, 'Spain! The most glorious country in God's universe, His admitted masterpiece, His gem, His——' He broke off, his eloquence dashed by the sad music of Monsignor Cuxa's hæmorrhage.

An office in the Chapel of the Crucifix was about to begin, recalling to their duties the scattered employees of the staff.

Hovering by the collection-box for the Souls in Hades, the Moorish maid from the College of Noble Damosels, bound on an errand of trust as ancient as the world, was growing weary of watching the people come and go.

'I must have missed him beneath the trees of the Market Place,' she ruminated, straightening on her head a turban wreathed in blossoms.

It was the matter of a message from Obdulia and Milagros to the radiant youth whose lips they were so idyllically (if perhaps somewhat licentiously) sharing.

'Fo' sh'o dis goin' to put dose heiresses in a quandry,' she deliberated, oppressed by her surroundings.

Eastern in origin like the Mesquita of Cordoba, it was impossible to forget that the great basilica of Clemenza was a Mosque profaned.

Designed for the cult of Islàm, it made her African's warm heart bleed to behold it now. Would it were reconverted to its virginal state, and the cry of the muezzin be heard again summoning men to Muhammad's house! Yes, the restitution of the cathedral to Allah was Muley's cherished dream, and it consoled her, on certain days when she was homesick, to stand before the desecrated mihrab in worship, her face turned towards Africa, and palm-girt Marrakesh across the sea.

'I almost inclined to slip across to de Café Goya,' she breathed, moving aside for a shuffling acolyte, bearing a crucifix on a salver.

Led by the pious sisters of the noble order of the Flaming-Hood, the Virgin was returning to her niche.

She was arrayed as though bound for the Bull-ring, in a robe of peacock silk, and a mantilla of black lace.

'*Santissima! . . .*'

'*Elegantissima!*' Devotees dropped adoring to the floor.

Alone, the African remained erect.

'Muhammad mine, how long?' she sighed, turning entreating eyes to the cabbalistic letters and Saracenic tracings of the azulejos arabesques.

MIDNIGHT had ceased chiming from the Belfry tower, and the last seguidilla had died away. Looking fresh as a rose, and incredibly juvenile in his pyjamas of silver-grey and scarlet (the racing colours of Vittoria, Duchess of Vizeu), the Cardinal seemed disinclined for bed.

Surveying in detachment the preparatives for his journey (set out beneath an El Greco Christ, with outspread, delicate hands), he was in the mood to dawdle.

'These for the Frontier. Those for the train,' he exclaimed aloud, addressing a phantom porter.

Among the personalia was a passport, the likeness of identity showing him in a mitre, cute to tears, though, essentially, orthodox; a flask of Napoleon brandy, to be 'declared' if not consumed before leaving the Peninsula; and a novel, *Self-Essence*, on the Index, or about to be.

'A coin, child, and put them for me on the rack,' he enjoined the wraith, regarding through the window the large and radiant stars.

The rhythmic murmur of a weeping fountain filled momentously the night.

Its lament evoked the Chicklet's sobs.

'Did I so wrong, my God, to punish him? Was I too hasty?' the Primate asked, repairing towards an ivory crucifix by Cano; 'yet, Thou knowest, I adore the boy!'

He paused a moment astonished by the revelation of his heart.

'It must have been love that made me do it,' he smiled, considering the incident in his mind. Assuredly the rebuff was unpremeditated, springing directly from the boy's behaviour, spoiling what might have been a ceremony of something more than ordinary poignance.

It had come about so.

There had been held previously during the evening, after the Basilica's scheduled closing hour, a service of 'Departure,' fastidiously private, in the presence only of the little Ostensoir-swinger 'Chicklet,' who, missing all the responses, had rushed about the cathedral after mice; for which the Cardinal, his sensitiveness hurt by the lad's disdain and frivolity, had afterwards confined him alone with them in the dark.

'Had it been Miguilito or Joaquin, I should not have cared a straw for their interest in the mice! But somehow this one——' the Cardinal sighed.

Adjusting in capricious abstraction his cincture, he turned towards the window.

It was a night like most.

Uranus, Venus, Saturn showed overhead their wonted lights, while in the sun-weary cloisters, brightly blue-drenched by the moon, the oleanders in all their wonder—(how swiftly fleeting is terrestrial life)—were over, and the bougainvillæas reigned instead.

'It must have been that,' he murmured, smiling up at the cathedral towers.

Poor little Don Wilful. The chapter-mice, were they something so amusing to pursue? 'I've a mind, do you know, to join you, boy; I declare I feel quite rompish!' he told himself, gathering up, with a jocund pounce, a heavy mantle of violet cloth-of-gold.

'Tu-whit, tu-whoo.'

Two ominous owls answered one another across the troubled garden.

'I declare I feel——' his hand sought vaguely his heart: it went pit-a-pat for almost nothing now! 'The strain of the diocese,' he breathed, consulting a pier-glass of the period of Queen Isabella 'the Ironical.'

'The Court may favour Paul Orna, but in my opinion no one can rival Joey Paquin's "line"; I should like to see him "tailor" our Madonna; one of the worst and most expensively dressed little saints in the world,' his Eminence commented, folding toga-wise the obedient tissues about his slender form.

An aspect so correctly classic evoked the golden Rome of the Imperial Caesars rather than the so tedious Popes.

Repeating a sonorous line from Macrobius, the Cardinal measured himself a liqueur-glass of brandy.

Poor little Don Bright-eyes, alone in the obscurity. It was said a black dervish 'walked' the Coro—one of the old habitués of the Mosque.

'Jewel-boy. Yum-yum,' he murmured, setting a mitre like a wondrous mustard-pot upon his head. *Omnia vanitas;* it was intended for Saint Peter's.

'Tu-whit, tu-whoo!'

Grasping a Bishop's stave, remotely shepherdessy, his Eminence opened softly the door.

Olé, the Styx!

Lit by Uranus, Venus and Saturn only, the consummate tapestries on the stairs recording the Annunciation, Conception, Nativity, Presentation, Visitation, Purification and Ascension of the Virgin made welcome milestones.

' . . . Visitation, Purification.' The Primate paused on the penultimate step.

On a turn of the stair by the 'Conception,' a sensitive panel, chiefly white, he had the impression of a wavering shadow, as of someone following close behind.

Continuing, preoccupied, his descent, he gained a postern door. A few deal cases, stoutly corded for departure, were heaped about it. 'His Holiness, I venture to predict, will appreciate the excellence of our home-grown oranges, not to be surpassed by those of any land,' the Primate purred, sailing forth into the garden.

Oh, the lovely night! Oh, the lovely night! He stood, leaning on his wand, lost in contemplation of the miracle of it.

'Kek, kek, kex.'

In the old lead aqua-butt, by the Chapter-house, the gossiping bull-frogs were discussing their great horned and hoofed relations. . . .

'There was never yet one that didn't bellow!'

'Kek, kek, kex.'

'*Los toros,* forsooth!'

'A blessed climate. . . .' The Primate pursued his way.

It was in the face of a little door like the door of a tomb in the cathedral's bare façade (troubled only by the fanciful shadows of the trees) that he presently slipped his key.

Olé, the Styx!

He could distinguish nothing clearly at first beyond the pale forked fugitive lightning through the triple titanic windows of the chancel.

'Sunny-locks, Don Sunny-locks?' the Cardinal cooed, advancing diffidently, as though mistrustful of meeting some charwoman's pail.

Life had prepared him for these surprises.

Traversing on his crozier a spectral aisle, he emerged upon the nave.

Flanked by the chapels of the Crucifix, of the Virgin, of the Eldest Son of God, and of divers others, it was here as bright as day.

Presumably Don April-showers was too self-abashed to answer, perhaps too much afraid. . . . 'If I recollect, the last time I preached was on the theme of Flagellation,' the Primate mused, considering where it caught the moon the face of a fakir in ecstasy carved amid the corbels.

'A sermon I propose to publish,' he resolved, peering into the chapel of Santa Lucia. It was prepared, it seemed, in anticipation of a wedding, for stately palms and branches of waxen peach-bloom stood all about. 'Making circulation perilous,' the Primate mused, arrested by the determined sound of a tenacious mouse gnawing at a taper-box.

'An admirable example in perseverance!' he mentally told himself, blinking at the flickering mauve flowers of light in the sanctuary lamps.

Philosophising, he penetrated the engrailed silver doors connecting the chapel of the Magdalen.

The chapel was but seldom without a coffin, and it was not without one now.

Since the obsequies of the brilliant Princess Eboli it had enjoyed an unbroken vogue.

Besides the triumphal monument of the beloved of Philip II, the happy (though, perhaps, not the happiest) achievement of Jacinto Bisquert, there were also mural tablets to the Duchesses of Pampeluna (*née* Mattosinhos), Polonio (*née* Charona), and Sarmento (*née* Tizzi-Azza), while the urn and ashes of the Marchioness of Orcasitas (*née* Ivy Harris) were to be found here too, far from the race and turmoil of her native New York.

'Misericordia! Are you there, boy?' the Cardinal asked, eyeing abstractedly the twin hooded caryatides that bore the fragile casket white as frozen snow containing the remains of the all-amiable princess.

Folded in dainty sleep below, he perceived the lad.

Witching as Eros, in his loose-flowing alb, it seemed profane to wake him!

'... And lead us not into temptation,' the Primate murmured, stooping to gaze on him.

Age of bloom and fleeting folly: Don Apple-cheeks!

Hovering in benison he had almost a mind to adopt the boy, enter him for Salamanca, or, remoter, Oxford, and perhaps (by some bombshell codicil) even make him his heir.

'How would you like my Velasquez, boy?...' His Eminence's hand framed an airy caress. 'Eh, child? Or my Cano Crucifix?... I know of more than one bottle-nosed dowager who thinks she'll get it!... You know my Venetian-glass, Don Endymion, is among the choicest in Spain....'

There was a spell of singing silence, while the dove-grey mystic lightning waxed and waned.

Aroused as much by it as the Primate's hand, the boy started up with a scream of terror.

'Ouch, sir!'

'Olé, boy?'

The panic appeared to be mutual.

'Oufarella!...' With the bound of a young faun the lad was enskied amid the urns and friezes.

The heart in painful riot, the Primate dropped to a chair.

Ouching, Oléing and Oufarellaing it, would they never have done? Paternostering Phœbe Poco (shadowing her master) believed they never would. 'Old ogre: why can't he be brisk about it and let a woman back to bed?' she wondered.

Thus will egotism, upon occasion, eclipse morality outright.

'And always be obedient, dear child,' the Cardinal was saying; 'it is one of the five things in Life that matter most.'

'Which are the others, sir?'

'What others, boy?'

'Why, the other four!'

'Never mind now. Come here.'

'Oh, tral-a-la, sir.' Laughing like some wild spirit, the lad leapt (Don Venturesome, Don Venturesome, his Eminence trembled) from the ledge of A Virtuous Wife and Mother (Sarmento, *née* Tizzi-Azza) to the urn of Ivy, the American marchioness.

'You'd not do that if you were fond of me, boy!' The Cardinal's cheek had paled.

'But I *am* fond of you, sir! Very. Caring without caring: don't you know?'

'So you do care something, child?'

'I care a lot! . . .'

Astride the urn of Ivy—poised in air—the Chicklet pellucidly laughed.

'Tell me so again,' the Cardinal begged, as some convent-bell near by commenced sounding for office before aurora.

For behind the big windows the stars were fading.

'It's to-day they draw the Lottery, sir.'

'Ah; well, I had nothing in it . . .'

'ooo50—that's me!'

The Cardinal fetched a breath.

'Whose is it, boy?' He pointed towards the bier.

'A Poet, sir.'

'A Poet?'

'The name, though, he had escapes me. . . .'

'No matter then.'

'Where would his soul be now, sir?'

'Never mind, boy; come here.'

'In the next world I should like to meet the Cid, and Christopher Columbus!'

'Break your neck, lad, and so you will.'

'Pablo Pedraza too. . . .'

'Who's that, boy?'

'He was once the flower of the ring, sir; superior even to Tancos; you may recollect he was tossed and ruptured at Ronda; the press at the time was full of it.'

'Our press, dear youth, our press! ! ! . . .' the Primate was about to lament, but an apologetic sneeze from a chapel somewhere in the neighbourhood of the Eldest Son of God arrested him.

It seemed almost to confirm the legend of old, Mosque-sick 'Suliman,' said to stalk the temple aisles.

The Cardinal twirled challengingly his stave—*Bible* v. *Koran*; a family case; cousins; Eastern, equally, each; hardy old perennials, no less equivocal and extravagant, often, than the ever-adorable *Arabian Nights*! 'If only Oriental literature *sprawled* less, was more concise! It should concentrate its roses,' he told himself, glancing out, enquiringly, into the nave.

Profoundly soft and effaced, it was a place full of strange suggestion. Intersecting avenues of pillared arches, upbearing waving banners, seemed to beckon towards the Infinite.

'Will you be obliged to change, sir; or shall you go straight through?'

'Straight through, boy.'

'I suppose, as you cross the border, they'll want to know what you have to declare.'

'I have nothing, child, but myself.'

'If ooo5o is fortunate, sir, I hope to travel, too—India, Persia, Peru! !... Ah, it's El Dorado, then.'

'El Dorado, boy?' The Cardinal risked an incautious gesture.

'Oh, tral-a-la, sir.' Quick as Cupid the lad eluded him on the evasive wings of a laugh; an unsparing little laugh, sharp and mocking, that aroused the Primate like the thong of a lash.

Of a long warrior line, he had always regarded disobedience (in others) as an inexcusable offence. What would have happened before the ramparts of Zaragoza, Valladolid, Leon, Burgos, had the men commanded by Ipolito Pirelli in the Peninsular War refused to obey? To be set at defiance by a youngster, a mere cock-robin, kindled elementary ancestral instincts in the Primate's veins.

'Don't provoke me, child, again.'

From pillared ambush Don Prudent saw well, however, to effect a bargain.

'You'd do the handsome by me, sir; you'd not be mean?'

'Eh?...'

'The Fathers only give us texts; you'd be surprised, your Greatness, at the stinginess of some!'

'...?'

'You'd run to something better, sir; you'd give me something more substantial?'

'I'll give you my slipper, child, if you don't come here!' his Eminence warned him.

'Oufarella....'

Sarabandish and semi-mythic was the dance that ensued. Leading by a dozen derisive steps Don Light-of-Limb took the nave. In the dusk of the dawn it seemed to await the quickening blush of day like a white-veiled negress.

'Olé, your Purpleship!'

Men (eternal hunters, novelty seekers, insatiable beings), men in their natural lives, pursue the concrete no less than the ideal—qualities not seldom found combined in fairy childhood.

'Olé.'

Oblivious of sliding mantle the Primate swooped.

Up and down, in and out, round and round 'the Virgin,' over the worn tombed paving, through Saint Joseph, beneath the cobweb banners from Barocco to purest Moorish, by early Philip, back to Turân-Shâh—'Don't exasperate me, boy'—along the raised tribunes of the choristers and the echoing coro—the great fane (after all) was nothing but a cage; God's cage; the cage of God! . . .

Through the chancel windows the day was newly breaking as the oleanders will in spring.

Dispossessed of everything but his fabulous mitre, the Primate was nude and elementary now as Adam himself.

'As you can perfectly see, I have nothing but myself to declare,' he addressed some phantom image in the air.

With advancing day Don Skylark *alias* Bright-eyes *alias* Don Temptation it seemed had contrived an exit, for the cathedral was become a place of tranquillity and stillness.

'Only myself.' He had dropped before a painting of old Dominic Theotocópuli, the Greek, showing the splendour of Christ's martyrdom.

Peering expectantly from the silken parted curtains of a confessional, paternostering Phœbe Poco caught her breath.

Confused not a little at the sight before her, her equilibrium was only maintained by the recollection of her status: 'I'm an honest widow; so I know what men are, bless them!' And stirred to romantic memories she added: 'Poor soul, he had the prettiest teeth. . . .'

Fired by fundamental curiosity, the dame, by degrees, was emboldened to advance. All over was it, with him, then? It looked as though his Eminence was far beyond Rome already.

'May God show His pity on you, Don Alvaro of my heart.'

She remained a short while lost in mingled conjecture. It was certain no morning bell would wake him.

'So.' She stopped to coil her brier-wood chaplet about him in order that he might be less uncovered. 'It's wonderful what us bits of women do with a string of beads, but they don't go far with a gentleman.'

Now that the ache of life, with its fevers, passions, doubts, its routine, vulgarity, and boredom, was over, his serene, unclouded face was a marvelment to behold. Very great distinction and sweetness was visible there, together with much nobility, and love, all magnified and commingled.

'*Adios,* Don Alvaro of my heart,' she sighed, turning away towards the little garden door ajar.

Through the triple windows of the chancel the sky was clear and blue—a blue like the blue of lupins. Above him stirred the wind-blown banners in the Nave.

The Princess Zoubaroff

A COMEDY

DRAMATIS PERSONÆ

ADRIAN SHEIL-MEYER
ERIC TRESILIAN
LORD ORKISH
MONSIGNOR VANHOVE
REGGIE QUINTUS
ANGELO
NADINE SHEIL-MEYER
ENID TRESILIAN
LADY ROCKTOWER
GLYDA, *her daughter*
MARCHESA PITTI-CONTI
DANTE SILVIO PAOLAO, *her son*
MRS. NEGRESS
MRS. MANGROVE
PRINCESS ZOUBAROFF

The Princess Zoubaroff

ACT I

SCENE I

Florence. Early summer. The garden of the Casa Meyer. Oleanders, giant ilex, Judas-trees, flowering hibiscus. A few long green palms. In their blue shade a peacock or two. A pillared circle of bougainvillæa-wreathed arches, from which hangs a hammock R. and through which a portion of the house can be seen. Within the circle, a faded marble statue, representing an effigy of the Virgin Mary, and a miscellaneous array of easy-chairs, two or three, and a portable table holding magazines and books, extending down. A rustic arch L. leading to roadway. Distant prospect, Florence. Time, afternoon.

ADRIAN, ERIC

ERIC: Where are they?

ADRIAN: Nadine and Enid have gone hunting together.

ERIC: Hunting?

ADRIAN: For Antiques.

ERIC: Poking round for Antiques—and we've been barely married a week. [ADRIAN *shrugs.*] Our marriage is *manqué*!

ADRIAN: This little jaunt of ours ought to clear the air.

ERIC: Do you know, I believe Enid would be positively glad if I didn't return to her again?

ADRIAN: She seemed quite bright at lunch.

ERIC: Precisely.

ADRIAN [*laughing*]: Between ourselves, I begin to fear we've both made mistakes!

ERIC: I'm glad you can laugh.

ADRIAN: I can't help it.

ERIC: Thank goodness we shall start to-morrow without them.

ADRIAN: Yes. Nadine loathes the Engadine. Mountains depress her nature.

ERIC: Do all mountains?

ADRIAN: Anything she can't see over.

ERIC: Their rarified atmosphere braces me. I'm never so well as in it.

ADRIAN: It can be had, as well, at home. [*Picking up a book, which he scans*] 'She read romances night and day, and wished to live them,*

701

after a fashion of the shepherds of Astrea; she slept upon a sofa painted like grass, and in a room representing trees and sheepfolds; and when the Beloved arrived, she would softly recite the *Eclogues of Fontanelle,* would talk of tender flames, the sensitive heart, and dish up all the mawkishness of the Operas.'

ERIC: Princess Zoubaroff has been lending *mia moglie* some books.

ADRIAN: One's inclined to be diffident of her influence!

ERIC: Her heart's desire now, I'm told, is to make her Peace with heaven.

ADRIAN: I know of nothing more dangerous; but I can scarcely believe it.

ERIC: One hears strange stories of her—Rumours, in fact.

ADRIAN: She fascinates Nadine and Enid! And here they are.

SCENE II

Same. NADINE SHEIL-MEYER *loaded with bric-à-brac.* ENID TRESILIAN. *Both are ultra-beautifully dressed.* MRS. SHEIL-MEYER'S *hat is one mass of quivering grasses.*

NADINE: Don't bother.

ENID [*airily helping her*]: An imaginary footman helps.

ADRIAN: What have you been getting?

ENID: Such enthralling things.

ERIC: Let's see.

NADINE: No, no, no, no.

ADRIAN: Peevish!

ENID: She is fagged, I fear, by our expedition.

NADINE [*indignantly*]: I'm not.

ENID: We've been to Ishmael Levy!

ADRIAN: Ah! Beware of fakes.

ENID [*superiorly*]: He offered us a *Lucia bearing her Eyes upon a Dish* —a supposed original of Masaccio, and a fantastic Moreau like some strong perfume.

ADRIAN: He did?

ENID: A head and hands business.

ADRIAN: Oh?

ENID: And who should there enter as we were glancing round *but Blanche*!

ERIC: Blanche?

ENID: Blanche Negress.

ERIC: Who's she?

ENID: . . . But so charming and so different to the rest!

ERIC: Then she *must* be refreshing.

NADINE: What induced you to ask her here this evening, Enid, by the way?

ENID: Because I thought it might be fun. You know she writes things for the papers.

ADRIAN: What sort of things?

ENID: Oh, don't ask me what sort of things.

NADINE [*throwing her purchases down upon a table*]: She was telling us they charge her more at the Bretagne to board her Great Dane than they do for her maid.

ERIC: Perhaps it eats more.

NADINE: Talking of eating—do you wish for a collation at day-break before you start?

ADRIAN: No, thanks.

ENID: You're packed?

ERIC: Not quite.

ENID: Could I do anything?

ERIC: It's good of you, dear, but there's practically nothing to do.

NADINE [*inquisitively*]: I suppose you're feeling pleasurably excited at the thoughts of to-morrow?

ERIC: Why not?

ENID: Remember, won't you, Eric, to gather a little edelweiss if you should notice any.

NADINE: Yes; don't forget that.

ENID: Though no accidents, mind.

NADINE: Naturally.

ERIC [*nettled, his anger rising*]: Say out straight what you mean, can't you?

ENID: What I mean?

ERIC: I don't go in for *arrière-pensées*.

ENID: Really, Eric, your hypersensitiveness would try an arch-angel, I think.

ERIC: Oh! Would it?

NADINE [*disdainfully*]: Poor child, don't mind him! One knows his bow-wow ways.

ENID: I'll not be long, dear [*kissing her finger-tips to her*]. I've a very little letter I must write.

NADINE: Must you?

ENID [*moving towards house*]: Just a few hurried flying lines. ...

ERIC [*following her*]: And I've some business too! ...

SCENE III

ADRIAN, NADINE [their *Married* voices]

NADINE: I could laugh when I think of her answering congratlatory letters still!

ADRIAN: She's having rather a pale sort of honeymoon apparently.

NADINE: If she's neglected, whose fault is it?

ADRIAN: You surely don't think it's mine!

NADINE: I do.

ADRIAN [*ominously*]: You dare to say that?

NADINE [*with intention*]: Don't let's repeat Egypt!

ADRIAN [*shuddering*]: Not for the universe.

NADINE: He'd better look out. She's just in the mood for fireworks.

ADRIAN: Is she?—the deuce.

NADINE: I know Enid better than Eric. [*Mysteriously*] She and I were at school together.

ADRIAN: What possessed you to ask her here for her honeymoon?

NADINE [*sentimentally staring at the tip of her shoe*]: Because—I don't know!—I wished to lend her a little support. ... Chaperon her, so to speak, the difficult first days. Poor darling! She had nobody. She was very unhappy at home.

ADRIAN [*blatantly*]: Eric and I—we too were at school together.

NADINE: Bah! Don't talk to me of Eric.

ADRIAN: He was my friend.

NADINE: What do *I* care?

ADRIAN: You tiresome woman.

NADINE: How dare you call me 'tiresome'?

ENID [*returning*]: Excuse me, Nadine, but what is Charlotte's address?

NADINE: Coombe Court, Straithfieldsaye.

ENID: And Elsie?

NADINE: Five Rue Sganarelle. ...

ENID: Oh, thank you, dear. [*She goes in.*]

NADINE: I can't *bear* to see her look so bored.

ADRIAN: Bored!

NADINE: Poor little soul! It makes one weep to look at her.

ADRIAN: I never saw anyone so . . . [*looking*].

NADINE: What?

ADRIAN: Nothing.

NADINE [*putting up her sunshade*]: I believe you were going to insult her!

ADRIAN [*horror-struck*]: I!

NADINE [*in indignant yet not displeased tones*]: I fancy you were about to say something unkind.

ADRIAN [*pointedly*]: Oh, that I leave to your Florentine friends!

NADINE: To whom do you refer?

ADRIAN [*lighting a cigarette*]: I refer to Lord Orkish. . . .

NADINE: Ah!

ADRIAN: And to Mrs. du Wilson. . . .

NADINE: Oh!

ADRIAN: And to Zena Zoubaroff.

NADINE: Zena? But Zena *adores* Enid.

ADRIAN: Rot!

NADINE: She adores her.

[*The garden gate opens and the* PRINCESS ZOUBAROFF, *a very pale, vaguely 'sinister-looking' woman of about thirty-five enters. She wears a riding-habit, rather Vanloo, fringed with sables. In lieu of a riding-crop she holds a fan.*]

PRINCESS: I just looked in to say Good-bye!

SCENE IV

ADRIAN, NADINE, PRINCESS

ADRIAN [*gallantly*]: What a charming surprise!

NADINE: We were this moment speaking of you, dear!

PRINCESS [*coming forward*]: Of me? Oh? . . . And what were you saying of me?

NADINE: I was telling Adrian how fond of Enid you seemed.

PRINCESS: How could one help loving her?

ADRIAN [*solicitously*]: Well? And what have *you* been doing?

PRINCESS [*glowing*]: I'm just back from oh such a heavenly ride. Half way to Vallombrosa!

NADINE: But wasn't it grilling?

ADRIAN [*matter of fact*]: We may expect a storm before morning, I think.

PRINCESS [*drawing off her gloves*]: Rain is needed badly.

NADINE: It would do the young vines good.

ADRIAN: And the garden too. . . .

PRINCESS: Yours is a Paradise. . . . Those purple, tragic roses. . . . Tell me, how are they named?

ADRIAN: I forget.

PRINCESS [*poetically*]: I love the Flowers. They talk to me. I love the Birds. They sing to me!

NADINE: What have they told you—if it's not indiscreet?

PRINCESS [*elusively*]: They say that opera-cloaks this spring are going to make one seven good feet across the shoulders.

NADINE: Ah?

PRINCESS: And that sandals shortly are coming in. . . .

NADINE: What else?

PRINCESS [*stooping*]: Let me admire your heliotropes.

ADRIAN [*flatteringly*]: Your own garden, Princess, you know, is all our envy.

PRINCESS [*sighing*]: This year I'm very vain of my pomegranates!

ADRIAN: I don't wonder.

PRINCESS: My beloved garden. You should see it early, at break of day, when Dawn makes its white holes through the trees.

NADINE [*succinctly*]: Perhaps to-morrow they will.

PRINCESS: And so you're really off?

ADRIAN: Yes.

PRINCESS: To those ridiculous mountains?

ADRIAN: Why do you say ridiculous?

PRINCESS: Aren't they?

ADRIAN: Not that I'm aware of.

PRINCESS: I am always disappointed with mountains. There are no mountains in the world as high as I could wish.

ADRIAN: No?

PRINCESS: They irritate me invariably. I should like to shake Switzerland. [*Looks at her hands.*]

NADINE: You have the perfectest hands, Zena.

PRINCESS [*wistfully*]: Have I?

NADINE: You know you have.

PRINCESS: How Ingres admired my hands. He quite worshipped my little fingers.

The Princess Zoubaroff

Scene V

Same. ENID

ENID: I can't write letters while Eric is fidgeting about.

NADINE [*whispering*]: Wait till we're Alone to-morrow.

ENID: Yes. I think so. Oh, Zena! [*Goes to her.*]

PRINCESS [*regarding her with pensive interest*]: You look done-in, dear; totally done-in.

ENID: Do I?

PRINCESS: Those great fatigued eyes. . . .

NADINE: She does far too much! Last night she was chasing bats after midnight with a long white rosary.

PRINCESS: Have you seen yet all the inevitable sights?

ENID: Oh heavens, no. Beyond a few churches, I've seen nothing whatever.

PRINCESS: Really?

ENID: Imagine, I haven't been at all to the Bargello.

PRINCESS: I was there one morning lately with one of the Hope girls.

ENID: Oh?

PRINCESS: It was dreadful. She would *scream* at everything that attracted her, and fall upon her knees . . . and kiss and touch the things.

NADINE [*with decision*]: I consider the eldest Miss Hope's a disgrace to England! You see her wool-gathering about the streets garbed in an old violet velvet sack, her hat set crooked, crammed with flowers.

PRINCESS: Yes! And Tozhy too's a sight.

ENID: Tozhy?

PRINCESS: Mr. Hope—the 'Father' of the English colony, you know.

ENID: Of course. He is going to show me some time where one can get Venetian glass!

PRINCESS [*leaning on the back of a garden chair*]: I have passed through all the fads, I suppose, myself in furniture and pictures and books. And now all I ask for's a cell. Give me a room with nothing in it!

ENID: How horribly *dull*.

ADRIAN: It must need courage to be so eclectic?

PRINCESS: Not really. [*With vivacity*] I often think I would rather like to run a Convent.

ENID: Oh, Zena!

PRINCESS: For little girls—not for sour old women.

ADRIAN: Have you remarked the cosmopolitanised faces of the Nuns one meets hereabouts?

PRINCESS: No.

ADRIAN: It's so curious.

PRINCESS [*beating the air dreamily with her fan*]: Florence—I always say it's a place one drifts to in the end!

ADRIAN: It's a pity perhaps so many—what shall I say—people do.

PRINCESS [*with a swift, bright look*]: I hear Reggie Quintus is in the town—looking quite lawless.

ADRIAN: Reggie?

NADINE: Oh!

PRINCESS: Lady Rocktower *saw* him.

NADINE: One would like to be kind to the boy on account of his poor darling mother—but it's a little difficult to, all the same.

PRINCESS [*critically*]: He has the manners of one who has nothing to lose and perhaps something to gain.

NADINE: Perhaps.

PRINCESS: He's so good-looking—too good-looking for a man.

ADRIAN: I don't intend ever having anything to do with him.

PRINCESS: No? Well, perhaps you're wise.

ENID [*looking towards house*]: Why's Eric beckoning?

ADRIAN: I expect he wants his revenge at billiards!

NADINE [*sweetly*]: Go to him, then, won't you, dear? Don't mind us!

ADRIAN: I will.

[*Exit* ADRIAN *to house.*]

SCENE VI

PRINCESS, NADINE, ENID

ENID: This evening I feel so reckless, so reckless. I could wear a forehead-ornament besides a hat!

PRINCESS [*fingering*]: Where did you get that love of a gown?

ENID: It was part of my *corbeille.*

PRINCESS: My dear, you have the instinct for dress. I never saw anything so perfect!

NADINE [*exclaiming*]: Oh! . . .

ENID: Is there anything the matter?

NADINE: What have you done with your wedding ring?

ENID: I took it off.

NADINE: What for?

ENID: I don't mean to wear one.

PRINCESS: But—my dear!

NADINE: Nonsense. You must!

ENID: Why?

NADINE: I insist.

ENID: Oh, of course if you're really keen . . .

PRINCESS: Where is it?

ENID: On the dressing-table in my room.

NADINE: I'll go and find it at once.

[*Exit* NADINE to house.]

SCENE VII

PRINCESS, ENID

PRINCESS [*a short silence*]: He has not been cruel?

ENID: No.

PRINCESS: You will make a fatal mistake, dear Enid, if you allow him to go!

ENID [*unconvinced*]: Shall I?

PRINCESS: Remember the Foreign Colony here is a very hornets' nest. . . .

ENID: I can't help it!

PRINCESS [*putting an arm about her*]: How are you with him?

ENID: Since lunch he and I are on tolerable terms again.

PRINCESS: Since lunch? . . .

ENID: After all, it's really rather risible.

PRINCESS: I don't consider it risible in the *very* least.

ENID: Not?

PRINCESS [*emphatic*]: It's an unprecedented honeymoon—*even for Florence!*

ENID: Don't let's grow solemn.

PRINCESS: In my opinion, marriage was something altogether too excessive for such very light desires.

ENID: Desires. . . . [*Smiling wanly*] Both he and I are dead to any wish.

PRINCESS: Don't say so.

ENID: Ah, but I do.

PRINCESS: What made you accept him, then? Tell me.

ENID: It was purely a match of reason. At home I was generally in the way. Mamma and I were nothing but rivals. But let's not talk about it.

PRINCESS [*retrospective*]: As a raw girl, I'd a disrelish for marriage too. But my parents sensibly made me. And when my first husband died, why, I soon remarried ... and when he, poor fellow, succumbed—he was a world-renowned explorer—I was induced to listen again.... [*Slight pause.*] And I've been married in all *six times*!

ENID [*admiringly*]: What a wonderful accumulation of experience you must have, Zena!

PRINCESS: Yes. [*Grimly*] When I want to impress a stranger, I carry their miniatures on my wrists—three on each arm.

ENID: Your last marriage, was it happy?

PRINCESS: My last marriage, my dear, was one long game of hide-and-seek.

ENID: I feel discouraged!

PRINCESS: A husband, one must remember, is something of an *acquired* taste.

ENID: Are they all alike?

PRINCESS: Why, of course not!

ENID: Aren't they?

PRINCESS [*nibbling her fan*]: No. Really, you provoke me to laugh.

ENID: I've been married a week and it isn't at all what I thought it would be!

PRINCESS [*tenderly*]: Poor darling! How I would love to spoil you.

ENID: You dear. But you do....

PRINCESS: Not enough.

ENID: Oh, Zena!

PRINCESS [*caressing admiringly her hair*]: Not nearly enough, *Elf-locks*.

ENID [*coyly*]: I'm all foolish nerves to-night!

PRINCESS: Poor Angel, Baby, Waif....

ENID [*closing her eyes*]: What would you advise?

PRINCESS: Make the most of youth! Remember nothing lasts....

ENID: You think I should take a lover?

PRINCESS: No, no ... you'd regret it.

ENID: There's no telling.

PRINCESS: Eventually, of course, you'll build a bridge!

ENID: Impossible.

PRINCESS: Tfoo!

ENID: He's so altered.

PRINCESS: How?

ENID: His tastes!

PRINCESS: They jar?

ENID: Dreadfully. His Hellenism once captivated me. But [*opening her eyes gloomily as wide as she is able*] the *Attic* to him means nothing now *but Servants' bedrooms*.

PRINCESS: Servants' what!

ENID [*faintly*]: *Closets*.

PRINCESS [*behind her fan*]: Oh!

ENID: It's revolting.

PRINCESS [*philosophically*]: In life, to be happy, the first rule is to learn pretty extensively to ignore.

ENID: I suppose, dearest, you were never situated before as I am?

PRINCESS [*nodding*]: Yes, indeed! One of my husbands also left me!

ENID: Oh, Zena?

PRINCESS: Left me even sooner than yours!

ENID: It isn't credible!

PRINCESS: He said a thousand tender pretty things, called me a thousand charming names, and then, at the end of twenty-four hours, deserted me!

ENID: What did you do?

PRINCESS: What could I do?

ENID: If Eric deserts me, I dare say I could start an 'Art School' here. It would be rather fun.

PRINCESS: Darling Enid, anything rather than that!

ENID [*puzzled*]: But why?

PRINCESS: Because . . .

Scene VIII

Same. NADINE

NADINE [*flourishing wedding-ring*]: Here it is!

ENID: Oh, thank you, Nadine.

NADINE: Put it on.

ENID [*evasively*]: It's far too hot to wear a ring!

PRINCESS: Rubbish.

NADINE [*suppliant*]: For me, dearest. Say you will!

ENID: Very well then, I will!

PRINCESS [*overbrimming with quiet fun*]: How she dreads a scandal. . . .

NADINE [*her sensitive panic patently subsiding*]: Well, it's not quite pleasant, is it? And foreign servants are such fools! They'd think it was a *faux-ménage*, or something.

ENID: As if I care!

PRINCESS [*urbane*]: Were I she, I'd allow myself, perhaps, a little sneer. . . .

ENID: I don't mean to upset my expression on Eric's account.

PRINCESS: But only a little *tiny* one.

ENID [*toying listlessly with her ring*]: Oh, don't ask me, please, to wear another thing more! Even a sneer.

PRINCESS: For his good, one could wish he'd some interest. . . . A man should have aspirations, I always contend.

ENID: Ah, there, my dear, I'm with you. When I think that one of Caligula's horses was a Member of Parliament, and when I remember what a plain, simple cow rose to be, I own I'm mortified at Eric's unambition.

PRINCESS [*gasping*]: What did the plain, simple cow rise to be?

ENID: She rose to be an Empress.

NADINE: An Empress?

ENID: Or a Goddess, was it? I'm sure I forget.

[*A piano-organ is heard suddenly beyond the garden gate.*]

NADINE: Horrid to be outdone by animals.

ENID [*to dance-air, taking a few tripping steps*]: Well, my dears! It's been a week of wonders!

PRINCESS: What is that?

NADINE [*raising her voice a little because of the organ*]: She says it's been a week of wonders.

PRINCESS: Poor child! A week ago she was an insouciant girl!

NADINE: Insouciant!

PRINCESS [*watching the bride with a mistrustful eye*]: I only hope she won't take to narcotics!

NADINE: We must not let her brood.

[*The organ stops.*]

PRINCESS: One day soon, Enid, let us ride together.

ENID: There's nothing I'd like more, only I've nothing to ride, I'm afraid.

PRINCESS: I will find you a charming little horse.

ENID [*dropping to her knees upon the grass*]: What a darling you are!

PRINCESS [*plying her fan*]: Galloping down some green cattle-track in the cool of evening, child, you will soon forget your worries.

ENID [*nestling*]: Your habit smells of Arcady. . . .

PRINCESS: Of what?

ENID: Arcady.

PRINCESS: Beyond the Porta San Gallo I often dismount and walk.

ENID: Enchanting.

PRINCESS: There's a road bordered by wild acacias I yearn to show you.

ENID [*elated*]: Yes?

PRINCESS: And at its end there's a Calvary . . . and a church designed by Andrea Orcagna with the loveliest windows.

ENID: One might perhaps do a sketch or something?

PRINCESS: The green brightness of the glass is amazingly nice. And such touching mosaics there are. You'll see!

[*Enter through arch* L. LADY ROCKTOWER, *an uncommonly long and lean woman—once a well-known beauty.*]

SCENE IX

Same. LADY ROCKTOWER

LADY ROCKTOWER [*hand extended, advancing to* NADINE]: I wrote to you about a week ago asking you to dinner, and having received no answer I thought I would ascertain . . .

NADINE [*retaining* LADY ROCKTOWER'S *hand captive in her own an instant in token of contrition*]: Did I *never* answer?

LADY ROCKTOWER: Both Lord Rocktower and I will be so disappointed if you fail us to-morrow night!

NADINE: To-morrow night I fear we shall be without either Adrian or Eric.

LADY ROCKTOWER: Are they leaving Florence?

NADINE: Yes. . . .

LADY ROCKTOWER: Dear me! I didn't know.

NADINE: They're leaving us—and Italy.

LADY ROCKTOWER: I trust nothing serious!

NADINE: Nothing very.

LADY ROCKTOWER: That's right. [*To* ENID] *My dear,* what a foreign behind! I didn't recognise you at first!

ENID [*amused*]: How do you like my Cinquecento jacket?

LADY ROCKTOWER: Your fastidious, imaginative dresses would not suit everyone.

ENID: Fortunately.

LADY ROCKTOWER [*looking about her*]: Where's Glyda?

NADINE: I don't know!

LADY ROCKTOWER: She came a few yards with me, and suddenly exclaimed: 'Oh, bother,' and then rushed back.

PRINCESS: Your daughter, I expect, will be here directly.

LADY ROCKTOWER [*shaking hands with* PRINCESS *very cordially*]: Dear Princess! Although you live within a stone's throw, one sees simply *nothing* of you!

PRINCESS: Yes. *How is it,* I wonder?

LADY ROCKTOWER: I don't remember ever having seen you at my *Musicale*?

PRINCESS: Unfortunately. . . . But I hear it was quite wonderful. With Julie Bonbon and Emma Block. . . .

LADY ROCKTOWER: Who told you?

PRINCESS: Mr. Waterbird.

LADY ROCKTOWER: I must protest! He wasn't there.

PRINCESS: Oh ! . . . .

LADY ROCKTOWER: I can't be civil to a political traitor!

NADINE: My dear, in Politics there is no honour. Disraeli has said so.

LADY ROCKTOWER: Anyway I should never invite the Waterbirds. [*Cryptically*] I regard Mrs. Waterbird as *no acquisition*!

PRINCESS [*irrelevantly*]: I watched her in the mirror once acting a little pantomime behind my back.

NADINE [*adjusting a pin*]: They say she has three lovers. . . .

PRINCESS: Three?

ENID: Surely three lovers would be very inspiriting!

LADY ROCKTOWER: How is it, I'd like to know, you're parting so soon with yours? Were I a new-made wife, I'd hold my husband tight, grip his coat-tails and not let go!

ENID: His going is of little consequence really.

LADY ROCKTOWER: It's soon to play Penelope yet!

PRINCESS [*a shadow of recollection crossing her face*]: Were I driven to choose, I'd prefer neglect, I think, to surfeit.

LADY ROCKTOWER: That, I suppose, depends upon the man.

PRINCESS [*with a half-laugh*]: A husband's attentions *soon* grow savourless!

ENID [*her eyes raised towards the gallery*]: He married me in creaking shoes.

LADY ROCKTOWER: What?

ENID [*reminiscent, unearthly*]: His shoes creaked when he married me!

LADY ROCKTOWER: I conclude you've been catching *glimpses* of each other. . . .

ENID: Glimpses?

LADY ROCKTOWER [*shrewdly*]: I believe this is nothing but a touch of sex-antagonism which presently will pass.

ENID [*evidently pleased with the consequence of the situation*]: This morning my maid found three little grey ones—hairs.

NADINE [*sympathetically*]: Darling Enid! She talks like an old woman and she's a mere *fillette* still!

LADY ROCKTOWER: Were I you, my dear, I would go for him tooth-and-nail!

PRINCESS [*conciliatory*]: I always pour oil on troubled waters. Harmony for me.

ENID [*with importance*]: Three little grey ones. . . .

[*She goes up stage enumerating them upon her fingers, and disappears after a moment in the garden.*]

NADINE [*following her with a look*]: Now she has gone off into some jewelled Hades of her own.

LADY ROCKTOWER: I'm bewildered to know what to advise!

NADINE [*musingly*]: It's difficult to interfere—Enid and Eric vying in vanity with each other as they do.

LADY ROCKTOWER: They're not sufficiently different, one feels, to be happy together.

PRINCESS: Enid's clever of course, but she needs directing.

LADY ROCKTOWER [*irreflective*]: One comfort is there's no issue!

PRINCESS: My dear, give them time!

NADINE: It's quite dreadful to hear her refer to her wedding-day as *Black Tuesday*.

LADY ROCKTOWER: Thank Heaven! Marriage isn't indissoluble.

PRINCESS: They're unreckonably temperamental. Both of them. . . .

LADY ROCKTOWER: People of their sort oughtn't to marry.

title
The Princess Zoubaroff

NADINE: Last night she had a bad *crise de nerfs* and began calling sixteen 'the Old Age of Youth.'

PRINCESS [*fluttering her fan*]: Is she *only* sixteen?

NADINE [*ignoring the interruption*]: So this morning I sent into town for Dr. Mater.

LADY ROCKTOWER: I don't think much of Dr. Mater. He'll tell you of all sorts of things to avoid, things that *in any case* it would never occur to one to take!

PRINCESS: What did he say?

NADINE: He has ordered her milk and the wings of chickens.

[*Enter* GLYDA ROCKTOWER, *aged eleven. She is pale, plump, precocious —an attaching manner.*]

SCENE X

Same. GLYDA

PRINCESS: Ah! . . . *ecco-la!*

LADY ROCKTOWER: Wicked peach.

GLYDA [*standing legs apart and swinging insolently her skirts*]: I met some people in the lane.

LADY ROCKTOWER: Who?

GLYDA: Guess?

LADY ROCKTOWER: I can't.

GLYDA [*pirouetting, preening herself*]: Apollo—and Lord Orkish.

LADY ROCKTOWER: Apollo—who?

GLYDA: Reggie Quintus.

LADY ROCKTOWER: Oh!

GLYDA: I told them you were here. They're coming in.

[*Enter* LORD ORKISH. *He is, despite 'Exile' and a 'certain age,' all cheerfulness, gaiety and sweet good-humour. Behind him* REGGIE QUINTUS. *Incredibly young. Incredibly good-looking. No one would suppose him to have figured as hero already in at least one* cause célèbre—*his manner, which is somewhat 'subdued,' alternates between the demi-dazed and the demi-demure.*]

SCENE XI

Same. LORD ORKISH, REGGIE QUINTUS

LORD ORKISH: Do we intrude?

NADINE: Delighted.

LORD ORKISH: We've just been paying a *visite de digestion* on Comtesse Willie White, and are on our way to Salut at San Lorenzo.

NADINE: Then there's no immediacy, is there?

LORD ORKISH [*shaking hands*]: Why, none.

LADY ROCKTOWER: Perhaps you can inform me if Madame Gandarella is still at the Villa?

LORD ORKISH: Yes; and Santuzza.

NADINE [*laughing*]: That poor Santuzza. She has the most fearful English accent in the world. Where is it? What is it? Who could have taught her? I wonder.

LORD ORKISH: People are circulating such dreadful stories!

PRINCESS [*miraculously*]: What about?

LORD ORKISH: I'm so newsy. [*Irrepressibly*] I feel I must tell it to somebody, if only a lizard, or a butterfly, or a garden-snail!

NADINE: Sit down and tell us instead.

[*All but imperceptibly twilight begins to form.*]

LORD ORKISH: I've but just this afternoon heard the Alpmuriels are leaving one another! . . . Mrs. Alpmuriel, in fact, has already gone.

LADY ROCKTOWER, NADINE: Gone? [*Ensemble*] Where?

LORD ORKISH: Away.

LADY ROCKTOWER: Dear me!

LORD ORKISH [*impressionistically*]: Instead of surprising them—*comment dirai-je?*—he found them unmysteriously eating.

LADY ROCKTOWER: *Eating?*

LORD ORKISH: Only imagine! ! ! And he with his drawn sword—or a revolver, was it?

LADY ROCKTOWER: Oh!

LORD ORKISH [*playing extinct eyes*]: Sir Dolfin Lewis is defending her.

PRINCESS [*amused*]: And what else, Lord Orkish, did you hear at the Villa White?

LORD ORKISH: That the new American Ambassadress likes to be thought a little *grisette*.

LADY ROCKTOWER: I sat next her a short while ago at the Theatro Valli.

NADINE: You did not tell me you had been to Rome!

REGGIE [*in a voice which is rather like cheap scent*]: Perhaps you won't agree. But I consider Florence has fewer amenities than Rome.

NADINE: It depends what one means by amenities, quite.

REGGIE [*regarding thoughtfully his white compact hands*]: I always feel a sort of *malaise* in Florence. Why, I can't tell.

LADY ROCKTOWER [*austerely*]: I fear the morals of the town are not especially high!

LORD ORKISH: A neighbour of ours sent her little maid the other night across the Piazza for a bottle of French brandy, and she has not been heard of again.

NADINE: How dreadful!

ENID [*coming down with a watering-can of Pesaro pottery in her hand. She is smiling, and has tucked into her dress a huge blue passion-flower*]: I heard men's voices. . . .

NADINE: Lord Orkish has been regaling us with a whole rosary of piquant anecdotes.

ENID: Really.

NADINE [*to* LORD ORKISH]: You've such wonderful *entraînement*.

LORD ORKISH [*very simply*]: I'm never bored. I enjoy everything.

REGGIE: So do I too! I love society. Alone with my shadow I'm soon depressed.

NADINE [*rather nervously*]: And where have you been to, Reggie, this perfect age?

REGGIE [*bending his head a little on one side to inhale the scent of the tuberose flowers that are in his button-hole*]: I and a friend of mine, Claud Cloudley, we've been visiting all the P's.

NADINE: All the what?

REGGIE: Pavia, Parma, Padua, Perugia, Pisa——

PRINCESS: Is it a method?

REGGIE: Claud's such an extremist, you know. [*Lowering impressively his voice*]. They say when he kissed the Pope's slipper [*a gentle cough*] he went on to do considerably *more*. . . .

GLYDA [*intrigued*]: What's he like, Reggie?

REGGIE [*nonchalantly*]: He's rather good-looking in a sickly sort of way.

GLYDA [*disappointed*]: What a description!

ENID [*slyly*]: I expect he's very good looking!

REGGIE [*smiling*]: He's sickly.

PRINCESS: I remember him coming to see me once in England, with his dripping umbrella.

LORD ORKISH: Shall you be going to England, Princess, later on?

PRINCESS [*cooling her cheeks with a powder-puff*]: Perhaps, if I can afford it.

NADINE: To hear her speak, she might be a Poor Clare!

LADY ROCKTOWER [*vivaciously*]: Our villa is let for the coming villeggiatura to Madame Olga Wittena-Gemot, the famous singer, and my husband is rampant with me because Renaldo Renetti——

[*Re-enter* ERIC, *with billiard cue.*]

SCENE XII

Same. ERIC

ERIC [*to* ENID]: Shake me a cocktail, darling. Do.

ENID: Oh, don't ask me to do anything so violent, Eric. Where's Angelo?

NADINE [*who looks as though she would be also glad of some refreshment herself*]: What shall it be? West-Coast? Manhattan? Kiss-me-Quick?

ERIC: Let it be a Gloom-Raiser.

NADINE: There's no more absinthe, I fear.

ERIC: Then a Champagne-Cobbler.

NADINE [*generally*]: Will you excuse me?

[*Exit* NADINE *to house.*]

LADY ROCKTOWER: Now, I'm going to scold him!

ENID: No, Lady Rocktower.

LADY ROCKTOWER: And Princess Zoubaroff shall second me.

PRINCESS: Oh, please! I'm unrepresented. [*She drifts away.*]

ERIC: *Buona sera.*

[*He begins balancing his billiard cue in the palm of his hand.* ENID, *with an ironic glance, follows* PRINCESS *towards hammock, where* LORD ORKISH *and* REGGIE *have commenced rocking* GLYDA.]

ENID [*witheringly, withdrawing*]: He is the Eternal-masculine.

LADY ROCKTOWER [*toute entière à sa proie attachée*]: Heartless man; and so you're going to leave us?

ERIC [*inconsequently*]: For a time.

LADY ROCKTOWER: You propose, of course, returning?

ERIC [*with an air of detachment*]: I expect so!

LADY ROCKTOWER: I think Enid is a saint about it all. [*Warming*] For a honeymoon's a honeymoon, however one looks at it.

ERIC: Bored people do desperate things.

LADY ROCKTOWER [*fairly floored*]: Why on earth did you marry?

ERIC [*ceasing juggling*]: I was only half serious when I proposed.

LADY ROCKTOWER: And she accepted you?

ERIC: I never expected to be taken quite *au pied de la lettre*.

LADY ROCKTOWER: Fool!

ERIC: I beg your pardon?

LADY ROCKTOWER: I said insensate! [*He continues his experiments with the cue.*] [*Beside herself*] Come down to us a little more. Forsake those heights!

ERIC [*turning away*]: If I leave you for a moment will you forgive me?

ENID [*reapproaching*]: Lady Rocktower! Please——

LADY ROCKTOWER: He seems determined!

ENID: Let him go.

LADY ROCKTOWER [*susceptibly*]: He has nice eyes.

ENID: There's something agreeably piquant—*almost*—about his excessive leanness!

LADY ROCKTOWER: Perhaps so.

ENID: And I don't so *much* detest his big, bold nose!

LADY ROCKTOWER: Tell me, dear. Were you solicited besides?

ENID: Was I——

LADY ROCKTOWER: Did anyone else ask you?

ENID [*exaggerating*]: I should say so indeed. I might have married whom I liked.

LADY ROCKTOWER: You seem to have selected an enigma!

ENID [*playing with her passion-flower*]: I will say this for Eric, he isn't carnal.

LADY ROCKTOWER: He isn't carnal enough, my dear, from what *I* can see. [*Half to herself*] He must have the blood of an Esquimau!

ENID: I scarcely realised, I suppose, at the time of my marriage, I was taking him on for a *term of years*.

LADY ROCKTOWER [*prophetic*]: Oh! But it won't be years! A term of weeks, dear, more like, at the rate things go.

ENID: I think my nerves need Mozart.

[*Enter* ANGELO, *a boy of sixteen, fair, sleek, languishing, a 'Benozzo Gozzoli,' bearing a tray with lemonade, sorbets, fruit, etc. He wears a trim black livery with violet-coloured facings and shoulder-knots.*]

SCENE XIII

Same. ANGELO

LADY ROCKTOWER [*helping herself recklessly to strawberries*]: I will order a Novena said for you.

[*Attracted by* ANGELO *and the tinkle of ice,* GLYDA *and* REGGIE *come down, followed more leisurely by* LORD ORKISH *and* PRINCESS. *Later* NADINE. *The twilight deepens. Lights, here and there, shine from town.*]

REGGIE: I believe strawberries are the clue to my heart!

ENID: Are they?

REGGIE: I'm most awfully *friand* of fruit.

GLYDA [*circling butterfly about*]: I'm fond of grapes, and apricots if they're green. . . . I can't say I like *bananas*.

LADY ROCKTOWER: Fastidious child.

REGGIE: I adore them.

GLYDA: How much?

REGGIS [*wittily*]: As a Russian does Nice.

ENID. Angelo! [*Backing him down towards footlights.*]

ANGELO. Signora!

ENID [*sotto voce*].: Have you the key of your master's valise?

ANGELO [*passionately*]: Ah, Madonna!

ENID: Answer me.

ANGELO [*as before*]: Ah, Mamma mia!

ENID [*taking a sorbet*]: You haven't?

ANGELO: *Ah, caro dio!*

ENID: It doesn't matter.

ANGELO: *Ah, che roba!* [*He crosses stage,* **rolling his black eyes,** *passing* ADRIAN L.]

Scene XIV

Same. ADRIAN

ADRIAN [*to* ENID]: Have you seen Eric?

ENID [*sipping her sorbet*]: He was here a moment ago.

ADRIAN: Visitors! [*He seems disconcerted at sight of* REGGIE.]

PRINCESS [*continuing her conversation with* LORD ORKISH]: I sent my new photo quarter-face to the Cardinal, and he said——

ENID [*drinking still*]: You'll think of the edelweiss, won't you—if it's only a single sprig!

ADRIAN: Eh?

ENID: It would so touch Nadine . . . Poor angel! She's always wanting some rare, far thing.

ADRIAN: I know.

ENID [*lightly*]: So be, be a dear!

REGGIE [*deftly,* *to* LADY ROCKTOWER, *without interrupting at all*

ADRIAN *and* ENID]. They had hoped it was Tiepolo—but it's only Sebastian Ricci.

ADRIAN: But it isn't the season for edelweiss.

ENID: Nonsense!

ADRIAN: I promise you.

ENID: You needn't try to put me off with an excuse!

LORD ORKISH [*very deftly, to* PRINCESS]: Lady Audley's still at Cannes. I hear you wouldn't know her! She's grown so stout.

ENID [*asserting her voice pathetically in general appeal*]: Isn't it the season for edelweiss?

LADY ROCKTOWER: For edelweiss. I'm sure I don't know.

ENID [*setting down her glass*]: It is the season. It *is*.

GLYDA [*to* PRINCESS]: What is the music written on your fan?

PRINCESS: A gipsy song—a *chansonette*.

ENID [*obstinately*]: I will wager you what you like, edelweiss grows *all the year round*.

NADINE [*re-entering from house*]: I think I hear the front door bell!

ADRIAN: It's amazing you hear anything.

[*Enter* ANGELO, *followed by* BLANCHE.]

ANGELO [*announcing*]: Mrs. Negress. [*He goes out, looking over his shoulder, apparently at* REGGIE.]

SCENE XV

Same. BLANCHE NEGRESS. *Her hair, worn short, in wildest spirals, is tinged with white. She is dressed in grey, like a Béguine. She has a pannier of red lilies.*

BLANCHE: I walked along a pink footpath, through the olive-gardens, till I saw a dog, which *nearly* drove me back. I don't know why it should be, but Italian dogs fly at me as a rule!

ENID [*accepting pannier, which* BLANCHE *tends*]: It's nice, your coming.

NADINE: Do you know everybody? Lady Rocktower, Mrs. Negress—Lord Orkish, Mr. Quintus, Princess Zoubaroff—Zena, this is Blanche!

PRINCESS: Delighted.

LORD ORKISH: I expect it was *my* dog. I left one at the door. [*He moves up.*]

NADINE [*introducing*]: My husband.

BLANCHE [*genially*]: I think we've slept together once?

ADRIAN: I don't remember.

BLANCHE: At the Opera. During *Bérénice*!

ADRIAN: Why, of course.

NADINE [*glimpsing* ERIC]: Mr. Tresilian——

ERIC: I give you full permission to slay me.

ENID: Why should she wish to slay you?

NADINE: Hark to his guilty conscience!

PRINCESS [*to* BLANCHE]: I confess, with shame, I never read one of your books.

BLANCHE [*amiable*]: It took me four years to choose my *nom de guerre*—Mary.

PRINCESS [*with a cry*]: Are you Mary?

BLANCHE: I am.

PRINCESS: Oh, then, *Love's Visé*—I know. . . . And *Lesbia, or Would He Understand?* [*Her admiration is boundless.*]

ENID [*indicating books*]: By the way, Zena, I haven't thanked you properly——

PRINCESS: Were any of them interesting at all?

ENID: I should think so.

PRINCESS [*affectionately*]: *Cara*.

ENID [*with a look at* ERIC]: I'm glad I can still sometimes drug my senses with a book.

NADINE: I've been perusing *Lord Tiredstock's Memoirs*.

PRINCESS: His biography is the barest memoranda, but it's wonderful.

[REGGIE, *at table where are* PRINCESS'S *books, chuckles*.]

ENID: What is amusing you?

REGGIE [*convulsed*]: *Orfeo*.

ENID: What about it?

REGGIE: It's too cruel.

ENID: No.

REGGIE [*reading*]: 'Woman is an object that always makes man ridiculous.'

NADINE [*shrieking*]: Fiend!

REGGIE [*continuing*]: 'If she is ugly—oh! What a misery! If she is beautiful—oh! What a danger! and whether one takes her or leaves her one always repents one's action.'

LADY ROCKTOWER [*protesting*]: Well, really!

ENID: Aren't you ashamed to read such things aloud to *us*?

REGGIE: You said I might.

PRINCESS: Mercifully, very soon it will be too dark to read!

GLYDA [*indicating*]: Oh, do look at the sky!

NADINE: Extravagant, isn't it?

ERIC [*grumbling*]: Another airless night!

LADY ROCKTOWER: I'm quite glad, do you know, of my Resorgimento cape. [*Puts wrap on.*]

PRINCESS: It is lightening a little towards the town.

BLANCHE: Florence fascinates me at sundown with its scores of shimmering lights.

LADY ROCKTOWER: The evenings grow dark here so very beautifully.

GLYDA: There's a sickle moon.

PRINCESS: Where? Show me.

GLYDA: Can't you see it? There, through the trees. [*She turns to* BLANCHE.]

BLANCHE [*modestly*]: I fear I'm becoming too obese to look at the moon.

ADRIAN [*inviting*]: Then look, do, at the shadows instead.

BLANCHE [*staring*]: The shadows?

NADINE: Adrian sees shapes in everything. [*Laughing*] He calls the trees at the foot of the garden an 'obscene brigade.'

LADY ROCKTOWER: My dear, if they choose to grow that way . . .

PRINCESS [*indolently*]: Not a frond stirs. It's as if a spell held all fast.

ENID [*sniffing*]: Delicious. The fresh odour of the dew.

PRINCESS: My favourite tree is certainly the Cypress.

GLYDA [*taking her fan from her and using it*]: Why?

PRINCESS: It tells no tales!

NADINE: But monotonous, like all evergreens are.

BLANCHE [*blinking at a flash of summer lightning*]: There was a beautiful thunderstorm the evening I arrived.

ENID: At the 'Bretagne,' Blanche, you would see!

BLANCHE: Yes; my room is on the river.

LORD ORKISH [*returning*]: I don't know at all what the Arno is coming to. I was leaning on my window-sill [*laughs*], and there were some youths who appeared to be bathing without false modesty of *any* kind.

LADY ROCKTOWER [*covering her eyes with an elaborately becoroneted vanity-bag*]: How dreadful!

LORD ORKISH [*pursuing*]: I'm sure if I looked it was quite involuntary.

LADY ROCKTOWER [*sympathetically*]: I'm sure you couldn't help yourself from standing and looking.

NADINE [*sentimentally*]: I love the Arno at low water.

ADRIAN: It's always that. Beyond the town it's unnavigable for even a newspaper!

ERIC [*to* BLANCHE]: Enid was saying you write for one.

BLANCHE [*proudly*]: I write for several.

ERIC: Oh? Which?

BLANCHE: Mainly women's. . . . [*A little sadly*] I was instrumental *in a very large degree* in obtaining my sex the vote.

PRINCESS: You are one of our champions then?

BLANCHE: Yes.

LADY ROCKTOWER: I'm glad you believe in us!

BLANCHE: Men amuse me sometimes. [*Simply*] But I have never really loved one.

ERIC [*astonished*]: You have never loved *any* man?

BLANCHE: Never!

LADY ROCKTOWER [*nervously fastening a hook to her cape*]: It's a pleasure to meet now and again a woman of really advanced morals.

BLANCHE: I can safely say I prefer the society of other women to that of men.

PRINCESS: That's nice of you.

LADY ROCKTOWER [*to* NADINE]: Well, dear, I really must run. I wish I hadn't to!

NADINE: Must you?

ENID: Stay a little while. It's absurdly early yet.

LADY ROCKTOWER: There's to be a small *sauterie* this evening at the Harkovs'.

NADINE: We were asked, but I didn't feel like going.

ENID: I'm far too slack to go fagging up to Fiesole to-night.

LADY ROCKTOWER [*to* GLYDA]: Come, child!

NADINE: Good-bye. You'll come and see me sometimes, won't you?

LADY ROCKTOWER [*moving towards garden gate with* GLYDA]: Often, if you wish it.

ENID: Do!

LADY ROCKTOWER [*up stage, at a distance*]. To-morrow . . . let me see. Is there no charming church where we could go and sit?

The Princess Zoubaroff

Scene XVI

Same. Minus LADY ROCKTOWER *and* GLYDA

LORD ORKISH [*low, to* REGGIE]: And we ought to be toddling too.

REGGIE [*deaf, to* ERIC]: We might frivol round together one evening if you like.

ERIC [*primly*]: I should love to, only I've no leisure for anything just now.

PRINCESS [*observant, to* LORD ORKISH]: In Spain, I'm told, you must first court the husband to get round the wife.

LORD ORKISH [*appalled at so much cynicism*]: Madame! Madame!

BLANCHE [*to* ADRIAN, *designating something*]: What is that big brick pile?

ADRIAN [*looking*]: Where? You surely don't mean the Signoria?

BLANCHE: Such a sad, fateful sunset.

LORD ORKISH [*touching* REGGIE's *arm*]: Ready?

REGGIE [*backing out of Salut*]: I'm so sorry . . . but I clean forgot! I've a *rendezvous*.

LORD ORKISH: Where?

REGGIE: At the quag end of the Cascine.

LORD ORKISH: Which end's that?

REGGIE: The quag end? The far end. . . .

LORD ORKISH: We can go part of the way together.

NADINE [*coming down*]: Dear Lady Rocktower. She gets statelier every year. [*Seeing* LORD ORKISH *and* REGGIE *are preparing to depart*] What? You're off?

LORD ORKISH: It's getting late.

NADINE: Try and look in to-morrow.

REGGIE [*to* PRINCESS]: Bye-bye. I press your hand. [*Does so.*]

LORD ORKISH: I fear I'm engaged to-morrow.

NADINE: Tiresome creature!

LORD ORKISH [*as he goes up, accompanied by* REGGIE]: I'm attending a tertulia *chez Camille*!

NADINE [*graciously*]: Well, *Addio* for the present.

[*Exeunt, by garden gate,* LORD ORKISH *and* REGGIE.]

BLANCHE [*precipitately making after them*]: As they know the way, I think I'll go with them.

[*Exit* BLANCHE.]

The Princess Zoubaroff

Scene XVII

Same. Minus LORD ORKISH, REGGIE, BLANCHE

PRINCESS: It must be almost dinner-time!

ADRIAN: I expect you're hungry after riding so far.

PRINCESS: I am!

ERIC: That's right.

PRINCESS: This morning my French cook got locked, by mistake in the orchid-house, and I've had nothing to eat all day.

NADINE *and* ENID [*coming down*]: Stay and dine with us.

PRINCESS: Impossible.

ENID: Because?

PRINCESS: I must change.

NADINE: Look in after, then.

ENID: Yes, do, Zena.

PRINCESS [*considering*]: Perhaps I may peep in quite at the very end of the evening.

NADINE: We'll expect you.

PRINCESS [*going*]: I'll bring a little volume of Higher Mysticism with me—shall I?—that I think you'll *adore*.

ENID [*blowing her a kiss*]: How delightful.

PRINCESS: Till by and by.

[*Exit* PRINCESS.]

Scene XVIII

ADRIAN, ERIC, NADINE, ENID

ADRIAN [*to* ERIC]: Shall we finish our game?

ERIC: By all means.

ENID [*affronted*]: Are you going indoors?

ERIC [*with simpering ardour*]: *Auf Wiedersehen,* my deathless girl.

[*Exeunt* ADRIAN *and Eric*.]

Scene XIX

NADINE, ENID

ENID [*complaining*]: Why aren't the Nightingales singing, and why is there no moon?

NADINE: But there is, dearest. A delicate new one—all for us.

ENID: I mean a proper moon.

NADINE: My dear Enid [*focusing the moon with a black-rimmed eyeglass*], I see nothing improper about this one.

ENID: I meant a full moon, darling.

NADINE: I don't know why you should prefer it to be full. A full moon is perhaps rather vulgar?

ENID: Vulgar?

NADINE: Just a little.

[ANGELO *enters and takes away empty glasses, murmuring intermittently to himself below his breath.*]

ANGELO: *Ah poveretta! La povera signora. Ah che roba! Ah, Dio!* [*He is almost crying in his distress for* ENID.]

ENID: I suppose they leave early?

NADINE: I've no idea.

ENID: I shan't come down.

NADINE: Neither will I. I intend receiving his parting peck in bed.

ENID: Eric never gives me such tangible proofs of his affection.

NADINE: Doesn't he?

ENID: In the morning he just touches my hand—and then he just grazes it—*et encore!!*—again at night.

NADINE [*after an instant, pacing to and fro*]: You know, Enid, I consulted Dr. Mater this morning, after he'd seen you.

ENID: What about?

NADINE [*after another instant*]: My health is in a very delicate state, dear.

ENID [*alarmed*]: Darling Nadine!

NADINE: Yes, I may be obliged—but I won't tax your little ears with it just now.

ENID [*anxious to ascertain the facts*]: Is it anything dreadful?

NADINE: It depends what one means quite by dreadful. [*Hal hysterically*] Define dreadful!

ENID [*taking* NADINE'S *hand*]: I'm so sorry . . .

NADINE [*turning from her*]: Of course we may all be wrong. . . .

ENID [*with fervour*]: I do sincerely hope so!

NADINE: I must go and dress. . . .

ENID [*calling after her*]: Tell Ferguson, dear, as you're going in, my gown with the Camellias.

SCENE XX

ENID, *Sola. She stands a moment, lost in conjecture. All the bells of Florence ring out. From the Judas-tree a nightingale utters a trill. Another*

*replies. . . . All in an instant the air is full of the singing of birds, the
tintinnabulation of bells. The sky is abloom with stars.*

ENID [*to herself, aloud*]: What can she be going to have?

[*Moving towards a flower-plat she inhales, indolently, a flower. A gong
goes within. Right hand to hip, left raised to chevelure, she goes slowly
up.*]

ENID [*lifting roguishly towards the sky her face*]: It sounds almost
as though she were sickening for the Plague. . . .

THE CURTAIN FALLS

ACT II

SCENE I

*Same as Act I, only the trees have changed their tints. Some are orange,
some are scarlet. Red creepers. Autumn flowers.*

NADINE, *slightly overdressed in black, with a colossal hat of Piedmontese
cock's feathers, is seen with a couple of lace pocket-handkerchiefs tied
to two fingers* [*which she bobs and waggles*], *diverting her infant son.*

ENID, *from hammock* [*her gown is white, with clusters of sophisticated-
looking fruit hanging from it*], *is listlessly watching her.*

ENID [*breaking at last the 'September Silence'*]: Why did you have it?

NADINE [*with a sigh, half of pride, half of resignation*]: My dear, I
simply couldn't help myself. . . .

ENID: I thought you cleverer!

NADINE [*to the infant*]: Charles Augustus Frederic Humphrey
Percy Sydney!

ENID: At any rate, I'm glad the christening's over.

NADINE [*soulfully*]: Yes. But it was beautiful.

ENID [*despondently*]: And now this wretched party.

NADINE [*kissing little* CHARLES]: He is just like an opening orchid.

ENID [*sitting up—she has in her hand a crystal*]: Just like what?

NADINE [*rocking*]: Forgive a mother's selfishness.

ENID: I won't let him monopolise you, Nadine.

NADINE [*oblivious*]: His mania for pulling everything to pieces
makes me anxious for his happiness later on.

ENID [*looking round*]: Here is Mrs. Mangrove.

729

[*Enter* NURSE. *She is Scotch. Portly. A woman of fifty. One realises immediately she would have her theories, her 'little ways,' as regards Nursery matters.*]

SCENE II

Same. NURSE

NADINE: You shall take him, Nurse.

NURSE: Very good, marm. [*Taking child.*]

NADINE: Gently, mind.

NURSE [*bursting into song*]:

> The man in the moone drinks claret,
> Eates powdered beef, turnip and caret,
> But a cup of old Malaga sack
> Will fire the bushe at his backe.

ENID [*detached*]: I hope you enjoyed the christening, Nurse?

NURSE: To be sure, I seldom saw a bonnier.

NADINE [*privately, to* NURSE]: See that he——

NURSE: He doesn't want to again, marm, Lord bless you! [*She bustles off through the trees with the child nevertheless.*]

SCENE III

NADINE, ENID

NADINE [*distressed*]: I am afraid she cannot have seen very distinguished service.

ENID: In the last family that she was in, on Notting Hill, she told me the governess and the five children used to go out roller-skating through the London streets. . . .

NADINE [*crossing over to her*]: Have you made any further discovery, Enid, in the crystal at all?

ENID: It's difficult. . . . I ought to have something to hold.

NADINE [*drawing something from her dress*]: Here is the last letter he wrote to me.

ENID [*taking it*]: Thanks.

NADINE: I feel it may be the last he *ever* wrote. . . .

ENID [*airily*]: Something tells me they are the two that slipped.

NADINE [*closing her eyes, gesticulating*]: It's appalling to think of them both falling . . . sinking.

ENID: Tsch!

NADINE: You may **read** what Adrian says.

ENID [*humouring her*]: 'The walks—the walks are a continual delight. On all sides—turn where one will—beauty breaks on beauty. . . .'

NADINE [*euphoniously, with her lips*]: Beauty breaks on beauty. . . .

ENID [*resuming*]: 'Wonder leaps on wonder' [*her voice breaking a little*]. 'I think of you sometimes at Livorno, where the green waves roll in ceaselessly and the brown fishing-nets upon the beach lie drying in the sun.'

NADINE: Because I told him we might be going to Livorno.

ENID [*commenting*]: A more depraved-looking autograph I've seldom seen!

NADINE [*with authority*]: Now use the ball.

ENID [*after an instant*]: In the crystal I see a beautiful little giraffe.

NADINE: A giraffe.

ENID: Such a darling. Oh, and I can see a hut, a little house. . . . [*She begins to squeal.*]

NADINE: That must be the guide's dwelling.

ENID [*still gazing*]: I think it's an antelope, not a giraffe.

NADINE [*anxiously*]: What is it doing?

ENID [*straining*]: Nothing.

NADINE: There, that's enough for the present, I want you fresh for the party.

ENID [*returning letter*]: It's a mistake, I think, having ordered tea indoors.

NADINE: It saves a lot of bother.

ENID [*thoughtfully*]: Awkward if Monsignor Vanhove should call here to-day.

NADINE [*flurried, applying to her lips a cosmetic*]: Did Zena say he'd call?

ENID: She said he might.

NADINE: I believe she intends taking it.

ENID: What? The veil?

NADINE: I'm sure.

ENID [*thrilled*]: But *are* you?

NADINE: And what's more, my dear, she also intends us!

ENID [*giggling nervously*]: Oh, I could never be a nun.

NADINE: Couldn't you?

ENID: Could I? . . .

[*Enter* PRINCESS.]

NADINE: Ah, here is Charlie's new godmother.

The Princess Zoubaroff

Scene IV

Same. PRINCESS. *She wears something which is crocus-coloured, contrasting radiantly with the autumnal foliage of the trees, a foppish hat, a winter-day muff. . . . She is looking charmingly Carthaginian.*

PRINCESS [*coming forward*]: Charles Augustus Frederic—what are the others?

NADINE: Humphrey, Percy, Sydney.

PRINCESS [*frowning, shocked*]: Such a wicked, dissolute name!

ENID: Names. . . .

NADINE: *Cher amour.*

PRINCESS: Well, Charlie's mother [*taking* NADINE'S *hands*], you're happy? You're content?

NADINE [*soulful, ethereal as before*]: It was beautiful.

ENID [*matter of fact*]: Was Violet du Wilson present?

PRINCESS [*nodding*]: With a sort of starfish in her hair.

NADINE: Violet's changed. She has the look of a great sinner. . . .

PRINCESS: Poor little woman—I want her *so* much.

NADINE [*dropping her eyes*]: You want her? What for?

PRINCESS: For my community.

ENID: Oh, Zena!

PRINCESS: I want you too.

NADINE: Us?

PRINCESS: I mean to have you.

ENID: No.

PRINCESS [*giving* ENID *a brush in the face with her muff*]: Oh, yes I do.

ENID [*changing the subject*]: Who else did you see at Santa Maria Novella?

PRINCESS [*vaguely*]: The Harkovs, the Scharas, the Rocktowers. [*Laughing*] Even old Mr. Hope, who never goes anywhere. . . .

NADINE: I can't suffer Countess Harkov, I'm afraid. She thinks she has only to smile to stir up an ocean of passion.

PRINCESS: It's a pity now she's getting to look so bloated.

ENID [*meaningly*]: You don't want her, I hope!

PRINCESS [*Christian*]: I want everybody—at least——

ENID [*curiously*]: But have you found your site?

PRINCESS [*mysteriously*]: I'm in communication with the Vatican now.

NADINE: So you are actually in touch!

PRINCESS [*nodding*]: My prospectus, I may say, is practically approved. . . .

ENID: By the Holy Father?

PRINCESS [*evasively*]: Monsignor Vanhove would do anything for me.

NADINE: Where will you fix?

PRINCESS: Beyond Settignano, I think.

ENID: Zena!

PRINCESS: What?

ENID: It's too utterly Uganda.

PRINCESS: Uganda?

ENID: Far off.

PRINCESS: Nonsense . . . what does one want to be near to?

ENID [*racily*]: I don't know what one wants to be near, but I know that Settignano is dreadfully ungetatable.

PRINCESS: One can't attain soul-stillness, dearest, within earshot of trains and trams.

NADINE [*catching her infant's howl*]: No, nor within earshot of my son and heir!

[*Exit* NADINE *hurriedly to house.*]

SCENE V

ENID, PRINCESS

ENID [*hands to ears*]: *Should I, could I, might I, dare I* drown it?

PRINCESS [*by hammock, frankly smiling*]: I almost wish you could.

ENID [*shocked, surprised*]: How ungodmotherly, Zena, of you!

PRINCESS [*seating herself*]: The worst of it is the Holy Father may not consent to have a boy brought up among us. . . .

ENID [*wondering, artless*]: Among whom?

PRINCESS: A little girl would have been easier to receive. . . .

ENID: Where?

PRINCESS: In a Religious House.

ENID [*laughing*]: A young man of Charlie's age can go anywhere.

PRINCESS [*scrupulous*]: It might give the nuns thoughts.

ENID [*still laughing*]: Thoughts?

PRINCESS [*toying with the tassels on her muff*]: Sexual ones.

ENID: Oh . . . but an infant!

PRINCESS: All the same, dear, infants—and a nun is such a sensitive creature as a rule.

ENID: I can't see that it matters at all. [*After a hesitation*] It might do later!

PRINCESS: Of course, some of us will be widows.

ENID: *You,* dear, for one.

PRINCESS [*with a sigh*]: Looking back, how droll it seems.

ENID [*diffident, cautious*]: Looking back at what?

PRINCESS: At everything.

ENID: This mystic side to you, Zena, is it something new?

PRINCESS: No.

ENID: Your late husband—did he know of it?

PRINCESS [*lifting her shoulders slightly*]: He may have guessed.

ENID: Only 'guessed.'

PRINCESS: Racing, pigeon-shooting, billiards, and whist were his chief pleasures.

ENID: An egoist?

PRINCESS [*softly reminiscent*]: Nils was different. He knew ...

ENID: Who was Nils?

PRINCESS: He was my first.

ENID: Oh?

PRINCESS: I adored him. We *adored* each other. [*With a sigh*] He was the dearest of *all* my husbands.

ENID: Tell me about him.

PRINCESS: He was not strong. He required always enormous precautions.

ENID: I presume you nursed him.

PRINCESS [*whimsically*]: Such a strange, bored and beautiful face he had ... though harrowingly thin he was. [*Laughing*] I sometimes miss his clever imitations of farmyard noises.

ENID [*fascinated*]: Yes?

PRINCESS [*mirthlessly*]: Hee-haw—Cook-a-doodle-doo.

ENID: He must leave a blank. ...

PRINCESS: I remember he died just as the clock was striking midday. ...

ENID [*speechless*]: ... !

PRINCESS [*poignant-eyed*]: Such a charming, such a brilliant man. ... He begged me to mourn him in Chinese fashion—White.

ENID: Which, of course, you did?

PRINCESS: And then, when all the wreaths were spread [*demonstrating*], I danced a *gavotte* over his grave.

ENID: He was not the explorer?

PRINCESS: Oh no.

ENID: What was *he* like?

PRINCESS [*evasively*]: Poor Phil—I forget what it was I didn't like about him. . . .

ENID [*prompt*]: His beard.

PRINCESS: Phil had no beard.

ENID: Which was the one that had?

PRINCESS: Hugh. He broke my heart.

ENID [*after an instant*]: Oh, isn't God far off? Zena! Isn't He, dear?

PRINCESS [*unruffled, abbessish*]: No, Enid. I don't think He is—not very.

ENID: Don't you?

PRINCESS [*smiling*]: Certainly I don't.

ENID [*impulsive*]: Do you care to understand me better? [*Leaning against* PRINCESS] Well—I prefer *St. John of the Cross* to *St. Vincent de Paul*!

PRINCESS: So do I!

ENID [*a slight pause; count 'six'*]: I feel I don't want love exactly— but some thrilling friendship. . . .

PRINCESS [*arch, gay, diagnosing*]: You want God, dear.

ENID: God?

PRINCESS: That is what is lacking.

ENID [*as* NADINE *appears*]: If it only were that!

SCENE VI

Same. NADINE

NADINE: I found Angelo in the loggia licking the ices.

ENID: Oh, Nadine.

PRINCESS: Do you go to Doney or Giacosa?

NADINE: Giacosa.

ENID [*moving towards house*]: Oughtn't one to be going in?

NADINE [*following her*]: I suppose one should!

PRINCESS [*dawdling*]: Delightful, the early Dahlias.

NADINE [*to* PRINCESS]: Coming?

[*Exeunt* ENID *and* NADINE *to house. Re-enter* NURSE *from the right bearing little* CHARLES.]

The Princess Zoubaroff

SCENE VII

PRINCESS, NURSE, INFANT

PRINCESS [*observing their names, admiring the dahlias*]: Louis-Philippe, Mrs. Marvel—voluptuous Mrs. Marvel! [*Bending*] Principessa Valentine di Odescalchi—a new variety, is it?

NURSE: It's been a glorious day, your Highness, for your godson's christening!

PRINCESS: You made me jump!

NURSE [*holding up infant*]: He's a fine vigorous boy, marm!

PRINCESS: Very.

NURSE: Oh, he's such a lusty little devil!

PRINCESS: He's handsome enough!

NURSE [*tossing him*]: Oh, he's a little sly one.

PRINCESS [*shaking her muff at him*]: He never cried once as he was sprinkled!

NURSE: He never noticed. All the while he was being baptised he was making Turk's eyes at a couple of pig-tails.

PRINCESS: Such a crowd at Santa Maria I've seldom seen.

NURSE: Poor Mrs. Sheil-Meyer. People are so sorry for her.

PRINCESS: It's terrible, I know.

NURSE [*voluble, familiar*]: Begging your pardon, marm, but do you think the Master's really dead?

PRINCESS [*surprised*]: I'm much afraid so!

NURSE: I don't, then!

PRINCESS [*arrested*]: Ah?

NURSE: I'm just suspicious. [*Wisely*] The service I've seen . . .

PRINCESS [*vaguely*]: Well, all the papers . . .

NURSE [*contemptuously*]: The papers!

PRINCESS: And the enquiries that were made . . .

NURSE: I shouldn't wonder, now, if he's not in America.

PRINCESS: In America?

NURSE: He and his friend.

PRINCESS: What makes you think that?

NURSE [*beaming*]: Gracious powers! [*Darkly*] I've seen what I've seen!

PRINCESS [*raising a drooping dahlia upon its stick*]: Life?

NURSE: It's not for nothing I've gone about as I have!

PRINCESS: And you've no wish at all to settle down?

NURSE: It's all one to me!

PRINCESS [*tentatively*]: I seek a porteress for a house of piety!

NURSE: That wouldn't suit me!

PRINCESS [*reassuring*]: It's an easy enough position.

NURSE: A porter's place in a Sisterhood? [*Dryly*] You call it settling down?

PRINCESS: Think it over!

NURSE: Let all have their latch-keys, and maybe I will.

SCENE VIII

Same. REGGIE [*hatless, from house*]

REGGIE: I want to hide.

PRINCESS: Hide?

REGGIE: I hadn't thought it possible [*breathlessly*] to meet so many wicked people at a Nursery Tea.

PRINCESS: Who have you run away from?

REGGIE: A withered lily woman.

PRINCESS: There are so many withered lily women [*vaguely*] ... here in Florence.

REGGIE [*saluting* CHARLES]: Please, might I hold him, Nurse?

NURSE: Certainly, sir!

REGGIE [*taking* CHARLES, *considering him*]: He's such a profound-looking baby!

PRINCESS [*dreamily*]: He has *an Ocean* of sleep upon him. . . .

NURSE: Oh, he's a little rascal.

REGGIE [*to* PRINCESS]: I'm told you called me disreputable the other night!

PRINCESS: I'm sure I hardly recollect whether I called you reputable or disreputable—I don't remember.

REGGIE: Unkind.

PRINCESS [*motherly*]: And how are our actual prospects?

REGGIE [*candid*]: If I'm a little disappointed at present I believe always in my own eventual star.

PRINCESS: That's right!

REGGIE: I'm hoping to be a Cardinal's secretary soon.

PRINCESS: *Are* you?

REGGIE: Nothing's quite decided—but I think I've got the job.

PRINCESS: You'll get awfully bored, shan't you, going to conversaziones in the religious world?

REGGIE [*resigned*]: *Forse!*

PRINCESS: Until you assume your duties, I presume you'll remain in Florence?

REGGIE [*returning infant to* NURSE, *who parades slowly with it up and down*]: Lord Orkish has asked me to make his house temporarily my home.

PRINCESS [*after an instant*]: Is *Lady* Orkish coming out this year?

REGGIE: She's been.

PRINCESS: Been?

REGGIE: She only broke her journey on her way from Rome.

PRINCESS [*looking down while she speaks*]: She didn't stay long.

REGGIE: Long enough!

PRINCESS: For Lord Orkish?

REGGIE [*with feeling*]: It made my flesh *creep* to see him in the white custody of a wife.

PRINCESS [*with brio*]: S-s-s-sh! For shame!

REGGIE: I admire the Old Bean! He wears his degradation brilliantly, as though it were *an Order!*

PRINCESS: He talked across me at dinner once and I've not forgiven him for it!

REGGIE: It's awful, I know, when he begins about 'The Cabal that rose up against me!'

PRINCESS: Oh, I'm terrified of him then!

REGGIE [*perceiving* LORD ORKISH]: And, it appears, here we have him.

[*Enter* LORD ORKISH.]

SCENE IX

Same. LORD ORKISH

LORD ORKISH: I've come as an emissary to say that tea is being served in the house.

PRINCESS: I don't want tea, thanks.

LORD ORKISH: Perhaps you'd care for an ice?

PRINCESS [*emphatic*]: No.

REGGIE: Why do you say 'No' in such a voice?

PRINCESS: Never mind.

LORD ORKISH: Lady Wilson-Philipson has just arrived with an octet of daughters like cabbage-roses—so large, so pink, so fresh.

[*Violins sound faintly from house.*]

REGGIE: It's going to be a crush!

PRINCESS: I think I'll go in, as Monsignor Vanhove may perhaps be in the drawing-room.

[*Exit* PRINCESS *to house.*]

SCENE X

LORD ORKISH, REGGIE

LORD ORKISH: I missed you in the Piazza.

REGGIE: Mr. Hope offered me a lift up in his carriage.

LORD ORKISH [*leering a little*]: I wish people would offer *me* lifts.

REGGIE [*amiable*]: I'd as soon have walked.

LORD ORKISH [*dropping into a seat*]: Seen anything at all of his Eminence?

REGGIE [*emotionally*]: Not half an hour ago—in furs, and a soft tulle hat like an Oxford mist.

LORD ORKISH: You didn't attack him?

REGGIE [*shocked*]: *Me?* How could I?

LORD ORKISH: His pretensions to youth are a little ridiculous.

REGGIE [*seating himself on the ground*]: The first time I went to the Villa—I shall never forget—I think the electric fan just kept me from fainting.

[*Enter* ANGELO, *with a salver and ices.*]

SCENE XI

Same. ANGELO

LORD ORKISH [*refusing ice*]: No, *grazie*.

REGGIE: There is something medieval to me in his appearance.

LORD ORKISH: Medieval?

REGGIE [*refusing ice*]: It's his livery.

ANGELO [*smiling*]: The signora will be sad you do not like her ice.

REGGIE: What are they?

ANGELO: This lemon, this pistaccio——

REGGIE: And this?

ANGELO [*languid*]: *Chi lo sa?*

REGGIE [*venturing*]: Shall I regret it?

LORD ORKISH [*to* ANGELO, *fixing him*]: Were you ever in Naples?

ANGELO [*languid*]: Yes; oh yes.

LORD ORKISH: I seem to have seen you.

ANGELO [*displaying his teeth, smiling*]: Via Tavolini!

LORD ORKISH: I dare say.

ANGELO: As a boy I vend flowers.

LORD ORKISH: Via Tavolini?

ANGELO: Now and then I would pose.

REGGIE: Pose?

ANGELO [*gazing indolently over his shoulder-knots*]: I'm a model.

LORD ORKISH [*ironic*]: And so at last I behold a model footman!

ANGELO [*sighing*]: *Ah, caro dio!*

LORD ORKISH: The perfect servant?

ANGELO [*smiling*]: *Per Bacco!*

REGGIE: You prefer this to Naples?

ANGELO: No.

REGGIE: Nicer Naples.

ANGELO: I want to go to America.

LORD ORKISH: Why do you want to go to America?

ANGELO: *Chi lo sa?*

LORD ORKISH: Young rapscallion!

ANGELO [*rolling his eyes*]: New York.

LORD ORKISH: What should you do in New York?

REGGIE: Yes. [*Rapping it out quickly*] And what were you doing under the Piazza della Signoria Colonnades the other night?

ANGELO: Piazza della Signoria?

REGGIE: In ambuscade.

ANGELO: *Niente.*

REGGIE [*sceptic*]: *Niente?*

ANGELO [*terrorised*]: Ah, Jesu!

[*Exit* ANGELO, *to house.*]

SCENE XII

LORD ORKISH, REGGIE

LORD ORKISH: It's a pity he's lost his master. Adrian would, of course, have trained him!

REGGIE: Where can he be—he and Eric?

LORD ORKISH: Nobody knows. Where the foxes say good-night to each other, I should think.

REGGIE: It must be a little *triste* for Mrs. Sheil-Meyer.

LORD ORKISH: She seems perfectly resigned.

[*Four or five small children emerge from house and scatter like butterflies behind the various bushes.*]

REGGIE: To-day she is receiving the felicitations of half Florence.

LORD ORKISH: *Davvero*. So many *he's and she's* I never saw!

[*Enter the* MARCHESA PITTI-CONTI, *peering about as if looking for someone.*]

SCENE XIII

Same. MARCHESA PITTI-CONTI

MARCHESA [*calling*]: Dante, Dan-te Silvio Paolao. [*To* LORD ORKISH *and* REGGIE, *whimsically*] He has left his mother, my little bundle of a boy. . . .

REGGIE: He can't be very far.

MARCHESA: A *bambino*, it seems, has captured his fancy. [*Peeping down among the dahlias*] He is flirting something outrageously with the sweetest blonde.

LORD ORKISH: Yes?

MARCHESA: It is impossible to resist your English children.

LORD ORKISH [*paternal, trying to look less like a wolf*]: Pretty, attractive tots——

MARCHESA [*gracious*]: We Italian women, you know, have an inclination . . . an *inclination particulier* . . . [*a sigh*] for the English type!

LORD ORKISH: Ah, the English type! But not the English climate?

MARCHESA [*pronouncing every syllable crisply, distinctly*]: Oh, come! It is not so bad as it is painted. . . . I have some charming recollections of your country . . . of England. [*Sentimentally*] Salisbury on a summer morning. . . . De-licious! [*Introspective*] I remember I was de-lighted—as well—with Bath. . . .

LORD ORKISH: One can hardly judge Great Britain from Salisbury and Bath.

REGGIE [*simpering*]: Or even Stonehenge!

MARCHESA: I don't. [*Proudly*] I have been much further than that. I have been in Oxford and in Cambridge. [*Beginning to gesticulate*] And into the Hebrides even—yes! I have seen the modern Athens! But no! [*With a grimace*] Also Abbotsford I was at. [*Ecstatic, cultured*] Sir Valter Scott! [*Recollecting herself*] But Salisbury on a summer morning—Salisbury!

[*She drifts away, peering for her son among the dahlias as* ENID *comes down.*]

Scene XIV

Same. ENID. *Later, a little boy; then* GLYDA

LORD ORKISH: The Marchesa is raving of the surpassing splendours of Salisbury.

REGGIE: Salisbury on a summer morning ...

ENID: I suppose she's homesick. You know she was *née* Smith, and born in the Close.

LORD ORKISH: I didn't.

REGGIE [*irrepressible*]: She is like a toy-terrier that bit me.

ENID: S-s-s-s-s-sh! Don't *say* such dreadful things.

REGGIE: Exactly.

ENID [*crossing to hammock and lifting up forgotten crystal, which she proceeds with hierarchic care to wipe*]: They have a gorgeous place ... near Verona ... The Pitti-Contis ... which is mortgaged to the last sod.

LORD ORKISH: What, gazing still?

REGGIE: There's a new man now in the town.

ENID: Oh? Really? You must give me his address.

REGGIE: He lives in the last house of a little mysterious street. You would never find the way.

LORD ORKISH: Have you seen anything yourself, Mrs. Tresilian?

ENID [*staring straight before her as though she were Cassandra*]: To-day I saw a beautiful little giraffe.

LORD ORKISH: Queer.

ENID: Or a goat it may have been.

REGGIE [*yawning*]: I had a morning dream—I saw goats.

ENID [*uninterested. Changing the subject*]: In autumn the garden is as melancholy as any churchyard.

LORD ORKISH: Oh, don't say so!

REGGIE: Now is the time for Vallombrosa.

ENID: The forest must be beautiful now....

[*Enter, from behind a tree, a* CHILD.]

CHILD: Mother! Where is she?

ENID: I don't know, dear.... I expect she's in the house.

[*Exit* CHILD.]

LORD ORKISH: Wasn't that Violet's boy?

ENID: Oh no ... he's four—and has the air of a budding policeman.

[*Enter* GLYDA, *très affairée in a 'Botticelli' frock.*]

GLYDA: Aren't you going in for any refreshment?

REGGIE: Thanks. I've already had an ice!

GLYDA [*to* ENID]: The new American actress 'Ondelette' has offered to recite.

REGGIE [*bored*]: Oh?

GLYDA [*important*]: *The Prayer of Akhnaton to the Sun.* . . .

LORD ORKISH: She gave it only lately at the Harkovs'.

REGGIE: And I heard her do it at the Villa White, [*mimicking*] 'Oh, Akhnaton! Akhnaton!'

ENID [*shrewdly*]: I think the sunlight has gone to her head.

REGGIE [*taking crystal from* ENID]: Let me see.

ENID: Be careful.

REGGIE [*consulting crystal*]: A nigger! [*Shouts.*]

LORD ORKISH [*leaning over him*]: Only *one*?

[LORD ORKISH *and* REGGIE *appear enthralled.*]

GLYDA: Mama has had to go to a private exhibition; but she's coming on.

ENID [*vague*]: Of what?

GLYDA [*seating herself*]: Of Pictures.

ENID: Oh.

GLYDA: *Portraits* . . . all by women. Carriera, Kauffman, Morisot, Le Brun——

ENID: *Fade*, I should think.

GLYDA [*arch*]: It's such fun, though, in Italy, being a woman!

ENID: Why?

GLYDA: I don't know—but it's such fun!!

ENID: Well, you're only a little girl yet.

GLYDA: You should see the way I'm looked at.

ENID: Where?

GLYDA: Where! Oh, in the street—in church. The other day, in the railway-carriage coming back from Milan——

ENID: Well?

GLYDA [*confused*]: A young officer—oh, how he stared. My goodness!

ENID: The Italians, I find, are very easily impressed.

GLYDA [*ideal*]: Love's a dose of heaven!

ENID: You modern girls are far too cute.

GLYDA [*after a hesitation*]: I cannot resist telling you . . . I've seen him again. . . .

ENID [*vague*]: Who?

GLYDA: The officer!

ENID: What is this craving after *orange-blossom*? . . . They would persuade us, it seems, a woman's chief aim is a march to the altar.

GLYDA: He's deliciously dark—a regular raven, my dear.

ENID: What next?

GLYDA [*longingly*]: Beautiful, Tall, and Mysterious Man!

ENID: Oh.

GLYDA [*tenderly*]: It was in the Cascine . . .

ENID: He didn't speak?

GLYDA [*moved*]: No . . . but as he came towards me it was like a *strain* of music.

[*Enter, from house,* NADINE, PRINCESS *and* MONSIGNOR VANHOVE.]

Scene XV

Same. NADINE, PRINCESS *and* MONSIGNOR VANHOVE. *He is dressed in something subtly chic; he looks a lover of delicatessen.*

MONSIGNOR [*to* NADINE]: Ah! Rome, Rome, in the days of Julia Farnese . . .

NADINE [*distrait*]: I suppose it must have been.

PRINCESS [*to* ENID]: Come here, dear, and be introduced. . . . I want you to know each other.

NADINE [*to* LORD ORKISH *and* REGGIE]: They're dancing the *farandole.* Quick and choose your partner.

LORD ORKISH [*objecting*]: My dancing days are over quite.

NADINE [*taking him and* REGGIE *up stage*]: I'll not believe it!

[*Exeunt* LORD ORKISH *and* REGGIE *to house.*]

[*Re-enter* NURSE *and infant, accompanied by a squadron of small children. She holds a story-book. Crossing to pillared circle, she seats herself sedately below the Virgin with the children grouped about her.* GLYDA *shortly joins them.*]

Scene XVI

ENID, PRINCESS, MONSIGNOR VANHOVE, *then* NADINE

PRINCESS: And so the Pope lends his authority?

MONSIGNOR [*twirling his thumbs*]: We have his prayers, his wishes.

PRINCESS: His prayers, his wishes!

ENID: What could you want more, dearest?

PRINCESS [*holding out her hand to her—the one with the muff*]: You dear girl—and Nadine!

ENID [*sublime*]: She would never leave her child.

MONSIGNOR [*significantly*]: Whosoever doth not bear his cross, and come after me, cannot be my disciple.

PRINCESS [*with feeling*]: My dear Monsignor.

MONSIGNOR: And isn't it so?

PRINCESS [*exalted, audacious*]: I never wanted a child, I think, till now.

ENID [*frivolous, laughing*]: Will you not be such a cynic?

PRINCESS: My dear, I mean it.

ENID [*in an undertone*]: Peculiar devotion . . .

PRINCESS: And what is going on down in Rome?

MONSIGNOR: Few functions . . .

PRINCESS: It's full early yet.

MONSIGNOR [*blinking*]: There was a ball the other evening at the Grand Hotel.

PRINCESS: Oh, whose?

MONSIGNOR: The Longfields'.

PRINCESS: I hear she, Lady Longfield, is working havoc amongst the Cardinals, with her copper hair, large moist eyes and liquid voice.

MONSIGNOR: And she also subscribes to everything.

PRINCESS: It makes one feel so jealous.

MONSIGNOR [*suave*]: You are not forgotten.

PRINCESS: No!

MONSIGNOR: Cardinal Ventifiore very often speaks of you.

PRINCESS: He took me round Trastevere once. It stands out vividly in my mind like *a first infidelity*.

MONSIGNOR: And Dom Jonquil too.

PRINCESS: I remember him, a great jaded-looking boy, almost as pale as the young man in St. Mark's who shows one the Pala d'Oro.

ENID [*deliberatingly*]: I suppose, Zena, a long grey tangle of a veil?

PRINCESS: Where?

ENID: I was thinking of our uniforms.

PRINCESS: All that, of course, is in my prospectus.

NADINE [*coming down*]: Monsignor Vanhove! *Is* it true they intend to build a new Embassy? The front *quite* windowless, the back *all* glass?

MONSIGNOR [*blinking*]: It's the first I've heard of it.

NURSE [*serenely reading*]: 'Then the wicked witch smeared her little limbs with ram's-grease and twisted her round three times! In a trice, the walls of the humble cottage fell away, and the palace appeared before them.'

PRINCESS: Who told you, Nadine, about the Embassy?

NADINE: Mr. Hope.

PRINCESS: What should 'Tozhy' know?

NADINE [*looking round*]: I'm so nervous of him. Since his exile here he has become a sort of public loofah.

NURSE [*continuing—on the crest of her tale*]: 'From that same minute the princess determined to follow the dictates of her heart, and refused to listen any longer to the worldly maxims of the King and Queen.'

MONSIGNOR: Ah, sweet innocents!

NADINE [*indicating a child*]: See that little gollywog there? . . . She's the Pontiff's niece.

ENID: Oh?

NADINE: The Pope is her uncle.

MONSIGNOR: She will become florid in time, like her mother.

PRINCESS [*glancing towards the tree-tops*]: Hark to the birds! How happy they must be. *Singing, singing, singing.* Nearer to heaven than *we* are!

[*Enter* BLANCHE NEGRESS.]

SCENE XVII

Same. BLANCHE. *She is wearing a tailor-made 'Redfern' and a man's cravat.*

BLANCHE: I've come to know if I may enrol myself?

PRINCESS: Eh?

BLANCHE: I happened to hear you're starting a Sisterhood—not *too* strait-laced—and I wish to offer myself as a probationer.

PRINCESS: Certainly; if you've any Vocation at all!

BLANCHE: My work is over in the world, you see. I have nothing to fight for now.

PRINCESS: Are you even giving up your pen?

BLANCHE [*confused*]: No . . . but hotels and lodgings *are* such noisy places.

PRINCESS [*doubtfully*]: I see . . .

BLANCHE [*rather wildly*]: Noise! Noise! Noise!

PRINCESS: But are there no quiet rooms, back rooms, in back hotels—and in back places?

BLANCHE [*tragically*]: I hate a silence that isn't *real*.

PRINCESS [*graciously*]: Well, in the cypress-alleys of our Anchorage I trust you will find inspiration.

[*Enter* LADY ROCKTOWER]

BLANCHE: I'm sure I shall; I feel it.

Scene XVIII

Same. LADY ROCKTOWER

LADY ROCKTOWER: I was obliged to go to the P.V. of the women-artists.

NADINE [*offering hand*]: I adore Private Views!

LADY ROCKTOWER: This was *so* dull.

PRINCESS: Everybody's here!

LADY ROCKTOWER: Some things are such an index. [*Intensely*] Violet is parting with her *Rosalba.* . . .

NADINE: I wonder why?

PRINCESS: She's become so mercenary. She seems to have now a sort of *hunger* for money.

ENID: Disgusting!

LADY ROCKTOWER: I fancy she gives it . . .

MONSIGNOR [*alert*]: Ah?

LADY ROCKTOWER [*in an undertone*]: To a dall, dark man in the Pope's bodyguard!

BLANCHE [*breathlessly*]: I suppose her lover?

MONSIGNOR: In my opinion, a woman may accept the consolations of Bacchus as soon as accept a lover.

PRINCESS: Do you really think she may?

ENID: Still every now and then one's face needs transforming. And Love does it better than anything else!

MONSIGNOR: It depends, my child, upon the *sort*.

PRINCESS: I suppose when one's husband is fifty-seven . . .

LADY ROCKTOWER: My dear, even a man of fifty-seven is better than nothing at all.

BLANCHE: I don't agree.

LADY ROCKTOWER: No?

BLANCHE: I've been married, you know, too. Yet I sometimes think the simple comfort of a hot-water bottle . . .

PRINCESS [*laughing*]: Well, I'm going to speak to the Wilson-Philipsons! I see Vicky over there.

[*A few persons emerge from house as if to enjoy the scene, which begins to take on the aspect of sunset.*]

BLANCHE: I mean to be off-hand with her. She translates every one into terms of colour, and I hear she called me a dirty white.

NADINE: She's *guapa*, as they say in Spain!

LADY ROCKTOWER: Poor things, they live, no one quite knows how.

ENID: I passed them all the other evening in a covered bullock-cart in the Viale dei Colli.

NADINE: Oh?

ENID: I just *moaned* for joy! The big tears rolling!

[*Re-enter* MARCHESA PITTI-CONTI *with her son* DANTE. *He is sobbing. He has evidently been misbehaving himself. The* MARCHESA *seems furious—her English is perfect.*]

SCENE XIX

Same. Plus MARCHESA *and* DANTE SILVIO PAOLAO

DANTE [*sobbing*]: Boo-oo-oo! Ow-ow-ow!

MARCHESA: Did not your father give you the choice, wicked little boy [*pinching him*], of Oxford, Cambridge, Salamanca, Utrecht, Harvard, Glasgow, Edinburgh or Heidelberg?

DANTE: Boo-oo-oo!

LADY ROCKTOWER [*turning*]: Are you thinking of sending him to school?

MARCHESA: Ah, *chère madame* . . . !

LADY ROCKTOWER: *Il est gentil ce grand gosse.* [*To* ENID.] *Je trouve qu'il est en train de devenir charmant.*

ENID: *N'est ce pas?*

MARCHESA [*to* BLANCHE]: *Bonjour, chère amie.*

BLANCHE [*all there*]: *Come va?*

MARCHESA: *Bene, grazie ; e lei ?*

BLANCHE [*all there still*]: *Benissimo!* . . .

LADY ROCKTOWER: To what school—*a che scuola*—shall you send him?

MARCHESA [*very foreign*]: I do not know.

LADY ROCKTOWER: School, in my time, was not the soft place it is to-day.

MARCHESA: No?

LADY ROCKTOWER: As a young girl I used to be whipped with furze.

MARCHESA [*appalled*]: Ah, *chère madame* . . .

LADY ROCKTOWER [*cheerfully, rearranging the back of her dress*]: I was all gorse-marks often!

[*Re-enter* LORD ORKISH]

The Princess Zoubaroff

SCENE XX
Same. Plus LORD ORKISH

LORD ORKISH: Young Astix is in the loggia.

NADINE: Is he?

LORD ORKISH: People are making such a fuss.

NADINE: Absurd. His slender volume of verses, you could pass it under the door. . . .

LORD ORKISH [*with indifference*]: I dare say.

NADINE: Why aren't you dancing?

LORD ORKISH: I'm too old.

NADINE: Or too lazy, which?

MONSIGNOR: At the fall, Florence tends to make one sluggish.

LADY ROCKTOWER: Yes; the autumn here is certainly enervating Only this very morning, I said to Dr. Mater, in the Boboli Gardens: 'I have that *tired* feeling, Doctor, again,' I said: 'and I can't think what it can be.' 'Oh, Lady Rocktower,' he said to me, with his piercing glance, 'I assure you it's nothing but the change of season.'

MONSIGNOR: Exactly.

LADY ROCKTOWER: I'll be glad, though, I confess, for Lord Rocktower's sake, when winter sets in.

LORD ORKISH: And how is my old pal Harry?

LADY ROCKTOWER: We all thought him passing out a day or two ago. Doctor Mater told me—but oh, so sweetly, oh, so gently—he could do nothing more, when suddenly he sat up and asked for lobster soup. Lobster soup! There was none in the house, but within an hour the soup was made—and he was saved!

LORD ORKISH: Bravo!

LADY ROCKTOWER: Every time I let the Villa he seems to quite give way. [*With a sigh of resignation*] Lord Rocktower loves Florence and he loathes leaving it. . . .

LORD ORKISH: I don't wonder.

MARCHESA [*to* DANTE, *who is making grimaces at the Pope's niece*]: *Ma che, ma che!*

ENID [*to* DANTE]: Come, and I will gather you a few dahlias.

[*She takes* MARCHESA *and* DANTE *up stage towards a flower-plat, while* NADINE *and* MONSIGNOR *cross to pillared circle where* NURSE *is seated.* BLANCHE *during progress of scene has joined the little group which is watching sunset.*]

LORD ORKISH: I suppose, if Mrs. Sheil-Meyer withdraws from Society, the *next* villa to let will be this!

LADY ROCKTOWER: I've no patience at all with her if she does.

LORD ORKISH: The Princess Zoubaroff can be very persuasive.

LADY ROCKTOWER [*with vigour*]: It's all very fine for Zena, who is no longer in her springtime, to retire. Six husbands must have left her with the minimum of a heart! But for a young and pretty woman like Nadine Sheil-Meyer to give up the world, it's another matter.

LORD ORKISH: Mrs. Tresilian is sure to follow suit!

LADY ROCKTOWER: *Que de sottises!*

LORD ORKISH: From sympathy.

LADY ROCKTOWER: She trifles—she truffles—but I can't think she will.

LORD ORKISH [*sententious*]: The Princess is one of those who, when they cast their spell——

LADY ROCKTOWER: I always stick up for Zena Zoubaroff. I don't believe *half* I hear about her! Although I dare say a *good deal* is true!

[*They both laugh.*]

LORD ORKISH: It's a pity their husbands can't appear just to bring them to their bearing.

[*The* Farandole *is heard.*]

LADY ROCKTOWER: Oh, they're coming out!

SCENE XXI
General

Children, hand in hand, emerge from house. Making a ring, they proceed to dance about the garden Temple.

LORD ORKISH: Youth, youth.

PRINCESS [*approaching*]: I feel I want to dance!

LADY ROCKTOWER: My dear Zena!

PRINCESS: I've had Austrian waltzes whirling through my head all day.

[REGGIE *is seen in the background pirouetting with* MR. ASTIX, *the author— a wild young man who looks like the Publisher's Ruin.*]

LADY ROCKTOWER: Oh . . . look at Reggie.

LORD ORKISH [*moved*]: Dear, dear boy.

MONSIGNOR [*coming forward, benign*]: Everywhere delicious innocence!

PRINCESS [*boxing,* con amore, *with her muff each little girl upon the ears as she goes by*]: Nun! Nun! Nun!

THE CURTAIN FALLS

~~~ ACT III ~~~

SCENE I

*Same scene. A few of the trees have shed their leaves. It is winter. Through
the bare branches of the Judas-trees a calvary is visible at the extremity
of the garden.*

As the curtain rises, NURSE *is seen strolling to and fro, exercising baby
in his pram.*

ANGELO *follows at her heels, singing strenuously to the guitar.*

NURSE *and* INFANT, ANGELO

NURSE: You young Italians are all passion.

ANGELO [*rhapsodically, carolling*]: Tra-li-lal-la!

NURSE: Not so loud, you'll wake the child.

[*She takes from the pram a flask of Lachryma Christi and drinks.*]

ANGELO: *Sapristi!*

NURSE: My favourite vintage! Plenty of body ...

ANGELO: *Ah, che roba!*

NURSE: Yes, you Italians are dangerous fellows.... [*Sentimentally*]
You make me think of Dudley, Lord Bellforest's under-butler,
long ago. [*Drinks.*] Ah, I've been a buxom woman in my day, dear.
... A little bit of proper *simpatico* I was! And I'm good enough
yet, honey.... Some constitutions are just like this [*drinking*],
they improve with time. [*Falling into reflection*] She was forty-nine
years old when she had me—my dear mother. And then there were
two after that.

ANGELO [*shrugging*]: *Che volete?*

NURSE [*cogent*]: Which is more than most of them could say (or
do), your Tuscan Signoras!

ANGELO [*indignant*]: I am not Tuscan myself at all. [*Strumming
his guitar*] My home is in the South. Ah *bella* Taormina!

NURSE [*sentimentally*]: Well, it's all South to me, dear.

ANGELO [*shrugging*]: *Per Bacco.*

NURSE: This is South all right for me [*returning flask to pram*].

ANGELO [*yawning*]: How dull it is—*ah, dio.*

NURSE: It's queer enough, it's true, now the mistress has gone.

ANGELO: *Povera!*

NURSE: I like a place, I must say, where there's a bit of life. When
I was with the Honourable Mrs. Cortez, there was company if you

like! Valets, chauffeurs, Parisian maids ... gracious powers, you could take your choice. It was in her establishment [*sighs*] I met my Albert.

ANGELO: Albert?

NURSE: Mr. Mangrove—my *sposo*!

> [*She sighs several times heavily.*]

ANGELO [*with morbid interest*]: And was he *tutto* ... *tutto* ... ?

NURSE [*nodding*]: *Tutto, tutto!* That is to say, my dear, I never could bear him but in the one capacity. ... For he never had any mind, or any understanding. ... What was he [*snaps her fingers*] but that! !

ANGELO: Ah!

NURSE [*archly winking*]: But in the one capacity of love he was unexcelled.

> [*Baby begins to require attention.*]
> [*Enter* REGGIE *from roadway.*]

Scene II

Same. REGGIE

REGGIE [*dapper, smiling*]: I blew in only to say good-morning to little Charles.

NURSE: That's very kind of you, sir. [*Raising baby*] Sit up and say good-morning to Mr. Quintus!

REGGIE: He's a fine child, Nurse.

NURSE: He's a little beauty, sir, as I'm his sainted nanny! [*Confidential*] They won't have him inside the convent, heaven protect us, for fear he'd flurry the nuns!

REGGIE: Will you kiss me, Charles?

NURSE: Kiss the gentleman. ...

REGGIE: That's right.

NURSE: See how he's laughing.

REGGIE: The rogue! I fear he's a rogue, Nurse.

NURSE: He's a fine fellow.

REGGIE: No morals ! ! ! He has no morals, I fear. ...

NURSE: Oh! Why, sir, why now?

REGGIE: Born in Florence, a boy rarely has.

NURSE: Don't be hard on Florence, Mr. Quintus, it's not near so fast, I'm sure, as San Francisco.

REGGIE: I wonder?

ANGELO [*wistfully*]: Ah, America . . .

REGGIE: Still keen as ever on visiting the States?

ANGELO [*with all the languor of 'the South'*]: Yes; oh yes.

REGGIE [*twinkling mysteriously*]: Before you go, I must give you a letter of introduction to a multi-millionaire—who's rather a friend of mine!—in Memphis, Tennessee.

ANGELO [*delighted*]: *Tante grazie!*

REGGIE: *Niente.*

[*The bell tinkles. Murmuring his gratitude,* ANGELO *answers the garden-gate, after which he exits to house.*]

[*Enter, from roadway,* BLANCHE.]

SCENE III

Same. BLANCHE. *She looks hot and dishevelled. She bears a sack. She is dressed as a Nun. She gives one the impression rather of an escaped peacock.*

BLANCHE [*dropping her sack*]: They sent me to wait here, with the victuals. [*Groaning*] Out at Monte Serravizza there isn't a thing.

REGGIE: What? Are they coming up to the Villa to-day?

BLANCHE: Yes.

[NURSE, *on hearing this intelligence, briefly withdraws.*]

REGGIE: The whole cortège?

BLANCHE [*seating herself, mopping her brow*]: We came into Florence —shopping, or begging—God knows which . . .

REGGIE [*amused*]: A bit of both, I expect.

BLANCHE: My wretched nerves: has Baccio Bertucci been?

REGGIE: Baccio Bertucci?

BLANCHE: He promised.

REGGIE [*mystified*]: What?

BLANCHE [*occult*]: It can't be helped. I suppose we must go without.

REGGIE: Your Abbess, I'm told, is quite scoring as a Saint.

BLANCHE [*irritated*]: Tsch! Who said so?

REGGIE: The Rocktowers.

BLANCHE [*intensely*]: Life at Monte Serravizza is quite indescribable.

REGGIE: It must be wonderful.

BLANCHE: It's nothing but backbiting from morning to night.

REGGIE: Oh!

BLANCHE: The violence of religious jealousy, I know of nothing at all that can match it.

REGGIE: Violence?

BLANCHE: Zena's becoming much too tyrannical.

REGGIE [*perching himself on a garden-chair*]: Remember, these small sub-lunar trials will one day pass!

BLANCHE: I hope so, I'm sure.

REGGIE: Poor Mrs. Negress.

BLANCHE: To-day—as we were coming into Florence—I arranged my side hair [*simpering*] experimentally, and she was *furious*. What are you doing with *those whiskers*? she said to me. I won't have any whiskers here, arousing our thoughts. . . .

REGGIE: Oh. . . .

BLANCHE: While her head was scrubbed but yesterday with henna.

REGGIE: She was shampooed you say with henna!

BLANCHE [*stalking up and down, swaying her skirts from side to side like a Spanish dancer*]: And only the day before she ordered herself a crystal cincture from Paris.

REGGIE [*tossing his hat*]: Olé, Olé.

BLANCHE: Thoughts indeed!

REGGIE [*admiringly*]: Nobody can do outrageous things so naturally as she can!

BLANCHE: I admit she's clever. She hushed up the affair of May Winterbottom most successfully.

REGGIE [*awed*]: There's been a scandal?

BLANCHE: A scandal! ! The very night the first new novice arrived——

REGGIE: Well?

BLANCHE: Zena smelt smoke. Heavy smoke. All the corridors full of it, coming from the Sister's cell. She went to her door and oh the horror.

REGGIE [*breathless*]: What?

BLANCHE: May Winterbottom was smoking opium.

REGGIE: Pouf!

BLANCHE: Yes.

REGGIE [*rising carelessly*]: If the Princess should want a Pinturicchio for her chapel, by the way, I know where there's one to be found.

BLANCHE: Indeed.

REGGIE: A '*Iokanaan.*'

BLANCHE: Oh!

REGGIE: Or, I know of a topping Tintoret.

BLANCHE: Thanks ... but I fancy she's on the scent of a *Sainte Famille* herself.

REGGIE: I'd give a good deal for a permit of inspection!

BLANCHE [*abysmal*]: There's no bathroom yet in the convent ... you just get caught in the rain. ...

REGGIE: Disgusting!

BLANCHE [*with a battered smile*]: One of the few drawbacks.

REGGIE [*looking at his watch*]: Well, I must go. I have to meet Lord Orkish in the town.

[*Exit* REGGIE *through garden-gate. Re-enter, at same moment,* NURSE *from house.*]

NURSE: Perhaps you'd prefer, m'm, to rest inside?

BLANCHE: I'm quite happy here.

NURSE: You don't look so, m'm.

BLANCHE: No?

NURSE [*brightly*]: The Religious Life, it's not for everybody!

BLANCHE: No.

NURSE [*confidential*]: She tried to coax me into it. ... But I didn't feel the call.

BLANCHE: My work was over in the world, you see. I had nothing to fight for. [*To* ENID, *who enters*] I thought you were *never* coming.

SCENE IV

Enter from roadway ENID, *followed by* NADINE *and* PRINCESS. NADINE *runs to baby's pram.* PRINCESS [*she holds a tortoise-shell cat, like an unhappy 'Society' woman, in her arms*] *hovers a moment speaking to someone outside the gate. They look very pale, slim and Isis-like in their grain-coloured Nuns' toilettes.*

ENID [*coming down*]: Sorry to be late, old girl.

BLANCHE [*mortified*]: Old girl ...

ENID: We've been getting ribbons from Monte—such a subtle old-flowered-velvet, and yards and yards and *yards* of green Georgette ...

BLANCHE [*aggrieved, staring at her sack*]: What for?

ENID [*airily*]: Decoration.

PRINCESS [*in great good-humour*]: To-day, as a special treat, we're going back by auto!

BLANCHE: Hallelujah!

PRINCESS: Did you do all my little commissions?

BLANCHE: All except the candles.

PRINCESS: Tiresome.

ENID: You look hot.

BLANCHE: My face must be a looking-glass.

PRINCESS: Not that.

BLANCHE: Had that dreadful sack weighed much more I think I should have fainted.

PRINCESS [*a little guilty, excusing herself*]: My dear, I'm desolate you should have had to carry it at all about the streets, but what *could* I do?

BLANCHE [*containing herself*]: Reggie Quintus has just gone.

PRINCESS: Really? And I had wanted to see him.

BLANCHE: He was telling me of a Tintoret, or something.

ENID [*nodding*]: He's rather a judge.

NADINE [*leaning over pram, sorrowfully, to her son*]: My poor pigeon ... I warn you to expect nothing very much from life.

PRINCESS: What makes her so oppressed?

ENID: She's chagrined a little because I said her habit made her look hunched.

BLANCHE [*critically*]: Distorted. And so it does!

ENID: And she was dreaming again of Adrian.

PRINCESS: Once I get a decent cook she'll not have these nightmares.

[BLANCHE *draws away a little, joining* NADINE.]

ENID: I'm so glad I'm not haunted with Eric!

PRINCESS [*angelic, virtuous*]: May white dreams attend you always, dear. Amen.

ENID [*earnestly*]: Amen.

PRINCESS [*catching marvellously her breath, as if her spirit, freed, had shot from earth to heaven, and from heaven back again to earth*]: Ah!

ENID: Blanche seems nervy to-day.

PRINCESS [*fluttered, breathless yet*]: Yes; unstrung. . . .

ENID: She says she feels 'jumpy.'

PRINCESS [*with sudden brusqueness*]: Can you wonder her nerves are what they are when she's sipping alternate coffee and tea from seven in the morning to twelve at night?

[*Enter from house,* LADY ROCKTOWER.]

The Princess Zoubaroff

Scene V

Same. LADY ROCKTOWER. *She looks slightly embarrassed: her face is a trifle red. She is wearing the family pearls. She has a hole in her veil.*

LADY ROCKTOWER: I saw you go by and guessed you'd be here.
[ENID *retreats.*]

PRINCESS [*kissing her à la Sainte Thérèse*]: My dear Lady Rocktower?

LADY ROCKTOWER [*clutching her pearls*]: I've come only to know if, dear—by *any* chance—you could take my daughter in.

PRINCESS [*stiffening*]: Take her in?

LADY ROCKTOWER: Receive her.

PRINCESS: As a novice?

LADY ROCKTOWER: For a time.

PRINCESS [*uncomfortable, suspicious*]: I fear she'd not be happy at Monte Serravizza; I fear our austerities—our Rule—everything!

LADY ROCKTOWER [*candid, frank*]: Glyda's so difficult and so giddy, and it's precisely for that.

PRINCESS [*ethereal, exquisite*]: I was once heedless too!

LADY ROCKTOWER: I would like to marry my daughter straight from your Convent door.

PRINCESS [*still evasive*]: Marry her?

LADY ROCKTOWER [*with much dignity*]: Well—*un grand mariage!*

PRINCESS [*reassured a little*]: But . . . could one manage her?

LADY ROCKTOWER: I am sure you could. And oh [*her voice breaks*] I should be so grateful.

PRINCESS: From what you say, I gather she's given her heart to someone.

LADY ROCKTOWER [*making a clean breast of it*]: Poor child, she thinks herself in love with a young Italian lieutenant . . . though I thank God on my knees, dear Zena, she has scarcely caught a glimpse of his shadow . . . !

PRINCESS: You're certain of that?

LADY ROCKTOWER: Positive.

PRINCESS: I'll come over one morning and have a quiet chat with Glyda—she and I, quite cosy! [*Laughing a little*] Although, really, I'm most awfully busy at present with my liqueur.

LADY ROCKTOWER: What liqueur?

PRINCESS: I'm inventing a delightfully potent liqueur to be made by the Nuns. The Holy Father [*rippling*] was quite charmed with the

757

few distilled drops I sent. He pretends . . . he pretends it will inspire him for Life!

LADY ROCKTOWER: Yes?

PRINCESS: We mean to call it yellow-ruin. . . .

LADY ROCKTOWER: I had an audience—my fifth!—only the other day.

PRINCESS: My dear, you're always trotting to Rome!

LADY ROCKTOWER: I adore it in winter.

PRINCESS: Is there lots and lots going on?

LADY ROCKTOWER: The usual thing; there's been a function at the Quirinal which was dull, and another at the Embassy which was worse . . . and *apropos* of recent Diplomacy, Lady Winifred Wheeler has just presented Sir Walter Wheeler with a black child. Such a commotion as there's been over it all.

PRINCESS [*horror-struck*]: Black?

LADY ROCKTOWER: Well, dear, dark; but, *oh,* so dark!

PRINCESS [*laughing*]: And the du Wilsons are just starting a Nursery, too.

LADY ROCKTOWER: Poor little Violet . . . ! She made me such a wan, sensitive smile in the street just now.

PRINCESS: She seems to think she should be asked to paint herself for the Uffizi. [*Hilarious*] Really, I never saw such cheeks!

LADY ROCKTOWER: No, nor I. [*Laughing, going*] Look in Thursday at the Villa, if you're able. [*Persuasively*] Sonino is singing . . .

PRINCESS: Sonino? Oh, when Sonino sings one visualises everything one wishes!

LADY ROCKTOWER: She is to throw in her sob of love, and sing three solos, for a special charge.

PRINCESS: It's hard indeed to refuse, but we *never* go out at night. . . .

LADY ROCKTOWER: This once! Oh, and I nearly forgot, I wanted to ask you for that choice receipt. Cocks' combs . . . ?

PRINCESS: And the hearts of artichokes!

LADY ROCKTOWER [*smiling, committing it to memory*]: *And the hearts of artichokes!*

PRINCESS [*impressively*]: Crush well.

LADY ROCKTOWER: A more delicious dish . . . you must give it me when I come to you—the days I visit Glyda.

PRINCESS [*leaning on* LADY ROCKTOWER'S *arm, and accompanying her towards the gate*]: I'm allowing the novices on feast days to receive their friends in a charming cognac chiffon.

LADY ROCKTOWER: You all look so interesting, as it is!

PRINCESS [*very much pleased*]: Do we?

LADY ROCKTOWER: I almost envy you. . . .

PRINCESS: Dear Lady Rocktower, perhaps some day——

LADY ROCKTOWER [*as she goes out*]: Who knows? A husband's often a strain, and mine's not a world-loving nature very.

SCENE VI

Same. Minus LADY ROCKTOWER

NADINE [*advancing—during* LADY ROCKTOWER'S *visit she has withdrawn from view behind a tree*]: And how has he kept, Nurse, all the week?

NURSE: Well as could be, thank you, marm.

NADINE: Poor spirit—!

NURSE: Oh, he's a little rascal!

NADINE: His little laugh does one good.

ENID [*quizzingly*]: He's a remarkably hideous child. Like a remarkably hideous duck . . .

PRINCESS [*abbessish*]: Prioress! Prioress!

ENID [*dancing mischievously about the pram*]: Who ever had such a wobbly chin? Or such a nervous, uncertain nose?

NADINE: He's like his father!

ENID: Ugly . . . ugly . . . like papa.

NURSE [*crooningly*]: *Where's Daddy ? ? ?*

[*Enter, from garden-gate,* ADRIAN *and* ERIC. *They both are looking wonderfully recouped and rejuvenated—as though their extensive holiday had done them good. Which has benefited from his freedom most—which looks the handsomer—it is not easy to determine.*]

NADINE: When he starts pummelling the air with his little pinkie-winkie fists, with his little dimpled doigts, what ever can it be? I know he wants something. . . .

ADRIAN: Probably *his Father*!

[*Slow music: A short Intermezzo (of a particularly 'cloying' nature), coming from the Orchestra, concludes the scene.*]

SCENE VII

Same. ADRIAN, ERIC

NADINE [*the Intermezzo ended, very calmly through the hood of the pram*]: Oh, Adrian, so you have come back!

ADRIAN: As you see.

ENID [*to* ERIC]: You might have given us a sign.

ERIC [*shortly*]: 'Drian's been ill—we were unwilling to alarm you.

ENID [*with biting satire*]: Alarm us!

ADRIAN: Do you remember how scared you were in Egypt once?

NADINE: I can't say I do.

ADRIAN: There's no use to cut up rough.

NADINE [*trenchantly*]: You're unwanted.

ENID: Quite unwanted!

PRINCESS [*interposing*]: Your wives are Dedicated!

ADRIAN: I beg your pardon?

ENID [*to* NADINE]: Don't they jar.

ERIC [*catching her by the veil*]: Lor' lummie, what's this?

ENID [*furious*]: Don't touch me!

ERIC [*assertive*]: That's as *I* choose.

ENID [*freeing herself*]: Oh, the horrid man—he hit me.

PRINCESS: He *hit* you?

BLANCHE [*wailing*]: Sacrilege!

ENID [*smacking* ERIC *smartly with her rosary*]: Ah! Monster!

NURSE [*panting*]: Well, I never.

[ANGELO *appears.*]

NADINE [*crucified*]: S-s-s-sh! Avoid a *scena* before the servants.

ERIC: Aie. . . .

BLANCHE [*hysterically*]: Oh! This is awful.

ANGELO [*announcing*]: The auto . . .

ENID [*quietly, threatening him with her scourge*]: Oh, Eric . . . don't exasperate me more!

NADINE [*with the upturned glance of a martyr*]: I refuse to wrangle.

PRINCESS [*inviolate, evoking calvary*]: Come!

ENID [*doing a little picturesque skirmishing*]: Beast!

ERIC: The bitch bit me.

BLANCHE [*picking up her sack and making for the gate*]: My knees refuse to carry me.

NADINE: Yes. Let's go.

ADRIAN [*indifferent*]: As you please!

NURSE [*to* NADINE]: *I wish to give warning!*

NADINE [*callous*]: Very well.

PRINCESS [*to* NADINE *and* ENID]: Come, chicks!

NADINE [*in her vividest voice*]: Mind the *step*, Zena.

PRINCESS [*turning defiantly at gate*]: The Vatican shall hear of this!
[*Exeunt* PRINCESS, NADINE *and* ENID.]

SCENE VIII

ADRIAN, ERIC

ADRIAN [*dropping into a chair*]: I thought perhaps we should find they'd remarried or something, but I'll be cursed if I thought they'd console themselves as they have!

ERIC [*at pram*]: The boy must be yours?

ADRIAN [*blushing, confused*]: I *suppose* I'm his father . . .

ERIC: What on earth are you going to do with the little beggar?

ADRIAN: I shall look out for a school for him to-morrow.

ERIC: No really, Adrian?

ADRIAN [*loftily*]: I shall set at once about his education.

ERIC [*bending over pram*]: Isn't he just too fat for anything!
[*The outside bell is heard to ring.*]

ADRIAN: What's that?

ERIC [*uneasily*]: My God, if they should have returned. . . .
[*Re-enter* ANGELO. *He saunters languidly over to garden-door.*]
[*Voice of* LORD ORKISH, *off*]: I must have missed Mr. Quintus: and I know he comes here most days to play with the child.
[*Voice of* ANGELO, *off*]: The Master has come home!

LORD ORKISH [*entering*]: What?

SCENE IX

Same. LORD ORKISH

ADRIAN [*surprised*]: Henry . . . !

LORD ORKISH [*considerably moved, proffering his hand*]: My dear, dear fellow.

ERIC: Henry?
[*Under the peculiar circumstances, they very nearly all embrace.*]

LORD ORKISH [*wonder-struck*]: And how amazingly fit you look: you seem to have grown much younger.

ERIC [*smiling*]: We've had a top-hole time! 'Drian was seedy, though, at first.

ADRIAN: Nothing at all to speak of!

ERIC: I *refused* to let him die.

ADRIAN [*nodding*]: Eric soon nursed me round!

LORD ORKISH: And your estimable wives—you've heard of them, of course.

ADRIAN: Yes, and seen them too—what's more!

ERIC [*hilarious*]: They must have passed you. They went off in a taxi, a snug half-dozen.

LORD ORKISH: What? They've gone? They've left you? . . .

ADRIAN: Apparently.

ERIC: It's all I can do to believe it.

LORD ORKISH [*with feeling*]: Lucky chaps.

ERIC: Delicious to be so dispossessed . . .

LORD ORKISH [*leering a little*]: Well, they're not the first to come to Florence to turn themselves into prudes!

ADRIAN [*pointedly*]: As *you* very well know, dear Harry.

LORD ORKISH: I take it you'll live apart, as we do—Lady Orkish and I—by 'mutual consent.'

ERIC: Yes. 'Mutual consent.'

LORD ORKISH: No odious fuss.

ERIC: I hope not.

LORD ORKISH: I assure you, after the first day I never missed Bella.

ERIC [*stretching luxuriously his arms*]: To be free, to be single! ! !

ADRIAN [*addressing rapturously the garden*]: Dear lawn. My own beautiful trees.

LORD ORKISH: He's enchanted to be home. [*Sighing.*] Well, there's no spot on earth to compare with Florence!

[*The outside bell is heard to ring again.* ANGELO *answers it as before. Enter a tiny boy in buttons. He has with him a faggot of huge Church candles.*]

Scene X

Same. ANGELO, BOY

ANGELO [*having ascertained the boy's business. To* ADRIAN]: He comes from the Church-furnishers in Borgo Santi Apostoli.

ADRIAN: From where?

ANGELO: From Baccio Bertucci's. . . .

ADRIAN [*sharply, to boy*]: Be off with you.

ANGELO: He say the Signora order the candles!

ADRIAN: Tell him to hook it.

ANGELO [*clapping his hands*]: A Monte Serravizza—*la giù.*

ERIC [*pointing, in desperation*]: *Laggiù, laggiù.*

ANGELO: *Via, via.*

LORD ORKISH [*patting the child's head*]: Run away, there's a good little sinner.

[*Exit boy, followed by* ANGELO.]

SCENE XI

LORD ORKISH, ERIC, ADRIAN, INFANT, *then* ANGELO

ADRIAN: The Eleusinian priestesses weren't in it!

LORD ORKISH: Have you formed yet any plans?

ADRIAN: I shall stop here. It will amuse me infinitely to see what they'll do!

LORD ORKISH [*flippantly*]: I shouldn't wonder much if they weren't back in Lewis hats and diamonds before to-night.

ERIC [*terrified at the idea*]: Oh don't . . . if Enid puts in an appearance again I shall take the first express to Rome.

ADRIAN: You're safe enough, Eric; *Enid has no ties.*

ERIC: No ties?

ADRIAN [*with a touch of conceit*]: She isn't a mother!

LORD ORKISH: It must take an exceptionally 'good' woman to forsake husband, son, friends, society, to follow the Way of the Cross.

ADRIAN: It's quite on the cards that Nadine was only bored. Besides, she hasn't deserted her *friends* at all. I believe but for Princess Zoubaroff she'd be here now.

ERIC: The Princess seems to have fairly bewitched them!

LORD ORKISH [*humming pensively to himself*]: With a hey-ho-hey, and a nonny.

ADRIAN: You're right.

LORD ORKISH: I wish she'd rake in Bella.

ADRIAN: Perhaps she will.

LORD ORKISH: And the old white cat . . .

ADRIAN: What old white cat?

LORD ORKISH: The Countess Willie!

[*The baby begins to fidget.*]

ADRIAN [*wheeling the pram about*]: S-s-sh . . . maddening.

LORD ORKISH: I'd like to know what you'll do with him.

ADRIAN: To-morrow he goes to school.

LORD ORKISH: Does he? By George! Well, I always believe in a boy getting used to the world as soon as possible.

ADRIAN: To be duly prepared.

LORD ORKISH: I know of an incomparable little *Lycée* here in Florence. . . . [*Sighing blissfully*] Incomparable instructors: incomparable boys. Incomparable, incomparable. Everything incomparable.

ADRIAN [*rather doubtfully*]: I dare say.

LORD ORKISH: Just the thing.

ERIC: Whereabouts is it, Harry?

LORD ORKISH: Via Canta; a vermilion-gold brick Palace in the very heart of the town!

ADRIAN [*bending over pram with smiling raillery*]: We're probably very backward . . . we probably know nothing at all?

[*The baby howls. Re-enter* ANGELO.]

ANGELO: *E pronto il pranzo!*

ADRIAN [*lightly*]: You'll stay, *pranz*, Harry?

LORD ORKISH: Thanks.

ADRIAN [*menacingly to baby*]: Stop it!

ERIC: And you shall play us each at pills after, what?

ADRIAN: I hope the nuns haven't injured the cloth!

[*The bell rings violently.*]

ERIC [*paralysed*]: Oh, my God . . . if it should be . . .

[*The garden-gate opens slightly—a handful of leaflets fall inside.*]

LORD ORKISH: *Confetti?*

ADRIAN [*relieved*]: It's only a circular.

ERIC: I thought it was Enid.

LORD ORKISH [*optimistically*]: I wouldn't worry. So long as the Princess chooses, she'll not leave the Sisterhood, I'll be bound.

ERIC: I sincerely hope you're right.

LORD ORKISH [*chuckling to himself*]: And she'll guard her close, believe me!

ERIC [*to* ANGELO, *who has picked a leaflet up*]: What's it all about?

ANGELO [*thrilling with exaltation, as though what he read was for him an article of faith*]: Oggi: Cinema Reale: grande representazione! . . . Sappho—Gli Amanti di Mytelene.

ADRIAN [*with a gesture of impatience*]: Oh, throw it away.

ANGELO [*perusing still, his whole face alight*]: La Bella Courtezan .. La Pompadour ... Una Assassina d'Amore ... La Vita di Londra ...

ADRIAN [*with the pram moving towards the house, followed by* ERIC *and* LORD ORKISH]: By the by, I don't even know my child's name!

ERIC: He gives me the impression rather of *an Hermione* ...

ADRIAN: Hermione? Nonsense, Eric. He has an air of Claud. Or Gervase even.

ERIC: Gervase?

ADRIAN [*to baby*]: Hello, Gervase!

LORD ORKISH [*prosaically*]: His name's Charles.

ADRIAN [*disappointed*]: Charles!

LORD ORKISH: Charles Augustus Frederic Humphrey Percy Sydney.

ADRIAN: I intend calling my son *Gervase*.

ERIC: Why not Gerry?

ADRIAN: No; Gervase.

ERIC: Gerry!

[*Exeunt, Gerrying and Gervaseing one another to house.*]

ANGELO [*still perusing the leaflet, dawdling, in tones of sheerest ecstasy and joy*]: La Pompadour ... La Vita-Dollar. ...

Looking like some statue of Verrocchio, he raises his arms yearningly, murmuring, 'Dollar!' 'Dollar!' 'La Vita-Dollar!'

as

THE CURTAIN FALLS

Dedications

ODETTE
In all the world to the dearest of mothers

CAPRICE
To Stephen Hammerton

THE FLOWER BENEATH THE FOOT
To Madame Mathieu and Mademoiselle Dora Garnier-Pagès